LINDA HOWARD

LINDA LAEL MILLER
— and —
SHERRYL WOODS

Come Lie with Me

 *Silhouette Books*

Published by Silhouette Books
America's Publisher of Contemporary Romance

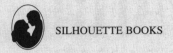 SILHOUETTE BOOKS

ISBN 0-373-48447-X

COME LIE WITH ME

Copyright © 2001 by Harlequin Books S.A.

The publisher acknowledges the copyright holders
of the individual works as follows:

COME LIE WITH ME
Copyright © 1984 by Linda Howington.

PART OF THE BARGAIN
Copyright © 1985 by Linda Lael Miller.

YESTERDAY'S LOVE
Copyright © 1987 by Sherryl Woods.

This edition published by arrangement with Harlequin Books S.A.

® and TM are trademarks of Harlequin Books S.A., used under license.
Trademarks indicated with ® are registered in the United States Patent
and Trademark Office, the Canadian Trade Marks Office and in other
countries.

Visit Silhouette at www.eHarlequin.com

Printed in U.S.A.

CONTENTS

COME LIE WITH ME
by Linda Howard

Chapter 1

The ocean had a hypnotic effect. Dione gave in to it without a struggle, peacefully watching the turquoise waves roll onto the blindingly white sand. She wasn't an idle person, yet she was content to sit on the deck of her rented beach house, her long, honey-tanned legs stretched out and propped on the railing, doing nothing more than watching the waves and listening to the muted roar of water coming in and going out. The white gulls swooped in and out of her vision, their high-pitched cries adding to the symphony of wind and water. To her right, the huge golden orb of the sun was sinking into the water, turning the sea to flame. It would have made a stunning photograph, yet she was disinclined to leave her seat and get her camera. It had been a glorious day, and she had done nothing more strenuous than celebrate it by walking the beach and swimming in the green-and-blue-streaked Gulf of Mexico. Lord, what a life. It was so sweet, it was almost sinful. This was the perfect vacation.

For two weeks she had wandered the sugar-white sands of Panama City, Florida, blissfully alone and lazy. There wasn't a clock in the beach house, nor had she even wound her watch since she'd arrived, because time didn't matter. No matter what time she woke, she knew that if she was hungry and didn't feel like cooking, there was always a place within walking distance where she could get something to eat. During the summer, the Miracle Strip didn't sleep. It was a twenty-four-hour party that constantly renewed itself from the end of school through the Labor Day weekend. Students and singles looking for a good time found it; families looking for a carefree vacation found it; and tired professional women wanting only a chance to unwind and relax beside the dazzling Gulf found that, too. She felt completely reborn after the past two delicious weeks.

A sailboat, as brightly colored as a butterfly, caught her attention, and she watched it as it lazily tacked toward shore. She was so busy watching the boat that she was unaware of the man approaching the deck until he started up the steps and the vibration of the wooden floor alerted her. Without haste she turned her head, the movement graceful and unalarmed, but her entire body was suddenly coiled and ready for action, despite the fact that she hadn't moved from her relaxed posture.

A tall, gray-haired man stood looking at her, and her first thought was that he didn't belong in this setting. P.C., as the vacation city was known, was a relaxed, informal area. This man was dressed in an impeccable three-piece gray suit, and his feet were shod in supple Italian leather. Dione reflected briefly that his shoes would be full of the loose sand that filtered into everything.

"Miss Kelley?" he inquired politely.

Her slim black brows arched in puzzlement, but she withdrew her feet from the railing and stood, holding out her hand to him. "Yes, I'm Dione Kelley. And you are...?"

"Richard Dylan," he said, taking her hand and shaking it firmly. "I realize that I'm intruding on your vacation, Miss Kelley, but it's very important that I speak with you."

"Please, sit down," Dione invited, indicating a deck chair beside the one she had just vacated. She resumed her former position, stretching out her legs and propping her bare feet on the railing. "Is there something I can do for you?"

"There certainly is," he replied feelingly. "I wrote to you about six weeks ago concerning a patient I'd like you to take on: Blake Remington."

Dione frowned slightly. "I remember. But I answered your letter, Mr. Dylan, before I left on vacation. Haven't you received it?"

"Yes, I have," he admitted. "I came to ask you to reconsider your refusal. There are extenuating circumstances, and his condition is deteriorating rapidly. I'm convinced that you can—"

"I'm not a miracle worker," she interrupted softly. "And I do have other cases lined up. Why should I put Mr. Remington ahead of others who need my services just as badly as he does?"

"Are they dying?" he asked bluntly.

"Is Mr. Remington? From the information you gave me in your letter, the last operation was a success. There are other therapists as well qualified as I am, if there's some reason why Mr. Remington has to have therapy this very moment."

Richard Dylan looked out at the turquoise Gulf, the waves tipped with gold by the sinking sun. "Blake Remington won't live another year," he said, and a bleak expression crossed his strong, austere features. "Not the way he is now. You see, Miss Kelley, he doesn't believe he'll ever walk again, and he's given up. He's deliberately letting himself die. He doesn't eat; he seldom sleeps; he refuses to leave the house."

Dione sighed. Depression was sometimes the most difficult aspect of her patients' conditions, taking away their energy and determination. She'd seen it so many times before, and she knew that she'd see it again. "Still, Mr. Dylan, another therapist—"

"I don't think so. I've already employed two therapists, and neither of them has lasted a week. Blake refuses to cooperate at all, saying that it's just a waste of time, something to keep him occupied. The doctors tell him that the surgery was a success, but he still can't move his legs, so he just doesn't believe them. Dr. Norwood suggested you. He said that you've had remarkable success with uncooperative patients, and that your methods are extraordinary."

She smiled wryly. "Of course he said that. Tobias Norwood trained me."

Richard Dylan smiled briefly in return. "I see. Still, I'm convinced that you're Blake's last chance. If you still feel that your other obligations are more pressing, then come with me to Phoenix and meet Blake. I think that when you see him, you'll understand why I'm so worried."

Dione hesitated, examining the proposal. Professionally, she was torn between refusing and agreeing. She had other cases, other people who were depending on her; why should this Blake Remington come before them? But on the other hand, he sounded like a challenge to her abilities, and she was one of those high-powered individuals who thrived on challenges, on testing herself to the limit. She was very certain of herself when it came to her chosen profession, and she enjoyed the satisfaction of completing a job and leaving her patient better able to move than before. In the years that she had been working as a private therapist, traveling all over the country to her patients' homes, she had amassed an amazing record of successes.

"He's an extraordinary man," said Mr. Dylan softly. "He's engineered several aeronautical systems that are widely used now. He designs his own planes, has flown as a test pilot on some top-secret planes for the government, climbs mountains, races yachts, goes deep-sea diving. He's a man who was at home on land, on the sea, or in the air, and now he's chained to a wheelchair and it's killing him."

"Which one of his interests was he pursuing when he had his accident?" Dione asked.

"Mountain climbing. The rope above him snagged on a rock, and his movements sawed the rope in two. He fell forty-five feet to a ledge, bounced off it, then rolled or fell another two hundred feet. That's almost the distance of a football field, but the snow must have cushioned him enough to save his life. He's said more than once that if he'd fallen off that mountain during the summer, he wouldn't have to spend his life as a cripple now."

"Tell me about his injuries," Dione said thoughtfully.

He rose to his feet. "I can do better than that. I have his file, complete with X rays, in my car. Dr. Norwood suggested that I bring it."

"He's a sly fox, that one," she murmured as Mr. Dylan disappeared around the deck. Tobias Norwood knew exactly how to intrigue her, how to set a particular case before her. Already she was interested, just as he had meant her to be. She'd make up her mind after seeing the X rays and reading the case history. If she didn't think she could help Blake Remington, she wouldn't put him through the stress of therapy.

In just a moment Mr. Dylan returned with a thick, manila envelope in his grasp. He released it into Dione's outthrust hand and waited expectantly. Instead of opening it, she tapped her fingernails against the envelope.

"Let me study this tonight, Mr. Dylan," she said firmly. "I can't just glance over it and make a decision. I'll let you know in the morning."

A flicker of impatience crossed his face; then he quickly mastered it and nodded. "Thank you for considering it, Miss Kelley."

When he was gone, Dione stared out at the Gulf for a long time, watching the eternal waves washing in with a froth of turquoise and sea-green, churning white as they rushed onto the sand. It was a good thing that her vacation was ending, that she'd already enjoyed almost two full weeks of utter contentment on the Florida panhandle, doing nothing more strenuous than walking in the tide. She'd already lazily begun considering her next job, but now it looked as if her plans had been changed.

After opening the envelope she held up the X rays one by one to the sun, and she winced when she saw the damage that had been done to a strong, vital human body. It was a miracle that he hadn't been killed outright. But the X rays taken after each successive operation revealed bones that had healed better than they should have, better than anyone could have hoped. Joints had been rebuilt; pins and plates had reconstructed his body and held it together. She went over the last set of X rays with excruciating detail. The surgeon had been a genius, or the results were a miracle, or perhaps a combination of both. She could see no physical reason why Blake couldn't walk again, provided the nerves hadn't been totally destroyed.

Beginning to read the surgeon's report, she concentrated fiercely on every detail until she understood exactly what damage had been done and what repairs had been made. This man *would* walk again; she'd make him! The end of the report mentioned that further improvement was prevented by the patient's lack of cooperation and depth of depression. She could almost feel the surgeon's sense of frustration as he'd written that; after all his painstaking work, after the unhoped-for success of his techniques, the patient had refused to help!

Gathering everything together, she started to replace the contents in the envelope and noticed that something else was inside, a stiff piece of paper that she'd neglected to remove. She pulled it out and turned it over. It wasn't just a piece of paper; it was a photograph.

Stunned, she stared into laughing blue eyes, eyes that sparkled and danced with the sheer joy of living. Richard Dylan was a sly one, too, knowing full well that few women would be able to resist the appeal of the dynamic man in the photograph. It was Blake Remington, she knew, as he had been before the accident. His brown hair was tousled, his darkly tanned face split by a rakish grin which revealed a captivating dimple in his left cheek. He was naked except for a brief pair of denim shorts, his body strong and well muscled, his legs the long, powerful limbs of an athlete. He was holding a good-sized marlin in the picture, and in the background she could make out the deep blue of the ocean; so he went deep-sea fishing, too. Wasn't there anything the man couldn't do? Yes, now there was, she reminded herself. Now he couldn't walk.

She wanted to refuse to take the case just to demonstrate to Richard Dylan that she couldn't be manipulated, but as she stared at the face in the photograph she knew that she would do just as he wanted, and she was disturbed by the knowledge. It had been such a long time since she'd been interested in any man at all that she was startled by her own reaction to a simple photograph.

Tracing the outline of his face with her fingertip, she wondered wistfully what her life would have been like if she'd been able to be a normal woman, to love a man and be loved in return, something that her brief and disastrous marriage had revealed to be impossible. She'd learned her lesson the hard way, but she'd never forgotten it. Men weren't for her. A loving husband and children weren't for her. The void left in her life by the total absence of love would have to be filled by her sense of satisfaction with her profession, with the joy she received from helping someone else. She might look at Blake Remington's photograph with admiration, but the daydreams that any other woman would indulge in when gazing at that masculine beauty were not for her. Daydreams were a waste of time, because she knew that she was incapable of attracting a man like him. Her ex-husband, Scott Hayes, had taught her with pain and humiliation the folly of enticing a man when she was unable to satisfy him.

Never again. She'd sworn it then, after leaving Scott, and she swore it again now. Never again would she give a man the chance to hurt her.

A sudden gust of salty wind fanned her cheeks, and she lifted her head, a little surprised to see that the sun was completely gone now and that she had been squinting at the photograph, not really seeing it as she dealt with her murky memories. She got to her feet and went inside, snapping on a tall floor lamp and illuminating the cool, summery interior of the beach house. Dropping into a plumply cushioned chair, Dione leaned her head back and began planning her therapy program, though of course she wouldn't be able to make any concrete plans until she actually met Mr. Remington and was better able to judge his condition. She smiled a little with anticipation. She loved a challenge more than she did anything else, and she had the feeling that Mr. Remington would fight her every inch of the way. She'd have to be on her toes, stay in control of the situation and use his helplessness as a lever against him, making him so angry that he'd go through hell to get better, just to get rid of her. Unfortunately, he really would have to go through hell; therapy wasn't a picnic.

She'd had difficult patients before, people who were so depressed and angry over their disabilities that they'd shut out the entire world, and she guessed that Blake Remington had reacted in the same way. He'd been so active, so vitally alive and in perfect shape, a real daredevil of a man; she guessed that it was killing his soul to be limited to a wheelchair. He wouldn't care if he lived or died; he wouldn't care about anything.

She slept deeply that night, no dreams disturbing her, and rose well before dawn for her usual run along the beach. She wasn't a serious runner, counting off the miles and constantly reaching for a higher number; she ran for the sheer pleasure of it, continuing until she tired, then strolling along and letting the silky froth of the tide wash over her bare feet. The sun was piercing the morning with its first blinding rays when she returned to the beach house, showered and began packing. She'd made her decision, so she saw no need to waste time. She'd be ready when Mr. Dylan returned.

He wasn't even surprised when he saw her suitcases. "I knew you'd take the job," he said evenly.

Dione arched a slim black brow at him. "Are you always so sure of yourself, Mr. Dylan?"

"Please, call me Richard," he said. "I'm not always so certain, but Dr. Norwood has told me a great deal about you. He thought that you'd take the job because it was a challenge, and when I saw you, I knew that he was right."

"I'll have to talk with him about giving away my secrets," she joked.

"Not all of them," he said, and something in his voice made her wonder just how much he knew. "You have a lot of secrets left."

Deciding that Richard was far too astute, she turned briskly to her cases and helped him take them out to his car. Her own car was a rental, and after locking the beach house and returning the car to the rental office, she was ready to go.

Later, when they were in a private jet flying west to Phoenix, she began questioning Richard about her patient. What did he like? What did he hate? What were his hobbies? She wanted to know about his education, his politics, his favorite colors, the type of women he had dated, or about his wife if he were married. She'd found that wives were usually jealous of the close relationship that developed between therapist and patient, and she wanted to know as much as she could about a situation before she walked into it.

Richard knew an amazing amount about Mr. Remington's personal life, and finally Dione asked him what his relationship was to the man.

The firm mouth twisted. "I'm his vice-president, for one thing, so I know about his business operations. I'm also his brother-in-law. The only woman in his life who you'll have to deal with is my wife, Serena, who is also his younger sister."

Dione asked, "Why do you say that? Do you live in the same house with Mr. Remington?"

"No, but that doesn't mean anything. Since his accident, Serena has hovered over him, and I'm sure she won't be pleased when you arrive and take all of his attention. She's always adored Blake to the point of obsession. She nearly went insane when we thought he would die."

"I won't allow any interference in my therapy program," she warned him quietly. "I'll be overseeing his hours, his visitors, the food he eats, even the phone calls he receives. I hope your wife understands that."

"I'll try to convince her, but Serena is just like Blake. She's both stubborn and determined, and she has a key to the house."

"I'll have the locks changed," Dione planned aloud, perfectly serious in her intentions. Loving sister or not, Serena Dylan wasn't going to take over or intrude on Dione's therapy.

"Good," Richard approved, a frown settling on his austere brow. "I'd like to have a wife again."

It was beginning to appear that Richard had some other motive for wanting his brother-in-law walking again. Evidently, in the two years since Blake's accident, his sister had abandoned her husband in order to care for him, and the neglect was eroding her marriage. It was a situation that Dione didn't want to become involved in, but she had given her word that she would take the case, and she didn't betray the trust that people put in her.

Because of the time difference, it was only midafternoon when Richard drove them to the exclusive Phoenix suburb where Blake Remington lived. This time his car was a white Lincoln, plush and cool. As he drove up the circular drive to the hacienda-style house, she saw that it looked plush and cool, too. To call it a house was like calling a hurricane a wind; this place was a mansion. It was white and mysterious, keeping its secrets hidden behind its walls, presenting only a grateful facade to curious eyes. The landscaping was marvelous, a blend of the natural desert plants and lush greenery that was the product of careful and selective irrigation. The drive ran around to the back, where Richard told her the garage area was, but he stopped before the arched entry in front.

When she walked into the enormous foyer Dione thought she'd walked into the garden of paradise. There was a serenity to the place, a dignified simplicity wrought by the cool brown tiles on the floor, the plain white walls, the high ceiling. The hacienda was built in a U, around an open courtyard that was cool and fragrant, with a pink marble fountain in the center of it spouting clear water into the air. She could see all of that because the inner wall of the foyer, from ceiling to floor, was glass.

She was still speechless with admiration when the brisk clicking of heels on the tiles caught her attention, and she turned her head to watch the tall young woman approaching. This had to be Serena; the resemblance to the photo of Blake Remington was too strong for her to be anyone else. She had the same soft brown hair, the same dark blue eyes, the same clear-cut features. But she wasn't laughing, as the man in the photo had been; her eyes were stormy, outraged.

"Richard!" she said in a low, wrathful tone. "Where have you been for the past two days? How dare you disappear without a word, then turn up with this…this gypsy in tow!"

Dione almost chuckled; most women wouldn't have attacked so bluntly, but she could see that this direct young woman had her share of the determination that Richard had attributed to Blake Remington. She opened her mouth to tell the truth of the matter, but Richard stepped in smoothly.

"Dione," he said, watching his wife with a cold eye, "I'd like to introduce my wife, Serena. Serena, this is Dione Kelley. I've hired Miss Kelley as Blake's new therapist, and I've been to Florida to pick her up and fly her back here. I didn't tell anyone where I was going because I had no intention of arguing over the matter. I've hired her, and that's that. I think that answers all of your questions." He finished with cutting sarcasm.

Serena Dylan wasn't a woman to be cowed, though a flush did color her cheeks. She turned to Dione and said frankly, "I apologize, though I refuse to take all of the blame. If my husband had seen fit to inform me of his intentions, I wouldn't have made such a terrible accusation.''

"I understand." Dione smiled. "Under the same circumstances, I doubt that my conduct would have been as polite."

Serena smiled in return, then stepped forward and gave her husband a belated peck on the cheek. "Very well, you're forgiven," she sighed, "though I'm afraid you've wasted your time. You know that Blake won't put up with it. He can't stand having anyone hover over him, and he's been pushed at and pounded on enough."

"Evidently not, or he'd be walking by now," Dione replied confidently.

Serena looked doubtful, then shrugged. "I still think you've wasted your time. Blake refused to have anything to do with the last therapist Richard hired, and he won't change his mind for you."

"I'd like to talk to him myself, if I may," Dione insisted, though in a pleasant tone.

Serena hadn't exactly stationed herself like a guard before the throne room, but it was evident that she was very protective of her brother. It wasn't all that unusual. When someone had been in a severe accident, it was only natural that the members of the family were overprotective for a while. Perhaps, when Serena found that Dione would be taking over the vast majority of Blake's time and attention, she would give her own husband the attention he deserved.

"At this time of day, Blake is usually in his room," Richard said, taking Dione's arm. "This way."

"Richard!" Again color rose in Serena's cheeks, but this time they were spots of anger. "He's lying down for a nap! At least leave him in peace until he comes downstairs. You know how badly he sleeps; let him rest while he can!"

"He naps every day?" Dione asked, thinking that if he slept during the day, no wonder he couldn't sleep at night.

"He tries to nap, but he usually looks worse afterward than he did before."

"Then it won't matter if we disturb him, will it?" Dione asked, deciding that now was the time to establish her authority. She caught a faint twitch of Richard's lips, signaling a smile, then he was directing her to the broad, sweeping stairs with his hand still warm and firm on her elbow. Behind them, Dione could feel the heat of the glare that Serena threw at them; then she heard the brisk tapping of heels as Serena followed.

From the design of the house, Dione suspected that all of the upstairs rooms opened onto the graceful gallery that ran along the entire U of the house, looking down on the inner courtyard. When Richard tapped lightly on a door that had been widened to allow a wheelchair to pass easily through it, then opened it at the low call that permitted entrance, she saw at once that, at least in this room, her supposition was correct. The enormous room was flooded with sunlight that streamed through the open curtains, though the sliding glass doors that opened onto the gallery remained closed.

The man at the window was silhouetted against the bright sunlight, a mysterious and melancholy figure slumped in the prison of a wheelchair. Then he reached out and pulled a chord, closing the curtains, and the room became dim. Dione blinked for a moment before her eyes adjusted to the sudden darkness; then the man became clear to her, and she felt her throat tighten with shock.

She'd thought that she was prepared; Richard had told her that Blake had lost weight and was rapidly deteriorating, but until she saw him, she hadn't realized exactly how serious the situation was. The contrast between the man in the wheelchair and the laughing man in the photo she'd seen was so great that she wouldn't have believed them to be the same man if it hadn't been for the dark blue eyes. His eyes no longer sparkled; they were dull and lifeless, but nothing could change their remarkable color.

He was thin, painfully so; he had to have lost almost fifty pounds from what he'd weighed when the photo had been taken, and he'd been all lean muscle then. His brown hair was dull from poor nutrition, and shaggy, as if it had been a long time since he'd had it trimmed. His skin was pale, his face all high cheekbones and gaunt cheeks.

Dione held herself upright, but inside she was shattering, crumbling into a thousand brittle pieces. She inevitably became involved with all her patients, but never before had she felt as if she were dying; never before had she wanted to rage at the injustice of it, at the horrible obscenity that had taken his perfect body and reduced it to helplessness. His suffering and despair were engraved on his drawn face, his bone structure revealed in stark clarity. Dark circles lay under the midnight blue of his eyes; his temples had become touched with gray. His once powerful body sat limp in the chair, his legs awkwardly motionless, and she knew that Richard had been right: Blake Remington didn't want to live.

He looked at her without a flicker of interest, then moved his gaze to Richard. It was as if she didn't exist. "Where've you been?" he asked flatly.

"I had business to attend to," Richard replied, his voice so cold that the room turned arctic. Dione could tell that he was insulted that anyone should question his actions; Richard might work for Blake, but he was in no way inferior. He was still angry with Serena, and the entire scene had earned his disapproval.

"He's so determined," Serena sighed, moving to her brother's side. "He's hired another therapist for you, Miss...uh, Diane Kelley."

"Dione," Dione corrected without rancor.

Blake turned his disinterested gaze on her and surveyed her without a word. Dione stood quietly, studying him, noting his reaction, or rather, his lack of one. Richard had said that Blake had always preferred blondes, but even taking Dione's black hair into consideration, she had expected at least a basic recognition that she was female. She expected men to look at her; she'd grown used to it, though once an interested glance would have sent her into panic. She was a striking woman, and at last she had been able to accept that, considering it one of nature's ironies that she should have been given the looks to attract men when it was impossible for her to enjoy a man's touch.

She knew what he saw. She'd dressed carefully for effect, realizing that her appearance would either be intimidating or appealing; she didn't care which, as long as it gave her an edge in convincing him to cooperate. She'd parted her thick, vibrant black hair in the middle and drawn it back in a severe knot at the nape of her neck, where she'd secured it with a gold comb. Gold hoop earrings dangled from her ears. Serena had called her a gypsy, and her warm, honey-tanned skin made it seem possible. Her eyes were cat's eyes, slanted, golden, as mysterious as time and fringed with heavy black lashes. With her high cheekbones and strong, sculptured jawline, she looked Eastern and exotic, a prime candidate for a lusty sheik's harem, had she been born a century before.

She'd dressed in a white jumpsuit, chic and casual, and now she pushed her hands into the pockets, a posture that outlined her firm breasts. The line of her body was long and clean and sweeping, from her trim waist to her rounded bottom, then on down her long, graceful legs. Blake might not have noticed, but his sister had, and Serena had been stirred to instant jealousy. She didn't want Dione around either her husband or her brother.

After a long silence Blake moved his head slowly in a negative emotion. "No. Just take her away, Richard. I don't want to be bothered."

Dione glanced at Richard, then stepped forward, taking control and focusing Blake's attention on her. "I'm sorry you feel that way, Mr. Remington," she said mildly. "Because I'm staying anyway. You see, I have a contract, and I always honor my word."

"I'll release you from it," he muttered, turning his head away and looking out the window again.

"That's very nice of you, but *I* won't release *you* from it. I understand that you've given Richard your power of attorney, so the contract is legal, and it's also ironclad. It states, simply, that I'm employed as your therapist and will reside in this house until you're able to walk again. No time limit was set." She leaned down and put her hands on the arms of his wheelchair, bringing her face close to his and forcing him to give her his attention. "I'm going to be your shadow, Mr. Remington. The only way you'll be able to get rid of me is to walk to the door yourself and open it for me; no one else can do it for you."

"You're overstepping yourself, Miss Kelley!" Serena said sharply, her blue eyes narrowing with rage. She reached out and thrust Dione's hands away from the wheelchair. ''My brother has said that he doesn't want you here!''

''This doesn't concern you,'' Dione replied, still in a mild tone.

''It certainly does! If you think I'll let you just move in here…why, you probably think you've found a meal ticket for life!''

''Not at all. I'll have Mr. Remington walking by Christmas. If you doubt my credentials, please feel free to investigate my record. But in the meantime, stop interfering.'' Dione straightened to her full height and stared steadily at Serena, the strength of her willpower blazing from her golden eyes.

''Don't talk to my sister like that,'' Blake said sharply.

At last! A response, even if it was an angry one! With secret delight Dione promptly attacked the crack in his indifference. ''I'll talk to anyone like that who tries to come between me and my patient,'' she informed him. She put her hands on her hips and surveyed him with a contemptuous curl to her mouth. ''Look at you! You're in such pitiful shape that you'd have to go into training to qualify for the ninety-eight-pound weakling category! You should be ashamed of yourself, letting your muscles turn into mush; no wonder you can't walk!''

The dark pupils of his eyes flared, a black pool in a sea of blue. ''Damn you,'' he choked. ''It's hard to do calisthenics when you're hooked up to more tubes than you have places for, and nothing except your face works when you want it to!''

''That was then,'' she said relentlessly. ''What about now? It takes muscles to walk, and you don't have any! You'd lose a fight with a noodle, the shape you're in now.''

''And I suppose you think you can wave your magic wand and put me into working order again?'' he snarled.

She smiled. ''A magic wand? It won't be as easy as that. You're going to work harder for me than you've ever worked before. You're going to sweat and hurt, and turn the air blue cussing me out, but you're going to work. I'll have you walking again if I have to half-kill you to do it.''

''No, you won't, lady,'' he said with cold deliberation. ''I don't care what sort of contract you have; I don't want you in my house. I'll pay whatever it takes to get rid of you.''

"I'm not giving you that option, Mr. Remington. I won't accept a payoff.''

"You don't have to give me the option! I'm *taking* it!''

Looking into his enraged face, flushed with anger, Dione abruptly realized that the photograph of the laughing, relaxed man had been misleading, an exception rather than the rule. This was a man of indomitable will, used to forcing things to go his way by the sheer power of his will and personality. He had overcome every obstacle in his life by his own determination, until the fall down the cliff had changed all that and presented him with the one obstacle that he couldn't handle on his own. He'd never had to have help before, and he hadn't been able to accept that now he did. Because he couldn't make himself walk, he was convinced that it wasn't possible.

But she was determined, too. Unlike him, she'd learned early that she could be struck down, forced to do things she didn't want to do. She'd pulled herself out of the murky depths of despair by her own silent, stubborn belief that life *had* to be better. Dione had forged her strength in the fires of pain; the woman she had become, the independence and skill and reputation she'd built, were too precious to her to allow her to back down now. This was the challenge of her career, and it would take every ounce of her willpower to handle it.

So, insolently, she asked him, "Do you *like* having everyone feel sorry for you?''

Serena gasped; even Richard made an involuntary sound before bringing himself back under control. Dione didn't waste a glance on them. She kept her eyes locked with Blake's, watching the shock in them, watching the angry color wash out of his face and leave it utterly white.

"You bitch,'' he said in a hollow, shaking voice.

She shrugged. "Look, we're getting nowhere like this. Let's make a deal. You're so weak, I'll bet you can't beat me at arm wrestling. If I win, I stay and you agree to therapy. If you win, I walk out that door and never come back. What do you say?''

Chapter 2

His head jerked up, his eyes narrowing as they swept over her slender form and graceful, feminine arms. Dione could almost read his thoughts. As thin as he was, he still outweighed her by at least forty, possibly even fifty, pounds. He knew that even if a man and a woman were the same weight, the man would be stronger than the woman, under normal circumstances. Dione refused to let a smile touch her lips, but she knew that these weren't normal circumstances. Blake had been inactive for two years, while she was in extremely good shape. She was a therapist; she had to be strong in order to do her job. She was slim, yes, but every inch of her was sleek, strong muscle. She ran, she swam, she did stretching exercises regularly, but most importantly, she lifted weights. She had to have considerable arm strength to be able to handle patients who couldn't handle themselves. She looked at Blake's thin, pale hands, and she knew that she would win.

"Don't do it!" Serena said sharply, twisting her fingers into knots.

Blake turned and looked at his sister in disbelief. "You think she can beat me, don't you?" he murmured, but the words were more a statement than a question.

Serena was tense, staring at Dione with an odd, pleading look in her eyes. Dione understood: Serena didn't want her brother humiliated. And neither did she. But she did want him to agree to therapy, and she was willing to do whatever was necessary to make him see what he was doing to himself. She tried to say that with her eyes, because she couldn't say the words aloud.

"Answer me!" Blake roared suddenly. Every line of him was tense.

Serena bit her lower lip. "Yes," she finally said. "I think she can beat you."

Silence fell, and Blake sat as though made of stone. Watching him carefully, Dione saw the moment he made the decision. "There's only one way to find out, isn't there?" he challenged, turning the wheelchair with a quick pressure of his finger on a button. Dione followed him as he led the way to his desk and positioned the wheelchair beside it.

"You shouldn't have a motorized wheelchair," she observed absently. "A manual chair would have kept your upper body strength at a reasonable level. This is a fancy chair, but it isn't doing you any good at all."

He shot her a brooding glance, but didn't respond to her comment. "Sit down," he said, indicating his desk.

Dione took her time obeying him. She felt no joy, no elation, in knowing that she would win; it was something she had to do, a point that she had to make to Blake.

Richard and Serena flanked them as they positioned themselves, Blake maneuvering himself until he was satisfied with his location, Dione doing the same. She propped her right arm on the desk and gripped her bicep with her left hand. "Ready when you are," she said.

Blake had the advantage of a longer arm, and she realized that it would take all of the strength in her hand and wrist to overcome the leverage he would have. He positioned his arm against hers and wrapped his fingers firmly around her much smaller hand. For a moment he studied the slim grace of her fingers, the delicate pink of her manicured nails, and a slight smile moved his lips. He probably thought it would be a cake walk. But she felt the coldness of his hands, indicating poor circulation, and knew the inevitable outcome of their little battle.

"Richard, you start it," Blake instructed, lifting his eyes and locking them with hers. She could feel his intensity, his aggressive drive to win, and she began to brace herself, concentrating all her energy and strength into her right arm and hand.

"Go," said Richard, and though there was no great flurry of movement between the two antagonists, their bodies were suddenly tense, their arms locked together.

Dione kept her face calm, revealing nothing of the fierce effort it took to keep her wrist straight. After the first moments, when he was unable to shove her arm down, Blake's face reflected first astonishment, then anger, then a sort of desperation. She could feel his first burst of strength ebbing and slowly, inexorably, she began forcing his arm down. Sweat broke out on his forehead and slipped down one side of his face as he struggled to reverse the motion, but he had already used his meager strength and had nothing in reserve. Knowing that she had him, and regretting her victory even though she knew it was necessary, Dione quickly settled the matter by forcing his arm down flat on the desk.

He sat in his wheelchair, a shattered expression in his eyes for a flashing moment before he closed himself off and made his face a blank wall.

The silence was broken only by his rapid breathing. Richard's face was grim; Serena looked torn between the desire to comfort her brother and a strong inclination to throw Dione out herself.

Dione moved briskly, rising to her feet. "That settles that," she said casually. "In another two months I won't be able to do that. I'll put my things in the room next to this one—"

"No," said Blake curtly, not looking at her. "Serena, give Miss Kelley the guest suite."

"That won't do at all," Dione replied. "I want to be close enough to you that I'll be able to hear you if you call. The room next door will do nicely. Richard, how soon can you have those changes made that I stipulated?"

"What changes?" Blake asked, jerking his head up.

"I need some special equipment," she explained, noting that the diversion had worked, as she'd intended it to. He'd already lost that empty look. She'd evidently made the right decision in being so casual about beating him at arm wrestling, treating the incident as nothing unusual. Now was not the time to rub it in, or to let him know that there were a lot of men walking the earth who couldn't match her in arm wrestling. He'd find out soon enough when they got into the weight-lifting program.

"What sort of special equipment?" he demanded.

She controlled a smile. His attention had certainly been caught by the possibility of any changes in his beloved home. She outlined her needs to him. "A whirlpool is a necessity. I'll also need a treadmill, weight bench, sauna, things like that. Any objections?"

"There might be. Just where do you plan to put all this?"

"Richard said he could outfit a gym for me on the ground floor, next to the pool, which will be very convenient, because you'll be doing a lot of work in the pool. Water is a great place for calisthenics," she said enthusiastically. "Your muscles still get the workout, but the water supports your weight."

"You're not putting in a gym," he said grimly.

"Read my contract." She smiled. "The gym is going in. Don't make such a fuss; the house won't be disfigured, and the equipment is necessary. An Olympic trainee won't be getting the workout you're facing," she said with quiet truth. "It's going to be hard work, and it's going to be painful, but you'll do it if I have to drive you like a slave. You can put money on it: You'll be walking by Christmas."

A terrible longing crossed his face before he brought his thin hand up to rub his forehead, and Dione sensed his indecision. But it wasn't in him to give in to anyone else easily, and he scowled. "You won the right to stay here," he said grudgingly. "But I don't like it, and I don't like you, Miss Kelley. Richard, I want to see that contract she keeps harping about."

"I don't have it with me," Richard lied smoothly, taking Serena's arm and edging her toward the door. "I'll bring it with me the next time I'm over."

Serena had time for only an incoherent protest before Richard had her out the door. Trusting Richard to keep his wife away, at least for the time being, Dione smiled at Blake and waited.

He eyed her warily. "Don't you have something else to do besides staring at me?"

"I certainly do. I was just waiting to see if you have any questions. If you don't, I need to be unpacking."

"No questions," he muttered.

That wouldn't last long, she thought, leaving him without another word. When he found out the extent of her therapy, he'd have plenty to say about it.

It was evidently up to her to find her way around the house, but because the design was so simple, she had no difficulty exploring. Her suitcases were sitting in the foyer, and she took them upstairs herself, finally examining the room she'd chosen for her own. It was a room for a man, done in masculine browns and creams, but it was comfortable and suited her; she wasn't picky. She unpacked, a chore that didn't take long because she didn't burden herself with a lot of clothing. What she had was good and adaptable, so she could use one outfit for several different things just by changing a few accessories. The way she traveled around, from one case to another, a lot of clothing would have been a hindrance.

Then she went in search of the cook and housekeeper; a house that size had to have some sort of staff, and she needed everyone's cooperation. It might have been easier if Richard had remained to introduce her, but she was glad that he'd taken Serena out of the way.

She found the kitchen without difficulty, though the cook who occupied it was something of a surprise. She was tall and lean, obviously part Indian, despite the pale green of her eyes. Though her age was impossible to determine, Dione guessed her to be at least in her fifties, possibly sixties. Her raven black hair didn't hint at it, but there was something in the knowledge in her eyes, the dignity of her features, that suggested age. She was as imperial as a queen, though the look she turned on the intruder into her kitchen wasn't haughty, merely questioning.

Quickly Dione introduced herself and explained why she was there. The woman washed her hands and dried them with unhurried motions, then held her hand out. Dione took it. "My name is Alberta

Quincy," the cook said in a deep, rich voice that could have been a man's. "I'm glad that Mr. Remington has agreed to therapy."

"He didn't exactly agree," Dione replied honestly, smiling. "But I'm here anyway, and I'm staying. I'll need everyone's cooperation to handle him, though."

"You just tell me what you want," Alberta said with pure confidence. "Miguel, who takes care of the grounds and drives Mr. Remington's car, will do as I tell him. My stepdaughter, Angela, cleans the house, and she'll also do as I say."

Most people would, Dione thought privately. Alberta Quincy was the most regal person she'd ever met. There wasn't much expression in her face and her voice was even and deliberate, but there was a force to the woman that most people wouldn't be able to resist. She would be an indispensable ally.

Dione outlined the diet she wanted Blake to follow, and explained why she wanted changes made. The last thing she wanted to do was offend Alberta. But Alberta merely nodded. "Yes, I understand."

"If he gets angry, put all the blame on me," Dione said. "At this point, I *want* him to be angry. I can use anger, but I can't work with indifference."

Again Alberta nodded her regal head. "I understand," she said again. She wasn't a talkative woman, to understate the matter, but she did understand, and to Dione's relief she didn't express any doubts.

There was one other problem, and Dione broached it cautiously. "About Mr. Remington's sister…"

Alberta blinked once, slowly, and nodded. "Yes," she said simply.

"Does she have a key to the house?" Gold eyes met green ones, and the communication between the two women was so strong that Dione had the sudden feeling that words were unnecessary.

"I'll have the locks changed," Alberta said. "But there'll be trouble."

"It'll be worth the benefits. I can't have his routine interrupted once I get him started on it, at least until he can see some improvement for himself and will want to continue with it. I think Mr. Dylan can handle his wife."

"If he even wants to any longer," Alberta said calmly.

"I think he does. He doesn't seem like a man to give up very easily."

"No, but he's also very proud."

"I don't want to cause trouble between them, but Mr. Remington is my concern, and if that causes friction, then they have to handle it as best they can."

"Mrs. Dylan worships her brother. He raised her; their mother died when Mrs. Dylan was thirteen."

That explained a lot, and Dione spared a moment of sympathy for both Serena and Richard; then she pushed thoughts of them away. She couldn't consider them; Blake would take all her concentration and energy.

Suddenly she was very tired. It had been a full day, and though it was only late afternoon, she needed to rest. The battle would begin in earnest in the morning, and she'd need a good night's sleep in order to face it. Starting tomorrow, her hands would be full.

Alberta saw the sudden fatigue that tightened Dione's features and within minutes had a sandwich and a glass of milk sitting on the table. "Eat," she said, and Dione knew better than to argue. She sat down and ate.

Dione's alarm clock went off at five-thirty the next morning. She rose and took a shower, her movements brisk and certain from the moment she got out of bed. She always woke instantly, her mind clear, her coordination in perfect sync. It was one reason why she was such a good therapist; if a patient needed her during the night, she didn't stumble around rubbing her eyes. She was instantly capable of doing whatever was required of her.

Something told her that Blake wouldn't be such a cheerful riser, and she could feel her heartbeat speeding up as she brushed her long hair and braided it in one thick braid. Anticipation of the coming battle ran through her veins like liquid joy, making her eyes sparkle and giving a rosy flush to her skin.

The morning was still cool, but she knew from experience that exertion would make her warm, so she dressed in brief blue shorts, a sleeveless cotton shirt with cheerful polka dots in red, blue and yellow, and an old pair of tennis shoes. She touched her toes twenty times, stretching her back and legs, then did twenty sit-ups. She was capable of many more than that, but this was only a quick routine to warm up.

She was smiling when she entered Blake's room after a quick tap on the door. "Good morning," she said cheerfully as she crossed the floor to the balcony and opened the curtains, flooding the room with light.

He was lying on his back, his legs positioned a little awkwardly, as if he'd tried to move them during the night. He opened his eyes, and Dione saw the flare of panic in them. He twitched and tried to sit up, groping at his legs; then he remembered and fell back, his face bleak.

How often did that happen? How often did he wake, not remembering the accident, and panic because he couldn't move his legs? He wouldn't do that for very much longer, she determined grimly, going over to sit on the bed beside him.

"Good morning," she said again.

He didn't return the greeting. "What time is it?" he snapped.

"About six o'clock, maybe a little earlier."

"What're you doing here?"

"Beginning your therapy," she replied serenely. He was wearing pajamas, she saw, and wondered if he were able to completely dress himself or if someone had to help him.

"No one's up at this hour," he grumbled, closing his eyes again.

"I am, and now you are. Come on; we've got a lot to do today." She rolled the wheelchair to the side of the bed and threw the covers back, revealing his pitifully thin legs clad in the pale blue pajamas. His feet were covered with white socks.

He opened his eyes and the anger was there again. "What're you doing?" he snarled, reaching out an arm to whip the covers back over himself again.

He didn't want her to see him, but she couldn't permit any modesty to interfere. Before long she'd be as familiar with his body as she was with her own, and he had to realize that. If he were ashamed of his physical condition, then he'd simply have to work to improve it.

She snatched the covers away again, and with a deft movement scooped his legs around until they were hanging off the side of the bed. "Get up," she said relentlessly. "Go to the bathroom before we get started. Do you need any help?"

Pure fire sparked from his blue, blue eyes. "No," he growled, so angry that he could barely speak. "I can go to the bathroom by myself, Mama!"

"I'm not your mother," she returned. "I'm your therapist, though the two do have a lot in common."

She held the chair while he levered himself into it; then he shot across the room and was in the adjoining bathroom before she could react. She laughed silently to herself. When she heard the lock click she called out, "Don't think you can lock yourself in there all morning! I'll take the door off the hinges if I have to."

A muffled curse answered her, and she laughed again. This was going to be interesting!

By the time he finally came out she had begun to think she really would have to take the door down. He'd combed his hair and washed his face, but he didn't look any more pleased with being awake than he had before.

"Do you have any underwear on?" she asked, not making any comment on the length of time he'd spent in the bathroom. He'd timed that very nicely, stalling as long as he could, but coming out just before she did something about it.

Shock froze his features. "What?" he asked.

"Do you have any underwear on?" she repeated.

"What business is it of yours?"

"Because I want your pajamas off. If you don't have any underwear on, you may want to put on a pair, but it really doesn't matter to me. I've seen naked men before."

"I'm sure you have," he muttered snidely. "I have underwear on, but I'm not taking my pajamas off for you."

"Then don't. I'll take them off for you. I think you learned yesterday that I'm strong enough to do it. But those pajamas are coming off, the easy way or the hard way. Which is it?"

"Why do you want them off?" he stalled. "It can't be so you can admire my build," he said bitterly.

"You're right about that," she said. "You look like a bird. That's why I'm here; if you didn't look like a bird, you wouldn't need me."

He flushed.

"The pajamas," she prodded.

Furiously he unbuttoned the shirt and threw it across the room. She could sense that he would have liked to do the same to the bottoms, but they were a bit more difficult to remove. Without a word Dione helped him back onto the bed, then pulled the garment down his thin legs and draped it over the arm of the wheelchair. "On your stomach," she said, and deftly rolled him over.

"Hey!" he protested, his face smothered in the pillow. He swept the pillow aside. He was shaking with fury.

She popped the elastic waistband of his shorts. "Calm down," she advised. "This will be painless this morning."

Her impertinent little gesture made his temper flare so hotly that his entire torso flushed. Smiling at his response, she began to firmly knead his shoulders and back.

He grunted. "Take it easy! I'm not a side of beef!"

She laughed. "How delicate you are!" she mocked. "There's a reason for this."

"Like what? Punishment?"

"In a word, circulation. Your circulation is terrible. That's why your hands are cold, and why you have to wear socks to keep your feet warm, even in bed. I'll bet they're icy cold right now, aren't they?"

Silence was her answer.

"Muscles can't work without a good blood supply," she commented.

"I see," he said sarcastically. "Your magical massage is going to zip me right onto my feet."

"No way. My magical massage is mere groundwork, and you should learn to like it, because you're going to be getting a lot of it."

"God, you're just loaded down with charm, aren't you?"

She laughed again. "I'm loaded down with knowledge, and I also come equipped with a thick hide, so you're wasting your time." She moved down to his legs; there was no flesh there to massage. She felt as if she were merely moving his skin over his bones, but she kept at it, knowing that the hours and hours of massage that she would give him would eventually pay off. She pulled his socks off and rubbed his limp feet briskly, feeling some of the chill leave his skin.

The minutes passed as she worked in silence. He grunted occasionally in protest when her vigorous fingers were a little too rough. A fine sheen of perspiration began to glow on her face and body.

She shifted him onto his back and gave her attention to his arms and chest and his hollow belly. His ribs stood out white under his skin. He lay with his eyes fixed on the ceiling, his mouth grim.

Dione moved down to his legs again.

"How much longer are you going to keep this up?" he finally asked.

She looked up and checked the time. It had been a little over an hour. "I suppose that's enough for right now," she said. "Now we do the exercises."

She took first one leg, then the other, bending them, forcing his knees up to his chest, repeating the motion over and over. He bore it in silence for about fifteen minutes, then suddenly rolled to a sitting position and shoved her away.

"Stop it!" he shouted, his face drawn. "My God, woman, do you have to keep on and on? It's a waste of time! Just leave me alone!"

She regarded him in amazement. "What do you mean, 'a waste of time'? I've just started. Did you really expect to see a difference in an hour?"

"I don't like being handled like so much putty!"

She shrugged, hiding a smile. "It's almost seven-thirty anyway. Your breakfast will be ready. I don't know about you, but I'm hungry."

"I'm not hungry," he said, and then a startled look crossed his face and she knew that he'd just realized that he *was* hungry, probably for the first time in months. She helped him to dress, though her aid managed to send him off into a black temper again. He was as sullen as a child when they entered the elevator that had been installed especially for him.

But the sullenness fled when he saw what was on his plate. Watching him, Dione had to bite her lip to keep from laughing aloud. First horror, then outrage contorted his features. "What's that mess?" he roared.

"Oh, don't worry," she said casually. "That's not all you're getting, but that's what you'll start off with. Those are vitamins," she added in a helpful tone.

They could have been snakes from the way he was staring at them. She had to admit that the collection was a little impressive. Alberta had counted them out exactly as Dione had instructed, and she knew that there were nineteen pills.

"I'm not taking them!"

"You're taking them. You need them. You'll need them even more after a few days of therapy. Besides, you don't get anything to eat until after you've taken them."

He wasn't a good loser. He snatched them up and swallowed them several at a time, washing them down with gulps of water. "There," he snarled. "I've taken the damned things."

"Thank you," she said gravely.

Alberta had evidently been listening, because she promptly entered with their breakfast trays. He looked at his grapefruit half, whole wheat toast, eggs, bacon and milk as if it were slop. "I want a blueberry waffle," he said.

"Sorry," Dione said. "That's not on your diet. Too sweet. Eat your grapefruit."

"I hate grapefruit."

"You need the vitamin C."

"I just took a year's supply of vitamin C!"

"Look," she said sweetly, "this is your breakfast. Eat it or do without. You're not getting a blueberry waffle."

He threw it at her.

She'd been expecting something like that, and ducked gracefully. The plate crashed against the wall. She collapsed against the table, the laughter that she'd been holding in all morning finally bursting out of her in great whoops. His hair was practically standing on end, he was so angry. He was beautiful! His cobalt blue eyes were as vivid as sapphires; his face was alive with color.

As dignified as a queen, Alberta marched out of the kitchen with an identical tray and set it before him. "She said you'd probably throw the first one," she said without inflection.

Knowing that he'd acted exactly as Dione had predicted made him even angrier, but now he was stymied. He didn't know what to do, afraid that whatever he did, she would have anticipated it. Finally he did nothing. He ate silently, pushing the food into his mouth with determined movements, then balked again at the milk.

"I can't stand milk. Surely coffee can't hurt!"

"It won't hurt, but it won't help, either. Let's make a deal," she offered. "Drink the milk, which you need for the calcium, and then you can have coffee."

He took a deep breath and drained the milk glass.

Alberta brought in coffee. The remainder of the meal passed in relative peace. Angela Quincy, Alberta's stepdaughter, came in to clear the mess that Blake had made with his first breakfast, and he looked a little embarrassed.

Angela, in her way, was as much of an enigma as Alberta was. She showed her age, unlike Alberta; she was about fifty, as soft and cuddly as Alberta was lean and angular. She was very pretty, could even have been called beautiful, despite the wrinkling of her skin. She was the most serene person Dione had ever seen. Her hair was brown, liberally streaked with gray, and her eyes were a soft, tranquil brown. She had once been engaged, Dione would learn later, but the man had died, and Angela still wore the engagement ring he'd given her so many years before.

She wasn't disturbed at all by having to clean egg off the wall, though Blake became increasingly restless as she worked. Dione leisurely finished her meal, then laid her napkin aside.

"Time for more exercises," she announced.

"No!" he roared. "I've had enough for today! A little of you goes a long way, lady!"

"Please, call me Dione," she murmured.

"I don't want to call you anything! My God, would you just leave me alone!"

"Of course I will, when my job is finished. I can't let you ruin my record of successful cases, can I?"

"Do you know what you can do with your successful record?" he snarled, sending the chair jerking backward. He jabbed the forward button. "I don't want to see your face again!" he shouted as the chair rolled out of the room.

She sighed and lifted her shoulders helplessly when her eyes met Angela's philosophic gaze. Angela smiled, but didn't say anything. Alberta wasn't talkative, and Angela was even less so. Dione imagined that when the two of them were together, the silence was deafening.

When she thought that Blake had had enough time to get over his tantrum, she went upstairs to begin again. It would probably be a waste of time to try his door, so she entered her room and went straight through to the gallery. She tapped on the sliding glass doors in his room, then opened them and stepped in.

He regarded her broodingly from his chair. Dione went to him and placed her hand on his shoulder. "I know it's difficult," she said softly. "I can't promise you that any of this will be easy. Try to trust me; I really am good at my job, and at the very worst you'll still be in much better health than you are now."

"If I can't walk, why should I care about my health?" he asked tightly. "Do you think I want to live like this? I would rather have died outright on that cliff than have gone through these past two years."

"Have you always given up so easily?"

"Easily!" His head jerked. "You don't know anything about it! You don't know what it was like—"

"I can tell you what it wasn't like," she interrupted. "I can tell you that you've never looked down at where your legs used to be and seen only flat sheet. You've never had to type by punching the keys with a pencil held in your teeth because you're paralyzed from the neck down. I've seen a lot of people who are a lot worse off than you. You're going to walk again, because I'm going to make you.''

"I don't want to hear about how bad other people have it! They're not *me!* My life is my own, and I know what I want out of it, and what I can't...what I *won't* accept.''

"Work? Effort? Pain?'' she prodded. "Mr. Remington, Richard has told me a great deal about you. You lived life to the fullest. If there were even the slimmest chance that you could do all of that again, would you go for it?''

He sighed, his face unutterably weary. "I don't know. If I really thought there was a chance...but I don't. I can't walk, Miss Kelley. I can't move my legs at all.''

"I know. You can't expect to move them right now. I'll have to retrain your nerve impulses before you'll be able to move them. It'll take several months, and I can't promise that you won't limp, but you *will* walk again...if you cooperate with me. So, Mr. Remington, shall we get started again on those exercises?''

Chapter 3

He submitted to the exercises with ill grace, but that didn't bother her as long as he cooperated at all. His muscles didn't know that he lay there scowling the entire time; the movement, the stimulation, were what counted. Dione worked tirelessly, alternating between exercising his legs and massaging his entire body. It was almost ten-thirty when she heard the noise that she'd been unconsciously listening for all morning: the tapping of Serena's heels. She lifted her head, and then Blake heard it, too. "No!" he said hoarsely. "Don't let her see me like this!"

"All right," she said calmly, flipping the sheet up to cover him. Then she walked to the door and stepped into the hallway, blocking Serena's way as she started to enter Blake's room.

Serena gave her a startled look. "Is Blake awake? I was just going to peek in; he usually doesn't get up until about noon."

No wonder he'd been so upset when I got him up at six! Dione thought, amused. To Serena she said blandly, "I'm giving him his exercises now."

"So early?" Serena's brows arched in amazement. "Well, I'm certain you've done enough for the day. Since he's awake early he'll be ready for his breakfast. He eats so badly. I don't want him to miss any meals. I'll go in and see what he'd like—"

As Serena moved around Dione to enter Blake's bedroom, Dione deftly sidestepped until she once more blocked the door. "I'm sorry," she said as gently as possible when Serena stared at her in disbelief. "He's already had his breakfast. I've put him on a schedule, and it's important that he stay on it. After another hour of exercise we'll come downstairs for lunch, if you'd like to wait until then."

Serena was still staring at her as if she couldn't believe what she was hearing. "Are you saying..." she whispered, then stopped and began again, her voice stronger this time. "Are you saying that I can't see my brother?"

"At this time, no. We need to complete these exercises."

"Does Blake know I'm here?" Serena demanded, her cheeks suddenly flushing.

"Yes, he does. He doesn't want you to see him right now. Please, try to understand how he feels."

Serena's marvelous eyes widened. "Oh! Oh, I see!" Perhaps she did, but Dione rather doubted it. Hurt shimmered in Serena's eyes for a moment; then she shrugged lightly. "I'll...see him in an hour, then." She turned away, and Dione watched her for a moment, reading wounded emotions in every line of her straight back. It wasn't unusual for the one closest to the patient to become jealous of the intimacy that was necessary between patient and therapist, but Dione never failed to feel uncomfortable when it happened. She knew that the intimacy was only fleeting, that as soon as her patient was recovered and no longer needed her services, she would go on to some other case and the patient would forget all about her. In Blake's case, there was nothing to be jealous of anyway. The only emotion he felt for her was hostility.

When she reentered the bedroom he twisted his head around to stare at her. "Is she gone?" he questioned anxiously.

"She's going to wait downstairs to eat lunch with you," Dione answered, and saw the relief that crossed his face.

"Good. She...nearly went to pieces when this happened to me. She'd be hysterical if she saw what I really look like." Pain darkened his eyes. "She's special to me; I practically raised her. I'm all the family she has."

"No, you're not," Dione pointed out. "She has Richard."

"He's so wrapped up in his work, he seldom remembers that she's alive," he snorted. "Richard's a great vice-president, but he's not a great husband."

That wasn't the impression Dione had gotten from Richard; he'd seemed to her to be a man very much in love with his wife. On the surface Richard and Serena were opposites; he was reserved, sophisticated, while she was as forceful as her brother, but perhaps they were each what the other needed. Perhaps her fire made him more spontaneous; perhaps his reserve tempered her rashness. But Dione didn't say anything to Blake. She began the repetitious exercises again, forcing his legs through the same motions.

It was tiring, boring work; tiring for her, boring for him. It made him irritable all over again, but this time when he snapped at her to stop, she obeyed him. She didn't want to browbeat him, to force her wishes on him in everything. He'd put in the most active morning he'd had since the accident, and she wasn't going to push him any further. "Whew!" she sighed, wiping her forehead with the back of her hand and feeling the moisture there. "I need a shower before lunch! Breaking off a little early is a good idea."

He looked at her, and his eyes widened in surprise. She knew that he didn't really see her all morning; he'd been preoccupied with his own condition, his own despair. She'd told him that he'd have to work hard, but now for the first time he realized that she'd be working hard, too. It wasn't going to be a picnic for her. She knew that she looked a mess, all sweaty and flushed.

"A bath wouldn't hurt you," he agreed dryly, and she laughed.

"Don't be such a gentleman about it," she teased. "You just wait. I won't be the only one working up a sweat before long, and I won't show you any mercy!"

"I haven't noticed you showing any, anyway," he grumbled.

"Now, I've been very good to you. I've kept you entertained all morning; I made certain you had a good breakfast—"

"Don't push your luck," he advised, giving her a black look, which she rewarded with a smile. It was important that he learn to joke and laugh with her, to ease the stress of the coming months. She had to become the best friend he had in the world, knowing as she did so that it was a friendship that was doomed from the outset, because it was based on dependence and need. When he no longer needed her, when his life had regained its normal pace, she would leave and be promptly forgotten. She knew that, and she had to keep a part of herself aloof, though the remainder of her emotions and mental effort would be concentrated entirely on him.

While she was helping him to dress, a process that didn't anger him as it had that morning, he said thoughtfully, "You'll be spending most of your time dressing and undressing me, it seems. If this is the routine you're going to be following it'll save a lot of time if I just wear a pair of gym shorts; I can put on a robe before we eat, and Alberta can bring trays up here."

Dione successfully hid her delight, merely saying, "That's your second good idea of the day." Secretly she was elated. From a practical standpoint he was right: It would save a lot of time and effort; however, it would also exclude Serena from most of their meals. That would be a big help.

If wasn't that she disliked Serena; if she had met her under different circumstances, Dione felt that she would have liked Serena very much. But Blake was her concern now, and she didn't want anyone or anything interfering with her work. While she was working on a case she concentrated on her patient to the extent that everyone else faded into the background, became gray cardboard figures rather than three-dimensional human beings. It was one of the things that made her so successful in her field. Already, after only one morning, Blake so filled her thoughts, and she was so much in tune with him, that she felt she knew him inside and out. She could practically read his mind, know what he was going to say before he said it. She ached for him, sympathized with him, but most of all she was happy for him, because she could look at his helplessness now and know that in a few months he would be strong and fit again. Already he was looking better, she thought proudly. It was probably due more to his anger than her efforts, but his color was much improved. He could stay angry with her for the entire time if it would keep him active and involved.

She was feeling satisfied with the morning's work as she walked

beside him into the dining room, but that feeling was shattered when
Serena plunged toward Blake, her lovely face bathed in tears.
"Blake," she said brokenly.

Instantly he was alert, concerned, as he reached for her hand.
"What is it?" he asked, a note of tenderness creeping into his voice,
a particular tone that was absent when he talked to everyone else.
Only Serena inspired that voice of love.

"The patio!" she wailed. "Mother's bench…it's ruined! They've
turned the pool into a madhouse! It looks awful!"

"What?" he asked, his brows snapping together. "What're you
talking about?"

Serena pointed a shaking finger at Dione. "*Her* gym! They've torn
up the entire patio!"

"I don't think it's that bad," Dione said reasonably. "It may be
disorganized now, but nothing should be torn up. Richard's overseeing the installation of the equipment, and I'm sure he wouldn't let
anything be damaged."

"Come see for yourself!"

Dione checked her watch. "I think we should have lunch first. The
patio isn't going anywhere, but the food will be cold."

"Stalling?" Blake inquired coldly. "I told you, Miss Kelley, that
I don't want this house changed."

"I can neither deny nor confirm what changes have been made,
because I haven't been outside. I've been with you all morning. However, I trust Richard's good sense, even if you don't," she said pointedly, and Serena flushed furiously.

"It isn't that I don't trust my husband," she began heatedly, but
Blake cut her off with a lifted hand.

"Not now," he said shortly. "I want to see the patio."

Serena fell into immediate silence, though she looked sulky. Evidently Blake was still very much the big brother, despite his obvious
ill health. His voice carried the unmistakable ring of command. Blake
Remington was accustomed to giving orders and having them carried
out immediately; his morning with Dione must have gone completely
against the grain.

It was the first time Dione had been on the patio, and she found it beautifully landscaped, cool and fragrant, despite the brutal Arizona sun. Yucca plants and different varieties of cactus grew in perfect harmony with plants normally found in a much more congenial climate. Careful watering explained the unusual variety of plants, that and the well-planned use of shade. White flagstones had been laid out to form a path, while a central fountain spewed its musical water upward in a perfect spray. At the back of the patio, where a tall gate opened onto the pool area, was a beautifully carved bench in a delicate pearl-gray color. Dione had no idea what type of wood it was, though it was gorgeous.

The patio *was* disorganized; evidently the workers Richard had hired had used the patio to store the pool furniture that was in the way, and also the materials that they didn't need at the moment. However, she saw that they had been careful not to disturb any of the plants; everything was placed carefully on the flagstones. But Serena ran to the lovely bench and pointed out a long gouge on its side. "See!" she cried.

Blake's eyes flashed. "Yes, I see. Well, Miss Kelley, it looks as if your workers have damaged a bench that I consider priceless. My father gave it to my mother when they moved into this house; she sat here every evening, and it's here that I see her in my mind. I want this whole thing called off before something else is ruined, and I want you out of my house."

Dione was distressed that the bench had been damaged, and she opened her mouth to apologize; then she saw the flash of triumph in Serena's eyes and she paused. To give herself time to think, she walked to the bench and bent down to examine the scarred wood. Thoughtfully she ran a finger over the gouge; a quick glance at Serena caught a hint of apprehension in those amazingly expressive eyes. What was Serena worried about? Looking back at the bench, the answer became readily apparent: The bench was undoubtedly damaged, but the gouge was old enough to have weathered. It certainly hadn't been done that morning.

She could have accused Serena of deliberately trying to cause trouble, but she didn't. Serena was fighting for the brother she loved, and though her battle was useless, Dione couldn't condemn her for it.

She would just have to separate Serena from Blake so her work could continue without a constant stream of interruptions. Richard would have to bring that laser brain of his into use and keep his wife occupied.

"I can understand why you're both upset," she said mildly, "but this gouge wasn't done tonight. See?" she asked, pointing at the wood. "It isn't a fresh scar. I'd guess that this has been here for several weeks."

Blake moved his wheelchair closer and leaned down to inspect the bench for himself. He straightened slowly. "You're right," he sighed. "In fact, I'm afraid I'm the culprit."

Serena gasped. "What do you mean?"

"A few weeks ago I was out here and I bumped the wheelchair into the bench. You'll notice that the gouge is the same height as the hub of my wheel." He rubbed his eyes with a thin hand that trembled with strain. "God, I'm sorry, Serena."

"Don't blame yourself!" she cried, rushing to his side and clutching his hand. "It doesn't matter; please don't be upset. Come inside and let's have lunch. I know you must be tired. It can't do any good for you to tire yourself out like this. You need to rest."

Dione watched as Serena walked beside the wheelchair, all concern and love. Shaking her head a little in amused exasperation, she followed them.

Serena remained close by Blake's side for the rest of the day, fussing over him like a hen with one chick. Blake *was* tired after his first day of therapy, and he let her coddle him. Though Dione had planned to have another session of exercise and massage, she let it go rather than fight a battle to do it. Tomorrow...well, tomorrow would be another story.

Richard arrived for dinner, a practice that Alberta had told Dione was the usual whenever Serena came over, which was every day. He watched silently as Serena hovered anxiously over Blake, and though Richard had the original poker face, Dione sensed that he wasn't happy with the situation. After dinner, while Serena got Blake settled in his study, Dione took the opportunity to speak privately to Richard.

They went out to the patio and sat on one of the benches that were scattered around. Dione looked up at the countless stars that were visible in the clear desert night. "I'm having a problem with Serena," she said without preamble.

He sighed. "I know. I've had a problem with her since Blake had his accident. I understand how she feels, but it's still driving me crazy."

"He said something today about raising her."

"Practically. Serena was thirteen when their mother died, and it was quite a shock to her. It was weeks before she could bear for Blake to be out of her sight; it must've seemed to her as if everyone she loved was dying. First her father, then her mother. She was especially close to her mother. I know that she's terrified something will happen to Blake, but at the same time I can't help resenting it."

"'Forsaking all others,'" Dione quoted, a little sadly.

"Exactly. I want my wife back."

"Blake said that you don't pay any attention to her, that you're wrapped up in your work."

He rubbed the back of his neck with restless fingers. "I have a lot of work to do, with Blake like he is. My God, what I wouldn't give to go home to just a little of the tender loving care that she smothers Blake with every day!"

"I spoke to Alberta about having the locks on the doors changed, but the more I think about it, the more I think it isn't such a good idea," she confessed. "Blake would be furious if anyone locked his sister out of his house. The problem is, I can't keep him on a schedule if she keeps interrupting."

"I'll see what I can do," he said doubtfully. "But any suggestion that will keep her away from Blake will go over like an outbreak of plague." He looked at her, and his teeth suddenly flashed white as he grinned. "You must have the steadiest nerves I've ever seen. Was it interesting today?"

"It had its moments," she replied, laughing a little. "He threw his breakfast at me."

Richard laughed aloud. "I wish I could've seen that! Blake's always had a hot temper, but for the past year he's been so depressed that you couldn't make him angry if you tried all day. It would've been like old times if I had been here to see him.''

''I hope I can get him to the point where he doesn't need to be angry,'' she said. ''I'm certain that he'll progress more rapidly if we aren't interrupted. I'm relying on you to think of something that'll keep Serena occupied.''

''If I could, I'd have used it before now,'' he said in disgust. ''Short of kidnapping her, I can't think of anything that will work.''

''Then why don't you?''

''What?''

''Kidnap her. Take her on a second honeymoon. Whatever it takes.''

''The second honeymoon sounds good,'' he admitted. ''But there's no way I can get free until Blake returns to work and takes over again. Any more ideas?''

''I'm afraid you'll have to think of something on your own. I don't know her that well. But I need privacy to work with Blake.''

''Then you'll have it,'' he promised after a moment's thought. ''I don't know what I'll do, but I'll keep her away as much as I can. Unless Blake's completely dead, it shouldn't take him long to realize that he'd rather have you fussing over him than his sister, anyway.''

At the obvious admiration in his voice, Dione shifted uncomfortably. She was aware of her looks, but at the same time she didn't want anyone to comment on them. Blake was her patient; it was out of the question for her to become involved with him in any sort of sexual relationship. Not only was it against her professional ethics, it was impossible for her. She no longer woke up in the middle of the night trying desperately to scream, her throat constricted by sheer terror, and she wasn't going to do anything to reawaken those nightmares. She'd put the horror behind her, where it had to stay.

Sensing her unease, Richard said, ''Dione?'' His voice was low, puzzled. ''Is something wrong?'' He put his hand on her arm, and she jumped as if she'd been stung, unable to bear the touch. He got to his feet, alarmed by her action. ''Dione?'' he asked again.

''I...I'm sorry,'' she murmured, wrapping her arms tightly around herself in an effort to control the trembling that had seized her. "I can't explain.... I'm sorry—"

"But what's wrong?" he demanded, reaching out his hand to her again, and she drew back sharply, jumping to her feet.

She knew that she couldn't explain, but neither could she stand there any longer. "Good night," she said rapidly, and walked away from him. She entered the house and almost bumped into Serena, who was stepping out onto the patio.

"There you are," she said. "Blake's gone to bed; he was so tired."

"Yes, I thought he would be," Dione said, gathering her composure enough to answer Serena evenly. Suddenly she felt very tired, too, and she was unable to stifle a yawn. "I'm sorry," she said. "It's been a long day."

Serena gave her an odd, considering look. "Then Richard and I will be leaving; I don't want to keep you up. I'll see Blake tomorrow."

"I'll be increasing his exercises tomorrow," Dione informed her, taking the opportunity to let Serena know that her presence would hinder rather than help. "It would be better if you waited until late afternoon, say after four."

"But that's too much!" Serena gasped. "He isn't strong enough!"

"At this point, I'm doing most of the work," Dione reassured her dryly. "But I'll be careful not to let him do too much."

If Serena heard the sarcasm that Dione couldn't quite suppress, she didn't let on. Instead she nodded. "I see," she said coldly. "Very well. I'll see Blake tomorrow afternoon."

Well, will wonders never cease, Dione thought wryly to herself as she made her way upstairs. All she'd had to do was mention that Blake would be busy, and though Serena hadn't been happy with the situation, she'd agreed to it.

After she'd gotten ready for bed, she tapped lightly on Blake's door; when she didn't hear an answer she opened the door just enough to peek inside. He was sound asleep, lying on his back, his head rolled against his shoulder. With only the light from the hallway on him, he looked younger, the lines of suffering not visible now.

Quietly she closed the door and returned to her room. She was tired, so tired that her limbs ached, but after she was in bed she found that sleep eluded her. She knew why, and lay awake staring at the ceiling, knowing that she might not sleep at all that night. Such a silly, trivial thing...just because Richard had touched her.

Yet it wasn't trivial, and she knew it. She might have pushed the nightmare away, she might have restructured her life completely, but her past was hers, a part of her, and it hadn't been trivial. Rape wasn't trivial. Since that night she hadn't been able to bear for anyone to touch her. She'd worked out a compromise with herself, satisfying her human need for warmth and touching by working with her patients, touching them, but she could bear the contact only as long as she was the one in control.

On the surface she had recovered completely; she had built a wall between who she was now and who she had been then, never dwelling on what had happened, literally forcing herself to gather together the shattered pieces of her life and, with fierce concentration and willpower, actually mending the pieces into a stronger fabric. She could laugh and enjoy life. More importantly, she had learned how to respect herself, which had been the hardest task of all.

But she couldn't tolerate a man's touch.

That night had effectively prevented her from marrying and having a family. Since that part of life was denied her, she ignored it, and never cried for what might have been. Instead she became a vagabond of sorts, traveling around the country and helping other people. While she was on a case she had an intense relationship full of love and caring, but without any sexual overtones. She loved her patients, and, inevitably, they loved her...while it lasted. They became her family, until the day when it was over and she left them with a smile on her face, ready to continue on to her next case and her next "family."

She had wondered, when she began her training, if she would ever be able to work with a man at all. The problem worried her until she decided that, if she couldn't, she would be handicapping her career terribly and made up her mind to do what was necessary. The first time she worked with a man she'd had to grit her teeth and use all her considerable determination to make herself touch him, but after a few minutes she had realized that a man who needed therapy obviously wasn't in any shape to be attacking her. Men were human beings who needed help, just like everyone else.

She preferred working with children, though. They loved so freely, so wholeheartedly. A child's touch was the one touch she could tolerate; she had learned to enjoy the feel of little arms going about her neck in a joyous hug. If there was one regret that sometimes refused to go away, it was the regret that she would never have children of her own. She controlled it by channeling extra devotion into her efforts for the children she worked with, but deep inside her was the need to have someone of her own, someone who belonged to her and who she belonged to, a part of herself.

Suddenly a muffled sound caught her attention, and she lifted her head from the pillow, waiting to see if it was repeated. Blake? Had he called out?

There was nothing but silence now, but she couldn't rest until she had made certain that he was all right. Getting out of bed, she slipped on her robe and walked silently to the room next door. Opening the door enough to look inside, she saw him lying in the same position he'd been in before. She was about to leave when he tried to roll onto his side, and when his legs didn't cooperate, he made the same sound she'd heard before, a half sigh, half grunt.

Did no one ever think to help him change his position? she wondered, gliding silently into the room on her bare feet. If he'd been lying on his back for two years, no wonder he had the temperament of a water buffalo.

She didn't know if he were awake or not; she didn't think so. Probably he was just trying to change positions as people do naturally during sleep. The light in the hallway wasn't on now, since everyone was in bed, and in the dim starlight coming through the glass doors she couldn't see well enough to decide. Perhaps, if he were still asleep, she could gently adjust his position without his ever waking up. It was something she did for most of her patients, a gesture of concern that they usually never realized.

First she touched his shoulder lightly, just placing her hand on him and letting his subconscious become accustomed to the touch. After a moment she applied a little pressure and he obeyed it, trying to roll to his right side, facing her. Gently, slowly, she helped him, moving his legs so they didn't hold him back. With a soft sigh he burrowed his face into the pillow, his breathing becoming deeper as he relaxed.

Smiling, she pulled the sheet up over his shoulder and returned to her room.

Blake wasn't like her other patients. Still lying awake over an hour later, she tried to decide why she was so determined to make him walk again. It wasn't just her normal devotion to a patient; in some way she didn't yet understand, it was important to her personally that he once again become the man he had been. He had been such a strong man, a man so vibrantly alive that he was the center of attention wherever he went. She *knew* that. She had to restore him to that.

He was so near to death. Richard had been correct in saying that he wouldn't live another year the way he was. Blake had been willing himself to die. She had gotten his attention that morning with her shock tactics, but she had to keep it until he could actually see himself progressing, until he realized that he could recover. She would never be able to forgive herself if she failed him.

She finally slept for about two hours, rising before dawn with a restless anticipation driving her. She would have loved to run on the beach, but Phoenix didn't have a beach, and she didn't know the grounds well enough to go trotting around them in the dark. For all she knew Blake had attack dogs patrolling at night. But despite her lack of sleep she was brimming with energy. She tried to burn off some of it by doing a brisk routine of exercises, but the shower she took afterward so refreshed her that she felt she was ready to tackle the world. Well, at least Blake Remington!

It was even earlier than it had been the morning before when she gave in to her enthusiasm and bounded into his room, snapping on the light as she did, because it was still dark.

"Good morning," she chirped.

He was still on his side; he opened one blue eye, surveyed her with an expression of horror, then uttered an explicit word that would have gotten his mouth washed out with soap if he'd been younger. Dione grinned at him.

"Are you ready to start?" she asked innocently.

"Hell, no!" he barked. "Lady, it's the middle of the night!"

"Not quite. It's almost dawn."

"*Almost?* How close to almost?"

"In just a few minutes," she soothed, then ruined it by laughing as she threw the covers off him. "Don't you want to see the sunrise?"

"No!"

"Don't be such a spoilsport," she coaxed, swinging his legs off the bed. "Watch the sunrise with me."

"I don't want to watch the sunrise, with you or anyone else," he snarled. "I want to sleep!"

"You've been asleep for hours, and you don't want to pass this sunrise up; it's going to be a special one."

"What makes this sunrise so special? Does it mark the beginning of the day you're going to torture me to death?"

"Only if you *don't* watch it with me," she promised him cheerfully, catching his hand and urging him upright. She helped him into the wheelchair and covered him with a blanket, knowing that the air would feel cool to him. "Where's the best place to watch it from?" she asked.

"By the pool," he grunted, rubbing his face with both hands and mumbling the words through his fingers. "You're crazy, lady; a certified lunatic if I've ever seen one."

She smoothed his tousled hair with her fingers, smiling down at him tenderly. "Oh, I don't know about that," she murmured. "Didn't you sleep well last night?"

"Of course I did!" he snapped. "You had me so tired I couldn't hold my head up!" As soon as the words left his mouth a sheepish expression crossed his face. "All right, so it was the best night I've had in two years," he admitted, grudgingly, it was true, but at least he said it.

"See what a little therapy can do for you?" she teased, then changed the subject before he could flare up at her again. "You'll have to lead the way to the pool; I don't want to go through the courtyard, since the workers have put so much of their equipment there. It could be tricky in the dark.''

He wasn't enthusiastic, but he put the chair in motion and led her through the silent house to the rear entrance. As they circled around the back to the pool, a bird chirped a single, liquid note in greeting of the new day, and his head lifted at the sound.

Had it been two years since he'd heard a bird sing?

Sitting beside the pool, with the quiet ripple of the water making its own music, they silently watched the first graying of dawn; then at last the first piercing ray of the sun shot over the rim of the mountains. There were no clouds to paint the sky in numberless hues of pink and gold, only the clear, clear blue sky and the white-gold sun, but the utter serenity of the new day made the scene as precious as the most glamorous sunrise she'd ever seen. As fast as that, the day began to warm, and he pushed the blanket down from his shoulders.

''I'm hungry,'' he announced, a prosaic concern after the long silence they had shared.

She looked at him and chuckled, then rose from her cross-legged position on the concrete. ''I can see how much you appreciate the finer things in life,'' she said lightly.

''If you insist on getting me up at midnight, naturally I'm hungry by the time dawn rolls around! Am I getting the same slop today that I had yesterday morning?''

''You are,'' she said serenely. ''A nutritious, high-protein breakfast, just what you need to put weight on you.''

''Which you then try your damnedest to beat off of me,'' he retorted.

She laughed at him, enjoying their running argument. ''You just wait,'' she promised. ''By this time next week you're going to think that yesterday was nothing!''

Chapter 4

Dione lay awake, watching the patterns of light that the new moon was casting on the white ceiling. Richard had worked miracles and informed her at dinner that night that the gym was now ready for use, but her problem was with Blake. Unaccountably he'd become withdrawn and depressed again. He ate what Alberta put before him, and he lay silent and uncomplaining while Dione exercised his legs, and that was all wrong. Therapy wasn't something for a patient to passively accept, as Blake was doing. He could lie there and let her move his legs, but when they started working in the gym and in the pool, he'd have to actively participate.

He wouldn't talk to her about what was bothering him. She knew exactly when it had happened, but she couldn't begin to guess what had triggered it. They had been sniping at each other while she gave him a massage before beginning the exercises, and all of a sudden his eyes had gotten that blank, empty look, and he'd been unresponsive to any of her gibes since then. She didn't think it was anything she'd said; her teasing that day had been lighthearted, because of his greatly improved spirits.

Turning her head to read the luminous dial of the clock, she saw that it was after midnight. As she had done every night, she got up to check on Blake. She hadn't heard the sounds that he usually made when he tried to turn over, but she'd been preoccupied with her thoughts.

As soon as she entered his room she saw that his legs had that awkward, slightly twisted look that meant he'd already tried to shift his position. Gently she put her left hand on his shoulder and her right on his legs, ready to move him.

"Dione?"

His quiet, uncertain voice startled her, and she leaped back. She'd been so intent on his legs that she hadn't noticed his open eyes, though the moonlight that played across the bed was bright enough for her to see him.

"I thought you were asleep," she murmured.

"What were you doing?"

"Helping you to roll over on your side. I do this every night; this is the first time you've been disturbed by it."

"No, I was already awake." Curiosity entered his tone as he shifted his shoulders restlessly. "Do you mean you come in here in the middle of every night and roll me around?"

"You seem to sleep better on your side," she said by way of explanation.

He gave a short, bitter laugh. "I sleep better on my stomach, or at least I did before. I haven't slept on my stomach in two years now."

The quiet intimacy of the night, the moonlit room, made it seem as if they were the only two people on earth, and she was aware of a deep despair in him. Perhaps he felt a special closeness with her, too; perhaps now, with the darkness as a partial shield, he would talk to her and tell her what was bothering him. Without hesitation she sat down on the edge of the bed and pulled her nightgown snugly around her legs.

"Blake, what's wrong? Something's bothering you," she said softly.

"Bingo," he muttered. "Did you take psychology, too, when you were in training to be Superwoman?"

She ignored the cut and put her hand on his arm. "Please tell me.

Whatever it is, it's interfering with your therapy. The gym is ready for you, but you aren't ready for it.''

''I could've told you that. Look, this whole thing is a waste of time,'' he said, and she could almost feel the weariness in him, like a great stone weighing him down. ''You may feed me vitamins and rev up my circulation, but can you promise that I'll ever be exactly like I was before? Don't you understand? I don't want just 'improvement,' or any other compromise. If I can't be back, one hundred percent, the way I was before, then I'm not interested.''

She was silent. No, she couldn't honestly promise him that there wouldn't always be some impairment, a limp, difficulties that would be with him for the rest of his life. In her experience, the human body could do wonders in repairing itself, but the injuries it suffered always left traces of pain and healing in the tissue.

''Would it matter so much to you if you walked with a limp?'' she finally asked. ''I'm not the way I would like to be, either. Everyone has a weakness, but not everyone just gives up and lets himself rot because of it, either. What if your position were reversed with say, Serena? Would you want her to just lie there and slowly deteriorate into a vegetable? Wouldn't you want her to fight, to try as hard as she could to overcome the problem?''

He flung his forearm up to cover his eyes. ''You fight dirty, lady. Yes, I'd want Serena to fight. But I'm not Serena, and my life isn't hers. I'd never really realized, before the accident, how important the quality of my life was. The things I did were wild and dangerous, but, my God, I was alive! I've never been a nine-to-five man; I'd rather be dead, even though I know that millions of people are perfectly happy and content with that kind of routine. That's fine for them, but it's not *me*.''

''Would a limp prevent you from doing all those things again?'' she probed. ''You can still jump out of airplanes, or climb mountains. You can still fly your own jets. Is the rhythm of your walk so important to you that you're willing to die because of it?''

''Why do you keep saying that?'' he asked sharply, jerking his arm down and glaring at her. ''I don't remember heading my wheelchair down the stairs, if that's what you're thinking.''

"No, but you're killing yourself just as surely in a different way. You're letting your body die of neglect. Richard was desperate when he tracked me down in Florida; he told me that you wouldn't live another year the way you were going, and after seeing you, I agree with him."

He lay in silence, staring up at the ceiling that he had already looked at for more hours than she could imagine. She wanted to gather him into her arms and soothe him as she did the children she worked with; he was a man, but in a way he was as lost and frightened as any child. Confused suddenly by the unfamiliar need to touch him, she folded her hands tightly in her lap.

"What's your weakness?" he asked. "You said that everyone has one. Tell me what torments you, lady."

The question was so unexpected that she couldn't stop the welling of pain, and a shudder shook her entire body. His weakness was obvious, there for everyone to see in his limp, wasted legs. Hers was also a wound that had almost been fatal, for all that it couldn't be seen. There had been a dark time when death had seemed like the easiest way out, a soft cushion for a battered mind and body that had taken too much abuse. But there had been, deep inside her, a bright and determined spark of life that had kept her from even the attempt, as if she knew that to take the first step would be one step too many. She had fought, and lived, and healed her wounds as best she could.

"What's wrong?" he jeered softly. "You can pry into everyone else's secrets, so why can't you share a few of your own? What are your weaknesses? Do you shoplift for kicks? Sleep with strangers? Cheat on your taxes?"

Dione shuddered again, her hands clenched so tightly that her knuckles were white. She couldn't tell him, not all of it, yet in a way he had a right to know some of her pain. She had already witnessed a lot of his, knew what he thought, knew his longing and despair. None of her other patients had demanded so much from her, but Blake wasn't like the others. He was asking for more than he knew, just as she was asking him for superhuman effort. If she put him off now, she knew in her bones that he wouldn't respond to her anymore.

His recovery depended on her, on the trust she could foster between them.

She was shaking visibly, her entire body caught up in the tremors that shook her from head to foot. She knew that the bed was vibrating, knew that he could feel it. His brows snapped together and he said uncertainly, "Dione? Listen, I—"

"I'm illegitimate," she grounded out, her teeth chattering. She was panting with the effort it took her to speak at all, and she felt a film of perspiration break out on her body. She sucked in her breath on a sob that shuddered through her; then with a grinding force of will she held her body still. "I don't know who my father was; my mother didn't even know his name. She was drunk, he was there, and presto! She had a baby. Me. She didn't want me. Oh, she fed me, I suppose, since I'm alive to tell about it. But she never hugged me, never kissed me, never told me that she loved me. In fact, she went out of her way to tell me that she hated me, hated having to take care of me, hated even seeing me. Except for the welfare check she got for me, she would probably have dumped me in a trash can and left me."

"You don't know that!" he snapped, heaving himself up on one elbow. She could tell that he was taken aback by the harsh bitterness in her voice, but now that she had started, she couldn't stop. If it killed her, the poison had to spew out now.

"She told me," she insisted flatly. "You know how kids are. I tried every way I knew how to make her love me. I couldn't have been more than three years old, but I can remember climbing up on chairs, then onto the cabinets so I could reach the whiskey bottle for her. Nothing worked, of course. I learned not to cry, because she slapped me if I cried. If she wasn't there, or if she was passed out drunk, I learned to eat whatever I could. Dry bread, a piece of cheese, it didn't matter. Sometimes there wasn't anything to eat, because she'd spent all the check on whiskey. If I waited long enough she'd go off with some man and come back with a little money, enough to get by until the next check, or the next man."

"Dee, stop it!" he ordered harshly, putting his hand on her arm and shaking her. Wildly she jerked away from him.

"You wanted to know!" she breathed, her lungs aching with the effort they were making to draw air into her constricted chest. "So you can hear it!... Whenever I made the mistake of bothering her, which didn't take much, she slapped me. Once she threw a whiskey bottle at me. I was lucky that time, because all I got was a little cut on my temple, though she was so angry at the wasted whiskey that she beat me with her shoe. Do you know what she told me, over and over? 'You're just a bastard, and nobody loves a bastard!' Over and over, until finally I had to believe it. I know the exact day when I learned to believe it. My seventh birthday. I'd started to go to school, you see, and I knew then that birthdays were supposed to be something special. Birthdays were when your parents gave you presents to show you how much they loved you. I woke up and went running into her room, sure that today was the day that she would finally love me. She slapped me for waking her up and shoved me into the closet. She kept me locked in the closet all day long. That's what she thought of my birthday, you see. She hated the sight of me."

She was bent over, her body tight with pain, but her eyes were dry and burning. "I was living in the streets by the time I was ten," she whispered, her strength beginning to leave her. "It was safer than home. I don't know what happened to her. I went back one day, and the place was empty."

Her rasping breath was the only sound in the room. He lay as if he had been turned to stone, his eyes burning on her. Dione could have collapsed, she was suddenly so tired. With an effort she drew herself upright. "Any more questions?" she asked dully.

"Just one," he said, and her body clenched painfully, but she didn't protest. She waited, wondering in exhaustion what he would ask of her next.

"Were you eventually adopted?"

"No," she breathed, closing her eyes, swaying a little. "I eventually wound up in an orphanage, and it was as good a place as any. I had food, and a place to sleep, and I was able to go to school regularly. I was too old for adoption, and no one wanted me as a foster child. My looks were too odd, I suppose." Moving like an old woman, she got to her feet and slowly left the room, knowing that the air was still heavy with questions that he wanted to ask, but she'd remembered enough for one night. No matter what she had accomplished, no matter how many years had passed since she was a lonely, bewildered child, the lack of her mother's love was still an emptiness that hadn't been filled. A mother's love was the basis of every child's life, and the absence of it had left her crippled inside just as surely as the accident had crippled Blake's legs.

Not surprisingly, she fell facedown on her bed and slept heavily, without dreaming, to awaken promptly when the alarm went off. She had learned, over the years, how to function even when she felt as if a part of her had been murdered, and she did so now. At first she had to force herself to go through the regular routine, but in only a moment the hard self-discipline had taken over, and she shoved the crisis of the night away. She would *not* let it drag her down! She had a job to do, and she'd do it.

Perhaps something of her determination was written on her face when she entered Blake's bedroom, because he promptly raised his hands and said mildly, "I surrender."

She stopped in her tracks and regarded him quizzically. He was smiling a little, his pale, thin face weary, but no longer locked in a mask of detachment. "But I haven't even attacked yet," she protested. "You're taking all the fun out of it."

"I know when I'm outgunned." He grimaced and admitted, "I don't see how I can give up without at least trying again. You didn't give up, and I've never been a man to back down from a challenge."

The hard knot of apprehension that had been tied in her stomach since he'd lapsed into depression slowly eased, then relaxed completely. Her spirits soared, and she gave him a blinding smile. With his cooperation, she felt that she could do anything.

At first he was capable of very little with the weights. Even the smaller ones were too much for him, though he kept gritting his teeth and trying to continue even when she wanted him to stop. *Stubborn* was too mild a word to describe him. He was hell-bent and determined to push himself to the limits of his endurance, which unfortunately wasn't far. It always took a long session in the whirlpool afterward to ease the pain from his tortured muscles, but he kept at it, even knowing that he was going to have to pay with pain.

To her relief he asked no more questions and in no way referred to what she'd told him of her childhood. Because of the extra demand he was making on his body, he was always sound asleep when she checked on him at night, so there were no repeats.

Over Serena's protests Dione also began giving him therapy in the pool. Serena was terrified that he'd drown, since his legs were useless and he obviously couldn't kick, but Blake himself overruled her objections. He'd said that he liked challenges, and he wasn't backing off from this one. With his engineering expertise, he designed and directed the construction of a system of braces and pulleys that enabled Dione to lower him into the pool and hoist him out when the session was ended, something that he would soon be able to do for himself.

One morning, after she'd been here a little over two weeks, Dione watched him as he devoured the breakfast that Alberta had prepared. Already it seemed that he was gaining weight. His face had fleshed out and wasn't as gray as it had been. He'd burned a little during the first few days he'd been in the sun, but he hadn't peeled, and now the light tan he'd acquired made his blue eyes seem even bluer.

"What're you staring at?" he demanded as Alberta removed the plate before him and replaced it with a bowl of fresh strawberries in cream.

"You're gaining weight," Dione told him with immense satisfaction.

"Shouldn't wonder," Alberta snorted as she left the room. "He's eating like a horse."

Blake scowled at her, but dipped his spoon into the bowl and lifted a plump strawberry. His white teeth sank into the red fruit; then his tongue captured the juice that stained his lips. "That's what you wanted, isn't it?" he demanded grumpily. "To fatten me up?"

She smiled and didn't reply, watching as he demolished the fruit. Just as he was finishing Angela glided in with a telephone, which she placed on the table before him. After plugging it in, she gave him a shy smile and left.

Blake sat there, staring at the phone. Dione hid a grin. "I think that means you have a call," she prompted.

He looked relieved. "Good. I was afraid you wanted me to eat it."

She chuckled and got to her feet. As he lifted the receiver and put it to his ear, she touched his shoulder lightly and murmured, "I'll be in the gym; come down when you're finished."

He met her eyes and nodded, already embroiled in conversation. She heard enough to know that he was talking to Richard, and just the thought of Richard was enough to pucker her brow in a line of worry.

Serena had been very good after that first day; she'd come to see Blake only in the late afternoon, when Dione had completed her schedule for the day. She'd also learned not to wait until too late to arrive, or Blake would already be asleep. Most nights, Richard also arrived for dinner.

Richard was a witty, entertaining man, with a dry sense of humor and a repertoire of jokes that often had her chuckling in her seat, but which couldn't be repeated when Blake or Serena asked what was so funny.

Dione couldn't say that Richard had been less than a gentleman. In no way had he said or done anything that could be termed suggestive. It was just that she could read the deepening admiration in his eyes, sense the growing gentleness in the way he treated her. She wasn't the only one who felt that perhaps Richard was becoming too fond of her; Serena was subtle, but she watched her husband sharply when he was talking with Dione. In a way, Dione was relieved; it meant that Serena was at least paying attention to her husband. But she didn't want complications of that sort, especially when there was nothing to it.

She didn't feel that she could say anything to Richard about it either. How could she scold him when he'd been nothing but polite? He loved his wife, she was sure. He liked and admired his brother-in-law. But still, he responded to Dione in a way that she knew she hadn't mistaken.

She'd been the object of unwanted attention before, but this was the first time that attention hadn't been obvious. She had no idea how to handle it. She knew that Richard would never try to force himself on her, but Serena was jealous. Part of Dione, the deeply feminine part of her, was even flattered by his regard. If Serena had been giving her husband the attention he deserved, none of this would be happening.

But they weren't important, she told herself. She couldn't let them be important to her. Only Blake mattered. He was coming out of the prison of his disability, more and more revealing himself as the man he'd been before the accident. In another month she hoped to have him standing. Not walking, but standing. Letting his legs get used to supporting the weight of his body again. What she was doing now was dealing with the basics, restoring him to health and building his strength up enough that he would be able to stand when she demanded it of him.

She ran hot water in a plastic container and set the flask of oil that she used down in it to warm it for the massage that she always gave him before he went in the pool, in an effort to protect him from any chill. Not that a chill was likely in the hundred-plus-degree heat of a summer day in Phoenix, she thought wryly, but he was so thin, still so weakened, that she didn't take any chances with him. Besides, he seemed to enjoy the feel of the warm oil being massaged into him, and he had little enough joy in his life.

She was restless, and she prowled aimlessly about the converted game room, pausing to stretch her body. She needed a good workout to release some of her energy, she decided, and positioned herself on the weight bench.

She liked lifting weights. Her aim was strength, not bulk, and the program that she followed was designed with that in mind. For Blake, she was altering the program enough to build up the bulk of his muscles without pumping him up like a Mr. Universe. Carefully regulating her breathing, concentrating on what she was doing, she began her sets. Up, down. Up, down.

She finished her leg sets and adjusted the system of pulleys and weights to what she wanted for her arms. Puffing, she began again. The demand she was making on her muscles reached a plateau that was almost pleasure. Again. Again.

"You damned cheat!" The roar startled her, and she jerked upright, alarm skittering across her features. Confused, she stared at Blake. He sat in his wheelchair, just inside the door, his face dark red and contorted with fury.

"What?" she spluttered.

He pointed at the weights. "You're a weight lifter!" he bellowed, so furious that he was shaking. "You little cheat. You knew the day you beat me at arm wrestling that you'd win! Hell, how many men *could* beat you?"

She blushed. "Not everyone," she said with modesty, which seemed to make him even angrier.

"I can't believe it!" He was yelling, getting louder and louder. "Knowing how it would make me feel that a woman could beat me at arm wrestling, you made a bet on it anyway, and you *rigged* it!"

"I never said that I wasn't good at it," she pointed out, trying to keep the laughter out of her voice. He looked wonderful! If sheer rage could have put him back on his feet, he'd have been walking right then. A giggle escaped her control, and at the sound of it he began pounding his fist on the arm of the wheelchair; unfortunately he was pounding on the controls, and the chair began jumping back and forth like a bronc trying to rid itself of an unwanted rider.

Dione couldn't help it; she gave up even trying to keep a straight face and laughed until tears ran down her face. She howled. She beat the weight bench with her fist in mute mockery of the way he'd pounded the wheelchair controls; she clutched her arms across her stomach, gasping for breath, and every new eruption of rage from him sent her off into renewed paroxysms.

"Stop laughing!" he thundered, his voice booming off the walls. "Sit down! We'll see who wins this time!"

She was so weak that she had to haul herself to the massage table where he'd propped his elbow and was waiting for her with a face like doom. Still giggling, she collapsed against the table.

"This isn't fair!" she protested, putting her hand in his grip. "I'm not ready. Wait until I stop laughing."

"Was it fair when you let me think I was wrestling a frail, *normal* woman?" he seethed.

"I'm perfectly normal!" she hooted. "You got beat fair and square, and you know it!"

"I don't know any such thing! You cheated, and I want a re-match."

"All right, all right. Just give me a minute." Quickly she squelched the remaining laughter that wanted to bubble out and flexed her hand in his. She began tightening her muscles. "Okay. I'm ready."

"On the count of three," he said. "One...twothree!"

It was fortunate that she was ready for the quick count he gave. She threw her entire body into the effort, realizing that the extra weight he'd gained and the few days of workouts that he'd had with the weights had increased his strength. Not by much, perhaps, but with the added impetus of his anger and the laughter that had weakened her, perhaps it would be enough to win the match for him.

"You cheated!" she accused in turn, gritting her teeth as she bore down with all her strength against the force of his arm.

"You deserved it!"

They panted and huffed and grunted for several minutes, and sweat began to run down their faces. They were close together, almost face to face, as their locked arms strained harder and harder. Dione groaned aloud. His initial burst of strength had been greater than hers, but not enough to make a quick end to it. Now it was a matter of stamina, and she thought that she could outlast him. She could have let him win, to soothe his ego, but it wasn't in her to trick him that way. If he won, it would be despite everything she could do.

Something of her determination must have shown in her face, because he growled, "Damn it, this is the part where you're supposed to let me win!"

She puffed, sucking in much-needed oxygen. "If you want to beat me, you're going to have to work for it," she panted. "I don't *let* anybody win!"

"But I'm a patient!"

"You're an opportunist!"

He ground his teeth and pushed harder. Dione ducked her head, a movement that placed her head in the hollow of his shoulder, and counteracted his move with everything she had. Slowly, slowly, she felt his arm begin to move back. The rush of strength that winning always gave her zoomed through her veins, and with a cry she slammed his arm down flat on the table.

Their panting breaths filled the room, and her heartbeat thundered in her ears like the hoofbeats of a galloping horse. She was still slumped against him, her head on his shoulder, and she could feel the pounding of his heart throughout his entire body. Slowly she pushed herself off him, letting her weight fall against the table. Like a rag doll, he slumped forward onto the table, too, his color fading almost to normal as he sucked in deep breaths of air.

After a moment he propped his chin on his folded arm and regarded her out of dark blue eyes that still held storm clouds.

Dione drew a deep breath, staring at him. "You're beautiful when you're angry," she told him.

He blinked in astonishment. Stunned, he stared at her for a long, long minute that hung suspended in time; then an odd little gurgle sounded in his throat. He gulped. The next sound was a full-throated roar of laughter. He threw his head back and clutched helplessly at his stomach. Dione began to giggle again.

He was rolling, howling with mirth, rocking back and forth. The abused controls of the wheelchair caught the impact of his fist again, and this time the jerky movements combined with his back and forth motion to pitch him out on his face. It was lucky that he wasn't hurt, because Dione couldn't have stopped laughing if her life had depended on it. She fell off her stool to lie beside him, drawing her legs up to her stomach. "Stop it! Stop it!" she shrieked as tears rolled down her face.

"Stop it! Stop it!" he mimicked, catching her and digging his fingers into her ribs.

In all her life, Dione had never been tickled. She'd never known what it was to play. She was so startled by the unbearably ticklish sensation of his fingers on her ribs that she couldn't even be alarmed at his touch. She was screaming her head off, rolling helplessly in an effort to get away from those tormenting fingers, when another voice intruded on them.

"Blake!" Serena didn't stop to interpret the scene before her. She saw her brother on the floor, she heard Dione screaming and she immediately assumed that a terrible accident had happened. She added her despairing cry to the din and dove for him, her desperate hands catching him and rolling him to her.

Though Serena wasn't supposed to be there during the day, Dione was grateful to her for the interruption. Shakily she rolled away from Blake and sat up, only then realizing that Serena was almost hysterical.

"Serena! There's nothing wrong," Blake was saying strongly, deliberately, having sensed his sister's state of mind before Dione had. "We were just playing around. I'm not hurt. I'm not hurt," he repeated.

Serena calmed down, her white face regaining some of its color. Blake pushed himself to a sitting position and reached for the blanket that usually covered his legs. As he covered himself, he demanded harshly, "What're you doing here? You know you're not supposed to come during the day."

She looked as if he'd slapped her, drawing back sharply and staring at him with a stunned look in her eyes. Dione bit her lip. She knew why he'd spoken so sharply. He'd become used to her seeing him, and in her presence he could sit around wearing nothing but a pair of briefs or gym shorts, but he was still sensitive about his body with everyone else, Serena most of all.

Serena recovered, lifting her chin proudly. "I thought this was supposed to be therapy, not play period." She lashed out as sharply as he had, and rose to her feet. "Excuse me for interrupting; I had a reason for seeing you, but it can wait."

Her outraged temper was evident in every line of her straight back as she marched out the door, ignoring Blake's rueful call.

"Damn!" he said softly. "Now I'll have to apologize. It's just so awkward explaining...."

Dione chuckled. "She's definitely your sister, isn't she?"

He eyed her warningly. "Don't be acting so cocky, young lady. I've found the weakness in your fortress, now. You're as ticklish as a baby!"

She prudently scooted out of his reach. "If you tickle me again I'll sneak up on you when you're asleep and pour ice water on you."

"You would, too, you wretch," he snorted, and glared at her. "I want a rematch in two weeks."

"You're a glutton for punishment, aren't you?" she asked gleefully, getting to her feet and contemplating the problem of getting him from the floor to the table.

"Don't even try it," he ordered, seeing the speculative look on her face as she looked at him. She smiled sheepishly, because she'd been about to try lifting him herself. "Call Miguel to help you."

Miguel was Blake's chauffeur, handyman and, Dione suspected, bodyguard. He was short and lean, as hard as rock, and his dark face was marred by a scar that puckered his left cheek. No one had said how Blake had acquired his services, and Dione wasn't sure she wanted to know. She didn't even know where Miguel was from; it could have been any Latin nation. She did know that he spoke Portuguese as well as Spanish and English, so she suspected that he was from South America, but again, no one volunteered the information and she didn't ask. It was enough that he was dedicated to Blake.

Miguel wasn't one for asking questions, either. If he was surprised to find his employer on the floor, none of that surprise was reflected on his face. Together he and Dione lifted Blake and put him on the table.

"Miguel, I need another contraption rigged for me in here like the one by the pool," Blake instructed. "We can bolt a bar across the ceiling, this way," he said, indicating the length of the room. "With the pulley arm swinging in any direction we want, and running the length of the bar, I can get myself up and down as I please."

Miguel studied the ceiling, getting in his mind exactly what Blake wanted. "No problem," he finally allowed. "Will tomorrow be soon enough?"

"If you can't do it any faster than that, I suppose it will."

"You're a brutal slave driver," Dione told him as she was massaging his back with the warm oil.

"I've been taking lessons from you," he murmured sleepily, burrowing his head deeper into the cradle of his arm. The comment earned him a pinch on his side, and he laughed. "One thing about it," he continued. "I haven't been bored since you bulldozed into my life."

Chapter 5

He was already awake the next morning when she went into his room; he was bending from the waist and rubbing his thighs and calves. She regarded him with satisfaction, glad that he was taking an active part in his recovery.

"I had a long talk with Serena last night," he grunted, not looking up from what he was doing.

"Good. I expect the apology was good for your soul," she said, slipping behind him and kneading his back and shoulders.

"She was upset. It seems Richard has been leaving again as soon as he takes her home at night, and she thinks he's seeing another woman."

Dione's fingers stilled. Was it possible? She hadn't thought him the type to sneak around. It seemed so tawdry, and Richard wasn't a tawdry man.

Blake swiveled his head around to look at her. "Serena thinks he's seeing you," he said bluntly.

She resumed the motion of her fingers. "What did you tell her?" she asked, trying to stay calm. She concentrated on the feel of his flesh under her hands, noting that he didn't feel as bony as he had at first.

"I told her that I'd find out and stop it if he was," he replied. "Don't look so innocent, because we both know that Richard's attracted to you. Hell, he'd have to be dead not to be. You're the type of woman who has men swarming around her like bees around a honey pot."

Richard had said much the same thing about Blake, she thought, and smiled sadly at how far they both were from the truth.

"I'm not seeing Richard," she said quietly. "Aside from the fact that he's married, when would I have time? I'm with you all day long, and I'm too tired at night to put forth the energy that sneaking around would take."

"Serena said that she saw you on the patio one night."

"She did. We were talking about you, not making love. I know that Richard's unhappy with Serena—"

"How do you know that?"

"I'm not blind. She's devoted the last two years to you and virtually ignored her husband, and naturally he resents it. Why do you think he was so determined to find a therapist for you? He wants you walking again so he can have his wife back." Perhaps she shouldn't have told him that, but it was time Blake realized that he'd been dominating their lives with his physical condition.

He sighed. "All right, I believe you. But just in case you start thinking how attractive Richard is, let me tell you now that the one thing I won't tolerate is for Serena to be hurt."

"She's a big girl, Blake. You can't run interference for her for the rest of her life."

"I can do it as long as she needs me, and as long as I'm able. When I think of how she was after our mother died…I swear, Dee, I think I'd kill to keep her from ever looking like that again."

At least she'd had a mother who loved her. The words were on Dione's lips, but she bit them back. It wasn't Serena's fault that Dione's mother hadn't been loving. Her burden of bitterness was her own, not something to be loaded onto someone else's shoulders.

She pushed it away. "Do you think he really is seeing someone else? In a way, I can't see it. He's so besotted with Serena that no one else registers."

"*You* register with him," Blake insisted.

"He's never said anything to me," Dione replied honestly, though she was still stretching the truth a little. "How do you know? Male intuition?"

"If you want to call it that," he murmured, leaning back against her as he tired. Her soft breasts supported his weight. "I'm still a man, even if I couldn't chase a turtle and catch it. I can look at you and see the same thing he sees. You're so damned beautiful, so soft and strong at the same time. If I could chase you, lady, you'd have the race of your life."

The soft words alarmed her in a way that was different from the panic she normally felt when faced with a prowling, hunting male. Her hands were still on his shoulders, and his weight was resting on her; his body was as familiar to her as her own, the texture of his skin, even the smell of him. It was as if he were a part of her, because she was building him, remaking him, shaping him into the gorgeous man he'd been before the accident. He was her creation.

She suddenly wanted to rest her cheek on his shaggy head, feel the silky texture of his hair. Instead she denied the impulse, because it was so foreign to her. Yet his head beckoned, and she moved her hand from his shoulder to touch the dark strands.

"You're beginning to look like a sheepdog," she told him, her voice a little breathless and tinged with the laughter that they shared so often now.

"Then cut it for me," he said lazily, letting his head find a comfortable position on her shoulder.

"You'd trust me to cut your hair?" she asked, startled.

"Of course. If I can trust you with my body, why not my hair?" he reasoned.

"Then let's do it now," she said, slapping his shoulder. "I'd like to see if you have ears. Come on, get off me."

A shudder rippled down him, and he turned his eyes to her, eyes as blue as the deepest sea, and as primal. She knew what he was thinking, but she turned her gaze away and refused to let the moment linger.

A nameless intimacy had enfolded them. She was jittery, yet she couldn't say that she was really frightened. It was...*odd,* and her forehead was furrowed with a pensive frown as she plied the scissors on his thick hair. He was a patient, and she'd learned not to be afraid of her patients. He'd gotten closer to her than she'd ever allowed anyone else to get, even the children who had tugged the most strongly at her heartstrings. He was the challenge of her career; he'd become so much to her, but he was still a man, and she couldn't understand why she didn't get that icy, sick feeling she normally got when a man got close to her. Blake could touch her, and she couldn't tolerate the touch of any other man.

Perhaps, she decided, it was because she knew that she was safe with him. As he'd pointed out, he wasn't in any condition to do any chasing. Sexually, he was as harmless as the children she'd hugged and comforted.

"You look like Michelangelo, agonizing over the final touches to a statue," he said provokingly. "Have you cut a big gap in my hair?"

"Of course not!" she protested, running her fingers through the unruly pelt. "I'm a very good barber, for your information. Would you like a mirror?"

He sighed blissfully. "No, I trust you. You can shave me now."

"Like heck I will!" With mock wrath she practically slapped the loose hair off his shoulders. "It's time for your session on the rack, so stop trying to stall!"

In the days that followed nothing else was said about the situation between Serena and Richard, and though the couple continued to have dinner with Blake and Dione, the coolness between them was obvious. Richard treated Dione with a warmth that never progressed beyond friendliness, though Dione was certain that Serena wasn't convinced that the situation between them was innocent. Blake watched everything with an eagle eye and kept Dione close by his side.

She understood his reasons for doing so, and as it suited her to be with him, she let him be as demanding of her company as he wanted. She liked being with him. As he grew stronger his rather devilish personality was coming out, and it took all her concentration to stay one step ahead of him. She had to play poker with him; she had to play chess with him; she had to watch football games with him. There were a million and one things that took his interest, and he demanded that she share them all. It was as if he'd been in a coma for two years and had come out of it determined to catch up on everything he'd missed.

He pushed himself harder than she ever would have. Because she could lift more weigh than he could, he worked for hours with the weights. Because she could swim longer and faster than he could, he pushed himself to do lap after lap, though he still couldn't use his legs. And every week they had a rematch at arm wrestling. It was their fifth match before he finally defeated her, and he was so jubilant that she let him have blueberry waffles for breakfast.

Still, she was nervous when she decided that it was time for him to begin using his legs. This was the crux of the entire program. If he couldn't see some progress now in his legs, she knew that he'd lose hope and sink into depression again.

She didn't tell him what she had planned. After he'd done his sets on the weight bench she got him back into the wheelchair and guided the chair over to the parallel bars that he would use to support himself while she reeducated his legs in what they were expected to do. He looked at the bars, then at her, his brows lifted in question.

"It's time for you to stop being so lazy," she said as casually as possible, though her heart was pounding so loudly it was a miracle he couldn't hear it. "On your feet."

He swallowed, his eyes moving from her to the bars, then back to her.

"This is it, huh? D day."

"That's right. It's no big deal. Just stand. No trying to walk. Let your legs get accustomed to holding your weight."

He set his jaw and reached out for the bars. Bracing his hands on them, he pulled himself out of the wheelchair.

The weight lifting came in handy as he pulled himself up, using only the strength in his shoulders and arms. Watching him, Dione noted the way his muscles bunched and played. He had real muscles now, not just skin over bone. He was still thin, too thin, but no longer did he have the physique of a famine victim. Even his legs had responded to the forced exercises she gave him every day by forming a layer of muscle.

He was pale, and sweat dripped down his face as Dione positioned his feet firmly under him. "Now," she said softly, "let your weight off your hands. Let your legs hold you. You may fall; don't worry about it. Everyone falls when he reaches this phase of therapy."

"I won't fall," he said grimly, throwing his head back and clenching his teeth. He was balancing himself with his hands, but his weight was on his feet. He groaned aloud. "You didn't say it would hurt!" he protested through his teeth.

Dione's head jerked up, her golden eyes firing with excitement. "Does it hurt?"

"Like hell! Hot needles—"

She let out a whoop of joy and reached for him, drawing back as she remembered his precarious balance. Unbidden, her eyes moistened. She hadn't cried since she was a child, but now she was so proud she was helpless against the tears that formed. Still, she blinked them back, though they shimmered like liquid gold between her black lashes as she offered him a tremulous smile. "You know what that means, don't you?"

"No, what?"

"That the nerves are working! It's all working! The massages, the exercises, the whirlpool...*your legs!* Don't you understand?" she shrieked, practically jumping up and down.

His head jerked around to her. All the color washed out of his face, leaving his eyes glowing like blue coals. "Say it!" he whispered. "Spell it out!"

"You're going to walk!" she screamed at him. Then she couldn't control the tears any longer and they trickled down her face, blurring her vision. She brushed them away with the back of her hand and gave a watery chuckle. "You're going to walk," she said again.

His face twisted, contorted by an agony of joy; he let go of the bars and reached for her, falling forward as his body pitched off-balance. Dione caught him, wrapping her arms tightly around him, but he was too heavy for her now, and she staggered and went down under his weight. He had both arms around her, and he buried his face in her neck. Her heart gave an enormous leap, her blood turned by icy terror into a sluggish river that barely moved. "No," she whispered, her mind suddenly blanking, and her hands moved to his shoulders to push him off.

There was an odd quivering to his shoulders. And there was a sound...it wasn't the same sound of her nightmares.

Then, like someone throwing a light switch and changing a room from dark to light, she knew that this was Blake, not Scott. Scott had hurt her; Blake never would. And the strange sound was the sound of his weeping.

He was crying. He couldn't stop the tears of joy any more than she'd been able to a moment before; the heaving sobs that tore out of him released two long years of torment and despair. "My God," he said brokenly. "My God."

It was like a dam bursting inside her. A lifetime of holding her hurts inside, of having no one to turn to for comfort, no one to hold her while *she* cried, was suddenly too much. A great searing pain in her chest rose into her throat and burst out in a choked, anguished cry.

Her body shuddered with the force of her sobs, and her enormous golden eyes flooded with tears. For the first time in her life she was being held close in someone's arms while she cried, and it was too much. She couldn't bear the bittersweet pain and joy of it, yet at the same time she felt as if something had changed inside her. The simple act of weeping together had torn down the wall that kept her isolated from the rest of the world. She had existed on only a surface level, never letting anything get too close to her, never letting herself feel too deeply, never letting anyone know the woman behind the mask, because the woman had been hurt so badly and feared that it could happen again. She'd developed quite a defense mechanism, but Blake had somehow managed to short circuit it.

He was different from every other man she knew. He was capable of loving; he was at once a laughing daredevil and a hard-hitting businessman. But most of all, he needed her. Other patients had needed her, but only as a therapist. Blake needed *her,* the woman she was, because only her personal strengths had enabled her to help him with her trained skills and knowledge. She couldn't remember anyone ever needing *her* before.

She cuddled him close to her, stunned by the slowly increasing warmth inside her that was gradually melting the frozen pain that had dominated her for so long. She wanted to weep some more, because she was both frightened and excited by her new freedom to touch and be touched. Her hand stroked his hair, her fingers lacing themselves in the silky waves, as his tears finally stopped and he lay sweetly, limply against her.

He lifted his head to look at her. He wasn't ashamed of the tears that wet his face and glittered in his blue eyes. Very gently he rubbed his wet cheek against hers, a subtle caress that mingled their happiness as well as their tears.

Then he kissed her.

It was a slow, wondering kiss, a gentle touch that sought but didn't pursue, a delicate tasting of her lips that lacked any aggressive, masculine need. She quivered in his arms, her hands automatically moving to his shoulders to shove him away if he progressed beyond the still-guarded borders of intimacy that she could accept. But he didn't try to deepen the kiss. He raised his mouth and instead touched his nose to hers, rolling his head back and forth in a light, brushing movement.

After a long moment he drew back slightly and let his gaze roam over her face with a certain curiosity. Dione couldn't look away from his eyes, watching the irises expand until they had almost swallowed the blue. What was he thinking? What caused that sudden flash of desperation that startled her, the shadow that crossed his face? His eyes lingered on the soft, trembling fullness of her lips, then slowly lifted to meet her gaze and lock in place. They stared at each other, so close that she could see her reflection in his eyes and knew that he could see himself in hers.

"Your eyes are like melted gold," he whispered. "Cat eyes. Do they shine in the dark? A man could get lost in them," he said, his voice suddenly rough.

Dione swallowed; her heart seemed to be rising to stick in her throat. Her hands were still on his shoulders; beneath the warmth of his flesh she could feel the flexing of his muscles as he levered himself up on his elbows, the weight of his body still pressed into hers from the waist down. She shivered, faintly alarmed by their posture, but too bemused by the emotional intimacy quivering between them to push him away.

"You're the loveliest thing I've ever seen," he murmured. "As exotic as Salome, as graceful as a cat, as simple as the wind…and so damned mysterious. What goes on behind those cat eyes? What are you thinking?"

She couldn't answer; instead she shook her head blindly as fresh tears made her eyes glitter. He sucked in his breath, then kissed her again, this time parting her lips and slowly penetrating her mouth with his tongue, giving her the time to decide if she would accept the caress. She was trembling in his arms, afraid to let herself be tempted by the gentle touch, yet she *was* tempted, terribly so. Her tongue moved hesitantly and touched his, withdrew, returned for another shy taste, and finally lingered. He tasted marvelous.

He deepened the kiss, exploring the ridges of her teeth, the softness of her mouth. Dione lay quietly beneath him, unaware of the growing force of his passion until suddenly his mouth turned hard and demanding, asking for more than she could give, reminding her abruptly and with chilling clarity how it had been with Scott—

The black pit of her nightmares loomed before her, and she squirmed under him, but he didn't feel the sudden tension in her body. His hands grasped her with the roughness of desire, and the last thread holding her control snapped.

She tore her mouth from his with a raw cry. "No!" she shrieked, sudden fear giving her strength. She shoved him away with all the considerable power of her arms and legs, and he rolled across the floor, bumping into the wheelchair and sending it flying across the room.

He pulled himself into a sitting position and seared her with a scathing, furious look. "Don't bother screaming," he snapped bitterly. "It's a cinch that nothing's going to happen."

"You can bet on it!" she snapped in return, scrambling to her feet and straightening her blouse and shorts, which had somehow become twisted. "I'm a therapist, not a…a convenience!"

"Your professional integrity is safe," he muttered. "From me, at any rate. You might want to try someone like Richard if you're really serious with your kisses, though I warn you right now, all of his parts are in working order and he might not be so easy to throw off!''

It was evident that his ego had been bruised, because she'd tossed him off so easily; he hadn't even noticed the wild expression that had touched her face. She gave silent thanks, then calmly retrieved the wheelchair and placed it beside him. "Stop feeling sorry for yourself," she said curtly. "We have work to do."

"Sure, lady," he snarled. "Anything you say. You're the therapist."

He pushed himself so hard for the rest of the day that Dione had to lose her temper with him that afternoon to make him stop. He was in the foulest mood she'd ever seen him in, surly and bleak. Even Serena was unable to coax him into a better mood that night over dinner, and he excused himself shortly afterward, uttering that he was tired and going to bed.

Serena's brows lifted, but she didn't protest. Richard got to his feet and said, "Let's go into the study for a minute, Blake. There are some things that I need to talk over with you; it won't take long."

Blake nodded briefly, and the two men left the room. Silence fell between Dione and Serena, who had never had much to say to each other.

Serena was apparently engrossed with the strappy white sandal she was dangling from her toes. Without looking up from it, she asked casually, "What's wrong with Blake tonight? He's like a hornet."

Dione shrugged. She wasn't about to tell Serena about the kisses that day, or the reason for Blake's ill humor. Instead she passed along the encouraging news that Blake, for some reason, hadn't. "He stood today. I don't know why he's so grouchy; he should be on top of the world."

Serena's eyes lighted up, and her pretty face glowed. "He stood?" she cried, dropping the sandal to the floor and sitting upright. "He actually stood?"

"He had his weight on his legs, yes, and he could feel it," Dione clarified.

"But that's wonderful! Why didn't he tell me?"

Again Dione shrugged.

Serena made a rueful face. "I know; you think I make too much of a fuss over him. I do; I admit it. I...I'm sorry for my attitude when you first came. I didn't think you'd be able to help him, and I didn't want him to get his hopes up, only to be disappointed again. But even if he doesn't walk again, I can see that therapy has been good for him. He's gained weight; he's looking so healthy again."

Surprised by the apology, Dione didn't know what to say beyond the conventional disclaimer, "That's all right."

"No, it isn't all right. Richard's barely speaking to me, and I can't say that I blame him. I've treated him like the invisible man for the two years since Blake had the accident. God knows how he's been as patient as he has. But now I can't get close to him again, and it's all my fault. Still, I'm irrational where Blake's concerned. He's my security, my home base."

"Perhaps Richard wants that distinction," Dione murmured, not really wanting to get into a discussion of Serena's marital problems. She hadn't forgotten that Serena thought Richard might be seeing another woman, namely herself, and she didn't think that involving herself with them would be smart. She liked Richard enormously, and Serena had behaved remarkably well since their bad beginning, but still, she felt uneasy discussing Richard as if she knew him a lot better than she actually did.

"Oh, I know he does! The trouble is, Blake's such a hard act for any man to follow. He was the perfect older brother," she sighed. "Strong, affectionate, understanding. When Mother died he became my rock. Sometimes I think that if anything happened to Blake, I'd die on the spot."

"Not a very considerate thing to do," Dione commented, and Serena looked at her sharply before giving a laugh.

"No, it wouldn't be, would it?"

"I've been jealous of you," Serena continued after a moment, when Dione showed no signs of picking up the conversational threads. "I'd been with Blake almost constantly since the accident; then you practically forbade me to come over except at a time *you* decided would be all right. I was livid! And almost from the beginning, Blake has been engrossed with his therapy, which has taken his attention away from me even when I am with him. He was so close to you, so obviously taken with you; you could get him to do all the things the other therapists couldn't even get him to think about.''

Dione shifted uncomfortably, afraid that Serena was going to start talking about Richard. It looked as if there was nothing she could do to prevent it, so she decided she might as well hold up her end of the conversation. Lifting her head, she turned somber golden eyes on the other woman.

"I knew you felt that way. I regretted it, but there was nothing I could do about it. Blake had to come first; you were interfering, and I couldn't let you do that.''

Serena arched her dark brows in a manner so like Blake's that Dione stared at her, taken by their similarities. "You were entirely right,'' Serena said firmly. "You were doing what you were supposed to do. It took about two weeks before I began to see the difference in Blake, and then I had to admit that I was resenting you on *my* behalf, not his. If I really loved Blake, then I had to stop acting like a spoiled brat. I'm sorry, Dione; I'd really like to be friends with you.''

Dione was startled again; she wondered briefly if Serena's apology had any ulterior motive, but decided to take the younger woman at face value. When all was said and done, she herself was there only temporarily, so anything Serena said wouldn't affect Dione beyond the moment. Lifelong friendships didn't come Dione's way, because she'd learned not to let anyone get too close to her. Even Blake— however close they might be right now, no matter how well she knew him or how much he knew about her—when this was all over, she would be gone and very probably never see him again. She didn't make a habit of keeping in touch with her ex-patients, though she did sometimes receive cards from some of them at Christmas.

"If you'd like,'' she told Serena calmly. "An apology really wasn't necessary.''

"It was for *me,*'' Serena insisted, and perhaps it had been. She was Blake's sister, and very like him. Blake didn't back down from anything unpleasant, either.

Dione was tired after the emotional impact of the day, and she didn't look in on Blake before she went to bed. The mood he'd been in, he was probably lying awake waiting for her to stick her head in so he could bite it off. Whatever was bothering him, she'd worry about it in the morning. She fell into a deep sleep, untroubled by dreams.

When she was jerked awake by her name being called, she had the feeling that the sound had been repeated several times before it penetrated her sleep. She scrambled out of bed as it came again. ''Dione!''

It was Blake, and from the horse strain in his voice, he was in pain. She ran to his room and approached the bed. He was writhing, trying to sit up. What was wrong with him? ''Tell me,'' she said insistently, her hands on his bare shoulders, easing him back.

''Cramps,'' he groaned.

Of course! She should have realized! He'd pushed himself far too hard that day, and now he was paying the price. She ran her hands down his legs and found the knotted muscles. Without a word she got on the bed with him and began to knead the cramps away, her strong fingers working efficiently. First one leg relaxed, then the other, and he sighed in relief. She kept massaging his calves, knowing that a cramp could return. His flesh was warm under her fingers now, the skin roughened by the hair on his legs. She pushed the legs of his pajamas up over his knees and continued with her massage. Perhaps he would go back to sleep under the soothing touch....

Abruptly he sat up and thrust her hands away from his legs. ''That's enough,'' he said curtly. ''I don't know what kind of a thrill you get out of handling cripples, but you can play with someone else's legs. You might try Richard; I'm sure he could do you more good than I can.''

Dione sat there astonished, her mouth open. How could he *dare* to say something like that? She'd pulled her nightgown up to give her legs more freedom of movement when she'd climbed on his bed, and now she thrust the cloth down to cover her long legs. ''You need slapping,'' she said, her voice shaking with anger. ''Damn it, what's wrong with you? You know I'm not seeing Richard, and I'm sick of you throwing him up to me! *You* called *me,* remember? I didn't sneak in here to take advantage of you.''

''You'd have a hard time doing that,'' he sneered.

''You're pretty sure of yourself since you've gotten stronger, aren't you?'' she said sarcastically. It made her doubly angry that he'd act like that after what they'd shared earlier. He'd kissed her. Of course, he couldn't possibly know that he was the only man to have touched her since she was eighteen, which had been twelve years before, but still...the injustice of it made her get to her knees on the bed, leaning forward as she jabbed a finger at him.

''You listen to me, Mr. Grouch Remington! I've been driving myself into the ground trying to help you, and you've fought me every step of the way! I don't know what's eating you and I don't care, but I won't let it interfere with your therapy. If I think your legs need massaging, then I'll do it, if I have to tie you down first! Am I getting through that hard head of yours?''

''Who do you think you are? God?'' he roared, his face darkening so much that she could see it even in the dim light that came through his windows. ''What do you know about what *I* want, what *I* need? All you think about is that damned program you've mapped out. There are other things that I need, and if I can't—''

He stopped, turning his head away. Dione waited for him to continue, and when he didn't she prompted, ''If you can't...what?''

''Nothing,'' he muttered sullenly.

''Blake!'' she said in utter exasperation, reaching out and grasping his shoulders and shaking him. ''What?''

He shrugged away from her grip and lay back down, his expression bleak as he turned his face back to the windows. ''I thought that learning to walk again would be the answer,'' he whispered. ''But it's not. My God, woman, you've been around me for weeks now, running around in almost nothing sometimes, and those see-through nightgowns of yours the rest of the time. Haven't you noticed yet that I can't...''

When his voice trailed off again Dione thought she'd explode. ''Can't what?'' she tried again, forcibly keeping her tone level.

"I'm impotent," he said, his voice so low that she had to lean closer to hear him.

She sat back on her heels, stunned.

Once he'd said the words aloud, the rest poured out of him in a torrent, as if he couldn't control it. "I didn't think about it before, because what was there to arouse me? It didn't matter, if I couldn't walk, but now I find that there's an opposite side of the coin. If I can't live life as a man instead of a sexless gelding, then it doesn't matter if I walk or not."

Dione's mind went blank. She was a physical therapist, not a sex therapist. It was ironic that he should even mention the subject to *her*, of all people. She was in the same boat he was in; perhaps she'd sensed that from the beginning, and that was why she hadn't been frightened of him.

But she couldn't let this prey on his mind, or he'd give up. Desperately she tried to think of something to tell him.

"I don't see why you'd even think you should be aroused by me," she blurted. "I'm a therapist; it's totally unethical for there to be any sort of relationship except a professional one between us. I certainly haven't been trying to seduce you, or even interest you! You shouldn't think of me like that! I...I'm more of a mother figure than I am anything else, so I'd think it was odd if you responded physically to me."

"You *don't* remind me of my mother," he said heavily.

Again she searched for something to say. "Did you really expect all of your capabilities to return immediately, just because you put your weight on your legs today?" she finally asked. "I would've been surprised if you had been...er, responding like that. You've had a lot on your mind, and you've been in terrible physical shape."

"I'm not in terrible physical shape now," he pointed out tiredly.

No, he wasn't. Dione considered him as he lay there, wearing only the bottoms of his pajamas. He'd started leaving off the tops several weeks ago. He was still lean, but now it was the leanness of a hard layer of muscle. Even his legs had fleshed out some as he gained weight, and thanks to the rigorous program he'd been following, he even had muscles in his legs, despite his inability to command move-

ment from them yet. He was a natural athlete anyway, and his body
had responded promptly to the training. His arms and shoulders and
chest were showing the benefits of weight lifting, and the hours in
the pool had given his skin a glowing bronze color. He looked incredibly healthy, all things considered.

What could she say? She couldn't reassure him that his mind and
body would recover and let him respond normally, because recovery
hadn't happened yet for her. She couldn't even say that she wanted
to "recover." Perhaps she missed out on a great deal of human
warmth by living the way she did, but she also avoided the pain of
human cruelty. Until the accident, Blake had led a charmed life. He
had loved, and been loved, by more women than he could probably
remember. To him, life wasn't complete without sex. To her, life was
much safer without it. How could she even begin to convince him of
something she didn't believe in herself?

At last she said cautiously, "You're better, yes, but you're not in
top physical condition yet. The body is a series of complementary
systems; when any part of it is hurt, all the systems cooperate in
helping to speed healing. With the therapy program you've been following, you've focused your mind and body on retraining your muscles. It's part of the recovery process, and until you've progressed
enough that such intense concentration isn't needed, I think you're
being unrealistic to expect any sexual responses. Let things happen
in their own time." After considering him for another minute, she
tilted her head sideways. "I estimate that you're at about sixty-five
percent of your normal strength. You're expecting too much."

"I'm expecting what any normal man expects in his life," Blake
said harshly. "You were bubbling over with self-confidence when
you promised me that I'd walk again, but you're not sure about this,
are you?"

"I'm not a sex therapist," she snapped. "But I do have common
sense, and I'm trying to use it. There's no physical reason why you
shouldn't be able to have sex, so I'd advise you to stop worrying
about it and concentrate on walking. Nature will take care of everything else."

"Stop worrying!" he muttered under his breath. "Lady, it's not the weather we're talking about! If I can't function as a man, what's the use in living? I'm not talking about just sex; there'd be no marriage for me, no children, and while I've never wanted to marry anyone yet, I've always thought that I'd like to have a family someday. Can't you understand that? Haven't you ever wanted a husband, children?''

Dione winced, physically shrinking away from him. He had an uncanny knack of hitting her where she was most vulnerable. Before she could stop herself, she blurted out thickly, "I've always wanted children. And I *was* married. It just didn't work out."

His chest rose and fell as he drew in a deep breath, and she could feel his gaze searching her face in the darkness. Surely he couldn't see anything more than an outline, since she was sitting out of the dim light coming through the windows, so why did she feel as if he could tell exactly how her lower lip was trembling, or see the sudden pallor of her cheeks?

"Damn," he said softly. "I've done it again, haven't I? Every time I say something, I stick my foot in my mouth."

She shrugged, trying not to let him know how thin her armor was. "It's all right," she murmured. "It was a long time ago. I was just a kid, too young to know what I was doing."

"How old were you?"

"Eighteen. Scott—my ex-husband—was twenty-three, but neither of us was ready for marriage."

"How long did it last?"

A harsh laugh tore from her throat. "Three months. Not a record-setting length of time, was it?"

"And since then? Haven't you been in love with anyone else?"

"No, and I haven't wanted to be. I'm content the way I am." The conversation had gone on long enough; she didn't want to reveal any more than she already had. How did he keep chipping away at the wall she'd built around her past? Most people never even realized it was there. She uncoiled her legs and crawled off the bed, tugging her nightgown down when it tried to crawl up to her hips.

Blake said a harsh expletive. "You're running, Dee. Do you realize how long you've been here without receiving a single phone call or a letter, without even going shopping? You've sealed yourself in this house with me and shut the world out. Don't you have any friends, any boyfriends on a string? What is it out there that you're afraid of?''

''There's nothing out there that frightens me,'' she said quietly, and it was true. All of her terrors were locked within herself, frozen in time.

''I think everything out there frightens you,'' he said, stretching out his arm and snapping on the bedside lamp. The soft glow drove away the shadows and illuminated her as she stood there in her white gown with her long, black hair streaming down her back. She looked medieval, locked away in a fortress of her own making. His blue eyes seared over her as he said softly, ''You're afraid of life, so you don't let anything touch you. You need therapy as much as I do; my muscles won't work, but you're the one who doesn't feel.''

Chapter 6

She didn't sleep that night; she lay awake, feeling the seconds and minutes ticking away, becoming hours. He was right; she *was* afraid of life, because life had taught her that she would be punished if she asked for too much. She had learned not to ask for anything at all, thereby risking nothing. She had denied herself friends, family, even the basic comfort of her own home, all because she was afraid to risk being hurt again.

It wasn't in her character to deny the truth, so she looked it in the face. Her mother wasn't a typical example of motherhood; her husband hadn't been a typical husband. Both of them had hurt her, but she shouldn't shut everyone else out because of them. Serena had made an overture of friendship, but Dione had backed away from it, doubting the other woman's motives. Those doubts were just an excuse for her own instinctive reaction to withdraw whenever anyone got too close to her. She had to take risks, or her life would be just a mockery, no matter how many patients she helped. She needed help just as much as Blake did.

But facing the truth and dealing with it were two very different things. Just the thought of lowering her defenses and letting anyone get close to her gave her a sick feeling. Even the little things were more than she had ever had, and more than she could handle. She'd never giggled with a girl friend far into the night, never gone to a party, never learned *how* to be with people in the normal manner. She'd had her back to the wall for her entire life, and self-protection was more than a habit: it was a part of her, branded into her cells.

Perhaps she was beyond changing; perhaps the bitter horror of her childhood had altered her psyche so drastically that she'd never be able to rise above the murky pit of her memories. For a moment she had a vision of her future, long and bleak and solitary, and a dry sob wrenched at her insides. But she didn't cry, though her eyes burned until her lids felt scorched. Why waste tears on years that stretched away emptily for as far as she could see? She was used to being alone, and at least she had her work. She could touch people through her work, giving them hope, helping them; perhaps it wasn't enough, but surely it was better than the sure destruction that awaited her if she allowed someone to hurt her again.

Suddenly a memory of Scott flashed into her mind and she almost cried out, her hands rising in the dark to push him away. The sickness in her changed to pure nausea, and she had to swallow convulsively to control it. For a moment she wavered on the edge of a black abyss, memories rising like bats from a rancid cave to dart at her; then she clenched her teeth on the wild cry that was welling up in her and reached out a trembling hand to turn on the lamp. The light drove away the horrors, and she lay staring at the shadows.

To combat the memories she deliberately pushed them aside and called up Blake's face as a sort of talisman against the evils of the past. She saw his blue eyes, burning with despair, and her breath caught. Why was she lying there worrying about herself, when Blake was teetering on the edge of his own abyss? *Blake* was the important one, not her! If he lost interest now, it would wreck his recovery.

She'd trained herself for years to push her personal interests and problems aside and concentrate entirely on her patient. Her patients had reaped the benefits, and the process had become a part of her inner defenses when things threatened to become too much for her. She used it now, ruthlessly locking out all thoughts except those of Blake, staring at the ceiling so intently that her gaze should have burned a hole in it.

On the surface the problem seemed to be simple: Blake needed to know that he could still respond to a woman, still make love. She didn't know why he couldn't now, unless it was because of the common-sense reasons she'd given him just a few hours before. If that were the case, as his health improved and he gained strength, his sexual interest would reawaken naturally, if he had someone to interest him.

That was a problem Dione chewed on her lower lip. Blake obviously wasn't going to start dating now; his pride wouldn't allow him to be helped in and out of cars and restaurants, even if Dione would allow him to disrupt his schedule so drastically, which was out of the question. No, he *had* to stay in therapy, and they were just now getting into the toughest part of it, which would require more time and effort, and pain, from him.

There simply was a shortage of available women in his life right now, a necessary shortage, but there nevertheless. Besides Serena, Alberta and Angela, there was only herself, and she automatically discounted herself. How could she attract anyone? If any man made a move toward her, she reacted like a scalded cat, which wasn't a good start.

A frown laced her brows together. That was true with all men...except Blake. Blake touched her, and she wasn't frightened. She had wrestled with him, romped on the floor with him...kissed him.

The idea that bloomed was, for her, so radical that when it first entered her consciousness she dismissed it, only to have it return again and again, boomeranging in her mined. Blake needed help, and she was the only woman available to help him. If she could attract him...

A shudder rose from her toes and flowed upward to shake her entire body, but it wasn't from revulsion or fear, except perhaps fear at her own daring. Could she do it? How could she do it? How could she possibly manage such a thing? It wouldn't do Blake any good if he made a pass at her and she ran screaming from the room. She didn't think she would do that with him, but just the thought of trying to attract a man was so foreign to her that she couldn't be sure. Could she tempt him enough to prove to him that he was a man?

She couldn't let the situation progress into anything concrete; she knew that not only was it something she wasn't ready for, but an affair with a patient was totally against her professional integrity. Besides, she wasn't Blake's type, so there was little chance of anything serious happening. She tried to decide if he would find her so lacking in expertise that she wouldn't appeal to him at all, or if his isolation for the past two years would blind him to her inexperience. He was fast leaving behind his morose preoccupation with his invalidism, and she knew that she wouldn't be able to fool him for long. Every day he became more himself—the man in the photo that Richard had shown her, with a biting intellect and a driving nature that swept everyone along with him like the force of a tidal wave.

Could she do it?

She trembled at the thought, but she was so shaken by what he'd said that night that she didn't push the idea away as she would have before. For the first time in her life Dione decided to try to attract a man. It had been so long since she'd cut herself off from sexual contact with anyone that she had no idea if she could do it without looking obvious and silly. She was thirty years old, and she felt as inexperienced and awkward as any young girl just entering her teens. Her brief marriage to Scott didn't count at all; far from trying to attract Scott, after her wedding night she'd gone out of her way to avoid him. Blake was a mature, sophisticated man, used to having any woman he wanted before the accident had robbed him of the use of his legs. Her only advantage was that she was the only available woman in his life right then.

She just didn't know how to arouse a man.

That unusual problem, one she'd never thought she'd face, was the reason she was standing hesitantly before the mirror the next morning, long past the time when she usually woke Blake. She hadn't even dressed; she was staring at herself in the mirror, chewing on her lower lip and frowning. She knew that men usually liked the way she looked, but were looks enough? She wasn't even blond, as Blake preferred his women to be. Her thick black hair swirled over her shoulders and down her back; she'd been about to braid it out of her way when she'd paused, staring at herself, and she still held the brush in her hand, forgotten, as she intensely surveyed the ripe figure of the woman in the mirror. Her breasts were full and firm, tipped with cherry nipples, but perhaps she was too bosomy for his tastes. Perhaps she was too athletic, too strong; perhaps he liked dainty, ultra-feminine women.

She groaned aloud, twisting around to study herself from the back. So many ifs! Maybe he was a leg man; she had nice legs, long and graceful, smoothly tanned. Or maybe... Her bottom, covered only by wispy, pink silk, was curvy and definitely feminine.

Her clothes were another problem. Her everyday wardrobe consisted mostly of things that were comfortable to work in: jeans, shorts, T-shirts. They were neat and practical, but not enticing. She did have good clothes, but nothing that could be worn while working and be practical, too. Her dresses weren't sexy, either, and her nightgowns were straight out of a convent, despite Blake's comment about her ''running around in see-through nighties.'' She needed new clothes, things that were sexy but not transparently so, and definitely a real see-through nightie.

She was so preoccupied that she hadn't heard the sounds of Blake in his bedroom; when his rumbling, early-morning voice broke into her thoughts with an ill-tempered, ''Lazybones, you overslept this morning!'' she whirled to face the door as it swung open and Blake rolled his wheelchair through the doorway.

They both froze. Dione couldn't even raise her arms to cover her bare breasts; she was stunned by the shock of his entrance, so lost in her thoughts that she was unable to jerk herself back to reality and take any action. Neither did Blake appear capable of moving, though good manners demanded that he leave the room. He didn't; he sat there with his blue eyes becoming even bluer, a dark, stormy expression heating his gaze as it raked down her almost naked body, then rose to linger over her breasts.

''Good Lord,'' he whispered.

Dione's mouth was dry, her tongue incapable of moving. Blake's intent look was as warm as a physical touch, and her nipples shrank into tiny points, thrusting out at him. He sucked in an audible breath, then slowly let his eyes dip lower, down the curve of her ribcage, the satiny smoothness of her stomach; his gaze probed the taut little indentation of her navel and finally settled on the juncture of her thighs.

An unfamiliar curling sensation low in her stomach frightened her, and she was finally able to move. She whirled away from him with a low cry, belatedly raising her arms to cover herself. Standing rigidly with her back to him, she said in a voice filled with mortification, "Oh, no! Please, get out!"

There was no obedient whir of an electric motor as he sent the wheelchair into motion, and she knew that he was still sitting there.

"I've never seen anyone blush all over before," he said, his voice deep and filled with an almost tangible male amusement. "Even the backs of your knees are pink."

"Get out" she cried in a strangled voice.

"Why are you so embarrassed?" he murmured. "You're beautiful. A body like that just begs for a man to stare at it."

"Would you please just leave?" she begged. "I can't stand here like this all day!"

"Don't hurry on my account," he replied with maddening satisfaction. "I like the back view as well as I did the front. It's a work of art, the way those long legs of yours sweep up into that perfect bottom. Is your skin as satiny as it looks?"

Embarrassment finally turned to anger and she stomped her foot, although it was largely a wasted effort, as the thick carpet muffled any sound her bare foot might have made. "Blake Remington, I'll get back at you for this!" she threatened, her voice trembling with anger.

He laughed, the deep tone vibrating in the quiet morning air. "Don't be such a sexist," he taunted. "You've seen me in only a pair of undershorts, so why be shy about my seeing you wearing only panties? You don't have anything to be ashamed of, but you have to know that already."

He evidently wasn't going to leave; he was probably enjoying himself, the wretch! She sidled around until she could reach her nightgown, where she had thrown it across the bed. She was careful to keep her back to him, and she was so fiercely preoccupied with reaching that nightgown that she didn't hear the soft whir of the wheelchair as it came up behind her. Just as she touched the nightgown a much larger hand appeared from behind and anchored the garment to the bed.

"You're beautiful when you're angry," he jibed, returning the teasing compliment she'd given him the day he'd become enraged when he had discovered that she lifted weights.

"Then I must be the world's most beautiful woman right now," she fumed, then added, "because I'm getting madder by the minute."

"Don't waste your energy," he crooned, and she jumped as his hard hand suddenly swatted her on the bottom, then lingered to mold the round, firm cheek with his long fingers. He finished with an intimate pat, then removed his hand from the nightgown.

"I'll be waiting for you at breakfast," he said smoothly, and she heard him chuckling as he left the room.

She wadded up the nightgown and threw it at the closed door. Her face felt as if it were on fire, and she pressed her cold hands to her cheeks. Furiously she considered ways of paying him back, but she had to stop short of physical harm, and that left out all the most delicious schemes she could imagine. It would probably be impossible to embarrass him in return; since he was in so much better condition now, she doubted if it would bother him if she saw him stark naked. In fact, from the way he'd acted that morning, he'd probably enjoy it and proudly let her look all she wanted!

She was seething, until the thought came to her that her scheme to attract him couldn't have gotten off to a better start. He hadn't been thinking about sex, really; he'd been indulging a streak of pure devilry, but the end result was that he'd become aware of her as a woman. There was the added advantage of the entire scene being totally spontaneous without any of the stiffness that would probably result from any effort she deliberately made.

That thought enabled her to get through the day, which was a difficult one. He watched her like a hawk, waiting for her to betray by either action or word that she was still embarrassed by the morning's incident. She was as cool and impersonal as she knew how to be, deliberately working him as hard as her conscience would allow.

He spent more time than the day before at the bars, balancing himself with his hands while his legs bore his weight. He kept up a continuous stream of cursing at the pain he endured, but he didn't want to stop, even when she decided to go on to other exercises. She moved his feet in the first walking motions they'd made in two years; sweat poured off of him at the pain in his muscles, unaccustomed to such activity.

That night the cramps in his legs kept him awake for hours, and Dione massaged him until she was so weary she could hardly move. There were no intimate discussions in the dark that night; he was in pain, barely getting relaxed after one cramp was relieved before another one would knot in his legs. Finally she took him down and put him in the whirlpool, which relieved the cramps for the night.

She really did oversleep the next morning, but she had been careful to lock her door before she went to bed, so she wasn't afraid of an interruption. When she did wake, she lay there with a smile on her face as she relished how he would react to the interruption in his route that she planned.

Over breakfast she said casually, "May I borrow one of your cars? I need to do some shopping today."

Startled, he looked up; his eyes narrowed thoughtfully. "Are you doing this because of what I said the other night?"

"No, of course not," she lied with admirable ease. "I do need some things, though. I'm not much on shopping, but like every woman I have necessities."

"Do you know anything about Phoenix?" he asked, reaching for the glass of milk that he now drank without protest at every meal.

"Nothing," she admitted cheerfully.

"Do you even know how to get downtown?"

"No, but I can follow signs and directions."

"No need to do that; let me give Serena a call. She loves shopping, and she's been at loose ends lately."

At first the thought of shopping in Serena's company dampened Dione's enthusiasm for her project, but she realized that she would probably need another woman's opinion, so she agreed to his suggestion. Serena did, too; he'd barely mentioned it to her over the phone before he hung up the receiver, a wry smile tugging at his chiseled mouth. "She's on her way." Then the smile gave way to a sharply searching look. "You didn't seem very enthusiastic," he remarked. "Did you have some other plans?"

What did he mean by that? "No, it's just that I had something else on my mind. I'm glad you thought of asking Serena; I could use her opinion on some things."

The searching look disappeared, to be replaced by one of lively curiosity. "What things?"

"Nothing that concerns you," she replied promptly, knowing that her answer would drive him crazy. He wanted to know the whys and wherefores of everything. He'd probably dismantled every toy he'd received as a child, and now he was trying to do the same thing to her. He probably did it to everyone. It was one of the characteristics that had made him such an innovative engineer.

As she quickly dressed for her shopping trip, she realized that lately Blake had shown signs of becoming more interested in his work again. He talked to Richard on the phone more than he had before, and designing the pulley system at the pool and in the gym had piqued his interest even more. Every night after dinner he made some mysterious doodles on a pad in his study, random drawings that resembled nothing Dione recognized, but Richard had seen the pad one evening and made a comment on it. The two men had then embarked on a highly technical conversation that had lasted until Dione put an end to it by signaling that it was time for Blake to go to bed. Richard had caught the signal and understood it immediately, giving her a quick wink.

The Phoenix heat prompted her to wear the bare minimum of clothing: a white sundress; the necessary underwear, which wasn't much; and strappy sandals. The weeks had slipped away, taking the summer with it, but the changing season wasn't yet reflected by any dip in the temperature. When she went downstairs to meet Serena, Blake gave her a quick comprehensive look that seemed to take inventory of every garment she had on. Dione shivered at the fleeting expression in his eyes. He knew what she looked like now, and every time he saw her he was imagining her without any clothes. She should probably be glad, as that was what she wanted, but it still made her uneasy.

Serena drove, as Dione knew absolutely nothing about Scottsdale or Phoenix. The pale blue Cadillac slipped as silently as oiled silk past the array of expensive millionaires' homes that decorated Mount Camelback. Overhead, a sparkle of silver in the pure blue of the sky, one of the innumerable jets from the air bases in the Phoenix area, painted a white streak directly above their path.

"Blake said you had shopping to do," Serena said absently. "What sort of shopping? Not that it matters; if it exists, I know a shop that carries it."

Dione gave her a wry glance. "Everything," she admitted. "Dresses, underwear, sleepwear, bathing suits."

Serena arched her slim, dark brows in an astonished movement. "All right," she said slowly. "You asked for it."

By the time they'd had lunch several hours later, Dione firmly believed that Serena knew the location of every shop in Arizona. They had been in so many that she couldn't keep straight just where she had bought what, but that didn't really matter. What mattered was the steadily growing mound of bags and packages, which they made regular trips to the car to stow in the trunk.

Dione systematically tried on dresses that made the most of her dark coloring and tall, leggy build. She bought skirts that were slit up the side to showcase her long, slender legs; she bought real silk hosiery and delicate shoes. The nightgowns she chose were filmy, flimsy pieces of fabric that were held on her body more by optimism than any other means. She bought sexy lace panties and bras, wickedly seductive teddies, shorts and T-shirts that clung to her body, and a couple of bikinis that stopped just short of illegal.

Serena watched all of this in amazed silence, offering her opinion whenever Dione asked it, which was often. Dione couldn't quite decide if a garment was sexy without being blatant, so she yielded to Serena's taste. It was Serena who chose the bikinis, one a delicate shell pink and the other a vibrant blue, both of which glowed like jewels on Dione's honey-tanned body.

"You know," Serena mused as she watched Dione choose a skin-toned teddy that, from a distance, made her look as if she had nothing on at all, "this looks like war."

Dione was feeling a little frantic and out of touch by that time, and she merely gave Serena a blank look.

"I could almost pity Blake for being the target of such firepower," the other woman continued, laughing a little. "Almost, but not quite. From the effort you're making, Dione, I think you're out for unconditional surrender. Are you in love with Blake?"

That got Dione's attention with the force of a punch in the jaw. In love? Of course not! It was impossible. Blake was her patient; falling in love with him would be against every professional ethic that she had. Not only that, how could she be in love with him? Couldn't Serena see that it was totally out of the question? she wondered distractedly. It was just that Blake's was such a demanding case. She'd rebuilt him almost literally, molded him from a basket case into a strong, healthy man; she couldn't let him give up now, couldn't let all of that sweat and effort go to waste.

But suddenly, seeing through Serena's eyes the staggering amount of clothing she'd bought in one day, she realized what a hopeless effort it was. How could she ever have imagined that she'd be able to physically attract Blake Remington? Not only did she not know how to do it, but she'd probably go into screaming hysterics if she succeeded!

She sagged into a chair, crumpling the flesh-colored teddy in her lap. "It's no use," she muttered. "It'll never work."

Serena eyed the teddy. "If he's human, it will."

"All of these props are useless, if the actors can't perform," Dione said in self-disgust. "I don't know how to seduce anyone, least of all a man who's been around as much as Blake has!"

Serena's eyes widened. "Are you serious? The way you look, you don't *have* to seduce anyone; all you have to do is stand still and let him get to you."

"Thanks for the pep talk, but it's not that easy," Dione hedged, unable to tell Blake's sister the entire story. "Some men like my looks, but I know that Blake's always preferred blondes. I'm not his type at all."

"How you can look in a mirror and still worry about not being blond is more than I can understand," Serena said impatiently. "You're...sultry. That's the only word I can think of to describe the way you look. If he hasn't made a pass at you yet, it's because you haven't given him a go-ahead signal. Those clothes will do it for you. Then just let things develop naturally."

If only they would! Dione thought as she paid for the teddy and a bottle of heady perfume that the saleswoman had sworn drove her husband mad with lust.

She didn't want Blake mad with lust, just aroused. What a dilemma for her to be in! Life was just full of little ironies, but she couldn't find this one very amusing.

Blake wasn't in evidence when they arrived back at the house, and Dione could only be thankful for that. She didn't want him to have any idea of the extent of her shopping trip. Angela silently helped Dione and Serena carry all the packages up to Dione's room, and when asked about Blake's whereabouts, the woman smiled shyly and murmured, "In the gym," before quickly walking out.

Serena gave a little laugh after Angela had left the room. "She's something, isn't she? I think Blake picked his entire staff on the basis of how much they talk, or rather, don't talk." Before Dione could make any comment, Serena changed the subject. "Do you mind if I stay for dinner? I know you probably want to start your campaign, but Richard told me this morning that he'd be late coming home tonight, and I'm at loose ends."

Far from being anxious to begin her "campaign," Dione was dreading it, and gladly asked Serena to stay. As she usually had dinner with them, Blake might think something was off if all of a sudden she stopped the practice.

While Serena went to the den to entertain herself, Dione made her way down to the pool and entered the gym. She stopped abruptly. Blake was on the bars, balancing himself with his hands, while Alberta was on her knees, moving his feet in walking motions. From the looks of him, he'd been hard at it since she'd left with Serena that morning, and poor Alberta was frazzled, too. Blake wore only a brief pair of blue gym shorts, and he'd tied his shirt around his forehead to keep the sweat from getting into his eyes. He was literally dripping as he strained, trying to force his muscles to do his bidding. Dione knew that he had to be in a great deal of pain; it was revealed in the rigid set of his jaw, his white lips. The fact that he'd enlisted Alberta's help instead of waiting for her to return said something about his determination, but she was afraid that he'd tried to do too much. He'd paid for his excesses the night before with agonizing cramps, and she had the feeling that tonight would be a repeat.

"Time for the whirlpool," she said easily, trying not to sound anxious. Alberta looked up with an expression of acute relief, and achingly got to her feet. Blake, on the other hand, shook his head.

"Not yet," he muttered. "Another half hour."

Dione signaled to Alberta, who quietly left the room. Taking a towel from the stack she always kept handy, she went up to him and wiped his face, then his shoulders and chest. "Don't push it so hard," she advised. "Not yet. You can do yourself more harm than good at this stage. Come on, into the whirlpool; give your muscles a rest."

He sagged against the bars, panting, and Dione quickly brought the wheelchair over to him. He levered himself into it; he seldom needed her help moving himself around now, since he was so much stronger. She switched the whirlpool on and turned around to find that he'd been staring at her bottom as she bent over. Wondering how much she'd exposed in the unaccustomed dress, she flushed pink.

He gave her a wicked little smile, then grasped the pulley and swung himself over the pool, letting himself down expertly in the water. He sighed in relief as the pulsing water eased his tired, strained muscles.

"I didn't expect you to be gone all day," he said, closing his eyes wearily.

"I only shop once a year." She lied without compunction. "When I shop, it's an endurance event."

"Who won, you or Serena?" he asked, smiling as he lay there, his eyes still closed.

"I think Serena did," she groaned, stretching her tight muscles. "Shopping uses an entirely different set of muscles than weight lifting does."

He opened one eye a slit and surveyed her. "Why not join me?" he invited. "As the old saying goes, 'Come on in, the water's fine.'"

It was tempting. She looked at the swirling water, then shook her head regretfully as she thought of the many things that she needed to do. She didn't have time to relax in a whirlpool.

"Not tonight. By the way," she added, changing the subject, "how did you talk Alberta into helping you with your exercises?"

"A mixture of charm and coercion," he replied, grinning a little. His gaze slipped over the bodice of her dress; then he closed his eyes again and gave himself up to the bliss of the whirlpool.

Dione moved around the room, putting everything in place and preparing for the massage she'd give him when he left the whirlpool, but her actions were purely automatic. Their conversation had been casual, even trivial, but she sensed an entirely different mood under the cover of their words. He was looking at her, he was seeing her, as a woman, not a therapist. She was both frightened and exhilarated at her success, because she'd expected it to take much longer before she got his attention. The intent way he stared at her was sending messages that she wasn't trained to interpret. As a therapist, she knew instinctively what her patient needed; as a woman, she was completely in the dark. She wasn't even completely certain that he wasn't staring at her with derision.

"All right, that's enough," he said huskily, breaking her train of thought. "I hope Alberta's not going to hold a grudge against me, because I'm hungry. Do you think she'll feed me?"

"Serena and I will let you have our scraps," Dione offered generously, earning a wryly appreciative glance from him.

A few minutes later he lay on his stomach on the table with a towel draped over his hips, sighing in contentment as her strong fingers worked their magic on his flesh. He propped his chin on his folded arms, the look on his face both absent and absorbed, a man concentrating on his inner plans. "How long before I'll be able to walk?" he asked.

Dione continued manipulating his legs as she considered the answer. "Do you mean until you take your first steps, or walk without aid?"

"The first steps."

"I'll take a stab and say six weeks, though that's only a rough guess," she warned him. "Don't hold me to it. You could do it in four or five, or it could be two months. It really depends on how well I've planned your therapy program. If you push too hard and injure yourself, then it'll take longer."

"When will the pain ease?"

"When your muscles are accustomed to your weight and the mechanics of movement. Are your legs still numb?"

"Hell, no," he growled feelingly. "I can tell when you're touching me now. But after those cramps last night, I'm not certain I want to feel."

"The price to pay," she taunted gently, and slapped him on the bottom. "Time to turn over."

"I like that dress," he said when he was lying on his back and could stare at her. Dione didn't glance up, consciously keeping the flexing of her fingers in an unbroken rhythm. When she failed to comment he pushed a little harder. "You've got great legs. I see you every day, dressed in next to nothing, but I hadn't realized how good your legs are until I saw you in a dress."

She quirked one eyebrow. That statement alone verified her suspicion that he hadn't been aware of her as a woman, not really. She half-turned her back to him as she rubbed her hands down the calf of his right leg, hoping that the vigorous massage would lessen any cramps he might have. When the warm touch of his hand rested on her bare thigh, under her skirt, she gave a stifled half scream and jerked up straight.

"Blake!" she yelped, pushing frantically at his hand in an effort to dislodge it from under her dress. "Stop it! What are you doing?"

"You're playing with *my* legs," he retorted calmly. "Turnabout's fair play."

His fingers were between her legs while his thumb was on the outside of her thigh, and she flinched from the feel of his hand as her other leg instinctively pressed against him to halt the upward movement. Her face flushed brightly.

"I like that," he said huskily, his eyes bright. "Your legs are so strong, so sleek. Do you know what you feel like? Cool satin."

She twisted, trying to loosen his grip, and to her dismay his fingers slid even higher. She sucked in a lungful of air and held it, going still, her eyes wide and alarmed as she tried to still the flare of panic in her stomach. Her heart lurched drunkenly in her chest.

"Let me go, please," she whispered, hoping that the trembling of her voice wouldn't be as noticeable if she didn't try to talk loudly.

"All right," he agreed, a little smile moving his lips. Just as she began to sag in relief, he added, "If you'll kiss me."

Now her heart was slamming so wildly that she pressed her hand to her chest in an effort to calm it. "I…just one kiss?"

"I can't say," he drawled, staring at her lips. "Maybe, maybe not. It depends on how well we like it. For God's sake, Dee, I've kissed you before. You won't be violating any sacred vow not to become involved with a patient. A kiss isn't what I'd term an involvement."

Despite her efforts to hold her legs together and trap his wandering hand, he somehow moved a little higher.

"It's only a kiss," he cajoled, holding his left hand out to her. "Don't be shy."

She wasn't shy, she was terrified, but she could still hold on to the thought that Blake wasn't Scott. That alone gave her the courage to lean down and touch her lips to his as lightly, as delicately, as a breath of air. She drew back and stared down at him. His hand remained on her leg.

"You promised," she reminded him.

"That wasn't a kiss," he replied. The expression in his eyes was intent, watchful. "A real kiss is what I want, not a child's kiss. I've been a long time without a woman. I need to feel your tongue on mine."

Weakly she leaned against the table. I can't handle this, she thought wildly, then stiffened as the thought formed in her brain. Of course she could; she could handle anything. She'd already been through the worst that could happen to her. This was just a kiss, that was all…

Though her soft, generous mouth trembled against his, she gave him the intimate kiss he'd requested, and she was startled to feel him begin to shake. He removed his hand from her leg and placed both arms around her, but he held her without any real force, only a warm sort of nearness that failed to alarm her. The hair on his bare chest was tickling her above the fabric of her sundress; the faintly musky smell of him filled her lungs. She became aware of the warmth of his skin, the roughness of his chin against her smooth skin, the light play of his tongue against hers. Her eyes had been open, but now they slowly closed, and she became lost in a world of sensation, the light only a redness against her lids, her senses of touch and smell intensified by the narrowing of her concentration.

That was what she wanted, she reminded herself dimly. She hadn't thought she would enjoy herself in the process, but the excitement that was beginning to course through her veins brought with it a warmth that could only be pleasure.

"God, you smell good," he breathed, breaking the kiss to nuzzle his face in the soft hollow of her throat. "What perfume is that?"

Giddily she remembered all the perfumes she'd tried. "It's a mixture of everything," she admitted in a bemused tone.

He chuckled and turned his head to claim her mouth again. This time the kiss was deeper, harder, but she didn't protest. Instead she kissed him back as strongly as he kissed her, and he finally fell back onto the table, gasping.

"You're taking advantage of a starving man," he groaned, and she gave a spurt of laughter.

"I hope Alberta doesn't feed you anything," she told him, and turned away to hide the color that she knew still tinted her cheeks. She fussed over several insignificant details, but when she turned back he wasn't paying attention to her. She disciplined her face into smoothness and helped him to dress, but there was a sense of determination about him that bothered her. It nagged at her all during dinner, where Serena entertained Blake with a wholly fictitious tale of their shopping trip.

What was he up to? She'd agonized over her scheme, gone to ridiculous lengths to put it into action, but somehow she still had the feeling that he was the one who was scheming, not her.

Chapter 7

"Dione, may I talk to you? In private, please." Richard's face was tight with strain, and Dione looked at him sharply, wondering at the bitterness that was so evident in his expression. She looked past him to the study door, and he read her mind.

"She's playing chess with Blake," he said heavily, thrusting his hands into his pockets and moving to the doors that opened onto the courtyard.

Dione hesitated only a moment, then followed him. She didn't want anything to be said about her being in his company, but on the other hand, she knew that Richard wasn't going to make a pass at her, and she resented feeling guilty for being friendly to him. Serena had continued her efforts at friendship, and Dione found that she really liked the younger woman; Serena was a lot like Blake, with his directness, his willingness to accept challenges. Sometimes Dione had the uneasy thought that Serena could check on her more easily under the guise of friendship, but more and more it seemed that the thought came from her own wariness, not any premeditated action on Serena's part.

"Aren't things going well?" she asked Richard quietly.

He gave a bitter laugh, rubbing the back of his neck. "You know they're not. I don't know why," he said wearily. "I've tried, but it's always in the back of my mind that she'll never love me the way she loves Blake, that I'll never be as important to her as he is, and it makes me almost sick to touch her.''

Dione chose her words carefully, picking them like wildflowers. ''Some resentment is only natural. I see this constantly, Richard. An accident like this really shakes up everyone connected to the patient. If it's a child who's injured, it can cause resentment between the parents, as well as the other children. In circumstances like these, one person gets the lion's share of the attention, and others don't like it.''

''You make me sound so small and petty,'' he said, one corner of his stern mouth curving upward.

''Not that. Just human.'' Her voice was full of warmth and compassion, and he stared at her, his eyes moving over her tender face. ''It'll get better,'' she reassured him.

''Soon enough to save my marriage?'' he asked heavily. ''Sometimes I almost hate her, and it's damned peculiar, because what I'm hating her for is not loving me the way I love her.''

''Why make her take all the blame?'' Dione probed. ''Why not put some of that resentment on Blake? Why not hate him for taking her attention?''

He actually laughed aloud. ''Because I'm not in love with him,'' he chuckled. ''I don't care what he does with his attention…unless he hurts you with it.''

Shock rippled through her, widening her enormous eyes. In the dimness of twilight they gleamed darkly gold, as deep and bottomless as a cat's. ''How can he hurt me?'' she asked, her voice husky.

''By making you fall in love with him.'' He was too astute, capable of summing up a situation in a glance. ''I've been watching you change these last couple of weeks. You were beautiful before, God knows, but now you're breathtaking. You…glow. Those new clothes of yours, the look on your face, even the way you walk…all of that has changed. He needs you now so intensely that everyone else is wiped out of his mind, but what about later? When he can walk again, will he still watch you as if his eyes are glued on you?''

''Patients have fallen in love with me before,'' she pointed out.

"I don't doubt that, but have you ever fallen in love with a patient before?" he asked relentlessly.

"I'm not in love with him." She had to protest the idea, had to thrust it away from her. She couldn't be in love with Blake.

"I recognize the symptoms," Richard said.

As sticky as the conversation was when they were discussing Serena, Dione infinitely preferred it to the current line, and she moved jerkily away. "I don't have any sandcastle built," she assured him, clenching her hands into fists in an effort to keep herself from trembling. "When Blake's walking, I'll move on to another job. I know that; I've known it from the beginning. I *always* get personally involved with my patients," she said, laughing a little. That was all it was, just her normal intense concentration on her patient.

Richard shook his head in amusement. "You see so clearly with everyone else," he said, "to be so blind about yourself."

The old, blind panic, familiar in form but suddenly unfamiliar in substance, clawed at her stomach. *Blind.* That word, the one Richard had used. No, she thought painfully. It wasn't so much that she was blind as that she deliberately didn't see. She had built a wall between herself and anything that threatened her; she knew it was there, but as long as she didn't have to look at it, she could ignore it. Blake had forced her on two occasions to face the past that she'd put behind her, never realizing what the ordeal had cost her in terms of pain. Now Richard, though he was using his coolly analytical brain instead of the gut instincts Blake operated on, was trying to do the same.

"I'm not blind," she denied in a whisper. "I know who I am, and what I am. I know my limits; I learned them the hard way."

"You're wrong," he said, his gray eyes thoughtful. "You've only learned the limits that other people have placed on you."

That was so true that she almost winced away from the thrust of it. Instinctively she pushed the thought away, drew herself up, marshaling her inner forces. "I think you wanted to talk to me about Serena," she reminded him quietly, letting him know that she wasn't going to talk about herself any longer.

"I did, but on second thought, I won't bother you with it. You have more than enough on your mind now. In the end, Serena and I will have to settle our differences on our own, so it's useless to ask anyone else's advice.''

Walking together, they reentered the house and went into the study. Serena was sitting with her back to them, though her posture of concentration told them exactly what expression was on her face. She hated to lose, and she poured all her energies into beating Blake. Although she was a good chess player, Blake was better. She was usually wild with jubilation whenever she managed to beat him.

Blake, however, looked up as Richard and Dione came in together, and a hard, determined expression pulled his face into a mask. His blue eyes narrowed.

Later that night, when she poked her head into his bedroom to tell him good-night, he said evenly, "Dee, Serena's marriage is hanging by a thread. I'm warning you: don't do anything to break that thread. She loves Richard. It'll kill her if she loses him."

"I'm not a home wrecker or a slut," she retorted, stung. Anger brought red spots to her cheeks as she stared at him. He had left the lamp on, evidently waiting until she told him good-night, as she usually did, so she could see exactly how forbidding he looked. Bewildered pain mingled with her anger to make her tremble inside. How could he even think... "I'm not like my mother," she blurted, her voice stifled, and she whirled, slamming the door behind her and fleeing to her own room despite the sound of her name being called demandingly.

She was both hurt and furious, but years of self-discipline enabled her to sleep dreamlessly anyway. When she woke hours later, just before her alarm went off, she felt better. Then she frowned. It seemed as if her subconscious could hear the echo of her name being called. She sat up, tilting her head as she listened.

"Dee! Damn it to hell!"

After weeks of hearing that particular note in his voice when he called her, she knew that he was in pain. Without her robe, she ran to his room.

She turned on the light. He was sitting up, rubbing his left calf, his face twisted in a grimace of pain. "My foot, too," he gritted. Dione seized his foot and forcefully returned his toes to their proper positions, digging her thumbs into the ball of his foot and massaging. He fell back against his pillow, his chest rising and falling swiftly as he gulped in air.

"It's all right," she murmured, moving her soothing hands up his ankle to his calf.

She devoted her attention to his leg, unaware of the fixed way he watched her. After several minutes she straightened out his leg and patted his ankle, then pulled the sheet over him. "There," she said, smiling as she looked up, but the smile faded as she met his gaze. Those dark blue eyes were as fierce and compelling as the sea, and she faltered in the face of his regard, her soft lips parting. Slowly his eyes dipped downward, and she was abruptly aware of her breasts, thrusting against the almost transparent fabric of her nightgown. A throbbing ache in her nipples made her fear that they had hardened, but she didn't dare glance down to confirm it. Her new nightgowns didn't hide a lot; they merely veiled.

Suddenly she couldn't withstand the force of his gaze, and she averted her eyes, her thick lashes dropping to shield her thoughts. His body was in her line of vision, and abruptly her eyes widened. She almost gasped, but controlled her reaction at the last second.

Jerkily she got to her feet, forgetting about how much the night-gown revealed. She'd accomplished her aim, but she didn't feel smug about it; she felt stunned, her mouth dry, her pulses hammering through her veins. She swallowed, and her voice was too husky to be casual when she said, "I thought you said you were impotent."

It was a moment before her words registered. He looked as stunned as she felt, then he glanced down at himself. His jaw hardened and he swore aloud.

A hot blush suddenly burned her face. It was ridiculous to stand there, but she couldn't move. She *was* fascinated, she admitted, completely bewildered by her reaction, or rather, her lack of it. As fascinated as a bird before a cobra, and that was a Freudian simile if ever she'd heard one.

"I must be psychic," he whispered rawly. "I was just thinking that that little bit of nothing you have on would rouse the dead."

She couldn't even smile. Abruptly, though, she was able to move, and she left the room as swiftly as she could without actually running.

That disturbing dryness was still in her mouth as she dressed, pulling out her old clothes rather than the clinging new garments she'd been wearing. There was no need to dress seductively now; that particular milestone was behind him, and she knew better than to play with fire.

The only problem was, she discovered as the days passed, that Blake didn't seem to notice that she'd reverted to her old clothes, her modest nightgowns. He didn't say anything, but she could always feel the blue fire of his gaze on her when they were together. In the course of therapy she was constantly touching him, and she gradually became accustomed to the way he'd wrap his fingers around her leg while she massaged him, or the frequency with which their bodies rubbed together when they were swimming.

Much sooner than she'd expected, he stood alone, not using his hands. He swayed for a moment, but his legs held and he regained his balance. He worked harder than any patient she'd had before, determined to end his dependency on the wheelchair. He paid for his determination every night with the torturous cramps that he suffered, but he didn't let up the killing pace he'd set for himself. Dione no longer organized his therapy; he pushed himself. All she could do was try to prevent him from doing so much that he harmed himself, and soothe his muscles at the end of every workout with massages and sessions in the whirlpool.

Sometimes she got a lump in her throat as she watched him straining himself to the limit, his teeth clenched, his neck corded with effort. It would soon be over, and she'd move on to another patient. He was already an entirely different man from the one she'd first seen almost five months before. He was as hard as a rock, tanned the color of teak, his body rippling with lean muscles. He'd regained all of his weight, and possibly more, but it was all muscle, and he was as fit as any professional athlete. She couldn't analyze the emotions that quivered through her when she watched him. Pride, of course, even some possessiveness. But there was also something else, something that made her feel warm and languid; yet at the same time she was more alive now than she'd ever been. She watched him, and she let him touch her, and she felt closer to him than she'd ever thought possible. She *knew* this man, knew his fierce pride, the daredevil in him that thumbed his nose at danger and laughingly accepted any challenge. She knew his swift, cutting intelligence, the blast of his temper, his tenderness. She knew the way he tasted, the strength of his mouth, the texture of his hair and skin beneath her hesitant fingers.

He was becoming so much a part of her that, when she allowed herself to think about it, it frightened her. She couldn't let that happen. Already he needed her less and less, and one day in the near future he would return to his work and she would be gone. For the first time the thought of moving on was painful. She loved the huge, cool hacienda, the smooth tiles underfoot, the serene expanses of white wall. The long summer days she'd spent in the pool with him, the laughter they'd shared, the hours of work, even the sweat and tears, had forged a bond that linked him to her in a way she didn't think she could bear.

It wasn't easy admitting that she loved him, but as the gilded fall days slipped past, she stopped trying to hide it from herself. She'd faced too much in the past to practice self-deception for long. The knowledge that at last she loved a man was bittersweet, because she didn't expect anything to come of it. Loving him was one thing; allowing him to love her was quite another. Her golden eyes were haunted as she watched him, but she threw herself into their remaining time together with a single-minded determination to gather all the memories she could, to let no shadows darken the time she had left. Like pieces of gold, she treasured his deep chuckles, the blistering curses he used whenever his legs wouldn't do as he wanted, the way the virile groove in his cheek deepened into a dimple when he would look up at her, elated, at every triumph.

He was so vitally alive, so masculine, that he deserved a woman in every sense of the word. She might love him, but she knew that she wouldn't be able to satisfy him in the way that was most important to him. Blake was a very physical man; that was a part of his character that became more and more evident with each passing day as he regained command of his body. She wouldn't burden him with the tangle of somber memories that lay just under the calm exterior she presented to the world; she wouldn't make him feel guilty that she'd come to love him. If it killed her, if it tore her to pieces inside, she'd keep their relationship on an even keel, guide him through the last weeks of his therapy, celebrate with him when he finally took those first, all-important steps, then quietly leave. She'd had years of practice in doing just that, devoting herself body and soul to her patient...no, the relentlessly honest side of her corrected. Never before had she devoted herself *body* and soul to anyone else, only to Blake. And he'd never know. She would smilingly say good-bye, walk away, and he'd pick up his life again. Perhaps sometimes he'd think of the woman who'd been his therapist, but then again, perhaps he wouldn't.

Her eyes were cameras, hungrily catching images of him and etching them permanently into her brain, her dreams, the very fiber of her being. There was the morning she went into his room and found him lying on his back, staring at his feet with fierce concentration. "Watch," he grunted, and she watched. Sweat beaded on his face, his fists clenched...and his toes moved. He threw his head back, giving her a blinding smile of triumph, and her built-in shutter clicked, preserving another memory; there was the scowl he gave her one night when she bested him in a long-fought game of chess, and he acted as outraged as he had when he'd discovered that she lifted weights. Laughing or frowning, he was the most beautiful thing that had ever happened to her, and she watched him constantly.

It simply wasn't fair that one man should be so rich with all the treasures of manhood, tempting her with his strength and laughter, when she knew that he was forbidden to her.

The depths of her fey golden eyes held a world of silent suffering, and though she was very controlled whenever she thought anyone was looking at her, in repose her features reflected the sadness she felt. She was so engrossed with the discovery of her love, and regret for what could never be, that she failed to notice the sharp blue eyes that watched her in return, read the pain she felt and determined to find the cause.

As the early days of November brought the sizzling Phoenix heat down into the comfortable mid-seventies, the milestone that she had dreaded, yet worked for so determinedly, was finally reached. He'd been on the bars all morning, literally dragging his feet along, and he was so wet with sweat that his dark blue shorts were soaked and clinging to him. Dione was exhausted by the effort of crouching beside him, moving his feet in the proper motions, and she sank to the floor.

"Let's rest a minute," she said, her voice muffled by fatigue.

His nostrils flared, and he made a sound that was almost a snarl. With his hands clenched around the bars, his teeth bared with determination, he flexed his muscles and bore down with the strain. His right foot moved erratically forward. A feral cry tore itself from deep in his chest and he sagged on the bars, his head falling forward. Trembling, Dione scrambled to her feet and reached out for him, but before she could touch him, he pulled his shoulders back and began the agonizing process with his left foot. His head arched back and he gulped in air; every muscle in his body stood out from the strain he was subjecting himself to, but at last the left foot moved, dragging more than the right foot had, but it moved. Dione stood rooted beside him, her face wet with silent, unnoticed tears as she watched him.

"Damn it," he whispered to himself, shuddering with the effort it cost him as he tried to take another step. "Do it again!"

She couldn't take it any longer; with a choked cry she hurled herself at him, wrapping her arms around his taut waist and burying her face in the sweaty hollow of his shoulder. He wavered, then regained his balance, and his sinewed arms locked around her, holding her so tightly that she moaned from the exquisite pain of it.

"You witch," he muttered thickly, burrowing his fingers under her tumbled mane of hair and twisting his hand in the black mass of it. He exerted just enough pressure to lift her face out of his shoulder and turn it up to him so he could see her wet cheeks, her drowning, glittering eyes and trembling lips. "You stubborn, beautiful witch, you all but jerked me out of that wheelchair by the hair on my head. Shhh, don't cry," he said, his tone changing to one of rustling tenderness. He bent his head and slowly kissed the salty tears from her lashes. "Don't cry, don't cry," he crooned, his lips following the tracks of her silvery tears down her cheek, sliding to her lips, where his tongue licked them away. "Laugh with me, lady; celebrate with me. Let's break out the champagne; you don't know what this means to me...lady...no more tears," he whispered, sighing the words against her face, her lips, and as the last one became sound he settled his mouth firmly over hers.

Blindly she clung to him, hearing the tone of his voice, though the words didn't make any sense. His arms were living shackles, holding her to him, his long, bare legs pressing against hers, her breasts crushed into the dark curls that decorated his chest, and she wasn't afraid. Not of Blake. The taste of him was wild and heady, his tongue strong and insistent as it moved into her mouth and tasted her deeply, possessively. Instinctively she kissed him in return, making her own discoveries, her own explorations. He bit gently at her tongue, then sucked it back into his mouth when she began a startled withdrawal. Dione's knees buckled and she sagged against him, which was enough to upset his precarious balance. He lurched sideways, and they stumbled to the floor in a tangle of arms and legs, but not once did he release her. Again and again his mouth met hers, demanding things that she didn't know how to give, and giving her a wild, alien pleasure that set her to trembling like a tree in a hurricane.

Her nails dug into his shoulders and she strained against him, mindlessly seeking to intensify the contact with him. Not once did she think of Scott. Blake filled her world. The sweaty male scent of him was in her nostrils, the slippery texture of his hot skin under her hands; the unbearably erotic taste of his mouth lay sweetly on her tongue. At some unknown point his kisses had slipped past celebration and become intensely male, demanding, giving, thrilling. Perhaps they'd never been celebration kisses at all, she thought fuzzily.

Suddenly he removed his mouth from hers and buried his face in the curve of her neck. When he spoke his voice was shaky, but husky with an undertone of laughter. "Have you noticed how much time we spend rolling around on the floor?"

It wasn't that funny, but in her sensitized state it struck her as hilarious, and she began to chuckle helplessly. He propped himself up on his elbow and watched her, his blue eyes lighted by a strange light. His hard, warm hand went to her stomach and slid under the thin fabric of her T-shirt top, resting lightly but soothingly on her bare flesh. The intimate but unthreatening touch calmed her almost immediately, and she quieted, lying there and watching his face with huge, fathomless eyes, in which her tears still glittered.

"This definitely calls for champagne," he murmured, leaning over to crush his lips lightly over hers, then withdrawing before the contact could start anew the searing fire of discovery.

Dione was under control again, and the therapist in her began to take over. "Definitely champagne, but first let's get off the floor." She rolled gracefully to her feet and extended her hand to him. He used his hands to place his feet in a secure position, then placed his forearm against hers, his hand cupping her elbow. She stiffened her arm, and he used the leverage to pull himself up, swaying for a moment before he found his balance.

"What now?" he asked.

Someone else might have thought he was asking about the immediate future, but Dione was so attuned to him that she knew he was asking about his progress. "Repetition," she replied. "The more you do it, the easier it'll be. On the other hand, don't push yourself too hard, or you could hurt yourself. People get clumsy when they're tired, and you could fall, break an arm or a leg, and the lost time would really hurt."

"Give me a time," he insisted, and she shook her head at his persistence. He didn't know how to wait; he pushed things along, impatient even with himself.

"I'll be able to give you a ballpark figure in a week," she said, not letting him push *her*. "But I'll definitely be able to keep my promise that you'll be walking by Christmas."

"Six weeks," he figured.

"With a cane," she threw in hastily, and then he glared at her.

"Without a cane," he insisted. She shrugged. If he set his mind to walking without a cane, he probably would.

"I've been thinking of going back to work," he said, startling her. She looked up and was tangled in the web of his blue gaze; it captured her as surely as a spider caught a helpless fly. "I could do it now, but I don't want to interfere with my therapy. What do you say about the first of the year? Will I be far enough along that working won't interfere with my progress?''

Her throat clogged. By the first of the year she'd be gone. She swallowed and said in a low but even voice, ''You'll be out of therapy by then and can resume your normal schedule. If you want to continue your exercise program, that's up to you; you have all of the equipment here. You won't have to work as hard as you have, because I was building you up from a very low point. All you have to do now, if you want to continue, is maintain the level you're at now, which won't require such intensive training. If you'd like, I'll draw up a program for you to follow to stay in your present shape.''

Blue lightning suddenly flashed from his eyes. ''What do you mean, for me to follow?'' he demanded harshly, his hand darting out to grip her wrist. Despite her strength, her bones were slender, aristocratic, and his long fingers more than circled her flesh.

Dione could feel her insides crumbling; hadn't he realized that when his therapy was completed, she'd be leaving? Perhaps not. Patients were so involved with themselves, with their progress, that the reality of other responsibilities didn't occur to them. She'd been living for weeks with the pain of knowing that soon she'd have to leave him; now he had to realize it, too.

''I won't be here,'' she said calmly, straightening her shoulders. ''I'm a therapist; it's what I do for a living. I'll be on another case by then. You won't need me anymore; you'll be walking, working, everything you did before...though I think you should wait a while before climbing another mountain.''

''You're *my* therapist,'' he snapped, tightening his grip on her wrist.

She gave a sad laugh. ''It's normal to be possessive. For months we've been isolated in our own little world, and you've depended on me more than you have on any other person in your life, except your mother. Your perspective is distorted now, but when you begin working again, everything will right itself. Believe me, by the time I've been gone a month, you won't even think about me.''

A dark red flush ran up under his tan. ''Do you mean you'd just turn your back on me and walk away?'' he asked in a disbelieving tone.

She flinched, and tears welled in her eyes. She'd gone for years without crying, having learned not to when she was a child, but Blake had shattered that particular control. She'd wept in his arms...and laughed in them. "It...it's not that easy for me, either," she quivered. "I get involved, too. I always...fall a little in love with my patients. But it passes.... You'll pick up your life and I'll move on to another patient—"

"I'll be damned if you're going to move in with some other man and fall in love with him!" Blake interrupted hotly, his nostrils flaring.

Despite herself, Dione laughed. "Not all of my patients are men; I have a large percentage of children."

"That's not the point." His flesh was suddenly taut over his cheekbones. "*I* still need you."

"Oh, Blake," she said in a half sob, half chuckle. "I've been through this more times than I can remember. I'm a habit, a crutch, nothing more, and I'm a crutch that you don't even need now. If I left today, you'd do just fine."

"That's a matter of opinion," he snapped. He shifted his grasp on her wrist and brought her hand up, cradling it to his beard-roughened cheek for a moment before touching his mouth to her knuckles. "You shoved your way into my life, lady, took over my house, my routine, *me*.... Do you think people forget volcanoes?"

"Maybe you won't forget me, but you'll discover, one day soon, that you don't need me anymore. Now," she said briskly, deliberately inserting cheer into her voice, "what about that champagne?"

They had champagne. Blake rounded up everyone, and between them they drank the entire bottle. Angela received the news of Blake's progress by gently crying; Alberta forgot herself so far as to give Dione a smile of self-satisfied complicity and drank three glasses of champagne; Miguel's dark face suddenly lighted, the first smile Dione had ever seen from him, and he toasted Blake with a silently raised glass, the two men's eyes meeting and communicating as memories flashed between them.

There was another bottle of champagne at dinner that night. Serena hurled herself into Blake's arms when he broke the good news to her, wrenching sobs of relief shaking her body. It took some time to quiet her; she was almost wild with the joy of it. Richard, whose face had become more and more strained as the weeks passed, suddenly looked as if the weight of the world had been lifted from his shoulders. "Thank God," he said with heartfelt sincerity. "Now I can have that nervous breakdown I've been putting off for two years."

Everyone laughed, but Blake said, "If anyone deserves a long vacation, it's you. As soon as I get back into harness, you're relieved of duty for at least a month."

Richard moved his shoulders tiredly. "I won't refuse it," he said.

Serena looked at her husband with determined cheerfulness. "How about Hawaii?" she asked. "We could spend the whole month lying on the beach in paradise."

Richard's mouth thinned. "Maybe later. I think I just need to be by myself for a while."

Serena drew back as though he'd slapped her, and her cheeks paled. Blake looked at his sister, reading the dejection in her, and anger brightened the dark blue of his eyes. Dione put her hand on his sleeve to restrain him. Whatever problems Richard and Serena were having, they had to work them out by themselves. Blake couldn't keep smoothing the path for Serena; that was a large part of the trouble. He was so important to her that Richard felt slighted.

In only a moment Serena gathered herself and lifted her head, smiling as though Richard's comment had completely missed her. Dione couldn't help but admire her grit. She was a proud, stubborn woman; she didn't need big brother to fight her battles for her. All she had to do was realize that for herself, and make Blake realize it, too.

Dinner was an astonishing melange of items that weren't normally served together, and Dione suspected that Alberta was still celebrating. When the cornish hen was followed by fish, she knew that the three glasses of champagne had been too much. She made the mistake of glancing at Blake, and the barely controlled laughter on his face was too much for her. Suddenly everyone at the table was laughing, effectively banishing the silence that had fallen after Richard's rejection of Serena.

To keep from hurting Alberta's feelings, they made a valiant effort at eating everything placed before them, though she'd evidently gotten carried away and prepared much more than she normally did. If she hadn't been such a good cook, even when she was tipsy, it would have been impossible.

They could hear occasional bursts of song from the kitchen, and just the thought of Alberta, of all people, singing, was enough to bring on fresh bouts of hilarity. Dione laughed until her stomach muscles were sore. The champagne was having its effect on them, too, and she suspected that anything would have made them laugh at that point.

It was much later than usual when Serena and Richard left, and if nothing else, the champagne had destroyed the distance between them. Richard had to support his wobbly wife for the short distance to the car, and Serena was frankly hanging on him, laughing like a maniac. Dione was still sober enough to be glad that Richard handled his alcohol well, since he was driving, but she was also tipsy enough to fall into gales of laughter at the thought that it was a good thing Blake was still in a wheelchair; he'd never have made it up the stairs if he'd been walking.

He insisted that she help him undress, and she put him to bed as if he were a child. As she leaned over him to adjust the sheet, he caught her hand and pulled it. After the champagne, her balance wasn't the best it had ever been, and she tumbled across him. He stopped her giggles by kissing her slowly, sleepily, then settling her in his arms. "Sleep with me," he demanded, then closed his eyes and fell immediately to sleep himself.

Dione smiled a little sadly. The lights were still blazing, and she was dressed in the royal-blue dress she'd put on to celebrate the occasion. She hadn't had *that* much to drink. After a few moments she gently extricated herself from his sleep-relaxed grip and slid from the bed. She turned out the lights, then made her way to her own room and removed the dress, dropping it carelessly on the floor. She, too, slept deeply, and woke the next morning with a headache that tempted her to just stay in bed.

With admirable, if painful, self-discipline, she got out of bed and showered, then went about her normal activities. The champagne hadn't affected Blake as much as it had her, and he was as clear-eyed as usual, ready to begin his exercises. After helping him to warm up, she left him to it and went to take a couple of aspirin.

Serena came in just as she was about to go downstairs—a radiant Serena, whose mouth seemed curved in a permanent smile. "Hi," she said cheerfully. "Where's Blake?"

When Dione told her, she said, "Good, I came to see you, not him. I just wanted to ask you how the chase is going."

It took a moment before Dione realized what she meant; her "scheme" to attract Blake had been so short-lived that, in retrospect, it seemed silly that she'd gotten so upset over something so trivial. Other worries had taken over her time and attention. "Everything's fine," she said, forcing herself to smile. "I think everything's fine with you, too. You look better than I'd expected you to look this morning."

Serena gave her a wink. "I hadn't had that much to drink," she admitted without a hint of shame. "It just seemed like too good an opportunity to pass up. You inspired me; if you could go after the man you wanted, why couldn't I? He's my husband, for heaven's sake! So I seduced him last night."

Despite her headache Dione chuckled. Serena grinned. "The war isn't won yet, but I've recaptured some lost territory. I've decided that I'm going to get pregnant."

"Is that wise?" So many things could go wrong. If the marriage failed, then Serena would be left to raise the child alone. Or Richard might stay because of the child, but that seemed like a hellish situation for all concerned.

"I know Richard," said Serena with confidence. "I've offended him, and it'll take him a while to forgive me, but I really think that he loves me. Having his baby will show him how much I love him, too."

"What he really needs is to know that you love him more than you love Blake,'' Dione said. She felt a little uneasy at giving advice; what did she know about handling a love life? Her own brief experience with marriage had been disastrous.

''I *do!* I love Richard in an entirely different way from the way I love Blake.''

''If you were faced with a situation where you could save one of them, but not both of them, which one would you save?''

Serena paled, staring at her.

''Think it over,'' Dione said gently. ''That's what Richard wants. Your wedding vows were to forsake all others.''

''You're telling me that I have to let Blake go, to cut him out of my life.''

''Not entirely; just change the amount of time that you devote to him.''

''I shouldn't have dinner over here every night, should I?''

''I'm sure Richard wonders which house you consider your home.''

Serena was a fighter; she absorbed Dione's words, and for a moment she looked frightened. Then her shoulders straightened and her chin went up. ''You're right,'' she said forcefully. ''You're a dear!'' She startled Dione by giving her a fierce hug. ''Poor Richard won't know what's hit him. I'm going to positively smother him with tender loving care! You can be the baby's godmother,'' she added with a wicked twinkle.

''I'll remember that,'' said Dione, but after Serena had left she wondered if Serena would remember. By that time, Dione would be long gone.

Chapter 8

The next day, without mentioning it to anyone, Dione began making arrangements to take another case. She'd give herself time to recover from the pain of losing Blake, time to adjust to waking up without knowing that he was in the next room. She'd begin at the end of January, she thought. Blake would be returning to work after the first of January, and she'd probably leave sometime around then.

Now that success was in his grasp, Blake pushed himself harder. Dione gave up even trying to rein in his energy. She watched him force himself along the bars, sweating, cursing steadily as an antidote against the pain and weariness, and when he was too tired to continue she'd massage his exhausted body, put him in the whirlpool, then give him another massage. She watched his diet more closely than ever, knowing how badly he needed extra nutrition now. When cramps knotted his legs in the night, she rubbed them out for him. There was no stopping him.

It was time for him to leave the wheelchair behind. She brought in a walker, a four-legged half cage that provided him with the balance and stability he needed, and the pleasure of getting around under his own power was so great that he gladly endured the slow pace, the strain.

He didn't mention Serena's sudden absence from the dinner table, though Alberta immediately adjusted both her menus and the amount she cooked. The full dinners almost ceased; instead she began preparing small, light dinners, and Dione often found the table set with candles and a decanter of wine. The intimate atmosphere was another spike that crucified her heart, but as Blake welcomed the pain of therapy, she welcomed the hurt of his company. This was all she had, and the days were trickling away so swiftly that she felt as if she were grasping at shadows.

On Thanksgiving Day, following Blake's directions, she drove them to Serena's house for dinner. Except for being transferred from the hospital to home, it was the first time he'd been out since his accident, and he sat turned to stone, his entire body tense as his senses struggled to take everything in. In two years Scottsdale had changed, cars had changed, clothing had changed. She wondered if the desert sky seemed bluer to him, the sun brighter.

"When will I be able to drive?" he asked abruptly.

"When your reflexes are fast enough. Soon," she promised absently. She seldom drove, and she had to concentrate on what she was doing. She jumped when his hand rested on her knee, then slid up under the skirt she was wearing to pat her thigh.

"Next week we'll start practicing," he said. "We'll go out in the desert, away from all the traffic."

"Yes, fine," she said, her voice taut with tension caused by the warm hand on her leg. He touched her constantly, bestowing kisses and pats, but somehow his hand seemed much more intimate when she had on a skirt.

A smile twitched at his lips. "I like that dress," he said.

She gave him a harried glance. He liked every dress she wore, evidently. He was definitely a leg man. He slid closer and bent his head to inhale the perfume she'd used in honor of the occasion, his warm breath caressing her collarbone just before he pressed his lips into the soft hollow. Simultaneously his hand slid higher, and the car wobbled dangerously before Dione straightened it.

"Stop it!" she fumed, pushing uselessly at his hand. "You're making me nervous! I don't drive that well anyway!"

"Then put both hands on the wheel," he advised, laughing. "I'm in the same car, remember? I'm not going to do anything that'll cause you to crash.''

"You wretch!" she shouted as his fingers began stroking back and forth over her thigh. "Damn it, Blake, would you stop it! I'm not a doll for you to play with!"

"I'm not playing," he murmured. His fingers circled higher.

Desperately Dione released the wheel and grabbed his wrist with both hands. The car veered sideways, and with a curse he finally moved his hand, grabbing the steering wheel and bringing the car back under control. "Maybe I'd better start driving *now*," he panted.

"You're going to be walking to Serena's!" she yelled, her face scarlet.

He threw his head back and laughed. "You don't know how good that sounds, lady! It would take me a while, but I could do it! God, I feel like a human being again!"

Abruptly she realized that his spirits were sky-high, the natural result of his victory and the experience of being away from the house. He was delirious with pleasure, drunk on his newfound freedom from the prison of his own body. Still, she was driving, and she was afraid that he was going to make her run into something.

"I mean it, stop fooling around!" she said sharply.

He gave her a lazy smile, a heart-stopping smile. "Lady, if I decided to fool around, you'd be the first to know."

"Why don't you go back to work tomorrow?" she demanded in sudden exasperation.

"We're closed for the holidays. I wouldn't have anything to do."

"I'm going to give you something to do," she muttered.

"Like what?"

"Picking your teeth up off the pavement," she said.

He threw his hands up in mock alarm. "All right, all right! I'll be good. Next thing I know, you'll be sending me to bed without my supper. I wouldn't really mind, though, because you always come to tuck me in, and I get to watch you running around in those thin nightgowns of yours that you think are so modest.... Serena's house is the solar redwood and rock one.'

He threw in the last sentence just as she opened her mouth to blast him again, and she maneuvered the Audi up the steep drive to where the house nestled against the mountain. By the time she'd gotten out of the car and gone around to help Blake wrestle with the walker, Serena and Richard had come out to greet them.

The steps were a problem for Blake, but he mastered them. Serena watched, an anxious look on her face, but she didn't run to help him. Instead she stayed firmly by Richard's side, her arm looped through his. Dione remained a step behind Blake, not out of servitude but to catch him in case he started to tumble. He looked over his shoulder at her and grinned. "Not bad, huh?"

"A regular goat," she replied, and only he caught her hidden meaning.

He gave her another of his breathtaking smiles. "Don't you mean mountain goat?"

She shrugged. "A goat is a goat is a goat."

His eyes promised retribution, but she felt safe from him for the time being. If he started anything on the drive back home, *she'd* get out and walk!

The traditional dinner had all of them groaning before it was over. Blake and Richard then retired to talk business, and Dione helped Serena clear the table. Serena had a cook, but she told Dione that everything had been prepared the day before and she'd given the cook the rest of the week off. "I don't mind being alone in the house with Richard," she said, laughing a little.

"Is Operation Manhunt going well?" asked Dione.

"At times." Serena laughed. "Sometimes I...ah...undermine his resistance. Then he'll freeze up on me again. But I think I'm winning the battle. He noticed that I've stopped going to Blake's every day."

"Did he ask you about it?"

"Richard? Not a chance! But he calls me almost every afternoon about some little something, as if he's checking on me."

They traded a few comments on the mule-headedness of men in general and finished cleaning the kitchen. When they finally emerged they discovered that the men were still deep in conversation about the company, with Richard going over some sort of electronic blueprint with Blake. Dione looked at Serena, and they both shrugged.

Kicking off their shoes, they sat down, and Serena used the remote control to turn on the television set, which revealed two football teams tearing into each other.

Within ten minutes the men had left their technical conversation and were sitting beside the women. Dione liked football, so she didn't mind watching the game, and evidently Serena shared the same fondness for it. At first Dione didn't pay attention to the hand that touched her shoulder, lying absently over it so that the fingers touched her collarbone. Gradually the touch firmed, shifted and exerted pressure. Without quite knowing how it had happened, she suddenly realized that she was leaning back in the circle of Blake's arm, resting against his chest while his arm kept her firmly anchored there.

The startled movement of her body brought a knowing smile to his lips, but he merely held her more closely than before. "Shhh. Just watch the game," he murmured.

She was so rattled that nothing sank into her consciousness, but eventually the warmth of his body began to relax her. He would behave himself here, so she was free to enjoy the sensation, let herself drown in the heady scent of his skin. All too soon she would have only the memories of him to take out and savor.

The time passed swiftly. Incredibly they became hungry again, so everyone raided the refrigerator and constructed enormous sandwiches of turkey, lettuce, tomato and anything else they could find. Blake's sweet tooth demanded feeding, and he devoured what was left of the strawberry pie. The atmosphere was easy, comfortable, and he commented on it when they were driving home late that night.

"Serena and Richard seem to have patched up their differences," he said, watching her sharply in the dim light from the dash.

"I think they're well on their way," she said, carefully keeping her tone bland. She wasn't about to divulge anything Serena had told her.

When they got home Dione looked him squarely in the eye and smiled. "I really don't think there's any need for me to tuck you in any longer," she said sweetly. "You're perfectly mobile now. I'll see you in the morning. Good night."

As she let herself into her room she heard him doing a perfect imitation of a chicken clucking, and she had to bite her lip to stifle her laughter. The monster!

But when he called her several hours later, jerking her out of a sound sleep, she didn't hesitate. She hurried to his room and flipped on the light switch. He was lying on his stomach, hopelessly tangled in the sheet as he tried to reach his left leg.

"Easy," she crooned, finding the cramp and briskly rubbing the muscle of his calf between her hands. He went limp with relief as the pain eased away.

"How much longer will this go on?" he muttered into his pillow.

"Until your muscles are used to the demands you're making on them," she said. "It's not as bad as it was. You seldom have a cramp in your right leg now."

"I know. My left leg drags more than the right. I'll always limp, won't I?"

"Who knows? It won't matter, though. You'll look smashing with a cane."

He laughed and rolled over on his back, tangling the sheet even more. Despite what she'd said earlier, Dione bent over him and automatically began straightening the sheet. "You managed to make a disaster area of your bed," she complained.

"I was restless tonight," he said, his voice suddenly strained.

Dione glanced up, and her hands froze at their task. He was staring at her, his gaze locked on her breasts. A look of such raw hunger was in his eyes that she would have flinched away if she'd had any strength in her limbs. But she continued to sit on the side of his bed, mesmerized by the way his gaze moved lovingly, longingly, over her female curves.

"Lady, what you do to me is almost criminal," he groaned in a shaky voice.

An odd tightening in her breasts made her close her eyes. "I've got to go," she said weakly, but for the life of her she couldn't make herself move.

"No, don't go," he pleaded. "Let me touch you...my God, I've got to touch you!"

Dione caught her breath on a sob as she felt his fingertips trace lightly over her breast, and she squeezed her eyes shut even more tightly than before. For a moment the awful unfamiliarity of a man's touch on her breast brought back a nightmare of pain and humiliation, and she made a choked sound of protest.

"Dee, honey, open your eyes. Look at me; look at how I'm shaking. Touching you makes me dizzy," he whispered fiercely. "I get drunk on the very smell of you."

Dione's eyes fluttered open, and she found that he'd moved closer, until his face was filling her vision. It was Blake's face, not Scott's, and his blue eyes were as dark and stormy as the sea, full of incredible hunger. His trembling fingers were still moving only lightly over her breasts, though the heat of his hand burned her even through her nightgown.

"That...that's enough," she said, her voice thin, wavering out of control. "This isn't right."

"I need you," he cajoled. "It's been so long...can't you tell how much I need you? Please. Let me touch you, really touch you. Let me unbutton this granny gown and see you."

Even as the words were tumbling harshly from his lips, his agile fingers were slipping the tiny buttons of her nightgown free of the buttonholes. The buttons ran down to her waist, and he undid every one of them while she sat helplessly transfixed by the primitive call of his need. Slowly, with rapt attention, he opened the gown and pushed it off her smoothly tanned shoulders, dropping the cloth around her arms and baring her to the waist.

"I've dreamed of this," he whispered harshly. "I saw you, that morning.... You were so perfect, so damned *female,* that you took my breath away." Gently he cupped a breast in his palm, curving his fingers over its ripe curve as if he were measuring the heft of it.

Dione began to tremble, wild little tingles of sensation shooting through her body. She didn't know what to do, how to handle him. She had no experience with men other than her husband, and that had been a horror from start to finish, nothing that compared to the sweet pain of Blake's touch. Sweet, yes...and not really pain. Incredible. Unknown. A primitive exultation raced along her veins, heating her blood, making her feel stupidly, happily weak. She wanted to sink down beside him on the bed, but she couldn't do that. Despite the joy her body was feeling, her mind was still locked away from even the possibility of it.

Now both of his hands were on her, holding her breasts together. His head bent, and she sucked in a convulsive breath, staring down at his dark hair with terrified fascination. His tongue darted out and washed a cherry nipple, then he blew his warm breath across it, watching with delight as it tightened and thrust out at him. "That's beautiful," he breathed, and tasted the other one.

At last she could move, and her fingers threaded through his hair. She thought dimly that she'd pull his head away, but instead her palms pressed against his warm skull and held him to her, held his mouth to the tender flesh he was suckling as fiercely as any starving infant.

He released her nipple from his mouth and lay back, his hands sliding to her ribs and drawing her with him, pulling her down until she lay half-across him. He began kissing her with short, hard kisses that stung her lips. "I need you," he panted. "Please. I want you so much. Let me make love to you."

Dione moaned, a high, keening sound that reflected both the tumult he'd stirred in her and her fear of going any further. "I can't," she cried, tears suddenly stinging her eyes. "You don't know what you're asking of me."

"Yes, I do," he whispered, moving his mouth down to the line of her jaw, nipping at her with his teeth. "I'm asking you to let me love you. I want you so much that I'm aching all over. I can't sleep for dreaming about you. Let me be a man with you; let me bury myself in you and forget about the past two years. Make me whole again," he pleaded.

She'd spent too long nurturing this man, agonized over him too much, felt his pain, celebrated his triumphs, loved him. How could she refuse him now? She'd be leaving soon, and she'd never know the heady taste of him again. But she was shaking, almost convulsed with the fear of what he'd do to her. For him, she'd bear it, this one last time. The scars that Scott had left on her mind had ruined her forever, kept her from feeling the total pleasure of a man, and when

Blake rolled, deftly placing himself above her, the nauseating panic that beat its wings in her stomach threatened to overtake her.

He saw the fixed expression in her enormous golden eyes and began to speak softly to her, making her realize his identity. With silent desperation she stared at him, her nails digging into his shoulders.

"It's all right," he murmured soothingly. "You know I won't hurt you; I'd never hurt you. Let's get you out of this," he said as he began thrusting the bunched cloth at her waist down over her hips, then stroking it away from her thighs. He leaned on his elbow and looked at her, drinking in and savoring all the details that he'd only dreamed about before. He steadied his shaking hand by flattening his palm on her stomach and sliding it over her satiny skin. One finger dipped into the tight little hollow of her navel, and she gasped again, but though her nails were digging so deeply into his shoulders that she'd broken the skin, the blind fear had left her face. Her eyes were locked on him, letting him know that for him, she would do this. Though she was afraid, she trusted him, and she would give him this one last gift, the pleasure of her body.

His hand slid lower, insinuating itself between her thighs and exploring, as he'd tried to do so many times before. She clenched her teeth in shock and tried to control her body's instinctive movement, but her thighs tightened as she tried to dislodge the alien touch.

"Honey, don't!" he cried. "I won't hurt you, I swear."

Dione swallowed and slowly regained control of herself, forcing her legs to relax. He was shaking all over, his body dewed with sweat, the color in his face as florid as if he burned with fever; she felt the heat of his skin beneath her hands and wondered vaguely if he weren't really fevered after all. His blue eyes were glittering wildly, and his lips were red, swollen. She removed one trembling hand from his shoulder and touched his face, placing her fingertips on his lips. "It's all right," she whispered thinly. "I'm ready."

"Oh, God, no, you're not," he groaned, kissing her fingers. "I wanted to wait, but I don't think I can."

"It's all right," she repeated, and with a muffled cry he moved to lie fully over her.

All of the love she felt for him welled up and made her body pliable for his touch; with her eyes wide open and locked on his face, she knew that this was Blake, and that she would do anything for him. Though her heart was slamming against her ribs with almost shattering force, though her entire body shook, she clutched his shoulders and drew him tightly to her.

He tried to be gentle, but the years of celibacy had destroyed a great deal of his normal self-control. When he parted her legs and felt the silkiness of her thighs cradle his hips, he moaned deep in his chest and took her with a single strong movement.

Hot tears burned her lids, then slid down her cheeks. This wasn't the agony she'd expected, but her body had been untouched for twelve years, and the pain and shock of his entry were all too real. To her astonishment, her flesh didn't flinch from him; she still lay soft and willing beneath him. She began to weep in earnest, not from the pain, which was already fading, but because suddenly she realized that Blake had given her as much as he was taking. He'd given her back her womanhood. The years had wrought their healing miracle, after all; it had taken Blake to make her realize it, Blake to make her love enough to overcome the past.

He lifted his head from her throat and saw the tears, and he paled. ''No,'' he croaked. ''Dee, what have I done? I'll stop—''

Inexplicably the tears mingled with laughter, and she caught him tightly, preventing the removal of his body. ''Don't stop!'' she said joyously, the words clogging in her throat. ''I didn't know…I had no idea! No, don't ever stop—''

He caught the babbling words in his mouth, kissing her wildly and deeply, relief making him drunk. ''I'm going to have to stop,'' he panted, beginning to move rhythmically on her. ''It's been over two years, darling. I don't think I can wait—''

''Then don't wait,'' she said softly, her eyes shining. ''This is for you.''

He kissed her again, even harder than before. ''The next one's for you,'' he promised hoarsely, just before he slid over the edge of control. Dione hugged him to her, accepting his body and his desperate, almost violent movements, cradling him, soothing him, and in a moment the storm had passed and he sagged against her.

She could feel the heavy pounding of his heart as he lay on her in the silent aftermath, feel the heat of his breath on her shoulder, the trickle of sweat that ran from his side and slipped down her ribs. She smoothed his tousled dark hair, adjusted his head more comfortably on her shoulder. He murmured something and his hand came up to cover her breast. She waited, lying there pressed into the bed by his weight, as his body relaxed and he drifted slowly, easily into sleep.

She stared up at the light that still blazed brightly; turning out the light hadn't occurred to either of them.

Exhaustion made her body heavy, but she couldn't sleep. The night had been a major turning point in her life, but she didn't know what direction to take. Or was it such a major turning point? Blake had taught her that she no longer needed to fear the touch of a man, but what difference did it make? If the man weren't Blake, then she didn't want him. It was the love that she felt for him that had enabled her to tear down her prison of fear, and without that love she simply wasn't interested.

Nor, she realized suddenly, could it ever happen again. She couldn't afford to let it happen. She was a therapist, and Blake was her patient. She'd violated her own professional code, totally forgotten the rules and standards that she'd set for herself. This was the worst mistake she'd ever made and she felt sick with remorse.

Whatever happened, she had to remember that soon she'd be leaving, that she was only a temporary part of Blake's life. She'd have to be stupid to jeopardize her career for something that she knew was only a moment out of time. I should have seen it coming, she thought tiredly. Of course Blake had been attracted to her; she was the only woman available to him. But she'd been so engrossed in her own misery and attraction that she hadn't realized that his actions hadn't been meant merely to tease.

Gently she shifted him to one side, and he was sleeping so deeply that he didn't flicker an eyelash. With slow, careful movements she sat up and reached for her discarded nightgown, pulling it over her head before she got to her feet. As she stood she winced at the unfamiliar soreness of her body, but forced herself to walk silently to the door and leave, turning out the light as she passed the switch.

In her own room she stared at her bed, but realized that it would be a waste of time to return to it. She'd never be able to sleep. Too many sensations, too many memories, were warring in her mind and body. Her bedside clock told her that it was a little after three; she might as well stay up the rest of the night.

She felt oddly empty, her regret candeling out the bittersweet plea- sure she'd found in his embrace and leaving her with nothing. For a short while, in his arms, she'd felt wildly alive, as if all her fetters had fallen away. Reality was something less than that. Reality was knowing that the night meant nothing to him beyond the immediate satisfaction of his sex-starved body. She'd seen it coming from a mile away and still hadn't had the sense to duck; no, she'd taken the punch full on the jaw.

But mistakes were something to learn from, better textbooks than anything that ever got put into print. She'd picked herself up before and gone on, and she'd do it again. The trick was to remember that there was an end to everything, and the end of her time with Blake was coming at her with the speed of a jet.

She cringed inwardly at the thought, and in agitation walked out to the gallery. The desert air was cold, and she shivered when it touched her heated skin, but she welcomed the shock of it. The night had been an emotional roller coaster, a ride that had left her stunned, bewildered. She'd gone from fear to acceptance, then to joy, followed by regret and a rerun of acceptance, and now she was afraid again, afraid that she wouldn't be able to pick up the pieces, afraid that life after Blake would be so hollow that it would be useless. Afraid, even, of the possibility that the fear he'd destroyed had been her strongest defense.

Chapter 9

The sudden lancing of light across the dark gallery made her heart leap into her throat, and she turned her head to the left to wearily eye the sliding doors to Blake's room, where the light was coming from. What had awakened him? When the glass doors remained closed, she turned back to stare out again into the blackness of the garden. She hoped he wouldn't come looking for her; she didn't think she could face him right then. Perhaps in the morning, when she was dressed in her familiar ''therapist uniform'' of shorts and a T-shirt and they were involved in the routine of exercise. Perhaps then she'd have herself under control and could act as if nothing unusual had happened. But now she felt raw and bleeding, every nerve exposed. Wearily she leaned her head against the railing, not even feeling how cold she'd become.

A whirr came to her ears and she lifted her head, frowning. It was coming from her room…then it stopped just behind her, and she knew. Blake had used the wheelchair, because he could get around faster in it than he could using the walker. Her entire body tensed as she listened to him getting out of the chair, struggling for balance, but she didn't dare look around. She kept her forehead pressed against the cold metal of the railing, hoping without belief that he'd realize she didn't want to be disturbed and leave her alone.

First she felt his hands, gripping her shoulders, then the hard, warm press of his body against her back and the stirring of his breath in her hair. "Dee, you're freezing," he murmured. "Come inside. We'll talk there, and I'll get you warm."

She swallowed. "There's nothing to talk about."

"There's everything to talk about," he said, a hardness that she'd never heard before in his voice making her shudder in reaction. He felt the ripple of her muscles under his fingers and pulled her closer to him. "Your skin is icy, and you're coming in with me now. You're in shock, honey, and you need to be taken care of. I thought I understood, but you threw me for a loop tonight. I don't know what it is you're hiding, what you're afraid of, but I'm damned well going to find out before this night is over."

"The night *is* over," she told him thinly. "It's morning now."

"Don't argue with me. In case you haven't noticed, I don't have a stitch of clothing on and I'm freezing, but I'm staying right here with you. If you don't come inside I'll probably catch pneumonia and undo all the progress you've worked for. Come on," he said, his tone changing into one of cajolery. "You don't have to be afraid. We'll just talk."

She shook her head, her long hair flying wildly and striking him in the face. "You don't understand. I'm not afraid of you; I never have been."

"Well, that's something," he muttered, dropping his arm to her waist and urging her to turn. She gave up and dully let him guide her inside, with his using her for balance. His pace was slow but remarkably steady, and he didn't really put any of his weight on her. He stopped to close the sliding doors, then guided her to the bed.

"Here, get under the covers," he ordered as he bent down to switch on the lamp. "How long have you been out there? Even the room is cold."

She shrugged; it didn't really matter how long it had been, did it? She did as he said and crawled into the bed, pulling the thick comforter up to her neck. Blake studied her pale, set expression for a moment, and his lips pressed grimly together. He lifted the cover and slid into the bed next to her, and she stared at him in shock.

"I'm cold, too," he said, and it was only half a lie. He slid his arm under her neck and curved his other hand around her waist, pulling her into the cocoon of his body heat. At first she was rigid; then the warmth began to penetrate her chilled skin and she started to shiver. His hand exerted just the slightest pressure and she moved with it, unconsciously pressing more closely to him in search of extra heat. When he had her settled, her head cradled on his shoulder and her legs tangled with his, he stroked the heavy black hair away from her face and she felt the pressure of his mouth on her forehead.

"Are you comfortable?" he murmured.

Comfortable wasn't the word for it; she was so tired that her limbs lay heavily, without strength. But she nodded, as he seemed to want an answer. What did it matter? She was just so tired....

After a moment he said with misleading mildness, "I thought you said you'd been married."

Surprise made her lift her head and stare at him. "I was." What did he mean?

Gently he threaded his fingers through her hair and forced her head back to his shoulder. "Then why was it so...painful for you?" he asked, his voice a rumble under her ear. "I damned near fainted, thinking that you'd been a virgin."

For a moment her mind was blank, struggling to understand what he was saying; then realization came abruptly and a hot flush warmed her cold cheeks. "I wasn't a virgin," she assured him huskily. "It's just that I haven't...it's been a long time."

"How long?"

With rising alarm she heard the determination in his voice, barely masked by the quietness of his tone. He meant to know everything, to uncover all her secrets. Twice before he'd torn away the protection of her forgetfulness, forcing her to remember the pains and failures that she'd tried so hard never to think of again. Did he like causing her pain?

"How long?" he repeated inexorably. "Talk to me, honey, because you're not leaving this bed until I know."

Dione closed her eyes in despair, swallowing in an effort to relieve the dryness of her mouth. She might as well tell him and get it over with. "Twelve years," she finally admitted, the words muffled against his skin because as she said them, she turned her face into his throat.

"I see." Did he? Did he really see? Could any man really understand what goes through a woman's mind when her body is violated? A wild bitterness sprang out of the well of pain that she usually kept covered. He didn't care if he explored the clock's workings until it could no longer tick, as long as he discovered what had made it tick in the beginning. Her hands stiffened against him and she pushed, but now he was much stronger than she was, and held her welded tightly to him, his body hard and unyielding against hers. After a moment she gave up the futile effort and lay beside him in rigid rejection.

He curved his long fingers over her smooth shoulder and tucked her even closer to him, as if to shield her. "Twelve years is a long time," he began easily. "You had to be just a kid. How old are you now?"

"Thirty." She heard the ragged edge of panic in her voice, felt the way her heart began to skitter, the increased rhythm of air rushing in and out of her lungs. She'd already told him too much; he could put the pieces of the puzzle together now and read the whole ugly story.

"Then you had to be just eighteen.... You told me that you got married when you were eighteen. Haven't you been in love since then? I know men have been attracted to you. You've got a face and body that turn my insides into melted butter. Why haven't you let someone love you?"

"That's my business," she cried sharply, trying again to roll away from him. He held her without hurting her, gently subduing her with his arms and legs. Goaded, maddened by the bonds that held her, she shrieked, "Men don't *love* women! They hurt them, humiliate them, then say, 'Whatsamatter? You frigid?' *Let me go!*"

"I can't," he said, his voice catching oddly. She was in no state to pay any attention to how her words had affected him; she began to fight in earnest, kicking at his legs, trying to scratch his face, her body arching wildly in an effort to throw herself off the bed. He snatched her hands away from his cheeks before she could do any damage, then wrestled her around until she was beneath him, his weight holding her captive.

"Dione, stop it!" he yelled. "Damn it, talk to me! *Were you raped?*"

"Yes!" she screamed, a sob tearing out of her throat. "Yes, yes, yes! Damn you! I didn't want to remember! Can't you understand that? It kills me to remember!" Another tearing, aching sob wrenched its way out of her chest, but she wasn't crying. Her eyes were dry, burning, yet still her chest heaved convulsively and the awful sounds, like someone choking on a pain too large to be swallowed, continued.

Blake's head fell back and he ground his teeth in a primal snarl, his neck corded with the rage that surged through him. His muscles trembled with the need to vent his fury physically, but a despairing whimper from the woman in his arms made him realize the need to control himself, to calm her. He held her and stroked her, sliding his palms down her body and feeling the marvelous tone of her sleek muscles even through the fabric of her gown. His lips nuzzled into her hair, moved on to discover the softness of her eyelids, the satin stretch of skin over her exotic cheekbones, the intoxicating bloom of her soft, generous mouth. He whispered to her, crooned endearments, reassured her with broken phrases that told her how lovely she was, how much he wanted her. He promised her with his words and his body that he wouldn't hurt her, reminding her over and over of the hour not long past when she'd trusted him enough to let him make love to her. The memory of that joining burned over his skin, but his need for her could wait. *Her* needs came first, the needs of a woman who had known too much pain.

Gradually she calmed; gradually she reached out to him, by slow degrees curling her arms around his muscular back. She was tired, so worn out from the emotional strain of the night that she was limp against him, but he had to know, so he said again, "Tell me about it."

"Blake, no," she moaned, turning her head weakly away from him. "I can't...."

"You can; you have to. Was that why you got divorced? Couldn't your husband handle what had happened to you?" His questions fell

on her like rocks, bruising her, and she flinched in his arms. He
caught her chin and turned it back to him so he could read the nuances of her expression. "What kind of bastard was he, to turn his
back on you when you needed him most? Did he think it was your
fault?"

A high, strained peal of laughter escaped her, and she shut it off
abruptly by clapping her hand over her mouth, afraid of the rising
hysteria in her. "He...oh, this is funny! He didn't have any trouble
handling what happened to me! *He* did it. My husband was the one
who raped me!"

Blake went rigid, stunned both by her words and the way she began
to laugh, gasping shrieks of laughter that again she shut off, visibly
clenching herself in an effort to regain control. She attained it, but
she used all of the inner strength she possessed, and as she lay in his
arms she could feel the emotion draining away from her, leaving her
heavy, spent...

"Tell me," he insisted, his voice so hoarse that she didn't recognize it.

Her heartbeat had changed from a frantic sledgehammer pounding
to a ponderous rhythm; dimly she wondered at it, but what did it
really matter? What did anything really matter? She'd had all she
could bear tonight....

"Dione," he prodded.

"I don't know why I married him," she said dully. "I don't think
I ever loved him. But he was handsome and he had money, something
I'd never had. He dazzled me with it. He bought me things, took me
places, told me how much he loved me. I think that was it; he told
me that he loved me. No one had ever told me that before, you see.
But I was still standoffish with him, and Scott couldn't stand that. I
don't think anyone had ever said no to him before. So he married
me."

Blake waited a moment for her to resume, and when she didn't he
jostled her lightly. "Go on."

Her eyelids lifted slowly. She stared at him with half-veiled eyes,
the glimmering, mysterious golden pools darkened to amber by the
shadow of her lashes. "On our wedding night, he hurt me," she said

simply. "He was so rough...I started fighting him. I was strong even then, and I knocked him off of me. He went wild.... He forced me to have sex with him, and he wasn't gentle. It was my first time, and I thought I was dying.

"I knew then that the marriage was an awful mistake, that I wanted out, but he wouldn't let me go. Every night I'd fight him again, and he'd force me again. 'He was going to teach me how to be a woman if he had to break every bone in my body,' he said. I couldn't stop fighting him," she muttered to herself. "I never could just lie there and let him get it over with. I *had* to fight back, or I felt like something in me would die. So I fought, and the more I fought, the rougher he got. He started...hitting me."

Blake cursed violently and she jumped, throwing her arm up to cover her face. She was so deep inside her bitter memories that she was reacting as she had then, defending herself. His curse changed into a groan and he cuddled her, coaxing her to lower her arm. "I'm sorry, darling, I didn't mean to startle you," he panted. "When he started hitting you, why didn't you turn him into the police?"

"I didn't know that he couldn't do that," she said tiredly. "I was so dumb; I read a lot of things about it afterward, but at the time I thought he had a legal right to do what he wanted with me, short of murder. He got worse and worse; he almost stopped wanting sex. He'd just start right in hitting me. Sometimes he'd go ahead and rape me, as roughly as he could, but most of the time he didn't."

"You stayed with him for three months? Isn't that how long you told me your marriage lasted?"

"Not even that long. That I stayed with him, I mean. I can't remember.... He pushed me down the steps one night, and I landed in the hospital with a broken arm and a concussion. I was there for several days, and a nurse figured out that I hadn't simply tripped while going down the steps. She talked to me, and a counselor talked to me. I didn't go back to Scott. When I was released from the hospital, the nurse let me stay with her."

She was calmer now, the memories easier to bear. In her normal voice she said, "Scott's family was horrified by what had happened, they were good people, and when I filed for divorce they forced Scott to go along with it. They gave me a lot of support, paid for my training as a therapist, kept Scott away from me, even got him into psychiatric counseling. It must have worked; he's remarried now, and they seem very happy. He has two daughters.''

"Have you kept in touch with him?" Blake asked incredulously.

"Oh, no!" she denied, shaking her head. "But while his mother was alive she kept track of me, sort of looked after me like a guardian angel. She never got over what had happened to me, as if it were her fault because Scott was her son. She told me when he remarried, and when her grandchildren were born. She died a couple of years ago."

"So he lived happily ever after, and you've been dragging a ball and chain around with you for all these years," he said angrily. "Afraid to let anyone touch you, keeping people pushed away at a safe distance...only half-alive!"

"I haven't been unhappy," she said wearily, her lashes sweeping down. She was so tired.... He knew all of it now, and she felt so empty, as if all the terror that had filled her for so long had seeped away, leaving her hollow and lost. The warmth of Blake's body was so comforting in the chilly room; the steady rumble of his heartbeat in his strong chest was so reassuring. She could feel the iron in the bands of flesh that wrapped around her, feel the security of his strength. She'd given him that strength; it was only right that she rely on it now. She turned her face against him, inhaling and tasting on her tongue the heady scent of his body. He smelled of man, of sweat, of a clean grassy scent that eluded her when she tried to search it out. He had the musky smell of sex, a reminder of the incredible night. With a slow, gentle sigh, she slept, all of her senses filled with him.

When she woke she was alone in the bed and the brightness of the room told her that the morning was almost over. She wasn't fortunate enough to forget, even for a moment, the events of the night. Her eyes went to the gallery, but the wheelchair was gone, and she wondered how Blake could have left her bed and taken the wheelchair without waking her; she was normally the lightest of sleepers, coming awake at any unusual noise. But she'd been so tired...she was still tired, her body heavy and clumsy feeling, her reactions slow.

She eased out of bed, wincing at the unfamiliar soreness of her body. How could she have been so stupid that she'd let Blake make love to her? She was trying to get through these last days with him with the least amount of emotional damage, and she'd made it impossibly complicated. She should never have tried to arouse him; she didn't know anything about handling men, or handling herself, if it came to that. He'd said, "I need you," and she'd melted. A real pushover, she told herself contemptuously. He must have seen her coming a mile away. Then, to top it all off, she'd told him about Scott.

She writhed inwardly with embarrassment. She'd managed for years to control herself, to keep herself from wallowing in the slimy pool of the past. So she hadn't been comfortable with men; what of it? A lot of women managed very well without men. When she thought of the way she'd clung to him, weeping and moaning, she wanted to die of shame. Her solitary nature hated the thought of displaying so much of herself to anyone, even the man who had taken up her days and nights for months.

Willpower had a lot to say for itself; it steadied her nerves, gave her the courage to shrug her shoulders and step into the shower as if there was nothing unusual about that morning. She dressed as she normally did, then went straight to the gym, where she knew she'd find Blake. There was no point in putting off their meeting, because time wouldn't make it any easier. It was best to face him and get it over with.

When she opened the door he glanced at her but didn't say anything; he was lying on his stomach, lifting weights with his legs, and he was counting. He was totally engrossed in the demands he was making of his body. With a slow but steady rhythm he lifted each leg in turn.

"How long have you been doing that?" Dione asked sternly, forgetting her discomfort as her professional concern surfaced.

"Half...an...hour," he grated.

"That's enough. Stop right now," she ordered. "You're overdoing it; no wonder your legs give you fits! What are you trying to do, punish your legs for the years they didn't work?"

He relaxed with a groan. "I'm trying to get away from the walker," he said irritably. "I want to walk alone, without leaning on anything."

"If you tear a muscle you're going to be leaning on something for a lot longer than necessary," she snapped back. "I've watched you push yourself past the bounds of common sense, but no more. I'm a therapist, not a spectator. If you're not going to follow my instructions, then there's no use in my staying here any longer."

His head jerked around, and his eyes darkened to a stormy color. "Are you telling me that you're leaving?"

"That's up to you," she returned stonily. "If you'll do as you're told and follow your training program, I'll stay. If you're going to ignore everything I say and do what you want, there's no point in my wasting my time here."

He flushed darkly, and she realized that he still wasn't used to giving in to anyone. For a moment she expected him to tell her to pack her bags, and she pulled herself up, braced for the words that would end her time with him. Then he clenched his jaw and snapped, "All right, lady, you're the boss. What's the matter with you today? You're as touchy as a rattler."

Absurd relief washed over her, at both her reprieve from exile and the familiar, comforting ill-temper apparent in his words. She could handle that; but she knew beyond a doubt that she wouldn't have been able to handle the situation if he'd made any reference to the intimacy of the night, if he'd tried to kiss her and act like a lover.

She was so determined to regain the therapist-patient relationship that during the day she resisted his teasing and efforts to joke with her, turning a cold face to his laughing eyes. By the time they had finished they were snarling at each other like two stray dogs. Dione, having eaten nothing all day, was so hungry that she was almost sick, and that only added to the hostility she felt.

Her body was rebelling against her misuse of it when it was finally time for dinner. On wobbly legs she made her way down the stairs, her head whirling in a nauseating manner that made her cling to the banisters. She was so preoccupied with the task of getting down the stairs in one piece that she didn't hear Blake behind her, didn't feel his searing blue gaze on her back.

She made it to the dining room and fell into her chair with relief at not having sprawled on the floor. After a moment Blake made his way past her and went into the kitchen; she was too sick to wonder at that, even though it was the first time she'd seen him enter the kitchen in the months she'd been living there.

Alberta came out promptly with a steaming bowl of soup, which she placed before Dione. "Eat that right now," she ordered in her gruff, no-nonsense voice.

Slowly Dione began to eat, not trusting her queasy stomach. As she ate, though, she began to feel better as her stomach settled; by the time she'd finished the soup the trembling in her body was subsiding and she wasn't as dizzy. She looked up to find Blake seated across from her, silently watching her eat. A wave of color heated her face, and she dropped her spoon, embarrassed that she'd begun eating without him.

"Lady," he said evenly, "you give the word *stubborn* a whole new meaning."

She lowered her eyes and didn't respond, not certain if he were talking about how hungry she'd been or something else; she feared it was the "something else," and she just couldn't carry on a calm, ordinary conversation about what had happened between them.

She made an effort to call a truce between them, though without lowering her guard an inch. She couldn't laugh with him; her nerves were stretched too tightly, her emotions were too ravaged. But she did smile and talk, and generally avoided meeting his eyes. In that manner she made it safely through the evening until it was time to go to bed and she could excuse herself.

She was already in bed, staring at the ceiling, when she heard him call. It was like an instant replay of the night before and she froze, a film of perspiration breaking out on her body. She couldn't go in there, not after what had happened the last time. He couldn't have cramps in his legs, because she'd heard him come up not five minutes before. He wasn't even in bed yet.

She lay there telling herself fiercely that she wouldn't go; then he

called her name again and years of training rose up to do battle with
her. He was her patient, and he was calling her. She could just check
and make certain that he was all right, and leave again if there was
nothing wrong.

Reluctantly she climbed out of bed, this time reaching for her robe
and belting it tightly around her. No more going into his room wearing only her nightgown; the thought of his hands on her breasts in-
terfered with the rhythm of her breathing, and an odd ache began in
the flesh that he had touched.

When she opened the door to his bedroom she was surprised to
see that he was already in bed. "What did you want?" she asked
coolly, not leaving her position by the door.

He sighed and sat up, stuffing his pillows behind his back. "We
have to talk," he said.

She froze. "If you like to talk so much, maybe you should join a
debating team," she retorted.

"I made love to you last night," he said bluntly, going straight to
the heart of the issue and watching as she flinched against the door.
"You had a rough deal with your ex-husband, and I can understand
that you're wary, but last night wasn't a total disaster for you. You
kissed me, you responded to me. So why are you acting today as if
I'd raped you?"

Dione sighed, shaking her long hair back. He'd never understand
something that she didn't really understand herself; she only knew
that, in her experience, caring led to pain and rejection. It wasn't so
much a physical distance she wanted from him as an emotional one,
before he took everything she had and left her only a shell, empty
and useless. But there was something he *would* understand, and at
last she met his eyes.

"What happened last night won't happen again," she said, her
voice low and clear. "I'm a therapist, and you're my patient. That's
the only relationship that I can allow between us."

"You're closing the barn door after the horse is already out," he
said with maddening amusement.

"Not really. You had doubts about your ability to have sex after
the accident, and that was interfering with your training. Last night

removed those doubts. That was the beginning and end of anything sexual between us.''

His face darkened. ''Damn it,'' he growled, all amusement gone. ''Are you telling me that last night was just a therapeutic roll in the hay?''

Her lips tightened at his crudity. ''Bingo,'' she said, and stepped out of his room, closing the door firmly behind her.

She returned to bed, knowing it was useless to think of sleep, but making the effort anyway. She had to leave. She simply couldn't stay until the first of the year, not with things as strained as they were now. Blake was almost fully recovered; time and practice would accomplish the rest of it. He didn't need her any longer, and there were other people who did.

Her bedroom door opened and he stood there, without the walker, moving slowly and carefully as he closed the door and crossed the room to her.

''If you want to run, I can't catch you,'' he said flatly.

She knew that, but still she lay where she was, watching him. He was nude, his tall, perfect body shamelessly exposed to her gaze. She looked at him and couldn't help feeling a thrill of pride at the ripple of muscles, the fluid grace of his body. He was beautiful, and she'd created him.

He lifted the sheet and got into bed beside her, immediately enveloping her in the warmth of his body. She wanted to sink into his flesh, but instead she made one more effort to protect herself. ''This can't work,'' she said, her voice cracking with pain.

''It already has; you just haven't admitted it yet.'' He put his hand on her hip and pulled her to him, nestling her against him down the entire length of his body. She sighed, her soft breath tickling the hairs on his chest; her body relaxed in traitorous contentment.

He tilted her chin up and kissed her, his lips gentle, his tongue dipping into her mouth briefly to taste her, then withdrawing. ''Let's get one issue settled right now,'' he murmured. ''I've been lying to you, but I thought it best to keep from frightening you. I wanted you since...hell, it seems like from the first time I saw you. Definitely since I threw my breakfast at you, and you laughed the most beautiful laugh I'd ever heard.''

Dione frowned. "Wanted me? But you couldn't—"

"That's what I've been lying about," he admitted, kissing her again.

She jerked back, her cheeks going scarlet. "What?" she gasped, mortified when she thought of the effort she'd made to arouse him, and the money she'd spent on seductive clothes.

Wryly he surveyed her furious face, but braved the wildcat's claws and pulled her back into his arms. "Several things you did made me think that you might have been mistreated," he explained.

"So you decided to show me what I'd been missing," she exploded, pushing at his chest. "Of all the sneaky, egotistical snakes in the world, you're at the top of the heap!"

He chuckled and gently subdued her, using the strength that she'd given him. "Not quite. I wanted you, but I didn't want to frighten you. So I pretended that I couldn't make love to you; all I wanted was for you to get to know me, learn to trust me, so I'd have a chance at least. Then you started dressing in those thin shirts and shorts, and I thought I'd go out of my mind. You damn-near killed me!" he said roughly. "You touched me constantly, driving me so wild I'd almost exploded out of my skin, and I'd have to hide my reaction from you. Didn't you wonder why I'd been working like a maniac?"

She sucked in a shaky breath. "Is that why?"

"Of course it is," he said, touching her lip with his finger. "I tried to get you used to my touch, too, and that only made my problem worse. Every time I kissed you, every time I touched your legs, I was driving myself crazy."

Closing her eyes, she remembered all the times when he'd stared at her with that peculiar, hot light in his eyes. A woman with any real experience would have known immediately that Blake wasn't impotent, but she'd been the perfect, all-time sucker for that line. "You must have laughed yourself sick at me," she said miserably.

"I haven't been in any shape to laugh, even if it had been a laughing matter. Which it wasn't," he said. "The thought that someone had hurt you made me so furious I wanted to tear the guy apart. Whoever he was, *he* was the reason you were frightened of me, and I hated that. I'd have done anything to make you trust me, let me love you.''

She bit her lip, wishing that she could believe him, but how could she? He made it sound as if he'd been so concerned for her, and all he'd really been concerned with was his own sexual appetite. She knew how touchy he'd been about letting even Serena see him while he was less than perfect; he wouldn't want to make love to a woman who might pity him for the effort it took him to walk, or, even worse, might want him because of a morbid curiosity. Dione was the one safe female of his acquaintance, the one who knew everything about him already and was neither shocked, curious, nor pitying. ''What you're saying is that you wanted sex, and I was handy,'' she said bitterly.

''My God, Dee!'' He sounded shocked. ''I'm not getting through to you, am I? Is it so hard for you to believe that I want *you*, not just sex? We've been through a lot together; you've held me when I hurt so much I couldn't stand it any longer, and I held you last night when you were afraid, but trusted me with yourself anyway. You're not just a sexual outlet for me; you're the woman I want. I want all of you: your temper, your contrariness, your strength, even your downright bitchiness, because you're also an incredibly loving woman.''

''All right, I absolve you,'' she said wearily. ''I don't want to talk about it now; I'm tired and I can't think straight.''

He looked down at her, and impatience flickered across his face. ''There's no reasoning with you, is there?'' he asked slowly. ''I shouldn't have wasted my time talking to you. I should have just shown you, like I'm going to do now.''

Chapter 10

Dione drew back sharply, her golden eyes flashing. "Do all men use force when a woman isn't willing?" she said between clenched teeth. "I warn you, Blake, I'll fight. Maybe I can't stop you, but I can hurt you."

He laughed softly. "I know you can." He lifted one of her fists and carried it to his lips, where he kissed each knuckle in turn. "Darling, I'm not going to force you. I'm going to kiss you and tell you how lovely you are, and do everything I can think of to give you pleasure. The first time was for me, remember, but the second time is for you. Don't you think I can show you?"

"You're trying to seduce me," she snapped.

"Mmmm. Is it working?"

"No!"

"Damn. Then I'll have to try something else, won't I?" He laughed again, and pressed his warm lips to her wrist. "You're so sweet, even when you're mad at me."

"I am not!" she protested, practically insulted by his compliment. "There's not a 'sweet' bone in my body!"

"You're sweet smelling," he countered. "And sweet tasting. And the feel of you is sweet torment. Your name should be Champagne instead of Dione, because you make me so drunk I barely know what I'm doing."

"Liar."

"What did I do for excitement before I met you?" he asked wryly. "Fighting with you makes mountain climbing pale in comparison."

The amusement in his voice was more than she could bear; she was so confused and upset, but he seemed to think it was funny. She turned her head away to hide the tears that welled up. "I'm glad you're getting such a kick out of this," she muttered.

"We'll talk about that later," he said, and kissed her. She lay rigidly in his arms, refusing to let her mouth soften and mold itself to his, and after a moment he drew back.

"Don't you want me at all?" he whispered, nuzzling her hair. "Did I hurt you last night? Is that what's wrong?"

"I don't know what's wrong!" she shouted. "I don't understand what I want, or what *you* want. I'm out of my depth, and I don't like it!" The frustration she felt with herself and with him came bubbling out of her, but it was nothing less than the truth. Her mind was so muddled that nothing pleased her; she felt violent, but without a safe outlet for that violence. She'd been violated, hurt, and though years had passed, only now was the anger breaking out of the deep freeze where she'd locked her emotions. She wanted to hurt him, hit him, because he was a man and the symbol of what had happened to her, but she knew that he was innocent, at least of that. But he had dominated her last night, manipulated her with his lies and his truths, and now he was trying to dominate her again.

Furiously she shoved at him, rolling him over on his back. Before he could react she was astride him, her face pagan with the raw force of her emotions. "If there's any seducing to be done, I'll do it!" she raged at him. "Damn you, don't you dare move!"

His blue eyes widened, and a rich understanding crossed his face. "I won't," he promised, a little hoarsely.

With a sensual growl she assaulted him, using her mouth, her hands, her entire body. A man's sexuality had always been denied to her, but now this man offered himself in spread-eagled sacrifice, and she explored him with voracious hunger. Much of his body she already knew; the sleek strength of his muscles under her fingers; the roughness of the hair on his chest and legs; the male scent that made her nostrils flare. But now she learned the taste of him as she nibbled at his ears, his chin, his mouth; she pressed her lips against the softness of his temple and felt his pulse hammering madly. She kissed his eyes, the strong column of his throat, the slope of his shoulder, the sensitive inside of his elbow.

His palms twitched as her tongue traced across them, and he groaned aloud when she sucked on his fingers. "Hush!" she said fiercely, crouching over him. She didn't want any break in her concentration. As she learned him, her body was coming alive, warming and glowing like something long frozen and slowly beginning to thaw. She moved upward, licked the length of his collarbone, then snaked her tongue downward through the curls of hair until she found the little nipples that hid there. They were tight, as hard as tiny diamonds, and when she bit them he shuddered wildly.

His flat stomach, ridged with muscles that were now writhing under her touch, beckoned her marauding mouth. She traced the arrow of downy hair, played a wet game of sneak attack with his navel, then slithered downward. Her silky hair draped across him as she kissed his legs from thigh to foot, biting the backs of his knees, dancing her tongue across his instep, then working her way back up.

He was shaking in every muscle, his body so taut that only his heels and shoulders were touching the bed. He was gripping the bedposts, his arms corded as he writhed in tormented ecstasy. "Please...please!" he begged hoarsely. "Touch me! Damn it, I can't take any more!"

"Yes, you can!" she insisted, panting for breath. She touched him, her hand learning him, stroking him, and something close to a howl broke from his throat.

Suddenly she knew. For such vital strength, for such tender power, there was only one resting place, and that was the mysterious depth of her femininity. Male and female, they had been created to join together, the two halves to make a whole. She felt breathless, stunned, as if suddenly the world had shifted and nothing was the same as it had been.

His body was a bow, taut and aching. "Take...me!" he rasped, both in plea and demand, and Dione smiled a radiant, mysterious smile that almost blinded him with the joy of it.

"Yes," she said, and with aching tenderness moved over him. She accepted him easily. He cried out, but lay still, letting her move as she wished. She looked at him, and golden eyes met blue, communicating wordlessly. She was awed by the rightness of their union, by the heated flares of pleasure that shot through her body. All the barriers were gone now; the fears and nightmares that had prevented her from letting herself enjoy the magic of giving herself to the man she loved had disappeared. She was sensual by nature, but events had taught her to deny that part of herself. No longer. Sweet heaven, no longer. He freed her, not only allowing her to be herself, but glorying in the woman she was. It was evident in the lost, rapt look he wore, the mindless undulating of his body.

She reveled in him. She adored him, she used him, she sank deeply into the whirlpool of the senses and welcomed the drowning. She was burning alive in the heat of her own body as the pleasure intensified and became unbearable, but still she couldn't stop. The moans and gasping cries that kept forcing themselves from his throat as he fought for control were matched by her own sounds of pleasure, until that pleasure became wildfire and she was consumed by it. She heard a wordless cry lingering in the night air and didn't recognize it was hers, or realize that it was joined by a deeper cry as Blake finally released himself from his sweet torture. She sank down, a long, long way, and sprawled weakly on him. His arms swept up and held her safely, securely in place.

He was kissing her, his mouth all over her face before finally settling on her lips and drinking deeply. She met his tongue with her own, and they lay together for a long time exchanging tired, leisurely kisses.

"You took me apart," he murmured.

"I put you together again," she said sleepily.

"I'm not talking about Humpty Dumpty, lady bird, I'm talking about what you did to me."

"Didn't you like it?"

"I loved it." A deep chuckle rumbled through his chest. "As if you had to ask." Then he sobered and pushed her hair away from her face so he could read her eyes. "Was it good for you?"

She smiled and ducked her head against him. "As if you had to ask."

"No bad moments?"

"None," she said, and yawned.

"Wretch, are you going to sleep on me?" he demanded in mock indignation, but his hands were tender as he stroked her. "You're tired, aren't you? Then sleep, darling. I'll hold you. Just don't move; I want to stay inside you all night."

She would have blushed, but she was too tired, too satisfied, and he made a wonderful bed. She was boneless, draped over him, protected by him. She eased into sleep with the steady throb of his heartbeat in her ear.

He woke her at dawn with his slow, tender movements. The room was chilled, but they were warm, heated by the excitement that began to curl inside. There was no urgency, no need to hurry. He talked to her and teased her, told her jokes that made her laugh, and her laughter somehow increased her inner heat. He knew her body as well as she knew his, knew how to touch her and make her writhe with pleasure, knew how to gradually move her up the plane to satisfaction. Her trust was a tangible thing between them, evident in her clear, shining eyes as she allowed him to handle her as he pleased. Even when he rolled her onto her back and pinned her with his weight, no shadow of ancient fear darkened her joy. He had earned her trust the night before when he had offered his own body for her enjoyment. How could she deny him the pleasure of hers?

There was pleasure for her, too, a deep and shining pleasure that took her breath away. It was so intense that she almost cried out her love for him, but she clenched her teeth on the words. The time with him was golden but transient, and there was no need to burden him with an emotion that couldn't be returned.

"I'd like to stay in bed with you all day," he whispered against her satiny skin. "But Alberta will be up here soon if we don't put in an appearance. She was worried about you yesterday, almost as much as I was."

She buried her hands in his thick, dark hair. "Why were you worried? You knew why I was upset."

"Because I never meant to upset you. I didn't want to remind you of anything that had hurt you, but I did. You were so pale and cold." He kissed the enticing slope of her breast and smiled at the ripple of response that was evident under her skin.

They showered together; then he sprawled on the bed and directed her dressing. He wanted her to wear the slinky, seductive shorts she'd worn before, and his eyes glittered as he watched her pull them on. He had to return to his room to dress, as he'd come to her stark naked, and stark naked he walked down the hall, moving slowly but with increasing confidence and grace. Tears of pride stung her eyes as she watched him.

"It's a beautiful day," Alberta said with an odd smugness as she served breakfast, and it was so unusual for Alberta to make small talk that Dione glanced at her sharply, but could read nothing in the woman's stoic face.

"Beautiful," Blake echoed gravely, and gave Dione a slow smile that started her blood racing.

Their workouts were leisurely and remarkably short; Blake seemed more interested in watching her than in lifting weights or walking on the treadmill. He was relaxed, satisfaction lying on him like a golden glow. Instead of trying to slow him down, Dione scolded him for doing so little. "I'm going to have to cut down on the amount you're eating if you aren't going to work any more than this."

"Whatever you say," he murmured, his eyes on her legs. "You're the boss."

She laughed and gave up. If he weren't going to work out, he might as well be walking. It was warmer out than it had been recently, so they walked around the grounds; the only support he used was his arm around her waist. She noticed that he was limping less; even his left leg moved without dragging as badly as it had.

"I've been thinking," he announced as they returned to the house. "There's no use in waiting until the first of the year before I go back to work. I'm going back Monday; I'll get myself accustomed to the place and what's going on, before Richard takes off."

Dione stopped and stared at him, her cheeks paling. He saw her expression and misunderstood it; he laughed as he hugged her to him. "I'm not going to hurt myself," he assured her. "I'll just work in the mornings. Half a day, I promise. Then I'll come home and put myself in your hands again, and you can work me until I drop if that's what you want."

She bit her lip. "If you're capable of returning to work, then there's no need for me to stay at all," she said quietly.

He frowned, his hands tightening on her. "There's all the need in the world. Don't even think about leaving me, honey, because I won't let you. You're part of me. We've already been through this once, and it's settled. You're staying here."

"Nothing's settled," she denied. "I have to work, to support myself—"

"By all means, work if you want," he interrupted. "But you don't *have* to. I can support you."

She jerked back, indignant color staining her face. "I'm not a call girl," she snapped. "Or a lap dog."

He put his hands on his hips. "I'll agree with that, but I'm not talking about either of those," he said, his own temper rising. "I'm talking about marriage, lady, the 'till death do us part' bit."

She couldn't have been more startled if he'd turned green before her eyes. She stared at him. "You can't mean that."

"Why can't I mean it?" he demanded irritably. "This is a hell of a reception for the only marriage proposal I've ever made."

She couldn't help it; she laughed at the anger in his tone, even though she knew inside that he would soon forget her. He was still involved in their intense, isolated therapist-patient relationship, with the added complication of their physical involvement. She'd known that making love with him was a mistake, but she hadn't suspected that he would carry it as far as considering marriage.

"I can't marry you," she said, shaking her head to reinforce her refusal.

"Why not?"

"It wouldn't work."

"Why wouldn't it work? We've been living together for almost half a year, and you can't say that we don't get along. We've had some great times. We fight, sure, but that's half the fun. And you can't say that you don't love me, because I know you do," he finished tightly.

Dione stared at him in silent dismay. She'd tried so hard not to let him know, but he'd seen through her pitiful defenses anyway. He'd demolished every wall that she'd built. She couldn't stay. She'd have to leave immediately, get away from him while she still could. "There's no sense in dragging this out," she said, pulling away from him. "I'll leave today."

Once she was free of his grip she knew that he wouldn't be able to keep up with her. Her conscience twinged at leaving him alone to make his way back to the house—what if he fell? But needs must when the devil drives, and her devil was driving her mercilessly. She went straight to her room and began pulling out her clothes. She was swift and efficient; she had all the clothes lying on the bed in neat stacks when she realized that the new clothes she'd bought made it impossible for her to fit everything into her two suitcases. She'd either have to leave them there, or buy another suitcase. If she bought another suitcase, she'd have to beg a ride from someone...no, where was her brain? She could always call a taxi. She didn't have to beg for anything.

"Dee, you're not leaving," Blake said gently from the doorway. "Put everything back and calm down."

"I have to leave. I don't have any reason to say." It had been a waste of breath for him to tell her to calm down. She was utterly calm, knowing what she had to do.

"I'm not reason enough to stay? You love me. I've known for quite a while. It's in your eyes when you look at me, your touch, your voice, everything about you. You make me feel ten feet tall, darling. And if I still needed proof, I had it when you let me make love to you. You're not a woman to give herself to any man without love. You love me, even if you're too stubborn to tell me the words."

"I told you," she said, her voice muffled with pain. "I always fall in love with my patients. It's practically required."

"You don't go to bed with all of your patients, do you?"

He already knew the answer to that. He didn't need the miserable little shake of her head, or the whispered, "No," to reassure him.

"It's not one-sided," he murmured, coming up behind her to wrap his arms around her middle. "I love you, so much I hurt. You love me, and I love you; it's only natural that we get married."

"But you *don't* love me!" she shouted, driven beyond control at hearing those precious words. It was unfair that she should be punished so much for loving him, but everything had to be paid for in coin. For daring to transgress, she would pay with her heart. She began to struggle against the bonds of flesh that held her, but he merely tightened his hold, not enough to hurt her, but she was securely restrained. After a moment of futile effort she let her head drop back against his shoulder. "You only think you love me," she wept, her voice thick with the tears lodged in her throat. "I've been through it before; a patient becomes so dependent on me, so fixated on me, that he confuses his feelings of need with love. It won't last, Blake, believe me. You don't really love me; it's just that I'm the only toy in your playground right now. When you go back to work you'll be seeing other women and everything will fall back into proportion. It would be awful if I married you and then you found out it had all been a mistake."

"I'm a man," he said slowly. "There have been other women who I wanted, other women who caught my interest, but give me credit for being intelligent enough to know the difference between the way I felt with them and the way I feel about you. I want to be with you, talk with you, fight with you, watch you laugh, make love with you. If that's not love, honey, no one will ever know the difference."

"I'll know the difference, and so will you."

He sighed impatiently. "You still won't listen to reason, will you? Then let's compromise. Are you willing to compromise?"

She eyed him warily. "It depends."

He smiled even as he shook his head. "You'd think I'm a mass murderer, the way you're looking at me. It's just a simple deal. You say that when I get out more and see other women to compare you to, I'll realize that I've just been infatuated with you. On the other hand, I say that I love you and I'll keep on loving you, regardless of how many other women I see. To settle the issue, all you have to do is stay until I've had a chance to make that comparison. Simple?''

She shrugged. ''I see what's in the deal for you; you win, either way. I know that you're planning to sleep with me, and I'm honest enough to know that if I stay, that's exactly how things will work out. If you decide that it was just a passing fancy after all, then you've lost nothing and had a bed partner while you thought about it.''

''There's something in it for you, too,'' he said, grinning.

The wicked gleam in his eyes gave him away. She could have kicked him, but it seemed that he could always make her laugh no matter how upset she was. ''I know, I know,'' she said, beginning to giggle. ''*I* get to sleep with *you*.''

''That's not such a bad deal,'' he said with blatant immodesty.

''You talk a good game, Mr. Remington,'' she said, still laughing despite all she could do to stifle it.

''That's not all I do well,'' he said, reaching for her and folding her against him. His lips found the slope of her throat and she shivered, her lashes falling to veil her eyes. ''Think of it as therapy,'' he encouraged. ''A sort of repayment for your own therapeutic knowledge. You gave me a reason to live, and I'll show you how to live.''

''Egotistical.''

''Truthful.''

''I can't do it.''

He shook her, then pulled her back to him and began to lay tender seige to her mouth, storming the barrier of her teeth and taking the treasure that lay beyond. ''You will do it,'' he insisted softly. ''Because you love me. Because I need you.''

''Past tense: You needed me. That's in the past. You're on your own, and you're doing fine.''

''I won't be doing fine if you leave me. I swear I'll put myself back in the wheelchair and not get out again. I won't go to work; I won't eat; I won't sleep. I need you to take care of me.''

''Blackmail won't work,'' she warned him, trying not to laugh again.

''Then I'll have to try another tactic. Please. Stay for me. I love

you, and you love me. What if *you're* wrong? What if I'm still as
wild for you ten years from now as I am today? Are you going to
throw that chance away just because you're afraid to believe it can
happen?''

The pain that seared her heart told her that at last he'd hit on the
real reason why she wanted to leave. She was afraid to believe in
love, because no one had ever loved her. She stared at him intently,
aware inside of herself that she had reached a personal milestone.
She could play it safe and run but people who played it safe never
knew the intoxication of going for it all, of putting their hearts on
the line. They never risked anything, so they never won anything.
Everything had to be paid for; she reminded herself of that once
again. All she could do was try. If she won, if by some miracle she
gained the golden apple, her life would be complete. If she lost,
would she really be any worse off than she was now? She already
loved him. Would leaving him now make the pain any less than
leaving him later?

''All right,'' she said huskily, aware of the bridges burning behind
her. She could feel the heat at her back. ''I'll stay with you. Don't
ask me to marry you, not yet. Let's see how it works out. An affair
is a lot easier to recover from when it goes sour than a marriage is.''

He quirked a dark eyebrow at her. ''You're not overconfident, are
you?''

''I'm…cautious,'' she admitted. ''Marriage was traumatic for me.
Let me take one hurdle at a time. If…if everything works out, I'll
marry you whenever you want.''

''I'll hold you to that,'' he murmured. ''I'd like to marry you now.
I'd like to make you pregnant right now, if I could. I was looking
forward to our devoting a lot of time to that project, but now I'll
have to take precautions. Our children will all come *after* we've been
married for at least nine months. No one's going to count their fingers
and smirk at our babies.''

Her eyes were such wide, huge golden pools of wonder, that they
eclipsed the rest of her face. The thought of children was so enticing
that she was tempted to tell him that she would marry him right then.
She'd always wanted children, wanted to be able to pour out the deep

reservoir of love that was dammed up inside her. The care and nourishment that she'd never received from her own mother were there, waiting patiently for a child of her own. Blake's child: blue eyes; dark hair; that engaging grin that brought out his hidden dimple.

But a child was the one thing she couldn't gamble with, so she didn't argue with him. Instead she offered quietly, "I'll see a doctor and get a prescription."

"No," he refused, steel lacing his voice. "No pills. You're not taking any risks, however slight, with your body. I can handle it without any risk at all, and that's the way we'll do it."

She didn't mind; the thought that he was willing to take responsibility for their lovemaking was a warm, melting one. She put her arms around him and nestled against him, drinking in his scent.

"Tell me you love me," he demanded, cupping her chin in his palm and lifting her face to him. "I know you do, but I want to hear it."

A tremulous smile quivered on her lips. "I love you."

"That's what I thought," he said with satisfaction, and kissed her as a reward. "Everything will be all right, darling. Just wait and see."

Chapter 11

She didn't dare to hope, but it seemed as if he might be right. He bought a slim black cane that looked more like a sexy prop than something that was actually used as support, and every morning Miguel drove him to work. At first Dione fretted every moment he was gone. She worried that he might fall and hurt himself, that he'd try to do too much and tire himself out. After a week she was forced to admit that he was thriving on the challenge of working again. Far from falling, every day he improved, walking faster and with less effort. Nor did she have to worry that he was pushing himself too hard; he was in excellent shape, thanks to her program.

She almost drove herself mad thinking of all the women he was in contact with every day; she knew herself how attractive he was, especially with that intriguing limp. When he came home the first day she all but held her breath, waiting for him to say cheerfully, "Well, you were right; it was just infatuation. You can leave now."

But he never said it. He returned home as eagerly as he went to work, and they spent the afternoons in the gym, or swimming if the day was warm. December was a pleasant month, with the afternoon temperatures often in the high sixties and low seventies, though at night it sometimes dipped close to freezing. Blake decided to have a heating unit put in the pool so they could swim at night, but he had so much on his mind that he kept putting it off. Dione didn't care if the pool was ever heated or not; why bother with swimming when the nights were better spent in his arms?

Whatever happened, whatever the ending that was eventually written to their particular story, she would always love him for freeing her from the cage of fear. In his arms she forgot about the past and concentrated only on the pleasure he gave her, pleasure which she joyously returned.

He was the lover who she had needed; he was mature enough to understand the rewards of patience, and astute enough to sometimes be impatient. He gave, he demanded, he stroked, he experimented, he laughed, he teased, and he satisfied. He was as happily fascinated with her body as she was with his, and that was the sort of open admiration that she needed. The events that had shaped her had made her wary of repressed emotion, even when that emotion was happiness, and the complete honesty with which Blake treated her gave her a secure springboard from which she launched herself as a woman, secure at last in her own femininity and sexuality.

The days of December were the happiest of her life. She had known peace and contentment, not a small accomplishment after the terror she'd survived, but with Blake she was truly happy. Except for the absence of a ceremony, she might already have been married to him, and each passing day the idea of being his wife became more firmly rooted in her mind, changing from impossible to implausible, then to chancy, then to a half-scared, hopeful "maybe." She refused to let herself progress beyond that, afraid of tempting the fates, but still she began to dream of a long stretch of days, even years, and she found herself thinking up names for babies.

He took her Christmas shopping, something she'd never done before in her life. No one had ever been close enough to her to either give or receive a gift, and when Blake learned this, he embarked on a crusade to make her first real Christmas one that would boggle the imagination. The house was decorated in a unique and not always logical blend of traditional and desert styles; every cactus found itself sporting gaily colored bows or even decorative glass balls, if the spines were large enough. He had holly and mistletoe flown in and kept in the refrigerator until it was time to put them up, and Alberta

entered into the spirit of the season by scouring cookbooks for traditional Christmas recipes.

Dione realized that they were all going to so much trouble for her,
and she was determined to throw herself into the preparations and
the happiness. Suddenly it seemed that the world was full of people
who cared, and those she cared for.

She'd been half-fearful that Blake would embarrass her by giving
her a lot of expensive gifts, and she was both delighted and relieved
when she began opening her gifts to find that they were small,
thoughtful and sometimes humorous. A long, flat box that could have
held a watch or an expensive bracelet instead yielded an array of tiny
charms that made her laugh aloud: a miniature barbell, a track shoe,
a sweatband, a Frisbee, a loving cup trophy and a little silver bell
that actually gave a tinny little chime when she shook it. Another
box held the charm bracelet that the charms were supposed to go on;
a third gift was a best seller that she'd picked up in a bookstore just
the week before, then replaced and forgotten to buy in the confusion
of shopping. A lacy black mantilla drifted over her head and she
looked up to smile at Richard, who was regarding her with an oddly
tender look in his cool gray eyes. Serena's gift made her gasp and
quickly stuff it back into the box, as Serena rolled with laughter and
Blake immediately came over to wrestle the box away from her and
hold up the contents: a very intimate garment with heart-shaped cut-
outs in strategic places.

"This was something you overlooked when you bought all those
clothes to wage war in," Serena said innocently, her blue eyes as
limpid as a child's.

"Ahhh, those clothes." Blake sighed in satisfaction.

Dione snatched the teddy…thing…whatever…away from him and
replaced it in the box, her cheeks fiery red. "Why is everyone watching me?" she asked uncomfortably. "Why aren't you opening your
own gifts?"

"Because you're so beautiful to watch," Blake replied softly, leaning down so only she could hear him. "Your eyes are shining like a
little girl's. I have something else for you to…ah, unwrap later on
tonight. Think you might be interested?"

She stared at him, her black pupils dilating until they almost obscured the golden rims. "I'm interested," she murmured, her body already quickening at the thought of the lovemaking they'd share later, when they were laying pressed together in his big bed.

"It's a date," he whispered.

The rest of the gifts were opened amid laughter and thank-yous; then Alberta served hot buttered rum. Dione seldom drank, having an aversion to alcohol that dated back to her earliest childhood, but she drank the rum because she was happy and relaxed and suddenly the old restrictions no longer mattered so much. The rum slid smoothly down her throat, warming her, and when that was finished she drank another.

After Serena and Richard had left, Blake helped Dione up the stairs with a steadying arm around her waist. He was laughing softly, and she leaned into him, letting him take most of her weight. "What's so funny?" she asked sleepily.

"You are. You're half-drunk, and you're beautiful. Did you know that you've had the sweetest, sleepiest smile in the world on your face for the last fifteen minutes? Don't you dare go to sleep on me, at least until after you've kept our date."

She stopped on the stairs and turned fully into his arms, winding herself around him. "You know I wouldn't miss that for the world," she purred.

"I'll see that you don't."

She let him talk her into wearing the scandalous teddy that Serena had given her, and he made love to her while she had it on, then even that scrap of fabric seemed to get in his way and he stripped it off her. "Nothing's as lovely as your skin," he whispered, stringing kisses like popcorn across her stomach.

She felt drugged, her mind a little fuzzy, but her body was throbbing, arching instinctively to meet the rhythmic thrusts that took her to bliss and beyond when he left off kissing her all over and possessed her again. When they were finished she lay weak and trembling on the bed, protesting with a murmur when she felt him leave her side.

"I'll be right back," he reassured her, and he was, his weight pressing the mattress familiarly. She smiled and moved her hand to touch him lightly, all without opening her eyes.

"Don't go to sleep," he warned. "Not yet. You haven't unwrapped your last present."

She propped her lids open. "But I thought that you were...when we made love, I thought that..." she mumbled in confusion.

He chuckled and slid an arm behind her back, urging her into a sitting position. "I'm glad you liked that, but I have something else for you." He placed another long, slim box in her hand.

"But you've already given me so much," she protested, awakening at the feel of the box.

"Not like this. This is special. Go ahead, open it."

He sat with his arm still around her, watching her face and smiling as she fumbled with the elegant gold wrapping, her agile fingers suddenly clumsy. She lifted the lid off and stared speechlessly at the simple pendant that lay on satin lining like a cobweb of gold. A dark red heart, chiseled and planed, was attached to the chain.

"That's a ruby," she stammered.

"No," he corrected gently, lifting it from the box and placing it around her neck. "That's my heart." The chain was long, and the ruby heart slid down her chest to nestle between her breasts, gleaming with dark fire as it lay against her honeyed skin.

"Wear that forever," he murmured, his eyes on the lush curves that his gift used as a pillow. "And my heart will always be touching yours."

A single, crystalline tear escaped the confines of her lashes, and rolled slowly down her cheek. He leaned over and caught it with his tongue. "An engagement ring wasn't good enough for you, so I'm giving you an engagement heart. Will you wear it, darling? Will you marry me?"

She stared at him with eyes so huge and deep that they drowned the entire world. For a month she'd shared his bed, trying to prepare herself for the day when she was no longer able to do so, savoring every moment with him in an attempt to store up pleasure as a squirrel stores acorns as insurance against a hard winter. She'd been certain that he would lose interest in her, but every day he'd turned to her and taken her in his arms, told her that he loved her. Perhaps the dream wasn't a dream, after all, but reality. Perhaps she could dare to believe.

"Yes," she heard herself say shakily as her heart and hungry yearnings overruled her head, and her head instantly tried to recover lost ground by adding, "but give me time to get used to the idea.... It doesn't seem quite real."

"It's real, all right," he muttered, sliding his hand along her rib-cage until a warm, full breast filled his palm. He studied the sheer perfection of her softly veined flesh, the taut little cherry tip that responded instantly to his lightest touch, and his body began to tighten with the familiar need that he could never quite satisfy. Gently he began to ease her down into a supine position. "I don't mind a long engagement," he said absently. "Two weeks is plenty of time."

"Blake! I was thinking in terms of months, not weeks!"

He looked up sharply; then as he saw the frightened uncertainty in her face, his gaze softened and his mouth eased into a smile. "Then name the day, darling, as long as it's within six months and you don't pick either Groundhog Day or April Fool's Day."

She tried to think, but her mind was suddenly fuzzy, entirely pre-occupied by the rough, wonderful rasp of his hard hands over her body. His finger slid between her legs and she gasped aloud, a hot twinge of pleasure shooting through her body. "May Day," she said, no longer really caring.

He was disconcerted, too, his senses caught by the rich beauty of the woman under his hand while he tried to make sense of her words. "Mayday?" he asked, puzzled and a little shocked. "You're asking for help?"

"No...May Day, not mayday," she explained, exaggerating the two words so he could hear the pause between them. "The first of May."

"What about it?" he murmured, dipping his head to taste the straining nipples that had been tempting him. He was rapidly losing all interest in the conversation.

"That's when we're getting married," she gasped, her body be-ginning a slow, undulating dance.

Those words made sense to him, and he lifted his head. "I can't persuade you to marry me before then?"

"I...don't know," she moaned. Her nails flexed into his shoulders. He could probably talk her into anything he wanted, the way she felt now. Though they had made love only a short while before, the need that was filling her was so urgent that it might have been years since he'd taken her. She turned to him, her sleek, soft body crowding him, and he knew without words what she wanted. He lay back, his hands guiding her as she flowed over him and engulfed him. She was wild when she loved him like that, her long black hair streaming down her back, falling across his face when she leaned forward. She worshipped him with the ancient, carnal dance of love, and the ruby heart lay on her breast like a drop of liquid fire.

For two days nothing intruded on the spell of happiness that held them enthralled. Everyone was pleased with the engagement, from the taciturn Miguel to a bubbling Serena. Alberta was as satisfied as if she'd arranged it all herself, and Angela hummed all day long. Serena passed along Richard's best wishes; evidently a wedding was just what everyone wanted, and Dione almost forgot why she'd been so cautious in the beginning.

On the third day Serena arrived for dinner, alone and pale, though she was composed. "I might as well tell you, before someone else does," she said quietly. "Richard and I are separated."

Dione stifled her gasp of shock. They had been getting along so much better for the past several weeks that she'd stopped being concerned with their situation. She looked swiftly at Blake, and was shocked again at the change in his expression. She had known him as laughing, loving, teasing, angry, even afraid, but never before had she seen him so deadly and intent. Suddenly she realized that she'd never really felt the force of his personality, because he'd always tempered his actions with consideration for her. Now the steel, the sheer power, was showing as he prepared to protect his sister.

"What do you want me to do?" he asked Serena in a calm, lethal tone.

Serena looked at him and even smiled, her eyes full of love. "Nothing," she said simply. "This is something I have to work out with Richard. Blake, please, don't let this interfere with your working relationship with him; this is more my fault than it is his, and it wouldn't be fair for you to take it out on him.''

"How is it your fault?'' he growled.

"For not growing up and getting my priorities straight until it was almost too late,'' she replied, a hint of the same steel lacing her sweeter voice. "I'm not giving up on him, not without a fight. Don't ask me any more questions, because I won't answer them. He's my husband, and this is a private matter.''

He regarded her silently for a moment, then gave a brief nod. "All right. But you know that I'll do whatever I can, whenever you ask.''

"Of course I do,'' she said, her face relaxing. "It's just that I have to do this on my own. I have to learn how to fight my own battles.'' As she spoke she flashed Dione a look that said, "See, I'm trying.'' Dione nodded in acknowledgement, then looked up to find that Blake had witnessed the little exchange and was also staring at her, a steel determination in his expression. Dione met his stare blandly; he could ask, but she didn't have to answer. If Serena wanted her brother to know that she was deliberately trying to put a distance between them, then she would tell him. If not, then he'd have to figure it out for himself. Richard and Serena didn't need any more interference in their marriage, and if Blake discovered that he was the basic cause of their separation, he was fully capable of taking it up with Richard.

Later that night, after he had made love to her with an intensity that left her dazed and sleepy, he said lazily, "What's going on between you and Serena? All those significant glances have to mean something.''

It was a sneak attack, she realized, struggling to gather her wits. He'd made love to her as usual, waited until she was almost asleep, and caught her unaware. To make the situation more even, she cuddled against him and slid her hand down his side in a long, slow caress. When she reached his thighs she was rewarded by the clenching of his entire body.

"It was nothing,'' she murmured, pressing soft, hot kisses on his chest. "Just a conversation we had the day she took me shopping for all those sexy clothes that you liked so much. She must have a secret fetish for indecent underwear. She picked out most of those barely there nightgowns, and then she gave me that teddy for Christmas.''

Hard fingers wrapped around her wrist, and he removed her hand from his body. Leaning over, he switched on the lamp and washed them with light. Dione watched him, knowing that he wanted to be able to read the nuances of expression that crossed her face. She tried to shield her thoughts, but an uneasy coldness began to creep over her skin as she stared into his piercing blue eyes.

''Stop trying to change the subject,'' he ordered sharply. ''Was Serena warning you away from Richard?''

That again! She stiffened, both angered and hurt by the way he had continually accused her of seeing Richard on the sly. How could he possibly think that of her? She had agreed to marry him only two days before, but for some reason she couldn't get it out of his mind that she might be involved with another man. She sat up, the sheet falling to her waist, but she was too angry to care if she were nude.

''What's with you?'' she demanded furiously. ''You sound like a broken record. What is it that makes you so suspicious of me? Why am I always the cause of any trouble between Serena and Richard?''

''Because Richard can never take his eyes off you when you're together,'' he replied, his mouth a hard line.

''I'm not responsible for Richard's eyes!'' The injustice of it made her want to scream.

''Aren't you?'' he snapped. ''Whenever you look at him, it's as if you're passing secret messages.''

''You just accused me of doing the same thing with Serena. Am I having an affair with her, too?'' Dione exploded. She clenched her fists in an effort to control the burgeoning fury in her. It would be stupid to lose her temper, so she forcibly sucked in a deep, calming breath and made her muscles relax.

Blake eyed her narrowly. ''If you don't have anything to hide, then why won't you tell me what Serena meant by what she said?'' he questioned.

Another sneak attack. She registered the hit and realized that again he'd caught her when her control was slipping. ''If you're so curious, why don't you ask her?'' she said bitingly, and lay down again, turning her back to him and pulling the sheet up to her chin.

She heard his breath hiss through his teeth a split second before the sheet was jerked away from her and thrown to the foot of the bed. An iron hand bit into her shoulder and turned her over, flat on her back. ''Don't turn your back on me,'' he warned softly, and the cold uneasiness in her turned into icy dread.

Silently, her face white and set, she threw his hand off her shoulder. She had never, *never,* been able to passively endure, even when resistance cost her additional pain. She didn't think; she reacted instinctively, the automatic resistance of someone fighting for survival. When he reached for her, angered by her rejection, she eluded his grasp and slid from the bed.

It didn't matter that this was Blake. Somehow, that made it worse. His image blurred with Scott's, and she felt a stabbing pain that threatened to drive her to her knees. She had trusted him, loved him. How could he have turned on her like that, knowing what he did about her? The sense of betrayal almost choked her.

He sprang from the bed and reached her as she stretched her hand out for the doorknob. He grabbed her elbow and spun her around. ''You're not going anywhere!'' he growled. ''Come back to bed.''

Dione wrenched herself away from his grip and flattened her body back against the door. Her golden eyes were blind, dilated, as she stared at him. ''Don't touch me,'' she cried hoarsely.

He reached for her again, then stopped abruptly when he looked at her and saw the fixed expression in her eyes. She was white, so pale that he expected her to slide into a faint at any moment, but she held herself tautly upright. ''Don't touch me,'' she said again, and his arms dropped heavily to his sides.

''Calm down,'' he said soothingly. ''It's all right. I'm not going to hurt you, darling. Let's go back to bed.''

She didn't move, her eyes still locked on him as she measured every move he made, however slight. Even the expansion of his chest with every breath he took made an impact on her senses. She saw the slight flare of his nostrils, the flexing of his fingers.

''It's all right,'' he repeated. ''Dee, we had an argument, that's all.

Just an argument. You know I'm not going to hit you.'' He extended his hand slowly to her, and she watched as his fingers approached. Without moving her body somehow drew in on itself, shrinking in an effort to avoid his touch. Just before he would have touched her, she slid swiftly to the side, away from the threatening hand.

Inexorably he followed, moving with her but not coming any closer. ''Where are you going?'' he asked softly.

She didn't answer; her eyes were wary now, instead of blindly staring. Blake held out both his hands to her, palms up in supplication.

''Honey, give me your hands,'' he whispered, desperation threading through his veins, congealing his blood. ''Please believe me; I'll never hurt you. Come back to bed with me and let me hold you.''

Dione watched him. She felt odd, as if part of herself were standing back and watching the scene. That had happened before with Scott, as if she somehow had to separate herself from the ugliness of what was happening to her. Her body had reacted mindlessly, trying to protect itself, while her mind had exercised its own means of protection by drawing a veil of unreality over what was happening. Now the same scene was being replayed with Blake, but it was somehow different. Scott had never stalked her, never talked to her in a crooning, husky voice. Blake wanted her to put her hands in his and go with him back to that bed, lie beside him as if nothing had happened. But what *had* happened? He had been angry, and he had grabbed her shoulder, throwing her to her back...no, that had been Scott. Scott had done that once, but they hadn't been in bed.

Her brow knitted, and she brought both hands up, rubbing her forehead. God, would she never be free of Scott, of what he had done to her? Blake's anger had triggered the memory of the other time, and though she hadn't confused their identities, she had been reacting to Scott, not Blake. Blake hadn't hurt her; he had been angry, but he hadn't hurt her.

''Dee? Are you all right?''

His beloved, anxious voice was almost more than she could bear. ''No,'' she said, her voice muffled behind her hands. ''I wonder if I'll ever be all right.''

Abruptly she felt his touch, his hands on her arms, slowly drawing her to him. She could feel the tension in him as he folded her into his arms. "Of course you will," he reassured her, kissing her temple. "Come back to bed with me; you're cold."

Abruptly she felt the cold, the chill of the night on the bareness of her body. She walked with him to the bed, let him put her between the sheets and draw the comforter up over her. He walked around to the other side, turned out the lamp and got into bed beside her. Carefully, as though he were trying not to startle her, he pulled her into his arms and held her tightly to his side.

"I love you," he said in the darkness, his low tones vibrating over her skin. "I swear, Dee, that I'll never again touch you in anger. I love you too much to put you through that again."

Hot tears burned her lids. How could he apologize for something that was, essentially, a weakness in her? How long would it take before he began to resent the flaw in her nature? He wouldn't be able to act naturally with her, and the strain would tear them apart. Normal couples had arguments, yelled at each other, knowing that their anger didn't harm the love between them. Blake would hold himself back, fearing another scene; would he come to hate her because he felt restricted by her? Blake deserved someone whole, someone free, as he was free.

"It would probably be better if I left," she said, the words trembling despite all she could do to hold her tone level.

The arm under her neck tensed, and he rose up on his elbow, looming over her in the darkness. "No," he said, and he achieved the firmness that she had striven for but failed to obtain. "You're where you belong, and you're going to stay here. We're getting married, remember?"

"That's what I'm trying to say," she protested. "How can we have any sort of life together if you're constantly watching what you say and do, afraid of upsetting me? You'd hate me, and I'd hate myself!"

"You're worrying about nothing," he said shortly. "I'll never hate you, so forget that line."

The edge in his voice cut her like a razor, and she fell silent, wondering why she had ever been fool enough to actually believe that they could have a normal life together. She should have learned by now that love wasn't meant to be a part of her life. Blake didn't love her; hadn't her common sense told her that from the beginning? He was infatuated with her, lured by the challenge of seducing her and the hothouse atmosphere that his intense therapy program had generated. Hothouses produced spectacular blooms, but she should have remembered that those blooms wouldn't flourish in the real world. They had to have that protected atmosphere; they withered and died when exposed to the often unfriendly elements of normal life.

Already the bloom of Blake's infatuation was dying, killed not by the attraction to another woman as she had feared, but by daily exposure to reality.

Chapter 12

Knowing that it was happening was one thing; preparing herself for it was another. Every time she glanced up and caught Blake watching her broodingly she had to turn away to hide the pain that twisted inside her. She knew that he was regretting his marriage proposal, but his pride wouldn't allow him to back out of it. Probably he would never ask to be released from the engagement; she would have to do the severing. She sensed that he still wasn't ready to admit that he'd been wrong, so she didn't try to take any action to break their engagement now. When the time came she would know, and she would free him.

New Year's passed, and, as he had planned, he began working full time. She could tell that he was always eager to leave the house, and he began to bring home a briefcase crammed with papers. Dione wondered if he brought work home so he would have an excuse to shut himself in the study and escape her company; then he mentioned that Richard had taken his suggestion and indulged in a month of vacation, and she felt guilty. He really was buried in paperwork without Richard to take part of the load off him.

One night he came to bed after midnight and groaned wearily as his body relaxed. Dione turned over and touched his cheek, trailing her fingers over his skin and feeling the prickle of his beard. ''Do you need a massage to relax?'' she asked quietly.

"Would you mind?" he sighed. "My neck and shoulders have a permanent kink in them from leaning over a desk. My God, no wonder Richard and Serena are having problems; he's had two years of this, and that's enough to drive any man crazy."

He rolled over on his stomach, and Dione pulled her nightgown up to her thighs, straddling his back and leaning forward to work her magic on his tight muscles. As her kneading fingers dug into his flesh he made a muffled sound of pain, then sighed blissfully as the tension left him.

"Have you seen Serena lately?" he asked.

Her fingers paused for a moment, then resumed their movement. "No," she replied. "She hasn't even called. Have you talked to her?"

"Not since the night she had dinner here and told us she and Richard had separated. I think I'll call her tomorrow. Ahhh, that feels good. Right there. I feel as if I've been beaten."

She rolled her knuckles up and down his spine, paying particular attention to the spot that he had indicated needed extra work. He made little grunting noises every time she touched a tender area, and she began to laugh. "You sound like a pig," she teased.

"Who cares? I'm enjoying this. I've missed the massages; several times I've started to call you and ask you to come to the plant to give me a rubdown, but it didn't seem like such a smart thing to do in a busy day."

"Why not?" she asked tartly, a little irritated that he considered her to be a traveling massage parlor, and a lot irritated that he hadn't followed through on his idea.

He laughed and rolled over, deftly keeping his body between her thighs. "Because," he murmured, "this is what usually happens to me during one of your massages. Let me tell you, I had a hell of a time keeping you from realizing what was going on when you thought I was impotent and were so sweetly trying to turn me on to prove that I wasn't."

She moved off him like a rocket, her entire body blushing. "What?" she yelled furiously. "You *knew* what I was doing, and you let me go ahead and make a fool of myself?"

He laughed uproariously, reaching out to pull her into his embrace. "It didn't take me long to figure it out," he admitted, still chuckling. "As if you needed sexy clothes to turn me on...but I couldn't let you know what you were doing to me without frightening you away. Honey, you weren't seducing me; *I* was seducing *you,* but I had to let you think it was the other way around."

She burned with embarrassment, thinking of the things she had done, the revealing clothes she had worn. Then she felt his hand on her breast, and the heat intensified, but no longer from shame. He hadn't made love to her for several days; he had been coming to bed late and falling asleep as soon as his head hit the pillow, and she had missed his touch.

"You don't really mind, do you?" he asked softly, pulling the nightgown over her head. "What are you doing with this thing on?"

"I get cold when you aren't in the bed," she explained, stretching her body in his arms, reveling in the rasp of his hair-roughed skin against hers.

With a growl he rolled her to her back and buried his face between her breasts. "I'm here now, so you don't need it," he said, his voice muffled by her flesh. He took her quickly, impatient after the days of abstinence. She held him even after he was asleep, her doubts momentarily eased by the passion of his lovemaking.

Serena called the next morning. "I've just talked to Blake," she said, laughing a little. "He practically ordered me to take you out to lunch. He said that you're going a little stir crazy with him so tied up at work. Does he really think I believe that?"

Dione laughed. "He thinks you're sitting there alone, brooding, and he wants you to get out of the house for a while. Shall we make him happy and go out to lunch?"

"Why not? I'll pick you up at twelve."

"I'm not brooding," Serena said firmly a few hours later as she bit into a crisp radish. "Richard wanted some time to himself, and I gave it to him. We didn't have an argument or anything like that. He's in Aspen. He loves to ski, and I've never learned how; he hasn't been since we were married, because he wouldn't do anything that I couldn't enjoy. I'm not athletic," she explained, grinning.

"You're not upset at all?"

"Of course I'm upset, but I'm borrowing a page from your book and keeping it all under control." She shrugged lightly. "We had a long conversation before he left, got everything out in the open. That's a first for Richard. He's so good at keeping his thoughts to himself that sometimes I want to scream. We decided that he's been under so much stress that the best thing to do was to get away from each other, let him relax and catch up on his sleep, before we did any more talking."

"Have you talked to him since he left?"

"No. That was part of the bargain. When he comes back we'll settle things once and for all."

Serena had changed a lot in the months since they had met, becoming a self-assured woman. Things might not work out for her, but she was facing the future with her chin up; Dione only hoped that she could do the same. While Blake was making love to her, she could forget that he was growing away from her, but they couldn't spend the rest of their lives in bed. The ruby heart rested warmly in the valley between her breasts; he had said that it was his heart, and she wouldn't be selfish. She would give his heart back to him.

"I know what we can do," Serena said firmly. "Let's go shopping! We can look for your wedding dress."

Shopping was Serena's cure-all, and Dione went along with it, though she couldn't work up any enthusiasm for any of the dresses that they looked at. How could she be concerned with a dress for a wedding that would never take place?

Blake was so tired when he came home that night that his limp was more pronounced, but he cross-examined her over dinner, asking for a word-for-word repetition of everything Serena had said, how she had looked, if she had seemed worried. Dione tried to reassure him, but she could tell that he was anxious about his sister.

The passion of the night before wasn't repeated; when he finally came to bed he threw his arm over her and went to sleep before his mumbled "good night" was out of his mouth. She listened to his steady breathing for a long time, unwilling to sleep and miss a moment of her time with him.

With calm resignation she made plans the next day for her future; she contacted Dr. Norwood and accepted a case, then booked a flight to Milwaukee. Her next patient was still hospitalized, but in three weeks he would be able to begin therapy, so that gave her three weeks to spend with Blake.

Every day he became more distant from her, more involved in his work, needing less from her. In her weak moments she tried to tell herself that it was just because he had so much work to do, but she couldn't believe that for long. She responded by doing as she had always done, shoving her pain and misery into a dark corner of her mind and building a wall around them. If it killed her, she would still leave him with her shoulders straight and not distress him by crying all over him. He wouldn't like that, and she wasn't the weepy type, anyway. She wouldn't just hit him with it; she would tell him that she was having doubts about their marriage, and that she thought it would be a good idea for them to spend some time apart. She would tell him that she'd taken another case, and that when it was finished they would discuss their situation. His conscience wouldn't bother him if she did it that way; he would be relieved that it was her idea.

She learned that Richard was back in town when he called her and asked if he could talk to her privately. She hesitated, and he said wryly, "Serena knows that I'm here. She suggested that I talk to you."

Why would Serena want Richard to talk to Dione? What could she possibly tell him that Serena couldn't say just as well? But a third party could sometimes see more clearly than the ones involved, so she agreed.

He drove over early that afternoon. He looked younger than he had, tanned from his weeks in Aspen in the winter sun, and far more relaxed. The lines of strain that had been in his face were gone, replaced by a smile.

"You're even more beautiful than before," he said, leaning down to kiss her cheek. She didn't shy away from him now; Blake had taught her that not all men were to be feared. She smiled up at him.

"You're pretty great looking yourself. I gather you've seen Serena?''

"We had dinner together last night. She sent me to you."

"But why?" Dione asked, bewildered. They walked out to the courtyard and sat down in the sun. With the walls of the house keeping any wind away from them, the cool January day was pleasant, and she didn't even need a sweater.

Richard leaned against the concrete back of the bench, crossing his ankle over his knee. She noticed idly that he was wearing jeans, the only time she'd ever seen him dressed so casually, and a blue pullover sweater that made his gray eyes seem blue. "Because she's a smart woman," he mused. "She's known from the beginning that I was attracted to you, and our marriage can't work if you're between us."

Dione's eyes widened. "What?" she asked weakly. "But...but Serena's been so friendly, so open...."

"As I said, she's a smart woman. She knew that you didn't return my interest. You've never been able to see anyone but Blake. How I feel about you is something that I have to work out."

She shook her head. "This is ridiculous. You don't love me; you never have. You're in love with Serena."

"I know," he admitted, and laughed. "But for a while I was pretty confused. Serena didn't seem to care if I was around or not, and there you were, so damned lovely that it hurt to look at you, so strong and sure of yourself. You knew what you wanted and didn't let anything stand in your way. The contrast was striking."

Was that how he had seen her? As strong and confident? Hadn't he realized that she was that way only in her profession, that privately she was crippled, afraid of letting anyone get close to her? It was strange that, as astute as Richard was, he hadn't seen her as she really was.

"And now?" she asked.

"I'll always admire you," he chuckled. "But this visit is just for Serena's peace of mind. You were right all along; I love her, and I've been punishing her because she relied on Blake instead of me. I freely admit to the illogic of it, but people in love aren't logical."

"She wanted you to be certain before you went back to her."

"That's right. And I am certain. I love skiing, but I spent the entire time I was in Aspen wishing that she was with me. You should hang out a shingle as a doctor in psychology," he said, laughing, and put his arm on her shoulder to hug her.

She walked him to the door and sent him on his way, glad that he'd ironed out his problems, but she was also depressed at the thought that she'd been involved in any way at all, however innocently. She walked back out to the courtyard and resumed her seat. She was tired, so tired of these months of emotional strain. She closed her eyes and lifted her face to the winter sun, letting her thoughts drift.

"How long had he been here?"

The harsh voice sliced through the air and she jumped, getting to her feet and whirling to face Blake. "You're early," she stammered.

"I know," he said, his voice as hard and cold as his face. "I haven't been able to spend much time with you lately, and when I managed to get everything cleared for today I decided to surprise you. I didn't mean to interrupt anything," he finished with a sneer.

A sick feeling in her stomach made her swallow before she answered. "You didn't," she said briefly, lifting her chin. Suddenly she knew that this was it, that he would use this as an excuse to break their engagement, and she couldn't bear to listen to him saying things that would break her heart. It would break anyway when she left, but she didn't want to have the memory of hard words between them.

"He hadn't been here over five minutes," she said remotely, lifting her hand to cut him off when he started to speak. "He and Serena have patched up their differences, and he wanted to talk to me. She sent him over, as a matter of fact, but you're welcome to call her if you don't believe me."

His eyes sharpened, and he took a step toward her, his hand reaching out. Dione backed away. It had to be now, before he touched her. He might not love her, but she knew that he desired her, and with them, touching led inevitably to sex. That was another thing she couldn't bear, making love with him and knowing it was the last time.

"Now is as good a time as any to tell you," she said, still in that remote voice, her face an expressionless mask. "I've accepted another case, and I'll be leaving in a few days. At least, those were my original plans, but now I think it would be best if I left tomorrow, don't you?"

His skin tightened over his cheekbones. "What are you saying?" he demanded fiercely.

"That I'm breaking our engagement," she said, fumbling with the delicate clasp at the back of her neck and finally releasing it. She took the ruby heart and held it out to him.

He didn't take it. He was staring at her, his face white. "Why?" he asked, grinding the word out through lips that barely moved.

She sighed wearily, rubbing her forehead. "Haven't you realized by now that you don't love me?"

"If you think that, why did you set a wedding date?" he rasped.

She gave him a thin smile. "You were making love to me," she said gently. "I wasn't in my right mind. I've known all along that you didn't love me," she burst out, desperate to make him understand. She couldn't hold out much longer. "I humored you, but it's time now for it to end. You've changed these past weeks, needing me less and less."

"Humored me!" he shouted, clenching his fists. "Were you also 'humoring me' when we made love? I'll be damned if you were!"

She winced. "No. That was real…and it was a mistake. I've never been involved with a patient before, and I'll never let it happen again. It gets too…complicated."

"Lady, I don't believe you!" he said in disbelief. "You're just going to waltz out of here as if nothing ever happened, aren't you? You're going to mark me down as a mistake and forget about me."

No, he was wrong. She'd never be able to forget him. She stared at him with pain-glazed eyes, feeling as if she were shattering inside. A sickening headache pounded in her temples, and when she held the necklace out to him again her hand was trembling. "Why are you arguing?" she asked raggedly. "You should be glad. I'm letting you off the hook. Just think how miserable you'd be, married to someone you don't love."

He reached out and took the necklace, letting the tiny gold links drip over his fingers like metal tears. The sun pierced the ruby heart, casting a red shadow that danced over the white bench beside her. Savagely he shoved it into his pocket. "Then what are you waiting for?" he shouted. "Go on, get out! What do you want me to do, break down and beg you to stay?"

She swayed, then steadied herself. "No," she whispered. "I've never wanted you to beg for anything." She moved slowly past him, her legs weak and unwilling to work as they should. She would pack and go to a hotel, and try to get an earlier flight rather than waiting until her original flight was scheduled. She hadn't imagined that it would be so difficult, or that she would feel so battered. This was worse, far worse, than anything Scott had ever done to her. He had hurt her physically and mentally, but he had never been able to touch her heart. It was killing her to leave Blake, but she had to do it.

Her headache was worse; as she stumbled around the bedroom trying to gather her clothing she had to grab at the furniture several times to keep from falling to her knees. Her mind was muddied, her thoughts jumbled, and nothing made much sense except the over-powering need she had to be gone. She had to leave before she was hurt any more, because she didn't think she'd be able to live if anything else happened.

"Stop it," a low voice commanded, and a hand caught her wrist, pulling her fingers away from the lingerie that she had been tossing carelessly into her suitcase. "You can pack later, when you're feeling better. You have a headache, don't you?"

She turned her head to look at him and almost staggered when her vision swayed alarmingly. "Yes," she mumbled.

"I thought so. I watched you practically crawl up the stairs." He put his arm around her waist, a curiously impersonal touch, and led her to the bed where they had shared so many nights. "Come on, you need a nap. You surprise me; I didn't think you were the type who lived on nerves, but this is a tension headache if I've ever seen one." His fingers moved down the front of her blouse, slipping the buttons out of their holes, and he eased the garment off her.

"I'm almost never sick," she apologized. "I'm sorry." She let him unsnap her bra and toss it aside. No, it wasn't a matter of *letting* him do anything. The truth was that she didn't feel capable of struggling with him over who would remove her clothes, and she badly needed the nap he had suggested. It wasn't as if he hadn't already seen every inch of her body. He eased her down on the bed and unfastened her slacks, sliding an arm under her and lifting her so he could pull them down over her hips. Her shoes came off with the slacks; then his hands returned and made short work of the filmy panties that were her last remaining garment.

Gently he turned her on her stomach, and she sighed as he began to rub the tight muscles in her neck. "I'm returning the favor," he murmured. "Just think of all the massages you've given me. Relax and go to sleep. You're tired, too tired to do anything right now. Sleep, darling."

She did sleep, deeply and without dreaming, sedated by his strong fingers as they rubbed the aching tension from her back and shoulders. It was dark when she woke, but her headache was gone. She felt fuzzy and disoriented, and she blinked at the dark form that rose from a chair beside the bed.

"Do you feel better?" he asked.

"Yes," she said, pushing her heavy hair away from her face. He tuned on the lamp and sat down on the edge of the bed, surveying her with narrowed eyes, as if gauging for himself how well she was feeling.

"Thank you for taking care of me," she said awkwardly. "I'll pack now, and go to a hotel—"

"It's too late to go anywhere tonight," he interrupted. "You've slept for hours. Alberta left a plate warming for you, if you feel like eating. I think you should try to eat something, or you'll be sick again. I didn't realize what a strain you had been under," he added thoughtfully.

She was hungry, and she sat up, holding the sheet to her. "I feel as if I could eat a cow," she said ruefully.

He chuckled softly. "I hope you'll settle for something less than a whole cow," he said, untangling a nightgown from the jumble of clothing that still littered the bed. He plucked the sheet away from her fingers and settled the nightgown over her head as impersonally as if he were dressing a child. Then he found her robe, and she obediently slid her arms into the sleeves while he held it.

"You don't have to coddle me," she said. "I feel much better. After food, I want a shower, and then I'll be fine."

"I like coddling you," he replied. "Just think of how many times you helped me to dress, how many times you coaxed me to eat, how many times you've picked me up when I lay sprawled on the floor."

He walked downstairs with her and sat beside her while she ate. She could feel his steady gaze on her, but the anger that had been there earlier was gone. Had it been only pride that made him lash out at her; did he now realize that she was right?

When she went back upstairs he was right behind her. She looked at him questioningly when he entered the bedroom with her. "Take your shower," he said, taking her shoulders and turning her in the direction of the bathroom. "I'll wait out here for you. I want to make sure you're okay before I go to bed."

"I'm fine," she protested.

"I'll stay," he said firmly, and that was that. Knowing that he was waiting, she hurried through her shower. When she came out of the bathroom he was sitting in the chair he'd occupied before, and he got to his feet.

"Bedtime." He smiled, pushing the robe off her shoulders. She hadn't fastened it, knowing that she would be taking it right off again, and it slipped to the floor. He leaned down and lifted her off her feet, then deposited her on the bed. She gasped and clutched at his shoulder.

"What was that for?" she asked, looking up at him.

"For this," he answered calmly, and kissed her. It was a deeply intimate kiss, his mouth opening over hers and his tongue moving in to touch hers. She dug her nails into his shoulder in surprise.

"Let me go," she said, pulling her mouth way from his.

"I'll let you go tomorrow," he murmured. "Tonight is mine."

He bent down to her again, and she rolled her head away; denied the sweet bloom of her lips, he found the sensitive slope where her neck met her shoulder and nipped at it with his teeth, making her gasp again. He dipped his hand into the bodice of her nightgown, rubbing his palm over the rich globes that had lured him.

"Blake...don't do this," she pleaded achingly.

"Why? You love me to touch your breasts," he countered.

She turned her head to look at him, and her lips were trembling. "Yes," she admitted. "But I'm leaving tomorrow. This...will only make it more difficult. I've accepted another job, and I have to go."

"I understand," he murmured, still stroking her flesh. "I'll put you on a plane tomorrow, if that's what you want, but we still have tonight together, and I want to spend it making love to you. Don't you like what we do to each other? Don't you like making me go out of my skull? You do. You make me wild, with your body like hot silk on me. One more night, darling. Let us have this last night together."

It was exactly what she hadn't wanted, to make love to him and know that she never would again, but the sensual promise he was making her with his hands and body was a heady lure. One more night, one more memory.

"All right," she whispered, beginning to unbutton his shirt. His hot flesh beckoned her, and she pressed her lips to him, feeling the curling hair under her mouth and the shiver that rippled over him. The intoxicating excitement that always seized her at his touch was taking over again, and she unbuckled his pants, helped him kick them away. He parted her legs and fit himself between them, the fever of feeling so high that no more preparation was needed, no more loving required to make her ready for him.

With a slow, smooth thrust he took her, and she adjusted her body to his weight and motion, letting the excitement well up like a cresting wave and take her away.

One more night. Then it would be finished.

Chapter 13

It didn't get any better. She had thought that it would get easier, even if the wound never quite healed, but from the time Blake saw her onto the plane at Sky Harbor Airport, the hurting never peaked, then declined. It stayed with her, eating at her. If she could forget about it during the day while she worked with Kevin, who was her new patient, it returned full force at night when she went to bed and lay there alone.

Milwaukee was at the opposite end of the world from Phoenix, or seemed like it. In a matter of a few hours she had exchanged a dry desert for several feet of snow, and she couldn't seem to get warm. The Colberts were nice, friendly people, anxious to do what they could to help her with Kevin, and Kevin was a darling, but he wasn't Blake. The childish arms that hugged her so spontaneously didn't satisfy the need she felt for strong, masculine ones, nor did the wet, loving kisses that Kevin and his little sister, Amy, gave her every night make her forget the kisses that had drowned her in a sea of sexual pleasure.

She had never thought that she would miss the fights that she and Blake had had, the loud and boisterous arguments, but she did. She missed everything about him, from his early-morning grumpiness to the wicked smile that lighted his face when he was teasing her.

With foolish desperation, she hoped that the last night they'd had together would result in a baby; he hadn't taken any precautions that night, and for almost three weeks she was able to dream, to pretend. Then she discovered that it wasn't to be, and her world turned that much darker.

When she received a large check in the mail, forwarded by Dr. Norwood, it was all she could do to keep from screaming aloud in pain when she saw his signature. She wanted to tear it up, but she couldn't. The check was for the agreed-upon money. She traced her fingertip over the bold, angular script. It was just as she had known it would be; once she was away from him, she became only a part of his past. She had done what was best for him, but she hadn't known that she would have to live the rest of her life on the fine edge of agony.

With grim determination she set about rebuilding the defenses that he had torn down. She had to have them, to push the pain and memories behind, to hold the darkness at bay. Someday, she thought, looking at the wintry gray sky, she would find pleasure in living again. Someday the sun would shine again.

She had been with the Colberts exactly one month when she was called to the telephone. Frowning in perplexity, she gave Kevin his coloring book and crayons to keep him occupied until she returned, then went out to the hall to answer the phone.

"It's a man," Francine Colbert whispered, smiling at her in delight; then she left to see what had happened to make Amy suddenly bellow as if she were being scalped.

Dione put the phone to her ear. "Hello," she said cautiously.

"I'm not going to bite you," a deep, rich voice said in amusement, and she slumped against the wall as her knees threatened to buckle under her.

"Blake!" she whispered.

"You've been there a month," he said. "Has your patient fallen in love with you yet?"

She closed her eyes, fighting down the mingled pain and pleasure that made her throat threaten to close. Hearing his voice made her weak all over, and she didn't know if she wanted to laugh or cry. "Yes," she gulped. "He's madly in love with me."

"What does he look like?" he growled.

"He's a gorgeous blond, with big blue eyes, not as dark as yours. He pouts for hours if he doesn't win when we play Go Fish," she said, and wiped a stray tear from her cheek.

Blake chuckled. "He sounds like real competition. How tall is he?"

"Oh, I don't know. About as tall as your average five-year-old, I suppose," she said.

"Well, that's a relief. I suppose I can leave you alone with him for a few more months."

She almost dropped the phone and had to grab the cord before it got away from her completely. Putting it back to her ear, she heard him say, "Are you still there?"

"Yes," she said, and wiped another tear away.

"I've been doing a lot of thinking," he said casually. "You told me over and over again that I didn't love you; you explained in great detail why I couldn't love you. But one thing that you never said was that you don't love me, and it seems to me that should have been your number-one reason for calling off a wedding. Well?"

What did he want? To reassure himself that she was all right, that she wasn't pining away? She bit her lip, then said weakly, "I don't love you."

"You're lying," he snapped in return, and she could feel his temper rising. "You're so crazy about me that you're standing there crying, aren't you?"

"No," she denied, fiercely dashing the wetness from her face.

"You're lying again. I've got a meeting waiting for me, so I'll let you get back to your patient, but I'm not through with you. If you thought you could end it by getting on a plane, you have a lot to learn about me. I'll be calling you again. Dream about me, honey."

"I will not!" she said fiercely, but she said it to a dial tone, and she *was* lying anyway. She dreamed about him almost every night and woke up with her pillow damp from the tears she'd shed in her sleep.

Thoroughly rattled, she returned to Kevin, and delighted him by losing a game of Go Fish.

Over the next few days her nerves gradually settled down, and she stopped jumping every time the phone rang. A blizzard shut the city down for two days, knocking out phone service and the electricity. The electricity was restored in a matter of hours, keeping them from freezing, but the phone service waited until clear skies had returned. She was out in the snow with Kevin and Amy, building a snowman for them with their inexpert but hilarious help, when Francine called her.

"Dione, you have a call! It's your friend again. Come on in; I'll bring the children in and get them dried off."

"Awww, Mommy," Kevin protested, but Francine was already pushing his little wheelchair inside and Amy followed obediently.

"Hello," Blake said warmly after she stammered out a hesitant greeting. "Are you pregnant?"

This time she was prepared and held on tightly to the receiver. "No. I...I thought about that, too, but everything's all right."

"Good. I didn't mean to get carried away. Serena *is* pregnant. She didn't waste any time when Richard came back. She was so excited at the possibility that she couldn't wait to take one of those early warning tests, or whatever you call them."

"I'm happy for her. How do you feel about being an uncle?"

"It's okay by me, but I'd rather be a father."

She cautiously leaned against the wall. "What do you mean?"

"I mean that when we get married I'm going to throw away my whole supply of—"

"We're not getting married!" she yelped, then glanced around to see if anyone had heard her. No one was in sight, so she guessed that Francine was still occupied with the children.

"Sure we are," he returned calmly. "On the first of May. You set the date yourself. Don't you remember? I was making love to you."

"I remember," she whispered. "But don't you remember? I broke the engagement. I gave your heart back to you."

"That's what you think," he said. "We're getting married if I have to drag you kicking and screaming back to Phoenix."

Again she was left listening to a dial tone.

She couldn't make any sense out of what he was doing. Sleep got harder and harder to attain, and she lay awake going over the possibilities. Why would he insist that they were getting married? Why couldn't he just let it go?

It was a week before he called her again, and Francine had an amused gleam in her eye when she handed her the phone. "It's that dishy guy again," she said as Dione lifted the receiver to her ear.

"Tell her thank you," Blake chuckled. "How are you, honey?"

"Blake, why are you calling me?" she asked in desperation.

"Why shouldn't I call you? Is it against the law for a man to talk to the woman he's going to marry?"

"I'm not going to marry you!" she said, and this time she bellowed it. Francine popped her head out of the kitchen and grinned at her.

Blake was laughing. "Sure you are. You already know all my bad habits and love me anyway; what could be better?"

"Would you listen to reason?" she yelled. "It's out of the question for me to marry you!"

"You're the one who's not listening," he countered. "You love me, and I love you. I don't know why you're so convinced that I can't love you, but you're wrong. Just think of the fun we're going to have while I show you how wrong you are."

"This is crazy," she moaned.

"No, this isn't crazy. You've got some crazy ideas, though, and you're going to get rid of them. You've convinced yourself that no one is going to love you, and you walked away from me, knowing that it was tearing me apart and half killing yourself at the same time. Your mother didn't love you, and Scott didn't love you, but they were only two people. How many people since then have loved you, and you pushed them away because you were afraid of getting hurt again? I'm not going to let you push me away, honey. Think about it."

"Some guy," Francine teased when Dione walked into the kitchen. Then she saw Dione's white face and quickly pushed a chair at her, then poured a cup of coffee. "Is something wrong?"

"Yes. No. I don't know." Dazed, she drank the coffee, then raised stunned golden eyes to the other woman. "He wants to marry me."

"So I gathered. What's so surprising about that? I imagine a lot of men have wanted to marry you."

"He won't take no for an answer," she said abstractedly.

"If he looks as great as he sounds, why would you want him to take no for an answer?" Francine asked practically. "Unless he's a bum."

"No, he's not a bum. He's...even greater than he sounds."

"Do you love him?"

Dione buried her face in her hands. "So much that I've been about to die without him."

"Then marry him!" Francine sat down beside her. "Marry him, and whatever problem is keeping you apart will be settled later. You'd be surprised how many problems people can settle when they're sleeping in the same bed every night and they wake up to the same face every morning. Don't be afraid to take the chance; every marriage is a gamble, but then so is walking across the street. If you didn't take the chance you'd never get to the other side."

Words tumbled around in Dione's mind that night as she lay sleeplessly in bed. Blake had said that she was afraid of getting hurt again, and it was the truth. But was she so afraid of getting hurt that she had deliberately turned her back on a man who loved her?

No one had ever loved her before. No one had worried about her, held her when she cried, comforted her when she was upset....

Except Blake. He had done all those things. Even Richard had thought she was strong and confident, but Blake had seen beneath the act, had realized how vulnerable she was, how easily hurt. Blake had replaced the memories of violence with the memories of love. When she dreamed of a man's touch now it was his touch she dreamed of, and it filled her with aching need.

Blake loved her! It was incredible, but she had to believe it. She had set him free, expecting him to forget her, but it hadn't happened like that. It wasn't a case of "out of sight, out of mind." He had gone to the trouble of finding out where she was, and he had given her time to think about a life without him before he called. He hadn't given up.

As the days passed she went through her routine with Kevin with a smile on her face, humming constantly. He was so willing to do anything she asked that it was a pleasure to work with him, and she knew that soon he wouldn't need her any longer. That automobile accident that had injured him was long forgotten, and all he was concerned with now was if he would be able to play ball by the time summer came.

"How's your patient doing?" Blake asked the next time he called, and Dione smiled at the sound of his voice.

"He's doing great. I'm about ready to graduate him to a walker."

"That's good news, and not just for him. That means you'll be able to take a long honeymoon."

She didn't say anything, just stood there smiling. No, Blake Remington didn't give up. Any other man would have thrown up his hands in disgust, but when Blake decided that he wanted something, he went after it.

"Have you fainted?" he asked warily.

"No," she said, and burst into tears. "It's just that I love you so much, and I miss you."

He drew a long, shuddering breath. "Well, thank God," he muttered. "I was beginning to think I really would have to kidnap you. Lady, it's going to take a lifetime of massages to make up for what you've put me through."

"I'll even sign a contract, if you want," she said, swiping at the tears.

"Oh, I want, all right. An ironclad contract. What day can I fetch you? If I know you, you have Kevin's schedule mapped out to the very day you kiss him good-bye and walk away, and I'm going to be there to meet you when you walk out the door. You're not getting out of my sight until you're Mrs. Remington."

"April twelfth," she said, laughing and crying at the same time.

"I'll be there."

He *was* there, leaning on the doorbell at nine o'clock sharp that morning, while a spring snowstorm dumped its white load on his unprotected head. When Francine opened the door he grinned at her. "I've come for Dione," Blake said. "Is she awake yet?"

Francine opened the door wider, smiling at the tall man with the slight limp who entered her house. There was a reckless air about him; he was the sort of man who didn't let the woman he loved walk away from him.

"She's trying to get everything packed, but the children are helping her and it could take a while," Francine explained. "I imagine they're both wrapped around her legs and crying."

"I understand the feeling," he muttered, and at Francine's questioning look he grinned again. "I'm one of her ex-patients," he explained.

"Take good care of her," Francine pleaded. "She's been so good to Kevin, keeping his spirits up, not letting him get bored. She's special."

"I know," he said gently.

Dione came around the turn of the stairs with two tearful children in her arms. She stopped when she saw Blake, and her entire face lighted up. "You came," she breathed, as if she hadn't dared to let herself really believe it.

"With bells on," he said, going up the steps in a graceful leap that made a mockery of the remaining limp. There was no way to get his arms around her without including the children, so he pulled all three of them to him and kissed her. Amy stuck her finger between their mouths and giggled.

Blake drew back and gave the little girl a rueful look, which she returned with wide-eyed innocence. "Are you the man who's taking Dee away?" Kevin asked tearfully, lifting his wet face from Dione's neck.

"Yes, I am," Blake replied gravely, "but I promise to take good care of her if you'll let me have her. I was her patient, too, and I need her a lot. My leg still hurts me at night, and she has to rub it."

Kevin could understand that, and after a moment he nodded. "All right," he sighed. "She's real good at rubbing legs."

"Kevin, let Dione put you down," Francine directed. When both of the children were on the floor, Amy wrapped her plump little arms around Blake's leg and looked up a long, long way to his face. He looked down at her, then lifted his eyes to Dione's face. "At least two,'' he said. ''And maybe even three, if you don't give me a daughter on your first two tries.''

''I'm thirty years old, remember,'' she said cautiously. ''Almost thirty-one.''

''So? You have the body of an eighteen-year-old, only in better shape. I should know,'' he murmured, the hot light in his eyes making her cheeks turn pink. In a normal voice he said, ''Are you packed?''

''Yes, I'll bring my suitcases down. You wait right here,'' she said hurriedly, turning and sprinting up the stairs. Her heart was galloping in her chest, and it wasn't from the stairs. Just seeing him again had been like getting kicked, except that it didn't hurt. She felt alive, truly alive; even her fingertips were tingling with joy. In eighteen days she would be getting married!

''Hurry it up!'' he called, and she shivered with delight. Picking up her two suitcases she ran down the stairs.

When they were in the car he sat for a long moment just looking at her. Francine and the children had said their last good-byes in the house, not coming out into the snow, so they were all alone. The snow had already covered the windows of the car, encasing them in a white cocoon.

''I have something for you,'' he murmured, reaching into his pocket. He withdrew the ruby heart and dangled it before her eyes. ''You might as well keep it,'' he said as he clasped it around her neck. ''It never did work right after you tried to give it back, anyway.''

Tears burned her eyes as the ruby heart slid down to its resting place between her breasts. ''I love you,'' she said unsteadily.

''I know. I had some bad moments when you first gave the heart back to me, but after I thought about it, I realized how frightened you were. I had to let you go to convince you that I loved you. Lady, that was the hardest thing I've ever done in my life, letting you get on the plane without me. Learning how to walk again was child's play compared to that.''

''I'll make it up to you,'' she whispered, going into his arms. His familiar scent teased her senses, and she inhaled it delightedly. The smell of him brought back hot, sunny days and the echo of laughter.

"Starting tonight," he threatened. "Or better yet, as soon as we can get to the hotel room I've booked for us."

"Aren't we flying back to Phoenix today?" she asked, lifting her head in surprise.

"In case you haven't noticed, we're in the middle of a snow-storm." He grinned. "All flights are grounded until it clears, which could be days and days. How would you like to spend days and days in bed with me?"

"I'll try to bear it," she sighed.

"Do you spell that b-a-r-e?" he asked, nuzzling her neck. Then, slowly, as if he had waited as long as he could, he closed his lips over hers. He kissed her for a long time, savoring the taste and feel of her, then pulled himself away with a visible effort.

"I'm able to drive now," he said unnecessarily as he put the car into gear.

"So I see."

"And I'm flying again. I tested a new engine last week—"

"Are you going to keep doing the dangerous stuff?" she inter-rupted.

He eyed her. "I've been thinking about that. I don't think I'll be taking as many chances as I used to. There's too much excitement going on at home for me to risk missing any of it."

She was swimming laps, the hot May desert sun beating down on her head. The exercise felt good to her body, stretching muscles that had felt cramped. She had missed the pool and the well-equipped little gym where she and Blake had played out so many of their crises. That morning she had gone to a Phoenix hospital and been hired on the spot; she would miss the intensity of a one-on-one therapeutic relationship, but the regular hours would permit her to be with Blake at night and still keep doing the work she loved.

"Hey!" a deep voice called. "Are you in training for the Olym-pics?"

She began treading water. "What are you doing home so early?" she asked, pushing her hair out of her eyes.

"That's a fine welcome," her husband of two weeks grumbled. He shed his coat and draped it over one of the chairs, then pulled his tie loose. Dione watched as he systematically undressed, dropping his clothes on the chair until he stood as naked as the day he was born. He came into the water in a neat, shallow dive, and reached her with a few powerful strokes of his arms.

"If you get caught like that, don't blame me," she warned.

"It's too hot for clothes," he complained. "Did you get the job?"

"Of course I got the job," she sniffed.

"Conceited." He put his hand on top of her head and ducked her, which didn't bother her at all. She was as good a swimmer under water as she was on top of it, and she kicked her graceful legs, darting away from him. He caught up with her when she reached the edge.

"You never did say why you're home so early," she said, turning to face him.

"I came home to make love to my wife," he replied. "I couldn't keep my mind on what I was doing; I kept thinking about last night," he said, and watched in fascination as her eyes grew heavy-lidded with memory.

He moved in closer to her and pressed his mouth to hers, his hand going to the back of her head and slanting her mouth across his. Their tongues met in mutual desire, and Dione quivered, letting her body float against his. Her legs twined with his and found them steady.

"You're standing," she said, lifting her mouth away.

"I know." His hand moved purposefully up her back and deftly unclipped her bikini top. He pulled it way from her and tossed it out of the pool. It landed on the tiles with a sodden plop. His fingers touched her breasts, cupping them together as he leaned forward and took another kiss.

With a moan she twined her arms around his neck; then she was wrapped around him like a vine. No matter how often he made love to her, it kept getting better and better as her body learned new ways of responding to him. The cool water lapped around them, but it didn't cool their hot skin. The fires within burned too brightly to be dampened by a little water.

He lifted her out of the water until her breasts were on a level with his mouth; then he feasted on the ripe curves that thrust so beguilingly at him. "I love you," he groaned, pulling at the ties that held the minuscule bikini bottom on her hips.

"Blake! Not here," she protested, but her body lay against his in sweet abandon. "Someone will see. Miguel...Alberta..."

"Miguel isn't here," he whispered, sliding her down the length of his body. "And no one can see what we're doing. The glare of the sun on the water takes care of that. Put your legs around my hips," he directed.

Suddenly she laughed aloud, throwing her head back and lifting her face to the hot Phoenix sun. "You're still a daredevil," she crooned, catching her breath as he took her with a long, delicious slide of skin against skin. "You love to take chances."

She clung to his shoulders, her senses dazzled, drenched in the beauty of the day. He watched her face, watched the wonderful play of emotions in her exotic eyes, watched them grow slumbrous, watching her teeth catch that full, passionate lower lip as she quivered with the desire he was carefully building in her. "Lady," he chanted. "Woman. You're all mine, aren't you?"

She laughed again, drunk with pleasure. She lifted her arms to the sun. "For as long as you want me," she promised.

"Then you'll go to your grave as my lady," he said. "And even that won't be the end of it."

PART OF THE BARGAIN
by Linda Lael Miller

For Laura Mast
Thank you for believing and being proud.

Chapter 1

The landing gear made an unsettling *ka-thump* sound as it snapped back into place under the small private airplane. Libby Kincaid swallowed her misgivings and tried not to look at the stony, impassive face of the pilot. If he didn't say anything, she wouldn't have to say anything either, and they might get through the short flight to the Circle Bar B ranch without engaging in one of their world-class shouting matches.

It was a pity, Libby thought, that at the ages of thirty-one and thirty-three, respectively, she and Jess still could not communicate on an adult level.

Pondering this, Libby looked down at the ground below and was dizzied by its passing as they swept over the small airport at Kalispell, Montana, and banked eastward, toward the Flathead River. Trees so green that they had a blue cast carpeted the majestic mountains rimming the valley.

Womanhood being what it is, Libby couldn't resist watching Jess Barlow surreptitiously out of the corner of her eye. He was like a lean, powerful mountain lion waiting to pounce, even though he kept his attention strictly on the controls and the thin air traffic sharing the big Montana sky that spring morning. His eyes were hidden behind a pair of mirrored sunglasses, but Libby knew that they would be dark with the animosity that had marked their relationship for years.

She looked away again, trying to concentrate on the river, which coursed beneath them like a dusty-jade ribbon woven into the fabric of a giant tapestry. Behind those mirrored glasses, Libby knew Jess's eyes were the exact same shade of green as that untamed waterway below.

"So," he said suddenly, gruffly, "New York wasn't all the two-hour TV movies make it out to be."

Libby sighed, closed her eyes in a bid for patience and then opened them again. She wasn't going to miss one bit of that fabulous view—not when her heart had been hungering for it for several bittersweet years.

Besides, Jess had been to New York dozens of times on corporation business. Who did he think he was fooling?

"New York was all right," she said, in the most inflamatory tone she could manage. *Except that Jonathan died,* chided a tiny, ruthless voice in her mind. *Except for that nasty divorce from Aaron.* "Nothing to write home about," she added aloud, realizing her blunder too late.

"So your dad noticed," drawled Jess in an undertone that would have been savage if it hadn't been so carefully modulated. "Every day, when the mail came, he fell on it like it was manna from heaven. He never stopped hoping—I'll give him that."

"Dad knows I hate to write letters," she retorted defensively. But Jess had made his mark, all the same—Libby felt real pain, picturing her father flipping eagerly through the mail and trying to hide his disappointment when there was nothing from his only daughter.

"Funny—that's not what Stace tells me."

Libby bridled at this remark, but she kept her composure. Jess was trying to trap her into making some foolish statement about his older brother, no doubt, one that he could twist out of shape and hold over her head. She raised her chin and choked back the indignant diatribe aching in her throat.

The mirrored sunglasses glinted in the sun as Jess turned to look at her. His powerful shoulders were taut beneath the blue cotton fabric of his workshirt, and his jawline was formidably hard.

"Leave Cathy and Stace alone, Libby," he warned with blunt savagery. "They've had a lot of problems lately, and if you do anything to make the situation worse, I'll see that you regret it. Do I make myself clear?"

Libby would have done almost anything to escape his scrutiny just then, short of thrusting open the door of that small four-passenger Cessna and jumping out, but her choices were undeniably limited. Trembling just a little, she turned away and fixed her attention on the ground again.

Dear heaven, did Jess really think that she would interfere in Cathy's marriage—or any other, for that matter? Cathy was her *cousin*—they'd been raised like sisters!

With a sigh, Libby faced the fact that there was every chance that Jess and a lot of other people would believe she had been involved with Stacey Barlowe. There had, after all, been that exchange of letters, and Stace had even visited her a few times, in the thick of her traumatic divorce, though in actuality he had been in the city on business.

"Libby?" prodded Jess sharply, when the silence grew too long to suit him.

"I'm not planning to vamp your brother!" she snapped. "Could we just drop this, please?"

To her relief and surprise, Jess turned his concentration on piloting the plane. His suntanned jaw worked with suppressed annoyance, but he didn't speak again.

The timbered land below began to give way to occasional patches of prairie—cattle country. Soon they would be landing on the small airstrip serving the prosperous 150,000-acre Circle Bar B, owned by Jess's father and overseen, for the most part, by Libby's.

Libby had grown up on the Circle Bar B, just as Jess had, and her mother, like his, was buried there. Even though she couldn't call the ranch home in the legal sense of the word, it was *still* home to her, and she had every right to go there—especially now, when she needed its beauty and peace and practical routines so desperately.

The airplane began to descend, jolting Libby out of her reflective state. Beside her, Jess guided the craft skillfully toward the paved landing strip stretched out before them.

The landing gear came down with a sharp snap, and Libby drew in her breath in preparation. The wheels of the plane screeched and grabbed as they made contact with the asphalt, and then the Cessna was rolling smoothly along the ground.

When it came to a full stop, Libby wrenched at her seat belt, anxious to put as much distance as possible between herself and Jess Barlowe. But his hand closed over her left wrist in a steel-hard grasp. "Remember, Lib—these people aren't the sophisticated if-it-feels-good-do-it types you're used to. No games."

Games. *Games?* Hot color surged into Libby's face and pounded there in rhythm with the furious beat of her heart. "Let go of me, you bastard!" she breathed.

If anything, Jess's grip tightened. "I'll be watching you," he warned, and then he flung Libby's wrist from his hand and turned away to push open the door on his side and leap nimbly to the ground.

Libby was still tugging impotently at the handle on her own door when her father strode over, climbed deftly onto the wing and opened it for her. She felt such a surge of love and relief at the sight of him that she cried out softly and flung herself into his arms, nearly sending both of them tumbling to the hard ground.

Ken Kincaid hadn't changed in the years since Libby had seen him last—he was still the same handsome, rangy cowboy that she remembered so well, though his hair, while as thick as ever, was iron-gray now, and the limp he'd acquired in a long-ago rodeo accident was more pronounced.

Once they were clear of the plane, he held his daughter at arm's length, laughed gruffly, and then pulled her close again. Over his shoulder she saw Jess drag her suitcases and portable drawing board out of the Cessna's luggage compartment and fling them unceremoniously into the back of a mud-speckled station wagon.

Nothing if not perceptive, Ken Kincaid turned slightly, assessed Senator Cleave Barlowe's second son, and grinned. There was mischief in his bright blue eyes when he faced Libby again. "Rough trip?"

Libby's throat tightened unaccountably, and she wished she could explain *how* rough. She was still stung by Jess's insulting opinion of her morality, but how could she tell her father that? "You know that it's always rough going where Jess and I are concerned," she said.

Her father's brows lifted speculatively as Jess got behind the wheel of the station wagon and sped away without so much as a curt nod or a halfhearted so-long. "You two'd better watch out," he mused. "If you ever stop butting heads, you might find out you like each other."

"Now, that," replied Libby with dispatch, "is a horrid thought if I've ever heard one. Tell me, Dad—how have you been?"

He draped one wiry arm over her shoulders and guided her in the direction of a late-model pickup truck. The door on the driver's side was emblazoned with the words "CIRCLE BAR B RANCH," and Yosemite Sam glared from both the mud flaps shielding the rear tires. "Never mind how I've been, dumplin'. How've *you* been?"

Libby felt some of the tension drain from her as her father opened the door on the passenger side of the truck and helped her inside. She longed to shed her expensive tailored linen suit for jeans and a T-shirt, and—oh, heaven—her sneakers would be a welcome change from the high heels she was wearing. "I'll be okay," she said in tones that were a bit too energetically cheerful.

Ken climbed behind the wheel and tossed one searching, worried look in his daughter's direction. "Cathy's waiting over at the house, to help you settle in and all that. I was hoping we could talk…"

Libby reached out and patted her father's work-worn hand, resting now on the gearshift knob. "We can talk tonight. Anyway, we've got lots of time."

Ken started the truck's powerful engine, but his wise blue eyes had not strayed from his daughter's face. "You'll stay here awhile, then?" he asked hopefully.

Libby nodded, but she suddenly found that she had to look away. "As long as you'll let me, Dad."

The truck was moving now, jolting and rattling over the rough ranch roads with a pleasantly familiar vigor. "I expected you before this," he said. "Lib…"

She turned an imploring look on him. "Later, Dad—okay? Could we please talk about the heavy stuff later?"

Ken swept off his old cowboy hat and ran a practiced arm across his forehead. "Later it is, dumplin'." Graciously he changed the subject. "Been reading your comic strip in the funny papers, and it seems like every kid in town's wearing one of those T-shirts you designed."

Libby smiled; her career as a syndicated cartoonist was certainly safe conversational ground. And it had all started right here, on this ranch, when she'd sent away the coupon printed on a matchbook and begun taking art lessons by mail. After that, she'd won a scholarship to a prestigious college, graduated, and made her mark, not in portraits or commercial design, as some of her friends had, but in cartooning. Her character, Liberated Lizzie, a cave-girl with modern ideas, had created something of a sensation and was now featured not only in the Sunday newspapers but also on T-shirts, greeting cards, coffee mugs and calendars. There was a deal pending with a poster company, and Libby's bank balance was fat with the advance payment for a projected book.

She would have to work hard to fulfill her obligations—there was the weekly cartoon strip to do, of course, and the panels for the book had to be sketched in. She hoped that between these tasks and the endless allure of the Circle Bar B, she might be able to turn her thoughts from Jonathan and the mess she'd made of her personal life.

"Career-wise, I'm doing fine," Libby said aloud, as much to herself as to her father. "I don't suppose I could use the sunporch for a studio?"

Ken laughed. "Cathy's been working for a month to get it ready, and I had some of the boys put in a skylight. All you've got to do is set up your gear."

Impulsively Libby leaned over and kissed her father's beard-stubbled cheek. "I love you!"

"Good," he retorted. "A husband you can dump—a daddy you're pretty well stuck with."

The word "husband" jarred Libby a little, bringing an unwelcome image of Aaron into her mind as it did, and she didn't speak again until the house came into sight.

Originally the main ranch house, the structure set aside for the general foreman was an enormous, drafty place with plenty of Victorian scrollwork, gabled windows and porches. It overlooked a sizable spring-fed pond and boasted its own sheltering copse of evergreens and cottonwood trees.

The truck lurched a little as Ken brought it to a stop in the gravel driveway, and through the windshield Libby could see glimmering patches of the silver-blue sparkle that was the pond. She longed to hurry there now, kick off her shoes on the grassy bank and ruin her stockings wading in the cold, clear water.

But her father was getting out of the truck, and Cathy Barlowe, Libby's cousin and cherished friend, was dashing down the driveway, her pretty face alight with greeting.

Libby laughed and stood waiting beside the pickup truck, her arms out wide.

After an energetic hug had been exchanged, Cathy drew back in Libby's arms and lifted a graceful hand to sign the words: "I've missed you so much!"

"And I've missed you," Libby signed back, though she spoke the words aloud, too.

Cathy's green eyes sparkled. "You haven't forgotten how to sign!" she enthused, bringing both hands into play now. She had been deaf since childhood, but she communicated so skillfully that Libby often forgot that they weren't conversing verbally. "Have you been practicing?"

She had. Signing had been a game for her and Jonathan to play during the long, difficult hours she'd spent at his hospital bedside. Libby nodded and tears of love and pride gathered in her dark blue eyes as she surveyed her cousin—physically, she and Cathy bore no resemblance to each other at all.

Cathy was petite, her eyes wide, mischievous emeralds, her hair a glistening profusion of copper and chestnut and gold that reached almost to her waist. Libby was of medium height, and her silver-blond hair fell just short of her shoulders.

"I'll be back later," Ken said quietly, signing the words as he spoke so that Cathy could understand too. "You two have plenty to say to each other, it looks like."

Cathy nodded and smiled, but there was something sad trembling behind the joy in her green eyes, something that made Libby want to scurry back to the truck and beg to be driven back to the airstrip. From there she could fly to Kalispell and catch a connecting flight to Denver and then New York....

Good Lord—surely Jess hadn't been so heartless as to share his ridiculous suspicions with Cathy!

The interior of the house was cool and airy, and Libby followed along behind Cathy, her thoughts and feelings in an incomprehensible tangle. She was glad to be home, no doubt about it. She'd yearned for the quiet sanity of this place almost from the moment of leaving it.

On the other hand, she wasn't certain that she'd been wise to come back. Jess obviously intended to make her feel less than welcome, and although she had certainly never been intimately involved with Stacey Barlowe, Cathy's husband, sometimes her feelings toward him weren't all that clearly defined.

Unlike his younger brother, Stace was a warm, outgoing person, and through the shattering events of the past year and a half, he had been a tender and steadfast friend. Adrift in waters of confusion and grief, Libby had told Stacey things that she had never breathed to another living soul, and it was true that, as Jess had so bitterly pointed out, she had written to the man when she couldn't bring herself to contact her own father.

But she wasn't in love with Stace, Libby told herself firmly. She had always looked up to him, that was all—like an older brother. Maybe she'd become a little too dependent on him in the bargain, but that didn't mean she cared for him in a romantic way, did it?

She sighed, and Cathy turned to look at her pensively, almost as though she had heard the sound. That was impossible, of course, but

Cathy was as perceptive as anyone Libby had ever known, and she often *felt* sounds.

"Glad to be home?" the deaf woman inquired, gesturing gently.

Libby didn't miss the tremor in her cousin's hands, but she forced a weary smile to her face and nodded in answer to the question.

Suddenly Cathy's eyes were sparkling again, and she caught Libby's hand in her own and tugged her through an archway and into the glassed-in sunporch that overlooked the pond.

Libby drew in a swift, delighted breath. There was indeed a skylight in the roof—a big one. A drawing table had been set up in the best light the room offered, along with a lamp for night work, and there were flowering plants hanging from the exposed beams in the ceiling. The old wicker furniture that had been stored in the attic for as long as Libby could remember had been painted a dazzling white and bedecked with gay floral-print cushions. Small rugs in complementary shades of pink and green had been scattered about randomly, and there was even a shelving unit built into the wall behind the art table.

"Wow!" cried Libby, overwhelmed, her arms spread out wide in a gesture of wonder. "Cathy, you missed your calling! You should have been an interior decorator."

Though Libby hadn't signed the words, her cousin had read them from her lips. Cathy's green eyes shifted quickly from Libby's face, and she lowered her head. "Instead of what?" she motioned sadly. "Instead of Stacey's wife?"

Libby felt as though she'd been slapped, but she recovered quickly enough to catch one hand under Cathy's chin and force her head up. "Exactly what do you mean by that?" she demanded, and she was never certain afterward whether she had signed the words, shouted them, or simply thought them.

Cathy shrugged in a miserable attempt at nonchalance, and one tear slid down her cheek. "He went to see you in New York," she challenged, her hands moving quickly now, almost angrily. "You wrote him letters!"

"Cathy, it wasn't what you think—"

"Wasn't it?"

Libby was furious and wounded, and she stomped one foot in frustration. "Of course it wasn't! Do you really think I would do a thing like that? Do you think Stacey would? He *loves* you!" *And so does Jess,* she lamented in silence, without knowing why that should matter.

Stubbornly Cathy averted her eyes again and shoved her hands into the pockets of her lightweight cotton jacket—a sure signal that as far as she was concerned, the conversation was over.

In desperation, Libby reached out and caught her cousin's shoulders in her hands, only to be swiftly rebuffed by an eloquent shrug. She watched, stricken to silence, as Cathy turned and hurried out of the sunporch-turned-studio and into the kitchen beyond. Just a moment later the back door slammed with a finality that made Libby ache through and through.

She ducked her head and bit her lower lip to keep the tears back. That, too, was something she had learned during Jonathan's final confinement in a children's hospital.

Just then, Jess Barlowe filled the studio doorway. Libby was aware of him in all her strained senses.

He set down her suitcases and drawing board with an unsympathetic thump. "I see you're spreading joy and good cheer as usual," he drawled in acid tones. "What, pray tell, was *that* all about?"

Libby was infuriated, and she glared at him, her hands resting on her trim rounded hips. "As if you didn't know, you heartless bastard! How could you be so mean...so thoughtless..."

The fiery green eyes raked Libby's travel-rumpled form with scorn. Ignoring her aborted question, he offered one of his own. "Did you think your affair with my brother was a secret, princess?"

Libby was fairly choking on her rage and her pain. "What affair, dammit?" she shouted. "We didn't *have* an affair!"

"That isn't what Stacey says," replied Jess with impervious savagery.

Libby felt the high color that had been pounding in her face seep away. *"What?"*

"Stace is wildly in love with you, to hear him tell it. You need him and he needs you, and to hell with minor stumbling blocks like his wife!''

Libby's knees weakened and she groped blindly for the stool at her art table and then sank onto it. ''My God...''

Jess's jawline was tight with brutal annoyance. ''Spare me the theatrics, princess—I know why you came back here. Dammit, *don't you have a soul?*''

Libby's throat worked painfully, but her mind simply refused to form words for her to utter.

Jess crossed the room like a mountain panther, terrifying in his grace and prowess, and caught both her wrists in a furious, inescapable grasp. With his other hand he captured Libby's chin.

''Listen to me, you predatory little witch, and listen well,'' he hissed, his jade eyes hard, his flesh pale beneath his deep rancher's tan. ''Cathy is good and decent and she loves my brother, though I can't for the life of me think why she condescends to do so. And I'll be *damned* if I'll stand by and watch you and Stacey turn her inside out! Do you understand me?''

Tears of helpless fury and outraged honor burned like fire in Libby's eyes, but she could neither speak nor move. She could only stare into the frightening face looming only inches from her own. It was a devil's face.

When Jess's tightening grasp on her chin made it clear that he would have an answer of some sort, no matter what, Libby managed a small, frantic nod.

Apparently satisfied, Jess released her with such suddenness that she nearly lost her balance and slipped off the stool.

Then he whirled away from her, his broad back taut, one powerful hand running through his obsidian hair in a typical gesture of frustration. ''Damn you for ever coming back here,'' he said in a voice no less vicious for its softness.

''No problem,'' Libby said with great effort. ''I'll leave.''

Jess turned toward her again, this time with an ominous leisure, and his eyes scalded Libby's face, the hollow of her throat, the firm roundness of her high breasts. ''It's too late,'' he said.

Still dazed, Libby sank back against the edge of the drawing table, sighed and covered her eyes with one hand. "Okay," she began with hard-won, shaky reason, "why is that?"

Jess had stalked to the windows; his back was a barrier between them again, and he was looking out at the pond. Libby longed to sprout claws and tear him to quivering shreds.

"Stacey has the bit in his teeth," he said at length, his voice low, speculative. "Wherever you went, he'd follow."

Since Libby didn't believe that Stacey had declared himself to be in love with her, she didn't believe that there was any danger of his following her away from the Circle Bar B, either. "You're crazy," she said.

Jess faced her quickly, some scathing retort brewing in his eyes, but whatever he had meant to say was lost as Ken strode into the room and demanded, "What the hell's going on in here? I just found Cathy running up the road in tears!"

"Ask your daughter!" Jess bit out. "Thanks to her, Cathy has just gotten *started* shedding tears!"

Libby could bear no more; she was like a wild creature goaded to madness, and she flung herself bodily at Jess Barlowe, just as she had in her childhood, fists flying. She would have attacked him gladly if her father hadn't caught hold of her around the waist and forcibly restrained her.

Jess raked her with one last contemptuous look and moved calmly in the direction of the door. "You ought to tame that little spitfire, Ken," he commented in passing. "One of these days she's going to hurt somebody."

Libby trembled in her father's hold, stung by his double meaning, and gave one senseless shriek of fury. This brought a mocking chuckle from a disappearing Jess and caused Ken to turn her firmly to face him.

"Good Lord, Libby, what's the *matter* with you?"

Libby drew a deep, steadying breath and tried to quiet the raging ten-year-old within her, the child that Jess had always been able to infuriate. "I hate Jess Barlow," she said flatly. "I hate him."

"Why?" Ken broke in, and he didn't look angry anymore. Just honestly puzzled.

"If you knew what he's been saying about me—"

"If it's the same as what Stacey's been mouthing off about, I reckon I do."

Libby stepped back, stunned. "What?"

Ken Kincaid sighed, and suddenly all his fifty-two years showed clearly in his face. "Stacey and Cathy have been having trouble the last year or so. Now he's telling everybody who'll listen that it's over between him and Cathy and he wants you."

"I don't believe it! I—"

"I wanted to warn you, Lib, but you'd been through so much, between losing the boy and then falling out with your husband after that. I thought you needed to be home, but I knew you wouldn't come near the place if you had any idea what was going on."

Libby's chin trembled, and she searched her father's honest, weathered face anxiously. "I...I haven't been fooling around with C-Cathy's husband, Dad."

He smiled gently. "I know that, Lib—knew it all along. Just never mind Jess and all the rest of them—if you don't run away, this thing'll blow over."

Libby swallowed, thinking of Cathy and the pain she had to be feeling. The betrayal. "I can't stay here if Cathy is going to be hurt."

Ken touched her cheek with a work-worn finger. "Cathy doesn't really believe the rumors, Libby—think about it. Why would she work so hard to fix a studio up for you if she did? Why would she be waiting here to see you again?"

"But she was crying just now, Dad! And she as much as accused me of carrying on with her husband!"

"She's been hurt by what's been said, and Stacey's been acting like a spoiled kid. Honey, Cathy's just testing the waters, trying to find out where you stand. You can't leave her now, because except for Stace, there's nobody she needs more."

Despite the fact that all her instincts warned her to put the Circle Bar B behind her as soon as humanly possible, Libby saw the sense in her father's words. As incredible as it seemed, Cathy would need her—if for nothing else than to lay those wretched rumors to rest once and for all.

"These things Stacey's been saying—surely he didn't unload them on Cathy?"

Ken sighed. "I don't think he'd be that low, Libby. But you know how it is with Cathy, how she always knows the score."

Libby shook her head distractedly. "Somebody told her, Dad— and I think I know who it was."

There was disbelief in Ken's discerning blue eyes, and in his voice, too. "*Jess?* Now, wait a minute..."

Jess.

Libby couldn't remember a time when she had gotten along well with him, but she'd been sure that he cared deeply for Cathy. Hadn't he been the one to insist that Stace and Libby learn signing, as he had, so that everyone could talk to the frightened, confused little girl who couldn't hear? Hadn't he gifted Cathy with cherished bullfrogs and clumsily made valentines and even taken her to the high-school prom?

How could Jess, of all people, be the one to hurt Cathy, when he knew as well as anyone how badly she'd been hurt by her handicap and the rejection of her own parents? How?

Libby had no answer for any of these questions. She knew only that she had separate scores to settle with both the Barlowe brothers.

And settle them she would.

Chapter 2

Libby sat at the end of the rickety swimming dock, bare feet dangling, shoulders slumped, her gaze fixed on the shimmering waters of the pond. The lines of her long, slender legs were accentuated, rather than disguised, by the old blue jeans she wore. A white eyelet suntop sheltered shapely breasts and a trim stomach and left the rest of her upper body bare.

Jess Barlow studied her in silence, feeling things that were at wide variance with his personal opinion of the woman. He was certain that he hated Libby, but something inside him wanted, nonetheless, to touch her, to comfort her, to know the scent and texture of her skin.

A reluctant grin tilted one corner of his mouth. One tug at the top of that white eyelet and...

Jess caught his skittering thoughts, marshaled them back into stern order. As innocent and vulnerable as Libby Kincaid looked at the moment, she was a viper, willing to betray her own cousin to get what she wanted.

Jess imagined Libby naked, her glorious breasts free and welcoming. But the man in his mental scenario was not himself—it was Stacey. The thought lay sour in Jess's mind.

"Did you come to apologize, by any chance?"

The question so startled Jess that he flinched; he had not noticed that Libby had turned around and seen him, so caught up had he been in the vision of her giving herself to his brother.

He scowled, as much to recover his wits as to oppose her. It was and always had been his nature to oppose Libby Kincaid, the way electricity opposes water, and it annoyed him that, for all his travels and his education, he didn't know why.

"Why would I want to do that?" he shot back, more ruffled by her presence than he ever would have admitted.

"Maybe because you were a complete ass," she replied in tones as sunny as the big sky stretched out above them.

Jess lifted his hands to his hips and stood fast against whatever it was that was pulling him toward her. *I want to make love to you,* he thought, and the truth of that ground in his spirit as well as in his loins.

There was pain in Libby's navy-blue eyes, as well as a cautious mischief. "Well?" she prodded.

Jess found that while he could keep himself from going to her, he could not turn away. Maybe her net reached farther than he'd thought. Maybe, like Stacey and that idiot in New York, he was already caught in it.

"I'm not here to apologize," he said coldly.

"Then why?" she asked with chiming sweetness.

He wondered if she knew what that shoulderless blouse of hers was doing to him. Damn. He hadn't been this tongue-tied since the night of his fifteenth birthday, when Ginny Hillerman had announced that she would show him hers if he would show her his.

Libby's eyes were laughing at him. "Jess?"

"Is your dad here?" he threw out in gruff desperation.

One shapely, gossamer eyebrow arched. "You know perfectly well that he isn't. If Dad were home, his pickup truck would be parked in the driveway."

Against his will, Jess grinned. His taut shoulders rose in a shrug. The shadows of cottonwood leaves moved on the old wooden dock, forming a mystical path—a path that led to Libby Kincaid.

She patted the sun-warmed wood beside her. "Come and sit down."

Before Jess could stop himself, he was striding along that small wharf, sinking down to sit beside Libby and dangle his booted feet over the sparkling water. He was never entirely certain what sorcery made him ask what he did.

"What happened to your marriage, Libby?"

The pain he had glimpsed before leapt in her eyes and then faded away again, subdued. "Are you trying to start another fight?"

Jerry shook his head. "No," he answered quietly, "I really want to know."

She looked away from him, gnawing at her lower lip with her front teeth. All around them were ranch sounds—birds conferring in the trees, leaves rustling in the wind, the clear pond water lapping at the mossy pilings of the dock. But no sound came from Libby.

On an impulse, Jess touched her mouth with the tip of one index finger. Water and electricity—the analogy came back to him with a numbing jolt.

"Stop that," he barked, to cover his reactions.

Libby ceased chewing at her lip and stared at him with wide eyes. Again he saw the shadow of that nameless, shifting ache inside her. "Stop what?" she wanted to know.

Stop making me want to hold you, he thought. *Stop making me want to tuck your hair back behind your ears and tell you that everything will be all right.* "Stop biting your lip!" he snapped aloud.

"I'm sorry!" Libby snapped back, her eyes shooting indigo sparks.

Jess sighed and again spoke involuntarily. "Why did you leave your husband, Libby?"

The question jarred them both: Libby paled a little and tried to scramble to her feet; Jess caught her elbow in one hand and pulled her down again.

"Was it because of Stacey?"

She was livid. "No!"

"Someone else?"

Tears sprang up in Libby's dark lashes and made then spiky. She wrenched free of his hand but made no move to rise again and run away. "Sure!" she gasped. "'If it feels good, do it'—that's my motto! By God, I *live* by those words!"

"Shut up," Jess said in a gentle voice.

Incredibly, she fell against him, wept into the shoulder of his blue cotton workshirt. And it was not a delicate, calculating sort of weeping—it was a noisy grief.

Jess drew her close and held her, broken on the shoals of what she was feeling even though he did not know its name. "I'm sorry," he said hoarsely.

Libby trembled beneath his arm and wailed like a wounded calf. The sound solidified into a word usually reserved for stubborn horses and income-tax audits.

Jess laughed and, for a reason he would never understand, kissed her forehead. "I love it when you flatter me," he teased.

Miraculously, Libby laughed too. But when she tilted her head back to look up at him, and he saw the tear streaks on her beautiful, defiant face, something within him, something that had always been disjointed, was wrenched painfully back into place.

He bent his head and touched his lips to hers, gently, in question. She stiffened, but then, at the cautious bidding of his tongue, her lips parted slightly and her body relaxed against his.

Jess pressed Libby backward until she lay prone on the shifting dock, the kiss unbroken. As she responded to that kiss, it seemed that the sparkling water-light of the pond danced around them both in huge, shimmering chips, that they were floating inside some cosmic prism.

His hand went to the full roundness of her left breast. Beneath his palm and the thin layer of white eyelet, he felt the nipple grow taut in that singular invitation to passion.

Through the back of his shirt, Jess was warmed by the heat of the spring sun and the tender weight of Libby's hands. He left her mouth to trail soft kisses over her chin, along the sweet, scented lines of her neck.

All the while, he expected her to stiffen again, to thrust him away with her hands and some indignant—and no doubt colorful—outburst. Instead, she was pliant and yielding beneath him.

Enthralled, he dared more and drew downward on the uppermost ruffle of her suntop. Still she did not protest.

Libby arched her back and a low, whimpering sound came from her throat as Jess bared her to the soft spring breeze and the fire of his gaze.

Her breasts were heavy golden-white globes, and their pale rose crests stiffened as Jess perused them. When he offered a whisper-soft kiss to one, Libby moaned and the other peak pouted prettily at his choice. He went to it, soothed it to fury with his tongue.

Libby gave a soft, lusty cry, shuddered and caught her hands in his hair, drawing him closer. He needed more of her and positioned his body accordingly, careful not to let his full weight come to bear. Then, for a few dizzying moments, he took suckle at the straining fount of her breast.

Recovering himself partially, Jess pulled her hands from his hair, gripped them at the wrists, pressed them down above her head in gentle restraint.

Her succulent breasts bore his assessment proudly, rising and falling with the meter of her breathing.

Jess forced himself to meet Libby's eyes. "This is me," he reminded her gruffly. "Jess."

"I know," she whispered, making no move to free her imprisoned hands.

Jess lowered his head, tormented one delectable nipple by drawing at it with his lips. "This is real, Libby," he said, circling the morsel with just the tip of his tongue now. "It's important that you realize that."

"I do...oh, God...Jess, *Jess.*"

Reluctantly he left the feast to search her face with disbelieving eyes. "Don't you want me to stop?"

A delicate shade of rose sifted over her high cheekbones. Her hands still stretched above her, her eyes closed, she shook her head.

Jess went back to the breasts that so bewitched him, nipped at their peaks with gentle teeth. "Do you...know how many...times I've wanted...to do this?"

The answer was a soft, strangled cry.

He limited himself to one nipple, worked its surrendering peak into a sweet fervor with his lips and his tongue. "So…many…times. My God, Libby…you're so beautiful…"

Her words were as halting as his had been. "What's happening to us? We h-hate each other."

Jess laughed and began kissing his way softly down over her rib cage, her smooth, firm stomach. The snap on her jeans gave way easily—and was echoed by the sound of car doors slamming in the area of the house.

Instantly the spell was broken. Color surged into Libby's face and she bolted upright, nearly thrusting Jess off the end of the dock in her efforts to wrench on the discarded suntop and close the fastening of her jeans.

"Broad daylight…" she muttered distractedly, talking more to herself than to Jess.

"Lib!" yelled a jovial masculine voice, approaching fast. "Libby?"

Stacey. The voice belonged to Stacey.

Sudden fierce anger surged, white-hot, through Jess's aching, bedazzled system. Standing up, not caring that his thwarted passion still strained against his jeans, visible to anyone who might take the trouble to look, he glared down at Libby and rasped, "I guess reinforcements have arrived."

She gave a primitive, protesting little cry and shot to her feet, her ink-blue eyes flashing with anger and hurt. Before Jess could brace himself, her hands came to his chest like small battering rams and pushed him easily off the end of the dock.

The jolting cold of that spring-fed pond was welcome balm to Jess's passion-heated flesh, if not his pride. When he surfaced and grasped the end of the dock in both hands, he knew there would be no physical evidence that he and Libby had been doing anything other than fighting.

Libby ached with embarrassment as Stacey and Senator Barlowe made their way down over the slight hillside that separated the backyard from the pond.

The older man cast one mischievously baleful look at his younger son, who was lifting himself indignantly onto the dock, and chuckled, "I see things are the same as always," he said.

Libby managed a shaky smile. *Not quite,* she thought, her body remembering the delicious dance Jess's hard frame had choreographed for it. "Hello, Senator," she said, rising on tiptoe to kiss his cheek.

"Welcome home," he replied with gruff affection. Then his wise eyes shifted past her to rest again on Jess. "It's a little cold yet for a swim, isn't it, son?"

Jess's hair hung in dripping ebony strands around his face, and his eyes were jade-green flares, avoiding his father to scald Libby's lips, her throat, her still-pulsing breasts. "We'll finish our...discussion later," he said.

Libby's blood boiled up over her stomach and her breasts to glow in her face. "I wouldn't count on that!"

"I would," Jess replied with a smile that was at once tender and evil. And then, without so much as a word to his father and brother, he walked away.

"What the hell did he mean by that?" barked Stacey, red in the face.

The look Libby gave the boyishly handsome, caramel-eyed man beside her was hardly friendly. "You've got some tall explaining to do, Stacey Barlowe," she said.

The senator, a tall, attractive man with hair as gray as Ken's, cleared his throat in the way of those who have practiced diplomacy long and well. "I believe I'll go up to the house and see if Ken's got any beer on hand," he said. A moment later he was off, following Jess's soggy path.

Libby straightened her shoulders and calmly slapped Stacey across the face. "How dare you?" she raged, her words strangled in her effort to modulate them.

Stacey reddened again, ran one hand through his fashionably cut wheat-colored hair. He turned, as if to follow his father. "I could use a beer myself," he said in distracted, evasive tones.

"Oh, no you don't!" Libby cried, grasping his arm and holding on. The rich leather of his jacket was smooth under her hand. "Don't you *dare* walk away from me, Stacey—not until you explain why you've been lying about me!''

''I haven't been lying!'' he protested, his hands on his hips now, his expensively clad body blocking the base of the dock as he faced her.

''You have! You've been telling everyone that I...that we...''

''That we've been doing what you and my brother were doing a few minutes ago?''

If Stacey had shoved Libby into the water, she couldn't have been more shocked. A furious retort rose to the back of her throat but would go no further.

Stacey's tarnished-gold eyes flashed. ''Jess was making love to you, wasn't he?''

''What if he was?'' managed Libby after a painful struggle with her vocal cords. ''It certainly wouldn't be any of your business, would it?''

''Yes, it would. I love you, Libby.''

''You love *Cathy!*''

Stacey shook his head. ''No. Not anymore.''

''Don't say that,'' Libby pleaded, suddenly deflated. ''Oh, Stacey, don't. Don't do this...''

His hands came to her shoulders, fierce and strong. The topaz fever in his eyes made Libby wonder if he was sane. ''I love you, Libby Kincaid,'' he vowed softly but ferociously, ''and I mean to have you.''

Libby retreated a step, stunned, shaking her head. The reality of this situation was so different from what she had imagined it would be. In her thoughts, Stacey had laughed when she confronted him, ruffled her hair in that familiar brotherly way of old, and said that it was all a mistake. That he loved Cathy, wanted Cathy, and couldn't anyone around here take a joke?

But here he was declaring himself in a way that was unsettlingly serious.

Libby took another step backward. ''Stacey, I need to be here, where my dad is. Where things are familiar and comfortable. Please...don't force me to leave.''

Stacey smiled. "There is no point in leaving, Lib. If you do, I'll be right behind you."

She shivered. "You've lost your mind!"

But Stacey looked entirely sane as he shook his handsome head and wedged his hands into the pockets of his jacket. "Just my heart," he said. "Corny, isn't it?"

"It's worse than corny. Stacey, you're unbalanced or something. You're fantasizing. There was never anything between us—"

"No?" The word was crooned.

"No! You need help."

His face had all the innocence of an altar boy's. "If I'm insane, darlin', it's something you could cure."

Libby resisted an urge to slap him again. She wanted to race into the house, but he was still barring her way, so that she could not leave the dock without brushing against him. "Stay away from me, Stacey," she said as he advanced toward her. "I mean it—stay away from me!"

"I can't, Libby."

The sincerity in his voice was chilling; for the first time in all the years she'd known Stacey Barlowe, Libby was afraid of him. Discretion kept her from screaming, but just barely.

Stacey paled, as though he'd read her thoughts. "Don't look at me like that, Libby—I wouldn't hurt you under any circumstances. And I'm not crazy."

She lifted her chin. "Let me by, Stacey. I want to go into the house."

He tilted his head back, sighed, met her eyes again. "I've frightened you, and I'm sorry. I didn't mean to do that."

Libby couldn't speak. Despite his rational, settling words, she was sick with the knowledge that he meant to pursue her.

"You must know," he said softly, "how good it could be for us. You needed me in New York, Libby, and now I need you."

The third voice, from the base of the hillside, was to Libby as a life preserver to a drowning person. "Let her pass, Stacey."

Libby looked up quickly to see Jess, unlikely rescuer that he was. His hair was towel-rumpled and his jeans clung to muscular thighs—

thighs that only minutes ago had pressed against her own in a demand as old as time. His manner was calm as he buttoned a shirt, probably borrowed from Ken, over his broad chest.

Stacey shrugged affably and walked past his brother without a word of argument.

Watching him go, Libby went weak with relief. A lump rose in her throat as she forced herself to meet Jess's gaze. "You were right," she muttered miserably. "You were *right*."

Jess was watching her much the way a mountain cat would watch a cornered rabbit. For the briefest moment there was a look of tenderness in the green eyes, but then his expression turned hard and a muscle flexed in his jaw. "I trust the welcome-home party has been scheduled for later—after Cathy has been tucked into her bed, for instance?"

Libby gaped at him, appalled. Had he interceded only to torment her himself?

Jess's eyes were contemptuous as they swept over her. "What's the matter, Lib? Couldn't you bring yourself to tell your married lover that the welcoming had already been taken care of?"

Rage went through Libby's body like an electric current surging into a wire. "You don't seriously think that I would...that I was—"

"You even managed to be alone with him. Tell me, Lib—how did you get rid of my father?"

"G-get rid..." Libby stopped, tears of shock and mortification aching in her throat and burning behind her eyes. She drew a deep, audible breath, trying to assemble herself, to think clearly.

But the whole world seemed to be tilting and swirling like some out-of-control carnival ride. When Libby closed her eyes against the sensation, she swayed dangerously and would probably have fallen if Jess hadn't reached her in a few strides and caught her shoulders in his hands.

"Libby..." he said, and there was anger in the sound, but there was a hollow quality, too—one that Libby couldn't find a name for.

Her knees were trembling. Too much, it was all too much. Jonathan's death, the ugly divorce, the trouble that Stacey had caused with his misplaced affections—all of those things weighed on her, but none were so crushing as the blatant contempt of this man. It was apparent to Libby now that the lovemaking they had almost shared, so new and beautiful to her, had been some sort of cruel joke to Jess.

"How could you?" she choked out. "Oh, Jess, how could you?"

His face was grim, seeming to float in a shimmering mist. Instead of answering, Jess lifted Libby into his arms and carried her up the little hill toward the house.

She didn't remember reaching the back door.

"What the devil happened on that dock today, Jess?" Cleave Barlowe demanded, hands grasping the edge of his desk.

His younger son stood at the mahogany bar, his shoulders stiff, his attention carefully fixed on the glass of straight Scotch he meant to consume. "Why don't you ask Stacey?"

"Goddammit, I'm asking *you!*" barked Cleave. "Ken's mad as hell, and I don't blame him—that girl of his was shattered!"

Girl. The word caught in Jess's beleaguered mind. He remembered the way Libby had responded to him, meeting his passion with her own, welcoming the greed he'd shown at her breasts. Had it not been for the arrival of his father and brother, he would have possessed her completely within minutes. "She's no 'girl,'" he said, still aching to bury himself in the depths of her.

The senator swore roundly. "What did you say to her, Jess?" he pressed, once the spate of unpoliticianly profanity had passed.

Jess lowered his head. He'd meant the things he'd said to Libby, and he couldn't, in all honesty, have taken them back. But he knew some of what she'd been through in New York, her trysts with Stacey notwithstanding, and he was ashamed of the way he'd goaded her. She had come home to heal—the look in her eyes had told him that much—and instead of respecting that, he had made things more difficult for her.

Never one to be thwarted by silence, no matter how eloquent, Senator Barlowe persisted. "Dammit, Jess, I might expect this kind of thing from Stacey, but I thought you had more sense! You were harassing Libby about these blasted rumors your brother has been spreading, weren't you?"

Jess sighed, set aside the drink he had yet to take a sip from, and faced his angry father. "Yes," he said.

"Why?"

Stubbornly, Jess refused to answer. He took an interest in the imposing oak desk where his father sat, the heavy draperies that kept out the sun, the carved ivory of the fireplace.

"All right, mulehead," Cleave muttered furiously, "don't talk! Don't explain! And don't go near Ken Kincaid's daughter again, damn you. That man's the best foreman I've ever had and if he gets riled and quits because of you, Jess, you and I are going to come to time!"

Jess almost smiled, though he didn't quite dare. Not too many years before the phrase "come to time," when used by his father, had presaged a session in the woodshed. He wondered what it meant now that he was thirty-three years old, a member of the Montana State Bar Association, and a full partner in the family corporation. "I care about Cathy," he said evenly. "What was I supposed to do— stand by and watch Libby and Stace grind her up into emotional hamburger?"

Cleave gave a heavy sigh and sank into the richly upholstered swivel chair behind his desk. "I love Cathy too," he said at length, "but Stacey's behind this whole mess, not Libby. Dammit, that woman has been through hell from what Ken says—she was married to a man who slept in every bed but his own, and she had to watch her nine-year-old stepson die by inches. Now she comes home looking for a little peace, and what does she get? Trouble!"

Jess lowered his head, turned away—ostensibly to take up his glass of Scotch. He'd known about the bad marriage—Ken had cussed the day Aaron Strand was born often enough—but he hadn't heard about the little boy. My God, he hadn't known about the boy.

"Maybe Strand couldn't sleep in his own bed," he said, urged on by some ugliness that had surfaced inside him since Libby's return. "Maybe Stacey was already in it."

"Enough!" boomed the senator in a voice that had made presidents tremble in their shoes. "I like Libby and I'm not going to listen to any more of this, either from you or from your brother! Do I make myself clear?"

"Abundantly clear," replied Jess, realizing that the Scotch was in his hand now and feeling honor-bound to take at least one gulp of the stuff. The taste was reminiscent of scorched rubber, but since the liquor seemed to quiet the raging demons in his mind, he finished the drink and poured another.

He fully intended to get drunk. It was something he hadn't done since high school, but it suddenly seemed appealing. Maybe he would stop hardening every time he thought of Libby, stop craving her.

Too, after the things he'd said to her that afternoon by the pond, he didn't want to remain sober any longer than necessary. "What did you mean," he ventured, after downing his fourth drink, "when you said Libby had to watch her stepson die?"

Papers rustled at the big desk behind him. "Stacey says the child had leukemia."

Jess poured another drink and closed his eyes. *Oh, Libby,* he thought, *I'm sorry. My God, I'm sorry.* "I guess Stacey would know," he said aloud, with bitterness.

There was a short, thunderous silence. Jess expected his father to explode into one of his famous tirades, was genuinely surprised when the man sighed instead. Still, his words dropped on Jess's mind like a bomb.

"The firewater isn't going to change the fact that you love Libby Kincaid, Jess," he said reasonably. "Making her life and your own miserable isn't going to change it either."

Love Libby Kincaid? Impossible. The strange needs possessing him now were rooted in his libido, not his heart. Once he'd had her— and have her he would, or go crazy—her hold on him would be broken. "I've never loved a woman in my life," he said.

"Fool. You've loved one woman—Libby—since you were seven years old. Exactly seven years old, in fact."

Jess turned, studying his father quizzically. "What the hell are you talking about?"

"Your seventh birthday," recalled Cleave, his eyes far away.

"Your mother and I gave you a pony. First time you saw Libby Kincaid, you were out of that saddle and helping her into it."

The memory burst, full-blown, into Jess's mind. A pinto pony. The new foreman arriving. The little girl with dark blue eyes and hair the color of winter moonlight.

He'd spent the whole afternoon squiring Libby around the yard, content to walk while she rode.

"What do you suppose Ken would say if I went over there and asked to see his daughter?" Jess asked.

"I imagine he'd shoot you, after today."

"I imagine he would. But I think I'll risk it."

"You've made enough trouble for one day," argued Cleave, taking obvious note of his son's inebriated state. "Libby needs time, Jess. She needs to be close to Ken. If you're smart, you'll leave her alone until she has a chance to get her emotional bearings again."

Jess didn't want his father to be right, not in this instance, anyway, but he knew that he was. Much as he wanted to go to Libby and try to make things right, the fact was that he was the last person in the world she needed or wanted to see.

"Better?"

Libby smiled at Ken as she came into the kitchen, freshly showered and wrapped in the cozy, familiar chenille robe she'd found in the back of her closet. "Lots better," she answered softly.

Her father was standing at the kitchen stove stirring something in the blackened cast-iron skillet.

Libby scuffled to the table and sat down. It was good to be home, so good. Why hadn't she come sooner? "Whatever you're cooking there smells good," she said.

Ken beamed. In his jeans and his western shirt, he looked out of place at that stove. He should, Libby decided fancifully, have been crouching at some campfire on the range, stirring beans in a blue enamel pot. "This here's my world-famous red-devil sauce," he grinned, "for which I am known and respected."

Libby laughed, and tears of homecoming filled her eyes. She went to her father and hugged him, needing to be a little girl again, just for a moment.

Chapter 3

Libby nearly choked on her first taste of Ken's taco sauce. "Did you say you were known and respected for this stuff, or known and feared?"

Ken chuckled roguishly at her tear-polished eyes and flaming face. "My calling it 'red devil' should have been a clue, dumplin'."

Libby muttered an exclamation and perversely took another bite from her bulging taco. "From now on," she said, chewing, "I'll do the cooking around this spread."

Her father laughed again and tapped one temple with a calloused index finger, his pale blue eyes twinkling.

"You deliberately tricked me!" cried Libby.

He grinned and shrugged. "Code of the West, sweetheart. Grouse about the chow, and presto—you're the cook!"

"Actually," ventured Libby with cultivated innocence, "this sauce isn't too bad."

"Too late," laughed Ken. "You already broke the code."

Libby lowered her taco to her plate and lifted both hands in a gesture of concession. "All right, all right—but have a little pity on me, will you? I've been living among dudes!"

"That's no excuse."

Libby shrugged and took up her taco again. "I tried. Have you been doing your own cooking and cleaning all this time?"

Ken shook his head and sat back in his chair, his thumbs hooked behind his belt buckle. "Nope. The Barlowes' housekeeper sends her crew down here once in a while."

"What about the food?"

"I eat with the boys most of the time, over at the cook shack." He rose, went to fill two mugs from the coffeepot on the stove. When he turned around again, his face was serious. "Libby, what happened today? What upset you like that?"

Libby averted her eyes. "I don't know," she lied lamely.

"Dammit, you *do* know. You fainted, Libby. When Jess carried you in here, I—"

"I know," Libby broke in gently. "You were scared. I'm sorry."

Carefully, as though he feared he might drop them, Ken set the cups of steaming coffee on the table. "What happened?" he persisted as he sat down in his chair again.

Libby swallowed hard, but the lump that had risen in her throat wouldn't go down. Knowing that this conversation couldn't be avoided forever, she managed to reply, "It's complicated. Basically, it comes down to the fact that Stacey's been telling those lies."

"And?"

"And Jess believes him. He said…he said some things to me and…well, it must have created some kind of emotional overload. I just gave out."

Ken turned his mug idly between his thumb and index finger, causing the liquid to spill over and make a coffee stain on the tablecloth. "Tell me about Jonathan, Libby," he said in a low, gentle voice.

The tears that sprang into Libby's eyes were not related to the tang of her father's red-devil taco sauce. "He died," she choked miserably.

"I know that. You called me the night it happened, remember? I guess what I'm really asking you is why you didn't want me to fly back there and help you sort things out."

Libby lowered her head. Jonathan hadn't been her son, he'd been Aaron's, by a previous marriage. But the loss of the child was a raw void within her, even though months had passed. "I didn't want you to get a firsthand look at my marriage,'' she admitted with great difficulty—and the shame she couldn't seem to shake.

"Why not, Libby?"

The sound Libby made might have been either a laugh or a sob. "Because it was terrible," she answered.

"From the first?"

She forced herself to meet her father's steady gaze, knew that he had guessed a lot about her marriage from her rare phone calls and even rarer letters. "Almost," she replied sadly.

"Tell me."

Libby didn't want to think about Aaron, let alone talk about him to this man who wouldn't understand so many things. "He had...he had lovers."

Ken didn't seem surprised. Had he guessed that, too? "Go on."

"I can't!"

"Yes, you can. If it's too much for you right now, I won't press you. But the sooner you talk this out, Libby, the better off you're going to be."

She realized that her hands were clenched in her lap and tried to relax them. There was still a white mark on her finger where Aaron's ostentatious wedding ring had been. "He didn't care," she mourned in a soft, distracted whisper. "He honestly didn't care..."

"About you?"

"About Jonathan. Dad, he didn't care about his own son!"

"How so, sweetheart?"

Libby dashed away tears with the back of one hand. "Th-things were bad between Aaron and me b-before we found out that Jonathan was sick. After the doctors told us, it was a lot worse."

"I don't follow you, Libby."

"Dad, Aaron wouldn't have anything to do with Jonathan from the moment we knew he was dying. He wasn't there for any of the tests and he never once came to visit at the hospital. Dad, that little boy cried for his father, and Aaron wouldn't come to him!"

"Did you talk to Aaron?"

Remembered frustration made Libby's cheeks pound with color. "I *pleaded* with him, Dad. All he'd say was, 'I can't handle this.'"

"It would be a hell of a thing to deal with, Lib. Maybe you're being too hard on the man."

"Too hard? *Too hard?* Jonathan was terrified, Dad, and he was in pain—constant pain. All he asked was that his own father be strong for him!"

"What about the boy's mother? Did she come to the hospital?"

"Ellen died when Jonathan was a baby."

Ken sighed, framing a question he was obviously reluctant to ask. "Did you ever love Aaron Strand, Libby?"

Libby remembered the early infatuation, the excitement that had never deepened into real love and had quickly been quelled by the realities of marriage to a man who was fundamentally self-centered. She tried, but she couldn't even recall her ex-husband's face clearly—all she could see in her mind was a pair of jade-green eyes, dark hair. Jess. "No," she finally said. "I thought I did when I married him, though."

Ken stood up suddenly, took the coffeepot from its back burner on the stove, refilled both their cups. "I don't like asking you this, but—"

"No, Dad," Libby broke in firmly, anticipating the question all too well, "I don't love Stacey!"

"You're sure about that?"

The truth was that Libby *hadn't* been sure, not entirely. But that ill-advised episode with Jess at the end of the swimming dock had brought everything into clear perspective. Just remembering how willingly she had submitted to him made her throb with embarrassment. "I'm sure," she said.

Ken's strong hand came across the table to close over hers. "You're home now," he reminded her, "and things are going to get better, Libby. I promise you that."

Libby sniffled inelegantly. "Know something, cowboy? I love you very much."

"Bet you say that to all your fathers," Ken quipped. "You planning to work on your comic strip tomorrow?"

The change of subject was welcome. "I'm six or eight weeks ahead of schedule on that, and the mechanicals for the book aren't due till fall. I think I'll go riding instead, if I can get Cathy to go with me.''

''What's a 'mechanical'?''

Libby smiled, feeling sheltered by the love of this strong and steady man facing her. ''It's the finished drawing that I turn in, along with the instructions for the colorist.''

''You don't do the colors?'' Ken seemed surprised at that, knowing, as he did, her love for vivid shades and subtle hues alike.

''No, I just do the panels and the lettering.'' It was good to talk about work, to think about work. Disdainful as he had been about her career, it was the one thing Aaron had not been able to spoil for her.

Nobody's fool, Ken drew her out on the subject as much as he could, and she found herself chattering on and on about cartooning and even her secret hope to branch out into portraits one day.

They talked, father and daughter, far into the night.

''You deserve this,'' Jess Barlowe said to his reflection in the bathroom mirror. A first-class hangover pounded in his head and roiled in his stomach, and his face looked drawn, as though he'd been hibernating like one of the bears that sometimes troubled the range stock.

Grimly he began to shave, and as he wielded his disposable razor, he wondered if Libby was awake yet. Should he stop at Ken's and talk to her before going on to the main house to spend a day with the corporation accountants?

Jess wanted to go to Libby, to tell her that he was sorry for baiting her, to try to get their complex relationship—if it *was* a relationship— onto some kind of sane ground. However, all his instincts told him that his father had been right the day before: Libby needed time.

His thoughts strayed to Libby's stepson. What would it be like to sit by a hospital bed, day after day, watching a child suffer and not being able to help?

Jess shuddered. It was hard to imagine the horror of something like that. At least Libby had had her husband to share the nightmare.

He frowned as he nicked his chin with the razor, blotted the small wound with tissue paper. If Libby had had her husband during that impossible time, why had she needed Stacey?

Stacey. Now, there was someone he could talk to. Granted, Jess had not been on the best of terms with his older brother of late, but the man had a firsthand knowledge of what was happening inside Libby Kincaid, and that was reason enough to approach him.

Feeling better for having a plan, Jess finished his ablutions and got dressed. Normally he spent his days on the range with Ken and the ranch hands, but today, because of his meeting with the accountants, he forwent his customary blue jeans and cotton workshirt for a tailored three-piece suit. He was still struggling with his tie as he made his way down the broad redwood steps that led from the loftlike second floor of his house to the living room.

Here there was a massive fireplace of white limestone, taking up the whole of one wall. The floors were polished oak and boasted a number of brightly colored Indian rugs. Two easy chairs and a deep sofa faced the hearth, and Jess's cluttered desk looked out over the ranchland and the glacial mountains beyond.

Striding toward the front door, in exasperation he gave up his efforts to get the tie right. He was glad he didn't have Stacey's job; not for him the dull task of overseeing the family's nationwide chain of steak-house franchises.

He smiled. Stacey liked playing the dude, doing television commercials, traveling all over the country.

And taking Libby Kincaid to bed.

Jess stalked across the front lawn to the carport and climbed behind the wheel of the station wagon he'd driven since law school. One of these times, he was going to have to get another car—something with a little flash, like Stacey's Ferrari.

Stacey, Stacey. He hadn't even seen his brother yet, and already he was sick of him.

The station wagon's engine made a grinding sound and then huffed to life. Jess patted the dusty dashboard affectionately and grinned. A car was a car was a car, he reflected as he backed the notorious wreck out of his driveway. The function of a car was to transport people, not impress them.

Five minutes later, Jess's station wagon chortled to an asthmatic stop beside his brother's ice-blue Ferrari. He looked up at the modernistic two-story house that had been the senator's wedding gift to Stacey and Cathy and wondered if Libby would be impressed by the place.

He scowled as he made his way up the curving white-stone walk. What the hell did he care if Libby was impressed?

Irritated, he jabbed one finger at the special doorbell that would turn on a series of blinking lights inside the house. The system had been his own idea, meant to make life easier for Cathy.

His sister-in-law came to the door and smiled at him somewhat wanly, speaking with her hands. "Good morning."

Jess nodded, smiled. The haunted look in the depths of Cathy's eyes made him angry all over again. "Is Stacey here?" he signed, stepping into the house.

Cathy caught his hand in her own and led him through the cavernous living room and the formal dining room beyond. Stacey was in the kitchen, looking more at home in a three-piece suit than Jess ever had.

"You," Stacey said tonelessly, setting down the English muffin he'd been slathering with honey.

Cathy offered coffee and left the room when it was politely declined. Distractedly Jess reflected on the fact that her life had to be boring as hell, centering on Stacey the way it did.

"I want to talk to you," Jess said, scraping back a chrome-and-plastic chair to sit down at the table.

Stacey arched one eyebrow. "I hope it's quick—I'm leaving for the airport in a few minutes. I've got some business to take care of in Kansas City."

Jess was impatient. "What kind of man is Libby's ex-husband?" he asked.

Stacey took up his coffee. "Why do you want to know?"

"I just do. Do I have to have him checked out, or are you going to tell me?"

"He's a bastard," said Stacey, not quite meeting his brother's eyes.

"Rich?"

"Oh, yes. His family is old-money."

"What does he do?"

"Do?"

"Yeah. Does he work, or does he just stand around being rich?"

"He runs the family advertising agency; I think he has a lot of control over their other financial interests too."

Jess sensed that Stacey was hedging, wondered why. "Any bad habits?"

Stacey was gazing at the toaster now, in a fixed way, as though he expected something alarming to pop out of it. "The man has his share of vices."

Annoyed now, Jess got up, helped himself to the cup of coffee he had refused earlier, sat down again. "Pulling porcupine quills out of a dog's nose would be easier than getting answers out of you. When you say he has vices, do you mean women?"

Stacey swallowed, looked away. "To put it mildly," he said.

Jess settled back in his chair. "What the hell do you mean by that?"

"I mean that he not only liked to run around with other women, he liked to flaunt the fact. The worse he could make Libby feel about herself, the happier he was."

"Jesus," Jess breathed. "What else?" he pressed, sensing, from Stacey's expression, that there was more.

"He was impotent with Libby."

"Why did she stay? Why in God's name did she stay?" Jess mused distractedly, as much to himself as to his brother.

A cautious but smug light flickered in Stacey's topaz eyes. "She had me," he said evenly. "Besides, Jonathan was sick by that time and she felt she had to stay in the marriage for his sake."

The spacious sun-filled kitchen seemed to buckle and shift around Jess. "Why didn't she tell Ken, at least?"

"What would have been the point in that, Jess? He couldn't have made the boy well again or transformed Aaron Strand into a devoted husband."

The things Libby must have endured—the shame, the loneliness, the humiliation and grief, washed over Jess in a dismal, crushing wave. No wonder she had reached out to Stacey the way she had. No wonder. "Thanks," he said gruffly, standing up to leave.

"Jess?"

He paused in the kitchen doorway, his hands clasping the woodwork, his shoulders aching with tension. "What?"

"Don't worry about Libby. I'll take care of her."

Jess felt a despairing sort of anger course through him. "What about Cathy?" he asked, without turning around. "Who is going to take care of her?"

"You've always—"

Jess whirled suddenly, staring at his brother, almost hating him. "I've always *what?*"

"Cared for her." Stacey shrugged, looking only mildly unsettled. "Protected her..."

"Are you suggesting that I sweep up the pieces after you shatter her?" demanded Jess in a dangerous rasp.

Stacey only shrugged again.

Because he feared that he would do his brother lasting harm if he stayed another moment, Jess stormed out of the house. Cathy, dressed in old jeans, boots and a cotton blouse, was waiting beside the station wagon. The pallor in her face told Jess that she knew much more about the state of her marriage than he would have hoped.

Her hands trembled a little as she spoke with them. "I'm scared, Jess."

He drew her into his arms, held her. "I know, baby," he said, even though he knew she couldn't hear him or see his lips. "I know."

Libby opened her eyes, yawned and stretched. The smells of sunshine and fresh air swept into her bedroom through the open window, ruffling pink eyelet curtains and reminding her that she was home again. She tossed back the covers on the bed she had once shared with Cathy and got up, sleepily making her way into the bathroom and starting the water for a shower.

As she took off her short cotton nightshirt, she looked down at herself and remembered the raging sensations Jess Barlowe had ignited in her the day before. She had been stupid and self-indulgent to let that happen, but after several years of celibacy, she supposed it was natural that her passions had been stirred so easily—especially by a man like Jess.

As Libby showered, she felt renewed. Aaron's flagrant infidelities had been painful for her, and they had seriously damaged her self-esteem in the bargain.

Now, even though she had made a fool of herself by being wanton with a man who could barely tolerate her, many of Libby's doubts about herself as a woman had been eased, if not routed. She was not as useless and undesirable as Aaron had made her feel. She had caused Jess Barlowe to want her, hadn't she?

Big deal, she told the image in her mirror as she brushed her teeth. *How do you know Jess wasn't out to prove that his original opinion of you was on target?*

Deflated by this very real possibility, Libby combed her hair, applied the customary lip gloss and light touch of mascara and went back to her room to dress. From her suitcases she selected a short-sleeved turquoise pullover shirt and a pair of trim jeans. Remembering her intention to find Cathy and persuade her to go riding, she ferreted through her closet until she found the worn boots she'd left behind before moving to New York, pulling them on over a pair of thick socks.

Looking down at those disreputable old boots, Libby imagined the scorn they would engender in Aaron's jet-set crowd and laughed. Problems or no problems, Jess or no Jess, it was good to be home.

Not surprisingly, the kitchen was empty. Ken had probably left the house before dawn, but there was coffee on the stove and fruit in the refrigerator, so Libby helped herself to a pear and sat down to eat.

The telephone rang just as she was finishing her second cup of coffee, and Libby answered cheerfully, thinking that the caller would be Ken or the housekeeper at the main house, relaying some message for Cathy.

She was back at the table, the receiver pressed to her ear, before Aaron spoke.

"When are you coming home?"

"Home?" echoed Libby stupidly, off-balance, unable to believe that he'd actually asked such a question. "I *am* home, Aaron."

"Enough," he replied. "You've made your point, exhibited your righteous indignation. Now you've got to get back here because I need you."

Libby wanted to hang up, but it seemed a very long way from her chair to the wall, where the rest of the telephone was. "Aaron, we are divorced," she reminded him calmly, "and I am never coming back."

"You have to," he answered, without missing a beat. "It's crucial."

"Why? What happened to all your...friends?"

Aaron sighed. "You remember Betty, don't you? Miss November? Well, Betty and I had a small disagreement, as it happens, and she went to my family. I am, shall we say, exposed as something less than an ideal spouse.

"In any case, my grandmother believes that a man who cannot run his family—she was in Paris when we divorced, darling—cannot run a company, either. I have six months to bring you back into the fold and start an heir, or the whole shooting match goes to my cousin."

Libby was too stunned to speak or even move; she simply stood in the middle of her father's kitchen, trying to absorb what Aaron was saying.

"That," Aaron went on blithely, "is where you come in, sweetheart. You come back, we smile a lot and make a baby, my grandmother's ruffled feathers are smoothed. It's as simple as that."

Sickness boiled into Libby's throat. "I don't believe this!" she whispered.

"You don't believe what, darling? That I can make a baby? May I point out that I sired Jonathan, of whom you were so cloyingly fond?"

Libby swallowed. "Get Miss November pregnant," she managed to suggest. And then she added distractedly, more to herself than Aaron, "I think I'm going to be sick."

"Don't tell me that I've been beaten to the proverbial draw,"

Aaron remarked in that brutally smooth, caustic way of his. "Did the steak-house king already do the deed?"

"You are disgusting!"

"Yes, but very practical. If I don't hand my grandmother an heir, whether it's mine or the issue of that softheaded cowboy, I stand to lose millions of dollars."

Libby managed to stand up. A few steps, just a few, and she could hang up the telephone, shut out Aaron's voice and his ugly suggestions. "Do you really think that I would turn any child of mine over to someone like you?"

"There is a child, then," he retorted smoothly.

"No!" Five steps to the wall, six at most.

"Be reasonable, sweetness. We're discussing an empire here. If you don't come back and attend to your wifely duties, I'll have to visit that godforsaken ranch and try to persuade you."

"I am not your wife!" screamed Libby. One step. One step and a reach.

"Dear heart, I don't find the idea any more appealing than you do, but there isn't any other way, is there? My grandmother likes you—sees you as sturdy peasant stock—and she wants the baby to be yours."

At last. The wall was close and Libby slammed the receiver into place. Then, dazed, she stumbled back to her chair and fell into it, lowering her head to her arms. She cried hard, for herself, for Jonathan.

"Libby?"

It was the last voice she would have wanted to hear, except for Aaron's. "Go away, Stacey!" she hissed.

Instead of complying, Stacey laid a gentle hand on her shoulder. "What happened, Libby?" he asked softly. "Who was that on the phone?"

Fresh horror washed over Libby at the things Aaron had requested, mixed with anger and revulsion. God, how self-centered and insensitive that man was! And what gall he had, suggesting that she return to that disaster of a marriage, like some unquestioning brood mare, to produce a baby on order!

She gave a shuddering cry and motioned Stacey away with a frantic motion of her arm.

He only drew her up out of the chair and turned her so that he could hold her. She hadn't the strength to resist the intimacy and, in her half-hysterical state, he seemed to be the old Stacey, the strong big brother.

Stacey's hand came to the back of her head, tangling in her freshly washed hair, pressing her to his shoulder. "Tell me what happened," he urged, just as he had when Libby was a child with a skinned knee or a bee sting.

From habit, she allowed herself to be comforted. For so long there had been no one to confide in except Stacey, and it seemed natural to lean on him now. "Aaron...Aaron called. He wanted me to have his...his baby!"

Before Stacey could respond to that, the door separating the kitchen from the living room swung open. Instinctively Libby drew back from the man who held her.

Jess towered in the doorway, pale, his gaze scorching Libby's flushed, tear-streaked face. "You know," he began in a voice that was no less terrible for being soft, "I almost believed you. I almost had myself convinced that you were above anything this shabby."

"Wait—you don't understand..."

Jess smiled a slow, vicious smile—a smile that took in his startled brother as well as Libby. "Don't I? Oh, princess, I wish I didn't." The searing jade gaze sliced menacingly to Stacey's face. "And it seems I'm going to be an uncle. Tell me, brother—what does that make Cathy?"

To Libby's horror, Stacey said nothing to refute what was obviously a gross misunderstanding. He simply pulled her back into his arms, and her struggle was virtually imperceptible because of his strength.

"Let me go!" she pleaded, frantic.

Stacey released her, but only grudgingly. "I've got a plane to catch," he said.

Libby was incredulous. "Tell him! Tell Jess that he's wrong," she cried, reaching out for Stacey's arm, trying to detain him.

But Stacey simply pulled free and left by the back door.

There was a long, pulsing silence, during which both Libby and Jess seemed to be frozen. He was the first to thaw.

"I know you were hurt, Libby," he said. "Badly hurt. But that didn't give you the right to do something like this to Cathy."

It infuriated Libby that this man's good opinion was so important to her, but it was, and there was no changing that. "Jess, I didn't do anything to Cathy. Please listen to me."

He folded his strong arms and rested against the door jamb with an ease that Libby knew was totally feigned. "I'm listening," he said, and the words had a flippant note.

Libby ignored fresh anger. "I am not expecting Stacey's baby, and this wasn't a romantic tryst. I don't even know why he came here. I was on the phone with Aaron and he—"

A muscle in Jess's neck corded, relaxed again. "I hope you're not going to tell me that your former husband made you pregnant, Libby. That seems unlikely."

Frustration pounded in Libby's temples and tightened the already constricted muscles in her throat. "I am not pregnant!" she choked out. "And if you are going to eavesdrop, Jess Barlowe, you could at least pay attention! Aaron wanted me to come back to New York and have his baby so that he would have an heir to present to his grandmother!"

"You didn't agree to that?"

"Of course I didn't agree! What kind of monster do you think I am?"

Jess shrugged with a nonchalance that was belied by the leaping green fire in his eyes. "I don't know, princess, but rest assured—I intend to find out."

"I have a better idea!" Libby flared. "Why don't you just leave me the hell alone?"

"In theory that's brilliant," he fired back, "but there is one problem: I want you."

Involuntarily Libby remembered the kisses and caresses exchanged by the pond the day before, relived them. Hot color poured into her face. "Am I supposed to be honored?"

"No," Jess replied flatly, "you're supposed to be kept so busy that you won't have time to screw up Cathy's life any more than you already have."

If Libby could have moved, she would have rushed across that room and slapped Jess Barlowe senseless. Since she couldn't get her muscles to respond to the orders of her mind, she was forced to watch in stricken silence as he gave her a smoldering assessment with his eyes, executed a half salute and left the house.

Chapter 4

When the telephone rang again, immediately after Jess's exit from the kitchen, Libby was almost afraid to answer it. It would be like Aaron to persist, to use pressure to get what he wanted.

On the other hand, the call might be from someone else, and it could be important.

"Hello?" Libby dared, with resolve.

"Ms. Kincaid?" asked a cheerful feminine voice. "This is Marion Bradshaw, and I'm calling for Mrs. Barlowe. She'd like you to meet her at the main house if you can, and she says to dress for riding."

Libby looked down at her jeans and boots and smiled. In one way, at least, she and Cathy were still on the same wavelength. "Please tell her that I'll be there as soon as I can."

There was a brief pause at the other end of the line, followed by, "Mrs. Barlowe wants me to ask if you have a car down there. If not, she'll come and pick you up in a few minutes."

Though there was no car at her disposal, Libby declined the offer. The walk to the main ranch house would give her a chance to think, to prepare herself to face her cousin again.

As Libby started out, striding along the winding tree-lined road, she ached to think that she and Cathy had come to this. Fresh anger at Stacey quickened her step.

For a moment she was mad at Cathy too. How could she believe such a thing, after all they'd been through together? How?

Firmly Libby brought her ire under control. *You don't get mad at a handicapped person,* she scolded herself.

The sun was already high and hot in the domelike sky, and Libby smiled. It was warm for spring, and wasn't it nice to look up and see clouds and mountaintops instead of tall buildings and smog?

Finally the main house came into view. It was a rambling structure of red brick, and its many windows glistened in the bright sunshine. A porch with marble steps led up to the double doors, and one of them swung open even as Libby reached out to ring the bell.

Mrs. Bradshaw, the housekeeper, stepped out and enfolded Libby in a delighted hug. A slender middle-aged woman with soft brown hair, Marion Bradshaw was as much a part of the Circle Bar B as Senator Barlowe himself. "Welcome home," she said warmly.

Libby smiled and returned the hug. "Thank you, Marion," she replied. "Is Cathy ready to go riding?"

"She's gone ahead to the stables—she'd like you to join her there."

Libby turned to go back down the steps but was stopped by the housekeeper. "Libby?"

She faced Marion, again, feeling wary.

"I don't believe it of you," said Mrs. Bradshaw firmly.

Libby was embarrassed, but there was no point in trying to pretend that she didn't get the woman's meaning. Probably everyone on the ranch was speculating about her supposed involvement with Stacey Barlowe. "Thank you."

"You stay right here on this ranch, Libby Kincaid," Marion Bradshaw rushed on, her own face flushed now. "Don't let Stacey or anybody else run you off."

That morning's unfortunate scene in Ken's kitchen was an indication of how difficult it would be to take the housekeeper's advice. Life on the Circle Bar B could become untenable if both Stacey and Jess didn't back off.

"I'll try," she said softly before stepping down off the porch and making her way around the side of that imposing but gracious house.

Prudently, the stables had been built a good distance away. During the walk, Libby wondered if she shouldn't leave the ranch after all. True, she needed to be there, but Jonathan's death had taught her that sometimes a person had to put her own desires aside for the good of other people.

But would leaving help, in the final analysis? Suppose Stacey did follow her, as he'd threatened to do? What would that do to Cathy?

The stables, like the house, were constructed of red brick. As Libby approached them, she saw Cathy leading two horses out into the sun—a dancing palomino gelding and the considerably less prepossessing pinto mare that had always been Libby's to ride.

Libby hesitated; it had been a long, long time since she'd ridden a horse, and the look in Cathy's eyes was cool. Distant. It was almost as though Libby were a troublesome stranger rather than her cousin and confidante.

As if to break the spell, Cathy lifted one foot to the stirrup of the Palomino's saddle and swung onto its back. Though she gave no sign of greeting, her eyes bade Libby to follow suit.

The elderly pinto was gracious while Libby struggled into the saddle and took the reins in slightly shaky hands. A moment later they were off across the open pastureland behind the stables, Cathy confident in the lead.

Libby jostled and jolted in the now unfamiliar saddle, and she felt a fleeting annoyance with Cathy for setting the brisk pace that she did. Again she berated herself for being angry with someone who couldn't hear.

Cathy rode faster and faster, stopping only when she reached the trees that trimmed the base of a wooded hill. There she turned in the saddle and flung a look back at the disgruntled Libby.

"You're out of practice," she said clearly, though her voice had the slurred meter of those who have not heard another person speak in years.

Libby, red-faced and damp with perspiration, was not surprised that Cathy had spoken aloud. She had learned to talk before the childhood illness that had made her deaf, and when she could be certain that no one else would overhear, she often spoke. It was a secret the two women kept religiously.

"Thanks a lot!" snapped Libby.

Deftly Cathy swung one trim blue-jeaned leg over the neck of her golden gelding and slid to the ground. The fancy bridle jingled musically as the animal bent its great head to graze on the spring grass. "We've got to talk, Libby."

Libby jumped from the pinto's back and the action engendered a piercing ache in the balls of her feet. "You've got that right!" she flared, forgetting for the moment her earlier resolve to respect Cathy's affliction. "Were you trying to get me killed?"

Watching Libby's lips, Cathy grinned. "Killed?" she echoed in her slow, toneless voice. "You're my cousin. That's important, isn't it? That we're cousins, I mean?"

Libby sighed. "Of course it's important."

"It implies a certain loyalty, don't you think?"

Libby braced herself. She'd known this confrontation was coming, of course, but that didn't mean she wanted it or was ready for it. "Yes," she said somewhat lamely.

"Are you having an affair with my husband?"

"No!"

"Do you want to?"

"What the hell kind of person do you think I am, Cathy?" shouted Libby, losing all restraint, flinging her arms out wide and startling the horses, who nickered and danced and tossed their heads.

"I'm trying to find that out," said Cathy in measured and droning words. Not once since the conversation began had her eyes left Libby's mouth.

"You already know," retorted her cousin.

For the first time, Cathy looked ashamed. But there was uncertainty in her expression, too, along with a great deal of pain. "It's no secret that Stacey wants you, Libby. I've been holding my breath ever since you decided to come back, waiting for him to leave me."

"Whatever problems you and Stacey have, Cathy, I didn't start them."

"What about all his visits to New York?"

Libby's shoulders slumped, and she allowed herself to sink to the fragrant spring-scented ground, where she sat cross-legged, her head down. With her hands she said, "You knew about the divorce, and about Jonathan. Stacey was only trying to help me through—we weren't lovers."

The lush grass moved as Cathy sat down too, facing Libby. There were tears shining in her large green eyes, and her lower lip trembled. Nervously she plied a blade of grass between her fingers.

"I'm sorry about your little boy," she said aloud.

Libby reached out, calmer now, and squeezed Cathy's hands with her own. "Thanks."

A lonely, haunted look rose in Cathy's eyes. "Stacey wanted us to have a baby," she confided.

"Why didn't you?"

Sudden color stained Cathy's lovely cheeks. "I'm deaf!" she cried defensively.

Libby released her cousin's hands to sign, "So what? Lots of deaf people have babies."

"Not me!" Cathy signaled back with spirited despair. "I wouldn't know when it cried!"

Libby spoke slowly, her hands falling back to her lap. "Cathy, there are solutions for that sort of problem. There are trained dogs, electronic devices—"

"Trained dogs!" scoffed Cathy, but there was more anguish in her face than anger. "What kind of woman needs a dog to help her raise her own baby?"

"A deaf woman," Libby answered firmly. "Besides, if you don't want a dog around, you could hire a nurse."

"No!"

Libby was taken aback. "Why not?" she signed after a few moments.

Cathy clearly had no intention of answering. She bolted to her feet and was back in the palomino's saddle before Libby could even rise from the ground.

After that, they rode without communicating at all. Knowing that things were far from settled between herself and her cousin, Libby tried to concentrate on the scenery. A shadow moved across the sun, however, and a feeling of impending disaster unfolded inside her.

Jess glared at the screen of the small computer his father placed so much store in and resisted a caveman urge to strike its side with his fist.

"Here," purred a soft feminine voice, and Monica Summers, the senator's curvaceous assistant, reached down to tap the keyboard in a few strategic places.

Instantly the profit-and-loss statement Jess had been trying to call up was prominently displayed on the screen.

"How did you do that?"

Monica smiled her sultry smile and pulled up a chair to sit down beside Jess. "It's a simple matter of command," she said, and somehow the words sounded wildly suggestive.

Jess's collar seemed to tighten around his throat, but he grinned, appreciating Monica's lithe, inviting body, her profusion of gleaming brown hair, her impudent mouth and soft gray eyes. Her visits to the ranch were usually brief, but the senator's term of office was almost over, and he planned to write a long book—with which Monica was slated to help. Until that project was completed, she would be around a lot.

The fact that the senior senator did not intend to campaign for reelection didn't seem to faze her—it was common knowledge that she had a campaign of her own in mind.

Monica had made it clear, time and time again, that she was available to Jess for more than an occasional dinner date and subsequent sexual skirmish. And before Libby's return, Jess had seriously considered settling down with Monica.

He didn't love her, but she was undeniably beautiful, and the promises she made with her skillfully made-up eyes were not idle ones. In addition to that, they had a lot of ordinary things in common—similar political views, a love of the outdoors, like tastes in music and books.

Now, even with Monica sitting so close to him, her perfume calling up some rather heated memories, Jess Barlowe was patently unmoved.

A shower of anger sifted through him. He *wanted* to be moved, dammit—he wanted everything to be the way it was before Libby's return. Return? It was an invasion! He thought about the little hellion day and night, whether he wanted to or not.

"What's wrong, Jess?" Monica asked softly, perceptively, her hand resting on his shoulder. "It's more than just this computer, isn't it?"

He looked away. The sensible thing to do would be to take Monica by the hand, lead her off somewhere private and make slow, ferocious love to her. Maybe that would exorcise Libby Kincaid from his mind.

He remembered passion-weighted breasts, bared to him on a swimming dock, remembered their nipples blossoming sweetly in his mouth. Libby's breasts.

"Jess?"

He forced himself to look at Monica again. "I'm sorry," he said. "Did you say something?"

Mischief danced in her charcoal eyes. "Yes. I offered you my body."

He laughed.

Instead of laughing herself, Monica gave him a gentle, discerning look. "Mrs. Bradshaw tells me that Libby Kincaid is back," she said. "Could it be that I have some competition?"

Jess cleared his throat and diplomatically fixed his attention on the computer screen. "Show me how you made this monster cough up that profit-and-loss statement," he hedged.

"Jess." The voice was cool, insistent.

He made himself meet Monica's eyes again. "I don't know what I feel for Libby," he confessed. "She makes me mad as hell, but…"

"But," said Monica with rueful amusement, "you want her very badly, don't you?"

There was no denying that, but neither could Jess bring himself to openly admit to the curious needs that had been plaguing him since the moment he'd seen Libby again at the small airport in Kalispell.

Monica's right index finger traced the outline of his jaw, tenderly. Sensuously. "We've never agreed to be faithful to each other, Jess," she said in the silky voice that had once enthralled him. "There aren't any strings tying you to me. But that doesn't mean that I'm going to step back and let Libby Kincaid have a clear field. I want you myself.''

Jess was saved from answering by the sudden appearance of his father in the study doorway.

''Oh, Monica—there you are,'' Cleave Barlowe said warmly. ''Ready to start working on that speech now? We have to have it ready before we fly back to Washington, remember.''

Gray eyes swept Jess's face in parting. ''More than ready,'' she replied, and then she was out of her chair and walking across the study to join her employer.

Jess gave the computer an unloving look and switched it off, taking perverse pleasure in the way the little green words and numbers on the screen dissolved. ''State of the art,'' he mocked, and then stood up and strode out of the room.

The accountants would be angry, once they returned from their coffee break, but he didn't give a damn. If he didn't do something physical, he was going to go crazy.

Back at the stables, Libby surrendered her horse to a ranch hand with relief. Already the muscles in her thighs were aching dully from the ride; by morning they would be in savage little knots.

Cathy, who probably rode almost every day, looked breezy and refreshed, and from her manner no one would have suspected that she harbored any ill feelings toward Libby. ''Let's take a swim,'' she signed, ''and then we can have lunch.''

Libby would have preferred to soak in the hot tub, but her pride wouldn't allow her to say so. Unless a limp betrayed her, she wasn't going to let Cathy know how sore a simple horseback ride had left her.

''I don't have a swimming suit,'' she said, somewhat hopefully.

''That's okay,'' Cathy replied with swift hands. ''It's an indoor pool, remember?''

''I hope you're not suggesting that we swim naked,'' Libby argued aloud.

Cathy's eyes danced. ''Why not?'' she signed impishly. ''No one would see us.''

"Are you kidding?" Libby retorted, waving one arm toward the long, wide driveway. "Look at all these cars! There are *people* in that house!"

"Are you so modest?" queried Cathy, one eyebrow arched.

"Yes!" replied Libby, ignoring the subtle sarcasm.

"Then we'll go back to your house and swim in the pond, like we used to."

Libby recalled the blatant way she'd offered herself to Jess Barlowe in that place and winced inwardly. The peaceful solace of that pond had probably been altered forever, and it was going to be some time before she could go there comfortably again. "It's spring, Cathy, not summer. We'd catch pneumonia! Besides, I think it's going to rain."

Cathy shrugged. "All right, all right. I'll borrow a car and we'll drive over and get your swimming suit, then come back here."

"Fine," Libby agreed with a sigh.

She was to regret the decision almost immediately. When she and Cathy reached the house they had both grown up in, there was a florist's truck parked out front.

On the porch stood an affable young man, a long, narrow box in his hands. "Hi, Libby," he said.

Libby recognized Phil Reynolds, who had been her classmate in high school. *Go away, Phil,* she thought, even as she smiled and greeted him.

Cathy's attention was riveted on the silver box he carried, and there was a worried expression on her face.

Phil approached, beaming. "I didn't even know you were back until we got this order this morning. Aren't you coming into town at all? We got a new high school..."

Simmonsville, a dried-up little community just beyond the south border of the Circle Bar B, hadn't even entered Libby's thoughts until she'd seen Phil Reynolds. She ignored his question and stared at the box he held out to her as if it might contain something squirmy and vile.

"Wh-who sent these?" she managed, all too conscious of the suspicious way Cathy was looking at her.

"See for yourself," Phil said brightly, and then he got back into his truck and left.

Libby took the card from beneath the red ribbon that bound the box and opened it with trembling fingers. The flowers couldn't be from Stacey, please God, they couldn't!

The card was typewritten. *Don't be stubborn, sweetness,* the message read. *Regards, Aaron.*

For a moment Libby was too relieved to be angry. "Aaron," she repeated. Then she lifted the lid from the box and saw the dozen pink rosebuds inside.

For one crazy moment she was back in Jonathan's hospital room. There had been roses there, too—along with mums and violets and carnations. Aaron and his family had sent costly bouquets and elaborate toys, but not one of them had come to visit.

Libby heard the echo of Jonathan's purposefully cheerful voice. *Daddy must be busy,* he'd said.

With a cry of fury and pain, Libby flung the roses away, and they scattered over the walk in a profusion of long-stemmed delicacy. The silver box lay with them, catching the waning sunlight.

Cathy knelt and began gathering up the discarded flowers, placing them gently back in their carton. Once or twice she glanced up at Libby's livid face in bewilderment, but she asked no questions and made no comments.

Libby turned away and bounded into the house. By the time she had found a swimming suit and come back downstairs again, Cathy was arranging the rosebuds in a cut-glass vase at the kitchen sink.

She met Libby's angry gaze and held up one hand to stay the inevitable outburst. "They're beautiful, Libby," she said in a barely audible voice. "You can't throw away something that's beautiful."

"Watch me!" snapped Libby.

Cathy stepped between her cousin and the lush bouquet. "Libby, at least let me give them to Mrs. Bradshaw," she pleaded aloud. "Please?"

Glumly Libby nodded. She supposed she should be grateful that the roses hadn't been sent by Stacey in a fit of ardor, and they *were* too lovely to waste, even if she herself couldn't bear the sight of them.

Libby remembered the words on Aaron's card as she and Cathy drove back to the main house. *Don't be stubborn.* A tremor of dread flitted up and down her spine.

Aaron hadn't been serious when he'd threatened to come to the ranch and "persuade" her to return to New York with him, had he? She shivered.

Surely even Aaron wouldn't have the gall to do that, she tried to reassure herself. After all, he had never come to the apartment she'd taken after Jonathan's death, never so much as called. Even when the divorce had been granted, he had avoided her by sending his lawyer to court alone.

No. Aaron wouldn't actually come to the Circle Bar B. He might call, he might even send more flowers, just to antagonize her, but he wouldn't come in person. Despite his dismissal of Stacey as a "soft-headed cowboy," he was afraid of him.

Cathy was drawing the car to a stop in front of the main house by the time Libby was able to recover herself. To allay the concern in her cousin's eyes, she carried the vase of pink roses into the kitchen and presented them to Mrs. Bradshaw, who was puzzled but clearly pleased.

Inside the gigantic, elegantly tiled room that housed the swimming pool and the spacious hot tub, Libby eyed the latter with longing. Thus, it was a moment before she realized that the pool was already occupied.

Jess was doing a furious racing crawl from one side of the deep end to the other, his tanned, muscular arms cutting through the blue water with a force that said he was trying to work out some fierce inner conflict. Watching him admiringly from the poolside, her slender legs dangling into the water, was a pretty dark-haired woman with beautiful gray eyes.

The woman greeted Cathy with an easy gesture of her hands, though her eyes were fixed on Libby, seeming to assess her in a thorough, if offhand, fashion.

"I'm Monica Summers," she said, as Jess, apparently oblivious of everything other than the furious course he was following through the water, executed an impressive somersault turn at the poolside and raced back the other way.

Monica Summers. The name was familiar to Libby, and so, vaguely, was the perfect fashion-model face.

Of course. Monica was Senator Barlowe's chief assistant. Libby had never actually met the woman, but she had seen her on television newscasts and Ken had mentioned her in passing, on occasion, over long-distance telephone.

"Hello," Libby said. "I'm—"

The gray eyes sparkled. "I know," Monica broke in smoothly. "You're Libby Kincaid. I enjoy your cartoons very much."

Libby felt about as sophisticated, compared to this woman, as a Girl Scout selling cookies door-to-door. And Monica's subtle emphasis on the word "cartoons" had made her feel defensive.

All the same, Libby thanked her and forced herself not to watch Jess's magnificent body moving through the bright blue water of the pool. It didn't bother her that Jess and Monica had been alone in this strangely sensual setting. It didn't.

Cathy had moved away, anxious for her swim.

"I'm sorry if we interrupted something," Libby said, and hated herself instantly for betraying her interest.

Monica smiled. Clearly she had not been in swimming herself, for her expensive black swimsuit was dry, and so was her long, lush hair. Her makeup, of course, was perfect. "There are always interruptions," she said, and then she turned away to take up her adoring-spectator position again, her gaze following the play of the powerful muscles in Jess's naked back.

My thighs are too fat, mourned Libby, in petulant despair. She took a seat on a lounge far removed from Jess and his lovely friend and tried to pretend an interest in Cathy's graceful backstroke.

Was Jess intimate with Monica Summers? It certainly seemed so, and Libby couldn't understand, for the life of her, why she was so brutally surprised by the knowledge. After all, Jess was a handsome, healthy man, well beyond the age of handholding and fantasies-from-afar. Had she really ever believed that he had just been existing on this ranch in some sort of suspended animation?

Cathy roused her from her dismal reflection by flinging a stream of water at her with both hands. Instantly Libby was drenched and stung to an annoyance out of all proportion to the offense. Surprising even herself, she stomped over to the hot tub, flipped the switch that would make the water bubble and churn, and after hurling one scorching look at her unrepenting cousin, slid into the enormous tile-lined tub.

The heat and motion of the water were welcome balm to Libby's muscles, if not to her spirit. She had no right to care who Jess Barlowe slept with, no right at all. It wasn't as though she had ever had any claim on his affections.

Settling herself on a submerged bench, Libby tilted her head back, closed her eyes, and tried to pretend that she was alone in that massive room with its sloping glass roof, lush plants and lounges.

The fact that she was sexually attracted to Jess Barlowe was undeniable, but it was just a physical phenomenon, certainly. It would pass.

All she had to do to accelerate the process was allow herself to remember how very demeaning Aaron's lovemaking had been. And remember she did.

After Libby had caught her husband with the first of his lovers, she had moved out of his bedroom permanently, remaining in his house only because Jonathan, still at home then, had needed her so much.

Before her brutal awakening, however, she had tried hard to make the rapidly failing marriage work. Even then, bedtime had been a horror.

Libby's skin prickled as she recalled the way Aaron would ignore her for long weeks and then pounce on her with a vicious and alarming sort of determination, tearing her clothes, sometimes bruising her.

In retrospect, Libby realized that Aaron must have been trying to prove something to himself concerning his identity as a man, but at the time she had known only that sex, much touted in books and movies, was something to be feared.

Not once had Libby achieved any sort of satisfaction with Aaron—she had only endured. Now, painfully conscious of the blatantly masculine, near-naked cowboy swimming in the pool nearby, Libby wondered if lovemaking would be different with Jess.

The way that her body had blossomed beneath his seemed adequate proof that it would be different indeed, but there was always the possibility that she would be disappointed in the ultimate act. Probably she had been aroused only because Jess had taken the time to offer her at least a taste of pleasure. Aaron had never done that, never shown any sensitivity at all.

Shutting out all sight and sound, Libby mentally decried her lack of experience. If only she'd been with even one man besides Aaron, she would have had some frame of reference, some inkling of whether or not the soaring releases she'd read about really existed.

The knowledge that so many people thought she had been carrying on a torrid affair with Stacey brought a wry smile to her lips. If only they knew.

"What are you smiling about?"

The voice jolted Libby back to the here and now with a thump. Jess had joined her in the hot tub at some point; indeed, he was standing only inches away.

Startled, Libby stared at him for a moment, then looked wildly around for Cathy and the elegant Ms. Summers.

"They went in to have lunch," Jess informed her, his eyes twinkling. Beads of water sparkled in the dark down that matted his muscular chest, and his hair had been towel-rubbed into an appealing disarray.

"I'll join them," said Libby in a frantic whisper, but the simple mechanics of turning away and climbing out of the hot tub eluded her.

Smelling pleasantly of chlorine, Jess came nearer. "Don't go," he said softly. "Lunch will wait."

Anger at Cathy surged through Libby. Why had she gone off and left her here?

Jess seemed to read the question in her face, and it made him laugh. The sound was soft—sensuously, wholly male. Overhead, spring thunder crashed in a gray sky.

Libby trembled, pressing back against the edge of the hot tub with such force that her shoulder blades ached. "Stay away from me," she breathed.

"Not on your life," he answered, and then he was so near that she could feel the hard length of his thighs against her own. The soft dark hair on his chest tickled her bare shoulders and the suddenly alive flesh above her swimsuit top. "I intend to finish what we started yesterday beside the pond."

Libby gasped as his moist lips came down to taste hers, to tame and finally part them for a tender invasion. Her hands went up, of their own accord, to rest on his hips.

He was naked. The discovery rocked Libby, made her try to twist away from him, but his kiss deepened and subdued her struggles. With his hands, he lifted her legs, draped them around the rock-hard hips she had just explored.

The imposing, heated length of his desire, now pressed intimately against her, was powerful proof that he meant to take her.

Chapter 5

Libby felt as though her body had dissolved, become part of the warm, bubbling water filling the hot tub. When Jess drew back from his soft conquering of her mouth, his hands rose gently to draw down the modest top of her swimsuit, revealing the pulsing fullness of her breasts to his gaze.

It was not in Libby to protest: she was transfixed, caught up in primal responses that had no relation to good sense or even sanity. She let her head fall back, saw through the transparent ceiling that gray clouds had darkened the sky, promising a storm that wouldn't begin to rival the one brewing inside Libby herself.

Jess bent his head, nipped at one exposed, aching nipple with cautious teeth.

Libby drew in a sharp breath as a shaft of searing pleasure went through her, so powerful that she was nearly convulsed by it. A soft moan escaped her, and she tilted her head even further back, so that her breasts were still more vulnerable to the plundering of his mouth.

Inside Libby's swirling mind, a steady voice chanted a litany of logic: she was behaving in a wanton way—Jess didn't really care for her, he was only trying to prove that he could conquer her whenever he desired—this place was not private, and there was a very real danger that someone would walk in at any moment and see what was happening.

Thunder reverberated in the sky, shaking heaven and earth. And none of the arguments Libby's reason was offering had any effect on her rising need to join herself with this impossible, overbearing man feasting so brazenly on her breast.

With an unerring hand, Jess found the crux of her passion, and through the fabric of her swimsuit he stroked it to a wanting Libby had never experienced before. Then, still greedy at the nipple he was attending, he deftly worked aside the bit of cloth separating Libby's womanhood from total exposure.

She gasped as he caught the hidden nubbin between his fingers and began, rhythmically, to soothe it. Or was he tormenting it? Libby didn't know, didn't care.

Jess left her breast to nibble at her earlobe, chuckled hoarsely when the tender invasion of his fingers elicited a throaty cry of welcome.

"Go with it, Libby," he whispered. "Let it carry you high... higher..."

Libby was already soaring, sightless, mindless, conscious only of the fiery marauding of his fingers and the strange force inside her that was building toward something she had only imagined before. "Oh," she gasped as he worked this new and fierce magic. "Oh, Jess..."

Mercilessly he intensified her pleasure by whispering outrageously erotic promises, by pressing her legs wide of each other with one knee, by caressing her breast with his other hand.

A savage trembling began deep within Libby, causing her breath to quicken to a soft, lusty whine.

"Meet it, Libby," Jess urged. "Rise to meet it."

Suddenly Libby's entire being buckled in some ancient, inescapable response. The thunder in the distant skies covered her final cry of release, and she convulsed again and again, helpless in the throes of her body's savage victory.

When at last the ferocious clenching and unclenching had ceased, Libby's reason gradually returned. Forcing wide eyes to Jess's face, she saw no demand there, no mockery or revulsion. Instead, he was grinning at her, as pleased as if he'd been sated himself.

Wild embarrassment surged through Libby in the wake of her passion. She tried to avert her face, but Jess caught her chin in his hand and made her look at him.

"Don't," he said gruffly. "Don't look that way. It wasn't wrong, Libby."

His ability to read her thoughts so easily was as unsettling as the knowledge that she'd just allowed this man unconscionable liberties in a hot tub. "I suppose you think...I suppose you want..."

Jess withdrew his conquering hand, tugged her swimsuit back into place. "I think you're beautiful," he supplied, "and I want you—that's true. But for now, watching you respond like that was enough."

Libby blushed again. She was still confused by the power of her release, and she had expected Jess to demand his own satisfaction. She was stunned that he could give such fierce fulfillment and ask nothing for himself.

"You've never been with any man besides your husband, have you, Libby?"

The outrageous bluntness of that question solidified Libby's jellylike muscles, and she reached furiously for one of the towels Mrs. Bradshaw had set nearby on a low shelf. "I've been with a thousand men!" she snapped in a harsh whisper. "Why, one word from any man, and I let him...I let him..."

Jess grinned again. "You've never had a climax before," he observed.

How could he guess a thing like that? It was uncanny. Libby knew that the hot color in her face belied her sharp answer. "Of course I have! I've been married—did you think I was celibate?"

The rapid-fire hysteria of her words only served to amuse Jess, it seemed. "We both know, Libby Kincaid, that you are, for all practical intents and purposes, a virgin. You may have lain beneath that ex-husband of yours and wished to God that he would leave you alone, but until a few minutes ago you had never even guessed what it means to be a woman."

Libby wouldn't have thought it possible to be as murderously angry as she was at that moment. "Why, you arrogant, *insufferable*..."

He caught her hand at the wrist before it could make the intended contact with his face. "You haven't seen anything yet, princess," he vowed with gentle force. "When I take you to bed—and I assure you that I will—I'll prove that everything I've said is true."

While Libby herself was outraged, her traitorous body yearned to lie in his bed, bend to his will. Having reached the edges of passion, it wanted to go beyond, into the molten core. "You egotistical bastard!" Libby hissed, breaking away from him to lift herself out of the hot tub and land on its edge with an inelegant, squishy plop, "You act as if you'd invented sex!"

"As far as you're concerned, little virgin, I did. But have no fear— I intend to deflower you at the first opportunity."

Libby stood up, wrapped her shaky, nerveless form in a towel the size of a bedsheet. "Go to hell!"

Jess rose out of the water, not the least bit self-conscious of his nakedness. The magnitude of his desire for her was all too obvious.

"The next few hours will be just that," he said, reaching for a towel of his own. Naturally, the one he selected barely covered him.

Speechless, Libby imagined the thrust of his manhood, imagined her back arching to receive him, imagined a savage renewal of the passion she had felt only minutes before.

Jess gave her an amused sidelong glance, as though he knew what she was thinking, and intoned, "Don't worry, princess. I'll court you if that's what you want. But I'll have you, too. And thoroughly."

Having made this incredible vow, he calmly walked out of the room, leaving Libby alone with a clamoring flock of strange emotions and unmet needs.

The moment Jess was gone, she stumbled to the nearest lounge chair and sank onto it, her knees too weak to support her. *Well, Kincaid,* she reflected wryly, *now you know. Satisfied?*

Libby winced at the last word. Though she might have wished otherwise, given the identity of the man involved, she was just that.

With carefully maintained dignity, Jess Barlowe strode into the shower room adjoining the pool and wrenched on one spigot. As he stepped under the biting, sleetlike spray, he gritted his teeth.

Gradually his body stopped screaming and the stubborn evidence of his passion faded. With relief, Jess dived out of the shower stall and grabbed a fresh towel.

A hoarse chuckle escaped him as he dried himself with brisk motions. Good God, if he didn't have Libby Kincaid soon, he was going to die of pneumonia. A man could stand only so many plunges into icy ponds, only so many cold showers.

A spare set of clothes—jeans and a white pullover shirt—awaited Jess in a cupboard. He donned them quickly, casting one disdainful look at the three-piece suit he had shed earlier. His circulation restored, to some degree at least, he toweled his hair and then combed it with the splayed fingers of his left hand.

A sweet anguish swept through him as he remembered the magic he had glimpsed in Libby's beautiful face during that moment of full surrender. *My father was right,* Jess thought as he pulled on socks and old, comfortable boots. *I love you, Libby Kincaid. I love you.*

Jess was not surprised to find that Libby wasn't with Cathy and Monica in the kitchen—she had probably made some excuse to get out of joining them for lunch and gone off to gather her thoughts. God knew, she had to be every bit as undone and confused as he was.

Mostly to avoid the sad speculation in Monica's eyes, Jess glanced toward the kitchen windows. They were already sheeted with rain.

A crash of thunder jolted him out of the strange inertia that had possessed him. He glanced at Cathy, saw an impish light dancing in her eyes.

"You can catch her if you hurry," she signed, cocking her head to one side and grinning at him.

Did she know what had happened in the hot tub? Some of the heat lingering in Jess's loins rose to his face as he bolted out of the room and through the rest of the house.

The station wagon, an eyesore among the other cars parked in front of the house, patently refused to start. Annoyed, Jess "borrowed" Monica's sleek green Porsche without a moment's hesitation, and his aggravation grew as he left the driveway and pulled out onto the main road.

What the hell did Libby think she was doing, walking in this rain? And why had Cathy let her go?

He found Libby near the mailboxes, slogging despondently along, soaked to the skin.

"Get in!" he barked, furious in his concern.

Libby lifted her chin and kept walking. Her turquoise shirt was plastered to her chest, revealing the outlines of her bra, and her hair hung in dripping tendrils.

"*Now!*" Jess roared through the window he had rolled down half-way.

She stopped, faced him with indigo fury sparking in her eyes. "Why?" she yelled over the combined roars of the deluge and Monica's car engine. "Is it time to teach me what it means to be a woman?"

"How the hell would I know what it means to be a woman?" he shouted back. "Get in this car!"

Libby told him to do something that was anatomically impossible and then went splashing off down the road again, ignoring the driving rain.

Rasping a swearword, Jess slipped the Porsche out of gear and wrenched the emergency brake into place. Then he shoved open the door and bounded through the downpour to catch up with Libby, grasp her by the shoulders and whirl her around to face him.

"If you don't get your backside into that car *right now*," he bellowed, "I swear to God I'll *throw* you in!"

She assessed the Porsche. "Monica's car?"

Furious, Jess nodded. Christ, it was raining so hard that his clothes were already saturated and she was standing there talking details!

An evil smile curved Libby's lips and she stalked toward the automobile, purposely stepping in every mud puddle along the way. Jess could have sworn that she enjoyed sinking, sopping wet, onto the heretofore spotless suede seat.

"Home, James," she said smugly, folding her arms and grinding her mud-caked boots into the lush carpeting on the floorboard.

Jess had no intention of taking Libby to Ken's place, but he said nothing. Envisioning her lying in some hospital bed, wasted away by a case of rain-induced pneumonia, he ground the car savagely back into gear and gunned the engine.

When they didn't take the road Libby expected, the smug look faded from her face and she stared at Jess with wide, wary eyes. "Wait a minute..."

Jess flung an impudent grin at her and saluted with one hand. "Yes?" he drawled, deliberately baiting her.

"Where are we going?"

"My place," he answered, still angry. "It's the classic situation, isn't it? I'll insist you get out of those wet clothes, then I'll toss you one of my bathrobes and pour brandy for us both. After that, lady, I'll make mad love to you."

Libby paled, though there was a defiant light in her eyes. "On a fur rug in front of your fireplace, no doubt!"

"No doubt," Jess snapped, wondering why he found it impossible to deal with this woman in a sane and reasonable way. It would be so much simpler just to tell her straight out that he loved her, that he needed her. But he couldn't quite bring himself to do that, not just yet, and he was still mad as hell that she would walk in the pouring rain like that.

"Suppose I tell you that I don't want you to 'make mad love' to me, as you so crudely put it? Suppose I tell you that I won't give in to you until the first Tuesday after doomsday, if then, brandy and fur rugs notwithstanding?"

"The way you didn't give in in the hot tub?" he gibed, scowling.

Libby blushed. "That was different!"

"How so?"

"You...you *cornered* me, that's how."

His next words were out of his mouth before he could call them back. "I know about your ex-husband, Libby."

She winced, fixed her attention on the overworked windshield wipers. "What does he have to do with anything?"

Jess shifted to a lower gear as he reached the road leading to his house and turned onto it. "Stacey told me about the women."

The high color drained from Libby's face and she would not look at him. She appeared ready, in fact, to thrust open the door on her side of the car and leap out. "I don't want to talk about this," she said after an interval long enough to bring them to Jess's driveway.

"Why not, Libby?" he asked, and his voice was gentle, if a bit gruff.

One tear rolled over the wet sheen on her defiant rain-polished face, and Libby's chin jutted out in a way that was familiar to him, at once maddening and appealing. "Why do you want to talk about Aaron?" she countered in low, ragged tones. "So you can sit there and feel superior?"

"You know better."

She glared at him, her bruised heart in her eyes, and Jess ached for her. She'd been through so much, and he wished that he could have taken that visible, pounding pain from inside her and borne it himself.

"I don't know better, Jess," she said quietly. "We haven't exactly been kindred spirits, you and I. For all I know, you just want to torture me. To throw all my mistakes in my face and watch me squirm."

Jess's hands tightened on the steering wheel. It took great effort to reach down and shut off the Porsche's engine. "It's cold out here," he said evenly, "and we're both wet to the skin. Let's go inside."

"You won't take me home?" Her voice was small.

He sighed. "Do you want me to?"

Libby considered, lowered her head. "No," she said after a long time.

The inside of Jess's house was spacious and uncluttered. There were skylights in the ceiling and the second floor appeared to be a loft of some sort. Lifting her eyes to the railing above, Libby imagined that his bed was just beyond it and blushed.

Jess seemed to be ignoring her; he was busy with newspaper and kindling at the hearth. She watched the play of the muscles in his back in weary fascination, longing to feel them beneath her hands.

The knowledge that she loved Jess Barlowe, budding in her subconscious mind since her arrival in Montana, suddenly burst into full flower. But was the feeling really new?

If Libby were to be honest with herself—and she tried to be, always—she had to admit that the chances were good that she had loved Jess for a very long time.

He turned, rose from his crouching position, a small fire blazing and crackling behind him. "How do you like my house?" he asked with a half smile.

Between her newly recognized feelings for this man and the way his jade eyes seemed to see through all her reserve to the hurt and confusion hidden beneath, Libby felt very vulnerable. Trusting in an old trick that had always worked in the past, she looked around in search of something to be angry about.

The skylights, the loft, the view of the mountains from the windows beyond his desk—all of it was appealing. Masculine. Quietly romantic.

"Perfect quarters for a wealthy and irresponsible playboy," she threw out in desperation.

Jess stiffened momentarily, but then an easy grin creased his face. "I think that was a shot, but I'm not going to fire back, Libby, so you might as well relax."

Relax? Was the man insane? Half an hour before, he had blithely brought her to climax in a hot tub, for God's sake, and now they were alone, the condition of their clothes necessitating that they risk further intimacies by stripping them off, taking showers. If they couldn't fight, what *were* they going to do?

Before Libby could think of anything to say in reply, Jess gestured toward the broad redwood stairs leading up to the loft. "The bathroom is up there," he said. "Take a shower. You'll find a robe hanging on the inside of the door." With that, he turned away to crouch before the fire again and add wood.

Because she was cold and there seemed to be no other options, Libby climbed the stairs. It wasn't until she reached the loft that her teeth began to chatter.

There she saw Jess's wide unmade bed. It was banked by a line of floor-to-ceiling windows, giving the impression that the room was open to the outdoors, and the wrinkled sheets probably still bore that subtle, clean scent that was Jess's alone...

Libby took herself in hand, wrenched her attention away from the bed. There was a glass-fronted wood-burning stove in one corner of the large room, and a long bookshelf on the other side was crammed with everything from paperback mysteries to volumes on veterinary medicine.

Libby made her way into the adjoining bathroom and kicked off her muddy boots, peeled away her jeans and shirt, her sodden underwear and socks. Goosebumps leapt out all over her body, and they weren't entirely related to the chill.

The bathtub was enormous, and like the bed, it was framed by tall uncurtained windows. Bathing here would be like bathing in the high limbs of a tree, so sweeping was the view of mountains and grassland beyond the glass.

Trembling a little, Libby knelt to turn on the polished brass spigots and fill the deep tub. The water felt good against her chilled flesh, and she was submerged to her chin before she remembered that she had meant to take a quick shower, not a lingering, dreamy bath.

Libby couldn't help drawing a psychological parallel between this tub and the larger one at the main house, where she had made such a fool of herself. Was there some mysterious significance in the fact that she'd chosen the bathtub over the double-wide shower stall on the other side of the room?

Now you're really getting crazy, Kincaid, she said to herself, settling back to soak.

Somewhere in the house, a telephone rang, was swiftly answered.

Libby relaxed in the big tub and tried to still her roiling thoughts and emotions. She would not consider what might happen later. For now, she wanted to be comforted, pampered. Deliciously warm.

She heard the click of boot heels on the stairs, though, and sat bolt upright in the water. A sense of sweet alarm raced through her system. Jess wouldn't come in, actually *come in,* would he?

Of course he would! Why would a bathroom door stop a man who would make such brazen advances in a hot tub?

With frantic eyes Libby sought the towel shelf. It was entirely too far away, and so was the heavy blue-and-white velour robe hanging on the inside of the door. She sank into the bathwater until it tickled her lower lip, squeezed her eyes shut and waited.

"Lib?"

"Wh-what?" she managed. He was just beyond that heavy wooden panel, and Libby found herself hoping...

Hoping what? That Jess would walk in, or that he would stay out? She honestly didn't know.

"That was Ken on the phone," Jess answered, making no effort to open the door. "I told him you were here and that I'd bring you home after the rain lets up."

Libby reddened, there in the privacy of that unique bathroom, imagining the thoughts that were probably going through her father's mind. "Wh-what did he say?"

Jess chuckled, and the sound was low, rich. "Let me put it this way: I don't think he's going to rush over here and defend your virtue."

Libby was at once pleased and disappointed. Wasn't a father *supposed* to protect his daughter from persuasive lechers like Jess Barlowe?

"Oh," she said, her voice sounding foolish and uncertain. "D-do you want me to hurry? S-so you can take a shower, I mean?"

"Take your time," he said offhandedly. "There's another bathroom downstairs—I can shower there."

Having imparted this conversely comforting and disenchanting information, Jess began opening and closing drawers. Seconds later, Libby again heard his footsteps on the stairs.

Despite the fact that she would have preferred to lounge in that wonderful bathtub for the rest of the day, Libby shot out of the water and raced to the towel bar. This was her chance to get dried off and dressed in something before Jess could incite her to further scandalous behavior.

She was wrapped in his blue-and-white bathrobe, the belt securely tied, and cuddled under a knitted afghan by the time Jess joined her in the living room, looking reprehensibly handsome in fresh jeans and a green turtleneck sweater. His hair, like her own, was still damp, and there was a smile in his eyes, probably inspired by the way she was trying to burrow deeper into her corner of the couch.

"There isn't any brandy after all," he said with a helpless gesture of his hands. "Will you settle for chicken soup?"

Libby would have agreed to anything that would get Jess out of that room, even for a few minutes, and he would have to go to the kitchen for soup, wouldn't he? Unable to speak, she nodded.

She tried to concentrate on the leaping flames in the fireplace, but she could hear the soft thump of cupboard doors, the running of tapwater, the singular whir of a microwave oven. The sharp *ting* of the appliance's timer bell made her flinch.

Too soon, Jess returned, carrying two mugs full of steaming soup. He extended one to Libby and, to her eternal gratitude, settled in a chair nearby instead of on the couch beside her.

Outside, the rain came down in torrents, making a musical, pelting sound on the skylights, sliding down the windows in sheets. The fire snapped and threw out sparks, as if to mock the storm that could not reach it.

Jess took a sip of the hot soup and grinned. "This doesn't exactly fit the scenario I outlined in the car," he said, lifting his cup.

"You got everything else right," Libby quipped, referring to the bath she'd taken and the fact that she was wearing his robe. Instantly she realized how badly she'd slipped, but it was too late to call back her words, and the ironic arch of Jess's brow and the smile on his lips indicated that he wasn't going to let the comment pass.

"Everything?" he teased. "There isn't any fur rug, either."

Libby's cheekbones burned. Unable to say anything, she lowered her eyes and watched the tiny noodles colliding in her mug of soup.

"I'm sorry," Jess said softly.

She swallowed hard and met his eyes. He did look contrite, and there was nothing threatening in his manner. Because of that, Libby dared to ask, "Do you really mean to...to make love to me?"

"Only if you want me to," he replied. "You must know that I wouldn't force you, Libby."

She sensed that he meant this and relaxed a little. Sooner or later, she was going to have to accept the fact that all men didn't behave in the callous and hurtful way that Aaron had. "You believe me now—don't you? About Stacey, I mean?"

If that off-the-wall question had surprised or nettled Jess, he gave no indication of it. He simply nodded.

Some crazy bravery, carrying her forward like a reckless tide, made Libby put aside her carefully built reserve and blurt out, "Do you think I'm a fool, Jess?"

Jess gaped at her, the mug of soup forgotten in his hands. "A fool?"

Libby lowered her eyes. "I mean…well…because of Aaron."

"Why should I think anything like that?"

Thunder exploded in the world outside the small cocoonlike one that held only Libby and Jess. "He was…he…"

"He was with other women," supplied Jess quietly. Gently.

Libby nodded, managed to look up.

"And you stayed with him." He was setting down the mug, drawing nearer. Finally he crouched before her on his haunches and took the cup from her hands to set it aside. "You couldn't leave Jonathan, Libby. I understand that. Besides, why should the fact that you stuck with the marriage have any bearing on my attitude toward you?"

"I just thought…"

"What?" prodded Jess when her sentence fell away. "What did you think, Libby?"

Tears clogged her throat. "I thought that I couldn't be very desirable if my o-own husband couldn't…wouldn't…"

Jess gave a ragged sigh. "My God, Libby, you don't think that Aaron was unfaithful because of some lack in you?"

That was exactly what she'd thought, on a subliminal level at least. Another woman, a stronger, more experienced, more alluring woman, might have been able to keep her husband happy, make him want her.

Jess's hands came to Libby's shoulders, gentle and insistent. "Lib, talk to me."

"Just how terrific could I be?" she erupted suddenly, in the anguish that would be hidden no longer. "Just how desirable? My husband needed other women because he couldn't bring himself to make love to me!"

Jess drew her close, held her as the sobs she had restrained at last broke free. "That wasn't your fault, Libby," he breathed, his hand in her hair now, soothing and strong. "Oh, sweetheart, it wasn't your fault."

"Of course it was!" she wailed into the soft green knit of his sweater, the hard strength of the shoulder beneath. "If I'd been better...if I'd known how..."

"Shhh. Baby, don't. Don't do this to yourself."

Once freed, Libby's emotions seemed impossible to check. They ran as deep and wild as any river, swirling in senseless currents and eddies, causing her pride to founder.

Jess caught her trembling hands in his, squeezed them reassuringly. "Listen to me, princess," he said. "These doubts that you're having about yourself are understandable, under the circumstances, but they're not valid. You are desirable." He paused, searched her face with tender, reproving eyes. "I can swear to that."

Libby still felt broken, and she hadn't forgotten the terrible things Aaron had said to her during their marriage—that she was cold and unresponsive, that he hadn't been impotent before he'd married her. Time and time again he had held up Jonathan as proof that he had been virile with his first wife, taken cruel pleasure in pointing out that none of his many girlfriends found him wanting.

Wrenching herself back to the less traumatic present, Libby blurted out, "Make love to me, Jess. Let me prove to myself—"

"No," he said with cold, flat finality. And then he released her hands, stood up and turned away as if in disgust.

Chapter 6

"I thought you wanted me," Libby said in a small, broken voice.

Jess's broad back stiffened, and he did not turn around to face her. "I do."

"Then, why…?"

He went to the fireplace, took up a poker, stoked the blazing logs within to burn faster, hotter. "When I make love to you, Libby, it won't be because either one of us wants to prove anything."

Libby lowered her head, ashamed. As if to scold her, the wind and rain lashed at the windows and the lightning flashed, filling the room with its eerie blue-gold light. She began to cry again, this time softly, wretchedly.

And Jess came to her, lifted her easily into his arms. Without a word, he carried her up the stairs, across the storm-shadowed loft room to the bed. After pulling back the covers with one hand, he lowered her to the sheets. "Rest," he said, tucking the blankets around her.

Libby gaped at him, amazed and stricken. She couldn't help thinking that he wouldn't have tucked Monica Summers into bed this way, kissed *her* forehead as though she were some overwrought child needing a nap.

"I don't want to rest," Libby said, insulted. And her hands moved to pull the covers down.

Jess stopped her by clasping her wrists. A muscle knotted in his jaw, and his jade-green eyes flashed, their light as elemental as that of the electrical storm outside. "Don't Libby. Don't tempt me."

She *had* been tempting him—if he hadn't stopped her when he did, she would have opened the robe, wantonly displayed her breasts. Now, she was mortally embarrassed. What on earth was making her act this way?

"I'm sorry," she whispered. "I don't know what's the matter with me."

Jess sat down on the edge of the bed, his magnificent face etched in shadows, his expression unreadable. "Do we have to go into that again, princess? Nothing is wrong with you."

"But—"

Jess laid one index finger to her lips to silence her. "It would be wrong if we made love now, Libby—don't you see that? Afterward, you'd be telling yourself what a creep I was for taking advantage of you when you were so vulnerable."

His logic was unassailable. To lighten the mood, Libby summoned up a shaky grin. "Some playboy you are. Chicken soup. Patience. Have you no passion?"

He laughed. "More than I know what to do with," he said, standing up, walking away from the bed. At the top of the stairs he paused. "Am I crazy?"

Libby didn't answer. Smiling, she snuggled down under the covers—she was just a bit tired—and placidly watched the natural light show beyond the windows. Maybe later there would be fireworks of another sort.

Downstairs, Jess resisted a fundamental urge to beat his head against the wall. Libby Kincaid was up there in his bed, for God's sake, warm and lush and wanting him.

He ached to go back up the stairs and finish what they'd begun that morning in the hot tub. He couldn't, of course, because Libby was in no condition, emotionally, for that kind of heavy scene. If he did the wrong thing, said the wrong thing, she could break, and the pieces might not fit together again.

In a fit of neatness, Jess gathered up the cups of cold chicken soup and carried them into the kitchen. There he dumped their contents into the sink, rinsed them, and stacked them neatly in the dishwasher.

The task was done too quickly. What could he do? He didn't like the idea of leaving Libby alone, but he didn't dare go near her again, either. The scent of her, the soft disarray of her hair, the way her breasts seemed to draw at his mouth and the palms of his hands—all those things combined to make his grasp on reason tenuous.

Jess groaned, lifted his eyes to the ceiling and wondered if he was going to have to endure another ice-cold shower. The telephone rang, startling him, and he reached for it quickly. Libby might already be asleep, and he didn't want her to be disturbed.

"Hello?"

"Jess?" Monica's voice was calm, but there was an undercurrent of cold fury. "Did you take my car?"

He sighed, leaning back against the kitchen counter. "Yeah. Sorry. I should have called you before this, but—"

"But you were busy."

Jess flinched. Exactly what could he say to that? "Monica—"

"Never mind, Jess." She sighed the words. "I didn't have any right to say that. And if you helped yourself to my car, you must have had a good reason."

Why the hell did she have to be so reasonable? Why didn't Monica yell at him or something, so that he could get mad in good conscience and stop feeling like such an idiot? "I'm afraid the seats are a little muddy," he said.

"Muddy? Oh, yes—the rain. Was Libby okay?"

Again Jess's gaze lifted to the ceiling. Libby was not okay, thanks to him and Stacey and her charming ex-husband. But then, Monica was just making polite conversation, not asking for an in-depth account of Libby's emotional state. "She was drenched."

"So you brought her there, got her out of her wet clothes, built a fire—"

The anger Jess had wished for was suddenly there. "Monica."

She drew in a sharp breath. "All right, all right—I'm sorry. I take it our dinner date is off?"

"Yeah," Jess answered, turning the phone cord between his fingers. "I guess it is."

Monica was nothing if not persistent—probably that quality accounted for her impressive success in political circles. "Tomorrow night?"

Jess sighed. "I don't know."

There was a short, uncomfortable silence. "We'll talk later," Monica finally said brightly. "Listen, is it okay if I send somebody over there to get my car?"

"I'll bring it to you," Jess said. It was, after stealing it, the least he could do. He'd check first, to make sure that Libby really was sleeping, and with luck, he could be back before she woke up.

"Thanks," sang Monica in parting.

Jess hung up the phone and climbed the stairs, pausing at the edge of the bedroom. He dared go no further, wanting that rumple-haired little hellion the way he did. "Libby?"

When there was no answer, Jess turned and went back down the stairs again, almost grateful that he had somewhere to go, something to do.

Monica hid her annoyance well as she inspected the muddy splotches on her car's upholstery. Overhead, the incessant rain pummeled the garage roof.

"I'm sorry," Jess said. It seemed that he was always apologizing for one thing or another lately. "My station wagon wouldn't start, and I was in a hurry..."

Monica allowed a flicker of anger to show in her gray eyes. "Right. When there is a damsel to be rescued, a knight has to grab the first available charger."

Having no answer for that, Jess shrugged. "I'll have your car cleaned," he offered when the silence grew too long, and then he turned to walk back out of the garage and down the driveway to his own car, which refused to start.

He got out and slammed the door. "Damn!" he bellowed, kicking yet another dent into the fender.

"Problems?"

Jess hadn't been aware of Ken until that moment, hadn't noticed the familiar truck parked nearby. "It would take all day to list them," he replied ruefully.

Ken grinned a typical sideways grin, and his blue eyes twinkled. He seemed oblivious of the rain pouring off the brim of his ancient hat and soaking through his denim jacket and jeans. "I think maybe my daughter might be at the top of the list. Is she all right?"

"She's…" Jess faltered, suddenly feeling like a high-school kid. "She's sleeping."

Ken laughed. "Must have been real hard to say that," he observed, "me being her daddy and all."

"It isn't…I didn't…"

Again Ken laughed. "Maybe you should," he said.

Jess was shocked—so shocked that he was speechless.

"Take my truck if you need it," Ken offered calmly, his hand coming to rest on Jess's shoulder. "I'll get a ride home from somebody here. And, Jess?"

"What?"

"Don't hurt Libby. She's had enough trouble and grief as it is."

"I know that," Jess replied, as the rain plastered his hair to his neck and forehead and made his clothes cling to his flesh in sodden, clammy patches. "I swear I won't hurt her."

"That's good enough for me," replied Libby's father, and then he pried the truck keys out of his pocket and tossed them to Jess.

"Ken…"

The foreman paused, looking back, his eyes wise and patient. How the hell was Jess going to ask this man what he had to ask, for Libby's sake?

"Spit it out, son," Ken urged. "I'm getting wet."

"Clothes—she was…Libby was caught in the rain, and she needs dry clothes."

Ken chuckled and shrugged his shoulders. "Stop at our place and get some of her things then," he said indulgently.

Jess was suddenly as confused by this man as he was by his daughter. What the hell was Ken doing, standing there taking this whole thing so calmly? Didn't it bother him, knowing what might happen when Jess got back to that house?

"See ya," said Ken in parting.

Completely confused, Jess got into Ken's truck and drove away. It wasn't until he'd gotten a set of dry clothes for Libby and reached his own house again that he understood. Ken trusted him.

Jess let his forehead rest on the truck's steering wheel and groaned. He couldn't stand another cold shower, dammit. He just couldn't.

But Ken trusted him. Libby was lying upstairs in his bed, and even if she was, by some miracle, ready to handle what was destined to happen, Jess couldn't make love to her. To do so would be to betray a man who had, in so many ways, been as much a father to him as Cleave Barlowe had.

The problem was that Jess couldn't think of Libby as a sister.

Jess sat glumly at the little table in the kitchen, making patterns in his omelet with a fork. Tiring of that, he flung Libby a beleaguered look and sneezed.

She felt a surge of tenderness. "Aren't you hungry?"

He shook his head. "Libby…"

It took all of her forbearance not to stand up, round the table, and touch Jess's forehead to see if he had a fever. "What?" she prompted softly.

"I think I should take you home."

Libby was hurt, but she smiled brightly. "Well, it *has* stopped raining," she reasoned.

"And I've got your dad's truck," added Jess.

"Um-hmm. Thanks for stopping and getting my clothes, by the way."

Outside, the wind howled and the night was dark. Jess gave the jeans and loose pink sweater he had picked up for Libby a distracted look and sneezed again. "You're welcome."

"And you, my friend, are sick."

Jess shook his head, went to the counter to pour coffee from the coffeemaker there. "Want some?" he asked, lifting the glass pot.

Libby declined. "Were you taking another shower when I got up?" she ventured cautiously. The peace between them, for all its sweet glow, was still new and fragile.

Libby would have sworn that he winced, and his face was unreadable. "I'm a clean person," he said, averting his eyes.

Libby bit the inside of her lower lip, suddenly possessed by an untimely urge to laugh. Jess had been shivering when he came out of that bathroom and unexpectedly encountered his newly awakened houseguest.

"Right," she said.

Jess sneezed again, violently. Somehow, the sound unchained Libby's amusement and she shrieked with laughter.

"What is so goddamn funny?" Jess demanded, setting his coffee cup down with an irritated thump and scowling.

"N-nothing," cried Libby.

Suddenly Jess was laughing too. He pulled Libby out of her chair and into his arms, and she deliberately pressed herself close to him, delighting in the evidence of his desire, in the scent and substance and strength of him.

She almost said that she loved him.

"You wanted my body!" she accused instead, teasing.

Jess groaned and tilted his head back, ostensibly to study the ceiling. Libby saw a muscle leap beneath his chin and wanted to kiss it, but she refrained.

"You were taking a cold shower, weren't you, Jess?"

"Yes," he admitted with a martyrly sigh. "Woman, if I die of pneumonia, it will be your fault."

"On the contrary. I've done everything but throw myself at your feet, mister, and you haven't wanted any part of me."

"Wrong." Jess grinned wickedly, touching the tip of her breast with an index finger. "I want this part..." The finger trailed away, following an erotic path. "And this part..."

It took all of Libby's courage to say the words again, after his brisk rejection earlier. "Make love to me, Jess."

"My God, Libby—"

She silenced him by laying two fingers to his lips. Remembering the words he had flung at her in the Cessna the day of her arrival, she said saucily, "If it feels good, do it."

Jess gave her a mock scowl, but his arms were around her now, holding her against him. "You were a very mean little kid," he muttered, "and now you're a mean adult. Do you know what you're doing to me, Kincaid?"

Libby moved her hips slightly, delighting in the contact and the guttural groan the motion brought from Jess. "I have some vague idea, yes."

"Your father trusts me."

"My father!" Libby stared up at him, amazed. "Is that what you've been worried about? What my father will think?"

Jess shrugged, and his eyes moved away from hers. Clearly he was embarrassed. "Yes."

Libby laughed, though she was not amused. "You're not serious!"

His eyes came back to meet hers and the expression in their green depths was nothing if not serious. "Ken is my best friend," he said.

"Shall I call him up and ask for permission? Better yet, I could drive over there and get a note!"

The taunts caused Jess to draw back a little, though their thighs and hips were still touching, still piping primitive messages one to the other. "Very funny!" he snapped, and a muscle bunched in his neck, went smooth again.

Libby was quietly furious. "You're right—it isn't funny. This is my body, Jess—mine. I'm thirty-one years old and I make my own living and I *damned well* don't need my daddy's permission to go to bed with a man!"

The green eyes were twinkling with mischief. "That's a healthy attitude if I've ever heard one," he broke in. "However, before we go up those stairs, there is one more thing I want to know. Are you using me, Libby?"

"Using you?"

"Yes. Do I really mean something to you, or would any man do?"

Libby felt as though she'd just grabbed hold of a high-voltage wire; in a few spinning seconds she was hurled from pain to rage to humiliation.

Jess held her firmly. "I see the question wasn't received in the spirit in which it was intended," he said, his eyes serious now, searching her burning, defiant face. "What I meant to ask was, are we going to be making love, Libby, or just proving that you can go the whole route and respond accordingly?''

Libby met his gaze bravely, though inside she was still shaken and angry. ''Why would I go to all this trouble, Jess, if I didn't want you? After all, I could have just stopped someone on the street and said, 'Excuse me, sir, but would you mind making love to me? I'd like to find out if I'm frigid or not.'''

Jess sighed heavily, but his hands were sliding up under the back of Libby's pink sweater, gently kneading the firm flesh there. The only sign that her sarcasm had rankled him was the almost imperceptible leaping of the pulsepoint beneath his right ear.

''I guess I'm having a little trouble understanding your sudden change of heart, Libby. For years you've hated my guts. Now, after confiding that your ex-husband put you through some kind of emotional wringer and left you feeling about as attractive as a sink drain, you want to share my bed.''

Libby closed her eyes. The motion of his hands on her back was hypnotic, making it hard for her to breathe, let alone think. When she felt the catch of her bra give way, she shivered.

She should tell him that she loved him, that maybe, despite outward appearances, she'd always loved him, but she didn't dare. This was a man who had thought the worst of her at every turn, who had never missed a chance to get under her skin. Allowing him inside the fortress where her innermost emotions were stored could prove disastrous.

His hands came slowly around from her back to the aching roundness of her breasts, sliding easily, brazenly under the loosened bra.

''Answer me, Libby,'' he drawled, his voice a sleepy rumble.

She was dazed; his fingers came to play a searing symphony at her nipples, plying them, drawing at them. ''I...I want you. I'm not trying to p-prove anything.''

''Let me look at you, Libby.''

Libby pulled the pink sweater off over her head, stood perfectly still as Jess dispensed with her bra and then stepped back a little way to admire her.

He outlined one blushing nipple with the tip of his finger, progressed to wreak the same havoc on the other. Then, with strong hands, he lifted Libby up onto a counter, so that her breasts were on a level with his face.

She gasped as he took languid, tentative suckle at one peak, then trailed a path with the tip of his tongue to the other, conquering it with lazy ease.

She was desperate now. "Make love to me," she whispered again in broken tones.

"Make love to me, *Jess,*" he prompted, nibbling now, driving her half-wild with the need of him.

Libby swallowed hard, closed her eyes. His teeth were scraping gently at her nipple now, rousing it to obedience. "Make love to me, Jess," she repeated breathlessly.

He withdrew his mouth, cupping her in his hands, letting his thumbs do the work his lips and teeth had done before. "Open your eyes," he commanded in a hoarse rumble. "Look at me, Libby."

Dazed, her very soul spinning within her, Libby obeyed.

"Tell me," he insisted raggedly, "that you're not seeing Stacey or your misguided ex-husband. Tell me that you see *me,* Libby."

"I do, Jess."

He lifted her off the counter and into his arms, and his mouth came down on hers, cautious at first, then almost harshly demanding. Libby was electrified by the kiss, by the searching fierceness of his tongue, by the moan of need that came from somewhere deep inside him. Finally he ended the kiss, and his eyes were smiling into hers.

Feeling strangely giddy, Libby laughed. "Is this the part where you make love to me?"

"This is it," he replied, and then they were moving through the house toward the stairs. Lightning crackled and flashed above the skylights, while thunder struck a booming accompaniment.

"The earth is moving already," said Libby into the Jess-scented wool of his sweater.

Jess took the stairs two at a time. "Just wait," he replied.

In the bedroom, which was lit only by the lightning that was sundering the night sky, he set Libby on her feet. For a moment they just stood still, looking at each other. Libby felt as though she had become a part of the terrible storm that was pounding at the tall windows, and she grasped Jess's arms so that she wouldn't be blown away to the mountaintops or flung beyond the angry clouds.

"Touch me, Libby," Jess said, and somehow, even over the renewed rage of the storm, she heard him.

Cautiously she slid her hands beneath his sweater, splaying her fingers so that she could feel as much of him as possible. His chest was hard and broad and softly furred, and he groaned as she found masculine nipples and explored them.

Libby moved her hands down over his rib cage to the sides of his waist, up his warm, granite-muscled back. *I love you,* she thought, and then she bit her lower lip lest she actually say the words.

At some unspoken urging from Jess, she caught his sweater in bunched fists and drew it up over his head. Silver-blue lightning scored the sky and danced on the planes of his bare chest, his magnificent face.

Libby was drawn to him, tasting one masculine nipple with a cautious tongue, suckling the other. He moaned and tangled his fingers in her hair, pressing her close, and she knew that he was experiencing the same keen pleasure she had known.

Presently he caught her shoulders in his hands and held her at arm's length, boldly admiring her bare breasts. "Beautiful," he rasped. "So beautiful."

Libby had long been ashamed of her body, thinking it inadequate. Now, in this moment of storm and fury, she was proud of every curve and hollow, every pore and freckle. She removed her jeans and panties with graceful motions.

Jess's reaction was a low, rumbling groan, followed by a gasp of admiration. He stood still, a western Adonis, as she undid his jeans, felt the hollows of his narrow hips, the firmness of his buttocks. Within seconds he was as naked as Libby.

She caught his hands in her own, drew him toward the bed. But instead of reclining with her there, he knelt at the side, positioned Libby so that her hips rested on the edge of the mattress.

His hands moved over every part of her—her breasts, her shoulders, her flat, smooth stomach, the insides of her trembling thighs.

"Jess…"

"Shh, it's all right."

"But…" Libby's back arched and a spasm of delight racked her as he touched the curls sheltering the core of her passion, first with his fingers, then with his lips. "Oh…wait…oh, Jess, no…"

"Yes," he said, his breath warm against her. And then he parted her and took her fully into his mouth, following the instinctive rising and falling of her hips, chuckling at the soft cry she gave.

A violent shudder went through Libby's already throbbing body, and her knees moved wide of each other, shaking, made of no solid substance.

Frantic, she found his head, tangled her fingers in his hair. "Stop," she whimpered, even as she held him fast.

Jess chuckled again and then went right on consuming her, his hands catching under her knees, lifting them higher, pressing them farther apart.

Libby was writhing now, her breath harsh and burning, her vision blurred. The storm came inside the room and swept her up, up, up, beyond the splitting skies. She cried out in wonder as she collided with the moon and bounced off, to be enfolded by a waiting sun.

When she came back inside herself, Jess was beside her on the bed, soothing her with soft words, stroking away the tears that had somehow gathered on her face.

"I've never read…" she whispered stupidly. "I didn't know…"

Jess was drawing her up, so that she lay full on the bed, naked and sated at his side. "Look it up," he teased, kissing her briefly, tenderly. "I think it would be under O."

Libby laughed, and the sound was a warm, soft contrast to the tumult of the storm. "What an ego!"

With an index finger, Jess traced her lips, her chin, the moist length of her neck. Small novas flashed and flared within her as her pulsing senses began to make new demands.

When his mouth came to her breast again, Libby arched her back and whimpered. "Jess…Jess…"

He circled the straining nipple with a warm tongue. "What, babe?"

No coherent words would come to Libby's beleaguered mind. "I don't know," she managed finally. "I don't know!"

"I do," Jess answered, and then he suckled in earnest.

Powerless under the tyranny of her own body, Libby gave herself up to sensation. It seemed that no part of her was left untouched, unconquered, or unworshiped.

When at last Jess poised himself above her, strong and fully a man, his face reflected the flashing lightning that seemed to seek them both.

"I'm Jess," he warned again in a husky whisper that betrayed his own fierce need.

Libby drew him to her with quick, fevered hands. "I know," she gasped, and then she repeated his name like some crazy litany, whispering it first, sobbing it when he thrust his searing magnificence inside her.

He moved slowly at first, and the finely sculptured planes of his face showed the cost of his restraint, the conflicting force of his need. "Libby," he pleaded. "Oh, God…Libby…"

She thrust her hips upward in an instinctive, unplanned motion that shattered Jess's containment and caused his great muscular body to convulse once and then assert its dominance in a way that was at once fierce and tender. It seemed that he sought some treasure within her, so deeply did he delve, some shimmering thing that he would perish without.

His groans rose above the sound of thunder, and as his pace accelerated and his passion was unleashed, Libby moved in rhythm with him, one with him, his.

Their bodies moved faster, agile in their quest, each glistening with the sheen of sweet exertion, each straining toward the sun that, this time, would consume them both.

The tumult flung them high, tore them asunder, fused them together again. Libby sobbed in the hot glory of her release and heard an answering cry from Jess.

They clung together, struggling for breath, for a long time after the slow, treacherous descent had been made. Twice, on the way, Libby's body had paused to greedily claim what had been denied it before.

She was flushed, reckless in her triumph. ''I did it,'' she exalted, her hands moving on the slackened muscles in Jess's back. ''I did it...I responded...''

Instantly she felt those muscles go taut, and Jess's head shot up from its resting place in the curve where her neck and shoulder met. *''What?''*

Libby stiffened, knowing now, too late, how grave her mistake had been. ''I mean, *we* did it...'' she stumbled lamely.

But Jess was wrenching himself away from her, searching for his clothes, pulling them on. ''Congratulations!'' he yelled.

Libby sat up, confused, wildly afraid. Dear God, was he going to walk out now? Was he going to hate her for a few thoughtless words?

''Jess, wait!'' she pleaded, clutching the sheet to her chest. ''Please!''

''For what, Libby?'' he snapped from the top of the stairs. ''Exhibit B? Is there something else you want to prove?''

''Jess!''

But he was storming down the stairs, silent in his rage, bent on escaping her.

''Jess!'' Libby cried out again in fear, tears pouring down her face, her hands aching where they grasped the covers.

The only answer was the slamming of the front door.

Chapter 7

Ken Kincaid looked up from the cards in his hand as the lights flickered, went out, came on again. Damn, this was a hell of a storm—if the rain didn't let up soon, the creeks would overflow and they'd have range calves drowning right and left.

Across the table, Cleave Barlowe laid down his own hand of cards. "Quite a storm, eh?" he asked companionably. "Jess bring your truck back yet?"

"I don't need it," said Ken, still feeling uneasy.

Lightning creased the sky beyond the kitchen window, and thunder shook the old house on its sturdy foundations. Cleave grinned. "He's with Libby, then?"

"Yup," said Ken, smiling himself.

"Think they know the sky's turning itself inside out?"

There was an easing in Ken; he laughed outright. "Doubt it," he replied, looking at his cards again.

For a while the two men played the two-handed poker they had enjoyed for years, but it did seem that luck wasn't running with either one of them. Finally they gave up the effort and Cleave went home.

With his old friend gone, Ken felt apprehensive again. He went around the house making sure all the windows were closed against the rain, and wondered why one storm should bother him that way, when he'd seen a thousand and never found them anything more than a nuisance.

He was about to shut off the lamp in the front room when he saw the headlights of his own truck swing into the driveway. Seconds later, there was an anxious knock at the door.

"Jess?" Ken marveled, staring at the haggard, rain-drenched man standing on the front porch. "What the hell...?"

Jess looked as though he'd just taken a first-rate gut punch. "Could I come in?"

"That's a stupid question," retorted Ken, stepping back to admit his unexpected and obviously distraught visitor. "Is Libby okay?"

Jess's haunted eyes wouldn't quite link up with Ken's. "She's fine," he said, his hands wedged into the pockets of his jeans, his hair and sweater dripping rainwater.

Ken arched an eyebrow. "What'd you do, anyway—ride on the running board of that truck and steer from outside?"

Jess didn't answer; he didn't seem to realize that he was wet to the skin. There was a distracted look about him that made Ken ache inside.

In silence Ken led the way into the kitchen, poured a dose of straight whiskey into a mug, added strong coffee.

"You look like you've been dragged backward through a knot-hole," he observed when Jess was settled at the table. "What happened?"

Jess closed his hands around the mug. "I'm in love with your daughter," he said after a long time.

Ken sat down, allowed himself a cautious grin. "If you drove over here in this rain just to tell me that, friend, you got wet for nothing."

"You knew?" Jess seemed honestly surprised.

"Everybody knew. Except maybe you and Libby."

Jess downed the coffee and the potent whiskey almost in a single gulp. There was a struggle going on in his face, as though he might be fighting hard to hold himself together.

Ken rose to put more coffee into Jess's mug, along with a lot more whiskey. If ever a man needed a drink, this one did.

"Maybe you'd better put on some dry clothes," the older man ventured.

Jess only shook his head.

Ken sat back in his chair and waited. When Jess was ready to talk, he would. There was, Ken had learned, no sense in pushing before that point was reached.

"Libby's beautiful, you know," Jess remarked presently, as he started on his third drink.

Ken smiled. "Yeah. I've noticed."

Simple and ordinary though they were, the words triggered some kind of emotional reaction in Jess, broke down the barriers he had been maintaining so carefully. His face crumbled, he lowered his head to his arms, and he cried. The sobs were deep and dry and ragged.

Hurting because Jess hurt, Ken waited.

Soon enough, his patience was rewarded. Jess began to talk, brokenly at first, and then with stone-cold reason.

Ken didn't react openly to anything he said; much of what Jess told him about Libby's marriage to Aaron Strand came as no real surprise. He was wounded, all the same, for his daughter and for the devastated young man sitting across the table from him.

The level of whiskey in Ken's bottle went down as the hour grew later. Finally, when Jess was so drunk that his words started getting all tangled up with each other, Ken half led, half carried him up the stairs to Libby's room.

In the hallway, he paused, reflecting. Life was a hell of a thing, he decided. Here was Jess, sleeping fitfully in Libby's bed, all alone. And just up the hill, chances were, Libby was tossing and turning in Jess's bed, just as lonely.

Not for the first time, Ken Kincaid felt a profound desire to get them both by the hair and knock their heads together.

Libby cried until far into the night and then, exhausted, she slept. When she awakened, shocked to find herself in Jess Barlowe's bed, she saw that the world beyond the windows had been washed to a clean sparkle.

The world inside her seemed tawdry by comparison.

Her face feeling achy and swollen, Libby got out of bed, stumbled across the room to the bathroom. Jess was nowhere in the house; she would have sensed it if he were.

As Libby filled the tub with hot water, she wondered whether she was relieved that he wasn't close by, or disappointed. A little of both, she concluded as she slid into her bath and sat there in miserable reverie.

Facing Jess now would have been quite beyond her. Why, why had she said such a foolish thing, when she might have known how Jess would react? On the other hand, why had *he* made such a big deal out of a relatively innocuous remark?

More confused than ever, Libby finished her bath and climbed out to dry herself with a towel. In short order she was dressed and her hair was combed. Because she had no toothbrush—Jess had forgotten that when he picked up her things—she had to be content with rinsing her mouth.

Downstairs, Libby stood staring at the telephone, willing herself to call her father and confess that she needed a ride home. Pride wouldn't allow that, however, and she had made up her mind to walk the distance when she heard a familiar engine outside, the slam of a truck door.

Jess was back, she thought wildly. Where had he been all night? With Monica? What would she say to him?

The questions were pointless, for when Libby forced herself to go to the front door and open it, she saw her father striding up the walk, not Jess.

Fresh embarrassment stained Libby's cheeks, though there was no condemnation in Ken's weathered face, no anger in his understanding eyes. "Ride home?" he said.

Unable to speak, Libby only nodded.

"Pretty bad night?" he ventured in his concise way when they were both settled in the truck and driving away.

"Dismal," replied Libby, fixing her eyes on the red Hereford cattle grazing in the green, rain-washed distance.

"Jess isn't in very good shape either," commented Ken after an interval.

Libby's eyes were instantly trained on her father's profile. "You've seen him?"

"Seen him?" Ken laughed gruffly. "I poured him into bed at three this morning."

"He was drunk?" Libby was amazed.

"He had a nip or two."

"How is he now?"

Ken glanced at her, turned his eyes back to the rutted, winding country road ahead. "Jess is hurting," he said, and there was a finality in his tone that kept Libby from asking so much as one more question.

Jess is hurting. What the devil did that mean? Was he hung over? Had the night been as miserable for him as it had been for her?

Presently the truck came to a stop in front of the big Victorian house that had been "home" to Libby for as long as she could remember. Ken made no move to shut off the engine, and she got out without saying good-bye. For all her brave words of the night before, about not needing her father's approval, she felt estranged from him now, subdued.

After forcing down a glass of orange juice and a slice of toast in the kitchen, Libby went into the studio Cathy and her father had improvised for her and did her best to work. Even during the worst days in New York, she had been able to find solace in the mechanics of drawing her cartoon strip, forgetting her own troubles to create comical dilemmas for Liberated Lizzie.

Today was different.

The panels Libby sketched were awkward, requiring too many erasures, and even if she had been able to get the drawings right, she couldn't have come up with a funny thought for the life of her.

At midmorning, Libby decided that her career was over and paced from one end of the studio to the other, haunted by thoughts of the night before.

Jess had made it clear, in his kitchen, that he didn't want to make love just to let Libby prove that she was "normal." And what had she done? She'd *gloated.*

Shame ached in Libby's cheeks as she walked. *I did it,* she'd crowed, as though she were Edison and the first electric light had just been lit. God, how could she have been so stupid? So insensitive?

"You did have a little help, you know," she scolded herself out loud. And then she covered her face with both hands and cried. It had been partly Jess's fault, that scene—he had definitely overreacted, and on top of that, he had been unreasonable. He had stormed out without giving Libby a chance to make things right.

Still, it was all too easy to imagine how he'd felt. Used. And the truth was that, without intending to, Libby had used him.

Small, strong hands were suddenly pulling Libby's hands away from her face. Through the blur, she saw Cathy watching her, puzzled and sad.

"What's wrong?" her cousin asked. "Please, Libby, tell me what's wrong."

"Everything!" wailed Libby, who was beyond trying to maintain her dignity now.

Gently Cathy drew her close, hugged her. For a moment they were two motherless little girls again, clinging to each other because there were some pains that even Ken, with his gruff, unswerving devotion, couldn't ease.

The embrace was comforting, and after a minute or two Libby recovered enough to step back and offer Cathy a shaky smile. "I've missed you so much, Cathy," she said.

"Don't get sloppy," teased Cathy, using her face to give the toneless words expression.

Libby laughed. "What are you doing today, besides being one of the idle rich?"

Cathy tilted her head to one side. "Did you really stay with Jess last night?" she asked with swift hands.

"Aren't we blunt today?" Libby shot back, both speaking and signing. "I suppose the whole ranch is talking about it!"

Cathy nodded.

"Damn!"

"Then it's true!" exalted Cathy aloud, her eyes sparkling.

Some of Libby's earlier remorse drained away, pushed aside by feelings of anger and betrayal. "Has Jess been bragging?" she demanded, her hands on her hips, her indignation warm and thick in her throat.

"He isn't the type to do that," Cathy answered in slow, carefully formed words, "and you know it."

Libby wasn't so certain—Jess had been very angry, and his pride had been stung. Besides, the only other person who had known was Ken, and he was notoriously tight-lipped when it came to other people's business. "Who told you?" she persisted, narrowing her eyes.

"Nobody had to," Cathy answered aloud. "I was down at the stables, saddling Banjo, and one of the range crews was there—ten or twelve men, I guess. Anyway, there was a fight out front—Jess punched out one of the cowboys."

Libby could only gape.

Cathy gave the story a stirring finale. "I think Jess would have killed that guy if Ken hadn't hauled him off."

Libby found her voice. "Was Jess hurt? Cathy, did you see if he was hurt?"

Cathy grinned at her cousin's undisguised concern. "Not a scratch. He got into an argument with Ken and left."

Libby felt a strong need to find her father and ask him exactly what had happened, but she knew that the effort would be wasted. Even if she could find Ken, which was unlikely considering the size of the ranch and all the places he could be, he wouldn't explain.

Cathy was studying the messy piece of drawing paper affixed to the art board. "You're not going to work?" she signed.

"I gave up," Libby confessed. "I couldn't keep my mind on it."

"After a night with Jess Barlowe, who could?"

Libby suddenly felt challenged, defensive. She even thought that, perhaps, there was more to the deep closeness between Jess and Cathy than she had guessed. "What do you know about spending the night with Jess?" she snapped before she could stop herself.

Cathy rolled her beautiful green eyes. "*Nothing.* For better or worse, and mostly it's been better, I'm married to Jess's brother—remember?"

Libby swallowed, feeling foolish. "Where is Stacey, anyway?"

she asked, more to make conversation than because she wanted to know.

The question brought a shadow of sadness to Cathy's face. "He's away on one of his business trips."

Libby sat down on her art stool, folded her hands. "Maybe you should have gone with him, Cathy. You used to do that a lot, didn't you? Maybe if you two could be alone...talk..."

The air suddenly crackled with Cathy's anger and hurt. "*He* talks!" she raged aloud. "I just move my hands!"

Libby spoke softly, gently. "You could talk to Stacey, Cathy—really talk, the way you do with me."

"No."

"Why not?"

"I know I sound like a record playing on the wrong speed, that's why!"

"Even if that were so, would it matter?" signed Libby, frowning. "Stacey knew you were deaf before he married you, for heaven's sake."

Cathy's head went down. "He must have felt sorry for me or something."

Instantly Libby was off her stool, gripping Cathy's shoulders in firm, angry hands. "He loves you!"

Tears misted the emerald-green eyes and Cathy's lower lip trembled. "No doubt that's why he intends to divorce me and marry you, Libby."

"No," insisted Libby, giving her cousin a slight shake. "No, that isn't true. I think Stacey is confused, Cathy. Upset. Maybe it's this thing about your not wanting to have a baby. Or maybe he feels that you don't need him, you're so independent."

"Independent? Don't look now, Libby Kincaid, but *you're* the independent one! You have a career...you can hear—"

"Will you stop feeling sorry for yourself, dammit!" Libby almost screamed. "I'm so tired of hearing how you suffer! For God's sake, stop whining and fight for the man you love!"

Cathy broke free of Libby's grasp, furious, tears pouring down her face. "It's too late!" she cried. "You're here now, and it's too late!"

Libby sighed, stepped back, stricken by her own outburst and by Cathy's, too. "You're forgetting one thing," she reasoned quietly. "I'm not in love with Stacey. And it would take two of us to start anything, wouldn't it?"

Cathy went to the windows and stared out at the pond, her chin high. Knowing that her cousin needed this interval to restore her dignity and assemble her thoughts, Libby did not approach her.

Finally Cathy sniffled and turned back to offer a shaky smile. "I didn't come over here to fight with you," she said clearly. "I'm going to Kalispell, and I wanted to know if you would like to come with me."

Libby agreed readily, and after changing her clothes and leaving a quick note for Ken, she joined Cathy in the shiny blue Ferrari.

The ride to Kalispell was a fairly long one, and by the time Cathy and Libby reached the small city, they had reestablished their old, easy relationship.

They spent the day shopping, had lunch in a rustic steak house bearing the Circle Bar B brand, and then started home again.

"Are you really going to give that to Jess?" Cathy asked, her eyes twinkling when she cast a look at the bag in Libby's lap.

"I may lose my courage." Libby frowned, wondering what had possessed her to buy a T-shirt with such an outlandish saying printed on it. She supposed she'd hoped that the gesture would penetrate the barrier between herself and Jess, enabling them to talk.

"Take my advice," said Cathy, guiding the powerful car off the highway and onto the road that led to the heart of the ranch. "Give him the shirt."

"Maybe," said Libby, looking off into the sweeping, endless blue sky. A small airplane was making a graceful descent toward the Circle Bar B landing strip.

"Who do you suppose that is?" Libby asked, catching Cathy's attention with a touch on her arm.

The question was a mistake. Cathy, who had not, of course, heard the plane's engine, scanned the sky and saw it. "Why don't we find out?"

Libby scrunched down in her seat, sorry that she had pointed out the airplane now. Suppose Stacey was aboard, returning from his business trip, and there was another uncomfortable scene at the airstrip? Suppose it was Jess, and he either yelled at Libby or, worse yet, pretended that she wasn't there?

"I'd rather go home," she muttered.

But Cathy's course was set, and the Ferrari bumped and jostled over the road to the landing strip as though it were a pickup truck.

The plane came to a smooth stop as Cathy parked at one side of the road and got out of the car, shading her eyes with one hand, watching. Libby remained in her seat.

She had, it seemed, imagined only part of the possible scenario. The pilot was Jess, and his passenger was a wan, tight-lipped Stacey.

"Oh, God," said Libby, sinking even further into the car seat. She would have kept her face hidden in her hand forever, probably, if it hadn't been for the crisp, insistent tap at her window.

Having no other choice, she rolled the glass down and squinted into Jess Barlowe's unreadable, hard-lined face. "Come with me," he said flatly.

Libby looked through the Ferrari's windshield, saw Stacey and Cathy standing nearby, a disturbing distance between them. Cathy was glaring angrily into Stacey's face, and Stacey was casting determined looks in Libby's direction.

"They need some time alone," Jess said, his eyes linking fiercely, warningly, with Libby's as he opened the car door for her.

Anxious not to make an obviously unpleasant situation any worse, Libby gathered up her bags and her purse and got out of the car, following along behind Jess's long strides. The station wagon, which she hadn't noticed before, was parked close by.

Without looking back at Stacey and Cathy, Libby slid gratefully into the dusty front seat and closed her eyes. Not until the car was moving did she open them, and even then she couldn't quite bring herself to look at the man behind the wheel.

"That was touching," he said in a vicious rasp.

Libby stiffened in the seat, staring at Jess's rock-hard profile now. "What did you say?"

The powerful shoulders moved in an annoying shrug. "Your wanting to meet Stacey on his triumphant return."

It took Libby a moment to absorb what he was implying. When she had, she slammed him with the paper bag that contained the T-shirt she'd bought for him in Kalispell and hissed, "You bastard! I didn't know Stacey was going to be on that plane, and if I had, I certainly wouldn't have been there at all!"

"Sure," he drawled, and even though he was grinning and looking straight ahead at the road, there was contempt in his tone and a muscle pulsing at the base of his jaw.

Libby felt tears of frustration rise in her eyes. "I thought you believed me," she said.

"I thought I did too," Jess retorted with acid amusement. "But that was before you showed up at the landing strip at such an opportune moment."

"It was Cathy's idea to meet the plane!"

"Right."

The paper bag crackled as Libby lifted it, prepared to swing.

"Do that again and I'll stop this car and raise blisters on your backside," Jess warned, without so much as looking in her direction.

Libby lowered the bag back to her lap, swallowed miserably, and turned her attention to the road. She did not believe Jess's threat for one moment, but she felt childish for trying to hit him with the bag. "Cathy told me there was a fight at the stables this morning," she dared after a long time. "What happened?"

Another shrug, as insolent as the first, preceded his reply. "One of Ken's men said something I didn't like."

"Like what?"

"Like didn't it bother me to sleep with my brother's mistress."

Libby winced, sorry for pressing the point. "Oh, God," she said, and she was suddenly so tired, so broken, and so frustrated that she couldn't hold back her tears anymore. She covered her face with both hands and turned her head as far away from Jess as she could, but the effort was useless.

Jess stopped the station wagon at the side of the road, turned Libby easily toward him. Through a blur, she saw the Ferrari race past.

"Let go of me!"

Jess not only didn't let go, he pulled her close. "I'm sorry," he muttered into her hair. "God, Libby, I don't know what comes over me, what makes me say things to hurt you."

"Garden-variety hatred!" sniffled Libby, who was already forgiving him even though it was against her better judgment.

He chuckled. "No. I couldn't ever hate you, Libby."

She looked up at him, confused and hopeful. Before she could think of anything to say, however, there was a loud *pop* from beneath the hood of the station wagon, followed by a sizzle and clouds of steam.

"Goddammit!" rasped Jess.

Libby laughed, drunk on the scent of him, the closeness of him, the crazy paradox of him. "This crate doesn't exactly fit your image, you know," she taunted. "Why don't you get yourself a decent car?"

He turned from glowering at the hood of the station wagon to smile down into her face. "If I do, Kincaid, will you let me make love to you in the back seat?"

She shoved at his immovable chest with both hands, laughing again. "No, no, a thousand times no!"

Jess nibbled at her jawline, at the lobe of her ear, chuckled huskily as she tensed. "How many times no?"

"Maybe," said Libby.

Just when she thought she would surely go crazy, Jess drew back from his brazen pursuits and smiled lazily. "It is time I got a new car," he conceded, with an evil light glistening in his jade eyes. "Will you come to Kalispell and help me pick it out, Libby?"

A thrill skittered through Libby's body and flamed in her face. "I was just there," she protested, clutching at straws.

"It shouldn't..."—Jess bent, nipped at the side of her neck with gentle teeth—"take long. A couple of days at the most."

"A couple of days!"

"And nights." Jess's lips were scorching their way across the tender hollow of her throat. "Think about it, Lib. Just you and me. No Stacey. No Cathy. No problems."

Libby shivered as a knowledgeable hand closed over one of her breasts, urging, reawakening. "No p-problems?" she echoed.

Jess undid the top button of her blouse.

Libby's breath caught in her throat; she felt heat billowing up inside her, foaming out, just as it was foaming out of the station wagon's radiator. "Wh-where would we s-stay?"

Another button came undone.

Jess chuckled, his mouth on Libby's collarbone now, tasting it, doing nothing to cool the heat that was pounding within her. "How about"—the third button gave way, and Libby's bra was displaced by a gentle hand—"one of those motels...with the...vibrating beds?"

"Tacky," gasped Libby, and her eyes closed languidly and her head fell back as Jess stroked the nipple he'd just found to pebble-hard response.

"My condo, then," he said, and his lips were sliding down from her collarbone, soft, soft, over the upper rounding of her bare breast.

Libby gasped and arched her back as his lips claimed the distended, hurting peak. "Jess...oh, God...this is a p-public road!"

"Umm," Jess said, lapping at her now with the tip of his tongue. "Will you go with me, Libby?"

Wild need went through her as he stroked the insides of her thighs, forcing her blue-jeaned legs apart. And all the while he plied her nipple into a panic of need. "Yes!" she gasped finally.

Jess undid the snap of her jeans, slid his hand inside, beneath the scanty lace of her panties.

"Damn you," Libby whispered hoarsely, "s-stop that! I said I'd go—"

He told her what else she was about to do. And one glorious, soul-scoring minute later, she did.

Red in the face, still breathing heavily, Libby closed her jeans, tugged her bra back into place, buttoned her blouse. God, what if someone had come along and seen her letting Jess...letting him play with her like that?

All during the ride home, she mentally rehearsed the blistering diatribe he deserved to hear. He could just go to Kalispell by *himself,* she would tell him. If he thought for one damned minute that he was going to take her to his condo and make love to her, he was sadly mistaken, she would say.

"Be ready in half an hour," Jess told her at her father's front door.

"Okay," Libby replied.

After landing the Cessna in Kalispell and making arrangements to rent a car, which turned out to be a temperamental cousin to Jess's station wagon, they drove through the small city to an isolated tree-dense property beyond. There were at least a million stars in the sky, and as the modest car rattled over a narrow wooden bridge spanning a creek, Libby couldn't help giving in a little to the romance of it all.

Beyond the bridge, there were more trees—towering ponderosa pines, whispering, shiny-leaved birches. They stopped in the driveway of a condominium that stood apart from several others. Jess got out of the car, came around to open Libby's door for her.

"Let's get rid of the suitcases and go out for something to eat," he said.

Libby's stomach rumbled inelegantly, and Jess laughed as he caught her hand in his and drew her up the darkened walk to the front door of the condominium. "That shoots my plans for a little fun before dinner," he teased.

"There's always after," replied Libby, lifting her chin.

Chapter 8

The inside of the condominium was amazingly like Jess's house on the ranch. There was a loft, for instance, this one accessible by both stairs and, of all things, a built-in ladder. Too, the general layout of the rooms was much the same.

The exceptions were that the floors were carpeted rather than bare oak, and the entire roof was made of heavy glass. *When we make love here, I'll be able to look up and see the stars,* Libby mused.

"Like it?" Jess asked, setting the suitcases down and watching her with discerning, mirthful green eyes.

Libby was uncomfortable again, doubting the wisdom of coming here now that she was faced with the realities of the situation. "Is this where you bring all your conquests?"

Jess smiled, shrugged.

"Well?" prodded Libby, annoyed because he hadn't even had the common decency to offer a denial.

He sat down on the stone ledge fronting the fireplace, wrapped his hands around one knee. "The place does happen to be something of a love nest, as a matter of fact."

Libby was stung. Dammit, how unchivalrous could one man be? "Oh," she said loftily.

"It's my father's place," Jess said, clearly delighting in her obvious curiosity and the look of relief she couldn't quite hide.

"Your father's?"

Jess grinned. "He entertains his mistress here, from time to time. In his position, he has to be discreet."

Libby was gaping now, trying to imagine the sedate, dignified Senator Barlowe cavorting with a woman beneath slanted glass roofs, climbing ladders to star-dappled lofts.

Jess's amused gaze had strayed to the ladder. "It probably puts him in mind of the good old days—climbing into the hayloft, and all that."

Libby blushed. She was still quite disturbed by that ladder, among other things. "You did ask the senator's permission to come here, didn't you?"

Jess seemed to know that she had visions of Cleave Barlowe carrying some laughing woman over the threshold and finding the place already occupied. "Yes," he assured her in a teasing tone, rising and coming toward her. "I said, 'Mind if I take Libby to your condo, dear old dad, and take her to bed?' And he said—"

"Jess!" Libby howled, in protest.

He laughed, caught her elbows in his hands, kissed her playfully, his lips sampling hers, tugging at them in soft entreaty. "My father is in Washington," he said. "Stop worrying."

Libby pulled back, her face hot, her mind spinning. "I'm hungry!"

"Umm," replied Jess, "so am I."

Why did she feel like a sixteen-year-old on the verge of big trouble? "Please...let's go now."

Jess sighed.

They went, but they were back, arms burdened with cartons of Chinese food, in less than half an hour.

While Jess set the boxes out on the coffee table, Libby went to the kitchen for plates and silverware. Scribbled on a blackboard near the sink, she saw the surprising words: "Thanks, Ken. See you next week. B."

A soft chuckle simmered up into Libby's throat and emerged as a giggle. Could it be that her father, her serious, hardworking father, had a ladyfriend who visited him here in this romantic hideaway?

Tilting her head to one side, she considered, grinned again. "Naaaah!"

But Libby's grin wouldn't fade as she carried plates, forks, spoons and paper napkins back into the living room.

"What's so funny?" Jess asked, trying to hide the hunk of sweet-and-sour chicken he had just purloined from one of the steaming cartons.

"Nothing," said Libby, catching his hand and raising it to his mouth. Sheepishly he popped the tidbit of chicken onto his tongue and chewed.

"You lie," Jess replied, "but I'm too hungry to press the point."

While they ate, Libby tried to envision what sort of woman her father would be drawn to—tall, short? Quiet, talkative?

"You're mulling over more than the chow mein," accused Jess presently in a good-natured voice. "Tell me, what's going on in that gifted little head?"

Libby shrugged. "Romance."

He grinned. "That's what I like to hear."

But Libby was thinking seriously, following her thoughts through new channels. In all the years since her mother's death, just before Cathy had come to live on the ranch, she had never imagined Ken Kincaid caring about another woman. "It isn't as though he's old," she muttered, "or unattractive."

Jess set down his plate with a mockingly forceful thump. "That does it. Who are you talking about, Kincaid?" he demanded archly, his wonderful mouth twitching in the effort to suppress a grin.

She perused him with lofty disdain. "Am I correct in assuming that you are jealous?"

"Jealous as hell," came the immediate and not-so-jovial response.

Libby laughed, laid a hand on his knee. "If you must know, I was thinking about my father. I've always kept him in this neat little cubicle in my mind, marked 'Dad.' If you can believe it, it has just now occurred to me that he's a man, with a life, and maybe even a love, of his own."

Mirth danced in Jess's jade eyes, but if he knew anything about

Ken's personal life, he clearly wasn't going to speak of it. "Pass the eggroll," he said diplomatically.

When the meal was over, Libby's reflections began to shift to matters nearer the situation at hand.

"I don't know what I'm doing here," she said pensively as she and Jess cleared the coffee table and started toward the kitchen with the debris. "I must be out of my mind."

Jess dropped the cartons and the crumpled napkins into the trash compactor. "Thanks a lot," he said, watching her attentively as she rinsed the plates and silverware and put them into the dishwasher.

Wearing tailored gray slacks and a lightweight teal-blue sweater, he was devastatingly attractive. Still, the look Libby gave him was a serious, questioning one. "What is it with us, Jess? What makes us behave the way we do? One minute, we're yelling at each other, or not speaking at all, and the next we're alone in a place like this."

"Chemistry?"

Libby laughed ruefully. "More like voodoo. So what kind of car are you planning to buy?"

Jess drew her to him; his fingertips were butterfly-light on the small of her back. "Car?" he echoed, as though the word were foreign.

There was a soft, quivering ache in one corner of Libby's heart. Why couldn't things always be like this between them? Why did they have to wrangle so fiercely before achieving this quiet accord? "Stop teasing me," she said softly. "We did come here to buy a car, you know."

Jess's hands pulled her blouse up and out of her slacks, made slow-moving, sensuous circles on her bare back. "Yes," he said in a throaty rumble. "A car. But there are lots of different kinds of cars, aren't there, Libby? And a decision like this can't be made in haste."

Libby closed her eyes, almost hypnotized by the slow, languid meter of his words, the depth of his voice. "N-no," she agreed.

"Definitely not," he said, his mouth almost upon hers. "It could take two—or three—days to decide."

"Ummm," agreed Libby, slipping deeper and deeper under his spell.

Jess had pressed her back against a counter, and his body formed an impassable barricade, leaning, hard and fragrant, into hers. He was tracing the length of her neck with soft, searing lips, tasting the hollow beneath her ear.

Finally he kissed her, first with tenderness, then with fervor, his tongue seeking and being granted sweet entry. This preliminary joining made Libby's whole entity pulse with an awareness of the primitive differences between his body and her own. Where she was soft and yielding, he was fiercely hard. Her nipples pouted into tiny peaks, crying out for his attention.

Seeming to sense that, Jess unbuttoned her blouse with deft, brazen fingers that felt warm against her skin. He opened the front catch on her bra, admired the pink-tipped lushness that seemed to grow richer and rounder under his gaze.

Idly he bent to kiss one peak into ferocious submission, and Libby groaned, her head falling back. Etched against the clear roof, she saw the long needles of ponderosa pines splintering the spring moonlight into shards of silver.

After almost a minute of pleasure so keen that Libby was certain she couldn't bear it, Jess turned to the other breast, kissing, suckling, nipping softly with his teeth. And all the while, he worked the opposite nipple skillfully with his fingers, putting it through delicious paces.

Libby was almost mindless by the time she felt the snap and zipper of her jeans give way, and her hands were still tangled in his dark hair as he knelt. Down came the jeans, her panties with them.

She could manage no more than a throaty gasp as his hands stroked the smooth skin of her thighs, the V of curls at their junction. She felt his breath there, warm, promising to cherish.

Libby trembled as he sought entrance with a questioning kiss, unveiled her with fingers that would not await permission.

As his tongue first touched the tenderness that had been hidden, his hands came to Libby's hips, pressing her down onto this fiery, inescapable glory. Only when she pleaded did he tug her fully into his mouth and partake of her.

Jess enjoyed Libby at his leisure, demanding her essence, showing no mercy even when she cried out and shuddered upon him in a final, soaring triumph. When her own chants of passion had ceased, she was conscious of his.

Jess still knelt before her, his every touch saying that he was worshiping, but there was sweet mastery in his manner, too. After one kiss of farewell, he gently drew her jeans and panties back into place and stood.

Libby stared at him, amazed at his power over her. He smiled at her wonder, though there was a spark of that same emotion deep in his eyes, and then lifted her off her feet and into his arms.

Say "I love you," Libby thought with prayerful fervor.

"I need you," he said instead.

And, for the moment, it was enough.

Stars peeked through the endlessly varied patterns the fallen pine needles made on the glass roof, as if to see and assess the glory that glowed beneath. Libby preened under their celestial jealousy and cuddled closer to Jess's hard, sheet-entangled frame.

"Why didn't you ever marry, Jess?" she asked, tracing a soft path across his chest with her fingers.

The mattress shifted as he moved to put one arm around Libby and draw her nearer still. "I don't know. It always seemed that marriage could wait."

"Didn't you even come close?"

Jess sighed, his fingers moving idly in her hair. "A couple of times I seriously considered it, yes. I guess it bothered me, subliminally, that I was looking these women over as though they were livestock or something. This one would have beautiful children, that one would like living on the ranch—that sort of thing."

"I see."

Jess stiffened slightly beneath the patterns she was making in the soft swirls of hair on his chest, and she felt the question coming long before he uttered it.

"What attracted you to Aaron Strand?"

Libby had been pondering that mystery herself, ever since her marriage to Aaron had begun to dissolve. Now, suddenly, she was certain that she understood. Weak though he might be, Aaron Strand was tall, dark-haired, broad in the shoulders. He had given the impression of strength and self-assurance, qualities that any woman would find appealing.

"I guess I thought he was strong, like Dad," she said, because she couldn't quite amend the sentence to a full truth and admit that she had probably superimposed Jess's image over Aaron's in the first place.

"Ummm," said Jess noncommittally.

"Of course, he is actually very weak."

Jess offered no comment.

"I guess my mistake," Libby went on quietly, "was in seeing myself through Aaron's eyes. He made me feel so worthless..."

"Maybe that made him feel better about himself."

"Maybe. But I still hate him, Jess—isn't that awful? I still hate him for leaving Jonathan in the lurch like that, especially."

"It isn't awful, it's human. It appears that you and Jonathan needed more than he had to give. Unconsciously, you probably measured him against Ken, and whatever else he is, your dad is a hard act to follow, Libby."

"Yes," said Libby, but she was thinking: *I didn't measure Aaron against Dad. God help me, Jess, I measured him against you.*

Jess turned over in a graceful, rolling motion, so that he was above her, his head and shoulders blocking out the light of the stars. "Enough heavy talk, woman. I came here to—"

"Buy a car?" broke in Libby, her tone teasing and full of love.

He nuzzled his face between her warm, welcoming breasts. "My God," he said, his voice muffled by her satin flesh, "what an innocent you are, Libby Kincaid!" One of his hands came down, gentle and mischievous, to squeeze her bottom. "Nice upholstery."

Libby gasped and arched her back as his mouth slid up over the rounding of her breast to claim its peak. "Not much mileage," she choked out.

Jess laughed against the nipple he was tormenting so methodically. "A definite plus." His hand moved between her thighs to assert an ancient mastery, and his breath quickened at Libby's immediate response. "Starts easily," he muttered, sipping at her nipple now, tugging it into an obedient little point.

Libby was beyond the game now, rising and falling on the velvet swells of need he was stirring within her. "I...Oh, God, Jess...what are you...ooooh!"

Somehow, Jess managed to turn on the bedside lamp without interrupting the searing pace his right hand was setting for Libby's body. "You are a goddess," he said.

The fevered dance continued, even though Libby willed herself to lie still. Damn him, he was watching her, taking pleasure from the unbridled response she could not help giving. Her heart raced with exertion, blood boiled in every vein, and Jess's lazy smile was lost in a silver haze.

She sobbed out his name, groping for his shoulders with her hands, holding on. Then, shuddering violently, she tumbled into some chasm where there was no sound but the beat of her own heart.

"You like doing that, don't you?" she snapped when she could see again, breathe again.

"Yes," replied Jess without hesitation.

Libby scrambled into a sitting position, blue eyes shooting flames. "Bastard," she said.

He met her gaze placidly. "What's the matter with you?"

Libby wasn't quite sure of the answer to that question. "It just...it just bothers me that you were...you were looking at me," she faltered, covering her still-pulsing breasts with the bedclothes.

With a deliberate motion of his hands, Jess removed the covers again, and Libby's traitorous nipples puckered in response to his brazen perusal. "Why?" he asked.

Libby's cheeks ached with color, and she lowered her eyes. Instantly Jess caught her chin in a gentle grasp, made her look at him again.

"Sweetheart, you're not ashamed, are you?"

Libby couldn't reply, she was so confused.

His hand slid, soothing, from Libby's chin to the side of her face. "You were giving yourself to me, Libby, trusting me. Is there shame in that?"

She realized that there wasn't, not the way she loved this brazen, tender, outlandish man. If only she dared to tell him verbally what her body already had.

He kissed her softly, sensing her need for greater reassurance. "Exquisite," he said. "Even ordinarily, you are exquisite. But when you let me love you, you go beyond that. You move me on a level where I've never even been touched before."

Say it now, Libby urged silently, *say you love me.*

But she had to be satisfied with what he had already said, for it was immediately clear that there would be no poetic avowals of devotion forthcoming. He'd said she was exquisite, that she moved him, but he'd made no declaration.

For this reason, there was a measure of sadness in the lovemaking that followed.

Long after Jess slept, exhausted, beside her, Libby lay awake, aching. She wanted, needed more from Jess than his readily admitted lust. So much more.

And yet, if a commitment were offered, would Libby want to accept it? Weren't there already too many conflicts complicating their lives? Though she tried to shut out the memory, Libby couldn't forget that Jess had believed her capable of carrying on with his brother and hurting her cousin and dearest friend in the process. Nor could she forget the wedge that had been driven between them the first time they'd made love, when she'd slipped and uttered words that had made him feel as though she'd used him to prove herself as a woman.

Of course, they had come together again, despite these things, but that was of no comfort to Libby. If they were to achieve any real closeness, more than just their bodies would have to be in accord.

After several hours, Libby fell into a fitful, dream-ridden sleep. When morning came, casting bright sunlight through the expanse of glass overhead, she was alone in the tousled bed.

"Lib!"

She went to the edge of the loft, peering down over the side. "What?" she retorted, petulant in the face of Jess's freshly showered, bright-and-shiny good cheer.

He waved a cooking spatula with a flourish. "One egg or two?"

"Drop dead," she replied flatly, frowning at the ladder.

Jess laughed. "Watch it. You'll get my hopes up with such tender words."

"What's this damned ladder for, anyway?"

"Are you this grouchy every morning?" he countered.

"Only when I've engaged in illicit sex the night before!" Libby snapped, scowling. "I believe I asked you about the ladder?"

"It's for climbing up and down." Jess shrugged.

Libby's head throbbed, and her eyes felt puffy and sore. "Given time, I probably could have figured out that much!"

Jess chuckled and shook his head, as if in sympathy.

Libby grasped the top of the peculiar ladder in question and gave it a vigorous shake. It was immovable. Her puzzlement made her feel even more irritable and, for no consciously conceived reason, she put out her tongue at Jess Barlowe and whirled away from the edge of the loft, out of his view.

His laughter rang out as she stumbled into the bathroom and turned on the water in the shower stall.

Once she had showered and brushed her teeth, Libby began to feel semihuman. With this came contrition for the snappish way she had greeted Jess minutes before. It wasn't his fault, after all, that he was so nauseatingly happy in the mornings.

Grinning a mischievous grin, Libby rummaged through the suitcase she had so hastily packed and found the T-shirt she had bought for Jess the day before, when she'd come to Kalispell with Cathy. She pulled the garment on over her head and, in a flash of daring, swung over the loft to climb down the ladder.

Her reward was a low, appreciative whistle.

"Now I know why that ladder was built," Jess said. "The view from down here is great.

Libby was embarrassed; she'd thought Jess was in the kitchen and thus unable to see her novel descent from the loft. Reaching the floor, she whirled, her face crimson, to glare at him.

Jess read the legend printed on the front of the T-shirt, which was so big that it reached almost to her knees, and laughed explosively. "'If it feels good, do it'?" he marveled.

Libby's glare simply would not stay in place, no matter how hard she tried to sustain it. Her mouth twitched and a chuckle escaped her and then she was laughing as hard as Jess was.

Given the situation, his words came as a shock.

"Libby, will you marry me?"

She stared at him, bewildered, afraid to hope. "What?"

The jade eyes were gentle now, still glistening with residual laughter. "Don't make me repeat it, princess."

"I think the eggs are burning," said Libby in tones made wooden by surprise.

"Wrong. I've already eaten mine, and yours are congealing on your plate. What's your answer, Kincaid?"

Libby's throat ached; something about the size of her heart was caught in it. "I...what..."

"I thought you only talked in broken sentences at the height of passion. Are you really as surprised as all that?"

"Yes!" croaked Libby after a struggle.

The broad shoulders, accentuated rather than hidden by a soft yellow sweater, moved in a shrug. "It seemed like a good solution to me."

"A solution? To what?"

"All our separate and combined problems," answered Jess airily. Persuasively. "Think about it, Lib. Stacey couldn't very well hassle you anymore, could he? And you could stay on the ranch."

Despite the companionable delivery, Jess's words made Libby's soul ache. "Those are solutions for me. What problems would marriage solve for you?"

"We're good in bed," he offered, shattering Libby with what he seemed to mean as a compliment.

"It takes more than that!"

"Does it?"

Libby was speechless, though a voice inside her kept screaming silly, sentimental things. *What about love? What about babies and leftover meatloaf and filing joint tax returns?*

"You dad would be happy," Jess added, and he couldn't have hurt Libby more if he'd raised his hand and slapped her.

"My dad? My *dad?*"

Jess turned away, seemingly unaware of the effect his convoluted proposal was having on Libby. He looked like exactly what he was: a trained, skillful attorney pleading a weak case. "You want children, don't you? And I know you like living on the ranch."

Libby broke in coldly. "I guess I meet all the qualifications. I do want children. I do like living on the Circle Bar B. So why don't you just hog-tie me and brand me a Barlowe?"

Every muscle in Jess's body seemed to tense, but he did not turn around to face her. "There is one other reason," he offered.

For all her fury and hurt, hope sang through Libby's system like the wind unleashed on a wide prairie. "What's that?"

He drew a deep breath, his hands clasped behind him, courtroom style. "There would be no chance, for now at least, of Cathy being hurt."

Cathy. Libby's knees weakened; she groped for the sofa behind her, fell into it. Good God, was his devotion to Cathy so deep that he would marry the woman he considered a threat to her happiness, just to protect her?

"I am so damned tired of hearing about Cathy," she said evenly, tugging the end of the T-shirt down over her knees for something to do.

Now Jess turned, looked at her with unreadable eyes.

Even though Libby felt the guilt she always did whenever she was even mildly annoyed with Cathy, she stood her ground. "A person doesn't have to be handicapped to hurt, you know," she said in a small and rather uncertain voice.

Jess folded his arms and the sunlight streaming in through the glass ceiling glittered in his dark hair. "I know that," he said softly. "And we're all handicapped in some way, aren't we?"

She couldn't tell whether he was reprimanding her or offering an olive branch. Huddling on the couch, feeling foolish in the T-shirt she had put on as a joke, Libby knotted her hands together in her lap. "I suppose that remark was intended as a barb."

Jess came to sit beside her on the couch, careful not to touch her. "Libby, it wasn't. I'm tired of exchanging verbal shots with you—

that was fine when we had to ride the same school bus every day, but we're adults now. Let's try to act as such.''

Libby looked into Jess's face and was thunderstruck by how much she cared for him, needed him. And yet, even a week before, she would have said she despised Jess and meant it. All that rancor they'd borne each other—had it really been passion instead?

''I don't understand any of this.''

Jess took one of her hands into both of his. ''Do you want to marry me or not?''

Both fear and joy rose within Libby. In order to look inward at her own feelings, she was forced to look away from him. She did love Jess, there was absolutely no doubt of that, and she wanted, above all things, to be his wife. She wanted children and, at thirty-one, she often had the feeling that time was getting short. Dammit, why couldn't he say he loved her?

''Would you be faithful to me, Jess?''

He touched her cheek, turning her face without apparent effort, so that she was again looking into those bewitching green eyes. ''I would never betray you.''

Aaron had said those words too. Aaron had been so very good with words.

But this was Jess, Libby reminded herself. Jess, not Aaron. ''I couldn't give up my career,'' she said. ''It's a crazy business, Jess, and sometimes there are long stretches of time when I don't do much of anything. Other times, I have to work ten- or twelve-hour days to meet a deadline.''

Jess did not seem to be dissuaded.

Libby drew a deep breath. ''Of course, I'd go on being known as Libby Kincaid. I never took Aaron's name and I don't see any sense in taking yours—should I agree to marry you, that is.''

He seemed amused, but she had definitely touched a sore spot. That became immediately obvious. ''Wait a minute, lady. Professionally, you can be known by any name you want. Privately, however, you'll be Libby Barlowe.''

Libby was secretly pleased, but because she was angry and hurt that he didn't love her, she lifted her chin and snapped, ''You have to have that Circle Bar B brand on everything you consider yours, don't you?''

''You are not a thing, Libby,'' he replied rationally, ''but I want at least that much of a commitment. Call it male ego if you must, but I want my wife to be Mrs. Barlowe.''

Libby swallowed. ''Fair enough,'' she said.

Jess sat back on the sofa, folded his arms again. ''I'm waiting,'' he said, and the mischievous glint was back in his eyes.

''For what?''

''An answer to my original question.''

Fool, fool! Don't you ever learn, Libby Kincaid? Don't you ever learn? Libby quieted the voice in her mind and lifted her chin. Life was short, and unpredictable in the bargain. Maybe Jess would learn to love her the way she loved him. Wasn't that kind of happiness worth a risk?

''I'll marry you,'' she said.

Jess kissed her with an exuberance that soon turned to desire.

Jess frowned at the sleek showroom sports car, his tongue making one cheek protrude. ''What do you think?'' he asked.

Libby assessed the car again. ''It isn't you.''

He grinned, ignoring the salesman's quiet disappointment. ''You're right.''

Neither, of course, had the last ten cars they had looked at been ''him.'' The sports cars seemed to cramp his long legs, while the big luxury vehicles were too showy.

''How about a truck?'' Libby suggested.

''Do you know how many trucks there are on the ranch?'' he countered. ''Besides, some yokel would probably paint on the family logo when I wasn't looking.''

Libby deliberately widened her eyes. ''That would be truly terrible!''

He made a face at her, but when he spoke, his words were delivered in a touchingly serious way. ''We could get another station wagon and fill the backseat with kids and dogs.''

Libby smiled at the image. ''A grungy sort of heaven,'' she mused.

Jess laughed. "And of course there would be lots of room to make love."

The salesman cleared his throat and discreetly walked away.

Chapter 9

"I think you shocked that salesman," observed Libby, snapping the seat belt into place as Jess settled behind the wheel of their rental car.

Jess shrugged. "By wanting a station wagon?" he teased.

"By wanting *me* in the station wagon," clarified Libby.

Jess turned the key in the ignition and shifted gears. "He's lucky I didn't list all the other places I'd like to have you. The hood, for instance. And then there's the roof..."

Libby colored richly as they pulled into the slow traffic. "Jess!"

He frowned speculatively. "And, of course, on the ladder at the condo."

"The ladder?"

Jess flung her a brazen grin. "Yeah. About halfway up."

"Don't you think about anything but sex?"

"I seem to have developed a fixation, Kincaid—just since you came back, of course."

She couldn't help smiling. "Of course."

Nothing more was said until they'd driven through the quiet, well-kept streets to the courthouse. Jess parked the car and turned to Libby with a comical leer. "Are you up to a blood test and a little small-town bureaucracy, Kincaid?"

Libby felt a wild, twisting thrill in the pit of her stomach. A marriage license. He wanted to get a marriage license. In three short days, she could be bound to Jess Barlowe for life. At least, she *hoped* it would be for life.

After drawing a deep breath, Libby unsnapped her seat belt and got out of the car.

Twenty minutes later, the ordeal was over. The fact that the wedding itself wouldn't take nearly as long struck Libby as an irony.

On the sidewalk, Jess caught her elbow in one hand and helped her back into the car. While he must have noticed that she was preoccupied, he was chivalrous enough not to say so.

"Stop at that supermarket!" Libby blurted when they'd been driving for some minutes.

Jess gave her a quizzical look. "Supermarket?"

"Yes. They sell food there, among other necessary items."

Jess frowned. "Why can't we just eat in restaurants? There are several good ones—"

"Restaurants?" Libby cried with mock disdain. "How can I prove what a great catch I am if I don't cook something for you?"

Jess's right hand left the steering wheel to slide languorously up and down Libby's linen-skirted thigh. "Relax, sweetheart," he said in a rather good imitation of Humphrey Bogart. "I already know you're good in the kitchen."

The obvious reference to last night's episode in that room unsettled Libby. "You delight in saying outrageous things, don't you?" she snapped.

"I delight in *doing* outrageous things."

"You'll get no argument on that score, fella," she retorted acidly.

The car came to a stop in front of the supermarket, which was in the center of a small shopping mall. Libby noticed that Jess's gaze strayed to a jewelry store down the way.

"I'll meet you inside," he said, and then he was gone.

Though Libby told herself that she was being silly and sentimental, she was pleased to think that Jess might be shopping for a ring.

The giddy, romantic feeling faded when she selected a shopping cart inside the supermarket, however. She was wallowing in gushy dreams, behaving like a seventeen-year-old virgin. Of *course* Jess would buy a ring, but only because it would be expected of him.

Glumly Libby went about selecting items from a mental grocery list she had been composing since she'd checked the refrigerator and cupboards at the condominium and found them all but empty.

Taking refuge in practical matters, she frowned at a display of cabbage and wondered how much food to buy. Jess hadn't said how long they would be staying in Kalispell, beyond the time it would take to find the car he wanted.

Shrugging slightly, Libby decided to buy provisions for three days. Because that was the required waiting period for a marriage license, they would probably be in town at least that long.

She looked down at her slacks and brightly colored peasant blouse. The wedding ceremony was going to be an informal one, obviously, but she would still need a new dress, and she wanted to buy a wedding band for Jess, too.

She pushed her cart along the produce aisle, woodenly selecting bean sprouts, fresh broccoli, onions. Her first wedding had been a quiet one, too, devoid of lace and flowers and music, and something within her mourned those things.

They hadn't even discussed a honeymoon, and what kind of ceremony would this be, without Ken, without Cathy, without Senator Barlowe and Marion Bradshaw, the housekeeper?

A box seemed to float up out of the cart, but Libby soon saw that it was clasped in a strong sun-browned hand.

"I hate cereals that crunch," Jess said, and his eyes seemed to be looking inside Libby, seeing the dull ache she would rather have kept hidden. "What's wrong, love?"

Libby fought back the sudden silly tears that ached in her throat and throbbed behind her eyes. "Nothing," she lied.

Jess was not fooled. "You want Ken to come to the wedding," he guessed.

Libby lowered her head slightly. "He was hurt when Aaron and I got married without even telling him first," she said.

There was a short silence before a housewife, tagged by two pre-schoolers, gave Libby's cart a surreptitious bump with her own, tacitly demanding access to the cereal display. Libby wrestled her groceries out of the way and looked up at Jess, waiting for his response.

He smiled, touched her cheek. "Tell you what. We'll call the ranch and let everybody know we're getting married. That way, if they want to be there, they can. And if you want frills and flash, princess, we can have a formal wedding later."

The idea of a second wedding, complete with the trimmings, appealed to Libby's romantic soul. She smiled at the thought. "You would do that? You would go through it all over again, just for show?"

"Not for show, princess. For you."

The housewife made an appreciative sound and Libby started a little, having completely forgotten their surroundings.

Jess laughed and the subject was dropped. They walked up one aisle and down another, dropping the occasional pertinent item into the cart, arguing good-naturedly about who would do the cooking after they were married.

The telephone was ringing as Libby unlocked the front door of the condo, so she left Jess to carry in their bags of groceries and ran to answer it, expecting to hear Ken's voice, or Marion Bradshaw's, relaying some message from Cathy.

A cruel wave of *déjà vu* washed over her when she heard Aaron's smooth, confident greeting. "Hello, Libby."

"What do you want?" Libby rasped, too stunned to hang up. How on earth had he gotten that number?

"I told you before, dear heart," said Aaron smoothly. "I want a child."

Libby was conscious of Jess standing at her elbow, the shopping bags clasped in his arms. "You're insane!" she cried into the receiver.

"Maybe so, but not insane enough to let my grandmother hand over an empire to someone else. She has doubts, you know, about my dependability."

"I wonder why!"

"Don't be sarcastic, sugarplum. My request isn't really all that unreasonable, considering all I stand to lose."

"It is unreasonable, Aaron! In fact, it's sick!" At this point Libby slammed down the receiver with a vengeance. She was trembling so hard that Jess hastily shunted the grocery bags onto a side table and took her into his arms.

"What was that all about?" he asked when Libby had recovered herself a little.

"He's horrible," Libby answered, distracted and very much afraid. "Oh, Jess, he's a monster—"

"What did he say?" Jess pressed quietly.

"Aaron wants me to have his baby! Jess, he actually had the gall to ask me to come back, just so he can produce an heir and please his grandmother!"

Jess's hand was entangled in her hair now, comforting her. "It's all right, Lib. Everything will be all right."

Then why am I so damned scared? Libby asked herself, but she put on a brave face for Jess and even managed a smile. "Let's call my dad," she said.

Jess nodded, kissed her forehead. And then he took up the grocery bags again and carried them into the kitchen while Libby dialed her father's telephone number.

There was no answer, which was not surprising, considering that it was still early. Ken would be working, and because of the wide range of his responsibilities, he could be anywhere on the 150,000 acres that made up the Circle Bar B.

Sounds from the kitchen indicated that Jess was putting the food away, and Libby wandered in, needing to be near him.

"No answer?" he asked, tossing a package of frozen egg rolls into the refrigerator-freezer.

"No answer," confirmed Libby. "I should have known, I guess."

Jess turned, gave her a gentle grin. "You did know, Libby. But you needed to touch base just then, and going through the motions was better than nothing."

"When did you get so smart?"

"Last Tuesday, I think," he answered ponderously. "Know something? You look a little tired. Why don't you climb up that ladder that bugs you so much and take a nap?"

Libby arched one eyebrow. "While you do what?"

His answer was somewhat disappointing. "While I go back to town for a few hours," he said. "I have some things to do."

"Like what?"

He grinned. "Like picking up some travel brochures, so we can decide where to take our honeymoon."

Libby felt a rush of pleasure despite the weariness she was suddenly very aware of. Had it been there all along, or was she tired simply because this subtle hypnotist had suggested it to her? "Does it matter where we honeymoon?"

"Not really," Jess replied, coming disturbingly close, kissing Libby's forehead. "But I like having you all to myself. I can't help thinking that the farther we get from home right now, the better off we're going to be."

A tremor of fear brushed against Libby's heart, but it was quickly stilled when Jess caught her right earlobe between gentle teeth and then told her in bluntly erotic terms what he had wanted to do to her on the supermarket checkout counter.

When he'd finished, Libby was wildly aroused and, at the same time, resigned to the fact that when she crawled into that sun-washed bed up in the loft, she would be alone. "Rat," she said.

Jess swatted her backside playfully. "Later," he promised, and then calmly left the condo to attend to his errands.

Libby went obediently up to the bedroom, using the stairs rather than the ladder, and yawned as she stripped down to her lacy camisole and tap pants. She shouldn't be having a nap now, she told herself, when she had things of her own to do—choosing Jess's ring, for one thing, and buying a special dress, for another....

She was asleep only seconds after slipping beneath the covers.

Libby stirred, indulged in a deliciously lazy stretch. Someone was trailing soft, warm kisses across her collarbone—or was she dreaming? Just in case she was, she did not open her eyes.

Cool air washed over her breasts as the camisole was gently displaced. "Ummm," she said.

"Good dream?" asked Jess, moistening one pulsing nipple to crisp attention with his tongue.

"Oooooh," answered Libby, arching her back slightly, her eyes still closed, her head pressed into the silken pillow in eager, soft surrender. "Very good."

Jess left that nipple to subject its twin to a tender plundering that caused Libby to moan with delight. Her hips writhed slightly, calling to their powerful counterpart.

Jess heard their silent plea, slid the satiny tap pants down, down, away. "You're so warm, Libby," he said in a ragged whisper. "So soft and delicious." The camisole was unlaced, laid aside reverently, like the wrapping on some splendid gift. Kisses rained down on Libby's sleep-warmed, swollen breasts, her stomach, her thighs.

At last she opened her eyes, saw Jess's wondrous nakedness through a haze of sweet, sleepy need. As he ventured nearer and nearer to the silk-sheltered sanction of her womanhood, she instinctively reached up to clasp the brass railings on the headboard of the bed, anchoring herself to earth.

Jess parted the soft veil, admired its secret with a throaty exclamation of desire and a searing kiss.

A plea was wrenched from Libby, and she tightened her grasp on the headboard.

For a few mind-sundering minutes Jess enjoyed the swelling morsel with his tongue. "More?" he asked, teasing her, knowing that she was already half-mad with the need of him.

"More," she whimpered as his fingers strayed to the pebblelike peaks of her breasts, plying them, sending an exquisite lacelike net of passion knitting its way through her body.

Another tormenting flick of his tongue. "Sweet," he said. And then he lifted Libby's legs, placing one over each of his shoulders, making her totally, beautifully vulnerable to him.

She cried out in senseless delirium as he took his pleasure, and she was certain that she would have been flung beyond the dark sky if not for her desperate grasp on the headboard.

Even after the highest peak had been scaled, Libby's sated body convulsed again and again, caught in the throes of other, smaller releases.

Still dazed, Libby felt Jess's length stretch out upon her, seeking that sweetest and most intimate solace. In a burst of tender rebellion, she thrust him off and demanded loving revenge.

Soon enough, it was Jess who grasped the gleaming brass railings lest he soar away, Jess who chanted a desperate litany.

Wickedly, Libby took her time, savoring him, taking outrageous liberties with him. Finally she conquered him, and his cry of joyous surrender filled her with love almost beyond bearing.

His breathing still ragged, his face full of wonder, Jess drew Libby down, so that she lay beside him. With his hands he explored her, igniting tiny silver fires in every curve and hollow of her body.

This time, when he came to her, she welcomed him with a ferocious thrust of her hips, alternately setting the pace and following Jess's lead. When the pinnacle was reached, each was lost in the echoing, triumphant cry of the other, and bits of a broken rainbow showered down around them.

Sitting Indian-style on the living-room sofa, Libby twisted the telephone cord between her fingers and waited for her father's response to her announcement.

It was a soft chuckle.

"You aren't the least bit surprised!" Libby accused, marveling.

"I figured anybody that fought and jawed as much as you two did had to end up hitched," replied Ken Kincaid in his colorful way. "Did you let Cleave know yet?"

"Jess will, in a few minutes. Will you tell Cathy for me, please?"

Ken promised that he would.

Libby swallowed hard, gave Jess a warning glare as he moved to slide an exploring hand inside the top of her bathrobe. "Aren't you going to say that we're rushing into this or something like that? Some people will think it's too soon—"

"It was damned near too late," quipped Ken. "What time is the ceremony again?"

There were tears in Libby's eyes, though she had never been happier. "Two o'clock on Friday, at the courthouse."

"I'll be there, dumplin'. Be happy."

The whole room was distorted into a joyous blur. "I will, Dad. I love you."

"I love you, too," he answered with an ease that was typical of him. "Take care and I'll see you Friday."

"Right," said Libby, sniffling as she gently replaced the receiver. Jess chuckled, touched her chin. "Tears? I'm insulted."

Libby made a face and shoved the telephone into his lap. "Call your father," she said.

Jess settled back in the sofa as he dialed the number of the senator's house in Washington, balancing the telephone on one blue-jeaned knee. While he tried to talk to his father in normal tones, Libby ran impudent fingertips over his bare chest, twining dark hair into tight curls, making hard buttons of deliciously vulnerable nipples.

With a mock-glare and a motion of his free arm, Jess tried to field her blatant advances. She simply knelt astraddle of his lap and had her way with him, her fingers tracing a path of fire around his mouth, along his neck, over his nipples.

Jess caught the errant hand in a desperate hold, only to be immediately assaulted by the other. Mischief flashed in his jade eyes, followed by an I'll-get-you-for-this look. "See you then," he said to his father, his voice a little deeper than usual and very carefully modulated. There was a pause, and then he added, "Oh, don't worry, I will. In about five seconds, I'm going to lay Libby on the coffee table and kiss her in all the best places. Yes, sir, by the time I get through with her, she'll be—"

Falling into the trap, Libby colored, snatched the receiver out of Jess's hand and pressed it to her ear. The line was, of course, dead.

Jess laughed as she assessed him murderously. "You deserved that," he said.

Libby moved to struggle off his lap, still crimson in the face, her heart pounding with embarrassment. But Jess's hands were strong on her upper arms, holding her in place.

"Oh, no you don't, princess. You're not getting out of this so easily."

"What—"

Jess smiled languidly, still holding her fast with one hand, undoing his jeans with the other. "You let this horse out of the barn, lady. Now you're going to ride it."

Libby gasped as she felt him prod her, hard and insistent, and fierce needs surged through her even as she raged at the affront. She was powerless, both physically and emotionally, to break away from him.

Just barely inside her, Jess reached out and calmly untied her bathrobe, baring her breasts, her stomach, her captured hips. His green eyes glittered as he stroked each satiny expanse in turn, allowing Libby more and more of him until she was fully his.

Seemingly unmoved himself, Jess took wicked delight in Libby's capture and began guiding her soft, trim hips up and down, endlessly up and down, upon him. All the while, he used soft words to lead her through flurries of silver snow to the tumultuous release beyond.

When her vision cleared, Libby saw that Jess had been caught in his own treachery. She watched in love and wonder as he gave himself up to raging sensation—his head fell back, his throat worked, his eyes were sightless.

Gruffly Jess pleaded with Libby, and she accelerated the up-and-down motion of her hips until he shuddered violently beneath her, stiffened and growled her name.

"Mess with me, will you?" she mocked, grinning down at him.

Jess began to laugh, between rasping breaths. When his mirth had subsided and he didn't have to drag air into his lungs, he caressed her with his eyes. In fact, it was almost as though he'd said he loved her.

Libby was still incredibly moved by the sweet spectacle she had seen played out in his face as he submitted to her, and she understood then why he so loved to watch her respond while pleasuring her.

Jess reached up, touched away the tear that tickled on her cheek. It would have been a perfect time for those three special words she so wanted to hear, but he did not say them.

Hurt and disappointed, Libby wrenched her bathrobe closed and tried to rise from his lap, only to be easily thwarted. Jess's hands opened the robe again, his eyes perused her and then came back to her face, silently daring her to hide any part of her body or soul from him.

With an insolent finger he brushed the pink buttons at the tips of her full breasts, smiled as they instantly obeyed him. Apparently satisfied with their pert allegiance, Jess moved on to trace patterns of fire on Libby's stomach, the rounding of her hips, the sensitive hollow at the base of her throat.

Jess seemed determined to prove that he could subdue Libby at will, and he only smiled at the startled gasp she gave when it became apparent that all his prowess had returned in full and glorious force.

He slid her robe off her shoulders then and removed it entirely. They were still joined, and Libby shivered as he toyed idly with her breasts, weighing them in his hands, pressing them together, thumbing their aching tips until they performed for him.

Presently Jess left his sumptuous playthings to tamper elsewhere, wreaking still more havoc, eliciting little anxious cries from a bedazzled Libby.

"What do you want, princess?" he asked in a voice of liquid steel.

Libby was wild upon him, her hands clutching desperately at his shoulders, her knees wide. "I want to be...under you. Oh, Jess... under you..."

In a swift and graceful motion, he turned her, was upon her. The movement unleashed the passion Jess had been able to contain until then, and he began to move over her and within her, his thrusts deep and powerful, his words ragged and incoherent.

As their very souls collided and then fused together, imitating their bodies, it was impossible to tell who had prevailed over whom.

Libby awakened first, entangled with Jess, amazed that they could have slept the whole night on that narrow couch.

A smile lifted one corner of her mouth as she kissed Jess's temple tenderly and then disengaged herself, careful not to disturb him. Heaven knew, he had a right to be tired.

Twenty minutes later, when Libby returned from her shower, dressed in sandals, white slacks and a lightweight yellow sweater, Jess was still sleeping. She could empathize, for her own slumber had been fathomless.

"I love you," she said, and then she went to the kitchen and wrote a quick note on the blackboard there, explaining that she had gone shopping and would be back within a few hours.

Getting into the rented car, which was parked in the gravel driveway near the front door, Libby spotted a cluster of colorful travel brochures fanned out on the opposite seat. Each one touted a different paradise: Acapulco, the Bahamas, Maui.

As Libby slid the key into the ignition and started the car, she grinned. She had it on good authority that paradise was only a few yards away, on the couch where Jess lay sleeping.

The day was a rich mixture of blue and green, set off by the fierce green of pine trees and the riotous blooms of crocuses and daffodils in quiet front yards. Downtown, Libby found a parking place immediately, locked the car and hurried on about her business.

Her first stop was a jewelry store, and while she had anticipated a great quandary, the decision of which wedding band to buy for Jess proved an easy one. Her eyes were immediately drawn to one particular ring, forged of silver, inset with polished chips of turquoise.

Once the jeweler had assured her the band could be resized if it didn't fit Jess's finger, Libby bought it.

In an art-supply store she purchased a sketching pad and a gum eraser and some charcoal pencils. Sweet as this interlude with Jess had been, Libby missed her work and her fingers itched to draw. Too, there were all sorts of new ideas for the comic strip bubbling in her mind.

From the art store, Libby pressed on to a good-sized department store. None of the dresses there quite struck her fancy, and she moved on to one boutique and then another.

Finally, in a small and wickedly expensive shop, she found that special dress, that dress of dresses, the one she would wear when she married Jess Barlowe.

It was a clingy creation of burgundy silk, showing off her figure, bringing a glow of color to her cheeks. There were no ruffles of lace or fancy buttons—only a narrow belt made of the same fabric as the dress itself. It was the last word in elegant simplicity, that garment, and Libby adored it.

Carrying the dress box and the heavy bag of art supplies, she hurried back to the car and locked her purchases inside. It was only a little after ten, and Libby wanted to find shoes that would match her dress.

The shoes proved very elusive, and only after almost an hour of searching did she find a pair that would do. Tired of shopping and anxious to see Jess again, Libby started home.

Some intuitive feeling made her uneasy as she drove toward the elegant condominium hidden in the tall trees. After crossing the wooden bridge and making the last turn, she knew why—Stacey's ice-blue Ferrari was parked in the driveway.

Don't be silly, Libby reprimanded herself, but she still felt alarmed. What if Stacey had come to try to talk her out of marrying Jess? What if Cathy was with him, and there was an unpleasant scene?

Determined not to let her imagination get the upper hand, Libby gathered up her loot from the shopping trip and got out of the car. As she approached the house, she caught sight of a familiar face at the window and was surprised all over again. Monica! What on earth was she doing here? Hadn't she left for Washington, D.C., with the senator?

Now Libby really hesitated. She remembered the proprietary looks the woman had given Jess as he swam that day in the pool at the main ranch house. Looks that had implied intimacy.

Libby sighed. So what if Jess and Monica had slept together? She could hardly have expected a man like him to live like a monk, and it wasn't as if Libby hadn't had a prior relationship herself, however unsatisfactory.

Despite the cool sanity of this logic, it hurt to imagine Jess making love with Monica—or with any other woman, for that matter.

Libby grappled with her purchases at the front door, reached for the knob. Before she could clasp it, the door opened.

Jess was standing there, shirtless, wearing jeans, his hair and suntanned chest still damp from a recent shower. Instead of greeting Libby with a smile, let alone a kiss, he scowled at her and stepped back almost grudgingly, as though he had considered refusing her entrance.

Bewildered and hurt, Libby resisted a primal instinct urging her to flee and walked in.

Monica had left the window and was now seated comfortably on the couch, her shapely legs crossed at the knee, a cocktail in her hand.

Libby took in the woman's sleek designer suit and felt shabby by comparison in her casual attire. "Hello, Monica."

"Libby," replied Monica with a polite nod.

The formalities dispensed with, Libby flung a hesitant look at Jess. Why was he glaring at her like that, as though he wanted to do her bodily harm? Why was his jawline so tight, and why was it that he clenched the towel draped around his neck in white-knuckled hands?

Before Libby could voice any of her questions, Stacey came out of the kitchen, raked her with guileless caramel eyes and smiled.

"Hello," he said, as though his very presence, under the circumstances, was not an outrage.

Libby only stared at him. She was very conscious of Jess, seething somewhere on the periphery of her vision, and of Monica, taking in the whole scene with detached amusement.

Suddenly Stacey was coming toward Libby, speaking words she couldn't seem to hear. Then he had the outright gall to kiss her, and Libby's inertia was broken.

She drew back her hand and slapped him, her dress box, purse and bag of art supplies falling to the floor.

Stacey reached out for her, caught her waist in his hands. She squirmed and flung one appealing look in Jess's direction.

Though he looked anything but chivalrous, he did intercede. "Leave Libby alone, Stacey."

Stacey paled. "I've left Cathy," he said, as though that settled everything. "Libby, we can be together now!"

Libby stumbled backward, stunned. Only when she came up against the hard barrier of Jess's soap-scented body did she stop. Wild relief went through her as he enclosed her in a steel-like protective embrace.

"Get out," he said flatly, addressing his brother.

Stacey hesitated, but then he reddened and left the condo in a huff, pulling Monica Summers behind him.

Chapter 10

Furious and shaken, Libby turned to glare at Jess. It was all too clear what had happened—Stacey had been telling more of his outrageous lies and Jess had believed them.

For a few moments he stubbornly returned her angry regard, but then he spread his hands in a gesture of concession and said, "I'm sorry."

Libby was trembling now, but she stooped to pick up her dress box, and the art-store bag. She couldn't look at Jess or he would see the tears that had clouded her eyes. "After all we've done and planned, how could you, Jess? How could you believe Stacey?"

He was near, very near—Libby was conscious of him in every sense. He moved to touch her, instantly stopped himself. "I said I was sorry."

Libby forgot that she'd meant to hide her tears and looked him full in the face. Her voice shook with anger when she spoke. "Sometimes being sorry isn't enough, Jess!" She carried the things she'd bought across the room, tossed them onto the couch. "Is this what our marriage is going to be like? Are we going to do just fine as long as we aren't around Stacey?"

Jess was standing behind her; his hands came to rest on her shoulders. "What can I say, Libby? I was jealous. That may not be right, but it's human."

Perhaps because she wanted so desperately to believe that everything would turn out all right, that a marriage to this wonderful, contradictory man would succeed, Libby set aside her doubts and turned to face Jess. The depth of her love for this erstwhile enemy still staggered her. "What did Stacey tell you?"

Jess drew in an audible breath, and for a moment there was a tightness in his jaw. Then he sighed and said, "He was sharing the glorious details of your supposed affair. And he had a remarkable grasp on what you like in bed, Libby."

The words were wounding, but Libby was strong. "Did it ever occur to you that maybe all women like essentially the same things?"

Jess didn't answer, but Libby could see that she had made her mark, and she rushed on.

"Exactly what was Monica's part in all this?" she demanded hotly. "Was she here to moderate your sexual discussion? Why the hell isn't she in Washington, where she belongs?"

Jess shrugged, obviously puzzled. "I'm not sure why she was here."

"I am! Once you were diverted from your disastrous course— marrying me—she was going to take you by the hand and lead you home!"

One side of Jess's mouth lifted in a grin. "I'm not the only one who is prone to jealousy, it appears."

"You were involved with her, weren't you?"

"Yes."

The bluntness of the answer took Libby unawares, but only for a moment. After all, had Jess said no, she would have known he was lying and that would have been devastating. "Did you love Monica?"

"No. If I had, I would have married her."

The possible portent of those words buoyed Libby's flagging spirits. "Passion wouldn't be enough?" she ventured.

"To base a marriage on? Never. Now, let's see what you bought today."

Let's see what you bought today. Libby's frustration knew no bounds, but she was damned if she was going to pry those three longed-for words out of him—she'd fished enough as it was. "I bought a wedding dress, for your information. And you're not going to see it until tomorrow, so don't pester me about it."

He laughed. "I like a woman who is loyal to her superstitions. What else did you purchase, milady?"

Libby's sense of financial independence, nurtured during the insecure days with Aaron, chafed under the question. "I didn't use your money, so what do you care?" she snapped.

Jess arched one eyebrow. "Another touchy subject rears its ugly head. I was merely curious, my love—I didn't ask for a meeting with your accountant."

Feeling foolish, Libby made a great project of opening the art-store bag and spreading its contents out on the couch.

Jess was grinning as he assessed the array of pencils, the large sketchbook. "Have I been boring you, princess?"

Libby pulled a face at him. "You could be called many things, Jess Barlowe, but you are definitely not boring."

"Thank you—I think. Shall we brave the car dealers of Kalispell again, or are you going to be busy?" The question was guileless, indicating that Jess would have understood if she wanted to stay and block out some of the ideas that had come to her.

After Aaron, who had viewed her cartooning as a childish hobby, Jess's attitude was a luxury. "I think I'd rather go with you," she said with a teasing smile. "If I don't you might come home with some motorized horror that has horns on its hood."

"Your faith in my good taste is positively underwhelming," he replied, walking toward the ladder, climbing its rungs to the loft in search of a shirt.

"You were right!" Libby called after him. "The view from down here is marvelous!"

During that foray into the jungle of car salesmen and gasoline-fed beasts, Libby spent most of her time in the passenger seat of Jess's rented car, sketching. Instead of drawing Liberated Lizzie, her cartoon character, however, she found herself reproducing Jess's image.

She imagined him looking out over the stunning view of prairies and mountains at home and drew him in profile, the wind ruffling his hair, a pensive look to his eyes and the set of his face. Another sketch showed him laughing, and still another, hidden away in the middle of the drawing pad, not meant for anyone else to see, mirrored the way Jess looked when he wanted her.

To field the responses the drawing evoked in her, Libby quickly sketched Cathy's portrait, and then Ken's. After that, strictly from memory, she drew a picture of Jonathan, full face, as he'd looked before his illness, then, on the same piece of paper, in a profile that revealed the full ravages of his disease.

She supposed it was morbid, including this aspect of the child, but to leave out his pain would have meant leaving out his courage, and Jonathan deserved better.

Touching his charcoal image with gentle, remembering fingers, Libby heard the echo of his voice in her mind. *Naturally I'm brave,* he'd told her once, at the end of a particularly difficult day. *I'm a Jedi knight, like Luke Skywalker.*

Smiling through a mist of tears, Libby added another touch to the sketch—a tiny figure of Jonathan, well and strong, wielding a light saber in valiant defense of the Rebel Alliance.

"That's terrific," observed a gentle voice.

Libby looked up quickly, surprised that she hadn't heard Jess get into the car, hadn't sensed his presence somehow. Because she couldn't speak just yet, she bit her lower lip and nodded an acknowledgment of the compliment.

"Could I take a closer look? Please?"

Libby extended the notebook and it was a gesture of trust, for these sketches were different from the panels for her comic strip. They were large pieces of her soul.

Jess was pensive as he examined the portraits of himself, Cathy, Ken. But the study of Jonathan was clearly his favorite, and he returned to it at intervals, taking in each line, each bit of shading, each unspoken cry of grief.

Finally, with a tenderness that made Libby love him even more than she had before, Jess handed the sketchbook back to her. "You are remarkably talented," he said, and then he had the good grace to look away while Libby recomposed herself.

"D-did you find a car you like?" she asked finally.

Jess smiled at her. "Actually, yes. That's why I came back—to get you."

"Me? Why?"

"Well, I don't want to buy the thing without your checking it out first. Suppose you hated it?"

It amazed Libby that such a thing mattered to him. She set the sketchbook carefully in the back seat and opened her car door to get out. "Lead on," she said, and the clean spring breeze braced her as it touched her face.

The vehicle in question was neither car nor truck, but a Land Rover. It was perfectly suited to the kind of life Jess led, and Libby approved of it with enthusiasm.

The deal was made, much to the relief of a salesman they had been plaguing, on and off, since the day before.

After some discussion, it was decided that they would keep the rental car until after the wedding, in case Libby needed it. Over a luncheon of steak and salad, which did much to settle her shaky nerves, Jess suggested that they start shopping all over again, for a second car.

Practical as it was, the thought exhausted Libby.

"You'll need transportation," Jess argued.

"I don't think I could face all those plaid sport jackets and test drives again," Libby replied with a sigh.

Jess laughed. "But you would like to have a car, wouldn't you?"

Libby shrugged. In New York, she had depended on taxis for transportation, but the ranch was different, of course. "I suppose."

"Aren't you choosy about the make, model—all that?"

"Wheels are wheels," she answered with another shrug.

"Hmmmm," Jess said speculatively, and then the subject was changed. "What about our honeymoon? Any place in particular you'd like to go?"

"Your couch," Libby said, shocked at her own audacity.

Again Jess laughed. "That is patently unimaginative."

"Hardly, considering the things we did there," Libby replied, immediately lifting a hand to her mouth. What was wrong with her? Why was she suddenly spouting these outlandish remarks?

Jess bent forward, conjured up a comical leer. "I wish we were on the ranch," he said in a low voice. "I'd take you somewhere private and make violent love to you."

Libby felt a familiar heat simmering inside her, melting through her pelvis. "Jess."

He drew some bills from his wallet, tossed them onto the table. "Let's get out of here while I can still walk," he muttered.

Libby laughed. "I think it's a good thing we're driving separate cars today," she teased, though secretly she was just as anxious for privacy as Jess was.

He groaned. "One more word, lady, and I'll spread you out on this table."

Libby's heart thudded at the bold suggestion and pumped color over her breasts and into her face. She tried to look indignant, but the fact was that she had been aroused by the remark and Jess knew it—his grin was proof of that.

As they left the restaurant, he bent close to her and described the fantasy in vivid detail, sparing nothing. And later, on the table in the condo's kitchen, he turned it into a wildly satisfying reality.

That afternoon, Libby took another nap. Due to the episode just past, her dreams were deliciously erotic.

As he had before, Jess awakened her with strategic kisses. "Hi," he said when she opened her eyes.

She touched his hair, noted that he was wearing his brown leather jacket. "You've been out." She yawned.

Jess kissed the tip of her nose. "I have indeed. Bought you a present or two, as a matter of fact."

The glee in Jess's eyes made Libby's heart twist in a spasm of tenderness; whatever he'd purchased, he was very pleased with. She slipped languid arms around his neck. "I like presents," she said.

Jess drew back, tugged her camisole down so that her breasts were bared to him. Almost idly he kissed each dusty-rose peak and then covered them again. "Sorry," he muttered, his mouth a fraction of an inch from hers. "I couldn't resist."

That strange, magical heat was surging from Libby's just-greeted breasts to her middle, down into her thighs and even her knees. She felt as though every muscle and bone in her body had melted. "You m-mentioned presents?"

He chuckled, kissed her softly, groaned under his breath. "I was momentarily distracted. Get out of bed, princess. Said presents await."

"Can't you just...bring them here?"

"Hardly." Jess withdrew from the bed to stand at its side and wrench back the covers. His green eyes smoldered as he took in the sleep-pinkened glow of her curves, and he bent to swat her satin-covered backside. "Get up," he repeated.

Libby obeyed, curious about the gifts but disappointed that Jess hadn't joined her in the bed, too. She found a floaty cotton caftan and slipped it on over her camisole and tap pants.

Jess looked at her, made a low growling sound in his throat, and caught her hand in his. "Come on, before I give in to my baser instincts," he said, pulling her down the stairs.

Libby looked around curiously as he dragged her across the living room but saw nothing out of the ordinary.

Jess opened the front door, pulled her outside. There, beside his maroon Land Rover, sat a sleek yellow Corvette with a huge rosette of silver ribbon affixed to its windshield.

Libby gaped at the car, her eyes wide.

"Like it?" Jess asked softly, his mouth close to her ear.

"Like it?" Libby bounded toward the car, heedless of her bare feet. "I love it!"

Jess followed, opened the door on the driver's side so that Libby could slide behind the wheel. When she did that, she got a second surprise. Taped to the gearshift knob was a ring of white gold, and the diamond setting formed the Circle Bar B brand.

"I'll hog-tie you later," Jess said.

Libby's hand trembled as she reached for the ring; it blurred and shifted before her eyes as she looked at it. "Oh, Jess."

"Listen, if you hate it..."

Libby ripped away the strip of tape, slid the ring onto her finger. "Hate it? Sacrilege! It's the most beautiful thing I've ever seen."

"Does it fit?"

The ring was a little loose, but Libby wasn't ready to part with it, not even to let a jeweler size it. "No," she said, overwhelmed, "but I don't care."

Gently Jess lifted her chin with his hand, bent to sample her mouth with his. Beneath the hastily donned caftan and her camisole, Libby's nipples hardened in pert response.

"There's only one drawback to this car," Jess breathed, his lips teasing Libby's, shaping them. "It would be impossible to make love in it."

Libby laughed and pretended to shove him. "Scoundrel!"

"You don't know the half of it," he replied hoarsely, drawing Libby out of the beautiful car and back inside the house.

There she gravitated toward the front windows, where she could alternately admire her new car and watch the late-afternoon sun catch in the very special ring on her finger. Standing behind her, Jess wrapped his arms around her waist and held her close, bending to nip at her earlobe.

"Thank you, Jess," Libby said.

He laughed, and his breath moved in Libby's hair and sent warm tingles through her body. "No need for thanks. I'll nibble on your ears anytime."

"You know what I meant!"

His hands had risen to close over her breasts, fully possessing them. "What? What did you mean?" he teased in a throaty whisper.

Libby could barely breathe. "The car...the ring..."

Letting his hands slip from her breasts to her elbows, Jess ushered Libby over to face the mirror above the fireplace. As she watched his reflection in wonder, he undid the caftan's few buttons and slid it slowly down over her shoulders. Then he drew the camisole up over her head and tossed it away.

Libby saw a pink glow rise over her breasts to shine in her face, saw the passion sparking in her dark blue eyes, saw Jess's hands brush upward over her rib cage toward her breasts. The novelty of watching her own reactions to the sensations he was stirring inside her was erotic.

She groaned as she saw—and felt—masculine fingers rise to her waiting nipples and pluck then gently to attention.

"See?" Jess whispered at her ear. "See how beautiful you are, Libby? Especially when I'm loving you."

Libby had never thought of herself as beautiful, but now, looking at her image in the mirror, seeing how passion darkened her eyes to indigo and painted her cheeks with its own special apricot shade, she felt ravishing.

She tilted her head back against the hard breadth of Jess's shoulder, moaned as he softly plundered her nipples.

He spoke with a gruff, choked sort of sternness. "Don't close your eyes, Libby. Watch. You're beautiful—so beautiful—and I want you to know it."

It was hard for Libby not to close her eyes and give herself up to the incredible sensations that were raging through her, but she managed it even as Jess came from behind her to bend his head and take suckle at one breast.

Watching him do this, watching the heightened color in her own face, gave a new intensity to the searing needs that were like storm winds within Libby. Her eyes were fires of ink-blue, and there was a proud, even regal lift to her chin as she watched herself pleasing the man she loved.

Jess drank deeply of one breast, turned to the other. It was an earthy communion between one man and one woman, each one giving and taking.

Presently Jess's mouth slid down over Libby's slightly damp stomach, and then he was kneeling, no longer visible in the magic mirror. "Don't close your eyes," he repeated, and Libby felt her satiny tap pants sliding slowly down over her hips, her knees, her ankles.

The wide-eyed sprite in the mirror gasped, and Libby was forced to brace herself with both hands against the mantel piece, just to keep from falling. Her breathing quickened to a rasp as Jess ran skilled hands over her bare bottom, her thighs, the backs of her knees. He heightened her pleasure by telling her precisely what he meant to do.

And then he did it.

Libby's release was a maelstrom of soft sobs that finally melded together into one lusty cry of pleasure. Jess was right, she thought, in the midst of all this and during the silvery descent that followed: she *was* beautiful.

Standing again, Jess lifted Libby up into his arms. Still feeling like some wanton Gypsy princess, she let her head fall back and gloried in the liberties his mouth took with the breasts that were thrust into easy reach.

Libby was conscious of an other-worldly floating sensation as she and Jess glided downward, together, to the floor.

Rain pattered and danced on the glass ceiling above the bed, a dismal heralding of what promised to be the happiest day of Libby Kincaid's life.

Jess slept beside her, beautifully naked, his breathing deep and even. If he hadn't actually spoken of his love, he had shown it in a dozen ways. So why did the pit of Libby's stomach jiggle, as though something awful was about to happen?

The insistent ringing of the doorbell brought Jess up from his stomach, push-up style, grumbling. His dark hair hopelessly rumpled, his eyes glazed, he stumbled around the bedroom until he found his robe and managed to struggle into it.

Libby laughed at him as he started down the stairs. "So much for being happy in the mornings, Barlowe," she taunted.

His answer was a terse word that Libby couldn't quite make out.

She heard the door open downstairs, heard Senator Barlowe's deep laugh and exuberant greeting. The sounds eased the feeling of dread that had plagued Libby earlier, and she got out of bed and hurried to the bathroom for a shower.

Periodically, as Libby shampooed her hair and washed, she laughed. Having his father arrive unexpectedly from Washington, probably with Ken and Cathy soon to follow, would certainly throw cold water on any plans the groom might have had for prenuptial frolicking.

When Libby went downstairs, her hair blown dry, her makeup in place, she was delighted to see that Cathy was with the senator. They were both, in fact, seated comfortably on the couch, drinking coffee.

"Where's Dad?" Libby asked when hugs and kisses had been exchanged.

Cleave Barlowe, with his elegant, old-fashioned manners, waited for Libby to sit down before returning to his own seat near Cathy. "He'll be here in time for the ceremony," he said. "When we left the ranch, he was heading out with that bear patrol of his."

Libby frowned and fussed with her crisp pink sundress, feeling uneasy again. Jess had gone upstairs, and she could hear the water running in the shower. "Bear patrol?"

"We've lost a few calves to a rogue grizzly," Cleave said easily, as though such a thing were an everyday occurrence. "Ken and half a dozen of his best men have been tracking him, but they haven't had any luck so far."

Cathy, sitting at her father-in-law's elbow, seemed to sense her cousin's apprehension and signed that she wanted a better look at Libby's ring.

The tactic worked, but as Libby offered her hand, she at last looked into Cathy's face and saw the ravages of her marital problems. There were dark smudges under the green eyes, and a hollow ache pulsed inside them.

Libby reprimanded herself for being so caught up in her own tumultuous romance with Jess as to forget that during his visit the day before, Stacey had said he'd left Cathy. It shamed Libby that she hadn't thought more about her cousin, made it a point to find out how she was.

"Are you all right?" she signed, knowing that Cathy was always more comfortable with this form of communication than with lip reading.

Cathy's responding smile was real, if wan. She nodded and with mischievous interest assessed the ring Jess had had specially designed.

Cleave demanded a look at this piece of jewelry that was causing such an "all-fired" stir and laughed with appreciation when he saw his own brand in the setting.

Cathy lifted her hands. "I want to see your dress."

After Jess had come downstairs, dressed in jeans and the scandalous T-shirt Libby had given him, the two women went up to look at the new burgundy dress.

The haunted look was back in Cathy's eyes as she approved the garment. "I can hardly believe you're marrying Jess," she said in the halting, hesitant voice she would allow only Libby to hear.

Libby sat down on the rumpled bed beside her cousin. "That should settle any doubts you might have had about my relationship with Stacey," she said gently.

Cathy's pain was a visible spasm in her face. "He's living at the main house now," she confessed. "Libby, Stacey says he wants a divorce."

Libby's anger with Stacey was equal only to her sympathy for his wife. "I'm sure he doesn't mean any of the things he's been saying, Cathy. If only you would talk to him..."

The emerald eyes flashed. "So Stacey could laugh at me, Libby? No, thanks!"

Libby drew a deep breath. "I can't help thinking that this problem stems from a lack of communication and trust," she persisted, careful to face toward her cousin. "Stacey loves you. I know he does."

"How can you be so sure?" whispered Cathy. "How, Libby? Marriages end every day of the week."

"No one knows that better than I do. But some things are a matter of instinct, and mine tells me that Stacey is doing this to make you notice him, Cathy. And maybe because you won't risk having a baby."

"Having a baby would be pretty stupid, wouldn't it? Even if I wanted to take the risk, as you call it. After all, my husband moved out of our house!"

"I'm not saying that you should rush back to the ranch and get yourself pregnant, Cathy. But couldn't you just talk to Stacey, the way you talk to me?"

"I told you—I'd be embarrassed!"

"Embarrassed! You are married to the man, Cathy—you share his bed! How can you be embarrassed to let him hear your voice?"

Cathy knotted her fingers together in her lap and lowered her head. From downstairs Libby could hear Jess and the senator talking quietly about the vote Cleave had cast before coming back to Montana for the wedding.

Finally Cathy looked up again. "I couldn't talk to anyone but you, Libby. I don't even talk to Jess or Ken."

"That's your own fault," Libby said, still angry. "Have you kept your silence all this time—all during the years I've been away?"

Cathy shook her head. "I ride up into the foothills sometimes and talk to the wind and the trees, for practice. Do you think that's silly?"

"No, and stop being so afraid that someone is going to think you're silly, dammit! So what if they do? What do you suppose people thought about me when I stayed with a man who had girl-friends?"

Cathy's mouth fell open. "Girlfriends?"

"Yes," snapped Libby, stung by the memory. "And don't tell my dad. He'd faint."

"I doubt it," replied Cathy. "But it must have hurt terribly. I'm so sorry, Libby."

"And I'm sorry if I was harsh with you," Libby answered. "I just want you to be happy, Cathy—that's all. Will you promise me that you'll talk to Stacey? Please?"

"I...I'll try."

Libby hugged her cousin. "That's good enough for me."

There was again a flash of delight in Cathy's eyes, indicating an imminent change of subject. "Is that car outside yours?"

Libby's answer was a nod. "Isn't it beautiful?"

"Will you take me for a ride in it? When the wedding is over and you're home on the ranch?"

"You know I will. We'll be the terror of the back roads—legends in our own time!"

Cathy laughed. "Legends? We'll be memories if we aren't care-ful."

Libby rose from her seat on the bed, taking up the pretty burgundy dress, slipping it carefully onto a hanger, hanging it in the back of the closet.

When that was done, the two women went downstairs together. By this time Jess and his father were embroiled in one of their famous political arguments.

Feeling uneasy again, Libby went to the telephone with as much nonchalance as she could and dialed Ken's number. There was no answer, of course—she had been almost certain that there wouldn't be—but the effort itself comforted her a little.

"Try the main house," Jess suggested softly from just behind her.

Libby glanced back at him, touched by his perception. Consoled by it. "How is it," she teased in a whisper, "that you managed to look elegant in jeans and a T-shirt that says 'If it feels good, do it'?"

Jess laughed and went back to his father and Cathy.

Libby called the main house and got a somewhat flustered Marion Bradshaw. "Hello!" barked the woman.

"Mrs. Bradshaw, this is Libby. Have you seen my father this morning?"

There was a long sigh, as though the woman was relieved to learn that the caller was not someone else. "No, dear, I haven't. He and the crew are out looking for that darned bear. Don't you worry, though—Ken told me he'd be in town for your wedding in plenty of time."

Libby knew that her father's word was good. If he said he'd be there, he would, come hell or high water. Still, something in Mrs. Bradshaw's manner was disturbing. "Is something the matter, Marion?"

Another sigh, this one full of chagrin. "Libby, one of the maids told me that a Mr. Aaron Strand called here, asking where you could be reached. Without so much as a by-your-leave, that woman came right out and told him you were in Kalispell and gave him the number. I'm so sorry."

So that was how Aaron had known where to call. Libby sighed. "It's all right, Marion—it wasn't your fault."

"I feel responsible all the same," said the woman firmly, "but I'll kick myself on my own time. I just wanted to let you know what happened. Did Miss Cathy and the senator get there all right?"

Libby smiled. "Yes, they're here. Any messages?"

"No, but I'd like a word with Jess, if it's all right."

Libby turned and gestured to the man in question. He came to the phone, took the receiver, greeted Marion Bradshaw warmly. Their conversation was a brief one, and when Jess hung up, he was laughing.

"What's so funny?" the senator wanted to know.

Jess slid an arm around Libby and gave her a quick squeeze. "Dare I say it in front of the creator of Liberated Lizzie, cartoon cavewoman? I just got Marion's blessing—she says I branded the right heifer."

Chapter 11

Libby stood at a window overlooking the courthouse parking lot, peering through the gray drizzle, anxiously scanning each vehicle that pulled in.

"He'll be here," Cathy assured her, joining Libby at the rain-sheeted window.

Libby sighed. She knew that Ken would come if he possibly could, but the rain would make the roads hazardous, and there was the matter of that rogue grizzly bear. "I hope so," she said.

Cathy stood back a little to admire the flowing silken lines of Libby's dress. "You look wonderful. Here—let's see if the flowers match."

"Flowers?" Libby hadn't thought about flowers, hadn't thought about much at all, beyond contemplating the wondrous event about to take place. Her reason said that it was insanity to marry again, especially to marry Jess Barlowe, but her heart sang a very different song.

Cathy beamed and indicated a cardboard box sitting on a nearby table.

At last Libby left her post at the window, bemused. "But I didn't..."

Cathy was already removing a cellophane-wrapped corsage, several boutonnieres, an enormous bouquet made up of burgundy rose-buds, baby's breath, and white carnations. "This is yours, of course."

Libby reached out for her bridal bouquet, pleased and very surprised. "Did you order these, Cathy?"

"No," replied Cathy, "but I did nudge Jess in the florist's direction, after seeing what color your dress was."

Moved that such a detail had been taken into consideration, Libby hugged her cousin. "Thank you."

"Thank Jess. He's the one that browbeat the florist into filling a last-minute order." Cathy found a corsage labeled with her name. "Pin this on, will you?"

Libby happily complied. There were boutonnieres for Jess and the senator and Ken, too, and she turned this last one wistfully in her hands. It was almost time for the ceremony to begin—where was her father?

A light tap at the door made Libby's heart do a jittery flip. "Yes?"

"It's me," Jess said in a low, teasing voice. "Are the flowers in there?"

Cathy gathered up the boutonnieres, white carnations wrapped in clear, crackly paper, made her way to the door. Opening it just far enough to reach through, she held out the requested flowers.

Jess chuckled but made no move to step past the barrier and see his bride before the designated moment. "Five minutes, Libby," he said, and then she heard him walking away, his heels clicking on the marble courthouse floor.

Libby went back to the window, spotted a familiar truck racing into the parking lot, lurching to a stop. Two men in rain slickers got out and hurried toward the building.

Ken had arrived, and at last Libby was prepared to join Jess in Judge Henderson's office down the hall. She saw that august room through a haze of happiness, noticing a desk, a flag, a portrait of George Washington. In front of the rain-beaded windows, with their heavy, threadbare velvet draperies, stood Jess and his father.

Everyone seemed to move in slow motion. The judge took his place, and Jess, looking quietly magnificent in a tailored three-piece suit of dark blue, took his. His eyes caressed Libby, even from that distance, and somehow drew her toward him. At his side stood the senator, clearly tired from his unexpected cross-country trip, but proud and pleased, too.

Like a person strolling through a sweet dream, Libby let Jess draw her to him. At her side was Cathy, standing up very straight, her green eyes glistening with joyous tears.

Libby's sense of her father's presence was so strong that she did not need to look back and confirm it with her eyes. She tucked her arm through Jess's and the ceremony began.

When all the familiar words had been said, Jess bent toward Libby and kissed her tenderly. The haze lifted and the bride and groom turned, arm in arm, to face their few but much-loved guests.

Instead of congratulations, they met the pain-filled stares of two cowboys dressed in muddy jeans, sodden shirts and raincoats.

Suddenly frantic, Libby scanned the small chamber for her father's face. She'd been so sure that he was there; he had seemed near enough to touch.

"Where—" she began, but her question was broken off because Jess left her side to stride toward the emissaries from the ranch, the senator close behind him.

"The bear..." said one of them in answer to Jess's clipped question. "We had him cornered and"—the cowboy's Adam's apple moved up and down in his throat—"and he was a mean one, Mr. Barlowe. Meaner'n the devil's kid brother."

Libby knew what was coming and the worn courthouse carpeting seemed to buckle and shift beneath her high-heeled burgundy sandals. Had it not been for Cathy, who gripped her elbow and maneuvered her into a nearby chair, she would have fallen.

"Just tell us what happened!" Jess rasped.

"The bear worked Ken over pretty good," the second cowboy confessed.

Libby gave a strangled cry and felt Cathy's arm slide around her shoulders.

"Is Ken dead?" demanded Cleave Barlowe, and as far as Libby was concerned, the whole universe hinged on the answer to that question.

"No, sir—we got Mr. Kincaid to the hospital fast as we could. But...but."

"But what?" hissed Jess.

"The bear got away, Mr. Barlowe."

Jess came slowly toward Libby, or at least it seemed so to her. As he crouched before her chair and took her chilled hands into his, his words were gentle. "Are you all right?"

Libby was too frightened and sick to speak, but she did manage a nod. Jess helped her to her feet, supported her as they left the room.

She was conscious of the cowboys, behind her, babbling an account of the incident with the bear to Senator Barlowe, of Cathy's quiet sobs, of Jess's steel arm around her waist. The trip to the hospital, made in the senator's limousine, seemed hellishly long.

At the hospital's admissions desk, they were told by a harried, soft-voiced nurse that there was no news yet and directed to the nearest waiting room.

Stacey was there, and Cathy ran to him. He embraced her without hesitation, crooning to her, smoothing her hair with one hand.

"Ken?" barked the senator, his eyes anxious on his elder son's pale face.

"He's in surgery," replied Stacey. And though he still held Cathy, his gaze shifted, full of pain and disbelief, to Libby. "It's bad," he said.

Libby shuddered, more afraid than she'd ever been in her life, her arms and legs useless. Jess was holding her up—Jess and some instinct that had lain dormant within her since Jonathan's death. "Were you there when it happened, Stacey?" she asked dully.

Stacey was rocking Cathy gently in his arms, his chin propped in her hair. "Yes," he replied.

Suddenly rage surged through Libby—a senseless, shrieking tornado of rage. "You had guns!" she screamed. "I know you had guns! Why didn't you stop the bear? Why didn't you kill it?"

Jess's arm tightened around her. "Libby—"

Stacey broke in calmly, his voice full of compassion even in the face of Libby's verbal attack. "There was too much chance that Ken would be hit," he answered. "We hollered and fired shots in the air and that finally scared the grizzly off." There was a hollow look in Stacey's eyes as they moved to his father's face and then Jess's, looking for the same understanding he had just given to Libby.

"What about the bear?" the senator wanted to know.

Stacey averted his eyes for a moment. "He got away," he breathed, confirming what one of the cowboys had said earlier at the courthouse. "Jenkins got him in the hind flank, but he got away. Ran like a racehorse, that son of a bitch. Anyway, we were more concerned with Ken at the moment."

The senator nodded, but Jess tensed beside Libby, his gaze fierce. "You sent men after the grizzly, didn't you?"

Stacey looked pained and his hold on Cathy tightened as her sobs ebbed to terrified little sniffles. "I...I didn't think—"

"*You didn't think?*" growled Jess. "Goddammit, Stacey, now we've got a wounded bear on the loose—"

The senator interceded. "I'll call the ranch and make sure the grizzly is tracked down," he said reasonably. "Stacey got Ken to the hospital, Jess, and that was the most important thing."

An uncomfortable silence settled over the waiting room then. The senator went to the window to stand, hands clasped behind his back, looking out. The cowboys went back to the ranch, and Stacey and Jess maneuvered their stricken wives into chairs.

The sounds and smells peculiar to a hospital were a torment to Libby, who had endured the worst minutes, hours, days, and weeks of her life in just such a place. She had lost Jonathan in an institution like this one—would she lose Ken, too?

"I can't stand it," she whispered, breaking the awful silence.

Jess took her chin in his hand, his eyes locking with hers, sharing badly needed strength. "Whatever happens, Libby, we'll deal with it together."

Libby shivered violently, looked at Jess's tailored suit, her own dress, the formal garb of Cathy and the senator. Only Stacey, in his muddy jeans, boots, shirt and sodden denim jacket, seemed dressed for the horrible occasion. The rest of the party was at ludicrous variance with the situation.

My father may be dying, she thought in quiet hysteria, *and we're wearing flowers.* The smell of her bouquet suddenly sickened Libby, bringing back memories of Jonathan's funeral, and she flung it away. It slid under a couch upholstered in green plastic and cowered there against the wall.

Jess's grip tightened on her hand, but no one made a comment.

Presently the senator wandered out, returning some minutes later with cups of vending-machine coffee balanced on a small tray. "Ken is my best friend," he announced in befuddled tones to the group in general.

The words brought a startling cry of grief from Cathy, who had been huddled in her chair until that moment, behind a curtain of tangled, rain-dampened hair. "I won't let him die!" she shrieked, to the openmouthed amazement of everyone except Libby.

Stacey, draped over the arm and back of Cathy's chair, stared down at her, his throat working. "Cathy?" he choked out.

Because Cathy was not looking at him, could not see her name on his lips, she did not answer. Her small hands flew to cover her face and she wept for the man who had loved her as his own child, raised her as his own, been her strength as well as Libby's.

"She can't hear you," Libby said woodenly.

"But she talked!" gasped Jess.

Libby lifted one shoulder in a broken shrug. "Cathy has been talking for years. To me, anyway."

"Good God," breathed the senator, his gaze sweeping over his shattered daughter-in-law. "Why didn't she speak to any of us?"

Libby was sorry for Stacey, reading the pain in his face, the shock. Of course, it was a blow to him to realize that his own wife had kept such a secret for so long.

"Cathy was afraid," Libby explained quietly. "She is very self-conscious about the way her voice sounds to hearing people."

"That's ridiculous!" barked Stacey, looking angry now, paler than before. He bolted away from Cathy's chair to stand at the windows, his back to the room. "For God's sake, I'm her husband!"

"Some of us had a few doubts about that," remarked Jess in an acid undertone.

Stacey whirled, full of fury, but the senator stepped between his two sons before the situation could get out of hand. "This is no time for arguments," he said evenly but firmly. "Libby and Cathy don't need it, and neither do I."

Both brothers receded, Stacey lowering his head a little, Jess averting a gaze that was still bright with anger. Libby watched a muscle leap in her husband's jaw and stifled a crazy urge to touch it with her finger, to still it.

"Was Dad conscious when you brought him here?" she asked of Stacey in a voice too calm and rational to be her own.

Stacey nodded, remembering. "He said that bear was almost as tough as a Mexican he fought once, down in Juarez."

The tears Libby had not been able to cry before suddenly came to the surface, and Jess held her until they passed. "Ken is strong," he reminded her. "Have faith in him."

Libby tried to believe the best, but the fact remained that Ken Kincaid was a mortal man, strong or not. And he'd been mauled viciously by a bear. Even if he survived, he might be crippled.

It seemed that Jess was reading her mind, as he so often did. His hand came up to stroke away her tears, smooth her hair back from her face. "Don't borrow trouble," he said gently. "We've got enough now."

Trying to follow this advice, Libby deliberately reviewed pleasant memories: Ken cursing a tangle of Christmas-tree lights; Ken sitting proudly in the audience while Cathy and Libby accepted their high school diplomas; Ken trying, and somehow managing, to be both mother and father.

More than two hours went by before a doctor appeared in the waiting room doorway, still wearing a surgical cap, his mask hanging from his neck. "Are you people here for Ken Kincaid?" he asked, and the simple words had the electrifying effect of a cattle prod on everyone there.

Both Libby and Cathy stiffened in their chairs, unable to speak. It was Jess who answered the doctor's question.

"Mr. Kincaid was severely injured," the surgeon said, "but we think he'll be all right, if he rests."

Libby was all but convulsed by relief. "I'm his daughter," she managed to say finally. "Do you think I could see him, just for a few minutes?"

The middle-aged physician smiled reluctantly. "He'll be in Recovery for some time," he said. "Perhaps it would be better if you visited your father tomorrow."

Libby was steadfast. It didn't matter that Ken was still under anesthetic; if she could touch his hand or speak to him, he would know that she was near. Another vigil had taught her the value of that. "I must see him," she insisted.

"She won't leave you alone until you say yes," Jess put in, his arm tight around Libby's shoulders.

Before the doctor could answer, Cathy was gripping Libby's hands, searching her cousin's face. "Libby?" she pleaded desperately. "Libby?"

It was clear that Cathy hadn't discerned the verdict on Ken's condition, and Libby's heart ached for her cousin as she freed her hands, quickly motioned the reassurances needed.

When that was done, Libby turned back to the doctor. "My cousin will want to see my father too."

"Now, just a minute…"

Stubbornly Libby lifted her chin.

Three hours later, Ken Kincaid was moved from the recovery room to a bed in the intensive-care unit. As soon as he had been settled there, Cathy and Libby were allowed into his room.

Ken was unconscious, and there were tubes going into his nostrils, an IV needle in one of his hands. His chest and right shoulder were heavily bandaged, and there were stitches running from his right temple to his neck in a crooked, gruesome line.

"Oh, God," whimpered Cathy.

Libby caught her cousin's arm firmly in her hand and faced her. "Don't you *dare* fall apart in here, Cathy Barlowe," she ordered. "He would sense how upset you are, and that would be bad for him."

Cathy trembled, but she squared her shoulders, drew a deep breath and then nodded. "We'll be strong," she said.

Libby went to the bedside, barely able to reach her father for all the equipment that was monitoring and sustaining him. "I hear you beat up on a bear," she whispered.

There was no sign that Ken had heard her, of course, but Libby knew that humor reached this man as nothing else could, and she went on talking, berating him softly for cruelty to animals, informing him that the next time he wanted to waltz, he ought to choose a partner that didn't have fur.

Before an insistent nurse came to collect Ken's visitors, both Libby and Cathy planted tender kisses on his forehead.

Stacey, Jess and Cleave were waiting anxiously when they reached the waiting room again.

"He's going to live," Libby said, and then the room danced and her knees buckled and everything went dark.

She awakened to find herself on a table in one of the hospital examining rooms, Jess holding her hand.

"Thanks for scaring the hell out of me," he said softly, a relieved grin tilting one corner of his mouth. "I needed that."

"Sorry," Libby managed, touching the wilting boutonniere that was still pinned to the lapel of his suit jacket. "Some wedding day, huh, handsome?"

"That's the wild west for you. We like excitement out here. How do you feel, princess?"

Libby tried to sit up, but the room began to swirl, so she fell back down. "I'm okay," she insisted. "Or I will be in a few minutes. How is Cathy?"

Jess smiled, kissed her forehead. "Cathy reacted a little differently to the good news than you did."

Libby frowned, still worried. "How do you mean?"

"After she'd been assured that you had fainted and not dropped dead of a coronary, she lit into Stacey like a whirlwind. It seems that my timid little sister-in-law is through being mute—once and for all."

Libby's eyes rounded. "You mean she was yelling at him?"

"Was she ever. When they left, he was yelling back."

Despite everything, Libby smiled. "In this case, I think a good loud argument might be just what the doctor ordered."

"I agree. But the condo will probably be a war zone by the time we get there."

Libby remembered that this was her wedding night, and with a little help from Jess, managed to sit up. "The condo? They're staying there?"

"Yes. The couch makes out into a bed, and Cathy wants to be near the hospital."

Libby reached out, touched Jess's strong face. "I'm sorry," she said.

"About what?"

"About everything. Especially about tonight."

Jess's green eyes laughed at her, gentle, bright with understanding. "Don't worry about tonight, princess. There will be plenty of other nights."

"But—"

He stilled her protests with an index finger. "You are in no condition to consummate a marriage, Mrs. Barlowe. You need to sleep. So let's go home and get you tucked into bed—with a little luck, Stacey and Cathy won't keep us awake all night while they throw pots and pans at each other."

Jess's remark turned out to be remarkably apt, for when they reached the condo, Stacey and his wife were bellowing at each other and the floor was littered with sofa pillows and bric-a-brac.

"Don't mind us," Jess said with a companionable smile as he ushered his exhausted bride across the war-torn living room. "We're just mild-mannered honeymooners, passing through."

Jess and Libby might have been invisible, for all the notice they got.

"Maybe we should have stayed in a motel," Libby yawned as she snuggled into Jess's strong shoulder, minutes later, in the loft bed.

Something shattered downstairs, and Jess laughed. "And miss this? No chance."

Cathy and Stacey were yelling again, and Libby winced. "You don't think they'll hurt each other, do you?"

"They'll be all right, princess. Rest."

Too tired to discuss the matter further, Libby sighed and fell asleep, lulled by Jess's nearness and the soft sound of rain on the glass roof overhead. She awakened once, in the depths of the night, and heard the sounds of another kind of passion from the darkened living room. A smile curved her lips as she closed her eyes.

Cathy was blushing as she tried to neaten up the demolished living room and avoid Libby's gaze at the same time. Stacey, dead to the world, was sprawled out on the sofa bed, a silly smile shaping his mouth.

Libby made her way to the telephone in silence, called the hospital for a report on her father. He was still unconscious, the nurse on duty told her, but his vital signs were strong and stable.

Cathy was waiting, wide-eyed, when Libby turned away from the telephone.

Gently Libby repeated what the nurse had told her. After that, the two women went into the kitchen and began preparing a quick break-fast.

"I'm sorry about last night," Cathy said.

Standing at the stove, spatula in hand, Libby waited for her cousin to look at her and then asked, "Did you settle anything?"

Cathy's cheeks were a glorious shade of hot pink. "You heard!" she moaned.

Libby had been referring to the fight, not the lovemaking that had obviously followed, but there was no way she could clarify this with-out embarrassing her cousin further. She bit her lower lip and con-centrated on the eggs she was scrambling.

"It was crazy," Cathy blurted, remembering. "I was *yelling* at Stacey! I wanted to hurt him, Libby—I really wanted to hurt him!"

Libby was putting slices of bread into the toaster and she offered no comment, knowing that Cathy needed to talk.

"I even threw things at him," confessed Cathy, taking orange juice from the refrigerator and putting it in the middle of the table. "I can't believe I acted like that, especially when Ken had just been hurt so badly."

Libby met her cousin's gaze and smiled. "I don't see what one thing has to do with the other, Cathy. You were angry with your husband—justifiably so, I'd say—and you couldn't hold it in any longer.''

''I wasn't even worried about the way I sounded,'' Cathy reflected, shaking her head. ''I suppose what happened to Ken triggered something inside me—I don't know.''

''The important thing is that you stood up for yourself,'' Libby said, scraping the scrambled eggs out of the pan and onto a platter. ''I was proud of you, Cathy.''

''Proud? I acted like a fool!''

''You acted like an angry woman. How about calling those lazy husbands of ours to breakfast while I butter the toast?''

Cathy hesitated, wrestling with her old fear of being ridiculed, and then squared her shoulders and left the kitchen to do Libby's bidding.

Tears filled Libby's eyes at the sound of her cousin's voice. However ordinary the task was, it was a big step forward for Cathy.

The men came to the table, Stacey wearing only jeans and looking sheepish, Jess clad in slacks and a neatly pressed shirt, his green eyes full of mischief.

''Any word about Ken?'' he asked.

Libby told him what the report had been and loved him the more for the relief in his face. He nodded and then executed a theatrical yawn.

Cathy blushed and looked down at her plate, while Stacey glared at his brother. ''Didn't you sleep well, Jess?'' he drawled.

Jess rolled his eyes.

Stacey looked like an angry little boy; Libby had forgotten how he hated to be teased. ''I'll fight with my wife if I want to!'' he snapped.

Both Libby and Jess laughed.

''Fight?'' gibed Jess good-naturedly. ''Was that what you two were doing? Fighting?''

''*Somebody* had to celebrate your wedding night,'' Stacey retorted, but then he gave in and laughed too.

When the meal was over, Cathy and Libby left the dirty dishes to their husbands and went off to get ready for the day.

They were allowed only a brief visit with Ken, and even though his doctor assured them that he was steadily gaining ground, they were both disheartened as they returned to the waiting room.

Senator Barlowe was there, with Jess and Stacey, looking as wan and worried as either of his daughters-in-law. Unaware of their approach, he was saying, "We've got every available man tracking that bear, plus hands from the Three Star and the Rocking C. All we've found so far is paw-prints and dead calves."

Libby was brought up short, not by the mention of the bear but by the look on Jess's face. He muttered something she couldn't hear.

Stacey sliced an ironic look in his brother's direction. "I suppose you think you can find that son of Satan when the hands from three of the biggest ranches in the state can't turn up a trace?"

"I know I can," Jess answered coldly.

"Dammit, we scoured the foothills, the ranges..."

Jess's voice was low, thick with contempt. "And when you had the chance to bring the bastard down, you let him trot away instead—wounded."

"What was I supposed to do? Ken was bleeding to death!"

"Somebody should have gone after the bear," Jess insisted relentlessly. "There were more than enough people around to see that Ken got to the hospital."

Stacey swore.

"Were you scared?" Jess taunted. "Did the big bad bear scare away our steak-house cowboy?"

At this, Stacey lunged toward Jess and Jess bolted out of his chair, clearly spoiling for a fight.

Again, as he had before, the senator averted disaster. "Stop it!" he hissed. "If you two have to brawl, kindly do it somewhere else!"

"You can bank on that," Jess said bitterly, his green gaze moving over Stacey and then dismissing him.

"What's gotten into the two of you?" Senator Barlowe rasped in quiet frustration. "This is a hospital! And have you forgotten that you're brothers?"

Libby cleared her throat discreetly, to let the men know that she and Cathy had returned. She was disturbed by the barely controlled hostility between Jess and his brother, but with Ken in the condition that he was, she had no inclination to pursue the issue.

It was later, in the Land Rover, when she and Jess were alone, that Libby voiced a subject that had been bothering her. "You plan to go looking for that bear, don't you?"

Jess appeared to be concentrating on the traffic, but a muscle in his cheek twitched. "Yes."

"You're going back to the ranch and track him down," Libby went on woodenly.

"That's right."

She sank back against the seat and closed her eyes. "Let the others do it."

There was a short, ominous silence. "No way."

Libby swallowed the sickness and fear that roiled in her throat. God in heaven, wasn't it enough that she'd nearly lost her father to that vicious beast? Did she have to risk losing her husband too? "Why?" she whispered miserably. "Why do you want to do this?"

"It's my job," he answered flatly, and Libby knew that there was no point in trying to dissuade him.

She squeezed her eyes even more tightly shut, but the tears escaped anyway. When they reached the condo again, Stacey's car and Cleave's pulling in behind them, Jess turned to her, brushed the evidence of her fear from her cheeks with gentle thumbs and kissed her.

"I promise not to get killed," he said softly.

Libby stiffened in his arms, furious and full of terror. "That's comforting!"

He kissed the tip of her nose. "You can handle this alone, can't you? Going to the hospital, I mean?"

Libby bit her lower lip. Here was her chance. She could say that she needed Jess now, she could keep him from hunting that bear. She did need him, especially now, but in the end, she couldn't use weakness to hold him close. "I can handle it."

An hour later, when Stacey and the senator left for the ranch, Jess went with them. Libby was now keeping two vigils instead of one.

Understanding Libby's feelings but unable to help, Cathy built a fire in the fireplace, brewed cocoa, and tried to interest her cousin in a closed-caption movie on television.

Libby watched for a while, then got out her sketchbook and began to draw with furious, angry strokes: Jess on horseback, a rifle in the scabbard of his saddle; a full-grown grizzly, towering on its hind legs, ominous muscles rolling beneath its hide, teeth bared. Try though she did, Libby could not bring herself to put Jess and that bear in the same picture, either mentally or on paper.

That evening, when Libby and Cathy went to the hospital, Ken was awake. He managed a weak smile as they came to his bedside to bestow tearful kisses.

"Sorry about missin' the wedding," he said, and for all his obvious pain, there was mirth in his blue eyes.

Libby dashed away the mist from her own eyes and smiled a shaky smile, shrugging. "You've seen one, cowboy, you've seen them all."

Ken laughed and the sound was beautiful.

Chapter 12

Having assured herself that Ken was indeed recovering, Cathy slipped out to allow Libby a few minutes alone with her father.

"Thanks for scaring me half to death," she said.

Ken tried to shrug, winced instead. "You must have known I was too mean to go under," he answered. "Libby, did they get the bear?"

Libby stiffened. The bear, the bear—she was so damned sick of hearing about the bear! "No," she said after several moments, averting her eyes.

Ken sighed. He was pale and obviously tired. "Jess went after him, didn't he?"

Libby fought back tears of fear. Was Jess face to face with that creature even now? Was he suffering injuries like Ken's, or even worse? "Yes," she admitted.

"Jess will be all right, Libby."

"Like you were?" Libby retorted sharply, without thinking.

Ken studied her for a moment, managed a partial grin. "He's younger than I am. Tougher. No grizzly in his right mind would tangle with him."

"But this grizzly isn't in his right mind, is he?" Libby whispered, numb. "He's wounded, Dad."

"All the more reason to find him," Ken answered firmly. "That bear was dangerous before, Libby. He's deadly now."

Libby shuddered. "You'd think the beast would just crawl off and die somewhere."

"That would be real handy, but he won't do it, Lib. Grizzlies have nasty dispositions as it is—their eyesight is poor and their teeth hurt all the time. When they're wounded, they can rampage for days before they finally give out."

"The Barlowes can afford to lose a few cows!"

"Yes, but they can't afford to lose people, Lib, and that's what'll happen if that animal isn't found."

There was no arguing that; Ken was proof of how dangerous a bear could be. "The men from the Three Star and the Rocking C are helping with the hunt, anyway," Libby said, taking little if any consolation from the knowledge.

"That's good," Ken said, closing his eyes.

Libby bent, kissed his forehead and left the room.

Cathy was pacing the hallway, her lower lip caught in her teeth, her eyes wide. Libby chastised herself for not realizing that Stacey was probably hunting the bear too, and that her cousin was as worried as she was.

When Libby suggested a trip to the Circle Bar B, Cathy agreed immediately.

During the long drive, Libby made excuses to herself. She wasn't going just to check on Jess—she absolutely was not. She needed her drawing board, her pens and inks, jeans and blouses.

The fact that she could have bought any or all of these items in Kalispell was carefully ignored.

By the time Libby and Cathy drew the Corvette to a stop in the wide driveway of the main ranch house, the sun was starting to go down. There must have been fifty horsemen converging on the stables, all of them looking tired and discouraged.

Libby's heart wedged itself into her throat when she spotted Jess. He was dismounting, wrenching a high-powered rifle from the scabbard on his saddle.

She literally ran to him, but then she stopped short, her shoes encased in the thick, gooey mud Montanans call gumbo, her vocal cords no more mobile than her feet.

"Ken?" he asked in a hoarse whisper.

Libby was quick to reassure him. "Dad's doing very well."

"Then what are you doing here?"

Libby smiled, pried one of her feet out of the mud, only to have it succumb again when she set it down. "I had to see if you were all right," she admitted. "May I say that you look terrible?"

Jess chuckled, rubbed the stubble of beard on his chin, assessed the dirty clothes he wore in one downward glance. "You should have stayed in town."

Libby lifted her chin. "I'll go back in the morning," she said, daring him to argue.

Jess surrendered his horse to one of the ranch hands, but the rifle swung at his side as he started toward the big, well-lighted house. Libby slogged along at his side.

"Is that gun loaded?" she demanded.

"No," he replied. "Any more questions?"

"Yes. Did you see the bear?"

They had reached the spacious screened-in porch, where Mrs. Bradshaw had prudently laid out newspapers to accommodate dozens of mud-caked boots.

"No," Jess rasped, lifting his eyes to some distant thing that Libby could not see. "That sucker might as well be invisible."

Libby watched as Jess kicked off his boots, flung his sodden denim jacket aside, dispensed with his hat. "Maybe he's dead, Jess," she blurted out hopefully, resorting to the optimism her father had tacitly warned her against. "Maybe he collapsed somewhere—"

"Wrong," Jess bit out. "We found more cattle."

"Calves?"

"A bull and two heifers," Jess answered. "And the hell of it is, he didn't even kill them to eat. He just ripped them apart."

Libby shivered. "He must be enormous!"

"The men that were with Stacey and Ken said he stood over eight feet," Jess replied, and his green eyes moved wearily over Libby's face. "I don't suppose I need to say this, but I will. I don't like having you here, not now. For God's sake, don't go wandering off by yourself—not even to walk down to the mailboxes. The same goes for Cathy.''

It seemed ludicrous that one beast could restrict the normal activities of human beings—in fact, the bear didn't seem real to Libby, even after what had happened to Ken. Instead, it was as though Jess was telling one of the delicious, scary stories he'd loved to terrify Libby with when they were children.

"That means, little one," he went on sternly, "that you don't go out to the barn and you don't go over to Ken's to sit and moon by that pond. Am I making myself clear?''

"Too clear,'' snapped Libby, following him as he carried the rifle through the kitchen, down a long hallway and into the massive billiard room where the gun cabinets were.

Jess locked the weapon away and turned to his wife. "I'm a little bit glad you're here," he confessed with a weary grin.

"Even tough cowboys need a little spoiling now and then," she replied, "so hie thyself to an upstairs bathroom, husband of mine, and get yourself a shower. I'll bring dinner to your room."

"And how do you know where my room is, Mrs. Barlowe?''

Libby colored a little. "I used to help Marion Bradshaw with the cleaning sometimes, remember?''

"I remember. I used to watch you bending over to tuck in sheets and smooth pillows and think what a great rear end you had.''

She arched one eyebrow. "Had?''

Jess caught her bottom in strong hands, pressed her close to him. "Have," he clarified.

"Go take your shower!" Libby huffed, suddenly conscious of all the cowboys that would be gathering in the house for supper that night.

"Join me?'' drawled Jess, persistent to the end.

"Absolutely not. You're exhausted.'' Libby broke away, headed toward the kitchen.

"Not *that* exhausted," Jess called after her.

Libby did not respond, but as she went in to prepare a dinner tray for her husband, she was smiling.

Minutes later, entering Jess's boyhood bedroom, she set the tray down on a long table under a line of windows. The door of the adjoining bathroom was open and steam billowed out like the mist in a spooky movie.

Presently Libby heard the shower shut off, the rustling sound of a towel being pulled from a rack. She sat down on the edge of Jess's bed and then bounded up again.

"Libby?"

She went cautiously to the doorway, looked in. Jess was peering into a steamy mirror, trying to shave. "Your dinner is getting cold," she said.

After flinging one devilish look at his wife, Jess grabbed the towel that had been wrapped around his hips and calmly used it to wipe the mirror. "I'll hurry," he replied.

Libby swallowed hard, as stunned by the splendor of his naked, muscle-corded frame as she had been on that first stormy night when they'd made love in the bedroom at Jess's house, the fevered motions of their bodies metered by the raging elements outside.

Jess finished shaving, rinsed his face, turned toward Libby like a proud savage. She could not look away, even though she wanted to. Her eyes were fixed on the rising, swelling shaft of his manhood.

Jess laughed. "I used to fantasize about this."

"What?" Libby croaked, her throat tight.

"Bringing the foreman's pretty daughter up here and having my way with her."

Libby's eyes were, at last, freed, and they shot upward to his face. "Oh, yeah?"

"Yeah."

"I thought you liked Cathy then."

He nodded. "I did. But even before she married Stacey, I thought of her as a sister."

"And what, pray tell, did you think of me as?"

"A hellion. But I wanted to be your lover, all the same. Since I didn't dare, I settled for making your life miserable."

"How very chivalrous of you!"

Jess was walking toward her now, holding her with the scorching assessment of those jade-green eyes even before his hands touched her. "Teenage boys are not chivalrous, Libby."

Libby closed her eyes as he reached her, drew her close. "Neither are men," she managed to say.

Her blouse was coming untucked from her jeans, rising until she felt the steamy air on her stomach and back. Finally it was bunched under her arms and Jess was tracing a brazen finger over the lines of her scanty lace bra. Beneath the fabric, her nipples sprang into full bloom, coy flowers offering their nectar.

"Y-your dinner," she reminded Jess, floating on the sensations he was stirring within her, too bedazzled even to open her eyes.

The bra slipped down, just on one side, freeing a hard-peaked, eager breast. "Yes," Jess breathed evilly, "my dinner."

"Not that. I mean—"

His mouth closed over the delicate morsel, drawing at it softly. With a pleased and somewhat triumphant chuckle, Jess drew back from the tender treat and Libby's eyes flew open as he began removing her blouse and then her bra, leaving her jeans as they were.

He led her slowly to the bed, but instead of laying her down there, as she had expected, Jess stretched out on his back and positioned her so that she was sitting up, astraddle of his hips.

Gripping her waist, he pulled her forward and lifted, so that her breasts were suspended within easy reach of his mouth.

"The age-old quandary," he breathed.

Libby was dazed. "What qu-quandary?"

"Which one," Jess mused. "How like nature to offer two when a man has only one mouth."

Libby blushed hotly as Jess nuzzled a knotted peak, a peak that ached to nourish him. "Oh, God, Jess," she whispered. "Take it...take it!"

He chuckled, flicked the nipple in question with an impertinent tongue. "I love it when you beg."

Both rage and passion moved inside Libby. "I'm...not... begging!" she gasped, but even as she spoke she was bracing herself with her hands, brushing her breast back and forth across Jess's lips, seeking admission.

"You will," he said, and then he caught the pulsing nipple between careful teeth, raking it to an almost unendurable state of wanting.

"Not on your wretched life!" moaned Libby.

"We'll see," he replied.

The opposite breast was found and thoroughly teased and Libby had to bite her lower lip to keep from giving in and pleading senselessly for the suckling Jess promised but would not give. He played with her, using his tongue and his lips, delighting in the rocking motion of her body and the soft whimpers that came from her throat.

The sweet torment became keener, and Libby both loved and hated Jess for being able to drive her to such lengths. "Make love to me... oh, Jess...make love...to me."

The concession elicited a hoarse growl from Jess, and Libby found herself spinning down to lie flat on the bed. Her remaining clothes were soon stripped away, her legs were parted.

Libby gasped and arched her back as he entered her in one ferocious, needing thrust. After gaining this warm and hidden place, Jess paused, his hard frame shuddering with restraint.

As bedazzled as she was, Libby saw her chance to set the pace, to take command, and she took it. Acting on an age-old instinct, she wrapped her legs around his hips in a fierce claiming and muttered, "Give me all of you, Jess—all of you."

He groaned in lusty surrender and plunged deep within her, seeking solace in the velvety heat of her womanhood. They were locked together for several glittering moments, each afraid to move. Soon enough, however, their bodies demanded more and began a desperate, swift rhythm.

Straining together, both moaning in fevered need, Libby and Jess reached their shattering pinnacle at the same moment, crying out as their two souls flared as one golden fire.

Twice after Jess lay still upon her, his broad back moist beneath her hands, Libby convulsed softly, whimpering.

"Some people are really greedy," he teased when, at last, her body had ceased its spasmodic clenching and unclenching.

Libby stretched, sated,. cosseted in delicious appeasement. "More," she purred.

"What did I tell you?" Jess sighed. "The lady is greedy."

"Very."

He rolled, still joined with Libby, bringing her with him so that she once again sat astraddle of him. They talked, in hushed and gentle voices, of very ordinary things.

After some minutes had passed, however, Libby began to trace his nipples with feather-light fingertips. "I've always wanted to have my way with the boss's son," she crooned, teasing him as he had teased her earlier.

She bent forward, tasted those hardening nipples, each in turn, with only the merest flick of her tongue. Jess groaned and grew hard within her, by degrees, as she continued to torment him.

"How like nature," she gibed tenderly, "to offer two when a woman has only one mouth."

Jess grasped her hips in inescapable hands and thrust his own upward in a savage demand.

Libby's release came swiftly; it was soft and warm, rather than violent, and its passing left her free to bring Jess to exquisite heights. She set a slow pace for him, delighting in the look in his eyes, the back-and-forth motion of his head on the pillow, the obvious effort it took for him to lie still beneath her.

He pleaded for release, but Libby was impervious, guiding him gently, reveling in the sweet power she held over this man she so completely loved. "I'm going to love you in my own way," she told him. "And in my own time."

His head pressed back into the pillows in magnificent surrender, Jess closed his eyes and moaned. His control was awesome, but soon enough it slipped and he began to move beneath Libby, slowly at first and then quickly. Finally, his hands tangling in her hair, he cried out and his body spasmed as she purposely intensified his pleasure. His triumph seemed endless.

When Jess was still at last, his eyes closed, his body glistening with perspiration, Libby tenderly stroked a lock of hair back from his forehead and whispered, "Some people are really greedy."

Jess chuckled and was asleep before Libby withdrew from him to make her way into the bathroom for a shower of her own.

The dream was very sexy. In it, a blue-gray dawn was swelling at the bedroom windows and Libby's breast was full in Jess's hand, the nipple stroked to a pleading state.

She groaned as she felt his hard length upon her, his manhood seeking to sheathe itself in her warmth. Jess entered her, and his strokes were slow and gentle, evoking an immediate series of tremulous, velvet-smooth responses.

"Good," she sighed, giving herself up to the dream. "So good..."

The easy strokes became demanding thrusts. "Yes," said the dream Jess gruffly. "Good."

"Ooooooh," moaned Libby, as a sudden and piercing release rocked her, thrusting her into wakefulness.

And Jess was there, upon her, his face inches from her own. She watched in wonder and in love as his features grew taut and his splendid body flexed, more rapidly now. She thrust herself up to receive the fullness of his love.

Libby's hands clasped Jess's taut buttocks as he shuddered and delved deep, his manhood rippling powerfully within her, his rasping moan filling Libby's heart.

Minutes later, a languid, hazy sleep overtook Libby and she rolled over onto her stomach and settled back into her dreams. She stirred only slightly when Jess patted her derriere and left the bed.

Hours later, when she awakened fully, Libby was not entirely certain that she hadn't dreamed the whole gratifying episode. As she got out of bed, though, to take a bath and get dressed, Libby knew that Jess had loved her—the feeling of lush well-being she enjoyed was proof of that.

The pampered sensation was short-lived. When Libby went downstairs to search out a light breakfast, she found Monica Summers sitting in the kitchen, sipping coffee and reading a weekly newsmagazine.

Even though Monica smiled, her dark gray eyes betrayed her malice. "Hello...Mrs. Barlowe."

Libby nodded uneasily and opened the refrigerator to take out an apple and a carton of yogurt. "Good morning," she said.

"I was very sorry to hear about your father," Monica went on, the tone of her voice totally belying her expression. "Is he recovering?"

Libby got a spoon for her yogurt and sat down at the table. "Yes, thank you, he is."

"Will you be staying here with us, or going back to Kalispell?"

There was something annoyingly proprietary in the way Monica said the word "us," as though Libby were somehow invading territory where she didn't belong. She lifted her chin and met the woman's stormy-sky gaze directly. "I'll be going back to Kalispell," she said.

"You must hate leaving Jess."

The pit of Libby's stomach developed an unsettling twitch. She took a forceful bite from her apple and said nothing.

"Of course, I'll be happy to...look after him," sighed Monica, striking a flame to the fuse she had been uncoiling. "It's an old habit, you know."

Libby suppressed an unladylike urge to fly over the table, teeth bared, fists flying. "Sometimes old habits have to be broken," she said, sitting very still, reminding herself that she was a grown woman now, not the foreman's little brat. Furthermore, she was Jess's wife and she didn't have to take this kind of subtle abuse in any case.

Monica arched one perfect eyebrow. "Do they?"

Libby leaned forward. "Oh, yes. You see, Ms. Summers, if you mess with my husband, I'll not only break the habit for you, I'll break a few of your bones for good measure."

Monica paled, muttered something about country girls.

"I am not a girl," Libby pointed out. "I'm a woman, and you'd better remember it."

"Oh, I will," blustered Monica, recovering quickly. "But will Jess? That's the question, isn't it?"

If there was one thing in the world Libby had absolutely no doubts about, at that moment anyway, it was her ability to please her husband in the way Monica was referring to. "I don't see how he could possibly forget," she said, and then she finished her apple and her yogurt, dropped the remnants into the trash, and left the room.

Marion Bradshaw was sweeping away residual dried mud when Libby reached the screened porch, hoping for one glimpse of Jess before she had to go back to Kalispell.

He was nowhere in sight, of course—Libby had not really expected him to be.

"How's Ken getting on?" Marion asked.

Libby smiled. "He's doing very well."

The housekeeper sighed, leaning on her broom. "Thank the good Lord for that. Me and Ken Kincaid run this place, and I sure couldn't manage it alone!"

Libby laughed and asked if Cathy was around.

Sheer delight danced in Mrs. Bradshaw's eyes. "She's where she belongs—upstairs in her husband's bed."

Libby blushed. She had forgotten how much this astute woman knew about the goings-on on the ranch. Did she know, too, why Jess had never gotten around to eating his dinner the night before?

"No shame in loving your man," Mrs. Bradshaw twinkled.

Libby swallowed. "Do you know if Stacey went with the others this morning?"

"He did. You go ahead and wake Miss Cathy right now, if you want to."

Libby was grateful for an excuse to hurry away.

Finding Stacey's room from memory, in just the way she'd found Jess's, she knocked briskly at the closed door, realized the foolishness of that, and turned the knob.

Cathy was curled up like a kitten in the middle of a bed as mussed and tangled as the one Libby had shared with Jess.

Libby bent to give Cathy's bare shoulder a gentle shake. Her cousin sat up, mumbling, her face lost behind a glistening profusion of tangled hair. "Libby? What...?"

Libby laughed and signed, "I'm going back to town as soon as I pick up some of my things at the other house. Do you want to go with me?"

Cathy's full lips curved into a mischievous smile and she shook her head.

"Things are going well between you and Stacey, then?"

Cathy's hands moved in a scandalously explicit answer.

"I'm shocked!" Libby signed, beaming. And then she gave her cousin a quick kiss on the forehead, promised to call Mrs. Bradshaw if there was any sort of change in Ken's condition, and left the room.

In Jess's room she found paper and a pen, and probably because of the tempestuous night spent in his bed, dared to write, "Jess. I love you. Sorry I couldn't stay for a proper good-bye, but I've got to get back to Dad. Take care and come to me if you can. Smiles and sunshine, Libby."

On the way downstairs, Libby almost lost her courage and ran back to rip up the note. Telling Jess outright that she loved him! What if he laughed? What if he was derisive or, even worse, pitying?

Libby denied herself the cowardice of hiding her feelings any longer. It was time she took responsibility for her own emotions, wasn't it?

The weather was crisp and bright that day, and Libby hummed as she drove the relatively short distance to her father's house, parked her car behind his truck and went in to get the things she needed.

Fitting extra clothes and her special set of pens and inks into the back of the Corvette proved easy enough, but the drawing board was another matter. She turned it this way and that way and it just wouldn't fit.

Finally Libby took it back inside the house and left it there. She would just have to make do with the kitchen table at the condo for the time being.

Libby was just passing the passenger side of Ken's truck when she heard the sound; it was a sort of shifting rustle, coming from the direction of the lilac hedge on the far side of the yard. There followed a low, ominous grunt.

Instinctively Libby froze, the hair tingling on the nape of her neck. Dear God, it couldn't be... Not here—not when there were men with rifles searching every inch of the ranch...

She turned slowly, and her heart leapt into her throat and then spun back down into the pit of her stomach. The bear stood within ten feet of her, on its hind legs.

The beast growled and lolled its massive head to one side. Its mangy, lusterless hide seemed loose over the rolling muscles beneath, and on its flank was a bloodcrusted, seeping wound.

In that moment, it was as though Libby became two people, one hysterically afraid, one calm and in control. Fortunately, it was this second Libby that took command. Slowly, ever so slowly, she eased her hand back behind her, to the door handle, opened it. Just as the bear lunged toward her, making a sound more horrifying than she could ever have imagined, she leapt inside the truck and slammed the door after her.

The raging beast shook the whole vehicle as it flung its great bulk against its side, and Libby allowed herself the luxury of one high-pitched scream before reaching for Ken's CB radio under the dashboard.

Again and again, the furious bear pummeled the side of the truck, while Libby tried frantically to make the CB radio work. She knew that the cowboys would be carrying receivers, in order to communicate with each other, and they were her only hope.

Fingers trembling, Libby finally managed to lift the microphone to her mouth and press the button. Her mind skittered over a series of movies she'd seen, books she'd read. *Mayday,* she thought with triumphant terror. *Mayday!* But the magic word would not come past her tight throat.

Suddenly a giant claw thundered across the windshield, shattering it into a glittering cobweb of cracks. One more blow, just one, and the bear would reach her easily, even though she was now crouching on the floorboard.

At last she found her voice. "Cujo!" she screamed into the radio receiver. "Cujo!" She closed her eyes, gasping, tried to get a hold on herself. *This is not a Stephen King movie,* she reminded herself. *This is reality. And that bear out there is going to tear you apart if you don't do something!*

"Libby!" the radio squawked suddenly. "Libby, come in!"

The voice was Jess's. "Th-the bear," she croaked, remembering to hold in the button on the receiver when she talked. "Jess, the bear!"

"Where are you?"

Libby closed her eyes as the beast again threw itself against the truck. "My dad's house—in his truck."

"Hold on. Please, baby, hold on. We're not far away."

"Hurry!" Libby cried, as the bear battered the windshield again and tiny bits of glass rained down on her head.

Another voice came in over the radio, this one belonging to Stacey. "Libby," he said evenly, "honk the horn. Can you do that?"

Libby couldn't speak. There were tears pouring down her face and every muscle in her body seemed inert, but she did reach up to the center of the wheel and press the truck's horn.

The bear bellowed with rage, as though the sound had hurt him, but he stopped striking the truck and withdrew a little way. Libby knew he wasn't gone, for she could hear him lumbering nearby, growling in frustration.

Jess's men converged with Stacey's at the end of the rutted country road leading to Ken's house. When the pickup truck was in sight, they reined in their horses.

"He's mine," Jess breathed, reaching for the rifle in his scabbard, drawing it out, cocking it. He was conscious of the other men and their nervous, nickering horses, but only vaguely. Libby was inside that truck—his whole being seemed to focus on that one fact.

The bear rose up in full view suddenly, its enormous head visible even over the top of the pickup's cab. Even over the repeated honking of the truck's horn, the beast's hideous, echoing growl was audible.

"Sweet Jesus," Stacey whispered.

"Easy," said Jess, to himself more than the men around him, as he lifted the rifle, sighted in carefully, pulled back the trigger.

The thunderous shot struck the bear in the center of its nose, and the animal shrieked as it went down. The impact of its body was so solid that it seemed to shake the ground.

Instantly Jess was out of the saddle. "Make sure he's dead," he called over one shoulder as he ran toward the truck.

Stacey and several of his men reached the bear just as Jess wrenched open the door on the driver's side.

Libby scrambled out from under the steering wheel, her hair a wild, glass-spattered tangle, to fling herself, sobbing, into his arms. Jess cradled her in his arms, carried her away from the demolished truck and inside the house. His own knees suddenly weak, he fell into the first available chair and buried his face in Libby's neck.

"It's over, sweetheart," he said. "It's over."

Libby shuddered and wailed with terror.

When she was calmer, Jess caught her chin in his hand and lifted it. "What the hell did you mean, yelling 'Cujo! Cujo!'"

Libby sniffled, and the fight was back in her eyes, a glorious, snapping blue. "There was this book about a mad dog...and then there was a movie..."

Jess lifted his eyebrows and grinned.

"Oh, never mind!" hissed Libby.

Chapter 13

Libby froze in the doorway of Ken's room in the intensive-care unit, her mouth open, her heart racing as fast as it had earlier, when she'd been trapped by the bear.

"Where is he?" she finally managed to whisper. "Oh, Jess, where is my father?"

Standing behind Libby, Jess lifted his hands to her shoulders and gently ushered her back into the hallway, out of sight of the empty bed. "Don't panic," he said quietly.

Libby trembled, looked frantically toward the nurses' station. "Jess, what if he…?"

There was a gentle lecture forming in Jess's features, but before he could deliver it, an attractive red-headed nurse approached, trim in her uniform. "Mrs. Barlowe?"

Libby nodded, holding her breath.

"Your father is fine. We moved Mr. Kincaid to another floor earlier today, since he no longer needs such careful monitoring. If you will just come back to the desk with me, I'll be happy to find out which room he's in."

Libby's breath escaped in one long sigh. What with spending perilous minutes cowering inside a truck, with a rogue bear doing its best to get inside and tear her to bits, and then rushing to the hospital to find her father's bed empty, she had had more than enough stress for one day. "Thank you," she said, giving Jess a relieved look.

He got rather familiar during the elevator ride down to the second floor, but desisted when the doors opened again.

"You're incorrigible," Libby whispered, only half in anger.

"Snatching my wife from the jaws of death has that effect on me," he whispered back. "I keep thinking that I might never have gotten the chance to touch you like that again."

Libby paused, in the quest for Room 223, to search Jess's face. "Were you scared?"

"Scared? Sweet thing, I was *terrified.*"

"You seemed so calm!"

He lifted one eyebrow. "Somebody had to be."

Libby considered that and then sighed. "I don't suppose we should tell Dad what actually happened. Not yet, at least."

Jess chuckled. "We'll tell a partial truth—that the bear is dead. The rest had better wait until he's stronger."

"Right," agreed Libby.

When they reached Ken's new room, another surprise was in store. A good-looking dark-haired woman was there plumping the patient's pillows, fussing with his covers. She wore well-cut jeans and a western shirt trimmed with a rippling snow-white fringe, and the way she laughed, low in her throat, said more about her relationship with Ken Kincaid than all her other attentions combined.

"Hello, Becky," said Jess, smiling.

Becky was one of those people, it seemed, who smile not just with the mouth but with the whole face. "Jess Barlowe," she crowed, "you black-hearted son-of-a-gun! Where ya been?"

Libby drew a deep breath and worked up a smile of her own. Was this the woman who had written that intriguing farewell on the condo's kitchen blackboard?

Deliberately she turned her attention on her father, who looked downright rakish as he favored his startled daughter with a slow grin and a wink.

"Who's this pretty little gal?" demanded Becky, giving Libby a friendly once-over.

For the first time, Ken spoke. "This is my daughter, Libby. Libby, Becky Stafford."

"I'll be!" cried Becky, clearly delighted. "Glad to meet ya!"

Libby found the woman's boisterous good nature appealing, and despite a few lingering twinges of surprise, she responded warmly.

"Did you get that bear?" Ken asked of Jess, once the women had made their exchange.

"Yes," Jess replied, after one glance at Libby.

Ken gave a hoot of delight and triumph. "Nail that son-of-a…nail that devil's hide to the barn door for me, will you?"

"Done," answered Jess with a grin.

A few minutes later, Jess and the energetic Becky left the room to have coffee in the hospital cafeteria. Libby lifted her hands to her hips, fixed her father with a loving glare and demanded, "Is there something you haven't told me?"

Ken laughed. "Maybe. But I'll wager that there are a few things you haven't told me, either, dumplin'."

"Who is Becky, exactly?"

Ken thought for a moment before speaking. "She's a good friend of mine, Libby. An old friend."

For some reason, Libby was determined to find something to dislike about Becky Stafford, difficult as it was. "Why does she dress like that? Is she a rodeo performer or something?"

"She's a cocktail waitress," Ken replied patiently.

"Oh," said Libby. And then she couldn't sustain her petty jealousy any longer, because Becky Stafford was a nice person and Ken had a right to like her. He was more than just her father, after all, more than just Senator Barlowe's general foreman. He was a man.

There was a brief silence, which Ken broke with a very direct question. "Do you like Becky, Lib?"

Like her? The warmth and humor of the woman still lingered in that otherwise dreary room, as did the earthy, unpretentious scent of her perfume. "Sure I do," said Libby. "Anybody with the perception to call Jess Barlowe a 'black-hearted son-of-a-gun' is okay in my book!"

Ken chuckled, but there was relief in his face, and his expression revealed that he knew how much Libby loved her husband. "How's Cathy?" he asked.

Remembering that morning's brief conversation with her cousin, Libby grinned. "She's doing fine, as far as I can tell. Bad as it was, your tussle with that bear seems to have brought Cathy and Stacey both to a point where they can open up to each other. Cathy actually talked to him."

Ken did not seem surprised by this last; perhaps he'd known all along that Cathy still had use of her voice. "I don't imagine it was peaceable," he observed dryly.

"Not in the least," confirmed Libby, "but they're communicating and…and, well, let's just say they're closer."

"That's good," answered Ken, smiling at his daughter's words. "That's real good."

Seeing that her father was getting very tired, Libby quickly kissed him and took her leave. When she reached the cafeteria, Becky was sitting alone at a table, staring sadly into her coffee cup.

Libby scanned the large room for Jess and failed to see him, but she wasn't worried. Probably he had gone back to Ken's room and missed seeing Libby on the way. Noticing the pensive look on Becky's face, she was glad for a few minutes alone with the woman her father obviously liked and perhaps even loved.

"May I sit down?" she asked, standing behind the chair that had probably been Jess's.

Becky looked up, smiled. "Sure," she said, and there was surprise in her dark eyes.

Libby sat down with a sigh. "I hate hospitals," she said, filled to aching with the memory of Jonathan's confinement.

"Me too," answered Becky, but her eyes were watchful. Hopeful, in a touchingly open way.

Libby swallowed. "My…my father has been very lonely, and I'm glad you're his friend."

Becky's smile was almost cosmic in scope. "That's good to hear," she answered. "Lordy, that man did scare the life out of me, going a round with that damned bear that way."

Libby thought of her own chance meeting with the creature and shivered. She hoped that she would never know that kind of numbing fear gain.

Becky's hand came to pat hers. "It's all right now, though, isn't it? That hairy booger is dead, thanks to Jess."

Libby laughed. Indeed, that "hairy booger" was dead, and she did have Jess to thank for her life. When she'd tried to voice her gratitude earlier, he had brushed away her words and said that she was his wife and, therefore, saving her from bears, fire-breathing dragons and the like was just part of the bargain.

As if conjured by her thoughts of him, Jess appeared to take Libby home.

The coming days were happy ones for Libby, if hectic. She visited her father morning and evening and worked on her cartoon strip and the panels for the book between times, her drawing board having been transported from the ranch by Jess and set up in the middle of the condo's living room.

Jess commuted between Kalispell and the ranch; many of Ken's duties had fallen to him. Instead of being exhausted by the crazy pace, however, he seemed to thrive on it and his reports on the stormy reconciliation taking place between Cathy and Stacey were encouraging. It appeared that, with the help of the marriage counselor they were seeing, their problems might be worked out.

The irrepressible Becky Stafford rapidly became Libby's friend. Vastly different, the two women nevertheless enjoyed each other—Libby found that Becky could draw her out when she became too burrowed down in her work, and just as quickly drive her back if she tried to neglect it.

"You did what?" Jess demanded archly one early-summer evening as he and Libby sat on the living-room floor consuming the take-out Chinese food they both loved.

Libby laughed with glee and a measure of pride. "I rode the mechanical bull at the bar where Becky works," she repeated.

Jess worked up an unconvincing scowl. "Hanging around bars these days, are you?" he demanded, waving a fortune cookie for emphasis.

Libby batted her eyelashes demurely. "Don't you worry one little bit,'' she said, feigning a musical southern drawl. ''Becky guards mah virtue, y'all.''

Jess's green eyes slipped to the V neck of Libby's white sweater, which left a generous portion of cleavage in full and enticing view. ''Does she now? And where is she, at this very moment, when said virtue is in immediate peril?''

An anticipatory thrill gyrated in the pit of Libby's stomach and warmed her breasts, which were bare beneath her lightweight sweater. Jess had loved her often, and well, but he could still stir that sweet, needing tension with remarkable ease. ''What sort of peril am I in, exactly?''

Jess grinned and hooked one finger in the V of her sweater, slid it downward into the warmth between her breasts. ''Oh, the most scandalous sort, Mrs. Barlowe.''

Libby's breath quickened, despite stubborn efforts to keep it even. ''Your attentions are quite unseemly, Mr. Barlowe,'' she replied.

He moved the wanton finger up and down between the swelling softness that was Libby, and sharp responses ached in other parts of her. ''Absolutely,'' he said. ''I mean to do several unseemly things to you.''

Libby tensed with delicious sensation as Jess's exploring finger slid aside, explored a still-hidden nipple.

''I want to see your breast, Libby. This breast. Show it to me.''

The outrageous request made Libby color slightly, but she knew she would comply. She was a strong, independent person, but now, in this sweet, aching moment, she was Jess's woman. With one motion of her hand, she tugged the sweater's neckline down and to one side, so that it made a sort of sling for the breast that had been softly demanded.

Not touching the rounded pink-tipped treasure in any way, Jess admired it, rewarding it with an approving smile when the confectionlike peak tightened into an enticing point.

Libby was kneeling now, resting on her heels, the cartons littering the coffee table completely forgotten. She was at once too proud to plead for Jess's mouth and too needing of it to cover herself.

Knowing that, Jess chuckled hoarsely and bent to flick at the exposed nipple with just the tip of his tongue. Libby moaned and let her head fall back, making the captured breast even more vulnerable.

"Unseemly," breathed Jess, nibbling, drawing at the straining morsel with his lips.

Libby felt the universe sway in time with his tender plundering, but she bit down hard on the garbled pleas that were rising in her throat. They escaped through her parted lips, all the same, as small gasps.

Her heartbeat grew louder and louder as Jess finally took suckle; it muffled the sounds of his greed, of the cartons being swept from the surface of the coffee table in a motion of one of his arms.

The coolness of the air battled with the heat of Libby's flesh as she was stripped of her sweater, her white slacks, her panties. Gently he placed her on the coffee table.

Entranced, Libby allowed him to position her legs wide of each other, one on one side of the low table, one on the other. Beyond the glass roof, in the dark, dark sky, a million silvery stars surged toward her and then melted back into the folds of heaven, becoming pinpoints.

Jess found the silken nest of her passion and attended it lovingly, stroking, kissing, finding, losing. Libby's hips moved wildly, struggling even as she gave herself up.

And when she had to have this singular gratification or die, Jess understood and feasted unreservedly, his hands firm under her bottom, lifting her, the breadth of his shoulders making it impossible for her to deny him what he would have from her.

At last, when the tumult broke on a lusty cry of triumph from Libby, she saw the stars above plummet toward her—or had she risen to meet them?

"Of course you're going to the powwow!" cried Becky, folding her arms and leaning over the platter of french fries in front of her. "You can't miss that and call yourself a Barlowe!"

Libby shrank down a little in the benchlike steak-house seat. As this restaurant was a part of the Barlowe chain, the name drew immediate attention from all the waiters and a number of the other diners, too. "Becky," she began patiently, "even though Dad's getting out of the hospital this afternoon, he won't be up to something like that, and I wouldn't feel right about leaving him behind."

"Leaving Ken behind?" scoffed Becky in a more discreet tone of voice. "You just try keeping him away—he hasn't missed a powwow in fifteen years."

Libby's memories of the last Indian powwow and all-day rodeo she had attended were hardly conducive to nostalgia. She remembered the dust, the hot glare of the summer sun, the seemingly endless rodeo events, the drunks—Indian and white alike—draped over the hoods of parked cars and sprawled on the sidewalks. She sighed.

"Jess'll go," Becky prodded.

Libby had no doubt of that, and having spent so much time away from Jess of late, what with him running the ranch while she stayed in Kalispell, she was inclined to attend the powwow after all.

Becky saw that she had relented and beamed. "Wait'll you see those Sioux Indians doing their war dances," she enthused. "There'll be Blackfoot, too, and Flathead."

Libby consoled herself with the thought of Indians doing their dances and wearing their powwow finery of feathers and buckskin and beads. She could take her sketchbook along and draw, at least.

Becky wasn't through with her conversation. "Did you tell Jess how you rode that electric bull over at the Golden Buckle?"

Libby tried to look dignified in the wake of several molten memories. "I told him," she said shyly.

Her friend laughed. "If that wasn't a sight! I wish I woulda took your picture. Maybe you should enter some of the events at the powwow, Libby." Her face took on a disturbingly serious expression. "Maybe barrel racing, or women's calf roping—"

"Hold it," Libby interceded with a grin. "Riding a mechanical bull is one thing and calf roping is quite another. The only sport I'm going to take part in is stepping over drunks."

"Stepping over what?" inquired a third voice, masculine and amused, from the table side.

Libby looked and saw Stacey. "What are you doing here?"

He laughed, turning his expensive silver-banded cowboy hat in both hands. "I own the place, remember?"

"Where's Cathy?" Becky wanted to know. As she had become Libby's friend, she had also become Cathy's—she was even learning to sign.

Stacey slid into the bench seat beside Libby. "She's seeing the doctor," he said, and for all his smiling good manners, he seemed nervous.

Libby elbowed her brother-in-law lightly. "Why didn't you stay there and wait for her?"

"She wouldn't let me."

Just then Becky stood up, saying that she had to get to work. A moment later, eyes twinkling over some secret, she left.

Libby felt self-conscious with Stacey, though he hadn't made any more advances or disturbing comments. She wished that Becky had been able to stay a little longer. "What's going on? Is Cathy sick?"

"She's just having a checkup. Libby..."

Libby braced herself inwardly and moved a little closer to the wall of the enclosed booth, so that Stacey's thigh wasn't touching hers. "Yes?" she prompted when he hesitated to go on.

"I owe you an apology," he said, meeting her eyes. "I acted like a damned fool and I'm sorry."

Knowing that he was referring to the rumors he'd started about their friendship in New York, Libby chafed a little. "I accept your apology, Stacey, but I truly don't understand why you said what you did in the first place."

He sighed heavily. "I love Cathy very much, Libby," he said. "But we do have our problems. At that time, things were a lot worse, and I started thinking about the way you'd leaned on me when you were going through all that trouble in New York. I liked having somebody need me like that, and I guess I worked the whole thing up into more than it was."

Tentatively Libby touched his hand. "Cathy needs you, Stacey."

"No," he answered gruffly, looking at the flickering bowl candle in the center of the table. "She won't allow herself to need me. After some of the things I've put her through, I can't say I blame her."

"She'll trust you again, if you're worthy of it," Libby ventured. "Just be there for Cathy, Stace. The way you were there for me when my whole life seemed to be falling apart. I don't think I could have gotten through those days without you."

At that moment Jess appeared out of nowhere and slid into the seat Becky had occupied before. "Now, that," he drawled acidly, "is really touching."

Libby stared at him, stunned by his presence and by the angry set of his face. Then she realized that both she and Stacey were sitting on the same side of the booth and knew that it gave an impression of intimacy. "Jess..."

He looked down at his watch, a muscle dancing furiously in his jaw. "Are you going to pick your father up at the hospital, or do you have more interesting things to do?"

Stacey, who had been as shocked by his brother's arrival as Libby had, was suddenly, angrily vocal. The candle leapt a little when he slammed one fist down on the tabletop and hissed, "Dammit, Jess, you're deliberately misunderstanding this!"

"Am I?"

"Yes!" Libby put in, on the verge of tears. "Becky and I were having lunch and then Stacey came in and—"

"Stop it, Libby," Stacey broke in. "You didn't do anything wrong. Jess is the one who's out of line here."

The long muscle in Jess's neck corded, and his lips were edged with white, but his voice was still low, still controlled. "I came here, Libby, because I wanted to be with you when you brought Ken home," he said, and his green eyes, dark with passion only the night before, were coldly indifferent now. "Are we going to collect him or would you rather stay here and carry on?"

Libby was shaking. "Carry on? *Carry on?*"

Stacey groaned, probably considering the scandal a scene in this particular restaurant would cause. "Couldn't we settle this somewhere else?"

"We'll settle it, all right," Jess replied.

Stacey's jaw was rock-hard as he stood up to let a shaken Libby out of the booth. "I'll be on the ranch," he said.

"So will I," replied Jess, rising, taking a firm grip on Libby's arm. "See you there."

"Count on it."

Jess nodded and calmly propelled Libby out of the restaurant and into the bright sunlight, where her shiny Corvette was parked. Probably he had seen the car from the highway and known that she was inside the steak house.

Now, completely ignoring her protests, he dragged her past her car and thrust her into the Land Rover beside it.

"Jess—damn you—will you *listen* to me?"

Jess started the engine, shifted it into reverse with a swift motion of his hand. "I'm afraid storytime will have to wait," he informed her. "We've got to go and get Ken, and I don't want him upset."

"Do you think I do?"

Jess sliced one menacing look in her direction but said nothing.

Libby felt a need to reach him, even though, the way he was acting, he didn't deserve reassurances. "Jess, how can you...after last night, how could you..."

"Last night," he bit out. "Yes. Tell me, Libby, do you do that trick for everybody, or just a favored few?"

It took all her determination not to physically attack him. "Take me back to my car, Jess," she said evenly. "Right now. I'll pick Dad up myself, and we'll go back to his house—"

"Correction, Mrs. Barlowe. *He* will go to his house. You, my little vixen, will go to mine."

"I will not!"

"Oh, but you will. Despite your obvious attraction to my brother, you are still my wife."

"I am not attracted to your brother!"

They had reached the hospital parking lot, and the Land Rover lurched to a stop. Jess smiled insolently and patted Libby's cheek in a way so patronizing that it made her screaming mad. "That's the spirit, Mrs. Barlowe. Walk in there and show your daddy what a pillar of morality you are."

Going into that hospital and pretending that nothing was wrong was one of the hardest things Libby had ever had to do.

Preparations for Ken's return had obviously been going on for some time. As Libby pulled her reclaimed Corvette in behind Jess's

Land Rover, she saw that the front lawn had been mowed and the truck had been repaired.

Ken, still not knowing the story of his daughter, his truck, and the bear, paused after stepping out of Jess's Land Rover, his arm still in a sling. He looked his own vehicle over quizzically. "Looks different," he reflected.

Jess rose to the occasion promptly, smoothly. "The boys washed and waxed it," he said.

To say the very least, thought Libby, who would never forget, try though she might, how that truck had looked before the repair people in Kalispell had fixed and painted it. She opened her mouth to tell her father what had happened, but Jess stopped her with a look and a shake of his head.

The inside of the house had been cleaned by Mrs. Bradshaw and her band of elves; every floor and stick of furniture had been either dusted or polished or both. The refrigerator had been stocked and a supply of the paperback westerns Ken loved to read had been laid in.

As if all this wasn't enough to make Libby's services completely superfluous, it turned out that Becky was there too. She had strung streamers and dozens of brightly colored balloons from the ceiling of Ken's bedroom.

Her father was obviously pleased, and Libby's last hopes of drumming up an excuse to stay the night, at least, were dashed. Becky, however, was delighted with her surprise.

"I thought you were working!" Libby accused.

"I lied," replied Becky, undaunted. "After I left you and Stacey at the steak house, I got a friend to bring me out here."

Libby shot a glance in Jess's direction, knew sweet triumph as she saw that Becky's words had registered with him. After only a moment's chagrin, however, he tightened his jaw and looked away.

While Becky was getting Ken settled in his room and generally spoiling him rotten, Libby edged over to her husband. "You heard her," she whispered tersely, "so where's my apology?"

"Apology?" Jess whispered back, and there was nothing in his face to indicate that he felt any remorse at all. "Why should I apologize?"

"Because I was obviously telling the truth! Becky said—"

"Becky said that she left you and Stacey at the steak house. It must have been a big relief when she did."

Heedless of everything but the brutal effect of Jess's unfair words, Libby raised one hand and slapped him, hard.

Stubbornly, he refused her the satisfaction of any response at all, beyond an imperious glare, which she returned.

"Hey, do you guys…?" Becky's voice fell away when she became aware of the charged atmosphere of the living room. She swallowed and began again. "I was going to ask if you wanted to stay for supper, but maybe that wouldn't be such a good idea."

"You can say that again," rasped Jess, catching Libby's arm in a grasp she couldn't have broken without making an even more embarrassing scene. "Make our excuses to Ken, will you, please?"

After a moment's hesitation and a concerned look at Libby, Becky nodded.

"You overbearing bastard!" Libby hissed as her husband squired her out of the house and toward his Land Rover.

Jess opened the door, helped her inside, met her fiery blue gaze with one of molten green. Neither spoke to the other, but the messages flashing between them were all too clear anyway.

Jess still believed that Libby had been either planning or carrying on a romantic tryst with Stacey, and Libby was too proud and too angry to try to convince him otherwise. She was also too smart to get out of his vehicle and make a run for hers.

Jess would never hurt her, she knew that. But he would not allow her a dramatic exit, either. And she couldn't risk a screaming fight in the driveway of her father's house.

Because she was helpless and she hated that, she began to cry.

Jess ignored her tears, but he too was considerate of Ken—he did not gun the Land Rover's engine or back out at a speed that would fling gravel in every direction, as he might have at another time.

When they passed his house, with its window walls, and started up a steep road leading into the foothills beyond, Libby was still not afraid. For all his fury, this man was too tender a lover to touch her in anger.

"Where are we going?" she demanded.

He ground the Land Rover into a low gear and left the road, now little more than a cow path, for the rugged hillside. "On our honeymoon, Mrs. Barlowe."

Libby swallowed, unnerved by his quiet rage and the jostling, jolting ascent of the Land Rover itself. "If you take me in anger, Jess Barlowe, I'll never forgive you. Never. That would be rape."

The word "rape" got through Jess's hard armor and stung him visibly. He paled as he stopped the Land Rover with a lurch and wrenched on the emergency brake. "Goddammit, you *know* I wouldn't do anything like that!"

"Do I?" They were parked at an almost vertical angle, it seemed to Libby. Didn't he realize that they were almost straight up and down? "You've been acting like a maniac all afternoon!"

Jess's face contorted and he raised his fists and brought them down hard on the steering wheel. "Dammit it all to hell," he raged, "you drive me crazy! Why the devil do I love you so much when *you drive me crazy?*"

Libby stared at him, almost unable to believe what she had heard. Not even in their wildest moments of passion had he said he loved her, and if he had found that note she'd left for him, betraying her own feelings, the day the bear was killed, he'd never mentioned it.

"What did you say?"

Jess sighed, tilted his head back, closed his eyes. "That you drive me crazy."

"Before that."

"I said I loved you," he breathed, as though there was nothing out of the ordinary in that.

"Do you?"

"Hell, yes." The muscles in his sun-browned neck corded as he swallowed, his head still back, his eyes still closed. "Isn't that a joke?"

The words tore at Libby's heart. "A joke?"

"Yes." The word came, raw, from deep within him, like a sob.

"You idiot!" yelled Libby, struggling with the door, climbing out of the Land Rover to stalk up the steep hillside. She trembled, and tears poured down her face, and for once she didn't care who saw them.

At the top of the rise, she sat down on a huge log, her vision too blurred to take in the breathtaking view of mountains and prairies and an endless, sweeping sky.

She sensed Jess's approach, tried to ignore him.

"Why am I an idiot, Libby?"

Though the day was warm, Libby shivered. "You're too stupid to know when a woman loves you, that's why!" she blurted out, sobbing now. "Damn! You've had me every way but hanging from a chandelier, and you still don't know!"

Jess straddled the log, drew Libby into his arms and held her. Suddenly he laughed, and the sound was a shout of joy.

Chapter 14

Drunken cowboys and Indians notwithstanding, the powwow of the Sioux, Flathead and Blackfoot was a spectacle to remember. Held annually in the same small and otherwise unremarkable town, the meeting of these three tribes was a tradition that reached back to days of mist and shadow, days recorded on no calendar but that of the red man's legends.

Now, on a hot July morning, the erstwhile cow pasture and ramshackle grandstands were churning with activity, and Libby Barlowe's fingers ached to make use of the sketchbook and pencils she carried.

Craning her neck to see the authentic tepees and their colorfully clad inhabitants, she could hardly stand still long enough for the plump woman at the admission gate to stamp her hand.

There was so much noise—laughter, the tinkle of change in the coin box, the neighing and nickering of horses that would be part of the rodeo. Underlying all this was the steady beat of tom-toms and guttural chants of Indian braves.

"Enjoy yourself now, honey," enjoined the woman tending the cashbox, and Libby jumped, realizing that she was holding up the line behind her. After one questioning look at the hat the woman wore, which consisted of panels cut from various beer cans and crocheted together, she hurried through the gate.

Jess chuckled at the absorbed expression on Libby's face. There was so much to see that a person didn't know where to look first.

"I think I see a fit of creativity coming on," he said.

Libby was already gravitating toward the tepees, plotting light angles and shading techniques as she went. In her heart was a dream, growing bigger with every beat of the tom-toms. "I want to see, Jess," she answered distractedly. "I've got to *see*."

There was love in the sound of Jess's laughter, but no disdain. "All right, all right—but at least let me get you a hat. This sun is too hot for you to go around bareheaded."

"Get me a hat, get me a hat," babbled Libby, zeroing in on a group of small Indian children, who wore little more than loincloths and feathers as they sat watching fathers, uncles and elder brothers perform the ancient rites for rain or success in warfare or hunting.

Libby was taken with the flash of their coppery skin, the midnight black of their hair, the solemn, stalwart expressions in their dark eyes. Flipping open her sketchbook, she squatted in the lush summer grass and began to rough in the image of one particular little boy.

Her pencil flew, as did her mind. She was thinking in terms of oil paints—vivid, primitive shades that would do justice to the child's coloring and the peacock splendor of his headdress.

"Hello," she said when the dark eyes turned to her in dour question. "My name is Libby, what's yours?"

"Jimmy," the little boy responded, but then he must have remembered the majesty of his ancestry, for he squared his small shoulders and amended, "Jim Little Eagle."

Libby made a hasty note in the corner of his sketch. "I wish I had a name like that," she said.

"You'll have to settle for 'Barlowe,'" put in a familiar voice from behind her, and a lightweight hat landed on the top of her head.

Libby looked up into Jess's face and smiled. "I guess I can make do with that," she answered.

Jess dropped to his haunches, assessed the sketch she'd just finished with admiring eyes. "Wow," he said.

Libby laughed. "I love it when you're profound," she teased. And then she took off the hat he'd given her and inspected it thoroughly.

It was a standard western hat, made of straw, and it boasted a trailing tangle of turquoise feathers and crystal beads.

Jess took the hat and put it firmly back on, then arranged the feathers so that they rested on her right shoulder, tickling the bare, sun-gilded flesh there in a pleasant way. "Did you wear that blouse to drive me insane, or are you trying to set a world record for blistering sunburns?" he asked unromantically.

Libby looked down at the brief white eyelet suntop and wondered if she shouldn't have worn a western shirt, the way Becky and Cathy had. The garment she had on had no shoulders or sleeves; it was just a series of broad ruffles falling from an elasticized band that fitted around her chest, just beneath her collarbone. Not even wanting to think about the tortures of a sunburn, she crinkled her nose and said, "I wore it to drive you insane, of course."

Jess was going to insist on being practical; she saw it in his face. "They're selling T-shirts on the fairway—buy one."

"Now?" complained Libby, not wanting to leave the splendors of the recreated Indian village even for a few minutes.

Jess looked down at his watch. "Within half an hour," he said flatly. "I'm going to find Ken and the others in the grandstands, Rembrandt. I'll see you later."

Libby squinted as he rose against the sun, towering and magnificent even in his ordinary jeans and worn cowboy shirt. "No kiss?"

Jess crouched again, kissed her. "Remember. Half an hour."

"Half an hour," promised Libby, turning to a fresh page in her sketchbook and pondering a little girl with coal-black braids and a fringed buckskin shift. She took a new pencil from the case inside her purse and began to draw again, her hand racing to keep up with the pace set by her heart.

When the sketch was finished, Libby thought about what she meant to do and how the syndicate that carried her cartoon strip would react. No doubt they would be furious.

"*Portraits!*" her agent would cry. "Libby, Libby, there is no *money* in portraits."

Libby sighed, biting her lower lip. Money wasn't a factor really, since she had plenty of that as it was, not only because she had married a wealthy man but also because of prior successes in her career.

She was tired of doing cartoons, yearning to delve into other mediums—especially oils. She wanted color, depth, nuance—she wanted and needed to grow.

"Where the hell is that T-shirt I asked you to buy?"

Libby started, but the dream was still glowing in her face when she looked up to meet Jess's gaze. "Still on the fairway, I would imagine," she said.

His mouth looked very stern, but Jess's eyes were dancing beneath the brim of his battered western hat. "I don't know why I let you out of my sight," he teased. And then he extended a hand. "Come on, woman. Let's get you properly dressed."

Libby allowed herself to be pulled through the crowd to one of the concession stands. Here there were such thrilling offerings as ashtrays shaped like the state of Montana and gaudy scarves commemorating the powwow itself.

"Your secret is out," she told Jess out of the corner of her mouth, gesturing toward a display of hats exactly like her own. The colors of their feather-and-bead plumage ranged from a pastel yellow to deep, rich purple. "This hat is not a designer original!"

Jess worked up an expression of horrified chagrin and then laughed and began rifling through a stack of colorful T-shirts. "What size do you wear?"

Libby stood on tiptoe, letting her breath fan against his ear, delighting as that appendage reddened visibly. "About the size of the palm of your hand, cowboy."

"Damn," Jess chuckled, and the red moved out from his ear to churn under his suntan. "Unless you want me to drag you off somewhere and make love to you right now, you'd better not make any more remarks like that."

Suddenly Libby was as pink as the T-shirt he was measuring against her chest. Coming from Jess, this was no idle threat—since their new understanding, reached several weeks before on the top of the hill behind his house, they had made love in some very unconventional places. It would be like him to take her to one of the small trailers brought by some of the cowboys from the Circle Bar B and follow through.

Having apparently deemed the pink T-shirt appropriate, Jess bought it and gripped Libby's hand, fairly dragging her across the sawdust-covered fairgrounds. From the grandstands came the deafening shouts and boot-stompings of more than a thousand excited rodeo fans.

Reaching the rest rooms, which were housed in a building of their own, Jess gave an exasperated sigh. There must have been a hundred women waiting to use the facilities, and he clearly didn't want to stand around in the sun just so Libby could exchange her suntop for a T-shirt.

Before she could offer to wait alone so that Jess could go back and watch the rodeo, he was hauling her toward the nest of Circle Bar B trailers at such a fast pace that she had to scramble to keep up with him.

Thrusting her inside the smallest, which was littered with boots, beer cans and dirty clothes, he ordered, "Put on the shirt."

Libby's color was so high that she was sure he could see it, even in the cool darkness of that camper-trailer. "This is Jake Peterson's camper, isn't it? What if he comes back?"

"He won't come back—he's entered in the bull-riding competition. Just change, will you?"

Libby knew only too well what would happen if she removed that suntop. "Jess..."

He closed the camper door, flipped the inadequate-looking lock. Then he reached out, collected her befeathered hat, her sketchbook, her purse. He laid all these items on a small, messy table and waited.

In the distance, over the loudspeaker system, the rodeo announcer exalted, "This cowboy, folks, has been riding bulls longer'n he's been tying his shoes."

There was a thunderous communal cry as the cowboy and his bull apparently came out of their chute, but it was strangely quiet in that tiny trailer where Jess and Libby stood staring at each other.

Finally, in one defiant motion of her hands, Libby wrenched the suntop off over the top of her head and stood still before her husband, her breasts high and proud and completely bare. "Are you satisfied?" she snapped.

"Not yet," Jess retorted.

He came to stand very close, his hands gentle on her breasts. "You were right," he said into her hair. "You just fit the palms of my hands."

"Oh," said Libby in sweet despair.

Jess's hands continued their tender work, lulling her. It was so cool inside that trailer, so intimate and shadowy.

Presently Libby felt the snap on her jeans, and then the zipper, give way. She was conscious of a shivering heat as the fabric glided downward. Protesting was quite beyond her powers now; she was bewitched.

Jess laid her on the narrow camper bed, joining her within moments. Stretched out upon her, he entered her with one deft thrust.

Their triumph was a simultaneous one, reached after they'd both traveled through a glittering mine field of physical and spiritual sensation, and it was of such dizzying scope that it seemed natural for the unknowing crowd in the grandstands to cheer.

Furiously Libby fastened her jeans and pulled on the T-shirt that had caused this situation in the first place. She gathered up her things, plopped her hat onto her head, and glared into Jess's amused face.

He dressed at a leisurely pace, as though they weren't trespassing.

"If Jake Peterson ever finds out about his, I'll die," Libby said, casting anxious, impatient looks at the locked door.

Jess pulled on one boot, then the other, ran a hand through his rumpled hair. His eyes smoldering with mischief and lingering pleasure, he stood up, pulled Libby into his arms and kissed her. "I love you," he said. "And your shameful secret is safe with me, Mrs. Barlowe."

Libby's natural good nature was overcoming her anger. "Sure," she retorted tartly. "All the same, I think you should know that every man who had ever compromised me in a ranch hand's trailer has said that selfsame thing."

Jess laughed, kissed her again, and then released her. "Go back to your Indians, you little hellion. I'll find you later."

"That's what I'm afraid of," Libby tossed back over one shoulder as she stepped out of the camper into the bright July sunshine. Almost before her eyes had adjusted to the change, she was sketching again.

Libby hardly noticed the passing of the hours, so intent was she on recording the scenes that so fascinated her: braves festooned with colorful feathers, doing their war and rain dances; squaws, plump in their worn buckskin dresses, demonstrating the grinding of corn or making their beaded belts and moccasins; children playing games that were almost as old as the distant mountains and the big sky.

Between the residual effects of that scandalous bout of lovemaking in the trailer and the feast of color and sound assaulting her now, Libby's senses were reeling. She was almost relieved when Cathy came and signed that it was time to leave.

As they walked back to find the others in the still-dense crowd, Libby studied her cousin out of the corner of her eye. Cathy and Stacey were living together again, but there was a wistfulness about Cathy that was disturbing.

There would be no chance to talk with her now—there were too many distractions for that—but Libby made a mental vow to get Cathy alone later, perhaps during the birthday party that was being held on the ranch for Senator Barlowe that evening, and find out what was bothering her.

As the group made plans to stop at a favorite café for an early supper, Libby grew more and more uneasy about Cathy. What was it about her that was different, besides her obviously downhearted mood?

Before Libby could even begin to work out that complex question, Ken and Becky were off to their truck, Stacey and Cathy to their car. Libby was still staring into space when Jess gently tugged at her hand.

She got into the Land Rover, feeling pensive, and laid her sketchbook and purse on the seat.

"Another fit of creativity?" Jess asked quietly, driving carefully through a maze of other cars, staggering cowboys and beleaguered sheriff's deputies.

"I was thinking about Cathy," Libby replied. "Have you noticed a change in her?"

He thought, shook his head. "Not really."

"She doesn't talk to me anymore, Jess."

"Did you have an argument?"

Libby sighed. "No. I've been so busy lately, what with finishing the book and everything, I haven't spent much time with her. I'm ashamed to say that I didn't even notice the change in her until just a little while ago."

Jess gave her a gentle look. "Don't start beating yourself up Libby. You're not responsible for Cathy's happiness or unhappiness."

Surprised, Libby stared at him. "That sounds strange, coming from you."

They were pulling out onto the main highway, which was narrow and almost as choked with cars as the parking area had been. "I'm beginning to think it was a mistake, our being so protective of Cathy. We all meant well, but I wonder sometimes if we didn't hurt her instead."

"Hurt her?"

One of Jess's shoulders lifted in a shrug. "In a lot of ways, Cathy's still a little girl. She's never had to be a grown-up, Libby, because one of us was always there to fight her battles for her. I think she uses her deafness as an excuse not to take risks."

Libby was silent, reflecting on Cathy's fear of being a mother.

As though he'd looked into her mind, Jess went on to say, "Both Cathy and Stacey want children—did you know that? But Cathy won't take the chance."

"I knew she was scared—she told me that. She's scared of so many things, Jess—especially of losing Stacey."

"She loves him."

"I know. I just wish she had something more—something of her own so that her security as a person wouldn't hinge entirely on what Stacey does."

"You mean the way your security doesn't hinge on what I do?" Jess ventured, his tone devoid of any challenge or rancor.

Libby turned, took off her hat and set it down between them with the other things. "I love you very, very much, Jess, but I could live without you. It would hurt unbearably, but I could do it."

He looked away from the traffic only long enough to flash her one devilish grin. "Who would take shameful liberties with your body, if it weren't for me?"

"I guess I would have to do without shameful liberties," she said primly.

"Thank you for sidestepping my delicate male ego," he replied, "but the fact of the matter is, there's no way a woman as beautiful and talented as you are would be alone for very long."

"Don't say that!"

Jess glanced at her in surprise. "Don't say what?"

It was his meaning that had concerned Libby, not his exact words. "I don't even want to think about another man touching me the way you do."

Jess's attention was firmly fixed on the road ahead. "If you're trying to make me feel secure, princess, it's working."

"I'm not trying to make you feel anything. Jess, before we made love that first time, when you said I was really a virgin, you were right. Even the books I've read couldn't have prepared me for the things I feel when you love me."

"It might interest you to know, Mrs. Barlowe, that my feelings toward you are quite similar. Before we made love, sex was just something my body demanded, like food or exercise. Now it's magic."

She stretched to plant a noisy kiss on her husband's cheek. "Magic, is it? Well, you're something of a sorcerer yourself, Jess Barlowe. You cast spells over me and make me behave like a wanton."

He gave an exaggerated evil chuckle. "I hope I can remember the hex that made you give in to me back there at the fairgrounds."

Libby moved the things that were between them into the backseat and slid closer, taking a mischievous nip at his earlobe. "I'm sure you can," she whispered.

Jess shuddered involuntarily and snapped, "Dammit, Libby, I'm driving."

She was exploring the sensitive place just beneath his ear with the tip of her tongue. "Umm. You like getting me into situations where I'm really vulnerable, don't you, Jess?" she breathed, sliding one hand inside his shirt. "Like today, for instance."

"Libby..."

"Revenge is sweet."

And it was.

Shyly Libby extended the carefully wrapped package that contained her personal birthday gift to Senator Barlowe. She had not shown it to anyone else, not even Jess, and now she was uncertain. After all, Monica had given Cleave gold cufflinks and Stacey and Cathy planned to present him with a bottle of rare wine. By comparison, would her offering seem tacky and homemade?

With the gentle smile that had won him so many hearts and so many votes over the years, he took the parcel, which was revealingly large and flat, and turned it in his hands. "May I?" he asked softly, his kind eyes twinkling with affection.

"Please do," replied Libby.

It seemed to take Cleave forever to remove the ribbons and wrapping paper and lift the lid from the box inside, but there was genuine emotion in his face when he saw the framed pen-and-ink drawing Libby had been working on, in secret, for days. "My sons," he said.

"That's us, all right," commented Jess, who had appeared at the senator's side. "Personally, I think I'm considerably handsomer than that."

Cleave was examining the drawing closely. It showed Jess looking forward, Stacey in profile. When the senator looked up, Libby saw the love he bore his two sons in his eyes. "Thank you," he said. "This is one of the finest gifts I've ever received." He assessed the drawing again, and when his gaze came back to meet hers, it was full of mischief. "But where are my daughters? Where are you and Cathy?"

Libby smiled and kissed his cheek. "I guess you'll have to wait until your *next* birthday for that."

"In that case," rejoined the senator, "why not throw in a couple of grandchildren for good measure?"

Libby grinned. "I might be able to come up with one, but a couple?"

"Cathy will just have to do her part," came the immediate reply. "Now, if you'll excuse me, I want to take this picture around and show all my guests what a talented daughter-in-law I have."

Once his father had gone, Jess lifted his champagne glass and one eyebrow. "'Talented' is definitely the word," he said.

Libby knew that he was not referring to her artwork and hastily changed the subject. "You look so splendid in that tuxedo that I think I'd like to dance with you."

Jess worked one index finger under the tight collar of his formal shirt, obviously uncomfortable. "Dance?" he echoed dryly. "Lead me to the organ grinder and we're in business."

Laughing, Libby caught at his free hand and dragged him into the spacious living room, which had been prepared for dancing. There was a small string band to provide the music.

Libby took Jess's champagne glass and set it aside, then rested both hands on his elegant satin lapels. The other guests—and there were dozens—might not have existed at all.

"Dance with me," she said.

Jess took her into his arms, his eyes never leaving hers. "You know," he said softly, "you look so wonderful in that silvery dress that I'm tempted to take you home and make damned sure my father gets that grandchild he wants."

"When we start a baby," she replied seriously, "I want it to be for us."

Jess's mouth quirked into a grin and his eyes were alight with love. "I wasn't going to tape a bow to the little stinker's head and hand it over to him, Libby."

Libby giggled at the picture this prompted in her mind. "Babies are so funny," she dreamed aloud.

"I know," Jess replied. "I love that look of drunken wonder they get when you lift them up high and talk to them. About that time, they usually barf in your hair."

Before she could answer, Ken and Becky came into the magical mist that had heretofore surrounded Libby and Jess.

"All right if I cut in?" Ken asked.

"How soon do you want a grandchild?" Jess countered.

"Sooner the better," retorted Ken. "And, Jess?"

"What?" demanded his son-in-law, eyes still locked with Libby's.

"The music stopped."

Jess and Libby both came to a startled halt, and Becky was so delighted by their expressions that her laughter pealed through the large room.

When the band started playing again, Libby found herself dancing with her father, while Jess and Becky waltzed nearby.

"You look real pretty," Ken said, beaming down at her.

"You're pretty fancy yourself," Libby answered. "In fact, you look downright handsome in that tuxedo."

"She says that to everybody," put in Jess, who happened to be whirling past with Becky.

Ken's laugh was low and throaty. "He never gets too far away from you, does he?"

"About as far as white gets from rice. And I like it that way."

"That's what I figured. Libby…"

The serious, tentative way he'd said her name gave Libby pause. "Yes?"

"Becky and I are going to get married," he blurted out, without taking a single breath.

Libby felt her eyes fill. "You were afraid to tell me that? Afraid to tell me something wonderful?"

Ken stopped, his arms still around his daughter, his blue eyes bright with relief and delight. Then, with a raucous shout that was far more typical of him than tuxedos and fancy parties, her father lifted her so high that she was afraid she would fall out of the top of her dress.

"That was certainly rustic," remarked Monica, five minutes later, at the refreshment table.

Libby saw Jess approaching through the crowd of guests and smiled down at the buttery crab puff in her fingers. "Are you making fun of my father, Ms. Summers?"

Monica sighed in exasperation. "This *is* a formal party, after all—

not a kegger at the Golden Buckle. I don't know why the senator insists on inviting the help to important affairs."

Slowly, and with great deliberation, Libby tucked her crab puff into Monica's artfully displayed cleavage. "Will you hold this, please?" she trilled, and then walked toward her husband.

"The foreman's brat strikes again," Jess chuckled, pulling her into another waltz.

Cathy was sitting alone in the dimly lit kitchen, her eyes fixed on something far in the distance. Libby was careful to let her cousin see her, rather than startle her with a touch.

"Hi," she said.

Cathy replied listlessly.

Libby took a chair opposite Cathy's and signed, "I'd like to help if I can."

Cathy's face crumbled suddenly and she gave a soft cry that tore at Libby's heart. Her hands flew as she replied, "Nobody can help me!"

"Don't I even get to try?"

A tendril of Cathy's hair fell from the soft knot at the back of her head and danced against a shoulder left bare by her Grecian evening gown. "I'm pregnant," she whispered. "Oh, Libby, I'm pregnant!"

Libby felt confusion and just a touch of envy. "Is that so terrible? I know you were scared before, but—"

"I'm still scared!" Cathy broke in, her voice unusually loud.

Libby drew a deep breath. "Why, Cathy? You're strong and healthy. And your deafness won't be the problem you think it will—you and Stacey can afford to hire help, if you feel it's necessary."

"All of that is so easy for you to say, Libby!" Cathy flared with sudden and startling anger. "You can hear! You're a whole person!"

Libby felt her own temper, always suppressed when dealing with her handicapped cousin, surge into life. "You know something?" she said furiously. "I'm sick of your 'Poor Cathy' number! A child is just about the best thing that can happen to a person and instead of rejoicing, you're standing here complaining!"

"I have a reason to complain!"

Libby's arms flew out from her side in a gesture of wild annoyance. "All right! You're deaf, you can't hear! Poor, poor Cathy! Now, can we get past singing your sad song? Dammit, Cathy, I know how hard it must be to live in silence, but can't you look on the positive side for once? You're married to a successful, gentle-hearted man who loves you very much. You have everything!"

"Said the woman who could hear!" shouted Cathy.

Libby sighed and sat back in her chair. "We're all handicapped in some way—Jess told me that once, and I think it's true."

Cathy was not going to be placated. "What's your handicap, Libby?" she snapped. "Your short fingernails? The fact that you freckle in the summer instead of getting tan?"

The derisive sarcasm of her cousin's words stung Libby. "I'm as uncertain of myself at times as you are, Cathy," she said softly. "Aaron—"

"Aaron!" spouted Cathy with contempt. "Don't hand me that, Libby! So he ran around a little—I had to stand by and watch my husband adore my own cousin for months! And I'll bet Jess has made any traumas you had about going to bed with a man all better!"

"Cathy, please..."

Cathy gave a guttural, furious cry of frustration. "I'm so damned tired of you, Libby, with your career and your loving father and your..."

Libby was mad again, and she bounded to her feet. "And my what?" she cried. "I can't help that you don't have a father—Dad tried to make up for that and I think he did a damned good job! As for a career—don't you dare hassle me about that! I worked like a slave to get where I am! If you want a career, Cathy, get off your backside and start one!"

Cathy stared at her, stunned, and then burst into tears. And, of course, Jess chose exactly that moment to walk in.

Giving Libby one scalding, reproachful look, he gathered Cathy into his arms and held her.

Chapter 15

After one moment of feeling absolutely shattered, Libby lifted her chin and turned from Jess's annoyance and Cathy's veiled triumph to walk out of the kitchen with dignity.

She encountered a worried-looking Marion Bradshaw just on the other side of the door. "Libby...Mrs. Barlowe...that man is here!"

Libby drew a deep breath. "What man?" she managed to ask halfheartedly.

"Mr. Aaron Strand, that's who!" whispered Marion. "He had the nerve to walk right up and ring the bell..."

Libby was instantly alert, alive in every part of her being, like a creature being stalked in the wilds. "Where is he now?"

"He's in the senator's study," answered the flushed, quietly outraged housekeeper. "He says he won't leave till he talks with you, Libby. I didn't want a scene, what with all these people here, so I didn't argue."

Wearily Libby patted Marion's shoulder. Facing Aaron Strand, especially now, was the last thing in the world she wanted to do. But she knew that he would create an awful fuss if his request was denied, and besides, what real harm could he do with so many people in the house? "I'll talk to him," she said.

"I'll get Jess," mused Mrs. Bradshaw, "and your daddy, too."

Libby shook her head quickly, and warm color surged up over her face. Jess was busy lending a strong shoulder to Cathy, and she was damned if she was going to ask for his help now, even indirectly. And though Ken was almost fully recovered from his confrontation with the bear, Libby had no intention of subjecting him to the stress that could result from a verbal round with his former son-in-law. "I'll handle this myself," she said firmly, and then, without waiting for a reply, she started for the senator's study.

Aaron was there, tall and handsome in his formal clothes.

"At least when you crash a party, you dress for it," observed Libby dryly from the doorway.

Aaron set down the paperweight he had been examining and smiled. His eyes moved over her in a way that made her want to stride across the room and slap him with all her might. "That dress is classy, sugarplum," he said in acid tones. "You're definitely bunk-house-calendar material."

Libby bit her lower lip, counted mentally until the urge to scream passed. "What do you want, Aaron?" she asked finally.

"Want?" he echoed, pretending pleasant confusion.

"Yes!" hissed Libby. "You flew two thousand miles—you must want something."

He sighed, leaned back against the senator's desk, folded his arms. "Are you happy?"

"Yes," answered Libby with a lift of her chin.

Again he assessed her shiny silver dress, the hint of cleavage it revealed. "I imagine the cowboy is pretty happy with you, too," he said. "Which Barlowe is it, Libby? The steak-house king or the lawyer?"

Libby's head began to ache; she sighed and closed her eyes for just a moment. "What do you want?" she asked again insistently.

His shoulders moved in a shrug. "A baby," he answered, as though he was asking for a cup of coffee or the time of day. "I know you're not going to give me that, so relax."

"Why did you come here, then?"

"I just wanted a look at this ranch. Pretty fancy spread, Lib. You do know how to land on your feet, don't you?"

"Get out, Aaron."

"Without meeting your husband? Your paragon of a father? I wouldn't think of it, Mrs. Barlowe."

Libby was off balance, trying to figure out what reason Aaron could have for coming all the way to Montana besides causing her added grief. Incredible as it seemed, he had apparently done just that. "You can't hurt me anymore, Aaron," she said. "I won't let you. Now, get out of here, please."

"Oh, no. I lost everything because of you—everything. And I'll have my pound of flesh, Libby—you can be sure of that."

"If your grandmother relieved you of your company responsibilities, Aaron, that's your fault, not mine. I should think you would be glad—now you won't have anything to keep you from your wine, women and song."

Aaron's face was tense. Gone was his easy, gentlemanly manner. "With the company went most of my money, Libby. And let's not pretend, sweetness—I can make your bright, shiny new life miserable, and we both know it."

"How?" asked Libby, poised to turn and walk out of the study.

"By generating shame and scandal, of course. Your father-in-law is a prominent United States senator, isn't he? I should think negative publicity could hurt him very badly—and you know how good I am at stirring that up."

Rage made Libby tremble. "You can't hurt Cleave Barlowe, Aaron. You can't hurt me. Now, get out before I have you thrown out!"

He crossed the room at an alarming speed, had a hold on Libby's upper arms before she could grasp what was happening. He thrust her back against the heavy door of the study and covered her mouth with his own.

Libby squirmed, shocked and repulsed. She tried to push Aaron away, but he had trapped her hands between his chest and her own. And the kiss went on, ugly and wet, obscene because it was forced upon her, because it was Aaron's.

Finally he drew back, smirking down at her, grasping her wrists in both hands when she tried to wriggle away from him. And suddenly Libby was oddly detached, calm even. Mrs. Bradshaw had been right when she'd wanted to let Jess know that Aaron was here, so very right.

Libby had demurred because of her pride, because she was mad at Jess; she'd thought she could handle Aaron Strand. Pride be damned, she thought, and then she threw back her head and gave a piercing, defiant scream.

Aaron chuckled. "Do you think I'm afraid of your husband, Libby?" he drawled. Incredibly, he was about to kiss her again, it appeared, when he was suddenly wrenched away.

Libby dared one look at Jess's green eyes and saw murder flashing there. She reached for his arm, but he shook her hand away.

"Strand," he said, his gaze fixed on a startled but affably recovering Aaron.

Aaron gave a mocking half-bow. It didn't seem to bother him that Jess was coldly furious, that half the guests at the senator's party, Ken Kincaid included, were jammed into the study doorway.

"Is this the part," Aaron drawled, "where we fight over the fair lady?"

"This is the part," Jess confirmed icily.

Aaron shrugged. "I feel honor-bound to warn you," he said smugly, "that I am a fifth-degree black belt."

Jess spared him an evil smile, but said nothing.

Libby was afraid; again she grasped at Jess's arm. "Jess, he really is a black belt."

Jess did not so much as look at Libby; he was out of her reach, and not just physically. She felt terror thick in her throat, and flung an appealing look at Ken, who was standing beside her, one arm around her waist.

Reading the plea in his daughter's eyes, he denied it with an almost imperceptible shake of his head.

Libby was frantic. As Jess and Aaron drew closer to each other, circling like powerful beasts, she struggled to free herself from her father's restraining arm. For all his weaknesses of character, Aaron Strand was agile and strong, and if he could hurt Jess, he would, without qualms of any kind.

"Jess, no!" she cried.

Jess turned toward her, his jaw tight with cold annoyance, and Aaron struck in that moment. His foot came up in a graceful arc and caught Jess in the side of the neck. Too sick to stand by herself or run away, Libby buried her face in Ken's tuxedo jacket in horror.

There were sounds—terrible sounds. Why didn't someone stop the fight? Why were they all standing around like Romans thrilling to the exploits of gladiators? Why?

When the sounds ceased and Libby dared to look, Jess was still standing. Aaron was sitting on the floor, groaning theatrically, one corner of his lip bleeding. It was obvious that he wasn't badly hurt, for all his carrying on.

Rage and relief mingled within Libby in one dizzying sweep. "Animals!" she screamed, and when she whirled to flee the ugliness, no one moved to stop her.

Libby sat on the couch in the condo's living room, her arms wrapped around her knees, stubbornly ignoring the ringing of the telephone. She couldn't help counting, though—that had become something of a game in the two days since she'd left the ranch to take refuge here. Twenty-six rings. It was a record.

She stood up shakily, made her way into the kitchen, where she had been trying to sketch out the panels for her cartoon strip. "Back to the old drawing board," she said to the empty room, and the stale joke fell flat because there was no one there to laugh.

The telephone rang again and, worn down, Libby reached out for the receiver affixed to the kitchen wall and snapped, "Hello!"

"Lib?" The voice belonged to her father, and it was full of concern. "Libby, are you all right?"

"No," she answered honestly, letting a sigh carry the word. "As a matter of fact, I'm not all right. How are you?"

"Never mind me—why did you run off like that?"

"You know why."

"Are you coming back to the ranch?"

"Why?" countered Libby, annoyed. "Am I missing some bloody spectacle?"

Ken gave a gruff sigh. "Dammit, Libby, do you love Jess Barlowe or not?"

Tears stung her eyes. Love him? These two days away from him had been hell, but she wasn't about to admit that. "What does it matter?" she shot back. "He's probably so busy holding Cathy's hand that he hasn't even noticed I'm gone."

"That's it. Cathy. Standing up for her is a habit with Jess, Lib— you know that."

Libby did know; in two days she'd had plenty of time to come to the conclusion that she had overreacted in the kitchen the night of the party when Jess had seemed to take Cathy's part against her. She shouldn't have walked out that way. "There is still the fight—"

"You screamed, Libby. What would you have done, if you'd been in Jess's place?" Without waiting for an answer, her father went on, "You're just being stubborn, and so is Jess. Do you love him enough to make the first move, Lib? Do you have the gumption?"

Libby reached out for a kitchen chair, sank into it. "Where is he?"

There was a smile in her father's voice. "Up on that ridge behind your place," he answered. "He's got a camp up there."

Libby knew mild disappointment; if Jess was camping, he hadn't been calling. She had been ignoring the telephone for two days for nothing. "It's nice to know he misses me so much," she muttered petulantly.

Having said his piece, Ken was silent.

"He does miss me, doesn't he?" demanded Libby.

"He misses you," chuckled Ken. "He wouldn't be doing his hermit routine if he didn't."

Libby sighed. "The ridge, huh?"

"The ridge," confirmed Ken with amusement. And then he hung up.

I shouldn't be doing this in my condition, Libby complained to herself as she made her way up the steep hillside. *But since the mountain won't come to me...*

She stopped, looked up. The smoke from Jess's campfire was curling toward the sky; the sun was hot and bright. What the devil did he need with a fire, anyway? It was broad daylight, for heaven's sake.

Muttering, holding on to her waning courage tenaciously, Libby made her way up over the rise to the top of the ridge. Jess was standing with his back to her, looking in the opposite direction, but the stiffness of his shoulders revealed that he knew she was there.

And suddenly she was furious. Hadn't she climbed up this cursed mountain, her heart in her throat, her pride God-only-knew-where? Wasn't the current situation as much his fault as her own? Hadn't she found out, the very day after she'd left him, that she was going to have his baby?

"Damn you, Jess Barlowe," she hissed, "don't you dare ignore me!"

He turned very slowly to face her. "I'm sorry," he said stiffly and with annoying effort.

"For what?" pressed Libby. Damned if she was going to make it easy!

Jess sighed, idly kicked dirt over his campfire with one booted foot. There was a small tent pitched a few feet away, and a coffeepot sat on a fallen log, along with a paperback book and a half-eaten sandwich. "For assuming that the scene with Cathy was your fault," he said.

Libby huffed over to the log, which was a fair distance from Jess, and sat down, folding her arms. "Well, praise be!" she murmured. "What about that stupid fistfight in your father's study?"

His green eyes shot to her face. "You'll grow horns, lady, before you hear me apologize for that!"

Libby bit her lower lip. Fighting wasn't the ideal way to settle things, it was true, but she couldn't help recalling the pleasure she herself had taken in stuffing that crab puff down the front of Monica Summers' dress at the party. If Monica had made one move to retaliate, she would have gladly tangled with her. "Fair enough," she said.

There was an uncomfortable silence, which Libby finally felt compelled to break. "Why did you have a fire going in the middle of the day?"

Jess laughed. "I wanted to make damned sure you found my camp," he replied.

"Dad told you I was coming!"

He came to sit beside her on the log and even though he didn't touch her, she was conscious of his nearness in every fiber of her flesh and spirit. "Yeah," he admitted, and he looked so sad that Libby wanted to cry.

She eased closer to him. "Jess?"

"What?" he asked, looking her squarely in the eyes now.

"I'm sorry."

He said nothing.

Libby drew a deep breath. "I'm not only sorry," she went on bravely, "I'm pregnant, too."

He was quiet for so long that Libby feared she'd been wrong to tell him about their child—at least for now. It was possible that he wanted to ask for a separation or even a divorce, but he might stay with her out of duty now that he knew. To hold him in that manner would break Libby's heart.

"When did you find out?" he asked finally, and the lack of emotion in his face and in his voice made Libby feel bereft.

"Day before yesterday. After Cathy said she was pregnant, I got to thinking and realized that I had a few symptoms myself."

Jess was silent, looking out over the trees, the ranges, the far mountains. After what seemed like an eternity, he turned to her again, his green eyes full of pain. "You weren't going to tell me?"

"Of course I was going to tell you, Jess. But, well, the time didn't seem to be right."

"You're not going to leave, are you?"

"Would I have climbed a stupid mountain, for pity's sake, if I wanted to leave you?"

A slow grin spread across Jess's face, and then he gave a startling hoot of delight and shot to his feet, his hands gripping Libby's and pulling her with him. If he hadn't caught her in his arms and held her, she would probably have fallen into the lush summer grass.

"Is it safe to assume you're happy about this announcement?" Libby teased, looking up at him and loving him all the more because there were tears on his face.

He lifted her into his arms, kissed her deeply in reply.

"Excuse me, sir," she said when he drew back, "but I was wondering if you would mind making love to me. You see, I'd like to find out if I'm welcome here."

In answer, Jess carried her to the tent, set her on her feet. "My tent is your tent," he said.

Libby blushed a little and bent to go inside the small canvas shelter. Since there wasn't room enough to stand, she sat on the rumpled sleeping bag and waited as Jess joined her.

She was never sure exactly how it came about, but within moments they were both lying down, facing each other. The weight of his hand was bliss on her breast, and so were the hoarse words he said.

"I love you, Libby. I need you. No matter how mad I make you, please don't leave me again."

Libby traced the strong lines of his jaw with a fingertip. "I won't, Jess. I might scream and yell, but I won't leave. I love you too much to be away from you—if I learned anything in the last two days, it was that."

He was propped up on one elbow now, very close, and he was idly unbuttoning her blouse. "I want you."

Libby feigned shock. "In a tent, sir?"

"And other novel places." He paused, undid the front catch of her bra.

Libby sighed, then gasped as the warmth of his mouth closed over the straining peak of her breast. The sensation was exquisite, sweeping through her, pushing away the weariness and confusion and pain. She tangled her fingers in his rumpled hair, holding him close.

Jess finally left the breast he had so gently plundered to remove his clothes, and then, more slowly, Libby's. When she lay naked before him in the cool shadows of the tiny tent, he took in her waiting body with a look of rapt wonder. "Little enchantress," he breathed, "let me worship you.

Libby could not bear to be separate from him any longer. "Be close to me, Jess," she pleaded softly, "be part of me."

With a groan, he fell to her, his mouth moist and commanding upon hers. His tongue mated with Libby's and his manhood touched her with fire, prodding, taking only partial shelter inside her.

At last Jess broke the kiss and lifted his head, and Libby saw, through a shifting haze, that he was savoring her passion as well as his own. She was aware of every muscle in his body as he struggled to defy forces that do not brook the rebellion of mere mortals.

Finally these forces prevailed, and Jess was thrust, with a raspy cry, into Libby's depths. They moved together wildly, seeking and reaching and finally breaking through the barriers that divide this world from the glories of the next.

Cathy assessed the large oil painting of Jim Little Eagle, the Indian child Libby had seen at the powwow months before, her hands resting on her protruding stomach.

Libby, whose stomach was as large as Cathy's, was wiping her hands on a rag reserved for the purpose. The painting was a personal triumph, and she was proud of it. "What do you think?" she signed, after setting aside the cloth.

Cathy grinned. "What do I think?" she asked aloud, sitting down on the tall stool behind Libby's drawing board. "I'll tell you what I think. I think you should sell it to me instead of letting that gallery in Great Falls handle it. After all, they've got your pen-and-ink drawings and the other paintings you did."

Libby tried to look stern. "Are you asking for special favors, Cathy Barlowe?"

Cathy laughed. "Yes!" Her sparkling green eyes fell to the sketch affixed to Libby's drawing board and she exclaimed in delighted surprise. "This is great!"

Libby came to stand behind her, but her gaze touched only briefly on the drawing. Instead, she was looking out at the snow through the windows of her studio in Ken and Becky's house.

"What are you going to do with this?" Cathy demanded, tugging at Libby's arm.

Libby smiled, looking at the drawing. It showed her cartoon character, given over to the care of another artist now. Liberated Lizzie was in an advanced state of pregnancy, and the blurb read, "If it feels good, do it."

"I'm going to give it to Jess," she said with a slight blush. "It's a private joke."

Cathy laughed again, then assessed the spacious, well-equipped studio with happy eyes. "I'm surprised you work down here at your dad's place. Especially with Jess home almost every day, doing paperwork and things."

Libby's mouth quirked in a grin. "That's *why* I work down here. If I tried to paint there, I wouldn't get anything done."

"You're really happy, aren't you?"

"Completely."

Cathy enfolded her in a hug. "Me, too," she said. And when her eyes came to Libby's face, they were dancing with mischief. "Of course, you and Jess have to understand that you will never win the Race. Stacey and I are ahead by at least a nose."

Libby stood straight and tried to look imperious. "We will not concede defeat," she said.

Before Cathy could reply to this, Stacey came into the room, pretending to see only Libby. "Pardon me, pudgy person," he began, "but has my wife waddled by lately?"

"Is she kind of short, with long, pretty hair and big green eyes and a stomach shaped rather like a watermelon?"

Stacey snapped his fingers and a light seemed to go on in his face. "That's a pretty good description."

"Haven't seen her," said Libby.

Cathy gave her a delighted shove and flung herself at her husband, laughing. A moment later they were on their way out, loudly vowing to win what Jess and Stacey had dubbed the Great Barlowe Baby Race.

Through with her work for the day and eager to get home to Jess, Libby cleaned her brushes and put them away, washed her hands again, and went out to find her coat. The first pain struck just as she was getting into the car.

At home, Jess was standing pensively in the kitchen, staring out at the heavy layer of snow blanketing the hillside behind the house. Libby came up as close behind him as her stomach would allow and wrapped her arms around his lean waist.

"I've just had a pretty good tip on the Baby Race," she said.

The muscles beneath his bulky woolen sweater tightened, and he turned to look down at her, his jade eyes dark with wonder. "What did you say?"

"We're on the homestretch, Jess. I need to go to the hospital. Soon."

He paled, this man who had hunted wounded bears and fire-breathing dragons. "My God!" he yelled, and suddenly they were both caught up in a whirlwind of activity. Phone calls were made, suitcases were snatched from the coat-closet floor, and then Jess was dragging Libby toward his Land Rover.

"Wait, I'm sure we have time—"

"I'm not taking any chances!" barked Jess, hoisting her pear-shaped and unwieldy form into the car seat.

"Jess," Libby scolded, grasping at his arm. "You're panicking!"

"You're damned right I'm panicking!" he cried, and then they were driving over the snowy, rutted roads of the ranch at the fastest pace he dared.

When they reached the airstrip, the Cessna had been brought out of the small hangar where it was kept and fuel was being pumped into it. After wrestling Libby into the front passenger seat, Jess quickly checked the engine and the landing gear. These were tasks, she had learned, that he never trusted to anyone else.

"Jess, this is ridiculous!" she protested when he scrambled into the pilot's seat and began a preflight test there. "We have plenty of time to drive to the hospital."

Jess ignored her, and less than a minute later the plane was taxiing down the runway. Out of the corner of one eye Libby saw a flash of ice blue.

"Jess, wait!" she cried. "The Ferrari!"

The plane braked and Jess craned his neck to see around Libby. Sure enough, Stacey and Cathy were running toward them, if Cathy's peculiar gait could be called a run.

Stacey leapt up onto the wing and opened the door. "Going our way?" he quipped, but his eyes were wide and his face was white.

"Get in," replied Jess impatiently, but his eyes were gentle as they touched Cathy and then Libby. "The race is on," he added.

Cathy was the first to deliver, streaking over the finish line with a healthy baby girl, but Libby produced twin sons soon after. Following much discussion, the Great Barlowe Baby Race was declared a draw.

*   *   *   *   *

YESTERDAY'S LOVE
by Sherryl Woods

For Nancy, whose rare combination
of zaniness and practicality makes her a very
special friend, and for Andy, who's brought her
happiness and romance.

Chapter 1

Tears streaming down her pale cheeks, Victoria flipped off the television by remote control and reached blindly for the box of tissues beside her on the huge brass bed. When her groping fingers met the empty slot, she muttered a soft expletive, tossed the useless container across the room and wiped away the tears with the back of her hand. *Now, Voyager* always did this to her.

"You'd think by now I'd be prepared, wouldn't you?" she said to the fluffy gray cat that was purring contentedly in her lap. How many times had she sobbed as a resigned Bette Davis pleaded with Paul Henried not to ask for the moon, when they already had the stars? Surely more than a dozen.

Of course, it wasn't just this movie that affected her that way, she noted ruefully. She'd cried through everything from *Jane Eyre* and *Camille* to *Terms of Endearment*. She'd even been known to sniffle a little when two obviously long lost lovers were reunited in a shampoo commercial.

Being a sentimental, hopeless romantic in a world of hardened cynics sometimes seemed to be a wretched curse. She recalled with more than a little dismay the number of times her embarrassed dates had exited a movie joking that they might be able to buy her diamonds, but they doubted they could afford to keep her supplied with Kleenex. Well, to hell with the emotionally uptight men of the world, she thought darkly. They'll all probably wind up with much deserved ulcers.

Climbing out of bed, she ignored Lancelot's outraged cry of protest at being displaced from his comfortable spot in her lap. After she pulled on the long, old-fashioned skirt and scoop-necked blouse she'd found during her last secondhand store excursion, she wandered barefoot into the kitchen. The fragrant scent of lilacs and freshly mowed grass was drifting in with the spring breeze that ruffled the curtains on the open windows. This was her favorite room in the decrepit old farmhouse she'd bought and begun remodeling bit by bit the previous year. Her parents had nicknamed her home Victoria's Folly, but once they'd seen what she'd accomplished with the kitchen, even they had to admit there was hope for the place.

Like the rest of the house, the kitchen had wide-plank hardwood floors, but in here she had stripped away layers of paint and wax and had polished the wood to a soft gleam. The huge windows, cleansed of the thick grime that had accumulated during years of neglect, now let in so much light that the room seemed bright even on the grayest Ohio winter day. She had scoured the once disreputable looking white tile countertops until they sparkled. The crumbling walls had been patched and painted a cheerful yellow, against which she had hung shiny copper pots and pans. She had refinished the round oak table and chairs in the middle of the room herself. And in the center of the table stood an antique blue-and-white water pitcher filled with daffodils from her garden.

"Okay, old guy, what shall we do about lunch?" she asked the cat who was now staring at her patiently from the sun-warmed windowsill. "Tuna? Liver? Chicken?" She waited for a responding meow. There was none. "You're not helping, Lancelot." She opened a can of the liver he seemed to love, wrinkled her nose in disgust and put it in his dish.

"You have no taste, cat," she said, as he arched haughtily and then made his way slowly to the dish of food she'd placed on the floor.

While Lancelot methodically devoured the liver, Victoria searched in the back of the huge, walk-in pantry for her picnic basket. The day was too incredibly gorgeous to waste one more minute of it indoors. She filled the wicker basket with chunks of Gouda and cheddar cheese, two freshly baked poppy seed rolls she'd bought at the bakery on her way home from her antique shop the previous afternoon, a bottle of chilled mineral water and a container of strawberries. She tossed a dog-eared volume of Elizabeth Barrett Browning's poetry in on top, took her floppy, wide-brimmed straw hat from the peg by the back door and set out across the rolling field behind the house. Lancelot, through with his meal, trailed at her heels sniffing hopefully amid the buttercups for the scent of a field mouse.

When she reached the huge, ancient oak tree that shaded the back corner of her property, she spread out her red-checked tablecloth and settled down for her picnic, barely noticing the taste of the food as she lost herself in the sad, poetic spell Browning had woven.

How do I love thee? Let me count the ways
I love thee to the depth and breadth and height
My soul can reach, when feeling out of sight
For the ends of Being and ideal Grace.

For the second time that day, she felt misty-eyed. Would she ever love someone this much, she wondered despondently. Nothing in her twenty-eight years indicated that she had the potential for such deep emotion. Certainly none of the men she'd met up until now had ever stirred a passionate response from her. Their kisses, their practiced touches had been mildly enjoyable, but nothing more. Maybe she was doomed to a life of lukewarm relationships. The thought was incredibly depressing, especially for someone who truly believed it was love that made the world go around.

Sighing heavily, she glanced up from the sonnet she'd been reading just in time to see Lancelot spring into the tree above her with surprising agility for a cat his size and age.

"Lancelot, no!" she shouted futilely, as he landed on a limb high above her head. "Lancelot, you know you're terrified of heights. Now what are you going to do?"

She shook her head as the cat uttered a pathetic meow.

"You got yourself up there," she reminded him unsympathetically. "Now get yourself down."

Lancelot seemed to shiver, then meowed again more loudly. He sounded pitiful, far too pitiful to ignore.

"Okay. Okay. I'm coming," she said resignedly, dropping her book onto the tablecloth and hiking up her skirt. She shinnied up the tree in the awkward, uneasy manner of someone who'd done this often in the past but never grown accustomed to it. To be perfectly truthful, she wasn't one bit fonder of heights than Lancelot was. To top it off, the minute she got near him, the cat backed out of her reach. "Lancelot, how can I rescue you if you keep moving away from me?"

She tested the strength of the limb and shifted until her body rested along the length of it. Stretching as far as she could, she tried again to grab the cat, whose cries had grown more shrill. Taking a deep breath, Victoria crept another few inches. "Here, Lancelot. Come on, fellow," she whispered encouragingly, just as she heard the branch creak and felt it waver beneath her. The tremor shook her confidence and her patience. "Lancelot, get over here right this minute!"

The cat didn't budge, but the limb dipped precariously and Victoria glanced nervously down at the ground. It seemed much farther away than she'd remembered. Clinging tightly to the branch while she tried to decide whether to risk a retreat or spend the next fifty years of her life right here living on bark, acorns and oak leaves, she looked off in the distance and spotted the welcome sight of someone heading in her direction.

With his determined, long-legged stride and squared jaw, the unfamiliar man looked like someone with a definite and probably unpleasant mission. Even from this distance and this crazy, sort of upside-down angle, she could tell he was physically impressive. His broad shoulders, beneath a pale blue shirt that was shadowed with perspiration, were obviously well formed and muscular. The tan slacks were slung low on slim hips, the fit emphasizing the curve of his thighs, the length of his powerful legs. His tie was askew, and he was carrying a tan jacket slung over his shoulder. He was definitely not dressed like someone who'd planned to go for a stroll in the country.

She shaded her eyes and squinted into the sun, studying what she could make out of the chiseled features of his face and the dark brown hair that needed cutting. Her breath caught in her throat.

"Good Lord, if I'm dreaming, don't let me wake up," she murmured under her breath as he approached, his expression growing puzzled as he noted the tablecloth, the picnic basket and the book.

"Hi," she said cheerfully, trying to keep a nervous tremor out of her voice. The last crack of the limb had tilted it until her head seemed nearly perpendicular to the blanket. As soft as the ground had seemed when she'd been sitting on it, she had no particular desire to land on it headfirst and test its resiliency.

Startled by the husky, whispered greeting, Tate McAndrews looked around for the person whose entrancing voice had seemed to come to him from the heavens.

"Up here."

He gazed up and stared into a pair of very wide, very blue eyes that glinted with suppressed laughter. His heart took an unexpected lurch.

"Hi, yourself," he said, his irritation at the rotten way the day had gone suddenly vanishing in the presence of such unabashed, impish humor. Perhaps this wild-goose chase he'd been sent on would have an unexpected dividend after all. "Do you always perch in trees after lunch?"

"Hardly," she said with a grimace that wrinkled her pert nose in a delightful way. "By the way, my name's Victoria Marshall and I'm very glad to see you. I seem to have gotten myself into a bit of a predicament."

Tate groaned and a pained expression replaced the quirk of amusement that had played about his lips. So much for any thoughts of pleasant diversions. His wild-goose chase had ended. "I should have known," he muttered.

"Is something wrong?"

He shook his head. "No. In fact, I was looking for you."

"You were? Do I know you?"

"Not yet, but you will," he mumbled ominously. "I'm Tate McAndrews. Internal Revenue Service."

Usually people panicked at the mere mention of the IRS, but Tate had to give Victoria Marshall credit. She didn't even flinch.

"Oh, that's nice," she said brightly and with such sincerity that Tate had to believe she had no idea what he was doing here. "But do you suppose you could help me get down before we continue this conversation? My head is beginning to spin."

"What are you doing up there in the first place?"

"Lancelot saw a squirrel."

"Lancelot? A squirrel?" He felt strangely light-headed, as though he were rapidly losing the capability of rational thought. It was either this unseasonably warm weather or this perky woman he'd discovered hanging upside down in a tree with her skirt hitched up in a decidedly provocative way. He preferred to think it was the weather.

"Lancelot is my cat. He's twelve and he mostly just lazes around now, but a squirrel will get to him every time."

"I see." Actually Tate didn't see at all. But he was beginning to understand that this assignment that Pete Harrison had foisted off on him was not going to be quite as easy and straightforward as he'd anticipated. He berated himself for not guessing that any woman who would demand that the IRS send her a refund for $15,593.12 more than she had paid in taxes was not exactly your run-of-the-mill evader. She was a kook. Everything that had happened in the last few minutes only confirmed the fact. She might be very attractive in an offbeat sort of way, but she was a kook nonetheless.

Still, she was also up in the tree, and he couldn't wrap up this absurd business about the refund until she came down. It would probably be best if she didn't do it headfirst and shake any more of her screws loose.

"Let go of the branch," he suggested.

"Are you crazy?" she replied in a horrified, hushed whisper, her eyes widening as the branch tipped a bit more. "I'm twelve feet off the ground. I'll break every bone in my body."

"Don't worry. I'm going to catch you."

"Then I'll break every bone in your body."

"I'll take my chances," he retorted. "Come on. Just let go and drop down."

"But what about Lancelot?"

"I don't think you need to worry about him," Tate replied dryly.

Victoria followed his gaze and saw that the traitorous cat was sitting serenely in the middle of the tablecloth eating the last of the Gouda cheese. "Lancelot, how could you?" she muttered.

"You might as well jump."

Sighing nervously, Victoria swung her legs around, allowing them to dangle as she clung tightly to the increasingly unsteady branch. She glanced down uneasily into Tate McAndrews's upturned face. "Are you sure about this?"

"I'm sure."

"Okay," she said, closing her eyes as she let go. There was no point in looking. It was up to Tate McAndrews to make good on his promise to catch her. She tried to think of herself as weightless, a butterfly floating on air, but it wasn't working. She felt as though she were plummeting like a rock. Her heart thudded against her ribs in anticipation of the crash landing that would leave them both in a tangle of broken bones.

Suddenly, just when she was sure it was too late, that she'd only imagined someone was going to save her from cracking her skull, she felt strong arms break her fall. As the breath whooshed out of her, her own arms instinctively circled Tate's shoulders. She hung on for dear life.

"You can open your eyes now," he said, his husky, laughter-filled voice a whisper of disturbing warmth against her flushed cheek.

Victoria wasn't sure she wanted to if it meant he would put her down. She was surprised to discover that she rather liked his tangy male scent, the rippling strength of his arms, the warmth that radiated through his clothes. He appealed to so many of her senses: touch, smell and—most definitely she decided, peeking at his chiseled profile—sight. The man was even more gorgeous than he'd appeared from her perch in the tree. Definitely romantic hero material, she thought, sighing unconsciously.

Tate heard the sigh and realized with a sense of shock that he was apparently having a very similar reaction. It was a reaction that was both unexpected and totally inappropriate. Ten years with IRS had hardened him, made him cynical about human nature in general and especially about the type of people who tried to bilk the government. They were thieves, and it was his job to catch them and see that they paid. Nothing more, nothing less. It was all very businesslike, very impersonal. Sometimes he spent months on a case, shadowing a subject's every move, getting to know the most intimate secrets of his or her life, but never before had he responded to one of them on a personal level.

Then again, he had to admit that none of his previous subjects had ever looked like Victoria Marshall. He lowered her gently to the checked tablecloth, then sat down beside her, unable to shift his gaze away. She was like no woman he had ever seen, except, perhaps, in a Renoir painting. She was wearing a long, ruffled cotton skirt in a bright shade of pink that made her seem daringly oblivious to the long red hair that framed her face in a profusion of untamed, golden-highlighted curls. Though those incredibly blue eyes met his gaze with an appealing, interested expression, she was fiddling nervously with a floppy, white straw hat. Her off-the-shoulder white blouse revealed an extraordinary amount of creamy flesh, he noted breathlessly before glancing quickly away only to encounter the enticing sight of her slender, bare feet peeking from beneath the folds of her skirt.

He drew a deep, shuddering breath. This wouldn't do at all. Obviously, Victoria Marshall was smarter than he'd thought. She was probably deliberately trying to appeal to him, to seduce him so that he'd forget all about the little matter of her bizarre tax return. She wouldn't be the first woman to try that. True, most of them were considerably more worldly than she seemed to be, but perhaps this wide-eyed innocence was all an act.

Victoria watched the play of expressions on Tate's face and wondered about them. Warmth. Anger. Determination. She had the feeling that he'd just made a decision about something or someone. Was it her? She didn't want to think so, because his brown eyes were glittering now with a cold hardness that she found almost frightening in its dark intensity.

"Did you bring my check?" she asked hopefully.

He shook his head. "Sorry. The IRS doesn't underwrite bad business debts. Why haven't you answered any of our letters?"

Victoria was puzzled. "I haven't seen any letters." She brightened. "Of course there is a stack of mail on the desk in the shop. They must be there. What were they about?"

"We're auditing you. You were supposed to report with all your records."

"Oh, dear. When?"

"Last week."

"Oh, dear," she repeated contritely. "Would you like some cheese?"

"What?"

"I asked if you would like some cheese," she explained patiently, holding out a chunk of the cheddar that Lancelot hadn't discovered during his raid on the picnic basket. "It's very good."

"Sure. Thanks. About the audit—"

"Couldn't we talk about that later?"

"Look, Ms. Marshall—"

"Call me Victoria."

Tate closed his eyes. His head was beginning to reel again. "Victoria. I drove all the way up here from Cincinnati to straighten out your tax problems. I don't have time to sit under a tree and eat cheese and make small talk with you." She blinked at him rapidly and his determination wavered.

"Much as I might like to," he added to soften the harsh effect of his very firm words. She'd looked as though she might cry and he couldn't stand that. He had come here to find out how much she'd been holding out on the government, not to make her cry.

"But I don't have any tax problems," she insisted stoutly. "I've always sent my return in right on time."

She hesitated, her very kissable pink lips pursed thoughtfully. "At least I think I have. I'm not sure. Paperwork is so boring, don't you think? Anyway, I'm almost certain that I haven't missed a single deadline. I make it a point to put a big red circle around April 15 on my calendar so I won't forget.''

''But you asked for a refund of money you'd never paid.''

She regarded him indignantly. ''How can you say that? I've paid year after year. This last year, when I opened my shop, I lost more money than I earned.''

Tate, to his dismay, was beginning to follow her logic. That scared the life out of him. Unleashed on an unsuspecting world, this woman would be dangerous. Beautiful, but kooky as they come. ''So you figured the government should reimburse you out of funds you'd previously paid?''

Her eyes sparkled, and she gave him a smile that could light up a skyscraper. ''Exactly.''

''It doesn't work that way.''

''It doesn't?''

''I'm afraid not.''

Her smile wavered. ''Oh. Well, I guess I'll get by. Business has been picking up lately. Now that it's spring more people seem to go for drives in the country. Most of them can't resist browsing through antiques.''

''Do they buy anything?''

She shrugged. ''Sometimes. More often than not, they drink a cup of coffee, chat awhile and then go on. That's part of the fun of owning an antique shop...meeting new people.''

''You give your customers coffee?''

The look she gave him was withering. ''Usually I have a home-made cake, too,'' she said defensively. ''Yesterday I had apple pie, but the crust was soggy. I haven't quite mastered pie crusts yet. I'm not sure what the problem is. Maybe the shortening.''

Tate shook his head. He'd obviously been dealing with powerful, cold-blooded corporations too long. He was not prepared to deal with someone who spent more money most days feeding her customers than she took in and then worried about the quality of her cooking on top of it.

''Do you suppose we could take a look at your records?'' he said, suddenly impatient to get this over with. He was getting some very strange feelings from this woman and, unfortunately, most of them were very unprofessional. Right now she was looking at him with wide, cornflower-blue eyes filled with hurt, as though he'd rejected her or worse. His pulse rate quickened, and he had the oddest desire to comfort her, to hold her and tell her he'd take care of everything. He drew in a ragged breath and reminded himself sternly that IRS agents, especially those with his reputation for tough, relentless questioning, did not comfort individuals they were about to audit.

"Of course," Victoria replied stiffly. Her first impression obviously had been correct: this man did have a mission, and it seemed he wasn't the type to be dissuaded from pursuing it. It was such a waste, too, she thought with a sigh. With his dashing good looks and trim build, he'd seemed exactly the sort of man she'd been waiting all her life to meet, the type who'd sweep a woman off her feet in the very best romantic tradition. Instead, he seemed to have the soul of a stuffy realist. He was going to wind up with ulcers by the time he hit forty, just like the rest of them.

Disillusioned and disappointed at having to abandon her fantasy so quickly, she gathered up the remnants of her picnic, perched her hat on top of her head and took off across the field, her long skirt billowing in the breeze. She didn't wait to see if Tate McAndrews followed. She knew instinctively that he wasn't about to let her out of his sight. He apparently thought she was some sort of criminal. She huffed indignantly at the very idea. A criminal indeed! Well, he could look at her records, such as they were, from now until doomsday, and he wouldn't find anything incriminating. Once he'd finished, he could apologize and go on his way.

She glanced over her shoulder and caught the frown on his face, the hard, no-nonsense line of his jaw. On second thought, he probably wouldn't apologize.

When they reached the house, Victoria opened the kitchen door and stood aside to allow Tate to enter.

"Why don't you have a seat? I'll get the papers and bring them in here," she suggested. "There's lemonade in the fridge, if you'd like some."

Lemonade? The corners of Tate's mouth tilted up as he watched her disappear into the main part of the house, the long skirt adding a subtle emphasis to the naturally provocative sway of her hips. He couldn't recall the last time anyone had offered him lemonade. Most of the women he knew had a Scotch on the rocks waiting for him when he walked in the door. He picked up two tall glasses from the counter by the sink, went to the refrigerator and filled them with ice. He found the huge pitcher of fresh-squeezed lemonade and poured them each a glass. He took a long, thirst-quenching swallow of the sweet-tart drink. It was perfect after that damnably hot trek through the field. He'd forgotten how good this stuff was. Maybe he was getting a little too jaded after all.

He sat on one of the high-backed chairs, tilted it on two legs and surveyed the room. It had a cheerful, homey feel to it. It was nothing like the pretentious glass and high-tech kitchens he was used to. In fact, he had a feeling Victoria Marshall had never heard of a food processor, much less used one. She'd probably squeezed every one of the lemons for this lemonade with her own hands. The thought proved disturbingly intriguing.

"Slow down, McAndrews. This woman is strictly off-limits," he muttered aloud. Not only was Victoria Marshall the subject of an official IRS investigation, she was totally inappropriate for him. He liked his women sophisticated, fashionable and, most of all, uncommitted. From what he'd seen of Victoria she was about as worldly as a cloistered nun. As for her fashion sense, it would have been fine about one hundred years ago. And, worst of all, she was definitely the type of woman who needed commitments. She'd been reading *Sonnets from the Portuguese*, for crying out loud.

But she was gorgeous. Fragile. Like the lovely old porcelain doll he remembered his mother keeping in a place of honor in her bedroom. That doll had been his great-grandmother's and would be passed along to his daughter if, as his mother reminded him frequently, he would only have the good sense to marry and settle down. He was suddenly struck by the fact that his mother probably would approve thoroughly of someone like Victoria.

"Uh-uh," he muttered emphatically, irritated at the direction his thoughts had taken. He'd better get this over with now before he did something absolutely ridiculous and totally out of character, such as asking Victoria Marshall for a date. His mother might cheer, but Pete Harrison would have his hide for that breach of ethics.

"Where the hell is she?" he groused, lowering the chair to all four sturdy legs with a thud and stalking out of the kitchen. As he went from room to empty room looking for her, his dismay grew. How could she live like this? The place was a shambles. No wonder she'd left him in the kitchen. The wallpaper in the rest of the downstairs was peeling, the floors were warped and weathered, as though they'd spent weeks under floodwaters, and there wasn't a stick of furniture in any of the rooms, unless you counted the old Victorian sofa which had stuffing popping out through holes in the upholstery. It looked as though it would be painfully uncomfortable under the best of repair.

"Victoria!"

"I'll be right down. I'm just trying to get everything together."

"I'll come up."

"Don't do that," she shouted back and he sensed an odd urgency in her voice. "The stairs—"

But before she could finish the warning, Tate had already reached the third step. As soon as he put his weight on it, he felt the stair wobble and heard the wood crack. His ankle twisted painfully and he fell backward, landing with a thud. The crash echoed throughout the house, followed by an explosion of exceptionally colorful curses as Tate lay on the floor, his ankle throbbing, his ego even more bruised than his body.

"Damn Pete Harrison and his so-called breeze of a case!" he growled ominously, completely undone by the emotional and physical shake-up of his life ever since he'd found Victoria Marshall in that damned tree. "I have a feeling I'd be in less danger checking out the head of the mob."

Chapter 2

Upstairs, Victoria listened to the cacophony of explosive sounds and winced. Obviously, her incomplete warning had been far too little, too late. Cautiously, she poked her head out the door of her makeshift office-storeroom and peered down into Tate McAndrews's scowling face.

"Are you okay?"

He was getting gingerly to his feet, testing his ankle. "Nothing's broken, if that's what you mean."

"I'm sorry. I tried to warn you."

"So you did," he admitted dryly. "How can you live like this?"

"Like what?" she asked, honestly puzzled by the question. She loved this old house and she'd never been happier anywhere else. It was exactly the sort of home she'd always dreamed of owning, a place with character, with all sorts of interesting nooks and crannies. It would be a terrific place for hide-and-seek.

"This place is falling apart."

She looked at the wobbly stairs, the tattered wallpaper and the dangling light bulb that Tate could see from the downstairs hall. Even she had to admit it didn't give the very best impression of the house. "You have to think in terms of potential," she suggested.

"Potential?"

"Like the kitchen," she explained, deciding that he needed concrete images. Men like Tate McAndrews always did. They seemed to have trouble dealing with the abstractions, with feelings and moods and ambiance.

"You mean the kitchen looked as bad as this?"

"Worse," she admitted. "It was my third project. It turned out rather well, don't you think?"

"You did the kitchen yourself?"

She wasn't sure whether she should be pleased or insulted by his incredulous tone. She decided to remain neutral. "You've seen my tax return. Does it look like I could afford to hire somebody?"

"I guess not."

"Well, then. Of course, if I'd gotten that refund...." Her voice trailed off forlornly.

"Forget it," he advised. "You said the kitchen was your third project. What were the others?"

"The bedroom and bathroom."

Despite himself, Tate was intrigued. Knowing he was going to hate himself later for allowing yet another distraction to keep him from wrapping up this audit and escaping to the relative safety of Cincinnati, he asked, "May I see?"

"Are you sure you want to risk the stairs?"

"Just tell me what the secret is."

"I've fixed every other one," she explained brightly, as though that were a perfectly sensible thing to do.

He looked down and saw what should have been obvious to him in the first place: every second step was made of new wood, polished and solid looking. The ones in-between were broken planks that looked no better than the floors he'd seen in the downstairs rooms. The third one was splintered where his weight had been too much for the dry-rotted wood.

"I should have guessed," he said, taking giant-sized steps to join her. "Lead on. You can warn me where the booby traps are."

"Careful," she whispered conspiratorially. "You'll hurt its feelings."

"Houses don't have feelings."

"Of course they do. They have feelings and personalities all their own."

"This one's obviously split," he murmured.

"What?"

"You know...a split personality. Repaired in some parts. Disastrous in others."

"Very funny."

"I thought it was."

"You would. You obviously have a cruel streak."

"I'll admit I'm not quite as tolerant as you appear to be," he retorted, giving her a grin that shattered her indignation into a thousand pieces. Victoria found herself smiling back at him helplessly.

"Do you want to see the rest or not?" she asked softly, her flashing blue eyes more challenging than her words. A flicker of desire had flared to life in Tate's eyes and Victoria felt a matching tremor of excitement so intense it startled her. So, she thought, this was what the fuss was all about. One minute you're leading a perfectly ordinary, placid existence, and the next minute some thoroughly impossible, sexy man turns up and turns your insides into warm honey. The sensation was both thrilling and frightening.

"Oh, I want," he replied in a low voice, his gaze drifting down over her slender neck and bare shoulders before halting in apparent fascination at the swell of her breasts. There was no doubt in her mind that he wasn't referring to a tour of the house. Victoria suddenly realized with a flush of embarrassment that her nipples were clearly visible beneath the light cotton of her blouse. Worse than that, they seemed to be responding merely to the appreciative warmth of his examination, swelling to an aching tautness. She suddenly felt claustrophobic and had the strangest desire to run. At the same time, she wanted very much to stay right here and see exactly what Tate Mc-Andrews had in mind and whether he meant to follow through on that dangerous glint she thought she'd read in his eyes.

Almost hesitantly, he reached toward her and her heart thundered in anticipation, while her head seemed to be shouting to her to get a grip on herself. Sighing regretfully, she decided that just this once she'd better listen to her head. Before Tate's fingers could touch her cheek, she whirled neatly around and stepped away from him.

"This is the bathroom," she said briskly, determined to keep the shakiness she felt from her voice. Just because Tate McAndrews was the sexiest creature she'd seen since her last viewing of Clark Gable in *Gone With the Wind*, that was no reason for her to go all wobbly and woolly-headed. The man was here to audit her, after all. It wasn't as though he'd asked her for a date. He'd only looked at her as though he'd wanted to...what? To kiss her senseless? And that was what had made her go weak in the knees. It was not a good way to begin a business relationship with an IRS agent, not unless you planned to follow through, which she most certainly did not.

With determinedly cool detachment she showed him the bathroom with its lovely old tiled walls and floor, its huge tub and the circular leaded window that let in shattered streams of bright sun during the day and soft moonlight at night. When they reached her bedroom, her composure slipped a little as she wondered idly what it would be like to have this virile man sharing her huge brass bed, the colorful, handmade quilt tossed anxiously aside in a tangled heap as a desperate, urgent passion made them oblivious to anything except each other. The prospect sent a disturbing shiver racing down her spine, and she blushed and turned away, avoiding his speculative gaze.

"Very nice," he murmured softly, and for one very disconcerting minute she wasn't sure whether he was talking about the bedroom or whether he had read her mind. The possibility that he, too, was looking at that bed and wondering who-knew-what unnerved her. She turned back to study him, a quizzical expression on her face, but he was looking innocently around the room.

"How long do you suppose it's going to take you to do the rest of the house?" he asked with nothing more than casual interest. Victoria wasn't sure whether to feel relieved or disappointed.

"At the rate I'm going, it should be finished by the twenty-first century," she admitted bleakly.

Her response seemed to make him angry for some reason. "You can't go on living like this."

"Of course I can," she retorted. "What's wrong with the way I live?"

"It's not safe."

"It's perfectly safe. Just because the wallpaper is peeling doesn't mean the house will fall down."

"I'm not so sure."

"Well, I am."

"Okay. Okay," Tate said resignedly. Obviously, there was no point in arguing. Besides, it was definitely none of his business how she lived…unless, of course, it happened to be beyond her reported means. From what he'd seen today, that was hardly likely.

"Where are those records you came up here to get?" he asked. "I think we'd better go over them and finish this up."

"They're in here," she said, walking down the hall to the door she'd pulled shut as he came up the stairs. "Why don't you go back down to the kitchen and wait for me?"

"Why? Do you have something to hide?" he asked, his highly trained and very suspicious mind instinctively surging into action.

She glared at him. "Of course not. It's just that I'm not sure you are ready for this."

"Ready for what? The room can't be in any worse shape than some of the others I've already seen. I think my system had become immune to the shock."

"It's not the room I'm concerned about."

"What then?"

"I have a feeling you have an orderly mind."

"I do. What does that have to do with anything?"

"My records aren't…" She hesitated. "…Well, they aren't exactly…orderly."

"What are they exactly?"

Victoria sighed and opened the door. "See for yourself."

Tate stepped into the room and immediately his eyes flew open, his eyebrows shooting up in horrified disbelief.

"Holy…!" His voice trailed off, and he stood there, seemingly unable to complete the thought. It was the cry of a wounded man and, for a fraction of a second, Victoria almost felt sorry for him.

"Maybe it would be better if you went back to the kitchen," she repeated in a consoling tone, pulling on his arm. "Have some more lemonade. I'll get what you need and bring it down."

"How? It would take an entire office of accountants to bring order to this...this chaos," he said weakly. He still seemed to be suffering from some sort of professional shock.

"It will only take me a little while," Victoria reassured him. "I know exactly where everything is."

He shook his head disbelievingly. "You couldn't possibly."

"Of course I do. I have a system."

He eyed her wonderingly. "This I have to see," he said, plucking a stack of old magazines off of the room's only chair and settling down to watch. "If you can locate the records you need for last year's tax return, I will buy you dinner in the most expensive restaurant in Cincinnati."

It seemed like a reasonable challenge, though Victoria wasn't at all sure it would be wise to spend an evening in the company of Tate McAndrews. Without even trying, he'd already stirred up all sorts of desires that only this afternoon she'd despaired of ever feeling. What on earth would happen over an intimate dinner? She'd probably fall head over heals in love with the man, and he'd go blithely along to his next audit. It was not a comforting prospect.

Still, she couldn't very well lose the bet on purpose. She had to prove to him that while her system of accounting might be a bit unorthodox by his standards, it was as effective as ledgers and computerized spread sheets.

"Okay, Mr. McAndrews, you're on," she replied determinedly. "How long do I have?"

Tate grinned at her complacently. "Oh, I think I can afford to be lenient. Take as long as you like."

"You really don't think I can do this, do you?"

"No."

"You haven't said what happens if I lose."

"You hire an accountant and get your finances straightened out."

"My finances are fine, thank you. I've never missed a mortgage payment. My electricity's never been turned off. And I don't even own a credit card.'' She absolutely refused to tell him that she'd lost them and never gotten around to obtaining replacements.

"Thank God," he murmured fervently under his breath.

She regarded him indignantly. "Are you insulting me?"

"Heaven forbid!"

"Then why did you say that?"

"Let's just say that individuals more organized than you seem to have gotten themselves in way over their heads by haphazardly buying with plastic."

To be perfectly truthful, that was exactly why Victoria had decided not to replace the credit cards. It wasn't that she'd overspent. It was that she had this silly habit of misplacing the bills so that she never knew whether they'd been paid or not. By buying with cash she was relatively certain that she, not the credit card company, owned her possessions.

She did not, however, intend to stand here and discuss the relative merits of plastic money with Tate McAndrews. Not when he'd just bet her that she couldn't turn over the receipts she needed to back up her tax return. Taking a deep breath, she surveyed the room and went to work, picking up, studying and then discarding stacks of paper that had been stashed in boxes and bags of every size and shape. Every so often, she triumphantly dumped something new in Tate's lap or at his feet, gloating at his increasingly bemused expression.

"There," she said at last, standing in front of him with her hands on her hips. "I think that's everything." It had taken her exactly twenty minutes.

Tate looked at the four shoeboxes, two bulging shopping bags, three manila envelopes and one beat-up purse that she'd deposited with him. "This is it?" he said skeptically. "Price Waterhouse would be impressed."

"Don't be sarcastic."

"Sorry. What exactly do I have here?"

"These two boxes have the receipts for everything I bought for the shop last year. These two are all the bills for fixing it up, the mortgage payments on the shop and so on."

"The shopping bags?"

"My cash register receipts. The envelopes have all of my other stuff. Medical bills. Interest payments. Insurance."

"I know I'm going to hate myself for asking, but what's in the purse?"

"Contributions to charity. You know like when you're driving along, and somebody's on a street corner collecting for muscular dystrophy and you give 'em a dollar."

"You actually kept track of that? I'm impressed," he said, opening the purse. He pulled out a Popsicle stick with "$2/M.D." scribbled on it, followed by a button from the heart fund drive clipped to a scrap of paper that said 50 cents. There were also stubs for at least a dozen charity raffles and the ends from three boxes of chocolate mint Girl Scout cookies. He groaned.

"What's wrong?" Victoria demanded. "It's all very clear."

"Yes. I suppose it is," Tate admitted. "It's just that I'm used to..."

"You're used to nice, tidy books with columns of numbers that all add up."

The way she put it sounded insulting, as though there was something wrong with believing in order. "I can't help it if I've been trained to respect reliable accounting methods. This is...it's..." He couldn't even find a word to express his utter dismay at her lackadaisical approach to record keeping.

"Mr. McAndrews," Victoria said, her cheeks flushed and her blue eyes flashing. "I have better things to do with my time than write a bunch of figures down in some book. They all add up the same whether they're in a book or in that shopping bag."

Tate's head was starting to pound. He was beginning to feel the way he had earlier when he'd understood her logic in expecting that ridiculous tax refund. "I suppose," he agreed without very much conviction. He stood up and tried to balance the stack of shoeboxes in one arm, while grabbing the two shopping bags and the purse with the other. He motioned toward the envelopes. "Can you get those?"

"Where are you going with this?"

"I'm going to take it into the office and try to make some sense of it. That's what an audit is all about. I have to assure the IRS that you haven't tried to cheat them.''

Victoria sighed. ''I haven't, you know,'' she said softly, her voice filled with something that sounded like disappointment at his continued disbelief.

Tate nodded. Ironically, he did believe her. No one whose head was as high in the clouds as Victoria Marshall's would ever dream of cheating on her taxes. And even if the thought had crossed her mind, he doubted if she could figure out how to do it.

Victoria followed him down the stairs and out to his car, noting that it was what she would have expected him to drive: a very conservative, American made, four-door sedan. Anyone with his precise, orderly mind definitely would not be into flash and dazzle. She was a little worried, though, about the effect the afternoon seemed to have had on him. He did not look like the same determined, self-confident man who'd walked into her life a few hours earlier. He appeared defeated somehow, though his brown eyes did twinkle a little when he said goodbye.

''What happened to dinner?'' she taunted. ''I did win the bet, you know.''

''As soon as I figure this out, I'll be in touch,'' he promised with a sizzling, sensual smile that sent her blood pressure soaring. ''And we'll celebrate your victory over IRS with champagne, caviar and beef Wellington.''

As he drove off, Victoria sighed. If he threw in candlelight and roses, she'd be a goner.

Chapter 3

The following morning, Victoria sat at the kitchen table for a long time, dreamily sipping a cup of tea and trying unsuccessfully to push disturbing and unexpectedly lusty thoughts of Tate McAndrews from her mind. The rumpled tan sports jacket he'd forgotten and left draped over the back of a chair was not helping matters. When she'd run her hand over the fine material, her fingers had picked up the lingering, tangy scent of his cologne. The clean, outdoorsy odor had brought back a sharp image of that brief, tantalizing moment when he'd caught her and held her in his arms.

Of all the men who might have wandered into her life and stirred up her untapped passions, Tate McAndrews was the worst possible choice. Tate was so…sensible, so practical. She had the distinct impression that he would never do anything impulsive. He would examine all the implications, evaluate the possible consequences and then, if it didn't seem too costly, he might indulge in a few minutes of simple fun.

She, on the other hand, was constantly getting sidetracked by interesting, unexpected things. Not once could she ever recall going from point A to point B without wandering off to explore along the way. She saw life in glorious, spectacular Technicolor. If what she'd seen yesterday was any indication, Tate seemed to view it in black and white, without the benefit of any grays.

Victoria sighed. It was definitely a mismatch. And yet.... She glanced over at the bright yellow wall phone, dared it to ring, then shook her head.

"You are losing it, Victoria," she muttered aloud. "It's barely 8:00 a.m. No man, however enchanted he might be, is likely to call at that hour, and Tate McAndrews did not seem the least bit enchanted." She paused thoughtfully, recalling those one or two looks that could have sizzled bacon to a crisp. She shook her head and dismissed them. "Uh-uh. The man thinks you are a certifiable nut. There is a very good chance he will not call at all...unless he remembers his jacket or decides to haul you in for income tax evasion. Forget about him."

Deep down she knew this was good advice. She also knew she wasn't likely to follow it. Unfortunately romantics never listened to their heads. Lancelot, who had finished his breakfast and retreated to the windowsill for his morning sunbath, meowed softly as though in complete agreement with her analysis of the absurdity of her behavior.

"Oh, shut up, cat! Don't you start on me," she grumbled irritably, slamming down her teacup and grabbing the morning paper. She turned the pages with a vengeance that caused more than one of them to tear. When the phone shrilled a moment later, she jumped nervously and stared at it, almost afraid to pick it up.

"Hello," she said at last, her voice soft, low and unintentionally sexy.

"Victoria? Is that you? You sound like you have a cold."

"Oh. Hi, Mom," she said, unconsciously trading sexiness for disappointed grumpiness.

"My goodness, that's certainly a cheerful greeting. What's wrong with you?"

"Nothing," she denied, trying to inject a little spirit into her voice before her mother rushed over with chicken soup and parental advice. "I'm fine. What's up?"

"I was just wondering if you'd like a little company at the shop today. I haven't seen you in a while."

"Three days."

"Well, it seems like longer."

Victoria chuckled. She knew how her mother loved to help out at the shop. She enjoyed meeting the people, and she absolutely loved haggling with them over a price. She said it made up for the frustration of having to pay outrageous prices without question in the local stores.

"Come on over, Mom. I should be there about ten."

"Why don't I stop by and pick you up? There's no point in driving two cars."

"I gather you're planning to spend the day?" Victoria teased.

Katherine Marshall refused to rise to the bait. "I thought I might as well. Your father had to go up to Columbus on business, and you did say you wanted to do some refinishing work in the back on that new washstand you bought last week."

"Why don't you say it, Mom?"

"Say what?"

"That you think you're better at the business side of running the shop than I am."

"Dear, surely even you must agree that you are a bit casual about making the best possible deal. I swear, sometimes I think you'd give something away just because someone admired it."

"I like my pieces to go to people who'll treasure them," she said defensively. "Not just to the highest bidder."

"Hasn't it ever occurred to you that the highest bidder must like something very much to pay so dearly for it?"

"I suppose. But it seems so..."

"Businesslike?"

"Okay, okay. You've made your point," Victoria said, wishing her mother didn't sound quite so much like Tate McAndrews. She had a feeling if the two of them ever joined forces, her life would become a boring, organized regimen of computerized bookkeeping. The very thought made her shudder. "If you promise to drop the lecture, you can come on over and pick me up."

"I'll be there in a few minutes," her mother replied tartly. "But I won't promise to keep my mouth shut."

She hung up before Victoria could respond.

As Victoria dressed in a pair of oversized, paint-splattered coveralls appropriate for the refinishing work she needed to do, she thought about her shop. Located just outside of town in the front of a large, converted barn, it had been open less than a year. She'd started the venture at her parents' enthusiastic urging. She'd accumulated so many interesting odds and ends at garage and farm sales that she'd run out of space to store them. In fact, her parents' garage had become so cluttered that for three months in the dead of a very snowy winter they'd been unable to get their car inside. At first they had dutifully admired the battered, scratched treasures she had dragged home. But after digging the car out of snowdrifts more than once, they had begun dropping subtle hints that these wonderful finds of hers would look much better ''someplace where they could be displayed to advantage. Perhaps even sold.''

The idea of selling something she'd discovered in a dusty old attic or in the back corner of some other shop had vaguely disturbed Victoria. She'd bought these things because she'd loved each and every one of them. Only after her mother had reminded her that she couldn't very well afford to hoard every antique in southern Ohio had she agreed to consider the idea. The more she'd thought about it, the better she had liked it.

Once the plan had taken hold in her mind, she went about it with her usual high-spirited enthusiasm, spending a small inheritance from her grandmother to rent the perfect, old, unused barn on the Logan property and to renovate it. At first she'd only been open on weekends, continuing to teach history during the week. Soon she had quit her job at the high school and kept the shop open Tuesdays through Sundays. Her mother willingly filled in whenever she needed to go to an auction or wanted to take some time off.

''Victoria!'' Her mother's shouted greeting broke into her reverie.

''I'll be down in a minute, Mom.'' She ran a brush hurriedly through her hair, then twisted it into a loose knot on top of her head. Golden-red curls promptly escaped in every direction. She tried taming a few of them, then gave it up as a lost cause. ''So, I look like Little Orphan Annie. I'm going to refinish a washstand, not try out for Miss Ohio.''

When she ran down the stairs and skidded to a halt in the kitchen a few minutes later, her mother was holding Tate's jacket out in front of her as though it were a live snake.

"This is not your father's," she said emphatically.

Victoria couldn't help grinning at her puzzled expression. "Nope," she said, opening the door of the refrigerator and sticking her head inside to scout around for some yogurt to take along for lunch.

"Victoria!"

She peeked around the side of the door. "Yes, Mother?"

"Whose jacket is this?"

Somehow Victoria did not want to explain about the IRS audit or about Tate. Her mother would want to hire an entire office of attorneys to defend her, and she wasn't quite up to fighting with her about it. "A friend's," she replied vaguely, sticking her head back in the refrigerator. She wasn't sure how long she could spend deciding between black cherry and lemon yogurt, but she was hoping it would be enough time to chill her mother's questions.

"What friend?"

She sighed. Obviously, her mother did not intend to drop the topic until her curiosity had been fully satisfied. Victoria gave up the idea of hiding and slammed the refrigerator door. Her nose had been getting cold anyway. "A man, Mother."

"I can tell it's a man, young lady. What are you trying to hide? Are you involved with someone? Is it serious? Why haven't your father and I met him?"

"Mother, I only met him myself yesterday."

Her mother's eyes widened. "You only met this man yesterday, and he's already leaving clothes lying around your house?"

"It is not what it seems."

Katherine Marshall looked at her skeptically. "Are you quite sure?"

"Now you sound disappointed, Mother. Are you that anxious to be rid of me?"

"I am not anxious to be rid of you. I would like to see you settle down with some nice, sensible young man who could take care of you."

The description certainly fit Tate, but Victoria was not about to get her mother's hopes up. Given the slightest provocation, her mother was capable of planning maneuvers that would terrify and subdue an entire company of marines, much less a lone IRS agent. "I do not need someone to take care of me. I have a home—"

"Such as it is."

Victoria shot her a reproachful glance. "I have a business—"

"Which you run like a front yard lemonade stand."

"And I have my friends—"

"Who are all nuttier than you are."

"Mother, I'm so glad you are on my side."

Katherine Marshall beamed at her, ignoring her sarcastic tone. "You should be dear. But I won't be around forever, and I'd like to know there's someone who'll look after you and keep you out of mischief when I'm gone."

"You're healthier than I am, so I don't think that's something we need to worry about today. Now could we drop this subject and get over to the shop? You may be missing a sale."

"Oh, dear. Of course, you're right." She put the jacket back on the chair. "But Victoria, I want you to promise me that you'll bring this young man of yours over to meet your father and me."

"Mother, I solemnly swear that if this man ever becomes *my young man*, you and Dad will be the first to hear. Just so you know, though, you will not have the power of a veto." Not that that was likely, she thought dryly.

When they pulled into the driveway at the shop a few minutes later, the young man in question was pacing around the barn much to her amazement and dismay. His very neat and very flattering navy pin-striped suit looked totally out of place in the rural setting. Victoria wondered curiously if he even owned a pair of blue jeans. Then she caught sight of the mud caked on his expensive leather shoes and winced. If Tate planned to keep up these visits, he obviously needed to get a new, more practical wardrobe before he destroyed the one he had.

"Is that the young man?" Katherine Marshall hissed, as her daughter opened the car door and got out. Victoria rolled her eyes heavenward. These were not the circumstances she'd had in mind for a second meeting with Tate McAndrews.

"Do you always show up for work an hour late?" he was demanding irritably, a scowl on his handsome face.

"I have an 'in' with the owner," she responded tartly, as she unlocked the door and stalked inside.

"That is no way to—"

"Run a business," Katherine Marshall chimed in. "I've been telling her that very thing myself. Hello. I'm Victoria's mother."

She held out her hand and waited expectantly. Tate took it, then looked in amazement from this trim, tidy woman with the firm handshake and no-nonsense style to Victoria in another one of her outrageous getups. He'd never have believed it. This woman seemed perfectly...normal. She would never keep her bills in shopping bags.

"Tate McAndrews," he told her. "I'm from—"

"Tate is a friend from Cincinnati," Victoria interrupted quickly, shooting him a warning glance. "I'm surprised to see you again so soon."

"I needed to talk to you about—"

"Dinner."

"Oh, is Victoria making you dinner tonight, Tate?" Katherine Marshall asked cheerfully. "How lovely. Why don't the two of you drop by the house for dessert?"

"Mother!"

"We'd love to, Mrs. Marshall."

"Are you out of your mind?" Victoria snapped at him, marching into the back room with Tate trailing after her.

"What's wrong with you? I was just trying to be polite."

"Don't you realize that if we go over there for dessert tonight, my mother will have the church reserved by next weekend? She already thinks we're involved," she told him, her brows lifting significantly. "That's in capital letters, by the way."

"Involved?" Tate repeated, his expression completely baffled. "You mean...?" His eyes widened as the implication finally registered. "Why on earth would she think that?"

"Your jacket."

"My jacket?" Tate was getting that spinning sensation in his head again.

"You left it in the kitchen. My mother, the protector of my virtue, found it there this morning. She's assumed the worst."

Tate burst out laughing. He couldn't help it. "You're kidding!"

"I do not kid about matters such as marriage and murder, particularly when they're my own."

"Can we expect to find your father on the front porch with a shotgun?"

Victoria gave him a withering glance. "Okay," she warned. "Make fun of me. But I'm telling you, before you know it, that woman in there is going to have you marching down the aisle."

"I'm a total stranger."

"She doesn't know that."

"She would not try to marry her daughter off to someone she doesn't even know."

"Tate, my mother may seem quiet and unassuming to you, but in her heart lurks the soul of a desperate matchmaker."

"Why should she be desperate? You're hardly over the hill."

"Thanks. But she seems to think I have all the characteristics of a woman who's going to spend her whole life in trouble up to her eyebrows without some man to protect her."

"That thought has crossed my mind, too."

"See what I mean?" she said triumphantly. "You're two of a kind. Once she finds that out, you and I will have no further say in this. You might as well go back to Cincinnati and start picking out silver patterns."

"Actually, I saw one out front I thought was rather nice," he taunted.

Victoria groaned and buried her head in her arms. "I don't believe this."

Tate was watching her closely, and something in the vulnerable curve of her neck got to him. Tentatively, he ran his fingers along the soft, tender skin. "I don't believe it, either," he said huskily.

She gazed up at him with luminous blue eyes and wondered why on earth she'd been putting up such a fuss. It wasn't as though Tate was some disgustingly ugly, boring toad. He was a handsome prince, if ever she'd seen one, but he was so blasted unsuitable. He would never pick daisies with her or wade barefoot in a stream or ride a merry-go-round, at least not without thinking twice about it.

He leaned down and brushed a soft kiss across her lips, igniting a flame that first flickered weakly, then burst into a glorious heat. "Oh," she sighed softly, as his lips captured hers again, this time more hungrily. Only their mouths touched, but it was a possessive branding.

Then, just when Victoria started seeing an entire kaleidoscope of colors, Tate stood up, his expression thoroughly confused and somewhat horrified. "I'm sorry."

"Why?" she asked curiously.

"I shouldn't have done that."

"Didn't you enjoy it?" For some reason, she couldn't resist teasing him. She knew exactly why he was so disturbed. His behavior had been both unpredictable and, from what she suspected about IRS regulations, unprofessional. Tate McAndrews did not strike her as the type to bend, much less break, the rules.

"Of course, I enjoyed it."

"Well, then?"

"It's just not..."

"Proper? I promise you I won't charge you with sexual harassment." She held up her hand solemnly, though her lips were twitching.

"That's not the point."

"Don't you ever do anything because it feels right at the moment?"

"Of course," he said stiffly, thinking of the majority of his relationships. They were all built on a flimsy base of such moments without a single solid thread to hold them together. That had never bothered him before. Why did it suddenly seem so shallow and unfulfilling?

"That's encouraging," Victoria was saying cheerfully.

"Is it? I'm not so sure," he said honestly.

"Tate, why did you come here today?"

"I needed to ask you a question about your tax return."

"Couldn't you have called?"

He looked at her oddly. "I suppose so."

"Why didn't you?"

He appeared genuinely puzzled. "I'm not sure."

Victoria patted his arm. "That's okay. Don't worry about it. Why don't you sit down, and I'll bring you a nice cup of tea, and we can discuss my taxes to your heart's content?"

Suddenly the idea of discussing taxes with Victoria bored him to tears. What he really wanted was to kiss her again and, quite probably, again.

"I think I'd better be going."

"But you just got here."

"No," he corrected. "You just got here. I've been here over an hour, and now I have to get back to work."

"But you haven't asked me any questions yet."

"I'll ask them over dinner."

Victoria's eyes widened. "You're still planning to come for dinner?"

"Of course." He grinned at her. "And for dessert with your parents."

"Maybe it would be better if I wrote a letter to the IRS and told them to forget about the $15,593."

"And twelve cents," he reminded her. "Uh-uh. It's too late."

She moaned. "I was afraid of that."

Tate leaned down and brushed a kiss across her forehead. "See you later."

Victoria nodded.

"And try not to get in any more trouble."

She nodded again as he walked through the door into the front of the shop. As she heard him laughing with her mother, Victoria sighed. "Why do I have the feeling I'm already in so much trouble it would take Indiana Jones and Superman to get me out?"

Chapter 4

Victoria had just stepped out of the bathtub when she heard the doorbell ring. She glanced at the clock as she padded across the bedroom to peer out the front window. It was six o'clock on the dot. Of course, Tate McAndrews would never be late. He'd probably arrived in the world precisely nine months to the second after his conception. Right now he was pacing impatiently outside, a frown wrinkling his very attractive brow as he stopped to test each board that creaked under his weight. She had a feeling she was in for another one of his lectures, this one a double-barreled poke at both her house and her tardiness.

Victoria knew that punctuality was considered a socially desirable trait, and she really meant to try harder to attain it, but events always conspired against her. Tonight, for example, she'd gotten home right on time, despite another afternoon shower that had turned the driveway at the shop into a sea of mud that had almost trapped her mother's car. She'd planned to fix a plain, but hearty stew and some homemade buttermilk biscuits for dinner, take a leisurely, fragrant bubble bath and find the perfect outfit for this absurd date Tate had trapped her into.

But as she'd started to dice the onions and chop the carrots, she'd glanced out the kitchen window and seen this glorious rainbow that disappeared right over the crest of the hill. She couldn't resist trying to find the end of it. By the time she'd run barefoot through the damp grass to the far side of the hill and back again, her schedule was all out of kilter...as usual.

She threw open the bedroom window and leaned out. "Come on in," she called down cheerfully. "The door's open."

Horrified by such a casual announcement indicating an absolute lack of concern for her own safety, Tate's gaze flew up and encountered those dancing blue eyes and a considerable amount of bare white flesh shimmering with droplets of water. His stern retort on the dangers of leaving her front door unlocked died on his lips as his heart lurched crazily. This woman's unabashed innocence was far more provocative than any planned seduction he'd ever encountered. How could she possible not know the effect she'd have leaning out that window with a blue towel precariously draped around her and that red halo of hair spilling over her creamy shoulders? Yet he knew with absolute certainty that she had no idea that she was even capable of provoking a very masculine response in him. It was one of her more charming traits.

Some of her other habits were... He tried to think of a kind description and couldn't. Infuriating was the first word that came to mind. Maybe also baffling or irresponsible, he thought, his anger returning. Like leaving her door unlocked as though the entire world were trustworthy. Didn't she read the newspapers?

"I'll be down in a minute," she promised, and Tate swallowed his irritation and resigned himself to a half hour—minimum—of waiting. He should have known her lateness this morning hadn't been an exception. A woman like Victoria would never be on time. He was probably lucky she was even home.

He walked in the front door and debated where he should wait. Poking his head in what he'd decided yesterday was the living room, he glanced again at the disreputable and uncomfortable looking sofa and promptly opted for the kitchen, where he'd expected to find all sorts of tantalizing smells coming from the oven and from pots simmering on the stove. A woman who prided herself on offering all sorts of delicacies to her customers would surely cook a spectacular dinner. His mouth had been watering all afternoon.

Instead of finding a gourmet feast, however, the only hints of dinner preparations were a diced onion and a bunch of partially chopped carrots scattered across a cutting board on the counter. The air was filled only with the sweet scent of lilacs and something else he couldn't quite identify. It smelled faintly fishy. He sniffed and his nose wrinkled in dismay. What on earth was it? Not dinner, he hoped.

He heard a soft, appealing meow and felt something nudging his ankles hopefully. A puff of gray fur wound itself between his legs. There was another meow, this one louder and definitely more demanding.

"Hey, old guy, are you starving, too?" he inquired, before suddenly realizing that the subtle odor had been that of cat food. "You can't be, you old fake. You've obviously been fed. Don't try to trick me into giving you a second dinner."

Lancelot, apparently sensing that he was wasting his friendliness, gave Tate a haughty look of disgust and walked away, his tail switching. Tate chuckled at the cat's indignant departure. Victoria and Lancelot were obviously two of a kind.

"If you don't mind, you could finish chopping the carrots." Victoria's musical voice drifted down to him. He had a feeling she could talk a man into chopping down trees. Carrots were no problem at all. "I won't be long."

Lured by the sound of that voice, Tate wandered out to the front of the stairs. "Anything else?"

"There are some potatoes around somewhere. You could try to find them and peel them."

"Do I get any clues?"

"About what?"

"Where they might be."

"They might be in the refrigerator," she suggested, as Tate started toward the kitchen again. "Wait. No. I think I put them in the pantry." He paused and waited. "On second thought, try under the sink."

He rolled his eyes heavenward and sighed. "Are the potatoes important?"

"Of course. I'm making a stew. It probably won't be very good, though. It should have been simmering for the last hour."

"What happened? Did you get held up at the shop?"

"No. I got home right on time, but there was this rainbow...." Her voice trailed off as Tate groaned and returned to the kitchen, reminding himself for the fiftieth time since yesterday that this woman was obviously not his type.

"So, why are you here, McAndrews?" he muttered under his breath. His pulse speeded up as an image of her scantily clad body flitted through his mind. He scowled. "That's a lousy answer."

He yanked open the refrigerator door and looked for the potatoes. He tried the pantry next, then checked the cabinet under the sink. He gave up, then accidentally found them when he opened the back door to let Lancelot out. They were sitting on the steps. He shrugged resignedly. "It's as good a place as any, I suppose."

By the time Victoria finally got downstairs, he had finished with the carrots and peeled the potatoes. The finished product didn't look quite right to him, but what did he know about peeling things? Apparently not much, judging from the quirk of amusement that tilted Victoria's soft, coral lips when she saw them. His earlier desire to sweep her straight into his arms returned with a nearly uncontrollable urgency, startling him into a subdued silence as he simply stared at her.

"You don't spend a lot of time in the kitchen, do you?" she said dryly, as she unceremoniously plopped his efforts into a huge pot, added some water, onions and already browned beef that she'd plucked from the refrigerator. Then she liberally sprinkled dibs and dabs of various spices over the top, her brow puckered in concentration.

"It shows?"

"It shows," she confirmed, glancing over at him. "Who fixes your meals for you?"

"I go out a lot."

"What about breakfast? Are you any better at that?"

"Not much."

"Then what...?" Her voice trailed off as he began to grin. "Never mind."

"I eat cereal," he informed her, as her cheeks turned decidedly pink. "At home."

"Oh," she said softly, an unfortunate tone of relief in her voice. He was still grinning...openly chuckling, in fact.

For the first time since he'd arrived, Victoria took a really good look at Tate. He was wearing the same shirt and suit pants he'd had on this morning. Even his tie was right in place, and his shoes had been polished to a high gloss without a trace left of this morning's muddy excursion around her barn. He had rolled up his sleeves to attack the potatoes and carrots, but that was the only concession to comfort he'd made.

His formality, combined with the odd way he was looking at her, made Victoria even more uncomfortable than she already had been about having this man back in her kitchen. There was a raw hunger in his eyes she couldn't quite identify, but it made her decidedly nervous. Maybe he was crazy about stew and couldn't wait for her to get dinner on the table. She gazed into his eyes again and blinked at the intensity. No, she thought, that look had nothing to do with food.

"Don't you ever wear anything besides a suit?" she finally asked, her voice far shakier than she would have liked.

"Sure, but not when I'm working."

She quirked a brow at him. "You're working now?"

"Of course. Until this audit is finished, any meeting we have is part of the investigation."

"Shouldn't I call an attorney or something, then?" she taunted.

That look in his eyes faded as he scowled at her. "I don't plan to arrest you, for heaven's sakes."

"You're going to charge me with tax evasion or fraud or something equally unpleasant."

"I told you yesterday, I believe you didn't do anything illegal. But once the case is opened, there are procedures we have to follow."

"You probably never speed either," she said wearily.

"Not often," he admitted, suddenly wishing he had at least a parking ticket he could tell her about.

"Haven't you ever wanted to break just one little rule?"

"There are reasons for rules."

"Do you always agree with those reasons?"

"Of course not."

"Then what do you do?"

"Try to get the rules changed."

Victoria tried to imagine Tate in the middle of a protest rally. Not even her vivid imagination could come up with an impression of that scene. He probably made an appointment, sat down and discussed things rationally, shook hands politely and waited for change to take place. The people he approached probably listened too. She had a feeling he could be a very persuasive man when he wanted to be.

He was sitting at the kitchen table now, his hands braced behind his head, leaning back in the chair and watching her again, laughter dancing in his dark brown eyes. She had a feeling he found her amusing and that irritated the daylights out of her. Despite her misgivings about all of this, she'd wanted to be beautiful and sexy and alluring tonight. She'd searched her closet and found a lovely old dress with tiny sprigs of bright yellow flowers on a beige background. It had a scooped neck, edged with antique lace, that drew attention to her full breasts and a wide satin sash that emphasized her tiny waist. For once, her hair had cooperated and fallen into shining waves. And now this infuriating man was laughing at her. She felt like smacking him in the mouth. Instead, she sliced through a tomato with a whack that jarred the counter.

Tate winced. "Remind me never to make you angry."

Victoria grinned. "You just did."

"How?" he asked.

"You were laughing at me."

"I was?"

"Weren't you?"

"I was smiling."

"At me."

Tate's head started spinning again. "Actually I was thinking about how unusual you are. I've never met a woman like you before.'' At the moment, he wasn't sure if that was good or bad.

''And that made you laugh.''

''Smile.''

''Whatever,'' she said airily. She hesitated for a minute, then confessed, ''I was going for sexy.''

''Ahh,'' he said softly as an even broader grin split his face. ''Now I see.''

The knife sliced through another tomato with a resounding thwack.

''You are sexy, you know,'' he said almost casually. Victoria promptly nicked her finger with the knife.

''Damn!''

''What happened?'' He was out of his chair and at her side in an instant.

''Nothing. Nothing at all.''

''Let me see.''

''It's just a little cut. I do this all the time,'' Victoria lied. There was no way she was going to let him think that he'd rattled her by telling her he thought she was sexy. It wasn't a complete lie, anyway. She did nick her fingers constantly. She had this dangerous habit of letting her mind wander while she was fixing meals.

''Let me see it,'' he repeated insistently, a look of steely determination in his eyes.

Reluctantly, she held out her hand. The tiny cut had already stopped bleeding.

''Do you have some antiseptic? And you'll need a bandage.''

''Don't be ridiculous. It's practically healed already.''

''Have you had a tetanus shot?''

Obviously he planned to ignore her protests and turn this into a case for a trauma unit, she thought resignedly. Maybe he was a frustrated paramedic.

''I think so.''

''When?''

''I don't know.''

''Then we ought to take you to the hospital,'' he said decisively, confirming her worst expectations.

"Tate McAndrews!" Victoria suddenly bellowed. "Sit down!"

Tate's eyes widened, but he sat back down. Victoria faced him with her hands on her hips. "Now will you please relax. Loosen your tie. Have a drink. Go upstairs and try to organize my bills. Anything, but please don't hover over me. I already have two perfectly good parents to do that."

"Did I touch a sore spot?" he asked innocently.

Victoria gave him a wobbly smile. "Well, they are a bit overly protective. You'll see."

"I brought them a bottle of Scotch, by the way."

"They don't drink."

Dismay suddenly filled Tate's eyes. That look of uncertainty, which gave a surprising impression of vulnerability, touched her. She wanted to pat his hand.

"I knew I should have brought candy," he muttered.

"You didn't need to bring anything."

"Of course I did. I read Miss Manners."

"If you're so worried about making a good impression on my parents, do me a favor."

"Anything."

"When we get over there tonight, don't say anything about working for the IRS or about this audit."

Tate looked at her oddly. "I gathered this morning that you wanted to keep this some deep, dark secret. Why? They're your parents."

"Exactly. They'll only worry, and I can handle it on my own."

"What if you can't?"

Victoria looked at him, a frown creasing her forehead. "You said you believed me."

"I do, but I'm not the only one involved."

"But you'll do the report. Won't they take your word for it?"

Tate hesitated. "Usually they do."

"Well, then. You see," she said, flashing him a wide smile that lit her blue eyes with glittering highlights. "I have nothing to worry about."

Tate couldn't bring himself to tell her that if Pete Harrison got even the tiniest inkling of the attraction he felt toward her, he'd put four other agents on the case to check out his work. Pete did not believe his agents should have human emotions. Anyone who did was suspect. In fact, if they could program computers to do the leg-work, instead of just the analysis, Pete would happily fire his entire staff.

Tate glanced at Victoria and felt his stomach muscles tighten at the perfect picture she presented. All of her worries over the audit were apparently forgotten thanks to her faith in his ability to protect her. She hummed cheerfully while stirring the stew. Norman Rock-well would have loved having her as a model. Her cheeks were flushed from the fragrant steam now rising from the pot. Golden-red curls framed her face. As she lifted the spoon to her mouth and tasted the stew, her lips pursed in an enchanting frown. Her hand hovered over the spice rack, then plucked out two bottles and sprinkled a dash of the contents into the pot. She tried the stew again and shook her head.

"It's still missing something. You taste it."

She dipped out a steaming spoonful and brought it to Tate, who obediently opened his mouth. Her eyes were on his lips as they closed over the spoon, and she ran her tongue over her own in an uncon-sciously sensual gesture that did all sorts of crazy things to Tate's pulse rate. He had a sudden urge to take the spoon out of her hand, pull her into his lap and taste the softness of her mouth for himself. Surely, it was more delectable than any stew. His eyes, filled with a raw yearning he couldn't disguise, lifted to meet hers, and he saw that she shared his hunger. He also saw that it seemed to startle her. She blinked and turned back to the stove, her hand shaking so badly that the spoon clattered against the side of the pot.

"I think the stew tastes fine," he said softly.

"Are you sure?"

"Absolutely."

She shrugged. "Okay. Then I think we're about ready. We were supposed to have biscuits, but I ran out of time."

She brought a loaf of homemade bread to the table instead and added a crock of fresh butter, then dished up huge steaming bowls of the stew. Over dinner, as the conversation veered off on one crazy tangent after another, Tate realized they had at least a few things in common, though hardly the sort of list that would qualify them for a computerized matchup. More important than their skimpy selection of mutual favorite things were the sparks that flew during lively discussions of their disagreements. Victoria had a razor sharp intelligence under that zaniness. She listened carefully to Tate's point of view and actually tried to understand it. Of course, she then dismissed it with some totally illogical argument that he could barely follow. When she started to make sense it scared the living daylights out of him.

Still, it was a beginning. But of what? A friendship? A brief romance? Surely it could be no more than that. They'd drive each other crazy, just as his parents had. His mother's disorganization, her off-the-wall logic and her absolute refusal to think beyond the moment had given his father fits. And, much as he loved his mother, Tate had agreed with his father. Life was supposed to have an order, a certain logic to it. You had to be able to count on things.

He glanced up at Victoria, who was stacking dishes haphazardly on the counter. She was definitely not a woman who knew the first thing about order. He sighed as a plate slipped off the counter and crashed to the floor.

''Let me help,'' he said, bending down to pick up the pieces.

''I've got it.''

Their hands closed over the same piece and their eyes met. The already charged atmosphere sizzled with electricity. Almost against his will, Tate leaned slowly forward and kissed her. He meant it only to be a light, teasing kiss, the sampling of her honeyed sweetness that he'd wanted all evening. Instead, it virtually crackled with passion. The piece of china fell back to the floor, as Victoria's hands slid slowly along his arms, finally coming to rest lightly on his shoulders. His own hands circled her tiny waist and lifted her to her feet, pulling her body tightly against his. The curves seemed to fit perfectly into his hard contours, as though a sculptor had carved them as a matching pair out of a single piece of marble.

As her body trembled in Tate's muscular arms, Victoria remembered every passionate movie kiss she'd ever envied. She sighed, unconsciously opening her mouth to Tate's exploring tongue, relishing the sensation. The kiss was sweet yet hungry, gentle yet demanding. A riptide of warm, exciting feelings flooded through her, bringing her body alive in a most disconcerting way. She wanted more, wanted Tate's lips to move beyond her mouth, wanted his hands to touch the breasts that were straining against the thin cotton of her dress. She also wanted him to stop, to give her time to catch her breath. These feelings were too new, too unexpected and far too powerful for her to deal with quite yet.

"Tate," she murmured, as his lips blazed a path down her neck. The fiery touch was even more intense, more nerve-shattering than she'd anticipated. She moaned softly. "Tate, please. It's nearly eight."

"So?"

"We promised my parents we'd be there by eight."

"They think we're involved, remember. They'll understand."

His lips were at the crest of her breasts, hovering over the creamy flesh. Victoria's body tensed in excited preparation for his touch, but she said firmly, "No, they won't."

Tate kept one arm securely around her, locking her body against his, as he glanced at his watch. "We're not due there for another fifteen minutes."

"It's a twenty-minute drive."

"We could speed."

"You said you never broke the law."

"I don't, but I think this is worth an exception."

"I will not be responsible for your fall from grace, Tate Mc-Andrews," she said saucily, slipping determinedly from his embrace. "Besides, we need to talk some more about this little visit we're about to pay to my parents. I don't think you have any idea what you're letting yourself in for."

"That's not exactly true," Tate denied with a weary sigh of resignation. "When I came down here yesterday, I didn't. Now I know I'm in trouble. Your parents are just the tip of the iceberg."

Chapter 5

On the drive to her parents' house, Victoria tried to think of some way to make Tate understand that he was about to undergo a third degree that would make one of his IRS investigations seem like child's play. Every time she opened her mouth to explain, he told her to quit worrying. She finally shut up, but she didn't stop fretting.

She wasn't sure what concerned her the most: her mother's delighted, if mistaken, impression that she and Tate were involved or the possibility that her parents would discover that he was auditing her taxes. Either one posed a minefield of hazards that the man next to her couldn't possibly have considered when he innocently accepted her mother's invitation. She still didn't understand why he'd agreed to do that, much less why he'd wrangled that dinner invitation from her, but right now she didn't have time to puzzle that part out. She was far more concerned with this sinking feeling of dread that she was about to end the evening with either an entirely inappropriate fiancé or a companion who'd been hog-tied and sternly lectured until he agreed to drop his inquiry into her financial affairs.

"Tate, maybe we should forget about this," she suggested hopefully. "I'll explain to my parents that your malaria flared up again, and you were in no condition to drop in."

The look he gave her was withering. "I don't have malaria."

"They don't know that."

He glanced over at her, his expression puzzled. "It's just a friendly visit. Why are you making such a big deal about it?"

"Because my parents are going to make a big deal about it and you don't seem to be prepared."

"I've been dating since junior high school and been asked every conceivable parental question. They will not rattle me."

"First of all," she reminded him, "this is not a date."

"It isn't?"

"You said yourself it was part of the investigation," she said irritably, then added pointedly, "an investigation I don't want them to know about."

Tate frowned. "Well, it is part of the investigation...in a way."

"What does that mean?"

"It's not exactly official."

"Meaning you don't usually drop in for dinner when you're auditing someone's taxes."

"Right."

"Then it's a date after all?" she asked weakly, her head swimming. Dear Lord, this was getting complicated. Maybe *she* could develop malaria and go home.

Tate's frustrated expression reminded her of the way she felt. "That's what I said in the first place," he told her, sounding puzzled. "Isn't it?"

"I suppose," Victoria muttered, then sighed. "Okay, then. How many times have you been asked what your intentions are on a first date?" she challenged, then shrugged in defeat. "Oh, forget it. If you're crazy enough to want to go through with this, far be it from me to try to stop you. Turn here."

Tate pulled into the driveway of a lovely old farmhouse surrounded by towering oaks that were beginning to bud. Pale green sparkled in the early moon-light against the dark backdrop of massive trucks and mighty branches. Unlike Victoria's ramshackle house, this one looked as though it had been in top condition for a hundred years, its appearance so solid and dependable that Tate was sure it could withstand another hundred.

As he turned off the car's engine, the front door flew open, and Katherine Marshall stood framed in the doorway, her simple cotton print dress topped by a ruffled apron, her cheeks flushed prettily and her hair—a shade darker than Victoria's—coiled into a neat bun. As Tate and Victoria approached, she positively beamed at them. Tate thought she looked exactly the way a mother should look—comfortable, warm and assured. She looked like a mother who would bake cookies. His own mother had burned the one batch she'd ever tried and hired a cook the same afternoon. She'd told Tate she'd rather take him hang gliding and leave the baking to someone else. Having a mother who wanted to be his pal had given him a rather distorted view of things. He'd always yearned to come home from school to someone a bit more traditional.

"Tate, how wonderful that you could come. Victoria's father and I are so looking forward to getting to know you."

Tate saw no hidden meaning in the friendly words, but Victoria mumbled, "I warned you," under her breath. As her mother linked arms with him and drew him into the living room, he shot Victoria a reproachful glance before gazing down at her mother with a smile.

That's all I need, Victoria thought in disgust. A couple of hundred-watt smiles like that and my mother will start buying frames for pictures of the grandchildren. As the evening wore on, her mouth settled into a grim line. Tate was actually enjoying himself and her parents were clearly infatuated. They couldn't seem to believe that she had finally brought home someone who was down-to-earth and seemingly financially stable, someone her father could talk to and her mother could...well, mother.

When Katherine brought out warm apple cobbler topped with mounds of melting vanilla ice cream, Victoria knew for certain that wedding bells were already pealing in her head. Homemade cobbler was her mother's specialty, prepared only when she wanted to use her biggest guns to make a sure kill. The last time she'd baked one the town scrooge had forked over ten thousand dollars to beautify a park. He was still grumbling about Katherine Marshall's sly, underhanded tactics.

Tate caught the dismayed expression on Victoria's face and briefly wondered about it. Then he dismissed it as her father deftly steered the conversation over a fascinating range of topics—from the intrigues of small-town politics to rampant, unrestricted development and poor zoning, from bank failures to the national debt. All were things Tate understood and felt comfortable with. He'd grown up discussing these subjects with his own father. It was both nostalgic and satisfying to find someone older with whom he could share his thoughts again. He'd missed that since his father's death.

As for Mrs. Marshall, she reinforced his earlier impression of her straightforward, brutally honest approach to life. She was clearly a perfectly contented homemaker, a self-assured woman who would never whimper about life's harsh realities or pretend they didn't exist. She'd roll up her sleeves and pitch in to make things better, always with that sparkling sense of humor that made her bright blue eyes, that were so like her daughter's, crinkle with laughter.

Despite Victoria's dire warnings, he found the Marshalls to be exactly the kind of people he most enjoyed. It was Victoria herself who baffled him. How such an unconventional, impractical woman could have turned up on that very sensible family tree was beyond him. Yet though her parents teased her unmercifully about her more unique friends and crazy lifestyle, it was obvious that they doted on and worried about her. It gave him a warm feeling to see this much love, given so freely and unconditionally.

There was one awkward moment, which began when Katherine Marshall asked how he and Victoria had met.

"Well," he began and shot Victoria a look that cried out for help. He was not used to prevaricating and had no idea what he could say that wouldn't violate his promise to avoid mentioning the audit. She let him sit and squirm uncomfortably under her mother's interested gaze for several horrible seconds.

"It was an accident, Mother," she said when his nerves had

stretched so taut he thought he'd have to blurt out the entire truth or explode.

Mrs. Marshall's eyes filled with concern. "An accident? You didn't wreck your car, did you? I've told you you should get rid of that old rattletrap. It's a menace."

"My car is not a menace and, anyway, it wasn't that kind of an accident. I'd just chased Lancelot up into a tree and got stuck. Tate came along and rescued me."

"Oh, my. How romantic," Mrs. Marshall said with a satisfied sigh, her eyes lighting with pleasure. "And how very fortunate that you happened by, Tate."

"Yes, that was a bit of luck, wasn't it?" Victoria said dryly. Tate refused to look her in the eye. He was terrified he would laugh and blow their tenuous credibility to smithereens.

Before he did, John Marshall tamped down the tobacco in his pipe with slow deliberation and said quietly, "Tell me, Tate, exactly what do you do for a living?"

"Ummm...I..."

"Tate's in finance," Victoria offered.

"Make a good living, do you?"

"Dad!"

Tate grinned. "Good enough."

"And you live in Cincinnati?"

"Yes."

"Like it there?"

"I've lived there all my life. It's a great city."

"You intend to stay there, then?"

"Well, yes, I suppose so."

"What about a family?" Katherine Marshall inquired, plopping another scoop of vanilla ice cream into his bowl and urging him to have a bit more cobbler.

Tate gulped. "I hadn't really thought about it," he said finally, as Victoria shot him an I-told-you-so look.

"A man can't wait too long to settle down," John Marshall said with all the subtlety of a rampaging rhino. He was obviously oblivious to Victoria's glare. Tate nodded politely, beginning to see exactly what he was up against. Oddly enough, the prospect of being bullied into a marriage with Victoria didn't terrify him nearly as much as it should have. Actually, the fact that it *didn't* was what scared him to death.

Despite the less than subtle nudging from the Marshalls, Tate found that he was having one of the best times of his life. From the incredible, mouth-watering apple cobbler to the gentle family teasing and intelligent conversation, he felt perfectly at home. Victoria, however, seemed to vacillate between amusement and nervousness. By the end of the evening, nervousness was winning out. The more Tate relaxed, the jumpier Victoria became. Soon he was certain that she'd been hoping they would all mix like oil and water. Then they'd never have to get together again.

When they were finally on the way home, after he'd promised to come back often, he questioned her about her odd attitude.

"You were hoping we'd hate each other, weren't you?"

"Why on earth would I want you to hate my parents?"

"You tell me."

She shook her head. "You're wrong. I expected you to like them. You're on the exact same wavelength," she said in a tone that made it sound as though they all were suffering from a similar incurable disease.

"Is that bad?"

She shrugged. "It is if you had other plans for the rest of your life."

"The marriage bit again," he said with a sigh. "It's crazy to worry about that. They can't push us into anything we don't want."

"Are you kidding? You are exactly what they've been looking for in a son-in-law. They're not about to let you get away. Didn't you notice the look of relief in my mother's eyes?" She glowered at him, then added with an air of resignation. "No, of course you didn't. You were too busy trying to figure out why I'm not more like them."

"The thought did cross my mind."

She looked so sad when he said that that he wanted to take it back.

"I don't know why I'm not," she said wearily, as if it were something she'd though about often. "I try to be more organized. I really do, but it seems to escape me. There are always so many more interesting things going on. Maybe I'm a throwback to my grandmother. Everyone thought she was a little cracked too, just because she didn't believe in sitting back and letting life slip by. She had the time of her life. She went out and grabbed what she wanted, without giving a hoot if it was considered proper. The rest of the family was absolutely scandalized by her antics, but when she died at eighty-one, she had no regrets.

"I'm not going to have any either," she added defiantly, her eyes flashing a challenge at him.

"I wouldn't want you to," Tate countered, meeting her gaze head-on without flinching. He wondered briefly why it was so important for her to believe that.

Victoria seemed to consider the sincerity of his claim, then nodded. "No, maybe not. But you do think I should do things by the rules. I can tell from that funny little look you get in your eyes every time I do or say something you don't approve of. I know what you think of my bookkeeping and my house. You think I should computerize my records and live in some tidy little apartment with a fully equipped kitchen, wall-to-wall carpeting and a dead bolt lock on the door." She shivered.

Tate grinned at her apparent idea of a fate worse than death. "Would that be so awful?"

"Don't you see?" she said plaintively. "It wouldn't be me. Filling in all those little numbers bores me, and I like light and space and character in a house. I even like the fact that mine's a mess right now, because when I'm finished fixing it up, I'll know how much I've accomplished."

Tate didn't know what to say to that. Victoria waited for a response, then sighed and regarded him as though he were hopeless. "You loved their house, didn't you?"

"I'm not sure what that has to do with anything, but yes," he admitted.

Not only had the exterior been in perfect condition, the inside had been spotless, freshly painted in soft colors and decorated with a sense of symmetry. There hadn't been a magazine out of place. He wouldn't have changed a thing, including the intriguing collection of photos of Victoria from infancy through adolescence. She'd been a golden-haired cherub at birth and her evolution into a wickedly impish redhead had charmed him. The house had fairly shouted of family and tradition and dependability.

He sighed aloud at the memory and a soft smile curved his mouth. "I thought it was lovely."

"See. I knew it," Victoria huffed and then retreated into silence. She didn't say another word on the ride home, until they pulled to a stop in front of her house. Even then, she only mumbled an agreement to be in his office the following afternoon at two to wrap up the audit. She was out of the car before he could even begin to figure out what was wrong with her, much less try to take her in his arms and recapture the wildfire and magic of those first tentative kisses they'd shared earlier in the evening.

All night long Tate thought about the evening with the Marshalls, going over and over everything that had happened in his usual methodical way, trying to figure out why Victoria's impish humor had vanished. The evening had started out so well, and he hadn't been mistaken about those kisses in her kitchen. She was more than attracted to him. She had wanted him as much as he wanted her. Yet when they'd returned to her house, alone again at last, she couldn't get away from him fast enough.

He spent all morning at his desk shuffling papers and thinking about Victoria. His frustration and confusion, along with the sharp sexual tension in his abdomen that threatened to embarrass him, mounted all afternoon. He glanced up at the clock. It was 2:30 and Victoria was late again.

"Damn it," he grumbled moodily. "Why the devil can't she at least learn to be on time? Doesn't she own a watch?"

"Problems?" Pete Harrison inquired from the doorway in his gruff, raspy voice. That voice, combined with his perpetual scowl, gave the impression that he was always angry. Tate was one of the few people on his staff who suspected he wasn't.

"I thought that crazy dame who wanted the refund was due in here this afternoon," he said, staring at Tate pointedly. "Where is she?"

"She's late."

Pete seemed about to growl, then said mildly, "Hey, McAndrews, don't worry about it. What'd you expect from a kook?"

Tate had expected this particular kook to at least make an attempt to be on schedule just this once, since it was her taxes they were trying to straighten out. For Pete's benefit, he simply shrugged his agreement. There was no point in letting his boss know that he'd like to wring the woman's pretty little neck. Pete would think the uncharacteristic display of emotion highly suspicious. He'd moved Tate quickly through the ranks precisely because of his cool, calm, objective demeanor. Murdering the subject of an audit simply because she was late for an appointment did not qualify as objective—much less rational—behavior.

Despite his efforts to control it, some of his irritation apparently showed on his face anyway because Pete was regarding him suspiciously. "You okay, McAndrews? Is there a problem with this case I ought to know about?"

"What kind of problem could there be? You said it. The woman's a kook," he said, immediately feeling disloyal. If she was that much of a kook, then why was he so damned attracted to her? Why had he been sitting at his desk all morning watching the clock and counting the hours until her arrival, instead of working on another file? Much as he hated to admit it, he could hardly wait to see how she'd look today. He wondered if he'd find her as alluring as ever. Even worse, he could hardly wait to see what crazy, quirky tangent her mind would take. None of this he could admit to Pete.

Aloud, he said only, "I'll have the whole thing wrapped up in a day or two."

Pete nodded. "Good. I need you on something else next week, so don't waste any time." Pete muttered something else about wasting taxpayer dollars investigating dingy females as he wandered away, leaving Tate to glare angrily at the sweeping second hand of the clock as though it were responsible for Victoria's tardiness.

He had started pacing around his office like a caged lion when the door swung open, and Victoria breezed in wearing a dress that must have been in vogue at the turn of the century. Tate was getting used to these out-of-date costumes of hers. He realized it somehow suited her with its puffed sleeves, fitted waist and mid-calf skirt. Still, he glanced cautiously down to check for high-button shoes, but her feet, thankfully, were clad in perfectly ordinary black patent pumps. From those tiny feet and well-turned ankles, his gaze rose to her face, hoping for at least some sign of remorse. Instead, to his absolute fury, her eyes were sparkling with childlike excitement. His breath caught in his throat. Her sheer delight was almost contagious.

"Guess what?" she asked breathlessly, oblivious to his foul-tempered mood. She'd had the most wonderful morning. It had made her forget all about the uncomfortable evening she'd spent under the hopeful eyes of her parents. Today's sky had been a shimmering, cloudless blue. The recently tilled and planted fields were turning green and had the most marvelous, earthy smell. It had been absolute heaven to drive along and look at the change that spring had brought to the landscape. It had been all she could do to resist the urge to stop and pick wildflowers, but an image of Tate's disapproving scowl had kept her speeding along the country roads.

"Where have you been?" Tate practically shouted at her, making her wince, even though she'd been half expecting such a tirade.

She decided it would be better to ignore the question and his tone. He'd obviously had a bad morning, but, once he'd heard about hers, that grumpy mood would vanish.

"Wait until I tell you about this terrific new antique shop I found," she announced enthusiastically. "The owner used to be a teacher, just like me, and he spent his summers driving around the country hunting for antiques. Now that he's retired, he decided to open a shop in his home. And he had the most marvelous old dresser. It's a mess right now. It must have fifteen layers of paint on it, but the construction is solid—I think it's cherry—and it has the most beautiful beveled mirror. I'm having it picked up tomorrow. I can hardly wait to get to work on it. Oh, Tate, wait until you see it.''

She gazed up at him expectantly, her smile wavering ever so slightly as she noticed that his scowl had not vanished as she'd hoped. ''Is something wrong? I thought you'd be excited.''

''You know I don't give a damn about antique dressers and beveled mirrors,'' he snapped. ''When you make an appointment for two o'clock, you're supposed to arrive at two o'clock. Not two-forty-five.''

''Ohhh. So that's it. Well, I'm here now, aren't I?'' she said brightly, flashing him another brilliant smile and sitting down. The man definitely needed to get his priorities in order. In fact that was what had troubled her all last night. He was so single-minded. He didn't have an impulsive bone in his very attractive body.

To make matters worse, he fit in so neatly with her family and, much as she loved them, they weren't wildly impulsive either. More than anything they wanted to see her settled down with someone like Tate. If her parents had their way, they'd offer him a dowry just to reassure themselves that he'd take her on. She'd seen that thank-goodness-we've-finally-found-someone look in their eyes even if Tate had been oblivious to it. He'd been so busy talking about strip zoning or something equally boring that he hadn't even noticed her mother practically measuring him for a tuxedo.

''Victoria,'' Tate began sternly, then sighed with frustration when he realized there was nothing he could say that would change her. ''Oh, never mind. Let's get this over with.''

But instead of proceeding in the brisk, businesslike manner he had in mind, Tate found that attempting to conduct a serious interview with Victoria was like trying to keep a toy train on a crooked track. She kept veering off in crazy, unexpected directions that at first infuriated, then delighted him. He listened raptly to one of her wild stories about leading her entire class of students in an all-night sit-in in the school cafeteria to give them a firsthand experience in Thoreau's concept of civil disobedience.

''What were you protesting?''

"The fact that they'd stopped serving hamburgers and fries."

"You staged a sit-in over hamburgers and French fries?"

"When you were a teenager, could you live without your daily ration of a burger, fries and a milk shake?"

"I can still live without them."

"I should have known," she said with a shake of her head. She studied him closely for several seconds, then smiled slowly. "Do you realize you haven't asked me a single dull question for the last half hour?"

"I haven't, have I?" he asked, his startled expression making her chuckle.

"It's wonderful," she told him approvingly.

"You won't think it's so wonderful when you have to go to court because I did a lousy job of finishing this audit and getting you off the hook."

"And the only way to do that is to ask boring questions?"

Tate nodded. "It would also help if I could get some straight answers."

"My answers are straight. I would never lie to you," she huffed.

"I'm not talking about lying. I'm talking about wandering all over the place with your answers until I'm so confused I find myself agreeing with you."

"Didn't it ever occur to you I might be right?"

"Not really."

"Thank you very much," she said, trying to keep the hurt out of her voice. She'd thought for a moment that Tate had actually approved of her. Instead, he'd only been laughing at her again. Well, that was just fine. She'd amuse him for another hour or so, straighten out this ridiculous mess, and then she'd drive home. That would be the end of it.

Except it wouldn't be. Something about this man appealed to her. Maybe it was nothing more than the crusader in her wanting to cure him of his stodginess and to discover if he had the stuff to be a true romantic hero. She sighed, wishing that was all there was to it. The real truth was that her suddenly traitorous body apparently didn't give a damn if he had the mind of a computer, as long as it could be held in those muscular arms and feel those sparks going off inside. She'd answer his ridiculous questions from now until doomsday just to reexperience the incredible feelings he aroused in her with one sizzling glance from those intense brown eyes. Right now those eyes were filled with laughter.

"You ready to try again?" he asked.

Victoria nodded reluctantly. "Fire away."

"I know I'm going to hate myself for asking this one, but explain to me how this contribution to somebody named Jeannie qualifies as charity."

Victoria couldn't help grinning at Tate's expression. He seemed to be holding his breath, obviously hoping for something he would consider a rational explanation. Well, this time she had one.

"Oh, that," she said airily. "Well, Jeannie is this friend of mine, who's trying to make it as an artist. You'll have to meet her sometime. She does ceramics. They're really quite special. She uses the loveliest blues and greens and grays." She paused thoughtfully, her lips pursed. "I can't quite figure out how she manages to get those shades, though I've watched and watched."

"Victoria," Tate said warningly.

She scowled, but went on. "Anyway, she wanted to help out Children's Hospital up in Columbus, only she didn't have any money. So I bought one of her pitchers, and she gave the money to the hospital," she concluded, gazing at him with eyes that seemed to expect him to understand how the leap from that transaction to her tax return made perfect sense. He supposed in her convoluted mind it did.

"Since the money went to the hospital, even though you gave it to Jeannie, you figured it was tax deductible," he said, trying not to scream.

"Exactly."

He shook his head. "Sorry."

"But the hospital qualifies as a charity," she protested vehemently.

"Jeannie doesn't."

"You don't know Jeannie," she mumbled.

"What does that mean?"

Her flashing gaze met his. "She's barely making ends meet, and she wanted to do something nice. I was only helping her out."

"And it was a wonderful gesture, but you can't deduct it," he said firmly.

"Oh, okay," she said, her voice edged with disgust. "Lordy, you people are picky."

"We're just following the rules."

Victoria sniffed and looked at him as though she'd like to tell him exactly what he could do with those rules. Tate promptly felt like an absolute rat and wished he'd gone into another profession. By the time the interview ended, he was worn out, and he knew his report to Pete Harrison was going to read like something from an anthology of science fiction.

Pete is never going to understand this, he thought, absolutely dazed and more intrigued than ever by this latest encounter with Victoria's logic. Something was happening to him and, for the life of him, he couldn't understand it. A sheer physical attraction he could deal with, but it was more than that. He was actually beginning to look forward to Victoria's slightly twisted train of thought. She was like the first crisp breeze of fall after a long, hot summer, a refreshing change that he'd never realized how much he'd longed for. Other women suddenly seemed so...ordinary. He grinned as he realized that he'd never before thought of that as an insult. He gazed at Victoria and something inside him seemed to snap. It was as though a belt that had been restricting the flow of blood had been suddenly loosened. He felt freer, happier than he'd felt in ages.

"Are we finished?" she asked him at last, blushing under his intense inspection.

"For now."

"And I can go?"

He stared at her, his expression clearly reflecting his disappointment. "Do you have to? I promised you a dinner."

Victoria's eyes widened. "You still want to take me?"

"Of course. I've been counting on it," he admitted, realizing it was true. He'd been thinking of nothing else all day long, and that was a first. Any woman who could get him to forget about his work, forget about business protocol for that matter, was a woman he needed to know better.

Or, he thought more rationally, one from whom he ought to be running like crazy.

He looked at Victoria, sitting across from him in her bright blue dress edged with black, her thick, red hair swept up in a Gibson girl style that emphasized her delicate features, and his breath came more rapidly...as though he'd already run a very long, very important race. And lost.

Chapter 6

Seated across from Tate in a lovely old restaurant where the lighting was seductively dim, the service impeccable and the food outrageously expensive, Victoria found herself relaxing and forgetting all about how totally inappropriate Tate was for her. The ambiance encouraged thoughts of romance. In fact, she had a feeling the tuxedo-clad waiters would escort anyone who seemed to be interested in anything else from the premises. Responding to the atmosphere, Tate's questions had lost the harsh edge of an inquisition and turned to more personal topics. It was as though he finally wanted to get to know her, not her tax status. He was going out of his way to be charming, displaying a surprising sense of humor and a willingness to poke fun at himself that she'd never suspected existed under the straitlaced exterior.

For the first time she had an idea of what it might be like to really date him, to feel his eyes sweep over her in a lingering visual caress, to hear his low voice whisper to her in a romantic undertone, to have him want her...and admit it. The idea intrigued her and a trembling responsiveness swept through her as she surveyed him in this new light.

Actually, she reminded herself, it wasn't so new. It was the way she had first viewed him from that tree and during those brief, tantalizing moments in his arms...right before they'd settled into their preassigned roles as righteous government worker and presumed tax evader. He had felt absolutely wonderful then, his body firm and solid and reassuring, his masculine muscles unyielding against her feminine softness. Just last night, his kisses had been the shattering, knee-weakening stuff of a torrid big screen love scene. A quiver of excitement flared at the memory, and suddenly she wanted more than anything to know that unique, bone-melting feeling again.

At first she hadn't the faintest idea of how to accomplish this without simply throwing herself into his arms. She could imagine his reaction to that. He wouldn't recover from the shock for days. Actually, the idea of startling Tate appealed to her, but she resisted it. Instead, she settled for a more traditional approach, a very feminine appeal. Tilting her head provocatively, she gazed unblinkingly into his eyes until she knew she had his undivided and, judging from the flush on his neck above his collar, slightly nervous attention. It turned out flirting wasn't quite as difficult as she'd thought it would be, and even without much practice her technique certainly seemed to be working fine.

"Tate," she began softly.

He cleared his throat and blinked, his brown eyes cautious. "Yes."

"Could we go someplace and dance?" She reached over and touched his hand beguilingly. "Please."

He regarded her incredulously. "You want to go to a disco?" he asked, sounding as shocked as if she'd declared a desire to have a fling in one of those adult motels with mirrors on the ceiling and king-size waterbeds.

"Of course not," Victoria replied indignantly. A disco was the last place she wanted to go. She wanted to be in the man's arms swaying to soft, romantic music, not twirling around under some blinding, flashing lights trying to find him in a crowd. "Isn't there someplace we can waltz?"

"Waltz?" His expression was bemused, as if he'd never heard the word before.

"Surely you're old enough to recall what that is. Ballroom dancing may be old-fashioned, but it hasn't vanished from the face of the earth. Can't you remember how to take a woman in your arms and move slowly around a room in time to the music?" Victoria teased.

"Of course, I remember," he retorted indignantly. "We had lessons in junior high. The boys all stood on one side of the room with sweaty palms and giggled, and the girls stood on the other side in their party dresses trying not to look desperate."

"You don't seem to remember much about the dancing part."

He shuddered. "I've blocked it from my mind."

"Well, unblock it and let's go someplace where I can prove to you that there's a very good reason for such an antiquated custom."

He paused thoughtfully, then shook his head. "I don't think there have been places like that in Cincinnati since the turn of the century."

"Of course there have. You just don't know where to find them," she charged.

"You may be right," he admitted, taking a deep breath. "Would you rather drive around and look for one or would you be willing to try my apartment instead?"

Actually, Tate thought, Victoria couldn't have given him a better opening. He'd been wondering all evening how he could entice her to come home with him so they could be alone. Blatantly suggesting that she stop by for a drink, with its implicit hint of a bedroom romp to follow, somehow bothered him. He felt as though he'd be betraying her parents' trust, which for him was an entirely new and not particularly welcome reaction. Even now, when Victoria was staring at him with come-hither eyes, he felt guilty as hell. He ought to be taking her out for a strawberry ice-cream soda, not trying to figure out how he could taste the strawberry pink of her lips in the privacy of his living room.

"That's certainly a better line than suggesting I stop by to see your etchings," she said, and he flinched as the all-too-perceptive dart struck home. But when he studied her expression more closely, he realized she actually seemed amused. She certainly didn't seem to be offended.

"Well then?" he prodded, ignoring the little voice that told him he was begging for trouble with a capital *T*.

Victoria took a deep breath. This was what she wanted, wasn't it? No man had ever made her feel quite as giddy as Tate McAndrews, and she wanted to explore that sensation, to discover what all the fuss was about. Tonight was as good a time as any. Once this tax audit was over with she might never see him again. Every true romantic deserved one wild night of explosive passion, and that was what Tate seemed to promise, if her thundering heartbeat was any indication.

"Why not?" she said boldly, ignoring the little tremor of trepidation that made her pulse lurch erratically. She also diligently silenced her ornery conscience which was reminding her that Tate McAndrews was not the right man to use for her romantic experimenting. If she happened to fall head over heels in love with him in the process, it could only lead to disaster. He was so completely unsuitable.

But he was also damnably attractive, she argued right back. Besides, she was too old to be meandering hesitantly through life as an untouched virgin. If Tate McAndrews could stir her hormones out of their previously dormant existence—and Lord knows he had—then she'd better find out why.

When they reached Tate's apartment, Victoria's mouth dropped open impolitely, and she stared around her in a sort of dazed wonder. For a moment she felt as though she were suffering from culture shock. His furniture had absolutely no character. It was upholstered in dull, serviceable colors, no doubt chosen because they wouldn't show dirt if anyone had the audacity to spill something. His paintings were formless splashes of hideous colors hung against plain white walls. The tables were all glass and chrome, and not a one of them had so much as a water mark to spoil the shiny surface. His plants were so full and green and healthy; it seemed as though they wouldn't dare to droop. In fact, everything was so disgustingly tidy, so perfectly placed and so horribly sterile, Victoria was convinced he must have a filing system for his trash. She would have given anything to find a speck of dust anywhere or one wilting leaf on a philodendron.

"Don't you ever feel like dropping your clothes on the floor?" she asked, her expression dismayed.

Tate grinned at her, his brown eyes flashing wickedly, as he removed his jacket with taunting deliberation. "Sure," he said softly, his gaze locking with hers. She felt as though she'd been frozen in the midst of a dream and couldn't wake up. The jacket fell to the floor and her eyes followed it, widening with disbelief. "Right now, for instance."

Suddenly her heart began drumming wildly in her chest, and she stared up at him in confusion. "That's not what I meant," she said, the words coming out as a choked whisper as passionate images of two nude bodies—hers and his—flickered to life in her brain. Liar, a little voice nagged. Judging from the Technicolor intensity of those images, it was exactly what she'd meant.

"Are you sure?" he taunted softly, taking a step toward her. He'd meant only to tease her, but all of a sudden the moment had turned breathlessly serious. He did want to undress, first Victoria and then himself, taking time to explore her body as she learned his. He wanted to know the feel of that creamy white skin under his fingers, to fill his hands with her breasts, to arouse the nipples into tight buds with his tongue, to feel her surrounding him with her moist femininity. He wanted her with a savage urgency that stunned him into immobility. He was afraid that if he took her in his arms, if he so much as kissed her, he wouldn't be able to stop until he knew every inch of her. And he could see from the half-frightened, half-hopeful expression in her blue eyes that she wasn't ready for that.

Victoria was shaking her head, reading the expression in Tate's eyes with unerring accuracy. But although she was telling him no, her pulse rate was definitely shouting yes, telling her to take all that he had to offer, to discover the hidden, untapped part of her own womanliness, to learn his masculine secrets. Confusing, contradictory thoughts roared through her head, warring for control of her actions.

How could her body yearn with such heated longing for someone her mind knew would be so wrong for her? Yet was he really wrong for her? He was strong, obviously dependable, sure of himself, in short the perfect balance for her zaniness. His instinctive protectiveness of her, even when he was most impatient, was certainly the stuff of romantic heroes, even though it tended to drive her crazy. Even now, she could tell that he was willing to follow her lead. He wanted her, but would take her only if she agreed, only if she came to him willingly and without reservations.

Lord knows, she had reservations. Why couldn't Tate have been someone else, someone more like herself? Then there would be no doubts at all. Even if he would unbend just a little, she thought, it would make all of this more understandable. For the first time in her life, her impulsive nature seemed to have abandoned her. With her first lover she would want much more than a fling, and with Tate that would be an absurd expectation. Even she knew better than to enter into a relationship with the hope of changing the other person. She'd heard enough accounts of marriages that had faltered because one partner suddenly realized those traits that had been merely bothersome during courtship were absolute hell to live with and that they weren't going to go away.

Suddenly it was all more than she could deal with. She wanted romance, candlelight and roses, impetuous adventures, laughter-filled days and passion-filled nights. She also wanted Tate, who promised no more than passion. She couldn't reconcile the two.

"I think I'd better go."

"Why?"

"This wasn't such a good idea."

"But we haven't danced yet," Tate said urgently, not wanting her to leave until he had at least held her in his arms. Surely he could keep himself under rigid control. He always had before. It wasn't until he had met Victoria that his control had snapped. Recently he'd found his temper flaring unexpectedly and his desires raging with such urgent abandon that it stunned him. Maybe if he burned an image of a disapproving Pete Harrison into his mind, he could regain his sense of balance, at least until he finished the audit.

"Danced?" she repeated blankly.

"You remember that quaint old custom," he teased lightly. "It's what we came here to do."

No, Victoria wanted to say. No matter what we said, we came here to make love and we both know it. But she knew she could never force those bluntly honest words past her suddenly quivering lips. Tate didn't see the tremor. He was walking to his stereo, selecting a tape and putting it on, as thought she had agreed to stay. When the soft strains of a ballad filled the air, he held out his arms. He looked so hopeful standing there that she couldn't refuse. Admit it, she chided herself, you don't even want to refuse. Her eyes locked with his, and she moved into his embrace, sighing softly just as he did when his arms closed securely around her.

The music surrounded them, drew them into its slow, provocative tempo. Victoria closed her eyes and gave herself up to the melody, to the wondrous sensation of feeling Tate's heart throbbing next to hers. She was captivated by that sure, steady beat, awed by her ability to alter it with a delicate touch of her fingers along the warm curve of his spine. Held by Tate, she knew the truly magical spell of romance for the first time and wondered again if she'd been wrong, if it could possibly work. She felt beautiful and graceful, as though she were floating on air.

"You're trying to lead," Tate murmured in her ear, the whisper of warm breath delicately tantalizing, even though his words startled her.

"I am not," she retorted indignantly, moving back to scowl up at him. He gave her an infuriating, crooked grin.

"Oh, yes, you are. What's the matter? Are you afraid I'm going to step on your toes?"

"Of course not."

"Then you don't trust me enough to follow me," he said flatly.

Victoria suddenly had a feeling he was talking about far more than dancing. "How can you say I don't trust you? I stayed here, didn't I?"

His gaze softened, and he touched a finger to her cheek, leaving behind a trail of fire and a blush of pink. "So you did. Are you sorry?"

She stared up at him solemnly. "No. I want to be here."

"In my arms?"

"In your arms."

He grinned again and her heart flipped over. "Then how about letting me lead?"

Victoria groaned. "Is your masculine ego being threatened?"

"Hardly. It's just easier if only one of us is in charge."

"Are we still talking about dancing?" Victoria asked dryly.

"I am." His expression was all innocence, though she had a feeling his comment was about as innocent as a million-dollar lawsuit.

"Are you sure you don't still have designs on straightening out my life?" she inquired edgily.

His eyes brightened, and he suddenly tilted her backward in an unexpected and breathtaking dip. "You're admitting it could do with a little reorganizing?"

"Let me up."

"First, admit it."

"I'll admit no such thing. My life is fine, Tate McAndrews!" It was impossibly difficult to say anything with conviction from this crazy angle, but she tried. He didn't seem to believe her.

"That's why you're in trouble with the IRS, why your business is haphazard at best, why your parents want to marry you off and why your house is tumbling down—because your life is under such perfect control?"

"You're being smug again."

"I am?"

"I hate it when you're smug."

"You hate it when I'm right."

"Leave me alone."

Tate put her solidly back on her feet and dropped his arms. He shrugged. "If that's what you want."

"It's what I want," she said, glaring at him defiantly, the spell broken. The man, she decided, had about as much romance in his soul as the author of a math textbook. He certainly didn't know how to pull off a seduction.

"Are you planning a dramatic exit?" he inquired, his lips twitching in a perfectly infuriating way.

"Now that you mention it, I don't think I'll give you the satisfaction." She walked to the door, turned back and gave him a haughty look of disapproval. "Good night, Mr. McAndrews," she said with prim politeness and shut the door softly behind her.

Tate stood and counted to ten. The doorbell rang. He opened it and found her standing there, her eyes flashing angrily.

"I'd like to call a cab, if you don't mind," she said stiffly.

His lips had stopped twitching and formed a full-blown, smug smile. "I'll drive you back to your car."

"That's not necessary."

"It is necessary," he said decisively, taking her arm and steering her from the apartment.

They drove across town in a silence so thick Tate felt like screaming. A few days ago that raging feeling of pure frustration would have been totally unfamiliar, but all of a sudden it was becoming a way of life. He didn't feel the least bit thrilled about it either. He had the oddest desire to shake Victoria until she agreed to shape up her life. The image of those hazardous stairs and peeling wallpaper sent shivers of fear and dismay along his spine. He had a feeling, though, she'd never admit to needing a bloody thing, least of all his help. She was the most stubborn, infuriating woman he'd ever met, and she obviously didn't know what was good for her.

Her parents were right. She needed him in her life. The only thing wrong with that theory was the very distinct probability that she'd drive him crazy in the bargain. He gazed over at her and discovered that she was staring straight ahead, her shoulders stiff, her mouth settled into a stern line. Perversely, he wanted to kiss her until her mouth curved into a sensual, lazy, satisfied smile again. He had a feeling if he tried, though, she'd slap him...and rightly so.

Victoria might be even wiser than her parents on this one, he decided reluctantly. It would be better if they never saw each other again and preserved their sanity. He could send her the outcome of the audit in the mail. Ironically, the minute he admitted to himself that she was absolutely wrong for him, that it would be wise to let her vanish from his life, he wanted her more than ever.

"Where's your car?"

"Near your office."

"Where near my office?" he said with more patience than he'd ever thought he was capable of.

"I don't know. In some lot. How many parking lots can there be around there?"

Tate groaned. There were half a dozen or more. Thank God she hadn't parked in a high-rise garage. They'd be driving up and down ramps the rest of the night.

"Couldn't you think of this as an adventure?" Victoria asked plaintively.

"Afraid not," he muttered as he circled the blocks in the vicinity of the IRS offices. Fortunately, at this hour it wasn't difficult to spot a dented blue Volkswagen sitting forlornly in the middle of a virtually empty lot. It reminded him of the sad expression in Victoria's eyes.

Don't start thinking like that, McAndrews, or you'll be right back where you started, he warned himself. He managed to keep his expression stern and unforgiving as Victoria climbed out hurriedly, dashed into her car and drove away with barely a wave. It wasn't until she'd gone out of sight that he began to experience something that was totally foreign to him. Finally, he realized it was sheer, heart-wrenching loneliness. He didn't like the feeling one bit.

Chapter 7

For the next ten days Tate suffered, agonizing over the separation from Victoria and, for the first time in his life, turning introspective. He analyzed the attraction he felt for her from every possible angle, dismissing it as sheer folly one minute, only to seize on the memory of her delightful laugh and beguiling smile the next. He was behaving in such an uncharacteristically sloppy, withdrawn way that his friends began asking first subtle, and then more pointed questions. They worried about an illness, a family problem, a financial reversal. No one seemed to suspect that a woman was involved. They all knew that Tate McAndrews would never allow a woman to disrupt his life so dramatically.

And his orderly life was most definitely being disrupted. In fact, it was in an unbelievable state of chaos. While he daydreamed, work piled up on his desk until even Pete commented on the disorganized clutter. At home he left unwashed coffee cups in the sink and clothes scattered on the floor. He didn't even seem to notice. One plant suddenly wilted and died, its bedraggled remains ignored. He opened magazines, stared uncomprehendingly at the pages and then dropped them. They stayed wherever they fell.

Only one image seemed to register fully in his mind—Victoria's. He pictured her as he'd first seen her, dangling precariously upside down from a tree branch. It was an enchanting, unforgettable image. He recalled the half-astonished, half-temptress look in her blue eyes when he'd kissed her for the first time, and his body began behaving like a teenager's, turning hot and ready at the mere memory of the way she'd felt in his arms. He was not used to having absolutely no control over his life, his thoughts or his body. Much more of this and he'd go stark raving bonkers, he thought desperately.

You can either forget her or do something, he told himself in the middle of Friday night as he tossed and turned restlessly amid a tangle of sheets. Since forgetting her seemed unlikely, he decided to accept the inevitable. He was going to have to kill this ridiculous obsession through overexposure. Every sensible bone in his body told him that spending more than a few hours with Victoria would drive him to distraction. He would be forced to acknowledge that she was absolutely wrong for him, and that would be the end of it. He could go back to doing his dishes and his work.

When the do-it-yourself home repair shop in his neighborhood opened Saturday morning, Tate was waiting. He selected lumber first, then hesitated about paint. Every conservative instinct in him shouted that he should buy white. He always bought white. It went with everything. Finally, he took a deep breath and pointed to what he considered to be an outrageous shade of blue...for a wall. It matched Victoria's eyes exactly. His hand shook, but he didn't back down. Since he wasn't about to leave anything to chance, he also bought a ladder, paintbrushes, rollers, turpentine and a complete assortment of nails and screws. At the checkout counter, he eyed the collection of items carefully, then went back for a hammer, a screwdriver and a saw.

"Gonna do a little work around the house?" the clerk said dryly.

"No, I'm going to build one," Tate replied grumpily, flinching at the figure that popped up on the cash register. Victoria was turning out to be a costly obsession in more ways than one. He handed over his credit card and wondered for the hundredth time if it made any sense at all for him to be doing this. Victoria wouldn't appreciate it.

In fact, she was probably going to resent it and throw him and his blue paint right back out the door.

"Too bad," he muttered under his breath. "You're not doing this for Victoria. You're doing it to save your sanity."

"What's that, mister?"

"Nothing."

Once everything was loaded into his car, he headed for Victoria's, his determination mounting. He was going to fix up that place of hers so he could stop worrying about it and get her out of his system in the process. It was going to be a wonderful, satisfying weekend.

By the time he arrived in her driveway, he was whistling cheerfully, envisioning the serenity that would return to his life in a few short days. It was worth the price of a little paint and lumber and the hard work.

At first he was surprised that Victoria didn't come out of her house as soon as his car stopped, but then he decided it was better that she hadn't noticed his arrival. It gave him time to get everything unloaded before she threw a fit. By the time he'd be ready to knock on the door and surprise her, it would be too late to send him packing.

He was about to lean the ladder against the side of the house when Lancelot suddenly wove between his legs, meowing a friendly greeting. Tate tripped over the cat and tumbled forward, the ladder crashing through a window. Lancelot's howl of protest was almost as loud as Tate's.

Victoria heard the noisy crash just as she rolled over and prepared to snuggle back under the covers to finish a perfectly delightful dream about a man who knew exactly how to win her heart, a man who was nothing in the world like Tate McAndrews. She had taken the day off and promised herself a few extra hours of sleep to make up for all of the restless nights she'd had since she and Tate had parted. She'd been furious at him, but that hadn't kept her from missing him terribly, and she hated herself for even noticing his absence.

"What in heaven's name was that?" she mumbled, suddenly wide awake. She waited for another crash, but heard only screeches that clearly came from Lancelot and mutterings that reminded her of

Tate's colorful carrying on when he fell through her stairs. Tate? She sat straight up in bed and listened more closely. No doubt about it. It was definitely Tate. She'd never heard such a wide vocabulary of expletives from anyone else. What on earth was he doing here at the crack of dawn on a Saturday morning? In fact, what was he doing here at all?

Wrapping a robe tightly around her, she ran to the window and peered out. The sight that greeted her was so unexpected, so ridiculously out of character, that it was all she could do to keep from laughing. Tate was lying on the ground his long legs tangled in a ladder, surrounded by scattered boards that resembled a giant's game of pick up sticks. His scowl as he tried to disengage himself was impressive and more than enough to convince her to save her laughter for later.

She ran down the stairs and threw open the door, her eyes widening in dismay as she noted the ladder protruding through the living room window. She knelt down and surveyed Tate quickly, looking for signs of blood, her hand brushing lightly over a bump on his forehead.

"Are you okay?"

"Fine," Tate said tightly.

She sat back on her heels then and regarded him quizzically, noting idly that he apparently did own one pair of jeans and that they fit like a well-worn glove. Instinctively her gaze surveyed the faded fabric, starting with its revelation of the hard muscles of his thighs, then moving upward to its taut stretch over his abdomen. She realized suddenly exactly where she was staring and blushed furiously. Fortunately, Tate didn't even seem to notice.

"Not that I'm not glad to see you, but exactly what do you think you're doing?" she said at last.

"I've come to help."

"With what? Demolishing my house?"

"No. Fixing it up," he explained, fighting to regain his sense of humor. He probably did look pretty ridiculous.

"You're off to a wonderful start," she said, glancing significantly at the shattered window. She sighed. "Tate, you really don't need to help. I thought we settled this the other night. I can do things for myself."

"I know you can," he agreed soothingly. Too soothingly. Victoria's suspicions flared to life. "I just thought maybe I could help. It'll go much faster if two of us work on it."

"Why does it matter so much to you how fast it goes?"

This was the tricky part. Tate knew he couldn't very well admit that he wanted to get her off his mind once and for all, so he settled for a half-truth. "I'm worried about your living like this. I'll feel better when you're settled."

It probably wouldn't do to analyze why he was worried about the way she lived in the first place. He just had to keep telling himself that once he stopped worrying, he would also stop thinking about her at all. He looked up, and his gaze met eyes that were filled with skepticism.

"Don't say it," he said.

"Don't say what?"

"Don't tell me again that it's none of my business how you live."

"It isn't."

"Maybe not, but I feel responsible."

"That's absurd."

He nodded. "I know it."

Suddenly Victoria grinned as she realized exactly how Tate must feel about finding himself in this position. He had probably never before done something that made as little sense as this. She could see from the confusion in his eyes that he didn't quite know what to make of it all now, either.

"As long as you're here, why don't you come on inside and have some breakfast?" she suggested.

"I have to finish unloading the car."

Victoria cringed. She couldn't afford too many more broken windows. "Leave it for now. I'll help you later."

Maybe it would be a good idea to have some coffee first, Tate decided. Not that this accident had been his fault. If that fool cat hadn't gotten in his way, Victoria would still be upstairs sleeping peacefully in her brass bed, her tousled red hair spread over the pillow, a sheet barely covering the curve of her breasts. He choked back a moan of pure frustration. He suddenly wanted, more than anything, to be in that bed with her.

Instead, he followed her docilely into the kitchen, trying not to notice the way her silk robe draped provocatively over her rounded rear. So far this was not exactly working out the way he'd intended. Instead of killing his interest, it was fanning it until he felt as though flames were shooting through his body.

"Why don't you go on and get dressed?" he suggested in a husky whisper. At her odd look, he cleared his throat and added, "I could start on breakfast, if you'll tell me what you want."

"I want everything," she said. "Breakfast on the weekend is my favorite meal. I want eggs and bacon and pancakes with maple syrup."

Tate stared at her blankly. "Umm, how about if I get the coffee started?" he offered.

Victoria grinned knowingly. "Terrific. I'll be back in a minute."

While she was gone, Tate tried not to imagine her slipping out of that robe, stepping into a hot shower and then slowly drying herself before dressing in skimpy little bikini pants and a lacy bra. He didn't succeed. He could visualize with breathtaking clarity every sensual movement. He nearly scooped the instant coffee into the pitcher of orange juice he'd found in the refrigerator. Forcing himself to concentrate, he got out the eggs, bacon and milk and set them carefully in a precise row on the counter. He found the dishes and neatly set the table. After first searching every cupboard, he finally retrieved the frying pan from the oven. He looked at the eggs and the pan, considered making an attempt to fix the eggs and shook his head.

"She wants breakfast, not a scientific experiment," he muttered and sat down to wait.

When Victoria came back into the kitchen a few minutes later, she was wearing a pair of paint-splattered cutoff jeans that barely covered her all-too-enticing bottom and a shirt that she seemed to have forgotten to button. It was tied around her middle, leaving an expanse of bare flesh that he wanted desperately to caress. He fought to focus his gaze elsewhere. It traveled to the silky curve of her neck. He wanted to touch his lips to that tender spot. His breath was coming in increasingly ragged gulps as he ripped his eyes away from that provocative sight. He told himself he should be staring out the window at the lilacs or checking out the fine job Victoria had done repairing the tiles, but he couldn't seem to move his gaze farther than the red plaid of her shirt as it fit snugly over the curve of her breast.

"I thought you were going to get dressed," he mumbled in a hoarse whisper, then could have kicked himself for virtually admitting that he was bothered by her appearance.

"I am dressed," she said, looking at him oddly.

"Barely."

"Did you want me to wear a formal gown while I work on the house?"

"No, but you could have put on...I don't know, something more...something less...."

Suddenly Victoria chuckled. "Which do you want?" she teased softly. "More or less?"

Tate glared at her. "Never mind. Wear whatever the hell you want."

"If I'm bothering you, I'll go back upstairs and change."

"You're not bothering me," he denied.

She took a step closer to him. "Are you sure?"

She smelled like a summer garden, Tate thought idly, his senses reeling. Troubled brown eyes looked up at her.

"Damn you," he muttered helplessly. "Come here."

Victoria stood perfectly still. The laughter that had filled her eyes only a moment before had died, replaced with a smoky desire. She shook her head slowly, a soft, knowing, entirely feminine smile tilting the corners of her mouth.

"You come here," she taunted.

Suddenly, with an agonized groan, Tate was out of his chair and pulling her into his arms. His lips burned against hers, demanding that they part, his tongue urgent in its quest for the tender, tentative touch of hers. His hands sought the bare skin at her waist and molded her body into his, relishing the way silk had turned to fire under his touch. Her hips instinctively tilted forward into the cradle of his, driving him nearly mad with longing. He wanted to take her right here in the middle of her kitchen. He wanted to rip that ridiculous outfit away from her body and expose every inch of flesh beneath it to his passion-sharpened gaze, to his hungry lips. He wanted to know that she was as crazy with this driving need as he was, to feel her responding to his lightest touch, crying out when the white-hot urgency of her arousal and desire matched his. He wanted.... Oh, Lord, he thought with a shuddering moan, he wanted her. He needed her.

"Victoria." Her name was uttered as half groan, half sigh as his lips burned against her neck, his tongue a moist brand that seared her. Her fingers danced through the thickness of his hair, skimmed the tight, muscled flesh of his shoulders, setting off a trembling in him that excited her beyond belief. Gone was Tate's intimidating self-control. Gone was that awesome straitlaced creature of habit, who seemed so far beyond her reach, so rigidly superhuman. This Tate was yielding, touchable and very, very human. In his arms, Victoria felt every inch a woman, a sensual, attractive woman who was all softness to his strength, all silk to his rougher denim.

Her skin was alive and tingling where his touch had branded her. Her lips burned against the hard, hair-roughened wall of his chest, and her tongue tentatively tasted flesh that was hot and damp from the fever of a passion she still couldn't quite believe. Her probing fingers, her thrusting hips, her thirsting mouth urgently sought to bring him beyond the point of denying her what she wanted so desperately. She knew instinctively that there might come a point when reason would return, when Tate's sensible nature would again seize control, and he would push her away, fighting against the pleasure they both wanted. She had to keep that from happening.

In the days they had been apart, she had made her decision. She knew that, if given another chance, she would take all that Tate had to offer for however long it lasted. She had forged a new strength to withstand any attempt he might make to change her. She believed with all her heart that she could have Tate, if she wanted him, without losing herself. If she wanted him...the words echoed distantly in her mind. Oh, yes, she wanted him, with every fiber of her being.

Her bare legs brushed against his thighs, against the hard evidence of his desire for her. She had worried that she might be a little frightened, a little tentative, when this moment finally came, but she wasn't. She was ecstatic, aggressive. Her heart was filled with so much joy, she thought she might burst, and she seemed to know exactly what to do, exactly how to excite him.

"Tate..."

"Hmmm." The low murmur barely interrupted the nearly unbearable, utterly sweet assault of his tongue on her aroused breast.

"Let's go upstairs."

"What's upstairs?" he mumbled from a daze of sensual delight.

Victoria smiled softly at his bemused state. "The bedroom."

"Bedroom?" He raised his head and his eyes widened, as though he had just realized where all of this was leading.

Sensing his slow return to sanity, Victoria stood on tiptoe and kissed him, dueling his tongue with her own, battling his sudden resistance. For a woman who'd never before seduced or been seduced—at least not successfully—she knew precisely how to work her will on him. In a matter of seconds, he was again moaning softly, holding her so tightly that her breasts crushed against his chest, her hips firmly in place against his seeking manhood. Even through two layers of clothing, hers and his, she could feel the heat, the throbbing need. There was no possible way he could pull away from her now.

Then the phone rang, and rang again, splintering the thick, passion-filled silence, shattering the moment of breathless insanity.

Chapter 8

The phone is *not* ringing," Tate mumbled determinedly, nibbling on Victoria's ear.

She gasped as the moist, feather-light touch sent a series of shock waves tripping along her spine. She'd never before realized that an ear was sensitive to anything more than sound. To her utter amazement and delight, it turned out that hers seemed to be a highly excitable erogenous zone. Unfortunately, it could also still enable her to hear the phone ringing.

"Yes, it is," Victoria countered, unable to keep a sigh of disappointment out of her voice. She'd been hoping to discover if her other ear was nearly as responsive as this one, and now she wouldn't find out…at least not this morning. She might be a romantic, but she could also be realistic. Tate's eyes might be glazed with passion right now, but his innate good sense was probably fluttering back to life. Passion could not stand up to a ringing phone, not after the fifth or sixth ring.

"Don't answer it," he urged, though his voice contained more hope than conviction.

Victoria gazed at him in feigned astonishment. "You actually want me to allow the phone to go on ringing? Shouldn't you be lecturing me on being responsible? It might be a problem at the shop. It could be your office. Someone might be sick. I might have won a sweepstakes. The sky might be falling.''

''Or it could be your father has ESP.''

She patted his hand consolingly. ''If he did, he'd be offering up a prayer of thanksgiving right now. You're falling right in with his plans.''

''I doubt that. Unless he's anxious to try out his shotgun.'' Tate muttered, running his fingers through his hair. ''Oh, answer the damn thing. The ringing is getting on my nerves.''

''Don't get testy. I'm sure it's not anything personal. Whoever's calling couldn't possibly know that we were about to,'' her voice faltered and she blushed. ''Do whatever it was we were about to do.''

He chuckled at her sudden confusion.

''Don't laugh at me,'' she grumbled, as she snatched up the receiver. ''I'm not in the habit of doing this.''

''Thank goodness,'' he said fervently, sighing and pulling her back into his arms.

Victoria scowled at him as she muttered into the phone, ''Hello.'' She winced at her tone; it was not her most pleasant. Not that it seemed to faze her caller, who hit her with a barrage of interested questions, then didn't even pause long enough for answers. It was just as well. With Tate's fingers now doing an erotic little dance across her stomach, Victoria was swept right back into a sensual daze that excluded the world and more mundane sensations. She barely heard the questions.

''What took you so long? You weren't still asleep, were you? Were you taking a bath? Oh, never mind. I just wanted to let you know I'd be by to pick you up in ten minutes.''

There was a pause, and Victoria finally realized some sort of response was expected. She murmured distractedly, ''Who is this?''

''What do you mean who is this?'' The voice was thick with righteous indignation. ''It's Jeannie. What's the matter with you?''

''Jeannie?''

"Jeannie?" Tate echoed, his brows lifting. "I should have known."

"Hush," Victoria hissed.

"What's going on over there, Victoria Marshall? Tell the truth. Remember, this is Jeannie. Your best friend. The friend who has read your diary and knows every one of your innermost secrets." She paused for added emphasis, then added significantly, "The friend who can read your mind."

I hope not, Victoria thought, suddenly tugging her blouse closed and trying to wriggle out of Tate's grasp. It seemed indecent somehow to have him kissing her, touching her so intimately, while her best friend was on the other end of the phone. Jeannie might not yet know this particular innermost secret, but she would definitely know something very peculiar was going on.

"I'm sorry," she apologized quickly. "I was just, umm, a little preoccupied." Tate drew her right back onto his lap and brushed his lips across the swell of pale skin revealed by the plunging V neck of her still-unbuttoned blouse. Tiny sparks sizzled straight through her, all the way down to her toes and Victoria couldn't help it: she gasped and then blushed furiously.

"Victoria Ann Marshall! Is someone with you? Is that what this is all about?" Jeannie was obviously too perceptive for her own good. She sounded pleased and very smug about her guess.

"If you've got something better to do, we can forget about the fair," she offered generously with a low, significant chuckle in her voice. Victoria wanted to strangle her. Or Tate. Or maybe both of them.

"Tell her yes," Tate was saying.

"Yes." She glared at him. "I mean no. What fair?"

"Never mind. Why don't I call you tomorrow?"

"No," she repeated adamantly, ignoring Tate's dismayed groan. It was ironic that her good sense had returned long before his had. She'd never even been aware that she had any. "What fair are you talking about?"

"The crafts fair," Jeannie explained patiently. "But don't worry about it. I can handle it alone."

"No. I'll help. I promised," Victoria said stoutly, a twinge of regret evident in her voice.

"Are you sure?"

"Yes." Maybe it was better this way, she thought, though at the moment she couldn't quite convince herself of that. Even if making love with Tate would be the mistake of a lifetime, she wanted to experience it. She had this awful feeling deep down inside that if they took more time to think about it, it would never happen. They'd both realize that there was no future for two people who were so incredibly mismatched. Her head believed that. Her heart wanted like crazy to believe that her head was wrong.

"Ten minutes then?" Jeannie was saying.

Tate's relentless fingers captured a nipple and a flash fire of blazing heat tore through her. "Make it a half hour," she said breathlessly.

Tate shook his head. "Not nearly enough," he whispered, as she hung up the phone.

"That's all we have, and I'm going to spend most of it taking a bath," she said briskly, absolutely amazed that she was apparently going to go upstairs, get dressed and walk right out of this house, when what she really wanted to do was throw herself straight back into Tate's arms. She must have a screw loose, just as he—and everyone else with the possible exception of her parents—seemed to think.

"With me?" he asked hopefully.

She grinned and shook her head sadly. "Not a good idea."

"Then you'd better make it a cold shower."

"Very funny."

Tate followed her up the stairs and sat down on the edge of her bed. Strangely, Victoria didn't feel the least bit uncomfortable about having him sitting there watching her as she got her clothes together. It was as though he belonged in this room, as though he'd been doing just this for years and years...as though they were married? The unexpected and all-too-pleasant thought sent a little tingle of excitement rippling through her. It was followed by a sharp stab of dis-

appointment. It will never happen, she told herself. Be honestly realistic for once in your life, even if it hurts like hell. Tate McAndrews
might be willing to have a fling with you because you're an attractive
oddity in his life, but that will be the end of it. He'll marry a member
of some country club who wears a cashmere sweater set, a double
strand of pearls and a tiny hat with a little veil as she struts off to
spend the afternoon analyzing the stock market.

"What am I supposed to do, while you're at this crafts thing?"
He sounded exactly like a kid left alone on a rainy day.

"You could come with me."

"And spend the day checking out pot holders and carved hunting
decoys? No way."

"Then you can stick around and fix the window or do whatever it
was you planned on doing when you came up here with all that
stuff."

"I'm not sure I like the options."

"You're the one who showed up without calling first."

"I thought you wanted me to learn to be more impulsive."

"I do," she said, brushing a kiss across his lips as she passed by
on her way to the bathroom. "One of the first things you learn when
you do the unexpected is that it may not turn out exactly the way
you expected."

Tate blinked at her uncomprehendingly. "What? How can you use
those words in the same sentence like that? No wonder you never
make any sense."

"I make perfect sense. You just haven't figured out how to listen
to me."

Tate stared at the bathroom door, then stood up and began ab-
sentmindedly straightening out the sheets. "There's a special way I
have to listen, too?" He shook his head as he fluffed the pillows and
put them neatly into place. "I'll never figure this out."

"Of course you will." Victoria opened the door and poked her
head out. "But you're too analytical. You need to listen with your
heart."

"Right now my heart is telling me that it would give anything to be behind that door with you."

"That's not your heart. That's your hormones."

"Maybe you ought to come back in here and give me a lesson in anatomy."

"Forget it, McAndrews. I gave up being a teacher," she retorted tartly. "Buy a book."

"I don't think a book will teach me the same lessons."

"Sure it will," she said, coming back into the room in another of her long skirts, this one a soft, silky green, and a scoop-necked blouse edged with multicolored rows of embroidery. "It just won't be as much fun." She looked from him to the bed, her eyes widening in surprise. "You made the bed."

Tate shrugged. "I needed to do something with my hands, since you weren't around."

"If you get bored while I'm gone, you could do the ironing," she suggested dryly, giving him a dazzling smile as she picked up her brush and drew it through a tangle of red hair.

"I didn't drive up here to play maid for you," he grumbled.

Victoria stopped brushing her hair and turned around and faced him, her expression puzzled. "Tate, why did you really come up here?" she asked slowly.

"I told you. I wanted to help you fix this place up."

She studied him intently. "Maybe," she said thoughtfully.

"What does that mean?"

"That might be part of it, but it's certainly not all." She shook her head sadly. "You still can't admit it, can you?"

"Admit what?" His expression was thoroughly bewildered.

"That you wanted to see me."

He coughed at her outspoken, thoroughly accurate remark. "Well…"

"Why is it so difficult for you to say it? Is it because you know as well as I do that this thing that seems to be happening between us is absurd?"

"It's true," he admitted regretfully. "We're not very well suited."

"No. We're not," she agreed candidly.

"Then why do I want to go on seeing you?" He sounded so confused and forlorn, Victoria almost wanted to take him in her arms and comfort him, but she knew exactly where that would lead. Suited or not, the chemistry between them was so volatile it made dynamite seem tamer than a Fourth of July sparkler. It could flare up with a mere look, much less an intimate caress.

"Because you want to get me into bed?" she suggested, watching his reaction in the mirror.

For a minute, Tate looked absolutely horrified. Then he looked guilty. Then he grinned. "Maybe you're right."

And wouldn't it be wonderful if she were? he thought. Maybe all it would take to stop this obsession would be one simple act of passion. He gazed at Victoria and recalled exactly how he had felt when she'd been in his arms. He'd been excited, yes, but more than that he'd wanted to hold her, protect her, cherish her. He'd never felt that way about a woman before. Most of the women he knew could take perfectly good care of themselves. As much as he hated to admit it, he knew those unexpectedly protective feelings he had about Victoria wouldn't go away once they'd made love. If anything, they'd deepen until he was caught up in a tangled web of desire and caring.

"Now we're getting somewhere," Victoria was saying triumphantly, and he wanted to warn her that she didn't have the vaguest idea what she was talking about, that this wasn't nearly as simple as she wanted to believe. This was no time to be starting a serious discussion like that, though, not with Jeannie—of the big heart, rotten cash flow and even lousier timing—about to pull into the driveway at any moment.

"Looks to me like we're not getting anywhere," he retorted, trying to keep his tone lightly teasing. "You're leaving."

"But I'll be back."

"And then?"

She sighed. "And then...I don't know." She looked him squarely in the eye and added softly, "Maybe we should both do some thinking about that, while I'm gone."

When she walked out of the bedroom, Tate stared after her in disbelief. Apparently, she did understand after all. She had realized that there were a lot of unanswered questions for the two of them, and she was as confused as he was about where or how to find the answers. Somehow that tiny sign of her own struggle with all of this reassured him tremendously. Not that he had the slightest idea why, he thought with a sigh.

"Who was he?" Jeannie asked as she set out an array of ceramic pitchers and bowls in her assigned booth at the fair. The morning sun was already taking the damp chill out of the air and making the muted blues and greens of her pottery glisten with silver-gray highlights.

"Who was who?"

"Don't play games with me, Victoria Marshall. Who was the man who had you so rattled you didn't even recognize my voice when I called?"

"What makes you think there was a man there?"

Jeannie groaned. "Your tone of voice for one thing. You always get this nervous little flutter in your voice when you're feeling guilty. I noticed it first when we were seven and you were trying to convince your mother we hadn't eaten an entire box of strawberries, even though we had red juice from head to toe."

Victoria glowered at her. Jeannie had been her friend for entirely too long and knew far too much. "What would I have to feel guilty about?"

"You tell me. Maybe it has something to do with the fact that you're denying the existence of a man, when I saw an incredibly gorgeous hunk walk into your back yard with a saw in one hand, a two-by-four in the other and bare shoulders that should be outlawed in the presence of unmarried females."

She studied Victoria closely. "Have you taken up with a handyman? It's nothing to be ashamed of, you know. In fact, it's about time you stopped being so blasted choosy. You've always wanted Clark Gable, Albert Schweitzer and a knight in shining armor all rolled into one. They don't make 'em like that anymore. I'm glad you've finally decided to settle for what's out there, just like the rest of us. You'll be much happier in the long run.''

Victoria burst out laughing at her friend's determined attempt to be broad-minded and encouraging in the face of what she obviously assumed to be Victoria's unexpected indiscretion. ''Thanks for your vote of confidence, but I don't need it. I have no intention of *settling* for anybody. As for Tate, he is not a handyman and, even if he were, I would never be ashamed of being involved with him.''

''Then you are involved,'' Jeannie said triumphantly. ''I'm so glad. It really is about time. What's he like? He certainly is scrumptious looking. Have your parents met him? When's the wedding?''

Victoria groaned. ''You're worse than my mother.''

''Then she has met him?''

''Oh, she's met him all right. For years I've thought her standards were tougher than the USDA's, but she practically branded Tate with her enthusiastic seal of approval on first sight. Before you even ask, he also has my father's blessing.''

''That must mean he can discuss politics and has a decent job.''

''He definitely has a job,'' Victoria replied dryly.

Jeannie regarded her curiously. ''The way you say that, it doesn't sound as if you're impressed.''

''Impressed is not the issue. He works for IRS.''

''Oh, my,'' Jeannie murmured, her voice an interesting blend of surprise and confusion. She managed to rally quickly, though, adding cheerfully, ''Well, that's certainly respectable.''

''Isn't it, though.''

''Why do I get the feeling that I'm missing something?''

''He is auditing my taxes,'' Victoria admitted casually, her eyes focused carefully on the large salad bowl she'd been fiddling with for the past five minutes.

''He's what?'' This time Jeannie didn't even attempt to cover her shock.

''It's ridiculous, of course,'' she mumbled with a wave of her hand. ''Something absolutely absurd about my making a claim for a refund the agency thinks is slightly exorbitant.''

Jeannie's hazel eyes widened, and the vase she was holding slid from her fingers. Victoria grabbed for it as it fell and placed it safely on a shelf in the back of the booth.

"Oh, my…" Jeannie said.

"Stop looking at me like that. I didn't do anything wrong."

"But if they're auditing you…"

"I did something stupid, not illegal. Tate says it should all be cleared up in a day or two."

"Are you sure? Do you trust him?"

Trust Tate? Victoria thought. Oddly enough, considering the rather unorthodox manner of their meeting and their short acquaintance, she did. She knew instinctively that she could trust him with her life. "I'm sure," she said confidently, then added dryly, "Just in case, though, if they cart me away to jail, you can bring me a hacksaw."

"It's not funny."

"You're telling me."

Jeannie studied her for several minutes, until Victoria thought she would scream. "What's wrong with you?" she finally demanded. "I'm not a criminal."

"I know that. I'm just trying to figure something out."

"What?"

"If he's auditing you, what's he doing in your backyard with his clothes off…?"

"Oh, for goodness' sakes," Victoria snapped indignantly. "He had his pants on."

"Whatever. He didn't look like he was checking out your financial records when I saw him."

"He wasn't. He's fixing up the house."

"He's what?" Jeannie exclaimed.

"Have you gone deaf?" Victoria muttered, her voice filled with growing irritation, even though she realized the whole thing did sound unbelievable.

"He's fixing up the house," she finally repeated.

"Is that a new government service?"

She glared at Jeannie. "No. He's worried about me. I've told him

I'm perfectly capable of fixing up my own house, but he doesn't think I'm doing it fast enough.''

"Ahh," Jeannie murmured, nodding with sudden understanding.

"What does that mean?"

"Clark Gable and a knight in shining armor all rolled up in one. Tell me, does this hunk have a brain?"

Victoria knew exactly where Jeannie was headed with that one. "Don't push it."

"Don't push what?" she replied innocently. "Unless I've lost every smidgen of intuition I ever had about you, you've fallen for this guy. Am I right?"

Victoria sighed. "You may be right."

Jeannie chuckled. "It's great to hear so much conviction in your voice."

"Well, it gets a bit confusing."

"I can imagine. An IRS agent doesn't sound like your type at all."

"He's not, at least not on the surface."

"But underneath?"

"Underneath there is something about him that I can't get out of my system. He drives me absolutely crazy one minute and the next I want to be in his arms. Does that make any sense?"

"Of course it does."

"It does?"

"You're in love." Jeannie was disgustingly gleeful.

"But he's so unsuitable."

"Apparently it doesn't matter."

"It should."

"Why?"

"Just because."

"Explain, Victoria Ann!"

"I've always wanted somebody who'd sweep me off my feet. Tate's at home sweeping off my porch."

"He sounds wonderful. When you're through with him, send him to my house."

"Not on your life!"

"You *are* a goner," Jeannie said delightedly. "I love it. I can hardly wait to meet him."

"You're not going to meet him," she said firmly.

"Why not?"

"I do not need another frustrated matchmaker actively plotting against me."

"Against you? Or for you?" Jeannie taunted.

"Oh, go spin your pottery wheel," Victoria retorted grumpily.

"I will," Jeannie said agreeably, smiling smugly. "I'll start on your wedding present."

Chapter 9

By four o'clock that afternoon every muscle in Tate's body, including some he'd never even been aware he had, ached. Instead of recommending expensive equipment and aerobics classes, fitness programs ought to be pushing the regular use of paintbrushes and a routine of ladder climbing. He'd gotten more exercise in one afternoon at Victoria's than he'd had in the last ten weeks at the gym.

He had replaced every one of the remaining broken stairs. The constant bending over to perform that task probably accounted for the dull, burning pain in his lower back. He'd also found the worst of the boards in the living-room floor, ripped them up and put in new ones. He'd had to yank, then stoop, over and over again, which most likely explained the tightness across his shoulders and the steady throbbing in the constricted muscles of his thighs and calves. He had patched the cracks in the walls and put on one coat of paint, constantly stretching over his head. His arms felt as though they weighed one hundred fifty pounds each and were going to fall off.

It had taken him a while to get the knack of all this unfamiliar home repair work. But he'd tackled the assignment with his usual methodical approach and, as he stood back and surveyed the nearly finished job, he was exhausted but triumphant and more than a little proud of what he'd accomplished. He had some small inkling now of what Victoria had been talking about. There was a lot of satisfaction to be had in working with your hands. The room was actually beginning to look habitable, though he was tempted to take Victoria's perfectly ugly sofa straight to a junkyard and put it out of its misery. He had a feeling, however, that Victoria would never forgive him. She probably believed the visible stuffing and threadbare upholstery gave it character.

He stretched and groaned. Surely the human body was not meant to do the sort of awkward physical contortions all of this activity had required. He looked at a paint roller lying on the floor and scowled. No more. His body couldn't take it. He would give anything for a long, hot shower that would soothe his tight muscles.

Well, why not? If he knew Victoria, she wouldn't be home for ages, and the bathroom had been one of her early projects. It probably had plenty of steaming hot water. He went out to the car and got the change of clothes he'd brought with him. Then, with a deep sigh of anticipation, he climbed the stairs, searching for her extra towels and went into the bathroom. He turned on the faucets full force, undressed, climbed into the tub and searched for the control to turn on the shower. There wasn't one. He looked up, hunting for the shower nozzle. Nothing. He practically cried, though he had to admit he wasn't surprised. Houses this age did not have showers, and women like Victoria preferred to soak in bubble baths anyway. The image of mounds of nearly transparent, shimmering bubbles strategically placed across Victoria's body suddenly appeared in his mind. It did not do a thing to relax him. In his mind those bubbles popped slowly and steadily, revealing more and more until his own body was taut with tension.

He muttered a low curse, plopped the stopper over the drain and watched the tub fill with almost unbearably hot water. When it was high enough, he sank down in it gratefully and felt the sore achiness begin to float away. He let his mind drift, dismayed that he still couldn't get it to focus on one of his more complicated work assignments. Instead, it was filled with more taunting images of Victoria.

He remembered her almost plaintive suggestion that he spend the day thinking about their relationship and what he wanted from it.

What did he want? He wanted the feeling of being vitally alive that he seemed to have discovered since meeting her. He wanted to learn to take chances, to explore life as she did with unabashed enthusiasm and excitement. Was it possible, though, to learn to do that? How could he give up a lifetime of caution and precise, carefully thought-out behavior? He had a feeling if he tried to be as impetuous as Victoria, he'd always fear that the police were only one step away. Yet that seemed better than never taking a dare. Without risks, life would certainly be safe and boring. He should know. He was coming to realize that his had become a tedious repetition of work, unsatisfying dinner dates and distant intimacy.

He grinned at the thought: distant intimacy. Now he was beginning to pair mismatched words just as Victoria did. They made sense, too. Despite the physical intimacy of his relationships, there had been a mental distance. Those women had never touched him, never captivated his heart as Victoria had. He had no idea why this was and perhaps it didn't require his understanding. Perhaps it was enough that it had happened. If one believed in a higher being controlling destiny, Tate thought, then one had to agree that in this case He had certainly worked in mysterious ways.

Suddenly he realized that the water had grown cool and the room was filled with the deepening shadows of twilight. He quickly got out of the tub, dressed in a fresh pair of jeans and a knit shirt and went downstairs. He'd made a decision while he was taking that bath, at first subconsciously and then with full awareness. Maybe later he'd attribute it to his mind becoming waterlogged, but right now it made sense. He was going to change, and he was going to start by fixing Victoria a gourmet dinner during which he could tell her all about the conclusions he'd reached about their future.

When Victoria finally got home, it was nearly seven o'clock, and she was almost surprised to find Tate still there. All day she'd been half fearing and half hoping that he'd realize how ridiculous this whole thing was and drive back home to Cincinnati where he belonged. Instead, here he was in the middle of the kitchen with flour on his nose, a recipe book open in front of him on the counter and dirty pans piled high in the sink. The place was an absolute mess. It was wonderful and amazing and horrible all at the same time.

"I know I've been encouraging you to be less orderly, but did you have to start practicing in my kitchen?" she teased. He barely looked up at her.

"Can it," he grumbled. "Don't interfere with the cook. I'm having enough trouble without your snide remarks."

"I hate to ask, but have you ever actually made a whole meal before? I had the impression that chopping carrots and peeling potatoes the other night was a first."

"It was."

"Then don't you think you should have started with something simple?"

"This was simple."

Victoria surveyed the mess disbelievingly. "Okay," she said wryly. "Then even simpler."

"Like hamburgers?"

"I was thinking more along the line of boiled eggs."

"Very funny."

Victoria leaned against the counter and gazed at him, suddenly serious. "Tate, what is this all about?"

"What does it look like? I'm fixing dinner. I figured you'd be too tired to do it."

"That's not what I mean and you know it."

He glanced over at her and shrugged. "Okay. I'm trying to prove to you that I can change, loosen up, experiment."

Victoria didn't have the heart to point out that fixing a meal was not exactly the same as flinging caution to the wind and going up in a hot air balloon. He seemed to consider it a breakthrough.

Instead, she asked simply, "Why?"

Tate returned her gaze solemnly. "Because you have more fun than I do."

Victoria chuckled. "That's probably true enough, but I had the distinct impression you didn't approve of my idea of fun."

"Well..."

"See what I mean?"

"No. What do you mean?" He glowered at her. "Are you suggesting that I can't change? I can do anything I put my mind to, Victoria Marshall. You are going to see a transformation the likes of which hasn't been seen since...since..."

"Since Count Dracula turned into a vampire?"

Brown eyes bored into her. "Hardly."

"Tate, don't you see? If you change, you won't be Tate McAndrews anymore. I can't ask you to do that for me."

"Then you admit you'd like me to change?"

"I'm not admitting anything. I'm just saying it never works, if you're changing for another person."

"I'm not. I'm doing it for me."

Victoria regarded him skeptically. "Tate, you'll never be comfortable taking life one minute at a time, the way I do. You're a planner."

"Maybe so. But isn't it possible that we might be able to compromise? Take life one *day* at a time?"

She grinned in spite of her misgivings. "That's some compromise."

"It is when you've had your entire life mapped out for the last ten years." He gazed at her, his eyes intense and filled with an intriguing blend of hope and desire. "Give me some time, Victoria. Please. Help me to know if there can be more to my life than auditing tax returns and going to the gym."

She shook her head. "Tate, I'm sure your life has more to it than that. You love your work and you've had fun in the past. You've certainly had other relationships, haven't you, relationships that made a whole lot more sense than this one ever could?"

"That's exactly my point. They've all made perfect sense. I've been with people like me, people so caught up in their careers and in doing the right thing that they don't take any chances. I've taken more chances today than I ever have in my life. It was wonderful.''

Victoria's eyes widened. "Chances? Here?" she asked anxiously. "Tate, what have you done? You didn't break any more windows, did you?"

"Of course not," he huffed. "Just wait until you see."

Victoria wasn't sure she had enough insurance to cover the possibilities or the stamina to withstand the shock. Still, she said bravely, "Let's go."

He shook his head. "Not now. After dinner, I'll take you on a tour."

"Don't you think you're being awfully optimistic?"

"What's that supposed to mean?"

"Do you actually think you're going to get a dinner out of this mess?"

"Just you wait, Victoria Marshall. You're going to regret making fun of me."

"I wasn't making fun of you. I was trying to be realistic."

"That has to be a first."

"Don't be snide. Where would you like me to sit?"

Like a maître d' Tate pulled out her chair, seated her and whipped open her napkin with an exaggerated flourish. He had just poured her a glass of wine, when the buzzer on the oven went off. Victoria's brows shot up. She hadn't even given him credit for being able to find the timer, much less knowing how to use it.

"Oh, dear," he muttered.

"What's wrong?"

"It's ready too soon. I haven't tossed the salad."

"We don't need a salad," Victoria soothed.

"Are you sure?"

"I'm sure."

"Okay," he said, relief evident in his voice. He opened the oven door and peered inside, his brow puckered in dismay.

"Now what's wrong?"

"It looks funny."

"What looks funny?"

"The soufflé."

"You made a soufflé?" Victoria couldn't keep the amazement out of her voice.

"Well, I thought I had, but it doesn't look like any soufflé I've ever seen."

"Let's see it."

With obvious reluctance Tate withdrew the casserole from the oven. Victoria eyed it curiously. There certainly wasn't any sign of a puffy golden top peeking over the rim of the dish. He walked over to the table and held it out.

"Does it need to cook some more?"

Victoria peered into the bowl and fought back the urge to giggle hysterically. It looked like a Florida sinkhole. The sides were barely three inches high and one shade beyond golden brown. The middle had simply caved in.

"I don't think baking will help it."

"Why not?"

"It's past help."

"But I've been checking it every few minutes. It seemed to be doing just fine."

Victoria's lips started twitching, and she gazed at Tate with blue eyes that sparkled with barely suppressed laughter. "You checked it every few minutes?" she said, her voice catching. "Were you careful not to slam the oven door?"

"What does that have to do with anything?"

"Tate, soufflés are very delicate. They can fall. Yours has taken a tumble."

"But I wanted it to be perfect."

"I'm sure it will taste fine," she said, though her voice lacked conviction. A moment later, with Tate gazing at her hopefully, she took a small bite, followed by a large gulp of wine.

"What's wrong with it?"

"Nothing," she denied. "It's a little hot."

"Of course it's hot. It just came out of the oven."

"That's not what I mean. Did you by any chance put any extra spices in it?"

"Extra spices?" He stared at her blankly. "No. I couldn't find the pepper shaker, so I used some of that red pepper instead, but that's all."

"Oh, my Lord," Victoria murmured.

"What?"

"Just taste it."

Tate scooped up a forkful, swallowed it and grabbed for his wineglass. His eyes watered.

"It's awful."

"Not awful exactly. Just spicy."

"We can't eat this. I'll make sandwiches."

Victoria stood up hurriedly. "No. You stay where you are. You've done enough. I'll make the sandwiches."

Tate grinned. "You don't trust me, do you?"

"Well, you did put hot pepper in a spinach soufflé."

"I wouldn't put it on the sandwiches."

"Maybe not, but humor me."

"Maybe we should take a look at the house first."

"Think that'll kill my appetite completely?"

Tate glared at her. "You're going to be sorry you said that."

"I hope so," Victoria muttered under her breath as she started toward the door.

"What did you say?"

She gave him a dazzling smile. "I said I can hardly wait."

Tate's tour started on the porch, where he pointed out the window he'd replaced. Then he showed her the stairs, all now solid-looking and even.

"I'm impressed," she admitted.

"Wait," he said, his brown eyes sparkling with an excitement that made her heart flip over. "Close your eyes."

"I won't be able to see if I close my eyes."

"Don't worry. I'll let you open them again. I just want you to experience the full effect all at once."

A nervous edginess crept into Victoria's voice. It was interesting that as Tate had grown more impulsive, she seemed to be growing increasingly cautious. "The full effect of what?"

"Close your eyes and come with me," Tate insisted, taking her hand. "Are they closed? They don't look closed."

"Tate, if I close them any tighter, I'll get wrinkles."

"They'll add character."

"I don't want character."

"Humph!"

Victoria noted that the hand clutching hers so tightly was much rougher than the hand that had caressed her that morning. For a moment she felt almost guilty about going off and leaving Tate alone to do all of this work. Then she visualized the mess in the kitchen and thought about how long it was likely to take her to repair the damage. Her guilt vanished. She'd say they were about even so far.

Suddenly they stopped and Victoria's nose twitched. Paint? She smelled paint. Suddenly she had this horrible vision of dull white walls. She'd known the minute she walked into his apartment that Tate's imagination did not stretch beyond white.

"Open your eyes," he said excitedly.

She took a deep breath and tried to prepare a properly enthusiastic response. After all, the man deserved some credit for trying. She opened her eyes. She rotated around in a tiny circle. Her brows rose ever so slightly. Her mouth dropped open.

"Tate, it's…"

"Do you like it?" he asked anxiously.

"It's so…blue."

"I thought it matched your eyes."

In that instant, with those softly spoken words, the room went from mere blue to incredible, spectacular and a dozen other adjectives it took to adequately describe the joy that shot through Victoria's heart. He'd bought the paint to match her eyes. If that wasn't the sweetest, most unexpected, most…romantic thing to do. She stood on tiptoe and threw her arms around him.

"Oh, Tate," she said, her eyes shining and turning a deeper, more intense blue than Tate had ever seen before. "It's the most beautiful room I have ever seen."

He knew then that every backbreaking moment had been worth it. The thrill of pleasing her, of surprising her was like no other emotion he'd ever experienced. He would climb mountains or tumble out of airplanes to keep that look on her face. Instead, he kissed her, his tongue flickering gently across her lips, teasing them into parting, urgently seeking her nectar, the uniquely sweet taste that was all Victoria.

With innocent abandon, she sighed and yielded to his embrace, like a child curling sleepily into the arms of a parent. But there was nothing childlike about her response in that moment of surrender. She was all woman in his arms, her body quivering under his deft touch as it roved over warm shoulders, curving spine, rounded buttocks and firm thighs. He felt the heat rising through her, matching his, blending with it until an urgent, white-hot fire raged between them.

Her hands were questing over his body, rippling along his muscles that were thirsting for her touch, tensed from the waiting, coiled even tighter when it came. They needed the release only she could bring. They needed to experience those delicate hands kneading, teasing, tempting him. He groaned aloud as her hand skimmed tentatively across the front of his jeans.

"No, babe," he pleaded. "Not yet." His control could take only so much.

"Tate, please don't stop," she pleaded. "I want you to love me."

"But we need to talk, remember. We need to think about what we want."

"I know what I want. I want to feel you inside me. I...I've never felt like this before, and I want it to be with you."

A thrill of pleasure soared through Tate, then hesitated and drifted down, turning into doubt. Could she possibly know what she was saying? Was she really willing to give her greatest gift to him? After all, she still thought they were mismatched and deep down so did he.

Nothing had happened to change that and making love would only confuse the issue.

She lifted his hand and placed it over her breast. He could feel the nipple harden. She gazed up at him, and there was a mute appeal in her eyes, an appeal it was taking every ounce of willpower he possessed to deny.

"Please," she whispered. "Please."

Tate buried his face in her hair, the golden-red curls surrounding him with fragrant silk. His body shuddered.

"Tate?"

"God help me, I want you too much to say no," he told her, scooping her into his arms and carrying her up the stairs. "We'll just have to sort it all out later."

When they reached the bedroom he carefully set Victoria on her feet, as though she were the fragile doll she'd once reminded him of. Then he turned down the covers on her brass bed, each hurried movement giving him a startling sense of déjà vu because he'd envisioned it so often in the last few days. She started to take off her blouse, but he stilled her hands.

"No," he said softly. "I want to do it."

Victoria saw the heated look of desire in his eyes and trembled. She had wanted this moment, wanted him so much and now it was happening. Her flesh burned, where his knuckles grazed it as he lifted her blouse over her head. His kisses fluttered across her shoulders, moist heat that seared soft satin. Her bra was unhooked and fell away and his lips replaced the lacy fabric, caressing, at first tenderly and then with an urgency that filled her breasts with an aching tautness. Waves of pleasure reached in and down, spiraling through her to some secret center of excitement that she'd never before realized she possessed.

Without her even knowing that Tate had touched it, her skirt slid to the floor, and her legs, which logic told her should have been cooled by the evening breeze, burned with an inner heat.

"You are so beautiful," he murmured softly, as his sure fingers skimmed over her anxious flesh, along the silken curve of her waist, over narrow hips and along firm thighs, drawn inevitably toward that trembling warmth between her legs. When his palm cupped her, Victoria gasped with surprise and delight. She'd had no idea what a man's touch would feel like there, no idea that it could create this breathless flutter of anticipation that was building into a thrill of tension that threatened to overtake her and send her senses reeling out of control.

"You're ready, aren't you?" She was so lost in the sensations flowing through her that Tate's voice seemed to come to her from a great distance.

Ready? She felt as though she'd been ready for a lifetime, waiting for this. "Yes," she murmured. "Oh, yes, Tate, I'm ready. I want you."

He slipped her pants off and then placed her gently on the bed. Victoria felt bereft without him, the fires inside were cooling, but as Tate yanked his shirt over his head, revealing his well-muscled chest with its scattering of crisply curling brown hairs, the flames built again. Victoria's fascinated eyes followed the movement of his hands as he unsnapped and then unzipped his jeans and slid them slowly down over lean hips, taking his briefs with them. Her breath caught in her throat at her first sight of him fully aroused for her. He was so utterly masculine, so incredibly virile. He was magnificent! She held out her arms to him and he came to her.

When flesh met flesh, Victoria's body responded with an urgency and eagerness that she could see from the look in Tate's eyes . His hands moved slowly over her, taunting her. Her body twisted and turned, alive with a yearning need to know it all, to feel the ultimate union of two highly different individuals into a uniquely special whole.

"Now, Tate, please," she pleaded.

"Shhh. I want to be sure you're ready," he soothed, his fingers gliding over the intense peak in which her arousal seemed to be centered to touch even warmer flesh. "I don't want to hurt you."

"You won't," she murmured softly against his chest, her lips moist and seeking, searching for a masculine nipple to feel the satisfying tension that could be aroused by a gentle flick of her tongue. "Nothing you could do could ever hurt me."

Tate knelt over her, poised, his eyes gazing down at her with love and desire and tenderness. Instinctively, Victoria's hips lifted to meet him, and the touch of that moistness lured him inside with a slow, steady thrust that hesitated only once, when a tiny cry escaped her lips.

"No, please," she said urgently, her hands on his hips drawing him to her, refusing to allow the retreat.

And then, once that instantaneous, tiny shock of pain was gone, she was filled with new waves of excitement that built to an incredible peak, calling to her, luring her to a place of awesome beauty and previously unimagined adventures. Suddenly she realized it was Tate's voice she heard, Tate calling out her name, as his body shuddered in an extraordinary moment of released passion, taking her with him on the most thrilling, romantic journey of all.

Chapter 10

As Victoria came slowly and reluctantly awake, she sensed that someone was staring intently at her. After awakening alone for twenty-eight years of her life, it was a most disconcerting feeling. It also felt wonderful to realize that Tate was next to her, and that it was his body causing that dip in the mattress, causing her to roll to his side. Smiling softly, she stretched and turned toward him, wanting to feel his arms around her again.

"Morning," she murmured quietly, not wanting to shatter the pleasant early morning hush of daybreak. She opened her eyes to meet his steady gaze, but as she took in the look of dismay on his face, her own gaze wavered. "What's wrong?"

"How could I do it? How could I be so stupid?"

"Do what?" She shook her head to try to clear the cobwebs. "Tate, I am not very good in the morning. You're going to have to try harder to make sense."

"How could I make love to you without protecting you?" he muttered, burying his face in his hands. If the eyes were the windows to the soul, Victoria thought, then Tate's soul was deeply troubled.

"You were a virgin, damn it. I never should have touched you. What if you get pregnant?" he said, then added decisively, "I'll marry you. That's all there is to it. We may have some problems adjusting at first, but we'll work it out. We ought to start thinking about a date.''

''Tate...''

His head snapped up. ''What?''

''Don't worry about it.''

''What do you mean don't worry about it? Of course I'm going to worry. I've never done anything this foolish and irresponsible before in my life. I never wanted to hurt you, and now I might have gone and gotten you pregnant. My God!''

''Tate, it's okay,'' she said soothingly, putting her cool hand on his bare shoulder. The flesh was warm, inviting. She felt him tremble, right before he decisively shrugged off her touch. He groaned aloud.

''Touching is not a good idea. That's what got us into this mess.''

''Tate McAndrews, I will not have you describing the most beautiful night of my life as a mess!'' Victoria snapped.

''Tell me that a few weeks from now when you're pregnant.''

''I am not going to get pregnant.''

''Do you have some sort of exclusive on luck?''

''No,'' she said patiently. ''But I took care of it. I saw a doctor...right after we met.'' She blushed. ''Well, not exactly right after, but soon...I mean once I knew....''

He gazed at her as though she'd announced that she'd been praying to a fertility god. ''You...''

''Saw a doctor,'' she repeated firmly. She grinned at him, noting the relief in his eyes. ''Someone had to be sensible,'' she added with a shrug.

Laughter bubbled up then, and Tate pulled her back into his arms. ''You are incredible, Victoria Marshall.''

''I've always thought so. I'm glad you've finally figured it out,'' she said, gasping when he nipped playfully at the taut peak of her breast. ''Tate!''

''Yes,'' he said innocently.

''What time is it?''

''I'm trying to make love to you, and you want to know what time it is?''

"I'm due at an auction at ten. I don't want to be late."

Tate moaned. "The woman who has never once in the two weeks I've known her been on time is worried about not being late to an auction. I can't decide whether to be astonished or insulted."

"Go for astonished. It's easier on the ego," she said as she rolled over top of him to see the clock for herself. "Whoops. It's nearly nine. I've got to get moving."

"You move much more, wiggle even one tiny finger, and you won't get out of this bed for a week," Tate announced in a voice so filled with urgency that Victoria froze.

"How do you expect me to get out of bed if I can't move?" she asked breathlessly, as her body became instantly aware of exactly how many interesting points of contact it had established with Tate's.

"I am going to do the moving. I am going to lift you ever so slowly so that you do not rub against me," he muttered, a low growl in his voice.

She wiggled.

"Victoria!"

She wiggled again and grinned. "Maybe I could be just a little late."

They arrived at the auction at noon. The yard of the farmhouse was crowded with familiar faces and the auctioneer's voice was filling the air with the rat-a-tat-tat patter that kept the bidding moving at a head-spinning pace. An excitement built inside Victoria, almost as great as that she'd experienced in Tate's arms. She loved exploring the rows of furniture and cartons of household goods at a farm sale, looking for some special treasure. Sometimes it seemed the more battered and decrepit the item, the more it appealed to her sense of discovery. She always wanted to learn what was under the paint or beneath the rust. Then she tried to imagine the lives it had touched. Maybe that was what made antiques so special to her, the fact they each had a history, stories they could tell about someone who had treasured them.

Because they were late, she didn't have time to do her usual advance survey of the items being offered. She signed up for a number so she could bid, then pulled Tate through the crowd.

"I'm starved," he murmured in her ear. "Can't we get something to eat?"

"You can. I'm working."

Tate's sharp gaze swept over the scene. "Are all of these people working?"

Victoria regarded him quizzically. "Tate, haven't you ever been to an auction before?"

"Never."

She shook head. "That's what happens when you spend your life playing games with rows of boring numbers. You miss all the fun."

"I thought you said this was work."

"It is for me. But a lot of these people just like to come and spend the day visiting with their friends. It's sort of like an old-fashioned community picnic."

His eyes lit up. "Picnic?"

Victoria grinned at his hopeful expression. "There are tables of food right over there. Go get something, if you're hungry."

He nodded and loped off through the crowd. When he returned a few minutes later he was carrying two plates piled high with hot dogs, homemade potato salad, coleslaw and slices of both cherry and apple pie. Victoria's eyes widened incredulously.

"I didn't want anything," she told him.

"Good," he said, grinning at her. "This was all for me. We never did have dinner last night, and you made me skip breakfast."

"We would have had time for breakfast, if you hadn't..." Her voice trailed off.

"Hadn't what?" he teased.

"Tate, please. You're distracting me."

"Am I?" he asked innocently. "Good."

"It is not good. I have to pay attention."

While Tate ate, Victoria studied the crowd, trying to pinpoint who the heavy bidders were and what they were buying. Only a handful seemed to be dealers or serious collectors. The rest were the usual assortment of auction followers, who bid erratically and frequently too high simply because an item appealed to them. Their unpredictability was what gave the auction its challenge. You had to know the value of every piece and set your limits, or you could be lured into a bidding war with someone to whom price was no object.

Tate watched with amazement as the intensity in Victoria's eyes mounted and her brow puckered into a tiny, fascinating frown. Somehow he'd thought of her business as a game, primarily because of her unique way of conducting it. He saw now that it was anything but a game to her. She took it seriously and, judging from the careful way she was watching the crowd, she knew what she was doing. Apparently she had to be as good a judge of people as she was of antiques.

He had been paying so much attention to Victoria that he'd lost track of what was happening on the makeshift stage set up under a huge oak tree. When she lifted the number she'd been holding in her lap, his gaze flew to the stage to see what she was trying to buy. It looked like a huge stack of unmatched dishes to him, and they were all in these glaringly bright shades of orange and red and blue. He couldn't imagine eating food off plates those colors.

"You're kidding!" he muttered aloud. "You want those things?"

"It's Fiestaware," Victoria said excitedly, as if that explained everything.

"Oh," he said and looked again. "It doesn't match."

"It doesn't have to," she said and flashed her card again. "Many collectors want a mix of colors. Others are looking for a single piece to fill in a set. I like to get as much as I can find."

The bidding had intensified, with only Victoria and two others remaining. Her card was waving in the air more frequently than a flash card at a high-scoring football game. Tate could barely tell from the auctioneer's rapid chatter exactly what the current price was, but it sounded outrageous to him. One of the remaining bidders dropped out, leaving only two. It was up to Victoria. She hesitated, then waved her card.

The other bidder promptly raised her offer and Victoria's face fell in disappointment. When the auctioneer looked back at her, she shook her head.

"You're going to drop out now?" Tate asked incredulously, as the auctioneer began his chant, "Going! Going!..."

Tate snatched Victoria's card and held it in the air.

"Tate, what are you doing?"

"You want it, you're going to have it," he said adamantly.

Victoria tried to snatch the card back. Tate held her hand up. When his bid was raised, he managed to wrestle the card away from Victoria long enough to wave it in the air. By now people around them were chuckling, but he didn't care. All he knew was that Victoria was going to have those dishes if it was the last thing he did.

"Tate McAndrews, stop it this minute," Victoria pleaded. "I can't afford to go any higher."

"I'll pay for the dishes."

"Tate," she said, his name coming out as a soft groan. "Please."

"You want them," he repeated insistently.

"Not for me."

His eyes flew open, and the card drifted back to his lap. "Not for you?"

"No. For the shop. I'm going to sell them."

"Oh. Of course," he said quietly, as the auctioneer said with a broad grin, "Sold to the gentleman...and lady...in the fifth row."

"Oh," Tate repeated, and this time his eyes were wide with shock. Victoria's lips were suddenly quivering, and then she was laughing, unable to control her mirth.

"Tate, you were wonderful."

"I feel like a fool."

"No," she said, kissing him. "You did something impetuous, totally crazy, absolutely impulsive, just to make me happy. I love you for it."

"You do?"

"I do," she said, grinning at him.

He chuckled and winked at her. "Should I do it again?"

"Don't you dare. We'll both go broke."

* * *

As the spring days lengthened toward a summery brightness, Tate spent more and more time with Victoria. They managed to avoid her inquisitive parents and an enthusiastically watchful Jeannie, though that was getting to be an uphill battle. One night, Victoria fully expected one of them to pop out of her closet just as she and Tate were rediscovering the magic that their bodies made together.

Though Victoria had tried to force Tate to include her in his life in Cincinnati, he'd been more insistent that he wanted to understand hers first. If he had told her once, he had told her a thousand times that he wanted to experience firsthand the lightheartedness that made her lips curve in a perpetual smile and her eyes sparkle like jewels in sunshine. When he said such uncharacteristically romantic things with a serious gleam in his eyes, her heart flipped over. She found herself doing exactly what she'd sworn not to. She fell more and more deeply in love.

Unfortunately, on top of that, none of her attempts to bring a sort of innocent pleasure, a more casual abandon into Tate's too-structured life went exactly according to plan. It was as though the same fate that had willfully thrown them together to fall in love had now decreed that it couldn't possibly work.

First, she had arrived at Tate's office in the middle of the day and dragged him on a picnic. It had gone beautifully once he'd stopped grumbling about the disruption in his busy schedule. She'd prepared a lovely lunch, brought along a book of poetry and found an idyllic setting. After they'd eaten, she'd leaned against a tree with Tate's head nestled in her lap, and started to read to him, her melodious voice filling the air with softly spoken, romantic words. It had been just about perfect…until a bee had settled on Tate's lip. She could still hear his startled shout, and she would never forget the frantic trip to the emergency room, once his lip had started swelling to at least three times its normal size.

"I'm sorry," she had said over and over again.

"No' yo' fau'," Tate mumbled thickly.

"Yes, it was. If I'd had any idea you were allergic to bees, I would have…"

"Wha'?"

"I don't know. I could have done something." She'd run her finger lightly across his lip and winced as she saw a flicker of pain in his eyes. "Oh, Tate."

"Shhh," he had said soothingly. "Don' worry abou' i'."

But she had worried and a few days later, when Tate had insisted on helping her plant her vegetable garden, she had practically pitched a fit, imagining him attacked by a whole swarm of bees and blowing up to the size of a hot air balloon.

"Victoria," he'd said patiently. "I'm sure the odds against my being stung again are a million to one."

"They are if you stay indoors."

"I'm helping with the garden." She knew that tone by now. She swallowed her doubts and gave him a shovel.

They had pulled weeds and cleared the patch of ground in the side yard, worked the rich black soil until it was absolutely perfect, added organic fertilizer and then put in rows of tiny tomato, corn and green bean plants.

"Where's the watermelon?" Tate had asked.

"I hate watermelon."

"I don't."

They had driven back to the garden store, where he had picked out three watermelon plants.

"Tate, one would be enough."

"What if it died?"

"Okay. Then two should do it."

"You might decide you like it."

Victoria had sighed. "Get three if you want them."

By the time she'd relented, he'd already paid for them. The man was completely stubborn.

It wasn't until later that night that they discovered the garden had been filled with poison ivy. For some unknown reason only Tate got a reaction to it. His arms were covered with a bright pink rash that he kept scratching until Victoria threatened to bandage his hands with adhesive tape.

"Tate, don't you think maybe we ought to do something in Cincinnati this weekend?" Victoria had suggested the previous night. "Maybe we could go to a movie."

"What would you do if you weren't with me?"

She'd shrugged. "I don't know. I never know exactly what I'm going to do until I'm practically in the middle of it."

"Well, if the weather's nice what would you probably do?"

"Go fishing, I suppose."

Tate had regarded her with a pained expression. "Fishing?"

"Sure."

"But what do you do while you're waiting for the fish to bite?"

"You don't *do* anything. It's so peaceful just to sit on the edge of the river and dangle your feet in the cold water and feel the sun touch your face. The sun feels almost as good as you do," she'd murmured, curving herself into his eagerly receptive body.

That had brought an abrupt halt to the discussion for the moment, but this morning she'd awakened to the sight of Tate standing by the bed with a sheepish expression on his face, a fishing pole in his hands and a hook caught in the seat of his jeans.

"Don't say it," he'd muttered, as she barely stifled a grin. "Just get it out."

After that she'd finally convinced him that they should drive to Cincinnati for a concert. It had taken them an hour to decide between a world famous violinist and an outrageous punk rock star with spiked pink hair and more mascara on his eyes than Victoria had ever worn in her life.

"But we both love classical music," Tate had argued. "Why would you even suggest we go to see this other jerk?"

"Have you ever seen a punk rock group?"

"No."

"Well, neither have I. It's time we did."

"Give me one good reason."

"It's an experience."

Tate couldn't find a single argument that could stand up to that kind of logic. "I'll call for tickets."

They never got to the concert, for which Tate would always be eternally grateful. They were on their way, in fact they were only a few miles away, when Victoria spotted a carnival.

"Oh, Tate we have to stop."

"We do?"

"Carnivals are such fun."

"No, they're not. They're grubby and cheap and disgusting."

"Tate, please."

"Oh, to hell with it." He couldn't resist it when she turned those blue eyes of hers on him with such a wide-eyed look of innocent entreaty. He vaguely understood now how men had been moved to conquer entire civilizations by the mere lift of some beguiling woman's brow. He was as helpless to refuse Victoria's wishes as a moth was to elude a flame. She was beaming at him now with that dazzling smile that warmed his heart and turned his determinedly rational head to absolute mush.

He parked the car, and they strolled hand in hand through the dusty lot onto the fairway. Raucous, tinny music filled the air with a cheerful noise. A Ferris wheel, decorated with bright lights, spun through the early evening sky, its stark reds and greens and blues streaking through the muted mauves of twilight. The distinctive scents of sticky, sweet cotton candy, fresh popcorn, garlicky sausage, hot dogs and pizza blended together to create a mouth watering effect. Barkers were trying to lure the crowd to try its luck pitching pennies, throwing hoops around milk bottles or shooting a moving target of tiny wooden ducks. Tate thought the whole thing had an air of awful unreality about it, but Victoria's expression was alive and excited, her eyes sparkling.

She drew him first to the cotton candy booth.

"You're not really planning to eat that stuff?" Tate asked, horrified by the puff of blue that was twirling around a paper cone.

"We're going to eat it," Victoria replied firmly, as he reluctantly paid for the candy. She pulled off a chunk and tried to feed it to him.

"That's nothing—" his protest began, as she poked some of the sticky blue mess in.

"—but sugar," he concluded, deciding it wasn't too awful. But it certainly had no nutritional content. "What a waste of calories."

"We didn't come here to diet. We came here to have a good time."

"And eating blue stuff is a good time?"

"Yes."

"If you say so," he said doubtfully. "What are we doing next for fun?"

"The Ferris wheel."

Tate's eyes surveyed the spinning wheel skeptically. "I don't think so. Those things aren't safe."

"Of course they are. How often have you read about one breaking?"

"Once would be enough, if you happened to be on it."

"Tate, it won't collapse."

"Do you have an in with the mechanic?"

"Buy the tickets."

"You want me to contribute to my own death? That's suicide."

"It's going to be murder, if you don't try to get into the spirit of this."

They were only stuck on top for forty-five minutes. Tate swore he would get even with Victoria, if it took him a lifetime.

"That's promising," she said, giving him a broad grin.

"It is? I didn't mean it to be."

"You're planning to spend a lifetime with me. Isn't that what you said?"

"Yes, but yours may end the minute we get back on the ground."

"Oh," she said softly, studying him quizzically. "Aren't you having a good time really?"

Actually, Tate supposed it wasn't the worst time he'd ever had in his life. Having the mumps at twenty-five had been pretty terrible, and having some idiot driver smash into the back of his new car twenty minutes after he drove it off the lot hadn't been too terrific. But this was definitely right up there among the top ten. He wasn't sure he ought to say that to Victoria, though. She was already upset enough about the bee and the poison ivy and the fish hook.

"I'm sure I'll have a great time once we're back down on the ground," he said with forced cheer.

"Right. We'll try the baseball toss, and you can win one of those huge teddy bears for me. I've always wanted someone to do that," she said wistfully.

At that moment Tate would have been willing to spend his next six lifetimes throwing baseballs until her entire house overflowed with those awful, ugly bears, if that was what she wanted.

His first three tosses were right on the mark, and Victoria's face was alight with laughter when the fat panda with the bright green bow around its neck was handed to her.

"Does he need a friend?" Tate asked.

"Of course," Victoria said solemnly. "Everyone needs a friend."

This time on the third toss, Tate wrenched his back and grimaced with pain.

"Tate, what is it?"

"Nothing."

"Tate, it is too something. You're holding your breath."

"Only so I won't scream."

"You hurt your back," Victoria guessed.

"It's nothing," he insisted. "I'm sorry about the bear."

"Don't worry about it. This one will be just fine. Lancelot will keep him company."

Tate suspected Lancelot would tear him to shreds, but he didn't want to put a damper on Victoria's enthusiasm.

"Is there anything else you wanted to do?"

"Let's see the fortune-teller."

"You're kidding!" Tate was incredulous. "You don't actually believe in that stuff?"

"Of course not, but it's fun."

"Just like the Ferris wheel."

"Don't be mean."

"Sorry."

They sat down in front of a woman with a yellow bandanna on her dark curls, golden hoops in her ears and red lipstick in a shade just this side of scandalous. She had dark, Gypsy eyes that told seductive tales and a contradictory, impish smile that teased like a child with a feather. Even Tate wanted to trust her. She spread the cards on the table, studied them intently, then hastily gathered them up. Her fingers moved so quickly that Tate wasn't even aware that her actions were peculiar until he heard Victoria's sharp intake of breath.

"What's wrong?" she asked hesitantly.

"Nothing," the woman said, though her tone was far from reassuring. "I made a mistake with the cards. I wish to try again."

"You saw something in the cards, didn't you?" Victoria insisted. "Tell me."

Tate reached over and took Victoria's hand. "Sweetheart, you said yourself it's only a game. Don't worry about it."

"It's not a game. She saw something, and I want to know what."

"I saw a tall, dark-haired, handsome man in your life."

"Brilliant," Tate muttered. The woman and Victoria glared at him.

"It was all wrong. It will never work out," she said, as Victoria's eyes filled with tears.

"I knew it," she murmured, looking at Tate. "I just knew it."

Tate wanted to throttle the woman. "Are you out of your mind? Can't you see you're upsetting her?"

"I only say what I see in the cards."

"Tate, I've always known it wouldn't work. We've been pretending, trying to turn a dream into reality."

Tate stared at her incredulously. "Victoria, this is the most ridiculous conversation I have ever had in my life. Are you trying to tell me that you're willing to let some crazy fortune-teller dictate what happens to us?"

"Sir, I am not crazy!"

"Oh, be quiet," Tate snapped. "You've done enough damage."

"I want to go home," Victoria said quietly.

"Victoria, please."

"I want to go home."

"Of all the simpleminded, ridiculous—"

"Now I'm simpleminded and ridiculous?"

Tate's head was reeling. "I don't believe this."

"Neither do I. I thought you were starting to love me a little bit, but you were just treating me like some circus freak show, weren't you?"

"What? Where the hell did that come from?"

"You've always thought I was just some dingy kook. Admit it."

"I thought you were unique, unusual, charming and wonderful. I do love you."

"You think that now, but when the novelty's worn off, you'll go right back to some prissy little career woman who buys her clothes in New York or Paris or someplace, instead of a secondhand store."

"Victoria, I don't give a damn where you buy your clothes."

"That's not the point."

"What is the point? I haven't been able to figure it out since we sat down at this stupid booth."

"We're all wrong for each other. Look at the last few weeks. You've tried. You really have tried, but you haven't had fun. Good heavens, you've been practically killed by a bee."

"Oh, for heaven's sakes," he said, rolling his eyes in disgust. "I was not practically killed."

"Whatever. And you got poison ivy. And you got a fish hook stuck in your rear. And you hurt your back tonight. If you keep trying to be more like me, you'll end up dead."

Tate sighed. He had a feeling there was no point in arguing with Victoria when she was in this state of mind. Maybe by the time they drove home, she'd be seeing things more rationally.

Or maybe by then, he'd at least figure out what the devil she was talking about.

Chapter 11

Victoria had heard the crazy, irrational words pouring out of her mouth and wanted to stop them, but she couldn't bring herself to be silent any longer. Deep down, she really believed what she had said: she and Tate were absolutely wrong for each other. The idea was hardly a new one. It had nagged at her from the very beginning, and their ill-fated attempt to make the relationship work had given her proof. The phony fortune-teller finally made her admit aloud to Tate and forced them both to face what they should have known from the start.

The last few weeks had been their impossible dream. In many ways she had been happier than she'd ever been in her life. She'd never laughed harder or shared more tender moments. Certainly she had never experienced any greater heights of passion. Tate had tried so hard to please her and ultimately, that was the problem. He had needed to try. If theirs were a match that was meant to be, shouldn't all of this have come naturally? Shouldn't their minds have been as perfectly attuned as their bodies obviously were?

When they finally pulled to a stop in her driveway, after the long, silent drive home from the carnival, she glanced over at Tate and found him staring straight ahead. A stormy expression was on his face, and his hands clutched the steering wheel with white-knuckled intensity. She noted idly that he hadn't turned off the engine. It seemed as if he could hardly wait for her to get out of the car before going on.

"Tate," she said softly.

"What?"

"I'm sorry."

"Sure."

"I am, but you know I'm right. You're trying to change. I'm trying to change. In the middle of all this changing, we're going to lose ourselves."

He scowled at her. "I have never asked you to change and, frankly, I haven't seen any signs that you've tried. You're still living with your head in the clouds, expecting everything to be romantic and wonderful without any effort. Sorry, honey, but that's not how it works in real life. People have to work at relationships. If you don't wake up and accept that, you're going to lead a very lonely life. That perfect fairy-tale hero on the white charger is never going to show up."

"I'm not waiting for some guy on a white charger," she huffed indignantly, though she wondered if he might not be right. Jeannie had accused her of the same thing often enough. But even if it were true, was it so terribly wrong to want someone who could capture her imagination and make it fly, who would soar with her through each day and fill it with color and light and laughter?

"Aren't you?" Tate was saying skeptically. "It seems to me you aren't about to be satisfied with some ordinary man who happens to love you. He doesn't wield a lot of flowery phrases or go out slaying dragons on his lunch hour."

"Is that what you think I want?"

"Of course it is. You've made that plain. No matter how hard I tried, I always disappointed you."

"That's not true. I loved you for trying."

"But it was never enough, was it?" he said sadly. "If it had been, some stupid fortune-teller couldn't have thrown you like this. She gave you an excuse to bow out, because my loving you and wanting to protect you and take care of you was never enough. You wanted the moon, and I could only give you the stars.''

His words, a paraphrase of those from her favorite movie which they'd watched together a few nights ago, shook Victoria to her very core. What had she done? Did she expect more than any woman had a right to ask of a man? Had she wanted him to do all of the changing, while she sat back and waited until he turned into an appropriate hero who plucked not only stars, but the moon, from the sky for her?

He was staring at her and to her amazement, his eyes were glistening with unshed tears. ''Well, I'm tired of trying,'' he said softly. ''Maybe that fortune-teller did us a favor, after all. I finally see that I've been wasting my time.''

''Oh, Tate,'' Victoria whispered, stunned now that it really was all crashing down around them. Somehow she'd expected Tate to argue with her, to fight for the relationship. At the carnival, he'd seemed so angry, so incredulous that she would throw it all away. But in the end apparently he'd also seen the truth of what she'd said. On the long drive home, all of the fight had drained out of him.

''I didn't mean for it to end this way,'' she said miserably. ''I thought for a while we could make it work. I really did.''

''So did I,'' he replied quietly, his gaze locking with hers, holding it, until Victoria felt her breath catch in her throat. ''Good night, Victoria.''

She hesitated for just a moment, not wanting to open the door of the car, not wanting to take that final step that would finish things between them. She started to say something, but Tate silenced her with a trembling finger held against her quivering lips.

''We've said enough,'' he said softly.

Victoria sighed and nodded. She got out of the car and closed the door quietly. The sound was more devastatingly final than if she'd slammed it. As Tate backed out of the driveway, she watched him go, hot, sorrowful tears at long last streaming down her cheeks.

''Goodbye,'' she murmured. When Lancelot wound between her legs, meowing softly, she picked him up and held him so tightly that he howled in protest. "Sorry, old guy," she apologized. "You're all I've got now."

No matter how many times in the next few weeks Victoria told herself that what had happened had been for the best, she was miserable. It might have been the right thing to do in the long run, but in the short run it was absolute hell. She thought continually about Tate's charge that her expectations had been unrealistic. Perhaps she had idealized romance in such a way that no mere human being could ever fulfill her dreams. Ironically, the more she mulled this over, the more she realized that Tate had fulfilled more of her dreams than she'd ever had any right to hope for. He'd been tender and caring and more than willing to tolerate—even indulge—her craziness. To her surprise, he'd even seemed to love her all the more because of it. So what if he'd been allergic to bees. He'd been willing to risk being stung to be with her. The same was true of all the rest of those crazy things they'd done together.

The problem, she finally admitted, hadn't been his acceptance of her at all. It had been her stupid inability to accept him. She had interpreted his dependability as stuffiness, his protectiveness as an attempt to dominate, his down-to-earth realism as an attempt to stifle her creativity. Even though she could see now that she had been the one lacking in imagination in terms of their relationship, she still felt that Tate was better off without her. Their differences ultimately would create strain, not excitement, and nothing anyone could say was likely to change her mind.

Goodness knows everyone had tried hard enough. Her parents were tired of watching her mope around. When her father's subtle, kindly questions drew no response, her mother had sat her down in the kitchen, poured her a cup of tea and demanded answers. When that didn't work, they had sent Jeannie over with strawberry shortcake, whipped cream, advice and sympathy so thick you could practically slice it with a knife. Victoria had eaten the shortcake, ignored the advice, choked on the sympathy and kept her innermost thoughts to herself.

After all of that, however, she did make an attempt to rally. She actually went to a farm sale, but instead of the excitement she usually felt, she became more depressed than ever. Images of Tate bidding wildly on the Fiestaware dishes just to please her teased her mind, taunted her with the realization that she'd had her storybook hero at her side and hadn't even known it.

On the day the envelope from the IRS arrived, Victoria broke down and cried for the first time since the night she and Tate had broken up. She couldn't even bear to open it. She was sitting behind the counter in the front of the shop, sniffling and wiping her eyes with the back of her hand when a woman in her mid-fifties breezed in. She was wearing a bright green jump suit and a colorful flowing scarf around her neck. At the sight of Victoria sobbing all by herself, a frown creased her brow, and the twinkle in her dark brown eyes died.

"Oh, dear," she said, clucking sympathetically. "Have you had bad news? Should I come back another time?"

Victoria waved the letter and shook her head, but she couldn't seem to stop the flow of tears. The woman reached into the huge bag she was carrying and dug around for several minutes. She pulled out a crumbling pack of peanut butter crackers, the nozzle for a garden hose, two paperbacks—one on astrology and another on the history of civilization—and a pair of bifocals before finally extracting a tissue and handing it to Victoria.

"Never can find things when you need them," she muttered under her breath, as Victoria realized with widening eyes that the woman's purse wasn't a handbag at all, but a plastic tote bag from Harrod's in a shade of olive-green that clashed horribly with her outfit. She put her glasses on and took the letter that Victoria had dropped on the counter.

"Do you mind?" she asked, peering over the top of the bifocals.

Victoria shook her head. What did it matter who read it? Either she was going to jail or she wasn't. What the letter really meant was that Tate hated her so much, he hadn't wanted to tell her in person. The woman was staring intently from the envelope to Victoria and back again as though she understood that. Suddenly Victoria forgot about her own pain and began to wonder who on earth this sympathetic, perceptive woman was.

"Who are you?" she asked at last.

"Lisa McAndrews," the woman replied matter-of-factly, as Victoria's pulse began to race.

"McAndrews? Tate's…"

"That's right, dear," she said with a bright smile that made her look like an impish girl. "I'm Tate's mother."

Victoria tried to snatch the letter back. She couldn't have Tate's mother finding out about this whole IRS mess. What on earth would the woman think of her?

"Don't be silly," Mrs. McAndrews said, holding the letter out of her reach. "There's no use your getting all upset over this, when you don't even know what it says."

She gave Victoria a sharp, considering glance. "But that's not what you're upset about anyway, is it?"

Startled, Victoria simply stared at her. "How did you know?"

"I'm a woman. I also know what a bullheaded fool my son can be."

Victoria shook her head miserably. "I'm the one who's been the fool."

"Scattering the blame around isn't going to help a thing, my dear, but if you miss him.…" She peered at Victoria over the top of her glasses. "You do miss him, don't you?"

"Terribly."

"Then why don't you do something about it?"

"It's not as simple as that. I really don't think there's any point. We're wrong for each other."

"Do you love him?" Tate's mother asked bluntly.

Victoria hesitated, but saw no reason not to be honest. "Yes."

"And he loves you."

"Did he say that?" Victoria asked hopefully.

"Well," Mrs. McAndrews admitted reluctantly. "Not in so many words."

Victoria sighed in disappointment. "No. He wouldn't."

"But he does. All the signs are there. Those ridiculously healthy plants of his are all dying, for heaven's sakes."

"His plants are dying?" Victoria's eyes lit up with a tiny glimmer of renewed hope. She couldn't have been happier if he'd sent her roses.

"And he came over after work the other day, and I noticed that his socks didn't match."

"His socks didn't match?" Her spirits began to skyrocket.

Lisa McAndrews chuckled. "I think you're beginning to catch on. The man's a basket case. If you don't do something about it soon, my sensible son is likely to quit his job and go hang out on a beach with a surfboard."

The very idea boggled Victoria's mind. "You're not serious?"

"Well," she said with a grin, "Perhaps that is a bit of an exaggeration, but he is at the end of his rope. Pete Harrison called me the other day and asked me if I thought Tate was under too much stress."

"Why on earth would his boss ask that?"

"He'd just turned down a complicated case that a few months ago he would have killed to get. He told Pete he was bored with the corporate cases. Needless to say, Pete was in a state of shock. Fortunately, he didn't guess that Tate's state of mind had anything to do with you, or your audit would have been held up for months while he went over it with a fine-tooth comb."

"How do you know that's not what he did anyway?"

"Come to think of it, you're right." She ripped open the envelope before Victoria could stop her. "Nope. You're in the clear. The government even apologizes for putting you to so much trouble." She clucked and her brows lifted. "And well they should. Anyone with half a brain can see that you're no criminal. That son of mine must have had a screw loose when he came down here and accused you of who-knows-what."

"He was just doing his job," Victoria defended.

"Frankly, I've always thought it was a lousy job. He'd be much better off if he found something with a little life to it. All those deadly little numbers, lined up in neat little rows...." Her voice trailed off, and she shuddered dramatically. "It gives me the chills."

"I know what you mean."

"Then save him from it," Mrs. McAndrews urged.

Victoria sighed. "I'm not sure we can make it work."

"You love each other," she reminded her simply. "After that, very little else matters."

"But we're so unsuitable."

"By whose standards? Certainly not mine. I led my husband on a merry chase, let me tell you. I think that's why Tate started out being so cautious with you. He was always convinced that his father and I were totally unsuited."

"I'm sure he didn't really believe that," Victoria said.

"Oh, yes, he did. I heard him say it to his father often enough, when he thought I wasn't listening."

"That's awful."

"No, it wasn't. Not really. He was just being protective. He was worried that my antics were going to drive his father over the edge." She grinned impishly. "Actually, we were a perfect match. I brought a lot of fun and craziness into his life, and he kept me out of jail. We were very much in love. I think you and Tate are, too. You can work it out.

"And just think," she added with a conspiratorial smile, "You'll never have to worry about balancing your checkbook again."

"Since you know about the audit, then you know I've never worried about that anyway," Victoria replied wryly. "Much to your son's dismay."

Lisa McAndrews threw her arms around Victoria and hugged her impulsively. "Go to him, my dear. I've always wanted a daughter-in-law just like you. We will have the most wonderful time."

They would, too, Victoria thought. She knew instinctively that she and Tate's mother were two of a kind, just as he was the son-in-law her parents had always dreamed of. That ought to count for something. Maybe this whole thing wasn't quite so crazy after all.

She gave Lisa McAndrews a dazzling smile.

"You're going to do it, aren't you?" the older woman said, her brown eyes twinkling just as Victoria had seen Tate's do on those occasions when she did something to delight him.

"I'm going to think about it."

"Don't think, dear. That's what got you in trouble in the first place. Listen to your heart," she advised, as she gathered her things and breezed out.

When she had gone, Victoria listened as hard as she could. Her heart was soaring.

Chapter 12

Tate stood in front of the steamed up bathroom mirror and took a good hard look at himself. Even through the foggy distortion, the image was enough to make him shudder. Today was his thirtieth birthday, and he looked like a man who'd been on a nonstop, three-week bender, and he hadn't even taken a drink. Not that he hadn't wanted to. Every time an image of Victoria had popped into his mind, he'd wanted to dull it with alcohol, but he'd forced himself to live with the vivid, beguiling impressions. They had dominated his days and taunted him in his dreams.

When Pete had told him to send the letter telling Victoria that the audit was complete and that there'd been no evidence of fraud or tax evasion, he'd thought that would be the end of it. He'd replace her case with another, her image with that of a new woman. Instead, the cases had bored him, and every woman he'd called had sounded so ridiculously sophisticated, so disgustingly normal and uninteresting, he'd hung up without ever asking for a date. He'd spent his evenings alone with his memories. Crazy, wacky, wonderful memories of the unexpected that always seemed to happen whenever Victoria was involved.

There would be no more of that, he solemnly told his reflection. His birthday was as good a day as any to start over, to get himself back on track again. Maybe he'd even quit his job and leave Cincinnati, check out new options and new horizons. The old ones had left him feeling increasingly dissatisfied ever since Victoria had opened his eyes to new possibilities.

An hour later he was sitting in his office trying to work up the courage to tell Pete he wanted to quit or, at the very least, transfer to another IRS office, when he heard a chorus of laughter floating through the outer offices. He opened the door and peered out to see what had brought on this totally unexpected, raucous sound. Pete frowned on joviality. In fact, right now Pete was standing outside his office, shaking his head and muttering dire curses under his breath.

"What's going on?" Tate asked.

"You tell me, McAndrews," he groused.

"What's that supposed to mean?"

"I think you'd better go check out the elevator."

"The elevator?" His head started spinning in that same crazy, light-headed way it always had when Victoria was up to something. It hadn't happened to him in weeks now.

He walked through the main office, noticing that everyone seemed to be either studiously ignoring him or grinning like the proverbial cat who'd just lunched on a very satisfying canary. When he reached the elevator, he began to understand why. The door was lodged open by a clown wearing a puffy, polka-dotted costume, a bright-orange fright wig and oversized shoes. One foot was propped against the left door, while the clown's very attractive rear poked against the right door. Both hands were frantically trying to pull a tangled bunch of helium-filled balloons through the doors before they smashed shut.

Tate started to chuckle at the perfectly incongruous sight, but the sound died in his throat as one of the balloons floated close enough for him to get a good look at it. He groaned softly and closed his eyes, hoping that when he opened them again, he'd discover that he'd only imagined that every one of the red, silver and blue balloons said "Happy Birthday, Tate" in bright green lettering. He peeked again. Nothing had changed. Without even counting, he knew there would be thirty balloons in that elevator. He prayed innocent, claustrophobic people weren't stuck in there with them.

His eyes squinted suspiciously and roved over the clown again, and his heart suddenly tripped a little faster. That rear end, poked out so provocatively, looked very familiar despite the baggy costume. Surely it couldn't be....

The clown offered him a lopsided grin. "Are you this Tate person?" an unfamiliar, squeaky little voice asked, throwing him. He stared at the clown more closely, his brow creasing in a puzzled frown. For a minute, he'd been so sure, but maybe his mind was playing tricks on him after all. He'd missed Victoria so much, his imagination had probably simply conjured her up for him. The clown, however, was very real and was waiting for an answer.

"I'm Tate," he admitted reluctantly.

"Sorry about the entrance," the clown squeaked. "But I'm a little new at this. If you could hold some of these?"

"Umm...of course," he said, blushing furiously as the new, unrestrained chuckles started again behind him. When he had all thirty balloons safely in tow, the clown released the elevator door and it slowly glided shut. The clown was inside. Tate was outside, staring at the elevator in confusion. A minute later, the door opened revealing an obviously embarrassed clown.

"Sorry. I was supposed to sing."

The clown cleared its throat and began a lusty, only slightly off-key rendition of "Happy Birthday to You." The entire office joined in, singing so loudly that Tate, for the life of him, couldn't be sure if it was Victoria's sweetly melodious voice he heard or not. Before he could make a grab for the clown and take a good hard look into those dancing, seemingly familiar blue eyes, the doors were shut again and the clown was gone.

"Do you suppose we could get some work done around here now?" Pete growled next to him, though there was a decided twinkle in his eyes.

Suddenly, Tate made a decision. He grinned at Pete, put the strings of the balloons into his hands and hopped on the next elevator. He thought if he lived to be a hundred, he would never forget the startled grin that had creased Pete's face, right before he'd resumed his more characteristic scowl.

When he reached the lobby, Tate wasn't sure exactly what he was going to do next. He only knew that he had to find that clown— Victoria, he was absolutely sure of it—and make things right between them somehow. As ridiculous as their relationship might be, their fight had been even more absurd. They loved each other, and two reasonably intelligent people should never have been separated by a fortune-teller and a deck of cards. Rational people in love could work things out, cards or no cards. Surely they could find a way to have both balloons and order in their lives.

He drove north as though he'd been sent to put out a raging fire, which, in a manner of speaking, he had. There had been a fire burning inside him for weeks now, and only Victoria had the power to quench the flames. He headed straight for Victoria's shop and found her mother chatting happily with a customer over coffee and cherry pie. He wondered briefly if the crust was soggy or if Victoria had finally mastered crusts.

Katherine Marshall glanced up at his entrance and beamed at him.

"It's about time," she chided gently.

"Where is she?"

"Have you tried the house? She seems to be hiding out there a lot lately."

"I'll have her back here by tomorrow," he promised.

"I'd rather you took her off on a long honeymoon."

He grinned. "I think that can be arranged, too."

When he got to the house, the battered blue Volkswagen was in the driveway. Feeling like an amateur detective, he walked over and laid his hand over the engine. It was still warm. She'd either been to the supermarket, or she'd been to Cincinnati. He was willing to lay odds on Cincinnati.

He knocked on the back door and marched in without even waiting for a response. He took the stairs two at a time. When he reached the top, he hesitated at the closed bathroom door, then shrugged, muttered under his breath and threw it open. Startled blue eyes flew up and met his in the mirror. Golden-red curls tumbled over her shoulders, which were still encased in an oversized clown's costume. He grinned. Her reflection grinned back at him hesitantly.

"You knew, didn't you?"

"Of course, I knew," he said confidently, as if he'd never had a second's doubt. "How many people do you think I know who'd get trapped in an elevator with thirty balloons?"

"Two that I can think of."

He chuckled. "You've met my mother."

Victoria nodded.

"I wondered how long it would take her to get to you."

Victoria knew that she would be forever grateful to Lisa Mc-Andrews for making her see that she and Tate shared all of the important values: love, respect, family loyalty. They just expressed them differently. She did wildly impulsive things for those she cared about. Tate expressed his caring in a more sedate manner, but the sentiment was just as strong, just as real.

"She was worried about you," she told Tate now.

"And you?"

"I was too busy being miserable and confused and mad at myself to worry about you."

"Me, too," he admitted. "I was being miserable and stubborn."

Victoria gave him a dimpled smile, that was emphasized by the rosy-red greasepaint on her cheeks. "You're very good at stubborn."

"You're not so bad yourself."

She turned around finally and took a step toward him, tilting her head to one side as she studied the face that she had missed so much. She reached out a finger and gently touched the dark circles under his eyes.

"My fault?"

"Nope. Mine."

She nodded. "Your mother says it doesn't matter whose fault it is, as long as we work it out."

"Wise woman, my mother."

Victoria grinned. "You might tell her that sometime. She's convinced you think she's a flake.

"She is."

"Tate!"

"That doesn't mean I don't love her, just like it doesn't mean I can't love you. It just took me a while to figure that out."

"Wise man," Victoria noted, gazing into his eyes, her heart warming at the answers she saw there, answers to all of her unasked questions. She grinned at him impishly.

"Did you like the balloons?"

Golden lights danced in his eyes. "I don't suppose you could have sent a card?"

She shook her head. "Boring. Would you have driven up here after me if you'd gotten some dumb old card in the mail?"

"Probably," he admitted. "But Pete wouldn't have had nearly as much fun."

"Pete?"

"I left the balloons with him."

"He must have loved that."

"Actually I think he did. You may be saving two men from boredom, instead of only one."

"I've always believed in getting a good deal."

"Since when?"

"Since I fell in love with a man who's keeping a close watch on my finances."

"Is that all you're interested in? My financial skills?"

She took another step closer and circled her arms around his neck. "Well, there is this other little skill I've noticed...."

"What's that?" he teased.

"Let me show you." Her lips brushed across his lightly, then returned with a firmer, hungrier touch. When his mouth opened and her tongue flicked across his teeth, she heard a moan rumble deep in his throat, and his arms tightened around her.

"Don't you ever leave me again," he whispered hoarsely. "I don't think I could stand it."

"There is one way to be sure I won't," she taunted, grinning at him impishly.

"What's that?"

"If I have to tell you, it doesn't count."

"Oh," he said. "That way."

She nodded, as Tate dropped dramatically to one knee.

"Victoria Marshall, will you marry me?" he asked solemnly.

She studied him considerably. "That's an awfully traditional proposal."

"Too traditional?" he teased, his brown eyes twinkling in the way that always made her feel as if he'd earned a Nobel prize.

"Much. I was thinking along the lines of a skywriter."

"Okay," he said agreeably. "Tell me where I can hire one."

"You'd really do that for me?"

"I would do almost anything for you. Don't you know that by now?" he asked as the phone rang. He groaned. "Not again."

"Hush," Victoria soothed. "I'll get rid of them."

She picked up the phone and talked briefly, her lips curving into a smile. "I'll tell him," she promised.

"Tell me what? Who was that?"

"It was your mother."

"How did she know I was here?"

"She said she knew it was only a matter of time."

"What did she want?"

"She had this great idea for our honeymoon."

"*She* had a great idea for *our* honeymoon? What made her think we were getting married?"

"She said that was only a matter of time, too."

Tate moaned. "Good Lord. What am I doing to myself? I'll never be able to cope with the two of you."

"Don't worry," Victoria consoled him. "You'll have my parents on your side."

"That may help some. What exactly did my mother have in mind for our honeymoon?"

"She wanted us to go on an archaeological dig."

"What?"

"With her."

"Victoria!"

"I think it would be fun."

"No. Uh-uh. Absolutely not. That would not be a honeymoon."

"Who says?"

Tate sighed. "Victoria do you know anything at all about archaeology?"

"No. Do you?"

"No."

"Then that's all the more reason for us to go."

"Victoria, I may not know much about digs, but I know a little about honeymoons. Mothers do not go."

"Who says? Miss Manners?"

"No. I do."

"Spoilsport."

Tate sighed. "How about if we go on our honeymoon alone and then go on an archaeological dig with my mother?"

"Oh, okay," she agreed finally. "I guess that makes sense."

"Thank goodness. Since you're so anxious to plan the honeymoon, does that mean you're accepting my proposal?"

"Oh," she said innocently, "Didn't I give you an answer?"

"You did not. Am I going to have to wait to see if I pass some other test?"

"Oh, you've passed all the tests," she said softly. "With flying colors."

"Hallelujah!" he said fervently. "Then you won't mind helping me up."

"Can't you get up?"

"No. I seem to have thrown my back out."

"Oh, Tate, not again."

"Again," he confirmed. "But it's okay. I'm getting used to it."

"Want me to kiss it and make it better?" she offered hopefully.

Tate regarded her skeptically. "Do you actually think that will work?"

"It's worth a try," she said, smiling at him suggestively.

"Now that you mention...."

Her delicate touch skimmed over him and suddenly his back did feel better. In fact his entire body felt as if it were floating on air. "Not bad, Victoria. Keep it up."

"I plan to," she promised. "For a lifetime."

* * * * *

LINDSAY McKENNA

continues her most popular series with a brand-new, longer-length book.

And it's the story you've been waiting for....

Morgan's Mercenaries:
Heart of Stone

They had met before. Battled before. And Captain Maya Stevenson had never again wanted to lay eyes on Major Dane York— the man who once tried to destroy her military career! But on their latest mission together, Maya discovered that beneath the fury in Dane's eyes lay a raging passion. Now she struggled against dangerous desire, as Dane's command over her seemed greater still. For this time, he laid claim to her heart....

Only from Lindsay McKenna and Silhouette Books!

"When it comes to action and romance, nobody does it better than Ms. McKenna."
—*Romantic Times Magazine*

Available in March at your favorite retail outlet.

Silhouette®
Where love comes alive™

In March 2001,

presents the next book in

DIANA PALMER's

enthralling *Soldiers of Fortune* trilogy:

THE WINTER SOLDIER

Cy Parks had a reputation around Jacobsville for his taciturn and solitary ways. But spirited Lisa Monroe wasn't put off by the mesmerizing mercenary, and drove him to distraction with her sweetly tantalizing kisses. Though he'd never admit it, Cy was getting mighty possessive of the enchanting woman who needed the type of safeguarding only he could provide. But who would protect the beguiling beauty from *him...?*

Soldiers of Fortune...prisoners of love.

#1 *New York Times* bestselling author

NORA ROBERTS

brings you more of the loyal and loving, tempestuous and tantalizing Stanislaski family.

The Stanislaski Sisters

Natasha and Rachel

Coming in February 2001

Though raised in the Old World traditions of their family, fiery Natasha Stanislaski and cool, classy Rachel Stanislaski are ready for a *new* world of love....

And also available in February 2001 from Silhouette Special Edition, the newest book in the heartwarming Stanislaski saga

CONSIDERING KATE

Natasha and Spencer Kimball's daughter Kate turns her back on old dreams and returns to her hometown, where she finds the *man* of her dreams.

Available at your favorite retail outlet.

Where love comes alive ™

PRAISE FOR THESE AWARD-WINNING AUTHORS

New York Times bestselling author
LINDA HOWARD

"Howard's writing is compelling."
—*Publishers Weekly*

"You can't read just one Linda Howard!"
—*New York Times* bestselling author
Catherine Coulter

New York Times bestselling author
LINDA LAEL MILLER

Named "The Most Outstanding Writer
of Sensual Romance"
by *Romantic Times Magazine*.

"Her characters come alive and walk right off
the pages and into your heart."
—*Rendezvous*

Award-winning author
SHERRYL WOODS

"Sherryl Woods always delivers a fast, breezy,
glamorous mix of romance..."
—*New York Times* bestselling author
Jayne Ann Krentz

"Sherryl Woods...writes with a very special warmth,
wit, charm and intelligence."
—*New York Times* bestselling author Heather Graham

Linda Howard

says that whether she's reading them or writing them, books have long played a profound role in her life. She cut her teeth on Margaret Mitchell and from then on continued to read widely and eagerly. In recent years her interest has settled on romantic fiction, because she's "easily bored by murder, mayhem and politics." After twenty-one years of penning stories for her own enjoyment, Ms. Howard finally worked up the courage to submit a novel for publication—and met with success! Happily, the Alabama author has been steadily publishing ever since, and has made numerous appearances on the *New York Times* bestseller list.

Linda Lael Miller

New York Times bestselling author Linda Lael Miller started writing at age ten and has made a name for herself in both contemporary and historical romance with over fifty published novels to her credit. Her bold and innovative style has made her a favorite among readers. She currently makes her home in Arizona.

Sherryl Woods

After writing more than seventy-five romances and mysteries in the last twenty years, Sherryl Woods has days when she wonders if she has anything left to say. But then a new character sneaks into her subconscious and starts telling her secrets. And because she loves to talk to real people once in a while, she also operates her own bookstore, Potomac Sunrise, in Colonial Beach, VA, where readers from around the country stop by to discuss her favorite topic—books. If you can't visit Sherryl at her store, then be sure to drop her a note at P.O. Box 490326, Key Biscayne, FL 33149.